Huguenot City

Anthony D. Murphy

PublishAmerica
Baltimore

ISBN: 1-4241-8920-9
PUBLISHED BY PUBLISHAMERICA, LLLP
www.publishamerica.com
Baltimore

Printed in the United States of America

Prologue

June 24, 1965

The two detectives pulled up to the scene in an unmarked Dodge Polara. The doorman knew from the look of the car and its two occupants that they were detectives. The driver was Frank Widelsky. He was a short, thickset, hard-looking man with a personality to match. He had a big head and virtually no neck. His face was broad, but his nose and eyes were small and it was easy to understand why his nickname in high school was "Moon face." He had on a green suit and a tan straw porkpie hat with a black band and small brown and red feather on it.

His partner was Phil Cairn, taller by half a foot than Widelsky was, and with enough charm for the two of them. He was a handsome man, but there was nothing pretty or boyish about his features. His nose was long and full and seemed to fit perfectly with his thick black eyebrows and full lips. His black hair was highlighted with thin streaks of gray, and his deeply tanned skin made his blue eyes look that much bluer. He had on a black suit with a white shirt and black and white diamond patterned tie.

He was arriving at the scene of a homicide, and if you didn't know he was a cop, you'd think he was the undertaker. He smiled, Widelsky didn't. They said nothing to the doorman, but let him lead the way. The doorman's hat was too big for his head and as they were going up in the elevator they studied him. The doorman was sweating and he kept repeating, "Terrible thing, just a terrible thing."

Before they got out of the elevator, Widelsky asked him, "You ever been in the movies?"

The doorman said, "I go to the RKO once in a while. Why?"

"I mean been in one?"

"No," the doorman said nervously.

"Okay, I was just asking."

Widelsky and Cairn followed the doorman to the apartment. Widelsky poked Cairn in the ribs with his elbow and said loud enough for the doorman to hear, "Looks like one of the fucking munchkins in the *Wizard of Oz*, doesn't he?"

The apartment door was open and there was a young patrolman standing in front of it. The two detectives flashed their badges, and Widelsky said, "Widelsky and Cairn, Major Case, where's your partner?"

"He's next door with the witness."

"We got a witness to the crime, great," Widelsky said, with just a little too much enthusiasm. "If we got a witness, we got a fucking suspect," he added sarcastically.

"There's no suspect. I mean nobody saw anyone, far as I know."

"Okay, glad we cleared that up. So now instead of telling me what you don't know, you can tell me what you do know. How'd you get the call?"

"It came over as an aided, a woman down."

"Who was in the apartment when you got here? It's all in your book, right?"

The patrolman opened his memo book and looked at his last entry. "The doorman, the lady next door, you know the one that called it in, the ambulance attendants, and eh, the two victims."

"Great, what'd you see when you came in?"

"The doorman was at the front door, and when we went inside to the bedroom, the neighbor was there, the ambulance attendants were working on the one victim and the other one was on the floor. They said she was dead. We didn't go in the room. Casey took the witness...excuse me," he said apologetically. "I mean, the neighbor who called it in, to her apartment. That's where he is now. She was crying and really upset. Sergeant Brown told me to keep a log of everyone coming and going. That's about it."

"Brown was here first, or after you?"

"When we saw it was a homicide. Casey called it in and asked for a boss."

"What phone didja use," Widelsky asked as he looked at his watch.

"The neighbor's phone, Casey made the call. I stayed in the apartment until the ambulance left."

"Okay, rookie, at least the academy's teachin' ya something useful these days." He then went into the apartment.

Cairn reached over and said, "Let me see your book. Sounds like you done okay." Cairn looked over the pages in the memo book and handed it back. "Widelsky and Cairn, let me spell it for you W-I-D-E-L-S_K-Y, Cairn, C-A-I-R-N. Got it?"

"Yes, sir."

"Anything else you saw?"

"Just some pictures on the floor, eight by tens. Looked like the dead lady's lying over a couple of them and there's one in her hand. She got a dent in her skull, but not much blood. Looked like whoever did it whacked her with an ashtray. There's a big one on the floor right near her head, and from what I could see there's some blood on it. We checked the rest of the apartment, but it looked clean. No signs of forced entry."

"All right, keep up the log until you're relieved. By the way, what's your name?"

"Patrolman Clay, Desmond Clay, my friends call me Desi."

"Okay, Desi, I'm Phil Cairn," he said as he extended his hand. "And you don't have to call me sir, I'm not a boss. Don't mind Widelsky, he don't like dead bodies and he always gives everyone taller than him a tough time."

Chapter One

June 18, 1965

Maria decided to wait until Henry left the house for work before she took her shower. She had made the morning coffee before he got up. When he was ready for his breakfast, she had already gone back to bed. He had his coffee alone and when he left for work he didn't bother saying goodbye. She'd gotten into one of her moods the night before and was angry with him, but he wasn't sure what it was really about, and it didn't matter to him much anyway.

Maria waited until she heard the apartment door open and close before she got out of bed. She heard the soft gush of air as the door closed and got up and put her robe on. She went over to the bedroom window and pulled back the drapes. The window afforded a clear view of Lincoln Boulevard, and she stood there waiting to see Henry leave the building. Reliving the litany of offenses he had committed against her had become as regular a part of her day as a morning cup of coffee. This morning was no different than any other morning, and if a good night's rest had reduced her anger, a mental recitation of the previous day's events would renew it.

Yesterday morning he had come into the bathroom and used the toilet while she was showering. She had locked the door. She always did. He didn't knock. He tried the door and when it wouldn't open, he asked her to let him in. He said he was in a hurry and was late for court. She unlocked the door and let him in. She was shampooing her hair and she heard him unbuckle his pants, then she heard the steady stream of his urine hitting the water in the toilet bowl. He sighed when he was finished and mumbled something about how good that felt. She was about to ask him not to flush the toilet, but before she could say anything, he flushed. The quick flush robbed the cold water from her shower and she had to stand on her toes at the back of the bathtub to keep from getting scalded. He fixed his pants, then opened the bathroom window all the way and left the room. The warm morning breeze pushed the curtains back and slowly the room aired out. She finished showering and reached for the bath towel hung on a hook behind the door at the same time Henry came back into the room. He pushed open the door and knocked her arm away and, without any apology, said, "I'm leaving now. You're not working late tonight, are you? We're eating at the club tomorrow night with the Sterns. It's lobster night. I told them we'd pick them up at seven. Tonight I'll meet you at Tsing's at six, see you then." He didn't wait for her reply. She said nothing, but at that moment she hated him.

Later that day when she was on her way home from work, the train she was on broke down. It happened in the tunnel that ran under the river and connected Huguenot City proper with the Upper Borough. The train was stuck for almost a half an hour. The weather above ground was in the seventies and sunny. Underground it was hot and humid. Maria had a seat, but the subway car she was in was crowded. The windows on the train were closed and it was hot and stuffy. She was happy for the seat, and to pass the time she started the crossword puzzle in the Huguenot City *News* she had bought at the mid-town station before boarding the train. She rarely read the paper, but always completed part of the crossword puzzle. An occasional headline would catch her interest and she would read the story, but as a rule, she found news stories repetitive and saw no point in reading the paper every day.

It was almost six-thirty when the train pulled into Monmouth Road. She knew that by the time she got to Tsing's Henry would be halfway through dinner. That was just one more thing about him she hated.

They ate out two nights a week, sometimes three. Occasionally, Henry asked her where she wanted to go, but normally he announced at breakfast or before he left for work where they would eat that night. Eating at Tsing's once a week was a perfect example. Maria disliked Chinese food. She even disliked Tsing more. She found him fawning, unctuous and insincere. Henry loved him. Dinner at Tsing's Chinese Garden was never served without an appearance by Tsing at their table. He would always find some little thing wrong at their table and apologize for the poor service and after correcting the error remind them of how he valued their business and was honored to serve them. Tsing's praise was always offered in a voice loud enough for the other customers to hear. Tsing would then bow over the table and whisper, "Of course, I have cook make special for you and missus. You the best, Mistah Wice, I tell cook put extra shrimp in your dish. Ha, ha!" Funny, she thought, you never knew if he was really insulting them when he pronounced their last name, "Wice."

The door to the ladies room was opposite the kitchen entrance, and on many occasions Maria had seen Tsing in the kitchen yelling at the cooks and dishwashers. She had seen him shake and strike his employees. She had seen the veins bulge in his neck and heard the high-pitched railing of his foreign harangue, and even though she didn't know what he was saying, there was no mistaking his anger. His vitriol was translated across the tired faces of his workers. They pushed their chins into their necks and lowered their eyes. The shoulders folded forward and the fingers fidgeted; to speak back in anger or defense meant unemployment. Tsing was the boss. That was the real Tsing and not the obeisant Oriental puppet he pretended to be. Maria had voiced her dislike often. Henry derided it. He said Tsing was a smart, tough businessman. He treated his customers well and he made his employees work. If the food was good and the price was right, who were they to complain? She ordered the lo mein, but she ended up only eating a little bit of it. Tsing came over to the table and made a fuss. He put his hands up and touched his chin with his fingertips and said, "Something wrong, Missus Wice? You not eating the lo mein?" She said she didn't feel well. Henry told Tsing to wrap it up; he'd take it home. Tsing said he wouldn't charge them for it. When they left, Henry went on about what a concerned and generous host Tsing was. Maria told him it was ten cents worth of greasy spaghetti with a couple of pieces of shrimp and vegetables thrown in and it was tasteless. Maria told Henry she wasn't eating there any more. Henry told her she was unreasonable, and furthermore, Tsing was a client. What was good for business was good for Henry. That was the end of the discussion and she didn't talk to him the rest of the evening.

Later in bed, he rolled against her and started to rub her breast. That was Henry's mating call. She had turned away from him and pushed his hand away. She didn't talk and he just rolled over and went to sleep. That was Henry, never an argument. The least talkative lawyer she had ever known.

Their apartment was on the eighth floor of the Excelsior. It was one of the finest apartment buildings on Lincoln Boulevard. Henry had moved into the building in 1941. That was a year before he had entered the Army. He kept it through the war, and when she married him in 1948 it reminded her of moving into an expensive hotel. He gave her a free hand to redecorate, but she had done little over the past seventeen years. Different draperies, new carpets and bedspreads were the only changes she had made. Most of his furnishings were tasteful, useful and expensive. Lincoln Boulevard was one of the most impressive streets in the Upper Borough. Its two service roads carried traffic north and south to all local streets, while the middle artery acted as a highway through the heart of the borough. Henry's law office was in the Boulevard Plaza at 888 Lincoln Boulevard. He was in walking distance of the Municipal Stadium and the Huguenot City criminal and civil court complex. He had season tickets for all the local teams, and judges, court clerks and administrative hearing officers were often his guests at the games. Every morning Henry left the apartment, crossed the street and waited for the Number One bus. If the bus didn't arrive right away, he hailed a cab. It was the same ride, thirty blocks or so. Bus or cab, it didn't matter

She was growing impatient waiting for him to leave, and she assumed he was deep in conversation with the doorman about some recent sporting event, probably baseball. Sports were a big part of Henry's life and a subject he loved to talk about; that is, if you knew something about them. She opened the window and took a deep breath of the warm June air. She felt a tightening around her temples and knew another migraine was on its way. Dr. Sklar had attributed the migraines to menopause, but she thought they were the byproduct of a life that had grown increasingly dismal with no prospect of improvement.

Henry was a major source of her discontent, and while she sucked in the clear morning air, hoping to mitigate the oncoming pain, she ran through the roll call of his recent sins: barging into the bathroom and flushing when she was in the shower, snoring all night in bed, giving her a hard time about Tsing and demanding that she like everything he liked. Everything in their marriage was taken for granted. The money she earned as a sales manager in Sable's for Lorient Cosmetics was hers to do as she pleased. Henry took nothing from her and gave everything; at least he did in economic terms. Clothes, housing, entertainment, club membership, cleaning woman, and every other expense was managed and paid for by Henry. Maria didn't shop for food like other women. She called in her order to the local grocer. The money she earned went into the bank or was spent on the things she wanted. That was Henry's way of maintaining power. He never said, "No," and more often than not he was the one offering while she was the one declining. Yet, there was a comfort to their existence that she could not deny, and going to Puerto Rico or Vegas two or three times a year wasn't such a tough thing to do.

Finally, Henry stepped from the courtyard onto the sidewalk and started across the busy thoroughfare. For just a moment she wished a car would come careening down the street and obliterate him. That wasn't about to happen, and she watched him cross the street. His gait was slightly opened-toed and he carried himself with a sense of confidence and openness. It was a warm day and he was wearing a loose-fitting summer suit. When he turned and stopped to wait at the bus stop, Maria could see the small swell of his growing paunch. He put his briefcase down and lit a cigarette. As he breathed the smoke in and released it, she could follow the rise of his stomach and it looked as if the front of his shirt was coming out of his pants. His thinning hair was slicked back across his head and the heavy splash of Vaseline hair tonic he used every morning made his bald spot shine in the harsh glare of the morning sun. Henry had turned fifty-three the month before and was starting to show his age. He had hurt his knee playing handball last December, and for the past six months he had stopped exercising entirely. The lack of vigorous exercise hadn't affected his habits and he still ate, smoked and drank as he always had. He had bought his summer suits at the Robert Hall two blocks from their apartment house. It was an impulse purchase and she chided him for not having gone to his regular tailor.

Henry Weiss was a pleasant man, and as he stood waiting for the bus, he looked up and could see Maria looking down from their eighth floor window. Was she watching because she couldn't let the day start without silently seeing him, or did she just want to make sure he was gone for the day? He would have preferred the former, but he knew it was the latter. Her moods of late seemed to be darker, more frequent and unnecessary. Life could be so good for the two of them. *Why bitch about every little thing?* he thought.

A Yellow Taxi came down the block and he stepped off the curb and waved it down. *Funny*, he mused, *the cab always beats the bus.* Maria always waited for the bus. She thought Henry was too extravagant. That, he knew, was a major difference between them. She wasn't cheap, but she hated waste. He liked to eat out and she liked to eat in. What she called food—salad, vegetables and almost no meat—he called rabbit feed. She told him his diet would kill him, and he told her it was a great way to die. Tonight was lobster night. She'd eat half a lobster and a bowl of salad. No bread, no potatoes, no linguine, no dessert. She would knock down a couple of glasses of wine and what if she had one too many? Then she'd pick at him. Tell him he ate and drank too much. Tell him if she was good and tight that he wasn't Rudy. The ghost of her first husband was always there. The teenage romance turned to tragedy.

11

She never spoke about him other than to speak his name, but Henry had seen the picture and the way Maria looked at it. Rudy was the love of her life and she was married to his memory. Henry was the crutch she used to get through life. His only way to contest that memory was to refuse to acknowledge that Rudy had ever existed. If she brought his name up, he offered no response. The time she showed him the pictures, he offered no response. He was always a good litigator and knew that the less you said about something the better off you often were. Yet, Maria was the most beautiful woman he had ever known. It was hard to believe she was fifty years of age. She looked thirty. Her hair was a mix of brown and gold that radiated with the light. Her skin was smooth and blemish free with no wrinkles and had a natural tint of honey that had such a healthful glow to it that, other than lipstick, she never needed to wear makeup. Diet and exercise, and the fact that she'd never been pregnant left her with a much younger woman's figure. Henry adored her for all the superficial reasons men adore beautiful woman. He knew it and he didn't care. She could be as cranky and bitchy as she wanted, and even if she did drink a little too much from time to time, there was no man whom he knew of at his age had a wife as good looking as his. It was a great source of pride, and the best part was that she was no kid. She had great legs, a small waist and big tits. She knew how to dress to show it all off, but not in a cheap way, and when she walked by, men looked. Shit, teenagers looked. Plenty of guys could dump the missus and marry some young babe, but the rub was always there that if you could pull that off you must have money and the money was the only reason you got the girl. His was the real article and he loved everything about her. She was an addiction he could never give up, and even if he had to satisfy his appetites elsewhere he would never leave her. The cab pulled to the corner of Lincoln Boulevard and Court Street and Henry got out. He walked across the busy boulevard and made a mental note to have Sophie, his secretary, send her some flowers that morning. He was looking forward to a nice night out and a peaceful weekend. Flowers always worked.

Henry was an attorney. He referred to himself as an L and T attorney. The L and T stood for landlord and tenant respectively. The fact that he had never, or wouldn't admit to having ever, represented a tenant made no difference. The Upper Borough of Huguenot City was his playing field. What were once several farms wedged between the calm waters of the sound to the east and the river to the west had grown by 1965, into a sprawling tract of apartment buildings and attached homes punctuated by parks and lined with elevated train lines. Huguenot City was founded in 1690 and incorporated as a city in 1888.

In 1896 it absorbed the hodgepodge of villages and hamlets that began at its southern and eastern boundaries and stretched for ten miles to the sandy beaches of the Atlantic coast. The new addition to the city was christened the Lower Borough. Shortly after the turn of the century the villages and hamlets to the north of Huguenot City were incorporated into the city as well and designated the Upper Borough. Strangely enough, there was no Middle Borough. The city had one mayor, one district attorney and three official political subdivisions for the purposes of council representation. Huguenot City proper was a bustling metropolis, but the Upper and Lower Burroughs were, at best, a collection of small villages passing as neighborhoods. Henry had been born and raised in Riverview. It was a verdant suburban section of the Upper Borough that was bordered by the river and just west of the sprawling working class neighborhood of Kingsbridge. As a child growing up, Henry had witnessed the urbanization of the Upper Borough. The construction of the elevated and underground train lines from Huguenot City into the Upper Borough had spawned a prolific and chaotic growth in the housing market. Farms vanished and apartment buildings sprung up on vacant lots like weeds and hordes of blue collar workers immigrated to the borough with the promise of spacious rooms, indoor plumbing, heat and hot water and nearby parks for their children to play in. The development of Lincoln Boulevard was the conception of city planners who understood that a thriving borough teeming with workers would create a commercial and professional class of people who would be loathe to live in the same apartment buildings and residential neighborhoods of single family homes as the people who butchered their meat, picked up their garbage and performed all of the other sweat-breaking and knuckle-busting jobs that make a civilization work. Lincoln Boulevard began as a concept around the newly built Municipal Stadium and Huguenot City Court complex, and in the ten years between 1918 and 1928 over a hundred luxury apartment buildings were constructed. The lawyers, doctors and businessmen who catered to the borough's inhabitants assumed a higher station in life and took their rightful place on the Boulevard. Those who preferred a more suburban locale moved to Riverview and took up residence in the many oversized single-family homes recently built. Henry's maturation from childhood to adulthood absorbed all of this and to him, the Upper Borough was still a farm. His practice cultivated landlords and small businessmen. He managed their properties and sometimes their problems. He helped them buy and sell their businesses and for his efforts he derived many benefits. He made money and lived well. He owned no property. He rented his office in the

Boulevard Plaza and from his window in a corner office he saw the courthouses, the stadium and the sea of apartment houses with the television antennas lining their roofs like tombstones in a cemetery that knew no boundaries. Not a day went by when he wouldn't stand by his office window and look out with appreciation at the buildings and the people; everything good that had happened in his life had happened in the Upper Borough.

Chapter Two

She watched the cab move down the street and when she could no longer see it, closed the drape, left the bedroom and went down the hallway to the living room. They didn't own a camera. Neither of them had come to the marriage with one and they had never felt the need to buy one. Maria looked around the living room, and on the mantle over the fireplace there were two framed black and white photos. One was of her and Henry in Havana in 1948 while they were on their honeymoon, and the other was taken at the Flamingo in Las Vegas in the mid 1950s. The Havana photo was her favorite. She was wearing a periwinkle blue cocktail dress. Henry was in a white dinner jacket and the photographer had captured them dancing just at a point when they were turning toward the camera, unaware of the photographer's presence. They were both smiling and the shot was very natural and relaxed. They looked like two people in love. The Flamingo picture had the two of them at a banquette. The table was covered with half-eaten plates of food and empty drink glasses. Henry had a cigarette in his hand and Maria had a wine glass in hers. It was the traditional nightclub shot, and Maria surmised that it was Henry's favorite. The only other photograph was on an end table, and that was of the two of them in evening clothes being received by the captain of a cruise ship on the Royale line when they had taken a trip to Bermuda some years ago. That was it; those were the only pictures she had of the two of them. Others had taken photographs at different affairs, but the only photographs she had were the ones in the living room.

Maria had a remarkable memory. It was inherited, she believed, from her father, and it proved to be the dominant characteristic of her personality. Remembering names and faces came easy to her, just as learning English, Spanish and French had been. But where others were able to remember the good times in their lives as being better than they were and, similarly were able to diminish and gloss over the bad times, Maria remembered everything just as it had occurred; and for her there was more bad than good.

She picked up the photo of them dancing, the one in Havana. She looked happy, and at the time, for the moment, she was. She held the frame in her hands and recalled how much fun they'd had on their honeymoon, what a good dancer Henry was, and how easy going and willing to please he had been. Still, from the very beginning she had doubts about how she really felt about him and how long the marriage would last. Henry had expressed no interest in her past. It was as if she hadn't existed before she met him and the only past was the time spent with him. She had met him in London in 1943. They went on a blind date with another couple. She was working as a civilian translator for the Royal Navy and he was assigned to the Army Corps of Engineers. They went out three more times and then he was transferred. He wrote her several times thereafter, friendly letters, nothing remotely romantic, and after the war was over he sent her his address in the States and offered a dinner invitation should she ever travel there. In 1946, she obtained a visa and moved to Washington, D.C. She secured a job as a French teacher in a private girl's academy and wasted no time in letting Henry know she had come to the States. Nine months later she abandoned the teaching position and moved to Huguenot City. It all happened quickly, and by January 1948 they were married and she was in Havana, in the periwinkle blue dress, on the cusp of happiness, or so she thought. She put the photo down and wiped the frame and glass with the hem of her nightgown. *That was so long ago; what happened to me?* she thought. *What happened?*

It was a beautiful June morning and here she was with a migraine approaching with all the threat of a hurricane, and instead of resting and clearing her mind, she was traipsing down her own bitter, memory lane. Why did she never buy a camera, why didn't she take pictures, she thought? And she knew the answer: there was nothing worth preserving in the marriage. A fact sadly proved, or so she thought, not long after they were married.

She recalled one incident in particular where Henry's cold disinterest in whom she had been really upset her. It was February of 1949, and they had only been married a year. Not much longer than she had been married to Rudy.

16

The fireplace burned gas instead of wood and had a receptacle for incense. Henry had bought sandalwood scented incense, and when the fireplace was on he would place a small pellet of the incense in a metal plate that sat over the grill. The scent was not overpowering and was very pleasant, and reminded her of the smell of the wood fire in her grandfather's bakery. Maria had poured them each a glass of wine and they were listening to music on the radio. Warm memories came back and she told Henry about the bakery and her childhood and how happy she had been and how she missed everyone so much. They were sitting on the couch, listening to the music and watching the fire glow. Maria asked Henry if he'd like to see some pictures of her family and her first husband Rudy. The pictures were over fifteen years old and everyone in them, with the exception of herself and her sister were dead. She had wanted to show him the album for some time, but she was unsure about how he would react since half of the pictures were of Rudy. She kept putting it off, waiting for the right moment. That night, she remembered thinking, was the right moment. She had thought about taking all of the pictures of Rudy out of the album, but felt that would have been dishonest. Rudy was dead and Henry was her husband. He would understand. Henry seemed reluctant at first, but after a brief silence he told her to go get the album.

She had told him the story of her family several times; her father's death in Africa in 1933, and the fire in the bakery that turned to a conflagration and consumed the apartments above, and with them her husband of nine months, mother, grandparents, aunt and uncle. She had told him all about it, but she had never put faces on the names. The faces were in the album and she wanted him to see them and, somehow, to acknowledge her history.

She then went to the bedroom and removed the album from the bottom drawer of her bureau. If nothing else, she believed Henry would be interested in what she looked like as a young woman; he so prized her looks. And from a rival's point of view, he would have some desire to measure himself against her first husband, even if it was only a picture and Maria's memory of him. After all, they were still practically children and she and Henry were mature adults.

She sat next to him on the couch, making sure to nestle to him closely. She opened the book and the first page was a large, slightly browned photo of Maria and Rudy on their wedding day. Henry said nothing. The book lay open on her lap for what seemed several minutes, but Henry offered no comment. She turned the page and the pictures were all of Rudy. Again, he said nothing. She turned to another page and pointed out family members, a big photo of the bakery with the large *Steinmetz Brothers* emblazoned in big black gothic letters above the shop window. Each picture, each comment by her received the same mute stare. Finally, when she had finished going through the book, she turned and said to him, "Don't you have any feelings? Do you have any interest in me at all?"

Henry's response was a simple shrug. "Hey, c'mon, you know I love you, that's the past. It's a book full of pictures of people I'll never meet or know. What do you expect me to say? Yes, they look like nice people. Yes, you looked beautiful and happy. Yes, your husband was a charming young fellow, so what. They're all dead and gone. I know you miss them, but I can't bring them back and there is nothing I can do or say that will change that. They're just pictures of strangers to me, nothing more. I'm not a sentimental man, I'm sorry if I hurt your feelings."

Reliving that moment was still painful, and she remembered silently getting up from the couch and returning to the bedroom to put the album away. She recalled the tears in her eyes and her disappointment with him. She remembered putting the album back and the strong desire she had to show him the second photo album in her drawer; the one in the green leather portfolio with the letters AK embossed in gold on the front of it. That was the album she'd like to show him and someday would.

It was a morning for feeling anger and melancholy and Maria's mind returned to a second incident concerning the photo album, an unpleasant scene she had with Henry's sister Gloria. It was around 1952, sometime before the November elections. One night they had Henry's brother and sister and their spouses to dinner. At that time in their marriage she saw little of them and was uncertain about her feelings toward them. Their marriage had been a civil ceremony, neither wanted a wedding, and the only witnesses were Henry's close friend Jack Stern and his wife Bobbi. Henry's mother and father had died some years ago, and Maria had never met them. Henry was fond of his brother and sister, but they all led busy lives and the three of them never got together more than three or four times a year.

His sister Gloria was the baby of the family. She and her husband Joel were public school teachers at the time. Gloria taught mathematics and Joel was a social studies teacher. Gloria loved to argue and never shut up. Joel was quiet and extremely well-mannered. He was clearly Gloria's opposite, and if Gloria went too far in making a point, which she almost always did, Joel was ready to offer a counterpoint and reduce whatever tension Gloria had created. Henry's brother Steven had followed in their father's footsteps and become a medical doctor. Steven had a general practice in Washburn, twenty minutes north of Huguenot City and had married his office nurse. Her name was Muriel and she incessantly talked about her children and Steven's practice; there seemed to be little else in her universe that interested her.

Dinner was finished and Maria cleared the dishes and served coffee. The three women were seated in the living room and the three men were at the dining room table playing cards. Muriel asked Maria if she still had any relatives in Europe. Maria told her that everyone was dead, and that the only one still living was her sister Alyss in Minnesota.

"Do you have pictures of any of them?" Muriel asked.

Maria knew that Muriel was just trying to make conversation and that she was looking for a diversion from Gloria's endless political lectures.

"Yes, I have an album. It's very old, but there isn't really much in it," Maria answered.

Muriel offered a warm smile and said, "Oh, it must be very difficult having no family. I'd be lost without my three sisters. I'd love to see the album. I just love old pictures."

Gloria, who had ignored Maria for most of the evening and dominated the dinner conversation either championing Stevenson's bid for the presidency or disparaging the government's case against the Rosenbergs, said, "Oh, yes, Maria, I'd love to see pictures of your family. Henry's never told us much about them. Have you, Henry?" she added.

Henry offered no comment and Maria, reluctantly, went to the bedroom to retrieve the album. Maria opened the dresser drawer and undid the linen cloth that covered the album. On top was the green portfolio. She was tempted to bring that out and show them, but she knew it was just a whim. She took out the photo album, carefully placed the linen cover back and closed the drawer. When she came down the hallway and turned to the living room, she was struck by the sight of Muriel and Gloria sitting on opposite ends of one of the couches. They looked like two misplaced bookends.

The smoke from Gloria's cigarette languidly climbed to the ceiling in a blue haze. She turned and smiled as Maria came down the stairs. Gloria's smile was predatory, and at times she had the look of a woman who was happiest planning an execution. Gloria was tall and lean, yet she didn't look skinny. There was certain shapeliness to her figure that was exceptionally attractive. Her hair was brown and wavy and fell freely to her shoulders. Her eyes were wide and deep brown, and they complemented her thin lips and broad smile. Her nose was long and slightly hooked, and the overall composition of her face was one

19

of feral beauty. Muriel, by comparison, was quite tame looking. She was short and bosomy and had a warm expressive smile. Her blond hair was washed and rinsed and touched up at the hairdresser's weekly and sprayed into place daily. She sat with her ankles crossed and her body language emanated a distinct sense of propriety and caution. She was very passive and abhorred conflict of any type. Her tiresome prattle about her children or Steven's practice wore thin, but she never meant any harm and truly wanted to be Maria's friend. She enjoyed people and, perhaps, in her own way, was far more secure in her world than Gloria was in hers.

Muriel turned to Maria and said, "Oh, I love old family albums. I'm dying to see what your family was like."

Gloria exhaled a long stream of smoke through her nostrils and added, "Yes, Maria, I'm quite anxious, too."

Maria sat down on the couch between the two women and placed the album on her lap. Henry, Steven and Joel were still seated at the dining room table and were engaged in a game of gin rummy. Muriel called to Steven to come and look at the photographs, but he told her he was playing cards and would look later. Maria opened it to the first page and showed them her wedding picture. Muriel immediately complimented her. "Maria, you made a beautiful bride. The gown's gorgeous. Was it hand made?"

"Yes, it was my mother's. Her mother and aunt made it for her." Neither Muriel nor Gloria offered any comment about Rudy. Maria turned the page and there was a group of photographs of Rudy in a gymnasium. He was in tights and was wearing a tee shirt. Maria told them that Rudy was an amateur gymnast and belonged to a gymnastic club. The photos were very flattering and showed off his sleek and muscular build. Rudy was very proud of his athletic ability, and in each of the photos he wore a big smile. It was if he was saying, "Look at me, look at me." He had dark brown hair and very light skin and deep dark eyes. The faded black and white photos failed to capture his color, but his musculature and confidence were evident.

Muriel was impressed. "He's very handsome. How old was he in these photos?"

Maria said that Rudy was two years older than she was, that Rudy was about twenty when those pictures were taken. Maria went on to tell them that the photographs were taken of Rudy and other gymnasts for a journal their club was sponsoring to raise money.

Gloria had said nothing to this point, then asked Maria, "What was his last name?"

Maria replied, "Kaval, Rudy Kaval."

"Is that a German name?" Gloria asked.

"No, it's Czech," replied Maria.

Gloria then turned the page and there were various photos of the family in different groups, and the photo of Maria's father in a safari outfit.

Gloria laughed. "Who's that? My God, what an outlandish outfit, and that mustache, it looks like something a Civil War general would have worn."

Maria bristled at the remark. "That outlandish man was my father."

"Oh, I'm only teasing," said Gloria. "I'm sure there are plenty of family photos we have that would give you a laugh. Please, he just looks a little comical. Was he going on a safari?"

"Well, in fact, he was leaving for a trip to Cameroon in Africa. My father was a language professor, and the government had hired him to accompany some officials on a trip to Cameroon about rubber plantations. My father was the translator. Many of the Cameroon officials spoke French and Bantu. My father was fluent in most European languages, and could also speak some Arabic and Bantu. He also had a wonderful sense of humor and the mustache, was a...well, it was his mustache. I never thought he looked comical," she added with a bit of emotion.

"Maria, don't get upset, Gloria's just kidding," Muriel plaintively said.

"Well, he died on that trip, and we only have a few pictures of him. I guess it is a funny photograph." Maria said with resignation. She did not want to have an argument with her sister-in-law.

Gloria then asked Maria, "What was your father's name?"

"Franz Dvorak," Maria answered.

"He was Czech, too?" Gloria asked.

"Czech and German. Both of my parents were Czech on one side and German on the other side. Prague has a very large German population, many of them Jewish, in fact, and it wasn't unusual for a Czech to marry a German. After all, is there any real difference among all the Europeans?" Maria said.

Muriel, who had nervously sat through this exchange, was quick to add, "You're so right, Maria. Why do we make so much out of what people are?"

Maria then followed, "For instance, Henry said your mother's family was from Germany and your father's from Austria. What's the difference?"

At that remark, Gloria expelled a great puff of smoke from her mouth, stubbed out her cigarette and said, "Rubbish! Our family is Jewish. Germany and Austria were just places they lived. No different than Jews in Spain or Japan for that matter. I would never think of myself as German or Austrian!"

she said with disdain. "Tell me, Maria, what year was it your father went on his fatal trip?"

"1933," Maria replied.

"…1933…weren't the Nazi's in control then? Was your father a Nazi? And when was it your family moved to Berlin? Didn't you tell me once that you moved there when you were ten?" Gloria asked in an accusatory tone.

Maria's faced reddened and she looked up to Henry for some relief, but he was deep in his card game with Steven, and Joel and appeared unaware of the mounting tension between them. While Maria knew her father had joined the Nazi party, she also knew that this occurred in 1932 before anyone was aware of the atrocities to follow, or so she thought. And her father being a gentle and kindhearted, though demanding man, would have never remained loyal to such a vile organization as the Nazi party had he lived to see what it would become. And, after all, he was only a member for a few months, then he died. She wanted to smash Gloria's face in, but simply replied, "No, he wasn't a Nazi, and I don't understand where this is going, Gloria."

Gloria didn't let up. "Maria, you seem very defensive. I just find your family and, if you must know, your own personal journey through life mysterious. I'm not saying suspicious, but mysterious. I'm just curious, and when you take such quick offense, I become that much more curious. In fact, I find it rather odd that you have no accent."

At that point Muriel volunteered to make another pot of coffee. All she wanted to do was get out of the room.

Maria frowned, and said, "What's mysterious? My father drowned, my husband and the rest of my family, those closest to me, you know, except for my sister, died in a terrible fire and I was left on my own at nineteen years of age. And, as for my accent," she said in a rising tone, "might I remind you that my father was a linguist. We spoke English in our home every day. Father was a great admirer of the United States and believed that English would someday be the universal language. And I've lived in English speaking countries since 1936."

"You don't have to get your water hot; I'm just interested in your past!" Gloria said without the slightest change in tone.

"What is this, an interrogation?" Maria replied indignantly.

"Just a friendly question and answer," Gloria offered. "And what happened to you and your sister?"

"I rented a room, and after several months of sitting around feeling sorry for myself, I got a job with an import/export company. The owner of the company was named Amos Koch and he had been a regular customer at the bakery. After the fire, he contacted me and asked me if I wanted to work for him as a translator. He knew I was fluent in Spanish and English. I went to work for him in January of 1935. He had a factory in Argentina where they canned meat. As for my sister, she was engaged to an American who worked for the Chicago *Tribune* and he was taking her to Chicago where he'd been reassigned."

"Then what?" Gloria said. "Was this Mr. Koch a Nazi? After all, wasn't Argentina one of the hot spots for Nazis on the run?"

"Of course he was. He and my father were Hitler's top advisers," replied Maria sarcastically. "Is that what you want to hear?"

"Oh, don't be so Goddamn defensive. It's just that I'm a little sensitive to what happened over there. Genocide is such an interesting subject, you know, and I'm one of those people who believe that the German people are all guilty. I know that sounds extreme, but I don't know how a country can go into the business of killing millions of people and its citizens not know what's going on." Gloria lit another cigarette and inhaled deeply. She got up and went to the window, and pointing into the night toward the skyline of silhouetted buildings, said, "Maybe I've been a little rude and accusatory, but I do have a problem with all that. It's as if everyone in Massachusetts and Connecticut was put to death over a period of time and no one noticed." She turned toward Maria. "Maria," she said, "I really mean it, how do you feel about all of this?"

Muriel came back in and said, "I plugged the pot in; it should be ready in about ten minutes. Who wants another cup?"

Henry, Steven and Joel each answered "I do."

Maria knew they had heard the whole conversation. She wished Henry had come to her defense, but it seemed no one ever wanted to tangle with Gloria.

Muriel sat back down on the couch.

Gloria said, "What I really want is another glass of wine." She then went over to the buffet in the dining room and poured a glass. While she was pouring the wine, she called out to Maria, "So tell me, Maria, how you feel?"

Maria put the album on the coffee table and looked over to Gloria. "It's a long story. I went to work for Mr. Koch, and after six months he told me he was moving his business to Argentina. He saw what was happening in Germany. His wife was Argentine and a Catholic, but Mr. Koch was Jewish. She left two months after I started working for him. It was a terrible time. The government was taking over Jewish businesses and there were rumors that Mr. Koch had supplied provisions to the allies in World War I. The company had offices in Argentina and Berlin, but almost all of his products were sold in Europe. He had a lot of money in German banks, and he couldn't get it out. In December of 1935, he closed the Berlin office and we left for France. So, I didn't know what was happening in Germany; I didn't know what was happening in my own life. I was only twenty and on my way to another country. We stayed in Paris for almost a year, then we went to London. He set up an office in London and I stayed there and he went back to Argentina. He rented a flat for me and paid the rent for a year. One month after he left, I received word that the London office was shutting down and that was the last I heard of him. I then got a job with the Royal Navy as a civilian translator and stayed with them until 1946, when I was able to obtain a visa and moved to Washington. Not very mysterious, was it?"

Gloria smirked. "I'm sure there are some juicy parts of the story you left out, weren't there? Why did you go to France together?"

Maria's cheeks reddened, and she replied, "Well, I did meet Henry in London in 1943, but you had better ask him about that."

"I meant Koch; how did Henry enter the story?" Gloria said with a slight sneer.

Maria ignored the remark and reached over to the album and turned to a new page. She sensed that Gloria's interest in it had faded, and she picked up the book and got up from the couch.

Muriel turned to her and asked, "Maria, could I just see the rest of the pictures?"

Maria smiled and answered, "Of course, go ahead."

Muriel picked up the book and went across the room to the leather chairs and sat in one and went through the rest of the album, but she never asked another question.

Gloria looked bored and then in a very sarcastic way, said, "That was very nice of your Mr. Koch friend to pay your rent for a year, wasn't it?"

Maria didn't immediately answer. She got up from the couch and walked toward the windows, and as she passed Gloria she said in a hushed, but angry tone, "You are such a bitch. You think you know everything; you think you know better than anyone else. You don't know what I went through, and maybe someday when you grow up I'll tell you about me!"

Gloria smiled at Maria, turned her head and said, "Henry, there's so much about Maria we don't know."

Henry put down his cards and looked toward the two women. "What you don't know can't hurt you. That's your problem, Glory; you just have to know everything, right, Joel?"

Joel laughed and said, "Problem with Gloria is that she's stuck in Huguenot Central High School teaching geometry to girls who refuse to answer any of her questions or pay her any attention. Tonight she has a captive audience and she wants a response."

They all had a laugh, then Henry said, "I can smell the coffee. C'mon, Maria, let's put out the dessert."

Maria took the album from Muriel and went to the bedroom to put it away. They were all laughing, Henry most of all. He was now calling Gloria the house detective. It was if her interrogation was just an innocent parlor game.

Maria remembered it all so vividly, and most of all she recalled Henry's mocking tone. It was the second time that morning she hated him.

Chapter Three

Almost thirteen years had passed since that unpleasant exchange with Gloria, and Maria never forgave her, but over the course of time the friction eased and they maintained a cordial relationship. They would kiss one another hello, but the physical exchange was interesting to watch. Each was apprehensive of the other, and the kiss was usually more of a touching of cheeks than a light pressing of the lips to the skin.

Maria liked it that way and she supposed that Gloria felt the same.

Gloria's passion for argument hadn't ebbed, and she remained a passionate advocate of practically everything that went against the status quo. She supported a host of liberal causes and was well informed on all the political issues of the day, but she was primarily a debater and there was scant evidence that she actively pursued her convictions beyond the voting booth. She was brash, outspoken and refreshingly guileless and, with experience, Maria learned how to read her and what it was she could do or say to either mollify Gloria or appease her.

There was one aspect of Gloria's personality and character that Maria admired, and it was Gloria's devotion to her children and, to a lesser extent, her students. She was a caring mother and teacher, and it was an area in her life where she was successful and totally resistant to praise. If her sons did well, it was because of their effort and not hers. If her students achieved successes, it wasn't because of endless hours of additional tutoring and coaching from Gloria, it was because the students worked hard and desired success. And it was that characteristic that was so evident in Gloria that was missing in her older brother.

Henry was self-indulgent and grossly superficial. There was nothing strident about him, because few things, if any, upset him. There was no urgency to Henry Weiss' life. He avoided controversy and kept most of his feelings to himself. Maria had informed him before their marriage that she didn't want to have children, at least not right away. Henry told her that was fine with him and never raised the subject again. They practiced birth control and Maria realized that her expressed desire prior to their marriage was probably exactly what Henry had wanted all along. He never talked about children, and now, at fifty, Maria was too old to have children and sorely regretted having not had them. A child would have created a bond between her and Henry, a bond that never existed. Her life seemed meaningless.

Dwelling on these thoughts increased the likelihood of the migraine worsening and she went to the bathroom and turned on the shower. She turned the cold water tap all the way on and didn't touch the hot water. She undressed and climbed into the shower and stood under the ice-cold spray. The cold water was a shock, but she was prepared for it and the shock often helped reduce the intensity of her headaches. A cold shower, light breakfast and brisk walk outdoors had proven to be a better remedy for her blinding migraines than the doctor's prescription of total rest and quiet. *I'll eat breakfast, get dressed and go for a walk to the river,* she thought. *Maybe that will make me feel better.*

Maria went into the kitchen and opened the refrigerator door. Several waxed paper containers that held the remnants of the past evening's dinner from Tsing's occupied the middle shelf. She moved them out of the way and found a container of strawberries. The container was half empty and held a mix of whole and half-eaten berries. Maria shook her head and took the container over to the sink. She took the whole berries out, washed them, placed them in a bowl and threw the remaining half eaten fruit in the garbage. She filled a cereal bowl with bran flakes and sliced the strawberries over them and added milk. She sat and ate her breakfast, and while she ate, she came to the conclusion that Henry would never change. His personal hygiene was faultless, but his manners, when no one was present but Maria, were boorish. The old adage that familiarity breeds contempt was alive in the Weiss household. At a restaurant or in the company of others he was a gentleman, but if they were home and alone, he scratched, burped, farted, picked his toenails or blew his nose into his table napkin without excuse or

27

embarrassment. It was common for Henry to go into the refrigerator and take a bite out of something, then put it back. She knew he figured it was something she wouldn't eat anyway, but it was a disgusting habit nonetheless. She didn't know if he just took her for granted, or he didn't care, but whatever the case, she was still there. Most importantly, she believed that Henry knew that she no longer loved him. She needed him, but she didn't love him. Although married, she was a kept woman, and her relationship with Henry was not any different than her relationship with Amos Koch. She often wondered if Henry had somebody else in his life.

Rudy had been her love and that was spoiled. What would Rudy be like now? They had been sworn to one another since their early teens. They could spend hours together and never say more than a few words, but still share a thousand thoughts. She remembered the hours they spent aimlessly walking the streets of Berlin. The fevered pitch their marathon coupling reached over the nine short months of their marriage. That too, would have ended and the reality of life together would have set in. Still, her teenage love, her young marriage had been such a time of joy, and why not she thought? The marriage was still young and fresh when it ended. Some marriages improve with age, but many she believed fall into disrepair like an old home that hasn't been maintained. Her marriage was in disrepair and she didn't care. Everything after Rudy was just the passage of time. She finished her cereal and came to the realization that she'd never be happy. Her life after Berlin had been spent waiting for something important to happen and while she waited, life went by.

She got up from the table and put the kettle on for tea. She cleaned the dishes and turned on the radio on the kitchen counter top. The rich baritone voice of the radio announcer filled the room and he was announcing the Housewife of the Day. *How silly radio is*, she thought. Every day on the Jack O. Riley morning show, or J.O.R. in the a.m., as he was known, one lucky listener was the recipient of the Housewife of the Day honor. The honoree's name was picked at random from the thousands of postcards contestants submitted weekly. The lucky lady, as J.O.R. liked to describe the winner, received a dozen roses from Fletcher's Florist in downtown Huguenot City and a gift certificate for twenty-five dollars to Sable's Department Store.

Maria worked at Sable's as the manager for Lorient Cosmetics and could never recall one of those Lucky Ladies cashing in their gift certificate at the Lorient counter. She asked a manager once why that was so. The answer was that the gift certificates were only redeemable in certain departments. The certificates could only be used for items that carried the Sable's label. It was an interesting concept, since the markup for Sable's items was steep; a gift certificate valued at twenty-five dollars might only cost the company seven dollars. Add in the advertising value and the extra money the "Lucky Ladies" often spent in the store and the promotion was a moneymaker. It was all so phony, but still, every week thousands of postcards were sent by hopeful housewives, yearning for that one minute interview with J.O.R. in the a.m. and the gift of flowers and a twenty-five dollar passport into Huguenot City's finest department store.

Silly or not, Maria enjoyed listening to the morning radio show. The station played mostly rock and roll, and Henry hated rock and roll. Every morning when he got up and went out to the kitchen for his coffee he would turn the radio on and find it tuned to J.O.R.'s station instead of his own morning choice of The Jackie Brown Morning Roundup. The roundup was a mix of news and popular standards—Sinatra, Nat King Cole, Peggy Lee and the hundred other middle of the road post World War II songbirds. Maria didn't care much for rock and roll, but the thrill of listening to Sinatra belt out *I Get A kick Out Of You* had waned years ago, and rock and roll annoyed Henry to no end, which made it all the more pleasurable to her ear.

She lowered the volume and took a pen and paper from the middle drawer under the kitchen counter, sat at the table and began making out her grocery list. When the list was completed, she called it into the Associated Market where they shopped for their groceries. After she was finished, she took her tea to the living room and sat on the couch. She surveyed the room, and said out loud, "I just love this apartment!"

The first time she saw the apartment was on her third date with Henry. They had gone to a dinner dance for the Bar Association, and after a night of dining, drinking and dancing, she told Henry she'd like to see his apartment. In fact, she told him she wanted to see his bedroom. She remembered walking in the door and seeing the sunken living room and the long row of uncovered windows with the moonlight brightening the room. Right then and there she knew she'd marry Henry, and even if the apartment had been the best part of the marriage, it was something that gave her great peace and comfort over the years.

The apartments in the Excelsior were very luxurious, particularly for the Upper Borough. Henry often said that their apartment rivaled ones you'd find on Huguenot Avenue, and they had it all for a third of the cost and within ten minutes of his office. When you came in the front door you were in a large foyer that led directly to the living room and to a hallway on the left that led to the two bedrooms and master bathroom and on the right that led to the dining room, kitchen, and pantry. They had a sunken living room, with one set of steps leading from the foyer and a second set leading to the dining room. The dining room was an open area just above the living room, and the nine-foot ceilings gave the apartment a cathedral-like spaciousness. The floors were oak parquet and were covered with various oriental carpets. The living room was long and wide, with four oversized windows facing Lincoln Boulevard, a fireplace at one end and the steps leading to the dining room at the other end. Two green leather chairs faced the fireplace, each with a round tea table to the far side and behind them toward the middle of the room two long tan crushed velour couches faced each other with a long glass coffee table between them. The windows had no treatments and faced west. Their placement on the eighth floor and the wide expanse of the boulevard made window coverings unnecessary.

Henry and Maria loved it when the afternoon sun bathed the apartment in sunlight, and even in the hottest weather when all windows were opened the apartment stayed cool. Maria could have sat there for hours, but she was expecting the grocery delivery by 11:00 a.m., and she wanted to be out of the apartment before the delivery boy came.

One of the attractions to the apartment was that it had a delivery entrance. There was a pantry off of the kitchen that opened to the service entrance. Their apartment line was the only one in the building that had this feature. There was a regular fire door with a lock at the rear of the kitchen. When you went through that door, you were in the pantry. The pantry had a box refrigerator, washing machine, dryer, shelves for groceries and a dumb waiter. They no longer used the dumb waiter to bring up packages or send out the garbage, and a cabinet they'd added some years ago covered the dumb waiter door. Normally, the delivery boy would bring the groceries up and ring the service bell. If they weren't going to be home, they would make arrangements with the doorman to let him up and buzz him into the pantry. The tip was added onto the grocery bill.

Walter Brown had been the delivery boy for as long as Maria could remember, and although there was never any need to see the delivery boy, over the years Maria had developed such a fondness for Walter that whenever she was home she would greet him and they would talk for a while. Walter aspired to be a songwriter and often he would sing his latest composition to Maria and wait for her reaction. He had a pleasant voice and Maria liked a lot of what he sang. She'd asked Henry if he could help Walter, and Henry had told her he'd ask around, but that was as far as that ever got.

Last week, when she was late getting ready for work, she called in the grocery order and expected to be gone before it arrived. She wasn't fully dressed when she heard the front doorbell ring. She hadn't heard the doorman call up to announce a visitor and she assumed it was either Henry, who was notorious for misplacing his keys, or her next-door neighbor, Mrs. Zimmerman. Edith Zimmerman loved to bake and it wasn't unusual for her to bake an extra coffee cake and drop it off for Henry. She'd known Henry since he moved into the building and, being considerably older, had always had a maternal affection for him. Maria didn't bother to look through the peephole, and when she opened the door she was surprised to see a tall, gangly teen standing there with two large boxes of groceries in his arms. She wasn't fully dressed and was wearing only her undergarments covered with a flimsy nightgown. She immediately realized that this was her grocery order, but didn't know why it wasn't Walter and had no idea why the boy was at her front door.

"Who are you?" she said as she clutched her nightgown and folded her arms across her chest.

The boy leered at her and said, "I'm here with your delivery. You called it in, didn't you?"

"Where's Walter, and why didn't you come up the service elevator?"

"Oh, someone's moving out and the elevator is tied up. Beery told me to wait, but then he wandered off and I figured I'd use the regular elevator and get this stuff up here. I have another delivery to make and my bike's sitting outside."

"Who's Beery, and you still didn't tell me what happened to Walter?"

He was still standing in the doorway holding the groceries. "Well, can I put these down somewhere first?"

"Please, come in."

As they walked in the apartment, the boy said, "Wow, this is some pad. My whole house could fit in your living room!"

Maria said nothing and led the way to the kitchen. She went to the far end of the kitchen and stood by the window. The sunlight was streaming through the kitchen window and Maria was suddenly conscious you could see right through her nightgown. She was also quite aware that the young man holding the boxes was staring at her. She was taken back by the brazen way he just stood there gaping at her. She turned and pulled down the kitchen shade and told him to put the boxes on the table.

He put them down, then smiled and said, "Walter got a promotion. He's the new produce manager. Old man Kimmel fired Balasco. He finally got wise that Balsaco's been stealing from him for years."

"How do you know that?" she queried.

"I been working there since December. Everyone knew Balasco and his son had a produce store on Eastborough Road."

He took his eyes off Maria and looked around the kitchen. On the counter top was a bowl of sourball candies. "Oh, I love these don't mind if I do, do ya?" he said as he leaned over the bowl and picked a few.

At that point Maria just wanted him gone, and she said to him, "Let me show you the service entrance." She was tempted to tell him to put the candies back, but he made her feel so uncomfortable that she just wanted him gone. She led him through the rear door of the kitchen into the pantry and explained what he was to do for future deliveries.

"Okay, so when I come, I get Beery and he lets me in the service entrance and I come up here and push the intercom, tell him I'm here and he buzzes me in, right?"

"Yes," she said, "but who's Beery?"

"Beery Cleary, your doorman."

"You mean Tim, don't you?" she said in a correcting tone.

"Yeah, Tim Cleary, the doorman. He lives in my building. We call him Beery. My old man calls him Sad Sack. Nobody calls him Tim. His old lady calls him Timmy, but he's Beery to me."

Maria had heard enough. She said thank you, opened the door and he left.

Well, that was last week, she thought. *What would happen this week?*

Maria got up from the couch and went into the bedroom. It was almost eleven and she realized that she had wasted much of the morning. She dressed for her walk. She had originally planned on walking through Kingsbridge, then up to Riverview and the river, but changed her mind and thought she'd go to the City Gardens instead. It wasn't as long a walk as going to the river was, but she knew the gardens would put her at peace. She put on a pair of Capri pants and a light cotton sweatshirt. She put on her tennis sneakers, wrapped a kerchief over her hair, applied some Sea and Ski sunscreen lotion to her face and hands, put on her dark sunglasses and went out the door.

As she was getting out of the elevator, she saw Tim the doorman talking with the delivery boy. Tim was a young man, somewhere in his early thirties. He was soft and doughy looking and had a ruddy complexion and a greasy forehead. His hair was a wispy light brown and was thinning. He had small fat little hands that were constantly fiddling with something; if it wasn't his tie or key ring, it was a rubber band or a paper napkin. He was, plainly speaking, unattractive. He was the type of man other men ignore; women order about and kids poke fun at. She knew he lived with his mother, and it was evident that he was a twelve-year-old boy trying to pass as a grownup.

She felt a knot in her stomach. There was something about this delivery boy she didn't like and as she approached she could hear him saying to Tim, "Man, you're such a ball breaker, Beery."

She could hear Beery's whining reply, "Danny those are the rules. Do you want me to call your boss?"

"Call my boss, listen asshole…" Danny caught sight of Maria approaching and stopped talking mid-sentence.

"Are you here with my delivery?"

"Yeah, me and Beery were just talking. We're neighbors ya' know" he answered smartly.

"Everything's fine, Mrs. Weiss," Tim nervously answered. "Just go around the side, Danny, and I'll buzz you in."

Maria smiled and went out through the courtyard. She knew that the delivery boy was trying to go through the front entrance again, and she had a mind to say something to him, but decided to leave that to Henry later. *Filthy little brat*, she thought. *God I'm almost an old woman,* she thought, *and this little punk wants another chance to look through my nightgown.*

Chapter Four

It took a moment for Danny Monaghan to recognize that the woman coming out of the elevator in the kerchief with the dark glasses and the sweatshirt was Maria. He'd been hoping to get through her front door again and possibly catch her in her nightgown. The image of her in her panties and bra underneath her nightgown with those little high-heeled slippers was burned in his mind. He had thought about her non-stop for the whole week. He wasn't sure if she was coming on to him or not, but she had left him in a state of throbbing sexual excitation.

He was hoping he could just bull his way past Cleary the doorman, but that failed. Cleary, for all of his weakness, or so Danny thought, wasn't about to let him go and it was obvious he'd have to use the delivery entrance. He was cursing at Cleary out of frustration, and when the elevator door opened he knew that Maria had heard him. He knew that was a mistake and he tried to gloss it over, but saw the cold look she gave him and wanted to strike out at Cleary and punch his face in for putting him in that position.

As Maria walked through the lobby, Cleary asked her if she was going for her walk. She answered yes with a smile at him, then went out to the courtyard. She ignored Danny and he followed her out of the building and called out, "Have a nice day, Mrs. Weiss."

She turned and gave him a look. It wasn't a smile, but it wasn't an angry look either, and he felt a little better. She turned out of the courtyard and went left on Lincoln Boulevard. Danny pushed the delivery bike out onto the street and watched her as she walked in the opposite direction. He went around to the delivery entrance and rang the intercom. Cleary answered, "Yes?"

Danny responded, "Beery, it's me, let me in you zit-faced virgin."

"Asshole," was the response from Cleary, the buzzer activated and Danny entered the building. He had two boxes. One was perishable items—milk, yogurt, butter, and meat, and the other was the grocery items—cereal, canned vegetables and some cookies. He got in the service elevator and went up alone. At the eighth floor he exited and directly opposite the elevator was the rear entrance to Maria's apartment. There was an intercom with two buttons. One was for the apartment and the other was for the doorman. He pushed the doorman's bell and Cleary answered, "That you, Monaghan?" he said.

"No, it's the fucking sandman, saloon face." Cleary didn't respond, but the buzzer sounded, the door unlocked and Danny entered the pantry.

The pantry was a small room, about eight feet by ten feet, if that. There was a square box refrigerator, counter, shelves, washer and dryer. The door to the apartment was closed and Danny put the perishables in the refrigerator and the dry goods on the counter. He knocked on the door and said, "Anyone home? Hello, Mr. Weiss, it's the delivery boy." He waited a few seconds and tried the door. The door was unlocked and he turned the knob and went into the apartment. He felt a surge in his stomach, almost like the feeling you get on a roller coaster or when you're on the roof up high and you lean over and think about what it would be like if you fell. The feeling in his stomach radiated to his groin and he felt himself getting an erection. He again said, "Hello, anybody home? The delivery's here."

He waited a few seconds and walked into the middle of the kitchen. He took a sour ball from the candy dish on the counter and peeled the wrapper off. He threw the wrapper on the floor and put the candy into his mouth. He walked into the dining room, then into the living room. He kept thinking about Maria and how she looked in her nightgown. He remembered when she stood in the sunlight in the kitchen and he saw through the gown. He'd seen naked woman in magazines, but that was the closest he'd ever been to seeing a woman naked, or almost naked, in real life. The thought was overpowering. Danny had been with girls and had some sexual experience, but most of it was cumbersome. Mary Breen—Hand-job Mary, as she was known in the neighborhood—had jerked him off a couple of times and let him feel her up, but she was fat and pimple faced and she made you tongue kiss her the whole time she was pulling at you. Danny hated the sulfur smell of her acne cream and the way the spittle would cake at the corners of her mouth. The worst thing was that Hand-job

Mary would hang all over you after it was over. His old girlfriend Diane would let him feel her up when they were dry humping but he could never get under her clothes, and sometimes an hour of kissing and grinding was just work and nothing else. *The girls got off on it,* he thought, *but all a guy got was a sore prick from rubbing against the zipper on his jeans.* A couple of the older guys talked about going to a whorehouse, but Danny had heard that's how you get the clap, and even though he had no idea what the clap was, he didn't believe they'd bring him along anyway. Most of his sexual experiences were what he fantasized about and right now the greatest fantasy of his life was Maria.

He edged his way down the hallway and saw the entrance to the two bedrooms and the bathroom off to the right. One of the bedrooms had a day bed, a chair and a television in it. The other room was obviously Maria and her husband's. There was a long bureau and a matching chest on chest. The bed occupied the wall space between the two windows and there were two closets. The bureau had a giant wall mirror over it and there was a mirrored tray with perfumes and cosmetics on one end of the bureau, a pretty music box on the other and a large ornate ashtray in the middle. Danny felt the bulge in his pants. He was scared and knew he should get out of the apartment before someone came home, or Beery came looking for him, but he couldn't help himself. It was as if some hidden force was pushing him on and he had to follow.

He opened a drawer in the bureau and inside of it were several neatly folded sweaters. He opened another drawer and there were some stockings and underwear. He took out a pair of the nylons and rubbed them against his face. He folded them neatly and put them back. He then took out a pair of Maria's panties and held them up. They were black and satiny and looked like the ones he'd seen her in that morning. He put his hands through the leg holes and stretched the panties across his face. He could see her in the kitchen and he imagined her taking the nightgown off and coming to him. It was dreamlike but very sensuous. He placed the crotch of the panties in his mouth and sucked at it. He took them out and placed them in his pocket. He wanted the nightgown, the one she was wearing last week; he just had to feel it and see it one more time.

He opened a bottom drawer and saw a pile of folded nightgowns. They were cotton and weren't the type you could see through. These were the kind his mother wore. He took them out and placed them on the floor. Beneath them was a tablecloth wrapped around something. He took the package out and undid the tablecloth. Wrapped inside of it was a green leather portfolio with the initials AK on it and underneath that was a photo album. He picked up the portfolio and opened it. There was a half sleeve inside the portfolio and placed in the sleeve was a packet of pictures. They were large pictures, eight by tens. He could see the back of the pictures and the name Amos Koch was stamped on them. He took the packet out and turned it around. The first photograph was of Maria. She was very young, maybe twenty or so and was draped in long, light-colored sheet of cloth. The pictures were black and white, but were not glossy. They were on thick paper and had a dull finish. Danny turned to the next photograph and in that one Maria was in the same pose, but the sheet of cloth was now off her shoulders and you could see the cleavage of her breasts. Maria was not smiling in the pictures and she had a distant look on her face.

Danny went from picture to picture and in each one more of Maria's body was a revealed. Her hair was swept up over her head in some shots and in others it fell loosely past her shoulders. In one picture her breasts were fully exposed and she was holding the sheet of cloth just below her naval with one hand covering her groin. When he turned to the last two pictures he was almost hyperventilating with excitement. In those pictures she was completely naked. One picture had her facing the camera with the sheet of cloth draped around her ankles and in the other picture one of her legs was raised and resting on an ottoman and her hands were splayed and pointed toward the brush of hair surrounding her vagina.

Danny started to rub his groin with his hand and then he heard a noise in the hallway. He panicked. What if someone came in and caught him? What would he do? He left everything on the floor and ran to the front door. If it started to open, he would run out the service door and go down the stairs. He stopped in the foyer by the front door. He listened for a second and heard an apartment door close. Then everything was quiet. He was safe. His heart was pounding and he was sweating, but he was safe. The sudden panic at the thought of getting caught had heightened his sexual feelings and his penis was pushing against the fabric of his dungarees more rigid than it had ever been. He knew what he was going to do, but first he wanted to put this treasure trove back where he'd found it. He carefully put everything back in the portfolio. He wrapped everything up in the tablecloth and placed it in the drawer. He put the nightgowns back in and closed the drawer. Danny then went to the bathroom and looked in the clothes hamper. There, under some men's dirty underwear was the sheer pink nightgown. He picked it out and held it up to the light. He then opened his belt buckle and dropped his pants and underpants to the floor. He took the nightgown and rubbed it up and down his legs and massaged his

37

penis with it. Then he dropped the nightgown back on top of the clothes hamper and took Maria's panties out of his pocket and masturbated into them, all the while imagining he was there alone with Maria. This was the most intense sexual experience of his life and he vowed he would share it again, share it somehow with Maria, even if was only old pictures of her.

He washed his hands and face in the bathroom. He rinsed out the panties and put them in his pocket. He put the nightgown back in the hamper under the dirty men's underwear. He looked around, and confident that everything was as he'd found it, he left.

Going down in the elevator he felt flushed and happy. This was the most exciting thing that had ever happened to him, and his mind was working feverishly on how to relive that experience again. He went out the service entrance, got on the delivery bike and went back to the supermarket. He'd been in the apartment for no more than ten minutes and he knew he'd gotten away without anyone being any the wiser.

Chapter Five

Henry's office was on the sixth floor. He was in suite 610. The front door had a frosted glass insert and in blocked gold letters it read LAW OFFICES. In smaller letters were the names Lee Futerman, Henry Weiss, John DeGiacomo, William Aneckstein, Joseph Schaller, listed one under the other. When you walked in the front office door there was a receptionist and behind her a small switchboard was mounted on the wall. A short hallway ran perpendicular to a second long hallway, with four offices facing the front of the building and four secretarial areas facing the inner walls opposite the offices. At one end of the hallway there was a doorway that led to a conference room and a small library, and at the other end of the hallway there was a doorway that led to a suite of three rooms Henry used for his office. The first room was where his secretary had her space and where he kept his legal files. A small bathroom was off to the right, and off to the left and facing Lincoln Boulevard was Henry's private office.

When Henry walked into the office, Sophie was bent over with her knees on the floor and her neck craned under her desk.

"Is that you, Poppy?" she called out.

"Good morning," Henry said cheerfully. "What are you looking for?"

"I put a check in the drawer yesterday and it got stuck in the back," she said as she came out from underneath the desk with a check in her hand and a big smile on her face. She was wearing a tight black skirt, a short sleeved red blouse with the two top buttons open, black stockings and black high heels. She reached over and fixed Henry's tie, took a step back and smoothed the wrinkles in her skirt with the palms of her hands. "Do you think I have too much black on today?" she asked earnestly.

Henry gave her an admiring smile, and said, "No, you look great. Now, enough about how you look," he said, changing the subject. "Do me a favor. First order of business today is to order flowers for Maria. Call the Valentine Florists and have them send over something."

Sophie frowned and sat down at her chair, "What's the matter, Poppy, the ice queen won't melt again?"

Henry laughed and waved her away with his hand as he walked back to his office, "Got to keep the peace, baby."

A few minutes later Sophie came into Henry's office with a cup of coffee for him. "I ordered the flowers. Anything else?" she said.

Henry leaned back in his chair and said, "Yeah, lots of things. First, we have that closing at eleven this morning. Is everything ready?"

"Of course, everything was ready last week. The title search is done and the loan officer from Commonwealth will be here with the check. All we have to do is notarize the papers and collect your fee."

He smiled. "You are the best. Now, here's the big question. Can you get your aunt to watch Joey for a few days next week?"

"Why?"

"I have to go to Montreal. Ancowitz is closing on a retail property up there and selling two properties he owns in Watertown. and I'm handling everything. but I'll need you."

"Need me for what? Don't you need a Canadian lawyer?"

"Hey, Montreal's cold, even in June, and I'll need someone to keep me warm. We can take the train up Tuesday morning. Morris' son Scott lives in Montreal and is handling the Canadian end of things."

"What about your precious wife? Doesn't she speak French?"

"She's working, and anyway I want to have some fun, and she's no fun."

"Aunt Lucy spends half her time at my house, so it's no big deal. What I'd like to know is when are you going to leave that bitch?"

"I can't. We've talked about this before. It's just too complicated."

"What's complicated? When was the last time you had sex with a woman? No wait, don't answer, it was Monday, right here in this office on that couch. I'm the one you're doing it with, honey, not her, and I know it. I'm the one who can make you do it anytime, anywhere. Don't forget that," she said as she turned and started walking out of his office.

Henry looked at her as she strutted out his office door and couldn't offer a word in disagreement. He and Maria's sex life was almost nonexistent and wasn't for his lack of trying. Maria just didn't seem interested. Sophie, on the other hand, never turned him away. She had a nice shape and everything she wore was just tight enough to show it off. She had a thick head of black hair that covered up too much of her face, and he knew she let it fall that way to hide the many pockmarks a ravaging case of teenage acne had left behind. It wasn't a pretty face, in fact, it was a hard face and it took time getting used to, especially when he compared her to Maria. But Sophie was right, she knew how to stoke a man's fires, and all he had to do was kiss her neck and rub her hips and she was his for the taking.

He got up from the desk and went out to her desk. She had a mirror in her hand and she was wiping the tears from her cheek. He put his hand under her chin and turned her face to him, "Baby, someday, but not now. We spend a lot of time together and I take good care of you and Joey, so please be patient." He bent down and kissed her forehead. He then lifted her up by her shoulders and drew her close to him.

At first she turned her head away, but he persisted and she started giggling. "Henry, it's Friday, we haven't done anything since Monday," she said, laughing. Then she took off his tie and undid his belt buckle and led him back into his office. "Hurry up and be quiet," she said as she slipped out of her skirt and undid her blouse.

It was quick and noisy. Sophie always told him to be quiet, but she was always noisy herself. Once the lovemaking started she didn't care who heard. In fact, she wanted people to hear what was going on, especially in Henry's office. Her dream was to have Maria come in and catch them, but Maria never came to the office. She knew Henry would never leave Maria. She knew Maria was incapable of loving Henry, or giving him the sexual comfort she did, and she also knew that she was nothing in Henry's eyes compared to Maria. And, at times, Henry was nothing in her eyes, nothing more than Joey's father.

Chapter Six

Maria walked east on Monmouth Road toward the City Gardens. The day was warming up and her migraine was fading. She passed under the elevated train line and turned into the campus of Jesuit University. She always took the longer walk through the Jesuit campus in order to avoid passing Grover Cleveland High School. The large groups of milling teenagers made her feel uneasy. She had been taking this walk for over ten years, and just last week she had remarked to Henry how the number of brown and black faces was growing among the Cleveland High School population. Henry's response took her by surprise. He said that the Upper Borough had about five years left before it was one big housing project teeming with spics and niggers. He had never talked like that before. Henry's aversion to discussing race, religion or politics was as strong as Gloria's penchant for them. Euphemistically, he might from time to time refer to Negroes and Puerto Ricans as wooly bullies and Kaffirs, but that was rare and was usually in response to some problem a landlord was having with his tenants. Henry's from the gutter reference had the bitter flavor of resentment and Maria imagined that as the Upper Borough was changing, so would Henry's law practice, and so would his life.

They were draining the salt marshes that bordered the edges of the northeast section of the Upper Borough, and Henry told her the city was going to build a mammoth housing project and that would create an exodus of white people from older neighborhoods. The Negroes and Puerto Ricans would take over those neighborhoods and the Upper Borough would be lost. Henry was a creature of the Upper Borough and he knew its neighborhoods well. He defended his statement by reciting the different neighborhoods that were once white and were now predominately colored or Puerto Rican. It was a different culture and landlords treated their properties differently, too. The attitude of many was to deliver as few services as possible and keep the turnover increasing for maximum rent increases and profits. Ancowitz Realty, his major client, was selling off its residential properties and buying commercial properties in the suburbs to the north of Huguenot City, and even in Canada, and it was only a matter of time before many of the landlords Henry represented either sold their holdings or let them slip into disrepair and he found himself defending slumlords and evicting welfare mothers.

Their own building was an example. When they first lived there, they had a doorman around the clock, two porters plus a superintendent. Now the doormen were on duty from 7:00 a.m. to midnight and there was one porter. The building was clean and well-maintained, but not to the degree it once was. Eventually the doorman would be gone and they'd have nothing more than an electric buzzer at the front entrance for security. He told her by 1970 they'd be in Riverview or downtown Huguenot City. Henry resigned himself to these changes in life and accepted them far more easily than Maria did. The thought of losing the apartment because the neighborhood changed was upsetting to Maria. She couldn't think of ever living anywhere else but at the Excelsior. Henry's remark about spics took her by surprise too, since she had imagined for some time that if Henry had another woman, it had to be Sophie Cruz.

Maria walked across the Jesuit campus and exited onto Floral Boulevard. She crossed the street and entered the City Gardens. She loved the gardens. It was over two hundred acres of beauty. Maria's favorite spot was the Rock Garden. The Rock Garden was an amalgam of natural habitats in miniature, the alpine, the heath, the forest, they were all represented there amid massive outcroppings of rock designed to create the different environments. Maria never read the signs describing the selected habitats or defining the various plants and flowers on exhibit. She enjoyed nature for what it was and the need to clutter her mind with definitions was unnecessary. She also loved to watch the other visitors to the gardens.

Her eye caught one couple that seemed out of place. They were a man and a woman. The man appeared to be in his late forties or early fifties. The woman was in her early twenties. They were holding hands and it was obvious from their body language that they were romantically involved. The man was dressed in a blue blazer and had on a blue button down shirt with a maroon knit tie, khaki pants and loafers. Everything about him said college professor. The woman was wearing a yellow cotton sundress that was bare at the shoulders with the hem slightly above the knees. She had heavy legs and was wearing flat brown sandals that didn't at all go with her dress. She wasn't very attractive, but she was young and that was the apparent attraction, or so she thought.

The professor, for that was how he was fixed in her mind, moved along the garden path from exhibit to exhibit. At each one he would stop to point to the plants or flowers and explain something to his companion. He would let go of her hand and his hand would move to the small of her back, sometimes she would laugh at something he said and other times she would lean over and kiss his cheek. They looked very happy.

Later on, Maria was at the City Garden Tea Room. She purchased an iced tea and a sandwich. She went outside to sit at a table and found herself across from the professor and the woman. He was now reading to her from a small book he'd taken from the side pocket of his blazer. Maria wondered whether it was a Shakespeare sonnet or some syrupy collection of poems the man had composed himself. The woman was staring dreamy-eyed and it was obvious she was smitten with her older consort. *How foolish women can be*, she thought, *especially when we're young.*

The City Garden Tea Room was a pleasant place to rest after touring the gardens, and as Maria watched the interaction of the older man and the younger woman, her thoughts reached back to her experiences with Amos Koch.

The fire had occurred in October of 1934. Maria started work with Koch in January of 1935. She translated correspondences from Spanish to German and English. The work was tedious and not very challenging. Koch spoke excellent English, Spanish and German, and for some odd reason he always spoke to her in English. In 1902, at the age of ten, he'd immigrated to Argentina with his parents. His father had secured a position managing a large cattle ranch for a German industrialist, and young Amos Koch found himself an apprentice gaucho on the Argentine pampas. When Amos was fourteen his mother died, and a year later his father bought a half share in a meat canning business and slaughterhouse. That was in 1907. His father's partner in the slaughterhouse was a man named Luis Garcia and it was under his name they sold canned beef and bouillon. Luis Garcia was a cruel man. He drank, gambled and whored his evenings away, and when there was time he beat his wife and cheated his partner at every chance he could. Amos' father was a judgmental man and his character was bereft of sentimentality or sympathy. He had no use for a partner he couldn't trust, and whether it was homicide or luck, no one ever knew, the senior Koch was neither surprised nor saddened when Luis Garcia was found dead with a broken neck on the slaughterhouse floor. That happened in 1909, and six months later Amos's father and Garcia's widow were married. The Garcia's had four daughters and within a year of the marriage the oldest daughter, Carmella, was pregnant with Amos's child. That was the only time in his life Amos could recall seeing his father cry. They were not tears of joy, but of shame. A hasty wedding was arranged and the newlyweds were then separated. Carmella was sent to Buenos Aires to live with her mother's sister for the duration of her pregnancy and Amos was sent on the road as a salesman for Garcia Premium Beef.

The onset of the World War proved a bonanza for the Koch family. Argentina was rich in beef and a long way from the battlefield. The canning company's business increased tenfold, and by the end of the war the Kochs were a very wealthy family and the product label was changed from Luis Garcia Premium Beef to Koch Beef, 'The Pride of the Pampas.' By 1920 Amos Koch and Carmella were the parents of two sons, and the young family was sent to Berlin to manage the growing interests of Levi Koch and Son Importing, Inc. Maria learned all of this her first month with Koch imports. Amos spent hours telling her about life in Argentina and there was always the underlying theme that his marriage was the consequence of biology and nothing more, and there was much about his life he regretted and much he wanted to do.

Maria found Amos interesting and found his confidences flattering. Here he was, a rich and successful businessman, intimately sharing the story of his life with a secretary young enough to be his daughter. This was a time of great emotional insecurity for Maria. The recent losses she had suffered seemed insurmountable, and her way of coping was to lose herself in work or other people. Taking into account his station in life and his role as the director of a large and thriving business, Maria knew that it was highly unusual, if not inappropriate, for Amos to show as much interest in her as he did and to reveal so much about his life as he did. It was, however, a welcome diversion and she looked forward to their daily conversations. In March of 1935 Carmella and his two sons two sons returned to Argentina. Amos was greatly concerned with the changing political climate in Germany and told Maria that by year's end he would relocate the business to France or England.

Maria rented a room in an old apartment house on Wallstrasse in the Mitte section of Berlin. The building was old and not well kept. There were four rooms on her floor, a bathroom and a kitchen. The bathroom and kitchen were shared by each of the roomers. The bathroom and kitchen were dirty and Maria took all of her meals out. She intended to speak with Koch about helping her to find better accommodations, but his revelation that he was moving from Germany put her in a position where she would soon be out of work and her lowly living quarters would be something of a luxury. She'd been having a recurring dream about the bakery for several months. In the dream she was alone in the bakery and all the shelves were empty and the store windows were broken. She walked through the bakery calling for her mother or Rudy, but there was no answer. It wasn't much of a dream, but she had it or variations of it repeatedly and she would always wake up in a panic, her heart pounding over the tragic realization that she was alone. One night she dreamed she was in the bakery and there was a cold draft running through it. She was calling for her mother and Rudy, but there was no answer. She heard a scratching sound and it grew louder and louder, and as she turned into the front room of the bakery she saw a rat in one of the showcases eating a loaf of bread. The rat looked at her, bared its teeth and ran away. Maria screamed. She was so frightened she woke up. She was breathing heavily but couldn't move. The light from the moon and a street lamp illuminated her room and as she lay with her head on the pillow and counted the cracks in the ceiling above she tried to calm herself. She was always afraid of rats and mice, and the sight of the greasy gray rat she saw in her dream left her in a cold sweat.

She lay there in bed calmly and suddenly she felt movement on the bed. It was a gentle rustling in the bedcover by her left hand. She froze. She couldn't lift her head up off the pillow, but she felt the presence of someone in the room. The light from the moon and street lamp created a field of shadows in her room and she knew something or someone that didn't belong there was with her. She wanted to scream, but she was so wracked with fear she couldn't. Suddenly the bed cover by her left hand moved again and her eye caught the image of a thin snake-like creature resting on the bed cover. She slowly moved her hand over to brush the object away when it moved. So quick was the movement that she jumped up in reaction and swatted at it with her hand. The snake moved quickly and it was not a snake at all, but the tail of a rat as large as a small kitten. Maria screamed and swung her fist at it and the rat lunged at her closed fist and bit her on the knuckles. It then jumped from the bed and scurried away. Maria got out of bed and turned on the lamp. Her window was open just a bit and she could feel an icy draft, the same draft she felt in her dream. Did the rat come in the window, under the door, or through and unseen hole was something she didn't know, what she did know was that she had to move. The wound was small and she treated it with some iodine and tied a handkerchief around her knuckles. She packed up her clothes in the two suitcases she owned and stood by the window until morning.

She had to rent a taxi to take her to work that morning. She brought the suitcases up to the area where she worked and placed them next to her desk. When Amos came in and saw them his face flushed. He asked her if she was leaving and she told him the story about the rat. He immediately called for his doctor to come to the office to treat her wound.

Later on that morning he called her into his office and offered her a cup of tea. Over tea he asked her where she was going to stay, and when she told him she had nowhere to go and was thinking of temporarily staying in a hotel. He told her that she could stay with him. He owned a large home on Oranienburgerstrasse in the old Jewish section of Berlin. It was where he had lived as a small child, and when he returned with his family in 1920 that was where he bought a home. He told Maria that his choice of where to live had proved a terrible mistake. Carmella was Roman Catholic and was devout in her faith. She didn't speak German and had no intention of learning the language or associating with her neighbors. The children's nurse, who stayed on long after her services were needed, the cook and the housekeeper were all Argentines. They, along with some members of the clergy she had befriended, made up Carmella's social circle in Berlin. Amos forged a social life of his own, but one without benefit of a spouse. Life in the Jewish quarter was somewhat friendless for him and residence there clearly identified him as a Jew and that was a designation he was uncomfortable with in 1935. He would soon be free of Germany he told her, but while he was still there he felt it would be a great benefit to Maria and a consolation to him if she moved into his home.

Maria was depressed, and the thought of returning to that cold room and having to worry about sharing her bed with vermin was unthinkable. She accepted his offer; all well knowing that Amos' interest in her was more than avuncular.

The Koch home was one of a series of limestone townhouses. Five steps led up to the oak framed stained-glass front door of Koch's house. A second set of steps led down to a basement service entrance. The first floor of Amos's home contained a parlor, a music room, dining room and kitchen area. The rooms were large and well furnished. The second floor was made up of three bedrooms, a library, sewing room and two bathrooms. Those rooms were large and well furnished, too. The third floor was the maid's quarters. Maria never ventured up there. Amos set her up in his older son's former bedroom. He called ahead and had the housekeeper make up the room. Maria had expressed her concern over the propriety of her moving into a married man's home and Amos dismissed her concerns by telling her that he told the household help, who were newly hired upon Carmela's departure, that Maria was his niece. Maria accepted his assurances, and upon seeing the house and the comparing it to where she had been living, she was grateful for his generous offer.

Amos and Maria traveled to and from the office together and ate their evening meals together. She knew that she had become a topic of much gossip in the office, and that many of her fellow workers thought her conduct shocking—a recently widowed woman setting up house with a married man while his wife was away was shocking—but she didn't care.

Amos Koch closed his Berlin office in November of 1935. All of the employees had been let go, and it was now just him and Maria. There was little business to conduct, and everything was being handled in Argentina. Amos' great concern now was selling his house and getting his money out of Germany. After the office closed, Maria announced that she would have to find a new job and find someplace to live. More than a year had passed since the fire, and the closing of Koch's office was almost as great a blow to her as her losses of the previous year. Nothing would ever bring Rudy or her family back, but life with Amos Koch had taken on a peaceful rhythm and the safety and comfort she found living with him had helped her to repress the anger and sorrow she felt over losing Rudy and the others. Amos had allowed her to live in his house, dine at his table, but he had respected her privacy and never compromised his position as her employer and overall benefactor by seeking her favor other than as a friend.

All of that changed in November 1935. They were having dinner and Amos was holding a glass of wine in his hand. He looked across the table at Maria and told her she was beautiful. He then told her that more than a year had passed since her husband's death and that it was time for her to stop mourning his loss and understand that she was a beautiful young woman and that her life was still in front of her. He then went on to tell her that he had loved her since he first walked into her family's bakery when she was a teenager. Maria blushed and thanked him for the compliment but told him this was all very confusing. He said, and she recalled his exact words, in his halting English, "There is no confusion. I love you. That's why you're here with me, in my home. In two weeks I'm leaving Berlin. You can come to Paris with me, or you can stay here. I have an apartment in Paris, there is one bed there and if you come with me. I expect you to share that bed with me. I'll await your decision." He then got up and left the table.

Maria finished her iced tea. Thinking about her time with Koch was tiring. She left the Tea Room and headed toward the exit of the gardens for her walk home. The professor and his date lingered behind. She wondered whether they had consummated their affection and how long it would be before the older man would grow weary with his young conquest and turn her away for someone else.

Chapter Seven

The closing was over in less than an hour. Sophie could have run the whole show without Henry being there. She had the business down to a science and she knew it. Henry was in his office reading the newspaper and Sophie came in.

"I'm going to the bank to make a deposit, then I'm off to Kroll's's to do some shopping. I'll be back around two. You still gonna be here, or are you going home for the weekend?" she said petulantly.

"I'm taking off around one or so; just waiting to hear from Morris about Montreal."

"Tell him to buy some property in Puerto Rico. Then you can meet my peoples," she said with an exaggerated accent on "my peoples." Then she bent over his desk and turned his chin up and kissed him on the tip of his nose. "Love you, Poppy."

"Don't I know," he sighed.

After Sophie left his office, Henry took his glasses off and put the newspaper down. He took a Pall Mall from the leather cigarette humidor Maria had bought him for his birthday several years ago and lit it up. He pulled in a long drag of smoke and let it out slowly. "God, she is one hard looking woman," he said out loud. Henry loved two women for all the reasons you're supposed to love one woman. Maria was beautiful, but distant and cold. She had a certain European sophistication he couldn't resist. He couldn't describe it, but it was a force that existed and it dominated him. There was nothing sophisticated about Sophie. She was trashy and cheap, and very much like the women he dated before he married Maria, cocktail waitresses, hat check girls, a few show girls. Nice legs, tight clothes and no desire for commitment. Let's have some fun, then go our own way. That was the way Henry liked things, but his life was growing more and more complicated. It was difficult sharing a bed with Maria. Most of the time she acted like you weren't there. When you could get a response it was mechanical; the price she paid to be with you and little more. *Still*, he thought, *she was someone he loved and would always love.*

Did he really love Sophie or was she just a convenience? Just before, when she bent down to kiss him he took a good look at her. He was wearing his reading glasses and up close every imperfection showed up: the faint mustache, the pockmarks and blackheads. He would see her every morning, sitting at her desk with a mirror in one hand and a tweezers in the other plucking her eyebrows and searching her chin and cheeks for those stray black stubs that seemed to pop up overnight. She was thirteen years younger than Maria. What would she look like at fifty? If he could pick out five things about her that repulsed him now, how long would it be before that raw sexual attraction he had for her burned out? Sophie was a problem.

It wasn't until Joey was two years old that she told Henry he was the father. Originally, he'd thought her old boyfriend Carl was the father. Carl's real name was Carlos Gomez, but he'd changed it to Carl Gomes when he opened a small business that sold and installed Venetian blinds, shades and drapes. He thought by Anglicizing his name he'd attract more business. When Sophie told him she was pregnant, Henry had immediately thought Carl was the father. Sophie had never hidden from Henry her relationship with Carl, and Henry, being married to Maria, never felt he was in any position to question Sophie's fidelity. Henry enjoyed the fact that Sophie had a boyfriend. It reduced the need for her to want more of his time than he could give her. He had never asked directly if Carl was the father, but it never crossed his mind that it could be him. He also didn't believe that Carl knew anything of his and Sophie's relationship, and when she told Henry that it was him and not Carl who was Joey's father, he was incredulous. Sophie told him that Carl was a member of the National Guard and had been on active duty and upstate when Joey was conceived. The only other man she'd been intimate with was Henry.

When Carl found out Sophie was pregnant, he offered to marry her. Carl assumed he was the boy's father and at the time Sophie found it expedient to let him believe that. She wouldn't marry him, but his name did go on the boy's birth certificate as the father. Carl was hurt by Sophie's denial of his offer of marriage and within a year of Joey's birth he was seeing another woman. Sophie, who by that time was totally devoted to Henry, told Carl he wasn't Joey's father and encouraged him to pursue his new love interest. Sophie's admission to Henry was the aftermath of a tense and heated argument that had as its genesis Henry's gift of flowers and candy on Valentines Day. He gave Sophie the candy and flowers and a two hundred dollar gift certificate to Sable's. Along with the gifts, he told her how much she meant to him and that he loved her. Her response was first to break out in tears and then to tell him he was just using her and that his gifts meant nothing to her. When Henry tried to explain that he was already married and that there was little he could do to change that, Sophie responded by informing him of Joey's parentage.

Henry's initial response was to sit back in his chair and shake his head saying, "This just can't be. It can't be. I know people. We could have done something. Why didn't you tell me?"

Sophie told him how scared she had been and how everything fell into place with Carl. She was thrilled at the thought of having Henry's child and believed in her heart that things would work out. She had vowed to herself to never tell him, but as time went on it became more difficult. After hearing the full story from Sophie, Henry's shock and anger dissipated. He understood his own culpability in the matter and he promised her he would help her in every way he could with providing for the boy, but there was simply no way he would legally acknowledge he was the boy's father. Soon after that, he accepted his responsibility and moved them from Fulton Avenue into a new middle income subsidized building on Kingsbridge Avenue. In addition to her salary, he paid her rent and any incidentals for Joey. The boy didn't know Henry was his father and that was fine with him. Sophie had, for the longest time, accepted that Maria was his wife and things wouldn't change. Yet, things were changing. Now Maria was the "Ice Queen" or the "Bitch." Sophie wasn't a kid any more and it was evident she wanted more from Henry than money and a quickie on the office couch.

Henry loved Sophie, but it was a selfish emotion. She was a terrific secretary. She had the real estate end of his practice down solid and practically ran it by herself. She was earthy and sexual, and she made him feel potent and virile. One time, early in their relationship, they went to dinner at the Crab King on Clam Island. The island was a quaint sailing, seafood and residential area of the Upper Borough that had been settled some two hundred years ago and was one of the last independent villages to be incorporated into Huguenot City during the depression. Clam Island was next to a large recreational area called

Clam Digger's Park that featured a beach on the sound and a large nature preserve. It was January and very cold out. As a Christmas gift, in addition to her bonus, he gave her a mink coat, and on that day she was wearing it. They were coming from a real estate closing in nearby Washburn.

It was a Thursday and Maria was working late at Sable's. Henry ordered crab cakes and Sophie ordered the Alaskan king crab legs. The waitress put a plastic bib around her and placed an enormous platter of crab legs on the table. He could still see her methodically cracking the crab legs and pulling the meat out and dipping it in the drawn butter sauce and putting chunk after chunk of it in her mouth. She must have eaten twenty of them, and he remembered asking her if she had a tip on a famine because he'd never seen her or anyone else, for that matter, attack a platter of crab legs like she did. Sophie was laughing and in great spirits, and told him she just liked crab legs. They were leaving the restaurant and she told him she had to go to the bathroom. He told her he'd get the car and he'd meet her outside. When she got in the car, she was all giggly and she told him she wanted to take a walk and digest that big dinner. He complained about the cold, but she wasn't worried as she had her new mink coat to keep her warm. Henry agreed and they drove over to the beach at Clam Digger's Park. There were no cars in the parking lot and they drove right up to the front entrance. Sophie and Henry got out of the car and took a walk along the promenade that ran alongside the beach and faced the sound. It was dark and windy, and after ten minutes Henry told Sophie they should go back to the car. Sophie asked him what was the hurry, then leaned against the promenade railing and opened her coat. She was naked from the waist up. She told Henry she'd wanted to take all of her clothes off and be totally naked with just the coat on, but she couldn't fit all of her clothes into her pocketbook. Henry approached her and cupped her breasts in his hands and told her she was crazy. She closed her coat and they went back to the car. When they got in the car, Sophie unbuckled his pants and drew his penis out from the slit in his boxer shorts. Soon her head was bobbing up and down with as much relish as she'd applied to the crab legs. It was an entirely unexpected erotic moment and Henry could still see the glow from the back of his car caused by his holding the brake pedal down while she pleasured him. Long after he climaxed, she was still kissing him and telling him how much she loved him. He often thought about that evening and the pleasure he knew they both derived from it. It was an experience of a kind he would never have with Maria. Sophie appealed to his vanity. She made life easier for him. And for all that he loved her but if she disappeared tomorrow his life wouldn't miss a step. He'd find a new secretary, maybe not as competent, but he'd get by. He'd miss the sex and probably think about it often, but there'd be someone new. He knew that there were still plenty of women just as sexually shallow as he was who'd be only too happy to help him spend his money and have a good time. He could live without Sophie, and more importantly, the inevitable day when he'd be forced to acknowledge he was Joey's father. *Ah, the ironies of life*, he thought, *Sophie needs me. I need Maria. Who does Maria need?* He didn't know the answer.

Chapter Eight

It was almost two in the afternoon when Maria returned home from her walk to the City Gardens. The migraine that had plagued her all day at varying degrees of intensity was almost gone and she thought if she laid down for an hour or two she would completely recover. The apartment door was unlocked when she got home, and when she walked in she saw Henry's suit jacket resting on the back of one of the dining room chairs. A large floral arrangement was sitting on the dining room table and she went over and examined it. The card said, "To Maria, love Henry." It looked like a funeral arrangement and Maria knew Henry had told Sophie to order it. It was a waste of money and she felt like telling him so, but her anger with him had cooled and she was in no mood for conversation. She didn't call out and say, "Hello or I'm home."

There was a linen closet in the hallway outside the bathroom and she went into it to get a fresh washcloth. She was going to dampen the washcloth with cold water and put it over her forehead and temples when she rested. The bathroom door was half closed. She pushed it open and heard Henry say, "Hey I'm in here and it doesn't smell like roses."

She stopped and looked at him. He was seated on the toilet bowl with his pants and underpants around his ankles. His left arm was resting on his left leg and the newspaper was spread across his lap. He was holding a square cardboard container that contained leftovers from the previous evening's dinner at Tsing's in his left hand and in his right hand he had a fork with strands of lo mien wrapped around it. She said nothing. She turned the cold-water tap in the bathtub on and wet the washcloth and left the bathroom and went to the bedroom.

She took off her tennis shoes and removed the sweatshirt and replaced it with a white tee shirt and lay down on the bed. She put the damp cloth over her head and closed her eyes. At that moment she wanted to block everything out of her mind. See nothing, hear nothing and think of nothing. She couldn't. Henry seated on the toilet bowl, eating his lunch and reading the newspaper was, to Maria, the perfect snapshot of their marriage. She was trying hard not to think and was hoping to drift off to sleep. It wouldn't happen.

Henry had bought a Zenith stereo console a few weeks ago. It had a spindle that you could put four or five LP albums on and when one record was finished playing the next record would drop and play. Henry's new pastime was to come home from work and put several albums on the stereo, turn up the volume, lay on the couch and let the music play. Henry loved popular music, particularly show tunes, and Maria, throbbing head and all, could clearly hear the overture to the musical Gypsy playing. Soon the brassy voice of Ethel Merman would fill the apartment and Henry would be in Heaven and Maria would be in Hell. She thought Ethel Merman was a loud, no talent entertainer. Henry thought she was one of the queens of Broadway. "Annie Get Your Gun," another big Merman musical and record in Henry's collection, was probably the next album and Maria, knowing she was in for an afternoon of Merman and company, got up and closed the bedroom door and asked Henry to lower the volume on the stereo.

She decided that they had to separate. She'd had this thought before, but never knew how to go about it, how to approach Henry and tell him the marriage was over. She had come to a point in her life where it was pathetically obvious that the only reason she stayed with him was for the comfortable lifestyle they enjoyed. It was so meaningless, and she was once again hatching a plan to start over. Henry's love for her and his pride in being a good provider had left her with a bank balance in excess of eighty thousand dollars. It wasn't a fortune, but it was enough to enable her to pick up and leave him without having to ask for anything. The only thing she had to ask for was his permission to divorce and, on that issue, she believed he would fight her. She meant too much to him and a divorce would be the ultimate rejection, something he could never acknowledge. She would wait until he went away on business, then she would go back to Europe. *It is, in the long run,* she thought, *the least I can do for Henry.*

Paris, Berlin, Prague, she'd lived in all of them and could certainly find a home there. She loved Paris, but her association with Koch tainted the memory of it. Maria's short life with Koch was an education she would have been better off not experiencing.

"I expect you to share that bed with me. I'll await your decision." How many times over the years had she wished she'd given a different answer to that request? How would her life have turned out? Would she have died during the war, an innocent victim? Would she have supported the Reich and Hitler? Would she have managed to flee to another country on her own? What did it matter, she thought, she gave him the answer he wanted and that set in motion everything else. She put her pillow over her head and tried to sleep. All day long her memory kept slipping back into the past, all day long she kept dredging up unpleasant memories, and now, when her migraine was starting to fade and she should be feeling better, the wretched memory of her affair with Amos Koch surfaced. It was a painful memory she could never escape. "I expect you to share that bed with me. I'll await your decision." She could hear his voice, the clipped, precise enunciation of each word and like a mantra it had played in her mind over and over during the years. Koch was always with her. She could recall it all so clearly.

His demand shocked her. They had just finished a simple meal of poached fish with spinach and carrots. There was little conversation during the meal except their remarks on how fresh the fish tasted. They were alike in many ways. They were both better listeners than talkers, and over the months she had lived with Koch she never felt like she had to talk just to make conversation. They both disliked heavy foods and were light eaters. Koch hated beef, he said Argentina was dripping in beef blood and either you loved it or hated it. Maria had grown up spending every day in the family bakery. She found the smell of bread and cakes baking suffocating. Most of all she had an aversion to sausage and fatty meats. The specialty of her family's bakery was sausage bread consisting of spicy bratwurst rolled in vinegar soaked cabbage leaves and baked inside a loaf of black bread with caraway seeds. Her mother spent all week making the sausage and on Friday nights they baked several hundred loaves for sale on Saturday.

He had told her all about his childhood in Argentina and his mistaken marriage, and she had told him all about Rudy. She felt comfortable with him and felt she knew him and that he cared for her. His blunt demand or offer or request, whatever it was, left her speechless. She was happy he got up from the table and left the room immediately after issuing it. Perhaps he thought she'd slap him? *Probably*, she thought, *it was a business ploy.* Amos Koch had built Koch Beef into a successful and large company because he was a skilled salesman and ruthless businessman. No opportunity went unexplored. Months of reading and translating correspondences for Koch Imports had taught her that Koch was a consumer, and when he wanted something he went after it. He didn't put the rat in her room or start the fire that killed her family, but he capitalized on those events and set in motion a simple plan that left her no reasonable alternative than to accede to his desires. Life without Koch meant unemployment and hard living conditions. She seized the opportunity and stunned him later on that evening with her answer.

Maria sat at the table after he left and had a second glass of wine. She then went to the music room. She had studied the piano as a child, but was not an accomplished musician. She had, however, mastered a number of pieces and could play them flawlessly. One was a group of compositions by Erik Satie titled *Gymnopiedes*. She sat down at Koch's piano and methodically and mechanically moved through the compositions. She loved the *Gymnopiedes* because she could play them without giving any thought to the music. The music filled the room and she was free to entertain all her thoughts. She remembered playing the music and determining that it would be she and not Koch and his wealth that would dominate their relationship.

Koch had told her many times that she was beautiful. Maria had always thought of herself as being attractive, but she'd never thought of her self as beautiful. Within her family and her upbringing there had never been any tolerance for such vanity. Her mother was considered the family beauty, but that was a minor attribute, an accident of nature that you could welcome, but one that contributed little toward the family's success. Maria's mother was best known for her sausage making ability and her wry wit. She was an outstanding baker, and a good wife and mother. Maria's mother was considered fortunate to have married Maria's father. He was something of a genius, and a successful teacher. His facility with learning and teaching languages. His services to the government were genuine accomplishments that brought honor to her family. She was the child of successful trade's people and none of that success had been achieved because someone was considered beautiful. When she had first gone to work for Koch, a number of men and women in the office had warned her to be careful of him. He had conducted numerous illicit affairs under the nose and with the apparent approval of his wife, and she was told that a young girl as beautiful as she was would surely be a prize he would wish to capture. She had initially dismissed these warnings, and by the time she moved into his house she'd stopped talking to her co-workers. They had assumed the worst; she knew it wasn't true, but she felt no need to explain herself to them. Of course, they were right. Koch had simply waited and done all he could to win her confidence and now when she was most vulnerable he issued his calculated offer. How could she say, "No?" But what made her such a prize?

Koch was rich and successful. He had leisure time; time to spend acquiring beautiful and tasteful things. Maria understood that Koch's interest in her was corporal. Within her family beauty was a luxury. It was a commodity not worth trading for, but in Koch's world it was a simple diversion he could afford. And as she finished playing the composition she decided that he would pay dearly for her services.

After dinner Koch had gone to his room. When Maria went upstairs, she saw that his bedroom door was slightly ajar and that the light was on. She went into her own room and changed into her nightgown. She then went to the bathroom and took a bath. After she bathed, she exited the tub and stood naked before the large oval mirror in the bathroom. She examined her body and tried to determine just what was it that Koch wished to possess. She had firm full breasts and a small waist. Her legs and backside were shapely and toned, and her face was unblemished and her features appealing. She turned and examined herself from different angles and agreed that she was attractive, if not beautiful. Rudy was gone and there would always be a void. How would she fill it? Koch was a handsome man. He was of average height and had a lean physique. His dress and hygiene were impeccable. He was rich, and the fact that he wanted her was stimulating. She felt a kind of power she had never felt before. Koch had offered an ultimatum of sorts and it was up to Maria to make him the supplicant. It was, quite simply, all about sex. He wanted to stuff his cock in her cunt, kiss her, suckle her and ride her the way a champion stud rides a prize mare. She'd not had a sexual feeling since before the fire. Any thought of love or physical congress had been unknown to her since the tragedy. But that night, in Koch's bathroom, as she stood naked before the mirror her sexuality returned. It was different, almost foreign. With Rudy it was always a union of one. Now she was a woman and she was on her own. She stood there before the mirror stimulating herself, and as her fingers massaged and tickled her cunt, she imagined Koch ramming his cock into her.

She grew excited and left the bathroom and went into Koch's bedroom. He was sitting up in bed reading a book. She came through the door and went over to his bed. She took the book from his hand and placed it on the nightstand. She sat down and leaned over and kissed him. She said nothing. She placed her

59

hand over his groin and felt him stiffen. He was in his pajamas, looking at her dumbfounded. She unbuttoned his pajama pants and straddled him. She felt herself flush with excitement and took hold of his hard penis and guided it into her. She knelt over him and arched her back and drove him as deeply into her as she could. She dug her fingers into his chest and moved up and down on him with hard thrusting motions. She felt him come. She kept riding him and telling him to push harder and harder into her. She was in frenzy, but it was a controlled frenzy. She could see him straining to stay erect, straining to satisfy her. Her orgasms came one after another, but she kept riding him, urging him to perform. He grew flaccid long before she was finished. His soft penis fell out of her and she tried to push it in and she kept telling him, "Please don't stop. Not now!" Koch was breathless and Maria climbed off him. She brushed his lips with her breasts, then kissed him firmly. "I think you know what my decision is," she said. And then she left the room.

When she went back to her bedroom, she knew that it was she who was in control and not Koch. She had planned it perfectly. Her goal was to make him climax as quickly as possible. Koch, the rich businessman and practiced lover, had reacted like an excited schoolboy having his first sexual experience. Maria went to sleep content with the fresh memory of her victory. Over the years she would recall with great satisfaction the picture of Koch's face, paralyzed with frustration as she squeezed his limp cock and implored him to stick it ever deeper into her.

It was a rich memory. She went to the bathroom and ran cold water over the washcloth. The thought of that night and her conquest of Koch had aroused her. The migraine was gone and it was the first time in months that she'd had a sexual yearning, and for a moment she toyed with the idea of inviting Henry into the bedroom, but then gave it a second thought and ran the water in the tub for a bath instead.

Chapter Nine

Ernie Lombardi was the delivery boy for the Associated Food Market located at the foot of Kingsbridge Road and Bailey Avenue. In addition to his duties as a delivery boy, he also stocked shelves and took grocery orders over the phone. The store was one of two owned by Bill and Harold Kimmel. Danny Monaghan was the delivery boy in the Kimmels' other store located further east on Kingsbridge Road near the Armory. It was late afternoon and Ernie was between deliveries. The phone rang in the front office that was adjacent to the checkout counters and separated from them by a glass window.

Gail, who was the store manager and emergency cashier, told Ernie to answer the phone. "Ernie, take that call. It's probably a delivery order."

Ernie went into the office and picked up the phone, "West Kingsbridge Market."

"That you, asshole?" answered Danny Monaghan.

"You must be talking to yourself again, dick face," Ernie said, laughing, then went on to say as Gail entered the office. "Okay, Mr. Gallagher, that's twelve quarts of Schlitz and three quarts of Pabst. And it's going to 212 West Kingsbridge Road, apartment 52C. I'll bring it right over." Ernie then wrote the information on a delivery slip and left the office. Gail followed him over to the refrigerator cooler and said, "Listen, wise guy, that better not be for you and your punk friends. Did Mr. Gallagher give a call back number?"

Ernie shot back, "No, but he's in the book. He calls almost every week."

"Yeah," she said, "every Friday, if I'm correct, around five."

"Guess, he likes to get a head start on the weekend."

"Well, you tell Mr. Gallagher there's an extra twenty cent delivery charge for every quart of beer. That's an extra three bucks, big shot. Payable in advance or you don't take the order."

Ernie dug into his pocket and took out a large lump of quarters and half dollars. He had about eight dollars in change, tip money he had earned earlier that afternoon, and he took four half dollar coins and four quarters and handed it to Gail. "You know, Mr. Gallagher's not gonna tip me after this," he said with genuine disappointment.

"Tough luck, buddy boy," she said with a smirk as she put the change in the pocket of her apron. "If he don't like it, tell him to buy his beer somewhere else." Gail then laughed and walked back to the office.

Ernie took twelve cold quarts of Schlitz and three cold quarts of Pabst beer and put them in a large reinforced cardboard carton. He picked up the heavy carton and went out the front door of the market and placed the carton in the oversized basket of the delivery bike. He turned the bike around and started to pedal up the steep incline of Kingsbridge Road.

On Kingsbridge Road, just east of 212 West Kingsbridge Road, midway up the hill was a large vacant lot that the neighborhood kids called Two-twelve. Sometime in the early 1930s, an enterprising builder had purchased the lot and begun the foundation for a large apartment building. The project never proceeded past the stone foundation, and as the economy of the Depression worsened, the project was cancelled. Over the course of two generations the abandoned building lot became a playground for the neighborhood kids. The scattered stone walls in various configurations were laid out in a complicated mosaic that was ideal for games of cowboys and Indians, cops and robbers, hide and seek and a host of other childhood diversions. As the children evolved into teenagers, the lot provided the shelter needed to harbor a first cigarette or bottle of beer. Danny Monaghan and Ernie Lombardi were the two toughest boys in a neighborhood clique of teenagers, who often referred to themselves as the Two-twelve Boys. Two-twelve was a place they could hang out far from the interference of nosy neighbors and meddling parents. Toward the back of the lot, bordering the rear of an apartment building on Heath Avenue was a large el shaped stone foundation. The foundation went up about twelve feet on both sides of the el and anyone behind the el could not be seen from the street or the east end of the apartment building at 212 West Kingsbridge Road. The Two-twelve Boys called the el The Spot, and it was their hangout. A cluster of elm trees covered the view from the Heath Avenue apartment buildings and private houses, and the boys had learned early on that within the shelter of the stone el they could be heard, but not seen. If they didn't make too much noise, no one would know they were there. If it was cold out, they could build a fire to stay warm and, again, as long as they weren't too noisy, no one bothered them. At the beginning of summer it was a cool and quiet retreat and ideal for an evening of beer drinking.

As Ernie passed the corner of Heath Avenue and Kingsbridge Road, he saw Danny Coleman and Billy Shaw sitting on the rear steps of P.S. 22. Coleman and Shaw waved to him and Coleman called out, "You got the stuff?"

Ernie responded, "Yeah, who do you know puts in an order like this but us? Meet me up at The Spot." Coleman and Shaw then took off down Heath Avenue and through the back yard of 2631 Heath for the shortcut into their hangout. Ernie pedaled halfway up the hill until he reached the north side of the apartment building and turned the delivery bike into the alleyway that ran next to the vacant lot. He wheeled the bike down the ramp and over to an opening in the fence that everyone used to enter the lot. He took the carton from the bike and handed it to Coleman and Shaw, who were already there waiting for him.

Ernie said to them, "Take the beer over to The Spot and put it in the Coffin. That fat bitch Gail knows this is for us. She made me give her an extra twenty cents for every quart of beer. She's such a bitch. I'm going over to the Gulf station on Bailey to get the ice. I'm getting two twenty-five pound blocks. Ray's supposed to get his brother to buy a couple of bottles of screwdriver mix and a half pint of Seagram's. I'll also get a couple of bottles of 7-Up from the soda machine. We should be all set"

Danny Coleman, who was called Little Danny and was Danny Monaghan's best friend, whipping boy and lackey, said, "Some big ass party we're throwing tonight. How much apiece?'

"Two dollars and twenty cents each. Let's hope the girls all come," Ernie said as he grabbed his crotch. "Maybe we'll get lucky." He giggled.

"Is Russian Annie coming?" asked Little Danny.

"Of course, it's Fagan's going away party and you know she likes him," said Ernie.

"What about Linda?" Billy Shaw inquired.

"Where you been? She broke up with him two nights ago. Guess she figured she'd need someone new with him going into the Navy and all that. You know what they say, if she's a cunt, she's a bitch," Ernie sneered.

"Danny's gonna be pissed off. He don't like her no more, don't like her at all," said Little Danny with emphasis.

63

"Like who?" Ernie said

"Russian Annie."

"You fergettin whose fucking party is this anyway?"

"Why doesn't Danny like Russian Annie?" Billy Shaw interjected.

"She's all right. It's her mother and grandmother that are crazy. Her grandmother's the Ukrainian Lady. That's what my granny and all the old ladies in the building call her. Sometimes she gets drunk and hangs out her kitchen window and curses out half the people in our building. If she sees the super, she throws stuff out the window at him. She's nuts, but very funny."

"Well, maybe she cursed out Danny's mother or father or something like that. He says Russian Annie's a whore and he don't wanna be around her," Little Danny added.

"Gimme a fucking break," replied Ernie. "Danny wants to get his hands on every chick he can. Truth is, Danny's old man is hammering Annie's mother Carla. I heard my mother telling my old man that the Milkman got caught by Louie the super screwing her on a table in the laundry room at 2810 last Saturday night. Story was all over the block."

"How'd your mother know that?" challenged Little Danny.

"You fergettin, mom's the crossing guard. Ain't nothing she don't find out worth finding out. My old man's a tight-lipped guinea, he don't say nothing, but my mother's an Irish washerwoman if ever there was one," Ernie said with pride as he climbed back on the bike and yelled over his shoulder as he pedaled away, "Get that shit in the Coffin 'fore it gets warm."

"Why do some people call Danny's old man the milkman?" Billy Shaw asked Little Danny as they both carried the carton of beer across the lot.

"You don't know?"

"If I fucking knew, I wouldn't ask."

"Danny's old man quit high school when he was sixteen and went to work as a milkman. His father was one and he got him the job. Anyway, he was working somewhere in the Lower Borough where there weren't no elevators and he had to carry all those heavy trays of milk up the stairs. That's how he got so strong. You ever see his forearms and hands? Like a fucking gorilla. When we was young, he used to be able to pick Danny and me up, one of us in each hand and spin us around. One time Danny told me, and don't repeat this story 'cause if you do I'll say it wasn't me, but he'll kick my ass 'cause of that's the way he is. Anyway, Danny's old man was crossing a rooftop to go to the other side of a building with deliveries when two niggers jumped out from behind a chimney and tried to rob him. Danny said his father put down his milk trays and knocked the first nigger on his ass and picked up the second one and threw him off the roof. Then he picked up his trays and went on his way. Didn't call the cops or nuthin. The other nigger got up and ran away."

"Yeah, I kinda heard that before, but I thought it was bullshit. Rumor was he killed a spook but I never knew he was a milkman. I only knew he was in construction. My father says Mike Monaghan's a small time hood."

"Just 'cause your old man's a parole officer don't mean he knows everything," Little Danny said defensively. "Me and Danny's lived across the hall from one another all our lives. His father's a wire latherer. Works all the time, and his mother goes to church every day. It ain't right and Danny don't like it when people talk about his family. So I don't care what your father says, and I'm not saying anything bad 'bout him 'cause I just know what I know and Danny's father has always been nice to me. You know?"

The two boys reached The Spot and put the carton down. Billy Shaw said to Little Danny, "No offense, I know you guys are tight, but the Monaghans are a strange family. How come his sister moved to England? Help me take the floor off the Coffin."

The Coffin was an oversized Coleman cooler the boys had stolen from the back of an unlocked Buick station wagon parked in a parking lot on Heath Avenue some months back. Little Danny, who was prized for his keen eye when it came finding something useful to steal, had seen it in the back of the car one night when they were going through the lot checking car doors to see if any were open and there might be some cigarettes or loose coins inside to steal. It was a Friday night and they carried the cooler back to the lot and put it in The Spot. The Two-twelve Boys took great pride in their maintenance of The Spot, and the addition of the Coleman cooler was one of their finest upgrades. A hole in the ground big enough to accommodate the cooler was dug. The hole was lined with tarpaper and bricks and the cooler was placed in it. The top three rows of brick were cemented in and there was a lip of brick several inches above ground level. A wooden hatch was nailed together from some loose pieces of lumber they found scattered around the lot and the cooler, secure in its new home, was christened the Coffin. An old rug they'd found thrown out for trash pick up was placed over the hatch and two benches made of wood planks nailed to wooden milk crates stood at ninety degree angles to the walls of the stone foundation. When everything was in place, the boys called it the Living Room.

In fact, just about everything and everyone in the neighborhood had a nickname. There was a large stone; eight feet up the wall, with an "L" painted on it. If you climbed the wall and pulled out the stone behind it you'd find several weathered girlie magazines. The stone-hiding place was called the Library. Inside the Coffin was a cotton comforter they had stolen from somebody's clothesline on the roof of one of the apartment houses on Bailey Avenue. When they had a party and there were girls in attendance, the comforter was spread out on the grass behind the foundation's walls. That was called the Bedroom, and if you wanted go and make-out and be alone with a girl you went to the Bedroom. In the corner of the el they had built a small fireplace from cinder blocks, and when the weather was cold they built a fire for warmth. Everything about The Spot was perfect, except, of course, when it rained. Rain was the great enemy. When it rained there was no place to go. You could hang out in the hallway of one of the apartment buildings or in the doorway of one of the stores on Kingsbridge Road, but it seemed someone was always chasing you away.

On school nights they could go to the gym at P.S. 22 and play basketball, but no place provided the refuge they found in The Spot. It was a treasured location and the younger kids in the neighborhood knew to stay away, the cops on patrol didn't care, and anyone over eighteen had better things to do than go trudging through a dirty, vacant building lot to see what a group of teenagers were up to.

Billy Shaw took the comforter out of the Coffin and spread it on the ground in the area they called the Bedroom. He winked at Little Danny and rubbed his hands over his jeans. "Maybe Russian Annie will give Fagan something to remember, whaddya think?"

"I just hope Danny don't start in on her," Little Danny said as he knelt down and placed the bottles of beer in the Coffin.

"This isn't Danny's party. Ernie's running the show and his best friend is Fagan. We got Mary, Russian Annie, Diane, Linda, Mary Kay and Denise coming tonight. None of those girls really like Mary or Annie so that should be fun enough. Fuck, Mary's gonna get drunk on one drink and go after Danny," Billy said, laughing.

"Oh shit! You're right. Danny doesn't like Diane no more. Danny's got a thing for Linda now that she dumped Fagan, and he ain't gonna want any of those girls thinking he's screwing around with Mary," Little Danny said as he sat on one of the benches and took out a pack of Kool non-filters. He lit one up and inhaled.

Billy Shaw sat down on the other bench and took out a pack of Marlboro's and put a cigarette in his mouth. He then took out his Zippo lighter and popped the lid and in one motion ran the lighter up his pants leg, igniting the wick and bringing the flame up to light his cigarette.

He then stood up and said, "The Iceman Cometh."

Striding across the lot was Ernie Lombardi carrying a cardboard box with two large blocks of ice in it. Ernie placed the box down and picked up one of the cinder blocks from the fireplace. He brushed the cinder block off, then raised it above his head and sent its point smashing down into the two ice blocks. He repeated the movement several times until the ice blocks had broken up into smaller shards of gleaming frozen water. Satisfied with his work, he lifted the lid to the Coffin and placed the ice over the quarts of beer.

As he was doing that, Ray Ferguson came huffing onto the scene with a brown shopping bag filled with clinking bottles.

"Whatcha got Raymondo?" Ernie asked.

"I got the ready-made screwdriver shit and a half-pint of Seagram's. Courtesy of Kingsbridge Liquors by way of my dear older brother Edward."

Ernie stood up and bowed and pointed his hand to the open cooler of beer and ice. "Please deposit your gifts, my good man."

"Yes, please do," joined in Billy Shaw. "For the Two-twelve Boys are going to rock tonight as we bid a fond farewell to Joseph Fagan, soon to be Seaman Fagan."

"And if he's lucky, the lovely Russian Annie will give him a special send-off," intoned Ernie.

"Yeah and if we're lucky, Danny won't ruin it for him," whined Little Danny.

"Don't worry, he gets out of line, I kick his ass. Just like that. He better act like his mother tonight and not his father," Ernie said with serious determination in his voice.

"What gives with his mother?" Billy Shaw, ever inquisitive, asked. "I mean, the fucking woman is always in church. The old man is a fucking wild man. My father says he does strong arm work for some bookie in Riverview. Shit, last year he walked into the Lounge and grabbed Beery Cleary and smashed his face right into the bar. He's beating people, and Danny's mother is practicing to be a nun. She has calluses on her knees from praying so much. That's how Danny got into Cathedral Prep. That's fucking irony," he said, shaking his head.

"Yeah, we know you go to prep school, showoff," Little Danny moaned and said in a falsetto voice. "That's fucking irony."

"Cut the shit," Ernie ordered. "It's almost six. We gotta be back by seven because that's the time I told all the girls to get here. So stop fighting, go home and eat and by the time youse get back everything will be ice cold for a hot time."

Ernie put the hatch back over the Coffin and placed the rug over that. The four boys then left the lot.

At five to seven Little Danny walked across the hall from his apartment and knocked on Danny Monaghan's door. Mrs. Monaghan opened the door and asked Little Danny in. Danny was seated at the kitchen table and was just finishing a plate of fried flounder and home fries. Mrs. Monaghan turned to Little Danny and said, "Daniel would you like a bit of flounder?"

Little Danny loved Mrs. Monaghan. He loved her sweet brogue and the gentle way about her. "No thanks, I just ate. We had egg salad and soup."

"Are you still hungry? I've plenty and you're a growing boy," she said as she straightened her apron.

"Ma, he don't wanna eat. We're going to a party for Joe Fagan, he's going into the Navy," Danny said as he pushed his empty plate away and wiped his mouth.

"Yeah, that's right, Mrs. Monaghan; we're late, but thanks anyway."

Danny got up from the table and went to the bathroom. He brushed his teeth and brushed back his hair. There was a jar of Dixie Peach pomade in the medicine cabinet and he smeared a dab in his palms and wiped his hands over the top of his thick brown hair. He stared in the mirror a moment and smiled in satisfaction with what he saw. "Ain't I fucking suave, just fucking too suave," he said out loud. He then took the top off the bottle of Canoe cologne he kept on the top of the toilet tank and splashed a generous amount over his face and neck. His toilet complete, he left the bathroom and bounded down the hallway. "All right, Mom, we're going," he said cheerfully.

"Now you both wait there one minute."

The two young men stood in the hallway by the front door in front of the gold-framed print of President John F. Kennedy that Mrs. Monaghan had hung in the hallway with a miniature picture of the Sacred Heart of Jesus squeezed into the lower right corner of the frame. She approached them, and in her right hand was a set of rosary beads. They were made of dark green glass and had been given to her by Father Dunphy, the Monsignor of St. John's parish. He had brought them back from a trip he'd taken to Fatima in Portugal and they were Mrs. Monaghan's most prized possession and rarely out of her reach. She took her right hand and placed it on Danny's left shoulder and her left hand on Little Danny's right shoulder and she told them to bow their heads.

"In the name of our blessed Lord Jesus and his mother the Virgin Mary and all the saints I ask for God's blessing for these two fine young men." She then took her hands off them and told them, "Repeat after me…in the name of the Father, and the Son and the Holy Spirit, Our Father, who art in Heaven, hallowed be thy name, thy kingdom come, Thy will be done, on earth as it is in Heaven, give us this day our daily bread, and forgive us our trespasses as we forgive those who trespass against us, lead us not…" Suddenly the front door to the apartment flew open and Little Danny was knocked into the wall. "Oh my God," shrieked Mrs. Monaghan.

It was Mike Monaghan. He wasn't drunk, but he'd been drinking. "For Christ sakes, Mary, I could hear you praying outside the God damn door. Let the boys go and make my dinner." He didn't greet either of the two boys and stamped down the hallway to the bathroom. He didn't bother to close the door and the forceful surge of his urine could be heard hitting the water in the toilet. "What's for dinner? I'm starving and I have to meet someone around eight, so let's get a move on," he yelled from the bathroom.

Mrs. Monaghan put her rosary beads into the pocket of her housedress and pushed the two boys out the door and made each of them make the sign of the cross. "Don't be too late, Danny, and have fun at your party."

"Your father scares the shit outta me sometimes," Little Danny said to Danny.

"Me too, my mother's always telling me to pray for him. But he's happy. She's got the problem," Danny responded.

"I love your mother; she's always been good to me."

"Yeah, I love her, you love her, my sister Kathy loves her, but my old man don't," Danny replied. "Don't ever repeat this, but before my sister left for England she told me my parents hadda get married. Shotgun thing, you know? That's why mom's always with the priests. My old man don't like all that religious shit and he breaks her balls about it all the time. Sometimes he gets real nasty and he calls her Irish Mary the Rosary Queen."

"Why?"

"If you can't figure it out, I ain't gonna waste my time telling you."

"Aw that's not nice," little Danny whined.

"Yeah, go tell my old man, tough guy," Danny said sarcastically.

"Sure thing, big guy, I wanna tell Mike Monaghan off—you're fucking crazy."

"That's how I feel, stupid," Danny said in a tone that suggested the conversation about his father was over.

ANTHONY D. MURPHY

As they were going out through the courtyard, Little Danny said, "You know Russian Annie and Hand-job Mary are gonna be there tonight."

"Yeah, Ernie told me. He thinks Fagan's gonna get in her pants. She's a fucking slut, but I don't think she goes that far. Anyway, it's Fagan's party. I'm staying clear of both of them. If Mary starts acting funny you gotta go with her. I might make a move for Linda, but I don't know. I got something else on my mind," he said devilishly.

"You got a new girl?"

"Better, but you can't tell a soul. If you do, I'll fucking kill you," Danny said menacingly.

Little Danny felt he'd learned more than he wanted to about the Monaghans and didn't want to burden himself with any more of Danny's revelations. Danny had a bad habit of letting Little Danny in on some small tidbit of gossip and swearing him to secrecy. That, however, always caused a problem since Danny would do the same thing with five other people and then when the news got out, as it always did, he would blame Little Danny for leaking the information. One of his nicknames for Little Danny was "Radio Free Kingsbridge." This was especially upsetting when the juicy tidbit pertained immediately to Danny Monaghan or members of his family. He made a futile attempt to change the subject and he asked Danny, "Do you think it's a mortal sin when we let your mother pray over us, then we go trying to find girls we can fuck?"

"It ain't a sin until we fuck one, and so far that hasn't happened."

"Yeah, but we're talking about it."

"Christ hates the sin, but loves the sinner. Didn't you ever hear that? We fuck up and we go to confession. And then we fuck up again," Danny said authoritatively. "Now, like I was saying before, and this is a fucking secret, do you understand? I think there's this older woman who wants to seduce me."

"You kiddin?"

"I was making a delivery last week up on Lincoln Boulevard, at the Excelsior. Right near Kingsbridge Road, real ritzy building and this woman opens the door and she's in this see-thru nighty. I take the groceries into the kitchen and I can see right through the fucking thing. She's standing by the window and I'm looking right at her in her panties and bra. Big bazoongas sitting in a black bra and black panties. She's just standing there and I'm fucking staring at her. I got a fucking hard on just looking at her. And she's just looking at me. Like I fucking know she's teasing me. You don't let someone in your house when you're in your underclothes unless you want them to see you. She's really good looking. And she's a woman. I know she wants me," he said excitedly. Just telling the story to Little Danny aroused him. He was almost wishing just Mary and Annie was coming to the party so he could get with Mary and find a little relief.

"How'd you know she wants you?"

"I can tell. There's some things about her I know, and she's that type. What a rack man, big fucking beautiful tits. You gotta see her, see what I mean," Danny went on. His mind was racing and he could see the pictures of her and he knew he'd be back, maybe not for her, but for the pictures. Danny always told Little Danny everything. They were closer than brothers, and although he bullied him and mocked him, Little Danny was his confidant in all things and the only person in the world he ever really felt comfortable with. Little Danny had always been his friend and would always be his friend. As they'd gone through life so far, no one picked on little Danny but Danny. No one bullied him or even teased him when Danny was around. If they chose up sides for a game, Little Danny was always chosen first by Danny. There were no secrets, but even so, he couldn't just yet tell him about the pictures. Once he got them he'd show him, but not until then.

"You're serious?"

Danny pulled a pair of woman's black panties from his dungaree pocket. They were folded like a handkerchief and Danny sniffed them. "I'm on a mission Little Dan," he sighed. "I know a woman when I see one."

Chapter Ten

Henry was sitting alone in the kitchen drinking a cup of coffee and listening to the morning radio. A recording of Matt Monro singing "I Get Along Without You Very Well" was playing and Henry was quietly singing along. Maria walked into the kitchen and Henry sang to her along with the crooner over the radio, "I get along without you very well, of course I do, except perhaps in spring…"

Maria smiled. "You'd do fine without me."

Henry laughed. "I'd be just like the fellow in the song, believe me I would."

"I think I'll have a cup of coffee this morning and a bowl of bran," Maria said, changing the subject. Maria was never drawn to popular music the way Henry was. He knew the lyrics to so many songs and loved to sing along. Maria liked to listen to music but she, despite her excellent memory, never paid much attention to the lyrics. She thought much of it was just plain sappy and repetitious. While Maria was getting her cereal, Henry poured her a cup of coffee. She ate and he sat down and finished his coffee.

After Maria was done eating she said to him, "You're off to Montreal this morning."

"That I am. We're catching the ten o'clock from La Rochelle Station."

"We're catching?" Maria questioned. "You're taking Sophie?"

"You could have come too," he replied. "She's essential to my practice. Ancowitz is buying a shopping center and different properties belong to different owners. It can be confusing and there is a lot of paperwork. Sophie's the best when it comes to those things."

"Yes, I know. You were singing her praises to Jack Stern the other night. The way you talk it sounds like you're the unessential one. When do you make her your partner?" she asked condescendingly.

Henry didn't say anything and poured Maria another cup of coffee. Maria was wearing an olive-colored skirt and a light yellow silk blouse. Her hair fell to her shoulders and looked soft and shiny in the morning wash of sunlight that poured through the kitchen window. She was standing by the counter sipping her coffee. She didn't sit down because she didn't want to wrinkle her skirt. Henry knew all of her eccentricities, and those surrounding her wardrobe and appearance were the most extreme. Once Maria was dressed, she didn't sit down until she got to work. When she rode the subway to work she stood the whole time. Even at work she was on her feet most of the day, and when she did sit it was on a high stool. It wasn't until she took the subway home that she actually sat down. Henry couldn't help but sit there and admire his wife. She took small bites of food and chewed carefully. There was nothing ravenous about her table manners. No matter the food or how hungry she was, it was always the same neat, measured approach to her meal. She leaned over the counter to sip her coffee and, again, every effort was made to neither wrinkle nor stain her clothing. Many women her age had filled out and swelled with age, or gotten too thin and stick-like, but Maria, somehow, remained pliant and youthful. Just to sit there and share a cup of coffee was a pleasant experience for him.

"I'm taking a taxi to the station. Are you coming with me?"

"I guess so. Are we picking up Sophie?"

"No, she's meeting me there. Would that be a problem?"

"No, not at all. I just haven't seen her for some time. Has her skin improved?"

"No, do you have some miracle cosmetic that will help her?" he asked sarcastically.

"Nothing would help her. Well, actually there are many things that would help her. She could try to change her diet, spend a week at our Forever Alive spa, have the enema treatment and try a little skin abrasion. That would help get the toxins out of her body and clean her face up some, I think." Maria answered in a professional and clinical manner.

Henry laughed. "My God, that's some sales pitch. You've met the woman, what, five times maybe six in the ten years or so that she's worked for me and you've worked out a beauty plan for her."

"That's what I do. I go to that spa twice a year. I've asked you to come. There's nothing wrong with cleansing your body," Maria chided.

"Oh yeah, the coffee enema treatment, every day for a week, right?"

"It works. Your girl couldn't afford the spa anyway. But she could use it."

"I think that's out of her league. She's not a movie star or a socialite"

Maria frowned at his remark, then said, "Not really, we have home spa treatments. Today we're doing a spa promotion. Some of the therapists and technicians from Forever Alive will be at Sable's. We give ten of our best customers a morning of health and beauty. They get there at eight and start the day with the coffee enema. Then they have a yoga class and learn some simple meditation practices. When I arrive, they get the pureed juice and green tea and I promote Forever Alive. Then we start the massages and facials with herbal scrubs and wraps. It's really delightful, and the treatment is no different than what you'd get at Forever Alive. Also, they give consultations on diet and beauty care. What type of skin you have and the type of diet best for it, that sort of thing. Next time we have a promotion spa day I'll invite Sophie. She'll think you're a very giving boss. Then, maybe she thinks that already."

Henry looked at Maria and smiled. She wasn't angry, but there did seem to be some hint of jealousy in her comments and he was secretly pleased by it. "You've never said more than ten words about Sophie, now you find out she's going to Montreal and suddenly you're interested in her. You've never even shown much interest in my practice, for that matter."

"Please, Henry. You are a lawyer and a good one I suspect, but I've no interest in what you do. It's dull. I'm not saying you're dull, but what you do doesn't appeal to me. Who your secretary is doesn't really matter to me either. I just find her very unattractive and cheap looking. I thought maybe I could be of some help, that's all," she responded as she put her cereal bowl and coffee cup in the sink. "What time is the taxi coming?"

"Eight forty-five, will you be ready?"

"I'm ready now," she answered.

Henry grabbed his travel suitor and held the door for Maria. As they were waiting for the elevator, she fixed his tie. "You really need to start buying shirts with a larger collar size," she said as she straightened his tie. "Some of the extra weight you put on went to your face and neck."

"I'm starting up my tennis game again. Playing with Doyle and Haas this coming Saturday and Sunday," he said as he examined himself in the mirrored wall that surrounded the elevator door opening.

"Well, I guess my weekend is planned."

"C'mon, it's summer. You know I go to the club every weekend. You work most Saturdays anyway," he said with a touch of annoyance in his voice. *God,* he thought, *the woman is happy to go for a walk and sit around the apartment reading a book all day. What am I supposed to do?*

They boarded the elevator, and as it was descending Henry asked her, "You've got to do me one favor. When Millie comes on Thursday, make sure she goes to Han Lee's and picks up my shirts. I left the ticket on my bureau. I was going to pick them up yesterday, but I forgot. There are seven shirts in my closet in that little hamper. Have her take those and pick up the clean ones. I packed my last three cleans ones and I'll have nothing for Friday."

"Millie has enough to do. I'll get your shirts."

"You pamper her way too much. She's our cleaning lady. I pay her well. She can run a few errands, too. It won't kill her."

"Henry, I work almost every Thursday from one until nine-thirty. Millie comes every Thursday at eleven. She loves to talk. If I'm lucky I get out the door by twelve so I can catch the train and get to work on time. It's much easier for me to drop off the shirts Thursday morning and pick up the clean ones than ask her to do it. She has a routine, and as long as we don't alter it, everything gets done. Whenever I add something new to her routine, she pesters me with a hundred questions about it. Last Thursday I sent her to Han Lees for the sheets. I was gone before she got back and if you noticed she never emptied the hamper in the bathroom. So, please, no added chores," she insisted.

"Fine," he said as the elevator doors opened and they walked out into the lobby.

Tim the doorman was at his post and greeted Henry and Maria. "Good morning, Mr. and Mrs. Weiss," he said with a big beaming smile on his face. "Here, Mr. Weiss, let me take your bag. Going on a trip I guess, there's cab waiting outside."

"Montreal, Tim, just for a couple of days. Mrs. Weiss is staying behind, so take care of her," Henry said as he drew two singles from his pocket and handed them to Tim.

"Montreal, that's where Jackie had his start, you know," Tim said referring to Jackie Robinson, who he knew was a favorite of Henry's.

"Right you are," Henry said as he waited for Tim to open the taxi door to let Maria in.

Maria got into the taxi slowly. She pulled on the hem of her skirt as she sat down and smoothed it out. It was a Checker cab and there was plenty of leg room in the passenger's compartment. She sat back in the seat and extended her legs and crossed them at the ankles.

Henry climbed into the taxi and waved goodbye to Tim. He told the driver to stop at Sable's, then to go on to La Rochelle Station. He put his hand on her thigh and told her, "I'm going to miss you, honey. Montreal's a beautiful place and we could have had a good time. We did the last time."

"I'm sure we would have," she said as she pushed his hand away from her. "Please, Henry, don't muss me up," she added.

Henry sat back in his corner of the car and folded his hands on his lap. He could see the driver continually looking into his rear view mirror and knew the guy was checking out more than the traffic. Henry wanted to ask her if she would miss him. He wouldn't though, because he knew that more than likely she'd say, "No" and he didn't want the driver to overhear that exchange. Instead, he said nothing, waiting for her to initiate the conversation, but she didn't and they rode silently into Huguenot City.

They made great time down the Upper Borough Expressway and over the West Avenue Bridge into Huguenot City, but the further they moved downtown the slower they went.

Maria was growing impatient and remarked, "This is why I always take the subway, it's faster, and cheaper, too!"

Neither Henry nor the cab driver answered her, but the driver either reflexively or in an attempt to please Maria increased his speed and engaged several maneuvers to pass cars and turn down different streets in a vain attempt to reach their destination sooner. Henry marveled to himself at Maria's ability to get men to do her bidding and sat smiling as they made better time.

The driver pulled up to the front of Sable's and Maria bent over and pecked Henry on the cheek before she got out of the cab. "Have a nice trip, I'll see you Thursday," she said warmly.

That little kiss made all the difference in the world to Henry. It was all he needed at that moment to demonstrate that she cared for him, even if it was just a little. He watched her exit the cab and walk down the street to the store entrance. She was wearing a pair of open toed sandals with just enough heel to add the proper contour to her legs, but not tire her legs from standing in them all day. The skirt was just tight enough to accent her figure, but there was nothing cheap or trashy—words she had used to describe Sophie about her outfit. *She was class, all class,* he thought.

"She your wife, buddy?" the cab driver asked.

"Yes, she is."

"She looks like Lee Remick, better than Lee Remick."

"You should have seen her when she was young."

"She don't look too old to me. I knew any better I'd a thought you we're her uncle."

"How old do you think she is?"

"Late thirties," was the cab driver's quick reply.

"She's fifty, my friend," Henry said definitively.

"Shit, my old lady's forty-five and she looks like she could be your wife's mother," the driver said with disgust. "You are one lucky fellow," he said with the emphasis on lucky.

"Tell me about it," Henry said with resignation.

They were stopped a block from La Rochelle Station and Henry saw Sophie trudging down the street carrying an oversized suitcase. "Jesus Christ," he said. "She took the subway. What's wrong with her? Please pull over," he said to the driver. "I'll get out here."

"Something wrong?" the driver asked.

"Nothing, just let me out here. It's my secretary."

They were half a block from the entrance to the station and the driver pulled over to the curb. He got out and went to the trunk and got Henry's suitor. Henry hurriedly paid the fare along with a generous tip and started down the block. He called out to Sophie several times, and as he got closer to her, she heard him and stopped. She gave him a big smile and wrapped her arms around his neck and gave him a long kiss on the lips.

"Don't say anything. I should have taken a cab, but I'm only a block from the subway. Why waste the money?"

"You don't listen."

Henry took Sophie's suitcase in one hand and his in another and said, "C'mon, let's find a porter. I'm too old to be carrying all this stuff."

Henry's cab driver was stalled in traffic and he watched the little scene between Henry and Sophie. *Jesus Christ*, he thought, *Goddamn guy has a wife that looks like a movie star and she's not out of sight for five minutes and the guy's kissing some hot chick in tight pants and catching a train with her to Montreal. Where did I go wrong?* he lamented.

Henry found a porter and told him they were taking the 10:00 a.m. to Montreal. Henry and Sophie went directly to the train and boarded. They went to the dining car and Henry ordered them coffee. No meals were served until the train departed. Sophie was dressed like a teenager. She looked cute, he thought, but there was something childish and unsophisticated about her look that annoyed him. Her hair was pulled back and tied with a red kerchief and you couldn't help but notice the set of gold earrings that were made up of a long chain with a globe about the size of a marble hanging at the bottom of the chain. She had on a pair of tight dungarees and a little top that stopped two inches above the waistband on her pants. She was wearing sharp pointed black suede shoes with small heels; they were the type of shoe popular with teenage girls. She'd gotten a lot of sun over the weekend and her skin was well tanned. The tanned skin and a little makeup did wonders for her complexion and she looked much better than usual. She looked cute and sexy, but she wasn't going to remind anyone of Lee Remick and that bothered him. What really bothered him was that she was genuinely happy to be with him and he would have given anything to have Maria feel that way.

Chapter Eleven

Maria was sorry she'd kissed Henry goodbye. She'd done it for the cab driver's benefit and not Henry's. The driver kept staring at her for most of the ride. His eyes were constantly checking the rearview mirror and she was sure it was her he was looking at. He was seedy looking and there was a faint stink of body odor and stale tobacco in the car that ruined what was otherwise a warm and fragrant June morning. The kiss was Maria's way of teasing the driver. She'd already kissed Henry before the driver pulled up to the curb. He saw her do it and when the cab stopped she got out and didn't even look at him or acknowledge him with a "Thank you or goodbye." That was her way of telling him he was insignificant. *You can leer and ogle all you want*, she thought, *but I'll just treat you like you don't exist.*

She'd been in a good mood when she woke up, but that was now gone. Henry's taking Sophie to Montreal had upset her more than she would have imagined. Just last week she was deciding to leave him for good because she thought their marriage was dead and now she was hurt and upset when confronted with a situation that clearly indicated what she had suspected for sometime: Henry was sleeping with Sophie. She told herself this was no surprise, when taking into consideration how cold she had been to him the last several years. Henry had always had an active libido and Maria should have realized that her lack of interest in sex in no way diminished his appetite. Maria never liked Sophie and from their first meeting it was evident that Sophie viewed her not as the boss's wife but as a rival. The handful of times Maria had been at Henry's office she found Sophie indifferent to her and noticeably indulgent, if not fawning, in her attentions to Henry. She sadly regretted mentioning the Forever Alive Spa and telling Henry she'd invite Sophie. She only said it because she wanted to remind Henry of just how homely she thought Sophie was. The irony of her jealousy was that an affair between Henry and Sophie was the obvious result of Maria's own disinterest in her husband. The thought of having his gum snapping secretary lapping up a day of high end beauty pampering at Sable's while Maria waited on her was sickening. Henry, who always enjoyed the magnanimous gesture, had, no doubt, already extended the invitation to Sophie and Maria was certain that Sophie would make sure Maria delivered on her promise. *Furthermore*, she thought, *the little bitch would view the invitation as an opportunity to get that much closer to me.* If Maria was going to lose Henry, she was going to lose him because that was what she wanted. She'd already lost Rudy and Amos Koch, and there was no way she'd permit Henry to abandon her.

Maria reached the third floor beauty salon at Sable's. She entered the spa room and found her ten wealthy and pampered clients wrapped in lush terry cloth robes sipping green tea and listening to a lecture on nutrition by Guy Roberts. Guy was a nutritionist and masseur by training and Lorient Cosmetics director of the Forever Alive Spa.

Guy interrupted his lecture and went over and embraced Maria. "We started twenty-five minutes late, so relax," he said. She apologized for interrupting him and went to the back of the room and poured herself a cup of tea and asked him to resume his program. There were two empty vinyl lounge chairs in the back of the room and a high backed stool. Maria went to the stool, but then took into account that Guy had a good forty minutes to go in his program and she sat down in one of the lounge chairs. She smoothed her skirt before she sat down, but she knew it'd wrinkle and she sat down nonetheless. It was a long morning and she needed time to relax.

The thought of Henry and Sophie traveling to Montreal by train brought back the memory of her own train trip from Berlin to Paris after she'd agreed to become Amos Koch's mistress. It was the morning after she had seduced Amos Koch. She'd gotten up and bathed and dressed, but didn't go downstairs for breakfast. She had gone to sleep in a euphoric mood, but upon awakening and reflecting on what she'd done the night before she didn't know exactly how Amos was going to interpret her actions. She had left him literally speechless and out of breath, and she was completely unsure about how to approach him.

She didn't want to appear brazen and overconfident, nor did she wish to act timid and uncertain. She sat on the edge of her bed and rehearsed in her mind what she would say to him when they next met. Her plan was to act casual and treat the incident as if it hadn't happened. She wasn't even going to mention Paris; instead she would let him make the next move.

There was a knock on the bedroom door and the Polish cook called out, "Miss Maria, breakfast." Her German was practically non-existent and most communications were limited to one or two simple words that had some connection to the matter at hand.

Maria didn't bother to answer. She looked in the mirror,, fixed her hair and left to go downstairs.

Maria entered the dining room and Koch was seated at the head of the table. He was reading the morning paper and there was a pot of tea in front of him. He raised his teacup toward her and smiled. "My deepest apologies, Maria," he said in his halting, but formal English. "It was wrong of me to try and compel you to my bed. I imagine that your treatment of me last night was symbolic of how I treated you and I ask your forgiveness. I want you to come to Paris with me, but our relationship must have as a foundation our mutual affection for one another," he stated with the utmost sincerity.

Maria always wondered, *What language does he think in before he translates it to English?*

The cook came in as Koch was speaking and when he finished, she said to Maria, "Eggs and prunes?" Maria had a soft-boiled egg and stewed prunes for breakfast every morning with tea.

She said, "Yes," to the cook and the cook smiled and left the room. She was grateful for the cook's intrusion, as it gave her time to think of a response. Koch's statement sounded rehearsed and Maria knew he'd given it a good deal of deliberation before delivering it. She smiled and put her head down and simply said, "I would like that too."

"Good, good. Now that we've settled that I have some news for you," Koch said as he stood up from his chair and moved toward Maria. He put his hand on her shoulder and squeezed it lightly. It didn't hurt, but Maria felt the pressure. "Tomorrow we leave for Paris. We'll pack this afternoon."

"But, Amos, this is all so sudden and unexpected," Maria remembered saying. She wanted to be with Koch, but wasn't ready to leave Berlin.

"I haven't much time. I own three warehouses here in Germany, fully stocked with my products, among other items of value and this afternoon they will be the property of a high government official. The financial loss is staggering, but it will enable me to leave Germany with a quarter of what I own. This official is anxious for me to leave the country and I have no desire to disappoint him."

"Your home here, all of your things, what will happen to them?"

"Sold, don't worry. Get your things together. I have two new trunks coming this afternoon and we'll pack our things," he said, then bent down, kissed her cheek and left the room.

Koch left the house shortly after that exchange and Maria returned to her room and collected her belongings. The thought of moving to France excited her, but Koch's news of their immediate departure unnerved her. She knew that she was politically naïve, but things in Berlin were turning and it was obvious to anyone who paid the least attention to civic affairs that a new regime had taken control of the country and Germany was headed in a new direction. Amos Koch was a shrewd man and was eager to cut his losses and escape before the new Germany consumed him.

Koch returned a little past noon and there were two men in work clothes with him. Each man was carrying an ornate brown leather trunk. The trunks matched one another and were four feet long by two feet wide by one and a half feet high. Koch directed the men to take the two trunks to Maria's bedroom. After the men left, Koch and Maria went up to her room.

Koch smiled at Maria and said, "Those warehouses I told you about. This is what they amounted to." He then took a black velvet cloth from his pocket and laid it on the top of a trunk. He unfolded it and withdrew from the apron inside sixteen sparkling stones. "Diamonds, difficult to imagine that a handful of crushed carbon could be worth so much," he said sadly.

Koch then unscrewed the handles from the two trunks. Inside of each handle was an empty brass cylinder. He inserted eight diamonds into each handle and reattached the handles to the trunks. "No matter what happens, we can't let these trunks out of our sight until we reach Paris."

"Will we be in danger?"

"If we remain in Berlin, only if we are here," he said with deep sadness.

Each trunk had a barrel combination lock. It was a tumbler with five numbered dials. The combinations were very simple. One was the odd trunk—1, 3, 5, 7, 9 and the other was the even trunk—2, 4, 6, 8, 0. The trunks seemed like any other piece of luggage, and he told her to put all of her belongings into the even trunk. He took the odd trunk into his room. Maria had one closet full of clothes and she told Koch that she didn't think everything would fit. He told her she could always buy more clothes in France and to take what she liked

82

and all that she deemed essential and to pack it. Everything else was to be left behind.

That night as she lay in bed, Koch came to her bedside. She was asleep and awakened with a start to the touch of someone gently stroking her arm. She wasn't surprised to find Koch there, and she said, "Oh, Amos, it's you. You startled me."

He was dressed in his pajamas. "I didn't mean to, but I had to come see you. Tomorrow we leave for France. My apartment is in the Hotel Montsouris on Rue Raymond Losserand. It is in a beautiful part of the city. Paris is a wonderful place and we'll be there together, but I must know before then— who you are?"

Maria looked at his face and there were tears in his eyes. "What do you mean?" she said as she sat up on the pillow.

"Last night you came into my room and you were very bold. Angry with me, I'm sure."

"Why would you think I was angry?"

"You were. And that is why I apologized this morning. My behavior was wrong. It was wrong of me to take advantage of my position and demand that you be my lover in exchange for my assistance."

Maria was moved by this act of contrition. "I was angry, but I was also interested. I would not have gone to you if I didn't want to."

Koch then bent down and kissed her. Maria was taken by his sweetness, his vulnerability and sensitiveness to her, and she returned the kiss. Maria moved off the bed and stood up. She was wearing a long flannel gown and she rolled it up and slipped it over her shoulders and head and put it on the floor. She stood naked before Koch. Unlike her fury of the previous evening, she was quiet and smiling.

Koch sat there on the bed staring at her. His eyes were wet with tears and he wiped at them and asked her to excuse his emotion.

Maria took his hands and placed them on her breasts. She said to him, "Be gentle."

Koch placed his hands around her hips and she moved closer to him. Slowly he licked at her breasts and lightly massaged her thighs. She pressed her fingers into his shoulders and he ran his tongue down her body past her navel and fell to his knees and delicately flicked his tongue at the opening of her vagina.

Maria came alive and lost track of the time as Koch rhythmically and slowly stroked his tongue deeper and deeper into the moistened groove of flesh that had been cold for so long. Maria's sighs and moans filled the room and Koch moved his tongue back up to her breasts and neck and gently they fell together onto the bed and he slipped into her, and as her legs gripped and wrapped around him she experienced a rush of pleasure that was at first familiar and then, as the intensity grew, the feeling was entirely new. Koch was now in control. Maria was out of breath and at a point where she had become so sensitive to his touch that she thought she would faint if he didn't stop. Koch shuddered and finally rolled to his side, but kept her in his arms. He was smiling and Maria began to laugh. "I think my life has started again."

"I'm happy and I promise you we'll be happy."

Maria got out of bed and put her nightgown back on. She sat on the side of the bed and touched Koch's cheek. "What about your wife?"

"I've told you much about Carmela, how Carmela and I came to be, but I've never told you how she feels about me."

"What do you mean?"

"Carmela's father was an animal. He raped her when she was fourteen, as he did her younger sister. The happiest day of her life was the day her father was found dead on the slaughterhouse floor. She was indifferent to her mother and the marriage to my father brought with it the excitement of adding me to their household. Carmela had always liked me and flirted with me. My bedroom was down the hall from hers, and I was young, just eighteen, and Carmela would come into my room, sometimes climb into bed at night, just to be near me. She would ask me if I cared for her and would I like to kiss her or touch her? Things that at that age a young man couldn't resist. One thing led to another and we became lovers. I was naïve and Carmela, for whatever reasons, planned to have my child, which she did. After the birth of Jonathan, my second son, Carmela had a conversion. She told me about her father's incestuous habits and how her mother had known about it and permitted it. Getting pregnant with my child was her way of getting back at her mother. She felt she had sinned, and as time went on she became more and more religious and more and more distant from me. I, for my part, had been unfaithful from the start. I felt I had been tricked into marriage, and in order to satisfy my father I did what was appropriate and married. We led different lives. I spent much time traveling for the business and it has only been the last five years that I've been home. She is a wonderful mother, but a wife in name only, and it is an arrangement that brings her contentment. She is back in Argentina with my sons and I am here. I live my own life and for now, you are a part of it," he finished by kissing her again and silently left the room.

Maria sat back in the chair and was aware of Guy Roberts droning on about the Forever Spa. She had been lost in her reverie for several minutes, but it seemed as if a lifetime had passed. She asked herself how much of the past she really remembered. *Was everything just as I recall or has time shaded my memory?* She didn't know, but in her heart there was a void that nothing or no one could fill. Guy was standing by a flip chart and Maria could see the bold printed message on the page SUGAR= FLAB and next to it was a caricature of a woman in a bikini. She had enormously fat thighs and a big belly. Guy was moving to the part of his program that outlines all the foods a diet shouldn't contain. "Eat these every day, and it doesn't matter how often you exercise, you'll be fat," he said with all the vigor and ardor of a football coach. This was where Guy was at his best. He could take a room full of pampered, wealthy and self-assured women and beat them down to a point where they viewed themselves as weak, slovenly, worthless relics of self indulgence and excess. It was an art. He chided them for their laziness and ignorance about health and nutrition. Not only were they harming themselves, but what about their husbands or lovers? Guy always added the lover's line, it was just a little racy and clearly suggested that Forever Alive would not only help you to be healthier, but sexier, too. He was now at the heart of his presentation and Maria, bored with the sales pitch she'd heard ten times, twenty times over, returned to her life with Koch.

The memories came streaming back like a series of snapshots. Her mind's eye would focus on an image of her and Koch, then some semblance of the conversation would return and she would relive the pain and shame of it all over again. She wanted to believe that it was much more than just sex, but in her heart that's all it was and ever would be and, for that, she never regretted what happened between them.

The trip to Paris was uneventful. Whatever fear she'd had about them leaving Germany safely or about the diamonds he'd hidden in the trunk handles was overcome by the boredom of the long train trip. Koch spent much of the trip writing letters to business associates, or reading a collection of short stories by Chekov. They took a taxi from the train station to the Hotel Montsouris. Most of the lodgings were two and three room apartments. The lobby was small, but well furnished, and off to the side was a dining room that served as a restaurant to guests and the public. Koch's apartment was large and expensively furnished. Maria was impressed by the luxury of it all and any shame she'd felt over becoming Koch's mistress paled in the face of all the material comfort Koch could provide.

Maria was overwhelmed by Koch's worldliness. She knew nothing about commerce or money. She was just a shop girl, and all she had to offer was her body. She remembered how weak and ignorant she felt in front of him and how the only leverage she had was her sex. Maria realized that she could leave him breathless and flaccid a hundred times over, but that power was transient and, no matter what, she would always be the subordinate in their relationship.

They spent eighth months in Paris, eight emotionally wearing months for Maria. Koch often left her alone to attend to his affairs, and though he spoke little French, he rarely requested her assistance as an interpreter. Sometimes he would be gone for upward of a week and she would be left alone to explore the city, go to movies or read silly romantic novels to pass the time until he returned. When he was with her, it was a honeymoon. He told Maria that he loved her and that after his father died he would divorce Carmela and they would marry.

Koch's two hobbies were hiking and photography. He owned a Voightlander Bessa camera and the walls of his home in Berlin were decorated with numerous photographs he'd taken of family and streetscapes. During their time in Paris he was preoccupied with taking photographs of street scenes. Catching a chestnut vendor stoking his coals on a busy thoroughfare or capturing a line of school children following the headmaster in the park were scenes that excited him. He used a closet in the apartment as a darkroom and Maria was amazed by the array of photography equipment and supplies he kept there. He developed his own pictures and Maria became his assistant. Koch catalogued all of his work in green leather portfolios with his initials embossed in gold on the cover. Maria praised his artistic eye and how the blackened image of a solitary tree at twilight against the darkening sky, or an old woman sweeping the walk in front of her house presented real and lasting images of the world that are present every day and everywhere, but go unnoticed.

Koch believed the photographer was as artistic as the painter. "The painter's art is to employ method and mechanics to reproduce reality. The photographer seizes reality and turns it into art. And true art is always beautiful and always truthful," he would repeatedly say.

Maria believed in Koch and believed he was an artist. Her feeling was so strong that it was she who asked him to photograph her in the nude. Maria thought of herself as a model, but instead of offering her likeness for the canvass, she asked him to photograph her.

Koch was excited by her offer and planned the sequence of poses. Each one revealing just a little more of her until finally she was completely naked and all that he found intoxicating and irresistible was revealed and recorded by the camera's eye. Koch was so impressed by the finished product that he had the photographs professionally finished and touched up. The processor had offered him a generous sum for the negatives, but Koch denied him.

Maria was as enthralled with the photographs as Koch was and was secretly pleased that the processor had wanted to buy the negatives. That was in June, and by the end of August of 1936 Maria and Amos Koch left for London.

The departure for London was as sudden and urgent as their departure for Paris was eight months earlier. Koch had been away on business for several days, and when he returned he directed Maria to gather up all of her things, as they were moving to London. Maria didn't question him and did as she was told. Koch advised her that they were taking an apartment in a townhouse in London and that he was considering making his permanent office in Glasgow. They would rent a small office in London on a temporary basis and he expected in six months to be in Scotland. Maria was completely dependent on Koch, and his dedication to her seemed so sincere that she found herself wishing his father would die so that he would divorce Carmela and marry her. Two new trunks were delivered to the apartment and in a matter of hours all of her belongings and much of his belongings, including business ledgers and some photography equipment were packed and posted to London in advance of their departure.

The townhouse was on Trebovir Road in London near Holland Park and Kensington Gardens. The house had been subdivided into six apartments and their apartment had a small sitting room, an even smaller kitchen, but a large bedroom and they had their own bathroom. Koch had rented a small office on Warwick Road within walking distance to their apartment. The land agent for the townhouse and office was an officious and overly talkative little man named Mr. Smyth. Koch told Maria that if he decided to situate his business in London, they would move to more spacious quarters. There was no room in the apartment for their luggage, and the only piece they brought to the apartment was the trunk with Maria's clothes. Koch removed some of his clothing from his trunk and brought it over, but everything else was left at the office on Warwick Road. Maria's life had taken on the appearance of an endless vacation.

Each evening Maria mapped out an itinerary for the next day. Where they would walk, what they would see. Koch seemed to have no interest in business and went by the office several times during those first two weeks, but he went early in the morning and usually returned in less than two hours. At the beginning of the third week he told Maria that he would be going to Glasgow the following week and that she would stay behind. That third week he went to business every day. Maria offered to go with him, but he told her there was no work for her to do. Once the correspondences started up again and he was actively shipping products there would be more work for her than she needed. He told her to enjoy herself and continue to acquaint herself with London. Maria had grown lazy. She was unsure of where their relationship was heading, but she enjoyed being a wealthy man's consort, and the thought of returning to the dull drudgery of daily office work was a prospect she was happy to delay.

It was a Sunday and they went for a picnic in Holland Park. Koch informed Maria that he was leaving for Glasgow the following day and would be gone for possibly a month. She was not to worry, and as soon as he was settled he would let her know whether to join him there or wait for his return. That night in bed he came to her. She told him that it was not a good time and they would have to wait until he returned from Glasgow.

Koch acted as if hadn't heard her and said, "How can I resist you?" His hands were then under her nightgown rubbing her thighs as he pressed his head to her breasts.

Maria tried to gently push him away, but he was insistent. "Not now," she quietly pleaded.

"We have fresh linen," was his reply as he licked her ear.

"You are incessant," she chided as her hand found its way inside his pajamas.

He stopped her hand and whispered in her ear, "There are other ways to say goodbye."

"I'm not in the mood," she said as she rubbed him.

"Please, please," he begged.

Maria was humiliated by his request. They had made love so often over the past nine months that she felt he should be more understanding. She had a headache and was sore and swollen and sex of any sort would be uncomfortable. He kept kissing her and telling her how much she meant to him. Finally, she acquiesced. She knelt on the bed and pushed him backward. She told herself it was easier than enduring his incessant pawing and petting. Despite his worldliness and confidence, Amos Koch was a spoiled child in the bedroom. He wanted what he wanted and Maria had never refused indulging his selfishness. After all, she recalled, there was no place for her to go. She was no better than an indentured servant, and with the growing fire of a migraine burning inside her head she ripped at the buttons on the fly on his pajamas and bent her head down. Soon his hands were cupped over her ears and she imagined he was milking a cow. It was over quickly, and when she was done Koch was still pulling at her head. She started to gag and in a fit of anger flung her head back. His response took her by surprise. As she was pulling her head back, he grabbed her hair and stopped her motion.

His face was menacing, and in his harshest voice he said, "This is no time for anger."

She didn't answer and he let go of her hair. She stumbled out of the bed and ran to the bathroom to cleanse herself.

When she returned to the bedroom, she found Koch in bed, snoring and fast asleep. The following morning Koch was dressed and ready to leave before Maria had gotten out of bed. He woke her up and told her he was leaving. He stood at the door to the apartment and held Maria at arm's length for a minute. "I'll carry in my heart your love and beauty wherever I go, sweet Maria," he said solemnly.

"Don't be so dramatic," she replied.

He then kissed her quickly, hugged her to his chest, turned and was gone.

After Koch left, Maria went for a walk. She stopped at a local restaurant, The Covey, which was located several blocks from the apartment. She and Koch had eaten there before. The owners were a Mr. and Mrs. Brown. They were a lovely couple and they served breakfast, lunch and afternoon tea. Mrs. Brown was very warm and she called her husband Brownie. He was quiet, but pleasant and often referred to her as Sweet. There was something about them that was genuine, and Maria could never imagine them being cross with one another.

Maria ordered tea and oatmeal. It was a cold morning for late September and she wanted something to warm her up. She watched the couple as they attended to their busy little business and she wondered if life would have been like that for her and Rudy had he lived. Would they have become the proprietors of her grandfather's bakery? Would they have happily spent their days waiting on customers and referring to one another in endearing terms? She believed they would have, and Rudy's absence had never felt more painful for her than it was that morning. It had been almost two years since the fire and all of a sudden she felt a terrible guilt. All she could think of was Rudy. Did she love Koch, or was it just his money? Life with Rudy had been so innocent, and his memory and all the dreams she had of what could have or would have been seemed worthless.

She finished her breakfast and hurried from the shop. The simple act of observing a happy middle aged couple going through their daily routine was crushing, and all the sorrow she had suppressed over the loss of her family came surging back and all she wanted was to be with them again.

Guy Roberts was exuberant and asked the ladies to give him five minutes, then Maria Weiss would make a short presentation about some special Lorient cosmetics, and after that the group would break up for their individual spa treatments. Maria got up from her lounge chair and excused herself. She went to the bathroom, took a towel and rinsed her face. She realized that she had been crying and she didn't want anyone to know. As she stood looking at herself in the mirror, her memory, again, returned to London in 1936 and she recalled what had followed that morning after she finished her breakfast and what had colored her life ever since and made her the woman she was.

Watching the Brown's at work, serving their customers and joking with them and one another had created such a feeling of melancholy that all Maria could do was think of her family. She recalled all the little nonsensical things that went on in the bakery and the small nuances of daily life that she'd once taken for granted and never acknowledged. It was a sense of belonging, and what she felt, with ever increasing intensity, was that she didn't belong, she didn't fit in, and she was just aimlessly going through life with no direction or goal. Koch could be warm and loving, and at other times indifferent to her, and the previous night's sexual episode was a cold and mercenary, but enlightening insight into just how wrong she'd been in accepting the role as Koch's lover. Now all she had of her family were photographs and memories. She decided to go to Koch's office on Warwick Road and retrieve her family photograph album. That, at least, brought her some comfort.

When she got to the office there was a small lorry outside and two men were loading the two trunks Koch had purchased in Paris. Mr. Smyth was standing in the doorway and there was a sign saying 'To Let' in the window. Maria was immediately stunned by what she saw. She approached Smyth and said, "Hello, Mr. Smyth."

"Oh, Miss Kaval, Mr. Koch's assistant. I'm so sorry that he's leaving us so soon. He called me yesterday and cancelled the lease. It was very nice of him to pay the full two months rent, and I daresay I'll have no problem renting this office. Very upright man, your Mr. Koch is," he said with an air of authority.

Maria couldn't believe what she was hearing, but was at such a loss for words that she just stared at Smyth.

"The lease for the flat on Trebovir is paid up through September next and I gather you'll be staying behind? Rather mysterious man Mr. Koch is," Mr. Smyth said, nodding his head and calling out to the workmen, "Now hurry, lads, there can be quite a bit of traffic from here to Southampton, and I want everything there by two. The *Hampshire* sets sail for Bermuda promptly at five, and you've another job late this afternoon."

Maria didn't immediately understand the reference "to Bermuda," but when she saw the other trunk from Berlin coming out next on a hand truck she said to Mr. Smyth, "Mr. Koch has some of my personal belongings in that trunk. I came down here this morning to get them."

"Didn't say anything of the sort to me, he didn't. And everything is locked and I haven't a key. Sorry, Miss Kaval, but I can't help you," he said officiously.

Maria remembered the combination and said, "I have the combination. It's just a family album and I don't know when I'll get up to Glasgow to see Mr. Koch. I must get these things now," she importuned.

"Glasgow," he guffawed. "Mr. Koch is on his way to Bermuda. Wouldn't take a steamer to Glasgow anyway."

"Please, it's just my picture album I want," she pleaded. It was clear to her Koch had lied and, as angry as she was at his duplicity, the recovery of her property took precedence over any display of emotion.

"Well, if you know the combination and nothing gets broken. Of course, I'll have to watch. Koch did entrust me with his things and he has been a most honorable gentleman."

"It will only take a minute. Could your men just bring it back inside?"

"Yes, lads don't load that last one, bring it back into the shop," Smyth ordered.

The workmen brought the trunk back in and Maria knelt down and fingered the lock 1,3,5,7, 9, she repeated as she moved the numbered cylinders. As she turned the last tumbler, the lock snapped open. She lifted the lid and the trunk was loaded with ledgers and some stationery with a packet of letters from Carmela Koch in Buenos Aires to Amos Koch at the Hotel Montsouris in Paris on top of the stationery. The letters were wrapped in a red ribbon. On the other side of the trunk was a stack of green leather bound portfolios. Underneath the portfolios was her family photograph album. Maria was happy to see her album and in shock over the letters from Carmela. Maria didn't touch the letters, but she did take out her photograph album, and said to Smyth, "Oh, thank God! It's here. See it's on the bottom."

"Hmm, doesn't seem too much of value in there. Well, get what's yours and lock it up. It's getting late," ordered Smyth as he walked back out the door.

Maria took out all of the green portfolios and piled them on the floor. Once her album was out, she started to put them back and remembered that one of them contained her nude photographs. She looked over her shoulder and saw Smyth and the two workmen standing on the sidewalk smoking. They weren't paying any attention to her and she looked through the portfolios until she found the one with her pictures. She took that and put it under her family album. She then took the packet of letters and put them in her coat pocket. She placed everything else back in the trunk, closed the lid and exited the store. She thanked Smyth and went on her way.

Maria returned to the apartment on Trebovir Road. The only things belonging to Koch that remained were an umbrella and his heavy tweed overcoat. Maria sat on the couch and opened the letters from Carmela. There were five of them, all written in Spanish, and they were all about the family and life in Buenos Aires. Adam, Koch's older son, and his wife Myrna had just had a baby boy in July and they named him after Amos. Jonathan and Adam were running the business down there and everything was going well. Carmela's mother and Amos' father were still living, and by the tone of Carmela's writing the Kochs were a loving and happy family and all were anxiously awaiting Amos' return. The last letter did make one reference to Maria, and that was nothing more than a rebuke to Amos for being too generous. "Six months severance is more than sufficient for your clerk, particularly since you have paid for her food and lodging this past year and received so little work from her," wrote Carmela. It was painfully obvious to Maria that Koch had made no secret of his relationship with her other than to omit its very personal nature.

Maria put the letters down and sobbed. What would Rudy think of her, what would her mother have said? They would have branded her a whore. She was thankful that Smyth was so taken with his authority that he failed to recognize that Koch had dumped her. Tossed her away like a used tissue, she thought. Now she was alone in London without work and virtually penniless. All of the anger she had against fate for taking her family and placing her in this condition was suddenly directed at Koch. She would have been better off in Berlin, and she knew it, but she was alone in London and Koch was on his way to New York, then to Argentina to join his family.

Smyth had mentioned the *Hampshire* sailing from Southampton at five that evening. It was almost eleven in the morning. Two weeks ago she'd gone to Southampton with Koch. He'd wanted to photograph the British frigate *Warrior*. They'd taken the tube from Kensington Garden, then a train to Portsmouth. The trains to Portsmouth left every hour and the entire trip from Trebovir wasn't more than two and a half hours if she made the right connections. The morning had started out damp and cool, but it was now raining. Maria knew that if she left now, she'd be able to intercept Koch before he sailed. She didn't know what she was going to say to him, but she had to see him and speak with him, let him know what an unspeakable fraud and coward he was before he left England. She took his umbrella and put on his tweed coat and left the apartment.

It was all fresh in her mind as she stood in the bathroom at Sable's. The tears were flowing freely from her eyes. She called out to Guy that she'd be a few more minutes. She stood there shaking and reliving her rage.

She arrived at the Main Road in Southampton at a little past two-thirty in the afternoon. It was raining and the docks were empty except for the dockworkers. She found the terminal for the White Star Line and saw the posting for the *Hampshire's* departure at five p.m. The terminal wasn't too crowded and it was evident that many of the passengers had already boarded the ship. There were customs officers up by the gangplank and she had no desire to talk with them.

She wandered the terminal looking for Koch, but he was not anywhere to be found. When she was last there, they had gone to an empty terminal that fronted where the frigate *Warrior* was berthed. Koch had taken photographs and told her he would like to take more but had run out of film. She left the White Star Line terminal and went down the road to the terminal for the frigate *Warrior*. There were several sightseers in the terminal and down at the end, where the windows faced the dock, was a photographer with a camera on a tripod. It was Koch. She knew his clothes and his movements and mannerisms, especially with the camera. He'd wanted more pictures of the *Warrior* and this was his last chance to get them.

She took up a position behind a steel column and watched him. She was aflame with anger, but afraid to approach him. After ten minutes or so she moved closer. She wanted to strike him with the umbrella. Last night he'd made her suck his cock, like a common whore, and today he had deserted her. As she approached, Koch started to put away his camera and tripod. It was getting late and he had to make his way to the *Hampshire*

Maria ducked behind another steel column. Her heart was pounding, fear and anger had gripped her and she didn't know what to do. Koch made his way through the terminal toward the exit. Maria followed. Halfway down he stepped into the public restroom. She followed him. He'd put his camera bag and tripod on the floor and was standing in front of the urinal urinating. Maria approached him from behind and whacked him across the back of his head with the umbrella.

He spun around and his penis was hanging from the opening in his pants and the urine was spraying. He instinctively covered his groin and looked at Maria with a look of shock. She saw his penis hanging and dripping urine. She said nothing, and before he could speak she plunged the tip of the umbrella into his face. The hard steel needle of the umbrella pierced his eye and went deep into his brain. Koch immediately crumbled to the floor. As he was falling, Maria pulled back the umbrella and left the bathroom. The terminal was almost empty and there was no one near the bathroom. She pulled the collar of the tweed coat up around her ears and walked quickly out of the terminal. It was raining heavily outside and she opened the umbrella and let the pounding September rain cleanse whatever bits of Koch's brain had spilled onto it. She went to the rail station and took the train back to London.

Maria dried her eyes and rinsed her face again. She went out into the spa room and greeted her clients. She felt better and was calmed by the memory of how well she slept that night in London after her return from Southampton.

Chapter Twelve

The Forever Alive spa day at Sable's ended at 3:00 p.m., and each of Maria's clients went home feeling far more refreshed and beautiful than she had when she arrived earlier in the day. Guy Roberts was in a great mood and broke open a bottle of champagne and poured glasses for Maria and his assistants.

"Great job, everyone, great, great job," he cheerfully expressed as he passed around the champagne. "Not only will we see all ten of those ladies up at Forever Alive, but you can bet the ranch twenty of their friends will be in tow."

Maria hadn't touched her champagne and was sitting in a chair, smiling, but looking very tired.

Guy went over to her. "Hey, what's wrong? You look beat."

"I'm just tired, it's been a long day."

"Know what you need? You need a Guy Roberts massage," he said, smiling as he took her hand and brought over to the room where the masseuse tables were set up.

"Oh no, I'm too tired for one of your workups."

"C'mon, I'll go easy on you. It's been two years since I gave you a good rub down, and I bet no man's hands have felt as good."

"All right, maybe a quickie."

"Quickie, did you say quickie?" he leered.

"You're incorrigible," Maria replied, laughing.

Maria went into the changing room and came out with a towel wrapped around her. She laid herself down on the table and said to Guy Roberts, "Get to work."

"Oh, the maestro will. Now, just close your eyes and relax. No talking. Listen to the music."

"That's Muzak, maestro, and I try not to listen to it all day."

"Well, it's all that's available, and right now I believe you're hearing the Hollywood Strings performing their priceless version of *I Want To Hold Your Hand*," said Guy as he patted Maria on her backside.

Maria felt his strong hands as they gently kneaded her shoulders. She felt relaxed, even to the point that she could hear the music in the background. The violins were pretty and the melodies pleasant, and the combination of soft music and Guy's magical hands working on her body lulled her into a dreamlike mood and she was neither awake nor asleep. She was lost in her dreams and thoughts and was no longer fully conscious of the music or Guy.

As always, her mind went back to the past. First she'd think of Rudy, he was her safety net. Guy's hands reminded her of Rudy's hands, strong and purposeful. They weren't stubby and thick, nor were they long and delicate. They were proportionate and powerful, if that was a description, and as Guy massaged her back and his hands probed deeper and deeper into her muscles she could feel Rudy's presence. But there was nothing tangible in that presence. It was, at best, a warm and distant memory and to dwell on it only made her unhappy because he would never return. If the memory of Rudy was fading, the same couldn't be said for Amos Koch.

Maria had never intended to murder Koch. It just happened and was, to her thinking, a natural response to the way he had treated her. His calculated use of her for sexual favors and companionship had been cleverly hidden beneath a veneer of false concern for her well-being and happiness. Maria knew that she was falling in love with Koch and she thought that he loved her too. It was all a lie and Smyth's innocent admission of Koch's sailing for Bermuda and her discovery of Carmela's letters was incontrovertible proof that she was nothing more than a pleasant diversion for Amos Koch. She had no idea how she found the strength and dexterity to plunge the hard metal tip of the umbrella into Koch's eye, but she did it and she felt cleansed by the experience.

The day after the murder she awoke early and went to The Covey for breakfast. Mrs. Brown inquired about her gentleman friend and Maria told her that Koch was her employer and had gone to Glasgow. Maria ate a hearty breakfast of eggs, toast and oatmeal that morning, and on the way back to the apartment she stopped and bought a copy of *The Times*. She planned on reading the classifieds and finding some employment. Her rent was paid in full for a year, but she still needed money to live, and her savings were only enough to keep her going for another six months or so. She arrived back at the apartment and laid the paper on the coffee table. In the lower right corner of the front page she saw a highlighted headline.

Southampton: Argentinean Businessman Murdered.

Her heart almost stopped, and the bold and blunt headline left her wracking in tears and sobs. She was afraid to read the story. She was afraid that somewhere in it she would be identified and requests for assistance from the public in apprehending her would be included too. She gained control of herself, and with as much fear and trepidation as a blind woman would have when crossing a busy street for the first time, she carefully made her way through the news story. She didn't remember the entire story, but there were several sentences that were unforgettable:

> *Southampton: Amos Koch, president of Koch Beef Imports, Ltd., was found murdered yesterday afternoon in a public restroom in a vacant terminal near Town Quay Dock in Southampton. Mr. Koch was scheduled to depart for Bermuda on the* Hampshire, *which had sailed from Southampton two hours before his body was found. An undisclosed government source related this may have been an assassination, and that Mr. Koch had strong ties to several prominent Nazi Party officials in Berlin, and he may have been involved in numerous financial improprieties. The manner of death has not been revealed, but this same source did assert that it was a quick, brutal and silent execution and was clearly the handiwork of professional killers.*

The article went on to discuss Koch Imports, and Maria was surprised at how successful, rich and well-known a man Amos Koch had been. She didn't fully understand the reference to Nazi Party officials or professional killers, but she was comforted by the article and any fears she had of being a suspect were erased. About an hour later her doorbell rang. Again she froze. She opened the door and was confronted by a young man in a messenger's uniform. He asked if she was Maria Kaval, and when she answered yes he asked her to sign for an envelope.

He left and Maria opened the envelope and inside was a letter addressed to her and twenty-four postdated bank drafts. The letter was on Koch's stationery and it read:

> *Dear Mrs. Kaval,*
>
> *Effective immediately, your service with Koch Imports is terminated. Two year's severance has been awarded at fifteen pounds per month and the enclosed bank drafts may be redeemed at any Bank of England office on the first business day of each month.*
>
> *Sincerely,*
> *Amos Koch*

Any lingering guilt or feelings of affection for Koch and remorse over his death were extinguished with that cold letter of dismissal. Two days after the murder she was visited by two men from Scotland Yard, a Sergeant Laffey and an Inspector Reed. The two policemen were middle-aged and rather nondescript. Their only interest was in Koch's business associates, and any French or German citizens he may have been dealing with since he arrived in London. Maria told them that Koch had been very secretive about his business dealings the past year and then she went on to brazenly tell the men that she had been Koch's lover. He had told her he was going to Glasgow on the day he was murdered. Maria went on to tell them that she didn't know about his plans to sail for Bermuda until the morning he left, and went on to tell them that she had made a trip to Southampton in a futile attempt to find him. She told them she was unsuccessful, and although saddened by his death, she was grateful he had given her two year's severance pay. She showed them Koch's letter of termination and the bank drafts. "He took what he wanted from me and then he discharged me with severance" she told the men without emotion.

They listened patiently, then Inspector Reed asked her, "Did Mr. Koch leave anything of his behind?"

"Just his tweed overcoat and his umbrella."

Reed looked over to an umbrella stand by the door. He went over to it and took out the umbrella. He placed the point on the floor and twirled it with his fingertips. "Nothing else?"

"No, nothing else. Is there something particular you're looking for?"

"Nothing particular. Sorry for the intrusion and your trouble," he said sympathetically. "Well, Sergeant Laffey, anything else you can think of?"

"No, no. Best be on our way. We'll be in touch if something else comes up. Imagine you'll remain here until the lease runs out. Very nice flat, nice area, convenient to many things," Laffey offered in what sounded like a verbalization of his stream of consciousness to his immediate surroundings.

Maria smiled and said, "Well, thank you. This has been quite a shock to me, but I must get on with my life and put this behind me."

"Yes, we all make mistakes," Reed said as he nodded his head and gave Maria a very concerned look.

"One thing," she said. "How was he killed?"

Laffey clasped his hands and looked to Reed, then he turned to her and said, "A well placed blow to the brain through the left eye. The quote in *The Times* was remarkably descriptive. Not the work of an amateur."

The two policemen then left the apartment.

Maria recalled the feeling of relief, if not outright pleasure at their departure and their total lack of interest in her. Murder can be such an easy thing she thought.

Guy was talking to her, but she refused to respond. He had her completely relaxed and she was happy she'd let him give her the massage. Guy was in love with her and had been so for many years. Even though she was ten years older than he, she knew her age didn't matter. Some years ago they had been up at Forever Alive for a week, and one night over too much wine he confessed his love for her. Maria told him he was sweet and she did care for him, but she was married and nothing would change that. Now, she thought, Henry was possibly deceiving her and the thought of his infidelity was crushing. This was why Koch was so on her mind lately. The image of Henry and Sophie having sex was more painful than her recurrent migraines. Maria's Achilles heel was that she always needed a man in her life. She didn't know why, but it was just that way. Life for her in-between Koch and Henry had been a series of lovers and while much of that occurred during the uncertain and terrifying years of World War II she had a dread of being alone. It was for that reason she would never leave Henry unless she had someone else to go to. Guy was an option, although she had no interest in adjusting to another man.

Sophie was the problem. *How can I kill Sophie?* she thought. *Murder can be such an easy thing, when carried out properly and if I do it and never tell anyone, then who'll ever know*, she thought as she found herself drifting off to sleep under the mesmerizing touch of Guy Roberts's hands.

Chapter Thirteen

Guy wanted Maria to go out to dinner with him that night, but she felt the beginning of one of her migraines and, as much as she enjoyed his company, she put him off until the following week when he'd be back in Huguenot City for another promotion of the spa. She took the subway home, and after a simple meal of two hard-boiled eggs and a half of a grapefruit she went to bed.

She awoke Wednesday morning around 6:00 a.m. and the first thing she thought of was the last thought she'd had going to bed the night before and that was Henry. If Maria had learned one thing over her life it was that you couldn't hide from the truth. In those last moments between consciousness and sleep, those fading moments when she confronted her life or some aspect of it, when there was no one left to lie to, no one to impress or deceive, when it was just her and the cold, imperfect reality of her existence, then she saw herself for what she was: a cold, conniving and frightened woman. She was afraid of death, afraid of facing life alone, afraid of living alone. She was selfish and self-centered, and since her union with Amos Koch she had used her physical attractiveness, a condition she never fully understood but accepted, to get men to take care of her.

Henry worshipped her, or so she thought, but he was, evidently, as self-centered and selfish as she was. There could be no other reason why he would have stayed with her as long as he did, especially since she had treated him, for so long, with such indifference. Henry was a generous man. He was also a terribly superficial man. Her beauty, her so-called cultured refinement, which was nothing more than a by-product of having been trained from birth to speak several languages, all played to Henry's vanity. Henry's long ago stated lack of interest in that part of her life that preceded their courtship was the wedge that prevented her from fully loving him or trusting him. After seventeen years of marriage it occurred to her that his love for her was waning and if there was a problem in their relationship it stemmed from her behavior, and not his. That was reality and it was the truth she could not deny.

There on that overcast and muggy June morning, with the dull ache of the migraine returning, Maria admitted to herself what she had tried so long to deny: She had to love her husband, because she couldn't live without him. Was it, now, too late? Was Sophie going to take her place? What could she do to repair their marriage? She was fifty. A fading beauty and in the blink of an eye she'd be an old lady. Sophie was much younger than she was, and her dedication to Henry, her congeniality and competence in the work place as his secretary were all attractive qualities that Maria couldn't compete against. Killing Sophie, she thought, was a possibility but how could she do it? How do you commit a murder and not get caught? It had worked for her once, but that was unplanned. She had no confidence she could do it again.

Despite the migraine, Maria went to work. All day long she wrestled with the idea of murdering Sophie. The more she thought about it the more improbable it became. She finally made up her mind to win Henry back. She didn't know if she'd lost him yet, but she believed if she hadn't, she was on the brink of losing him.

She arrived home at a little after six in the evening. Henry was staying at The Ritz-Carlton Montreal. They had gone to Montreal seven years ago. It was winter and they stayed at the Ritz-Carlton. Maria loved the hotel. It was a luxury hotel and it was built in 1912 at a time when no expense was spared in the name of luxury. Everyone spoke French, and Maria was Henry's guide and translator. It was winter and they went ice-skating. That was one of the few things they had in common. As children they both skated often, and as adults they could still put on skates and comfortably negotiate the ice. They had a wonderful time, and as Maria reflected back she became incensed with the thought of Henry enjoying that provincial and captivating city, staying with his Puerto Rican whore in their hotel.

Henry had left her the phone number for the hotel and she dialed long distance and was connected with the hotel's switchboard. She asked for Henry's room, and after two rings Sophie answered the phone.

"Hola," Sophie said in Spanish.

"Sophie, is that you?"

"Yes, who is calling?" Sophie coquettishly said.

"It's Mrs. Weiss, is my husband there?" Maria demanded, not at all pleased to find Sophie on the other end of the phone in Henry's hotel room.

Sophie put her hand over the phone and said to Henry, "It's Maria. I didn't recognize her voice. She sounds a little pissed. I wonder why?"

Henry walked over and took the phone from Sophie. "Hey, Maria, how are you, sweetheart?" As he was talking, Sophie undid the zipper to his pants and pulled his penis out and started to pet it while she mimed Henry's every word to Maria.

"What's she doing in your room?"

Henry pushed Sophie away, and while putting himself back in order, said to Maria, "Working, sweetheart. This turned out to be a much bigger deal than I thought. There's five different property owners involved and twice as many lawyers. Canada's another country and, ah, what the hell, it's a real pain in the ass. That's the best way I can sum it up," he said with some exasperation in his voice, hoping he could mollify her objection to Sophie being in his room. There was a pause in the conversation and he added, "It's a good thing you didn't come because you wouldn't have seen much of me,"

"Well, I miss you," Maria said softly. "And I thought tomorrow I'd make you a nice shrimp coquille and a chocolate cream pie to welcome you back. Would that be agreeable?"

"It's only a couple of days, but if it makes you feel any better, I miss you too. Now the dinner sounds great, but I won't be back until late. At this point, I'm planning on flying back tomorrow night. The train took nine hours and there's no way we're gonna catch the morning train. We should close on Ancowitz's properties by the afternoon. There's a train leaving at eight tomorrow evening, but that doesn't arrive in La Rochelle Station until around five or six Friday morning. Ancowitz says we can catch a flight tomorrow evening at seven-thirty and be back on the ground around nine, nine-thirty. That should get me home around ten. A little late for dinner, don't you think?"

"Okay, I can wait until Friday night. I just feel like I've been neglecting you lately and I thought it would be nice to make one of your favorite meals, and we could have a nice night together."

"Why do you feel like that?'

"I just do. Sometimes I forget how much you mean to me. Well, I won't keep you. I love you and I'll see you tomorrow."

"Yeah, I love you too, honey. See you tomorrow," Henry responded with just a trace of hesitancy before he said, "I love you too."

Sophie was listening to every word uttered by Henry, and even though the call didn't take more than a minute from beginning to end, by the time Henry hung up the receiver she was packing her suitcase and screaming at him.

"I love you too, honey," she mimicked. "You fucking piece of shit. Why didn't you tell her the truth? I love you too, honey and oh, by the way, just fifteen minutes ago I was fucking the pants off Sophie. Yeah, Sophie, you know my whore and the mother of my seven-year-old son Joey. Oh, sweetheart, I didn't tell you that. Well, I've been doing it with Sophie ever since you stopped doing it with me. You're a fucking shit bag Jew bastard. That's all you are. You and all your fucking kikes," she screamed at him between sobs and gasps.

"C'mon, calm down. Why do you talk like that? Is that what I am, a 'fucking Jew cocksucker' or whatever it is you said?"

"No, you got it wrong. I'm the Jew cocksucker. I've been sucking your cock for how long? I'm the fool and now it's over. The only reason you brought me up here was to fuck me. That's all I am to you. It's over. You can go home to your little mannequin queen and fuck her in the icebox she calls a cunt. Better you can go fuck yourself, 'cause I'm through with you!"

"Sophie, baby. Please stop it. I told you, how many times, have some patience, someday we'll work it out. Relax, just relax and listen to yourself," he said, almost begging.

"Fuck you, fuck your mother, fuck your father, your sister and your little fucking princess of a wife," she added in a calmer voice. "I'll see you in court. Everyone's going to find out your Joey's father," she said, pointing her finger at him.

"What's that going to prove? I take care of you and him. I do my part. You tricked me, don't forget? If I had known, we could have fixed it and there'd be no Joey. And that's the truth."

Henry walked over to the window and lit a cigarette. Sophie finished packing her suitcase. She went to the bathroom to wash her face, and Henry went over to her and said, "And furthermore, I don't appreciate all that Jew and Kike shit. You're better than that." He then put on his suit jacket and walked to the door. "I have a meeting with Ancowitz, I'll be back in an hour."

"I'm leaving now," she shot back.

"Suit yourself you fucking maniac," he mumbled to himself as he slammed the door shut and went down the hallway.

What a head case, he thought. *Maria's my wife, what does she expect? Does she really believe I'd leave Maria? What do I do now? Maria calls out of the blue and it's like we rolled the clock back fifteen years. She couldn't have been nicer and I know Sophie read my face. She knows me too well. God, if I could just make Sophie disappear,* he thought. "But it ain't gonna happen, it just ain't gonna happen," he said aloud as he stepped into the elevator.

Chapter Fourteen

The overnight train from Montreal arrived in La Rochelle Station at 5:30 a.m. Sophie was exhausted from the trip. She didn't sleep the whole ride and spent all of her time blankly staring out the window and mordantly thinking of various ways to kill Maria.

She took the subway from the station to her apartment in the Upper Borough, and as she neared home, her mood temporarily brightened at the thought of seeing Joey. Her son was the centerpiece of her life. Everything revolved around him, and just being away from him for two days had upset her emotional equilibrium and, no doubt, added to her vicious outburst the previous evening with Henry. She sadly regretted calling him a 'Jew mother-fucker and a kike' because she knew how much he detested that type of talk and how hurtful and senseless it was. Whether she'd caused irreparable harm to their relationship or not was yet to be known, but she'd said what she said and now she had to deal with it.

That fucking bitch Maria, she thought, *I hate her so much. She doesn't love him, but she won't let him go. I should have never gone with him to Montreal. That was a challenge and it didn't take much for her to show me who was the boss.* "I'm not done with that fucking pig, yet," she said to herself as she went through the door to the apartment.

It was almost seven in the morning and her Aunt Lucy was sitting at the kitchen table drinking a cup of coffee.

"Tia," Sophie said as she put her suitcase down and went over to hug and kiss her aunt.

"What a surprise. I thought you were coming in tonight?"

"I did my thing and Henry didn't need me anymore. I missed Joey and didn't feel like spending a day alone up there with nothing to do. Is Joey awake?"

"I was just going to wake him up."

"I'll get him up. Did he behave?"

"He always behaves. And when I put him to bed, he gives me a big hug and says, 'Te amo tia,' it's so cute," she gushed.

Sophie went down the hall to Joey's room and went in. She sat down on the side of the bed and watched her son as he lay sleeping. Joey had thick dark brown hair and an angelic face. He was, in her eyes, beautiful, and to others a cute and handsome child. Sophie thought he had Henry's smile, and he was tall for his age, something she was excited about because so many Puerto Rican men were short and stocky. She was hoping he'd grow to be tall like his father, and it appeared that if he continued to grow at the rate he was growing, that would be the case. She bent down and kissed him on the cheek and tickled his stomach. "Wake up, sweetie," she cooed.

Joey turned his head and opened his eyes. When he saw his mother he jumped up and wrapped his arms around her and hugged her tightly. "Mommy," he squealed with delight. "You're back. Did you bring me anything?" he asked as he hugged and kissed her.

"I have some things in my bag, but nothing until you're washed and dressed. Hurry up, and I'll make you breakfast before school," she ordered as she kissed him again.

The boy jumped out of bed and went to the bathroom. Sophie could hear the water in the sink running and she went out to the kitchen to make him some French toast.

"Well, I was only gone two days, did I miss anything?"

"Nothing much. A letter came from P.S. 7 day camp on Tuesday. I opened it because Joey was all excited. He has the same counselor as last year. There's some other information about swimsuits and bathing caps and what trips they'll take. It's on your bureau. Camp starts Monday, and the last day of school is tomorrow. Yesterday he went to his friend Jimmy Cullen's house after school. His mother called me in the morning and asked if he could come over. She picked him up and he stayed all day and for dinner. Her daughter brought him home at eight. She's a beautiful girl, her daughter. She has red hair, but it's that soft blonde red, green eyes and so nice. Joey gave her a big kiss. He's a Romeo, and so young." She laughed.

"Oh, I know. The girl's name is Erin. She's only fourteen, but so pretty. I use her to babysit Joey sometimes. The Cullen's are very nice, and Jimmy's his best friend. They're going to day camp together."

While Joey had breakfast, Sophie took a quick shower and changed her clothes. She took him to school and made arrangements with her aunt to pick him up at dismissal. She said she was going in to the office and would be home around three or so.

Joey was finishing the second grade at St. John's grammar school. As they walked up Kingsbridge Avenue on the way to school, Joey talked non-stop about the end of school and day camp that was beginning the following week. Sophie's black mood was lightened by the exuberant presence of her son. Joey was a happy, well-adjusted little boy. He did well in school and he had friends. He was outgoing and bright, with limitless energy and possessed a sweet and obedient disposition that made being around him a pleasure. She could do nothing to jeopardize his future or their relationship. Murdering Maria, getting caught and going to prison was not in Joey's best interests, nor Sophie's. Her desire to expunge Maria from Henry's life was intense, but she couldn't do so at the risk of ruining her son's life. She kissed him goodbye in front of the school and told him to be a good boy.

Sophie went down to Broadway and waited for the number twenty bus to bring her over to Lincoln Boulevard.

She exited the bus at Jersey Avenue, just two blocks west of Lincoln Boulevard. She went to a diner and bought a cup of coffee to go and walked over to St. Jerome's Park. The park was on Jersey Avenue between Kingsbridge and Monmouth Roads. It was a pretty little park, with benches and trees and six tennis courts. The morning was heating up, and Sophie took a seat on a bench in the shade and drank her coffee.

On the trip up to Montreal with Henry he had suggested that Sophie and Joey move to Riverview. He said he could get her a nice apartment in the Riverview Gardens and they could send Joey to Elysian or the Fieldmere School. Elysian and The Fieldmere School were both expensive private schools, and Henry suggested that the level of education would far exceed anything Joey would receive at St. John's. Sophie was pleased by Henry's interest in Joey's education and his offer to finance an expensive private school education, but she was intimidated by the thought of Joey mixing with students who would clearly be from a different social level than he was from. Actually, Joey would have no problem interacting with his classmates. It was Sophie who would feel out of place and, furthermore, she rationalized, Joey loved St. John's and already had a group of friends. *Why upset the apple cart*, she thought. She loved the Kingsbridge Arms where they lived and was quite content with everything in her life except her relationship with Henry. As generous as Henry's offer was, it didn't portend any intimate contact between Henry and Joey.

She had just shown him Joey's First Holy Communion pictures and Henry seemed puzzled by Joey's outfit. Joey was wearing a dark blue jacket and white short pants with a big white silk bow tie and white gloves with the rosary beads draped over them. He looked very solemn, and as Henry studied the pictures he couldn't deny that Joey was his son. There was an unmistakable likeness between father and son, and Henry's recognition of that likeness surely was the catalyst for his recommendation that they move to Riverview and Joey enroll in a school superior to the one he was presently attending. She wanted Henry to play an active role in Joey's life, but it had to be something more than paying the bills and deciding what schools he should attend.

Henry was weak. Sophie loved him, but she knew he was the type of man who would try to buy his way out of every difficulty. He loved Maria, something that was painfully obvious in his telephone conversation with her in Montreal. Sophie couldn't believe how his face lit up at whatever it was Maria was saying on the other end of the phone. It infuriated her that he could fold so easily, and when he said to Maria, "I love you, too" it was said with such sincerity that Sophie knew she was simply the girlfriend. What Sophie didn't know was what Maria said to him and why she said it.

Sophie's presence in Montreal must have rattled Maria. *Maria's a very proud woman,* Sophie thought. *She carries herself well and won't tolerate an insult. I have to put her in her place, and I know exactly what I'll do,* she thought. She opened her pocketbook and took out the packet of pictures from Joey's Holy Communion. It was Thursday. She knew Maria went to work late on Thursdays and she decided that she'd wait outside the apartment building until Maria came out. She'd follow her to the subway, get on the train with her and while they were riding downtown she'd give Maria one of Joey's pictures and tell her Henry was the father. *Just like that,* she thought, *and I'll do it just before the train comes to a stop and while she's standing there wide-eyed and in disbelief, I'll get off the train. Fuck them both,* she thought. *I can work for anybody and I don't need that bastard's money. I'll take him to court and he'll pay and I'll find a new man.*

Content that her scheme to shame them both was the answer to all her problems, she left the park and walked south on Jersey Avenue toward Monmouth Road. There was a sporting goods store there and she wanted to buy Joey a new bathing suit, cap and a baseball glove. Camp started Monday, and it was important her little baby had everything he needed. She had plenty of time to kill before Maria left for work. *Time's all I need to kill today. Nobody goes to jail for killing time*, she thought.

Chapter Fifteen

It was almost eleven in the morning and Maria was having her morning tea. She was going to work a half-day and planned on leaving for work at her usual time of noon. Her migraine was back, and she contemplated taking the entire day off, but Millie her cleaning lady was due any minute and there'd be no peace or quiet in the apartment with Millie at work. She was making out her grocery list and was going over the extra ingredients she needed for the shrimp coquille and the chocolate cream pie. She was happy that they had put the special meal off until tomorrow because she knew she would be sick tonight and in no mood for cooking a big meal or doing anything else, particularly making love. *I can make the pie, that's it*, she told herself.

She dialed the number for the Associated Market and a familiar voice answered the phone. It was the delivery boy, the one she didn't like.

"Hello, this is Mrs. Weiss."

"Oh, hi, it's Danny Monaghan, your delivery boy. What can I do for you?"

"I want to give you my grocery order. Do you have a pencil and paper ready?"

"Right here, shoot, I'm ready," was his friendly response.

He sounded very pleasant over the phone, and Maria thought that maybe she had been too hasty in forming a negative opinion of him. *After all*, she thought, *I was the one half naked and he is a teenage boy*. She gave him her list of things and made him read it back. He had everything correct, then she told him to pay special attention to one more item.

"You have to go next door to Joe's Fish Market. Tell the man behind the counter that you want to place an order for Henry Weiss. Now write that down, the man in the store knows my husband and he'll bill Mr. Kimmel for my order. I want one pound of extra jumbo shrimp. I want the shrimp cleaned, the veins taken out and then I want him to butterfly each one. Now tell me what you're going to do?"

"Before I fill your order I'm going to Joe's Fish market and I'm gonna tell Benny, he's the guy behind the counter all the time, that Henry Weiss wants one pound of extra jumbo shrimp. You want the shrimp cleaned, the veins taken out and he has to butterfly each one. He can bill my boss for the shrimp and that's it."

"Very good, now remember, it's very warm today and I don't want the cream or shrimp to spoil. Don't fill my order until you know the shrimp is ready. Please. Take my order, pick up the shrimp and deliver it right away. Make sure you put all the cold goods in the refrigerator in the pantry. And don't stop to annoy Mr. Cleary when you make the delivery, do you understand?"

"Yeah, I know I was being a wise guy last week. Don't worry, I won't bother him anymore," he said contritely.

"I'm happy to hear that."

"Is there any rush on this order?"

"No, we'll be out all day. Just get it here before six."

"Okay."

"Thank you, Danny," Maria said, then hung up the phone.

No sooner had she hung up the phone than the buzzer to the service entrance sounded and Millie Campos came walking into the pantry, then the kitchen. Millie was a small, talkative woman. She was from the Philippines, and she and her husband had immigrated to the U.S. right after the war. Millie had five daughters. All of them were married and she had fifteen grandchildren. It seemed as if one of them was always sick, and every time Millie showed up to clean the apartment and do the laundry she would launch into a long monologue about how she spent the night nursing one of her sick grandchildren and hadn't had any sleep herself in over twenty-four hours.

It was a familiar complaint, and Maria's stock reply was always the same, "I don't know how you do it." That line always elicited a smile from Millie, and no matter how tired she was or claimed to be, she always exerted more than enough energy to put the apartment in order and leave it clean and tidy before she left.

"Mrs. Weiss how are you?"

"I'd be fine if my migraine went on hiatus, but it hasn't and if you must know the truth I'm dying."

"Menopause, I went through the same thing. My grandchildren were just being born then, my God, I don't think I could have went through menopause and cared for all these children. How many times have I said, I have five daughters, four of them nurses and not one can properly care for a sick child?" Millie lamented in an exasperated voice. "Put some ice on your temples before you go to work. It will ease the pain. Believe me I know," she added. "Also, you need sensible shoes. Stop wearing high heels. See these white crepe soled shoes I'm wearing? It's what all the nurses in busy emergency rooms and hospital wards wear. Good shoes are easy on the spine and that prevents headaches. Believe me they do!" she said emphatically as she lifted her right foot and showed off the shoes to Maria.

"Millie, you're probably right, but I don't think they'd be too happy down at Sable's if I was wearing those shoes and trying to sell beauty at the same time."

"Wear a lab coat, it goes with the shoes," Millie retorted. "Then you can tell them you're a beauty doctor."

Maria was in no mood for Millie's banter, and she didn't follow up with any comment about the shoes. She put her teacup in the sink and said to Millie, "Could you do me one special favor? Henry left seven of his dress shirts, they're on my bed, to be cleaned at Han Lees and a ticket for his clean ones. I'm too sick to run the errand. Would you get them for me?"

"Of course, it's no problem. I was at Sonja's all night with her youngest. He has the flu, Sonja was working a late shift and her husband is a nincompoop and can't do a thing. I was up half the night. Let me get started with the kitchen and the laundry. I didn't have breakfast, so I'll take the shirts and go to the little luncheonette on Kingsbridge Road and have a something to eat."

Maria was happy there was no argument. She went into the hall closet and got out her pocketbook. She opened it and took ten dollars from her wallet and handed it to Millie and said, "Use that for the shirts and your lunch. I'm going to get dressed and try to get to work."

Millie said thanks and busied herself in the kitchen. Maria went to her bedroom and got dressed for work.

Chapter Sixteen

Danny hung up the phone, sat back in his chair and sighed. He looked at Maria's grocery list and smiled. She made him feel so horny that he was tempted to go into the bathroom and masturbate, but he thought he'd wait until he got to her apartment. When she said no one would be home he felt a surge of blood in his groin. She sounded pretty friendly, and he imagined himself having sex with her. *Maybe that's what she wants*, he thought, but he didn't know.

Ever since he found her pictures he couldn't think of anything but her. Fagan's going away party was a blast, but he didn't drink much, and when Linda Kelly came on to him he made out with her, but kept himself in check. He was the gentleman in every way, and he could tell she appreciated it. Funny, now she was calling him up and asking him out. Russian Annie and Hand-job Mary got drunk that night in a hurry. They drank down the bottled screwdriver mix like it was orange soda. Annie was off in the Bedroom with Fagan and puked all over him. Mary was so drunk she fell asleep and didn't wake up until one of the guys tried to put his dick in her mouth. The rumor going around was that Billy Shaw or Little Danny jerked off in her face, but he'd already left before that happened and word was out that Mrs. Breen had gone to the cops so none of the guys was talking. Linda and the rest of the girls made fun of them and Danny was only too happy to see the two neighborhood sluts make fools of themselves. He hated Annie because everyone in the neighborhood knew his father was messing around with her mother.

The day before Fagan's party, Louie, their building superintendent, came to the apartment and asked to speak with Danny's mother. Danny overheard part of the conversation and it wasn't nice. Louie lived above the building's laundry room, and several weeks ago, on a Saturday night, he heard noise in the laundry room. He thought someone was breaking into the coin machines and went down to investigate. When he got there, he found Danny's father and Annie's mother having sex on the table they use to fold the clothes. Louie told them to get out and closed the door and left. He told Mrs. Monaghan that if something like that ever happened again he would have them evicted. Everyone in the building knew about it and he told her she should be ashamed of her husband. Louie then left the apartment, and as he was going out the door he said to Mrs. Monaghan, "Don't forget what I said. I'm not afraid of your husband, I run a good building."

Danny's relationship with his father was complicated. He feared and admired his father, and was often embarrassed by his behavior. The many arrests over the years, and his absenteeism from the home for softball, carousing and womanizing left Danny with a belief that his father would support them, but was only too happy to be anywhere else but home. Half the neighborhood was scared stiff of him, and the other half kissed his ass like he was some big shot. When Danny went with Hand-job Mary or got drunk and picked on Little Danny or other kids he was acting just like his father. He loved his mother, and he knew that the one thing she wanted was for him not to turn out like his father. Somehow, and he didn't fully understand it, his infatuation with Maria, his determination to establish a connection with her was the way his father would behave. If he wanted something, he went after it. In this case, all he wanted were Maria's pictures. No one else interested him right now, and Maria had become an obsession. If he could get the pictures he could find a way to get her. Maybe it was a silly fantasy, but today was going to be the day he'd steal the pictures. Deep down he knew that the pictures would be the extent of their relationship, but that was okay. Someday he would have a woman like Maria, he'd live in a building like the Excelsior, the superintendent would call him Mr. Monaghan and all the delivery boys and doormen of the world would be jerking themselves off every night dreaming about his wife.

She told him they wouldn't be home, and there would be no obstacles to prevent him from making his score. Danny merrily went up to Joe's Fish Market to place her order. Benny, the fish man, told him to come back around noon and the order would be ready. Danny went back to the Associated and made a delivery. He returned twenty minutes later and filled a cart with groceries from Maria's list. He checked the groceries out, boxed them and put the charge slip in the cashier's office. He went up to the fish market and stood outside the front window. He was hoping the fish man would see him and expedite Maria's order. He was in a hurry to get to the Excelsior.

Sophie was sitting on a park bench in Lincoln Park. The park was situated on Lincoln Boulevard just south of Kingsbridge Road. It was a beautiful urban oasis with trees and benches and flower gardens. Sophie passed it every day on the bus on her way to and from work. She'd bought Joey a Johnny Podres model baseball mitt at the Monmouth Athletic shop on Jersey Avenue. The salesman looked like he was a college student, was very friendly and appeared very knowledgeable about baseball gloves. Sophie explained to him that Joey was seven and going to day camp. He had a glove from her brother, but he complained that it was too small. The salesman told her that Joey probably had a hardball glove and what he needed was a glove for softball. The model he sold her could be used for either hardball or softball, and was already broken in. It cost fourteen dollars, but he assured her it was worth it. Sophie confessed to the salesman that Joey was her only son and she wanted the best for him. *If the glove cost five dollars more than then the other gloves, so be it,* she said to herself. She wanted the best. She also bought two bathing suits and the bathing cap the camp required.

She was sitting on the park bench with the bag from the sporting goods store on her lap. The big clock on the Dollar Savings Bank at the corner of Lincoln Boulevard and Monmouth Road read eleven-fifteen.

She left the park and walked across Kingsbridge Road to the Excelsior. She entered the lobby and saw the doorman sorting mail and putting it in numbered slots. He turned and put down a handful of mail and greeted her. The doorman was small and pudgy, and appeared the nervous type. He seemed self-conscious, averted his eyes from hers, stared at her chest, and said, "Can I help you, ma'am?"

"Yes, did Mrs. Weiss leave for work, yet? I work for her husband and I wanted to talk with her."

"No, she should be down soon. She usually leaves around noon on Thursdays. Do you want me to ring her?"

"No, that's all right, I'll wait outside."

Tim Cleary watched Sophie leave the building. He was immediately taken with her. She reminded him of his first trip to Cuba, and of all the trips since to Puerto Rico. Tim loved Latin women. Sophie was wearing tight dungarees and she had on an oxford shirt with the shirttails tied in a knot above her waist. She was carrying a big handbag and a shopping bag. She had on dark red lipstick and her fingernails were painted to match. As she walked toward the front door, Tim stared hungrily at her ass and admitted to himself he'd have paid twenty dollars, right then and there just to hold that ass in his hands for five minutes. *Three and a half months until my next vacation, one week out of fifty-two, makes it all worthwhile in the end,* he thought. Tim watched her until she was through the doors and no longer in sight. He then went back to sorting the mail and dreaming of vacations and hookers who'd do anything for a price.

Sophie stood in front of the building and took a package of cigarettes from her pocketbook. She lit one up, leaned against a car that was parked at the curb. The Excelsior was an impressive building. The brickwork was ornate, and multiple designs had been worked into the building's façade. The courtyard wasn't big, but there was a large street lamp in the middle of it with six large lighted globes hanging from wrought iron arms. The lamp was in the middle of a small circular garden, and the garden was packed tightly with colorful impatiens and pansies. The front entrance had two large brass and glass doors set into a wide frame of glistening marble. The building stood out from every other building on the block, and Sophie could only imagine that the apartments were just as nice. Her own building couldn't compare, and even though it was new, clean and modern, it lacked the character and craftsmanship of the Excelsior. She wondered to herself if that was the same difference between herself and Maria?

It was 11:45 and Maria hadn't gotten dressed for work. She had on her undergarments and stockings, but hadn't the energy to put on her dress or fix her hair.

Millie came into the bedroom and told her she'd cleaned the kitchen and put on the wash and would now take Henry's shirts to the laundry and get some lunch. Maria told her the envelope with her day's wages was on the dining room table. Millie told Maria that she hoped she felt better and left the apartment through the service entrance. Years ago Henry had given Millie a key for the service entrance, and she always entered and left the apartment through that exit. Millie took the service elevator down to the lower level and exited the building. She walked up the alleyway to the street and turned south on Lincoln Boulevard toward Kingsbridge Road. It was a little muggy out, but she liked that type of weather. She passed a woman leaning against a car smoking a cigarette. She smiled at the woman, but the woman ignored her and

Millie went on her way. *It's too much effort for some people to smile, they should have my problems,* she thought.

Right after Millie left, Maria put on her dress, shoes and fixed her hair. She took four aspirin and had two glasses of water. The migraine was at that brain numbing, unbearable stage, and for the second time that morning she contemplated calling in sick and going to bed. She told herself if it didn't let up she'd leave work early, but there was no point in not attempting to get through the day. She put the bottle of aspirin into her handbag and left the apartment.

When she got to the lobby, Tim greeted her in his slightly obsequious, but nonetheless, genuine and friendly manner. "Good morning Mrs. Weiss, how are you today?"

"I've been better."

"Oh, I almost forgot, there's a woman outside waiting for you, says she works with Mr. Weiss."

"Where?"

"Outside, at least that's where she said she'd be," he cautiously advised. "I told her I'd ring you, but she said not to bother. Is there a problem, should I do something?"

"No, no problem, I just don't know who this could be. My husband has a secretary, but she's with him in Montreal."

"I'll follow you out just in case. You never know, lotta crazy people in the world today."

Tim led the way through the lobby, and when they entered the courtyard he pointed out Sophie, who was leaning against a car. "That's her. Do you know her?"

"Yes," Maria bristled. "It's Henry's secretary."

Maria approached Sophie and said, "What do you want?"

"We have to talk. There's a lot going on you should know."

Maria walked to the corner and waited for the light to change. She turned to Sophie, who was following her, and said, "I can't imagine anything we would have in common or anything important we have to talk about."

Maria started across the street, and Sophie walked in front of her, turned around and crossed the street walking backward. Sophie's plan to be cool and casual and spring the picture on Maria while they were on the train was falling apart. She felt her blood rising and her voice was inching up a pitch. "You're kidding, tell me you're kidding? Nothing in common, how's Henry Weiss for starters?" she said accusingly.

"Henry's my husband and you're his secretary, that's our only connection."

They reached the other side of the street, and Maria started down the stairs to the entrance for the subway. Sophie was now alongside of her and her voice had not only increased several pitches, but she was also shouting. "Don't play that game with me, honey. You know what's going on, don't tell me you don't," she shouted.

Maria stopped on the stairs and put her hands to her temples. "Sophie, I suffer from migraines. Right now I'd rather be dead, that's how much pain I'm in. I'm trying to go to work. Please, leave me alone. Whatever problems you have, you have with my husband. I can't help you, please go away and stop making a scene." Maria continued down the stairs and went up to the turnstile and put in a token. She walked down to the platform and waited for the train.

Sophie had to buy a token from the token booth clerk, and after she went through the turnstile she went over to where Maria was standing and said, "You don't get it. I'm not going away. I've been more of a wife to Henry than you've ever been. He tells me all about you. You're a cold, fucking bitch. A spoiled bitch," she sneered.

Maria turned and looked down the platform. They were the only two people waiting for the train. It was midday and the high schools and colleges had already begun their summer recesses. Maria was no longer listening to Sophie. The volume of Sophie's verbal attack had increased, along with the coarseness of her language. Maria wondered how Henry could keep the company of such a foul and vulgar woman. *In another minute the train will arrive and I can leave her behind. She's Henry's problem. I'm not going to deal with her,* she resolved in her mind.

Sophie quieted down for a moment and put the shopping bag she was carrying down on the ground between her legs and reached into her handbag.

Maria stepped back, fearful that Sophie was going to pull out a knife or a gun and attack her.

Sophie took out an envelope. She withdrew a photograph of a young boy and glared at Maria. It was a photograph of a young boy and he was wearing a Holy Communion outfit and had a set of rosary beads clasped in his white-gloved hands. Sophie waved the photo in front of Maria's face. "Take a look, a good fucking look. That's my son. Look at him, you bitch, look at him. Who do you see?" she said as she pressed the photograph in Maria's hand.

Maria looked at the picture and she saw the resemblance to Henry. She wanted to sit down at that moment, if not faint. It was clear that the boy was Henry's, and his existence was what had Sophie so distressed. Maria felt her head was about to explode and, what she had perceived as the small inconvenience of dealing with her husband's mistress, had suddenly manifested itself as a major problem. She had the photograph in her hand, and without looking at it further she dropped it to the ground and said, "I don't know what you're talking about. Please leave me alone."

As she was speaking, Sophie went down to her knees to pick up the photograph. Maria could hear the distinctive sound of the train approaching, and as Sophie was kneeling with her back to Maria, near the edge of the platform, she decided to push her onto the tracks and into the path of the oncoming train. She took a step forward and stopped. From the corner of her eye she saw a little gleam of silver and a dark figure approaching. It was a police officer. He was colored and in the dark light of the subway station and deep blue of his uniform he was almost invisible except for the gleaming silver badge on the left side of his uniform shirt.

The officer approached and said, "Ladies, is there a problem?"

The light from the train lit up the tunnel and the sound of the squealing brakes shrieked through the station as it pulled in and stopped.

Maria smiled at the officer, and said, "This woman is bothering me. She works for my husband. I wish she would leave me alone."

The doors to the train opened and Maria stepped onto the train. Sophie threw Joey's photograph at her and said, "You forgot this, bitch."

The doors to the train closed and Maria picked up the photograph. As the train left the station, Maria put the photograph in her pocketbook without looking at it. She turned her head and watched Sophie and the policeman until the train had entered the tunnel and they were out of view.

Maria's heart was pounding and her temples were throbbing. She was sweating and her hands were cold and clammy. *My God*, she thought. *I was about to push her to her death and I would have done so in front of a policeman. What would have happened to me?*

No sooner had the train sped up, then it came to a screeching halt again at the next station. It was stopped at Monmouth Road and Lincoln Boulevard. Maria exited the train. She couldn't go on, and decided to go back to the apartment. Her encounter with Sophie had left her numb, and all she wanted to do was crawl into bed and go to sleep.

The police officer was able to calm Sophie down. He wrote her name and address in his memo book and told her she could be arrested for disturbing the peace. Sophie apologized, picked up her bags and walked to the subway exit. The cop called out to her, "Miss, just for the record, what was the other lady's name?"

Sophie turned and shouted back, "Maria Weiss, W-E-I-S-S, like in ice." The cop didn't answer and Sophie went back up the stairs and onto Lincoln Boulevard. It was just a little past noon, and she didn't want to go home. All morning she had worked herself up for that triumphant moment when she revealed the truth to Maria, but her plan had failed. Nothing, absolutely nothing moved Maria. Henry would, in all probability, fire her and she'd end up in a long and tawdry paternity suit with a man who was on a first name basis with every judge, living or dead, or so he always said, in the Upper Borough. "Well, I've still got Joey and that's more than either of those two have," she said to herself.

Sophie walked south on Lincoln Boulevard. It was hot and muggy, and she figured an afternoon in the coolness of Loew's Grand Palace watching a movie might improve her mood. *After all*, she told herself, *it couldn't hurt.*

At five minutes to noon Danny left Joe's fish Market with Maria's shrimp. He went back to the Associated, picked up her grocery order, put everything into the delivery bike and started for The Excelsior. He stopped at the hot dog vendor's wagon at Kingsbridge and Lincoln Boulevard and bought two hot dogs with mustard, sauerkraut and onions and a Dr. Brown's cream soda. He was waiting for the light to cross the street and saw Maria and another lady walking to the stairs for the subway. She was half a block away, but Danny stopped to admire her. She was wearing a yellow dress, kind of like the one Marilyn Monroe wore in the *Seven Year Itch* and he thought she looked just as sexy. Danny pulled the bike into the courtyard and stepped into the lobby.

"Hey, Sad Sack," he yelled to Tim. "Buzz me in the service entrance." He didn't wait for Tim to answer, but he knew he had heard him. He went around to the alleyway and wolfed down the hot dogs and the bottle of soda. He let out a loud belch and waited for Tim to buzz him into the building. He went up the elevator, and when he got to the door he pushed the intercom button and said, "Hurry up, saloon face, I ain't got all day." He had his hand on the doorknob and he felt the pulsating hum of the buzzer as the door unlocked. Danny took great care to place the groceries needing refrigeration into the refrigerator. He put the dry goods on the counter, then approached the door to the kitchen. He turned the knob, and much to his relief and satisfaction the door opened and he was in the apartment.

"Hey, anyone home? It's Danny with the delivery from Associated," he called out. No one answered.

Danny went straight to Maria's bedroom. He opened the bottom drawer in her bureau where the pictures were and took out the nightgowns.

Underneath them, wrapped in the linen cloth were the two albums. He took out the green leather portfolio and opened it. There were all of Maria's pictures. He opened another drawer and saw several pairs of gloves and a stack of boxes. He opened one of the boxes, and it contained a pair of women's stockings. The stockings were folded neatly and wrapped in tissue paper. He decided to leave those alone because he would never be able to put them back the way he'd found them. One of the pairs of gloves was white and made of lace. He put them on, and even though they were too small for his hands he was able to squeeze into them. There was a mirrored tray, music box and ashtray on the top of the bureau. He moved them to the side and made enough room to lay out all of Maria's pictures in one neat row. He went into her underwear drawer and took out a pair of white satiny-looking panties. He took his pants and underpants off. He put his underwear on her bed and put on Maria's underwear. He left the bedroom and went to the bathroom. He was looking for her pink nightgown, the sheer one, but he couldn't find it. There was a jar of cold cream on the windowsill with some other creams and lotions. He had an erection and it was bulging out through Maria's panties. The tightness of the panties hurt a little, but it was a good hurt and he enjoyed the sensation. He took the top off the cold cream jar and peeled the panties down to his thighs. He jabbed his erect penis into the cold cream jar several times and spread the glistening cream over it. He pulled the panties up, smoothed out the cream in the jar, put it back on the windowsill and went back to the bedroom.

He went into the closet. One had all men's things and he closed the door. The other was Maria's, and he looked at her clothes. The closet was wide and deep, and there were at least fifty shoe boxes neatly piled on the floor. He opened one and found a pair of yellow high heels inside of it. He sniffed the shoe, then measured it against his foot. He wanted to put the shoe on, but he knew it wouldn't fit. He fantasized that it wasn't him in Maria's clothes, but her there with him. He licked the inside of her shoe, then he put it away. He went back to the bathroom and looked in the hamper. He was looking for her dirty clothes, particularly a pair of panties. The hamper was bare. He went back to the bedroom and studied the nude photographs of Maria. He fondled himself through her panties and imagined that the lacy-gloved hands rubbing against him were Maria's. He couldn't recall ever being that happy or excited before. She had said they'd be out all day. He wasn't going to rush and was going to make sure he left no evidence behind.

He closed the bedroom door and took the black panties he stolen the previous week out of his front pocket and put them in his mouth. He sucked on them and started to slowly rub his penis.

Millie's trip to Han Lee's Chinese Hand Laundry and Jeno's Luncheonette had taken forty minutes and it was almost 12:30 when she got back to the building. Tim Cleary was standing in front of the building talking with one of the tenants. Millie waved to him and asked him to buzz her in the service entrance.

"Come in the front, it's easier," Tim called out to her.

"That's okay, I have the service door key."

"All right, just a minute."

Millie entered the apartment through the service entry. She saw that the groceries had been delivered and wondered where the delivery boy was because his bike was still downstairs parked in the alleyway. *Maybe he has more than one delivery*, she speculated. She opened the unlocked pantry door and walked into the kitchen. *Let me put Mr. Weiss' shirts away, change the sheets*, she thought, *and then I'll scrub the bathroom, fold the clothes and be on my way.* She walked down the hall and her new crepe soled shoes didn't make a sound. The bedroom door was closed, but she paid it no mind, as Henry and Maria were forever leaving doors half open and things undone. *That's what happens when you don't have to clean up after yourself*, she mused.

Danny had the fully nude photograph of Maria in his left hand. He was licking at it and slowly masturbating himself. He had the black panties in his hand and they were covering his penis. He was too lost in his fantasy to hear Millie open the door. Millie opened the door and let out a gasp. Her first glimpse was of Danny naked from the waist down except for a pair of tight underwear bunched around his thighs. He was wearing white gloves and had a black cloth in one hand and his penis was erect and exposed. There were pictures all over the top of the bureau, and Millie, in her shock, grabbed one of the pictures and screamed at Danny, "Who are you, what are you doing here?" She was too frightened and shocked to run, and she stood her ground and demanded he explain himself to her.

Danny didn't know what to do, and without thinking he reached over to the end of the bureau and picked up the ashtray and flung it at Millie's head. When he threw the ashtray, he bumped into the bureau and two of the pictures he'd had leaning against the mirror at the far edge of the bureau fell to the floor.

The point of the ashtray thudded into her left temple and she fell against the bureau, then slid to the floor, falling over the two photographs of Maria. He heard a faint gurgle, but she wasn't moving. Danny pulled the panties up, then put his own pair of underwear on over them. He put on his dungarees and buckled his belt, all the while watching Millie as she lay motionless on the floor.

He was in a panic and kept telling himself to stay calm. Maria had said to him "We'll be out all day." He kept repeating that to himself. He took the black panties and wiped down the edges of the drawers. Everything he'd touched before he put on the lace gloves, he wiped down. Millie still wasn't moving and he was certain she was dead. There was one photograph in her hand. He reached down to take it out, but her fingers were locked on both sides of the photo and he couldn't move them. It was a picture of Maria with her breasts exposed. Two other pictures were under her body, but he was afraid to touch her. He took the remaining photographs and put them in the green portfolio and placed it on the bed. He went to the bathroom to clean up any mess he'd made in there with the cold cream. He couldn't get caught, "I have all day, all day," he repeated over and over.

When Maria exited the subway station at Monmouth Road, she crossed over Lincoln Boulevard and started the walk northbound to her apartment. It was four long blocks, and the combination of her migraine and her run in with Sophie had drained her of all her energy. Nothing would have made her happier than to have pushed Sophie onto the train tracks and under the oncoming train. Sophie was, in Maria's mind, a vile little creature who deserved to die. *Who was this little whore to try and ruin my life?* she thought.

When she reached Lincoln Park, she sat on a bench for ten minutes. She would have stayed longer, but another woman sat down next to her and initiated a mindless conversation Maria was too tired and sick to even politely pursue. She got up and continued home. When she reached the building, Tim Cleary was standing outside.

He gave her a grave look of concern and went over and took her by the arm. "Are you all right, Mrs. Weiss? You look very sick?"

"Just my migraine, Tim, I had to get off the train."

"Do you need anything? Should I call Dr. Sklar? I know he's your doctor."

"No, but thanks, you're a very sweet young man, Tim. I'm going upstairs to bed, but thanks for your concern."

Tim walked Maria to the elevator and went up with her to her floor. When they got there, Maria told him she'd be fine and she got off and he went back down.

Danny had cleaned everything up as best he could. Millie was on the floor, and he knew she was dead. He sat on the floor next to her, careful not to touch her or get close to the pool of blood that had formed by her head. He was crying and praying to God that she would revive, but his prayers went unanswered and he sat there in shock over what he'd done. *This is an evil mortal sin,* he thought. *My poor mother, after putting up with my father all her life, I go and do this.* "All because some fucking cunt in her underwear teases me," he cried. He had put the green portfolio and the remaining photographs in a paper bag. "I came for these fucking pictures, and I'm taking them, and that's that," he said to himself. He was just about to step over Millie's body when he heard the front door open. He didn't know what to do and ran over to Maria's closet, opened the door and hid inside.

Maria walked in the apartment and called out to Millie, "Millie, hello, Millie are you still here?" There was no answer and she turned toward her bedroom. She took several steps down the hall when she saw Millie lying motionless on the floor. She let out a faint cry and ran into the bedroom. "Millie, Millie, what happened?" She knelt down and saw the photograph in Millie's hand and the other two under her. She saw the ashtray and the blood on it. She picked up the ashtray and tried to understand what had occurred. The pain from her migraine was intensifying and she felt faint. She heard a noise in her closet, stood up and went toward the closet door. Before she could take a second step the door burst open and a figure rushed at her. Everything was a blur and she felt the blow of the figure's elbow as it hit her in the chest. She staggered back, then everything went black. She felt herself falling. It was the same sensation you have in a dream when you're falling, except this sensation cleared her migraine and she fell and fell until she lost consciousness.

Chapter Seventeen

He knew the elbow had sent her reeling and he hoped he hadn't killed her, too. He pulled the lace gloves off, stuffed them into his pocket and ran down the hallway toward the pantry with the black panties in his hand. He was wearing her white panties and he could feel them cutting into his skin. He pushed the pantry door shut and wiped the knob with the panties. In the second it took to do that he listened to hear if Maria was chasing him, but he heard nothing. He went out the service entrance and took the elevator down. *So far*, he thought, *no one had seen him.*

When he got to the alleyway, he casually got on the bike and pedaled slowly toward the exit on to Lincoln Boulevard. He pedaled across the sidewalk and across the boulevard. He didn't look left or right, but kept his eyes focused straight ahead. When he reached the west side of the boulevard, he turned south toward Kingsbridge Road and headed back to the food market.

When he got back to the Associated Market his boss, Mr. Kimmel, asked him where'd he'd been. He told him that he stopped for a couple of frankfurters and a soda before he made the delivery and ate them afterward. He was rehearsing every step and accounting for every minute since he had left with the delivery. He knew the cops would be around, and he wanted everything to sound as original and casual as possible. The portfolio with the pictures was in a brown grocery bag in the basket of the delivery bike. He had originally planned on hiding the pictures underneath the Coffin at their hangout in the 212 Lot and showing them to his pals at their next drinking party, but that was out.

He couldn't hide them in his room because his mother was a snoop and was always going through his stuff.

Kimmel told him to get moving, as the deliveries were backing up. He excused himself and went to the bathroom and removed Maria's panties. He had the black ones and the gloves folded in one pocket and he folded the white ones and put them in another pocket. He had to dump the panties and gloves, but he couldn't give up the pictures. The next three deliveries were for addresses going west on Kingsbridge Road toward the 212 Lot.

He went to a building on College Avenue and dropped off two boxes of groceries at two different apartments. Each of the customers gave him a seventy-five cent tip, and all he could think of was how happy he would have been on any other day before this one to have received two nice tips like that. The next delivery was to a building on Armory Avenue. He only received a quarter as a tip, but the building had an incinerator and he dropped both pairs of panties and the gloves down the incinerator chute.

He left the Armory Avenue building and pedaled furiously west for four bocks until he was past Kingsbridge Terrace and heading toward the 212 Lot. He parked the bike and took the paper bag with the pictures and went to the Spot. There was no one there and he lifted the wooden hatch that covered the Coffin. He worked the Coleman cooler out of its bed of bricks, and while he was tugging one side and then the other he thought to himself how ridiculous this all was. The cooler was the Coffin and their hangout was the Spot, and all they did was smoke and drink and talk about sex and girls and give stupid code names and nicknames to everything and everybody. All those things he now rationalized had driven him to murder. When he had freed the cooler, he was surprised to find that the layer of bricks it rested on had been overrun with a thin film of ground water. He put the cooler back in its hole and went to the east end of the lot.

He went over to a rotten, but still standing tree that was barely visible behind a cluster of wild Elm saplings that abounded in the lot. He remembered that the tree backed up to a small stone wall and that years ago when they were playing Irish cops with the older boys he'd often used the hollowed out trunk as a hiding place. The hollowed out area of the trunk was dry and musty. He placed several flat stones on the ground and the paper bag containing the portfolio of Maria's picture against the inside of the trunk on top of the stones. Barring a monsoon rainfall, he was confident the pictures would stay protected from the elements until he could think of a better place to hide them.

His treasure hidden, he ran back to his bike and headed back to work. He was having a nightmare, and all he wanted was his mother's warm touch to make it go away, but with each breath and push of his legs against the pedals he knew he was awake and that there was nothing his mother and all her prayers could do to reverse the damage he'd caused. He thought of some of his classmates at Cathedral Prep, the ones he always poked fun at, the ones who thought they had a vocation and a calling from Christ, and he wished he had been like them. *I'm no better than my father*, he thought.

Chapter Eighteen

Phil Cairn smiled at Desmond Clay, and said, "I'm going to the neighbor's apartment. Don't let anyone in there until the ME gets here. That includes the crime scene detectives. If they arrive first, you give me a holler. There's no rush here, and we want to do this by the numbers. Got it?" he said with emphasis.

"Yeah, I read yuh."

Cairn opened the door to Edith Zimmerman's apartment and went inside. He was in a foyer and there was a telephone stand with a black phone on it, and next to it a chair. Widelsky, Patrolman Casey and Edith Zimmerman were down the hall sitting in the living room. Cairn called out, "Frank, it's Phil. Ask the lady if I can use her phone?"

"Go right ahead," was the response from Edith Zimmerman.

Cairn dialed the number to the Lincoln Boulevard Precinct, identified himself and asked for Sergeant Kreppell in the major case squad. He was put on hold, and after what seemed like an hour, but wasn't more than a minute, an irritated voice from the other end of the phone barked, "That you, Phil? What's the story?"

"Hey, Sarge, yeah, it's me, Phil. The story is we got us a whodunit and a homicide. Two ladies, one dead and the other was already on her way to Borough Med. They said she's in a coma, but I didn't see her. I don't know much more than that right now."

"All right, Brown filled me in. He says the dead one's got a hole in her head from an ashtray and the other one was barely breathing, but he just took a quick look and beat it outta the room."

"Shit, lotta people took a quick look and beat it outta that room."

"What are you gonna do? It's a homicide; somebody's gotta take a look. How many people you figure have walked on the scene?"

"We got the neighbor who discovered it, the doorman, the two ambulance attendants, the two responding cops, Sergeant Brown and Widelsky, although the two cops and Widelsky never went past the doorway."

"Nothing out of the ordinary, hold the scene. I have our elite Borough Major Case forensic specialists on their way along with the ME. Let the ME in there first with Hogan and Smith. They all work together very well. Smith can take his pictures before anything is touched. and Hogan can look for any evidence. Then the ME can play with the body before he packages it up for his shop. Do you follow me?"

"Not for nothing. Sarge," Cairn said with just a touch of annoyance in his voice. "I know how to handle a crime scene, give me some credit please."

"Pardon me. I forgot you and Mr. Personality were big time Huguenot City detectives until they farmed you out to us up here in Sticksville."

"Yes, sir. Any thing else, you'd like to tell me?"

"Plenty, I'm sending Murphy and DeMarco over to canvass the building. I'm also sending two detectives to the hospital to check on the lady in the coma and to scrape her fingernails and impound her clothes. But before I can do all of that and still supervise the 3:30 p.m. lineup for the City Park rapist, I would like some names so we can make some notifications. Headquarters has this thing about wanting immediate notification on all homicides, and nobody likes it when I tell them the victim is a Jane Doe. And the captain, you know him, don't you? Captain Grimsley? He has this thing about notifications to the loved ones of the recently deceased. So do you have that information?" Kreppell demanded.

"We're getting it. I just called to see if forensics and the ME were coming," Cairn said defensively.

"Nice talking to you, call back when you have something to say," Kreppell said abruptly, then hung up without waiting for Cairn to answer.

Fucking prick, Cairn thought. *Christ we been in the Upper Borough one fucking year and we're still treated like shit. Fucking farmers, all of them,* he cursed to himself.

Cairn put down the phone and walked to the living room. Edith Zimmerman had collected herself and smiled as he came in.

"How're we doing?" Cairn asked, while giving Edith Zimmerman his warmest smile.

"Oh, what a terrible shock!"

Widelsky added," Yes, it is, but you've been very helpful. Patrolman Casey, will take you to the drugstore to finish that errand you started out on. Won't you, Case?"

"Sure thing, c'mon, sweetheart, you're in good hands."

"I really don't want to bother you, but if you don't mind."

"It's no problem," Casey said reassuringly.

"Mrs. Zimmerman, would you mind if we used your apartment for a bit? Just to make some more phone calls and take our notes?" Widelsky asked.

"Please, make yourselves at home. I'll do anything I can to help."

Patrolman Casey and Mrs. Zimmerman left for the drugstore. Cairn sat down on the couch and griped to Widelsky "That Goddamn Kreppell. I call him up to check in with him and he starts breaking my balls. You know? Big time Huguenot City detectives, all that crap, then he starts managing the crime scene over the fucking phone like I'm some rookie or something. What a prick."

"Tell me about it."

"What else did he want?"

"Names, facts, all the usual stuff. But please give me a chance to get it, you know?" Cairn said with a look of disgust on his face.

"You know what it is? We're second grade detectives and these assholes up here are third grade, and they all know Greason got his stars and we're going back downtown. That's all it is. So stop worrying."

"Well, I'm happy you figured that all out. Now, did the lovely Mrs. Zimmerman shed any light on this little dance of death?"

"She was as helpful as she could be," answered Widelsky as he opened his steno book. "I took very good notes, and I'm happy to say that once Casey learned she didn't see a suspect he was bright enough not to ask any questions. Figured that's our job. It's what I love about guys who've been around a long time and are ready to pull the plug. Why engage in police work? Leave that for the real cops, y'know?"

"You must mean Kreppell?"

"Whatever. Now, listen up and don't interrupt. Edith and Arthur Zimmerman have lived in this apartment since 1931. The apartment next door, where the homicide occurred, is the domicile of Henry Weiss and his lovely wife Maria. She's the one they took to the hospital. Henry moved into the building in 1941. He was an assistant district attorney in the Upper Borough, but by the time he moved here he was a successful attorney specializing in real estate. Edith, that's Mrs. Zimmerman, said that Henry was a very good looking and eligible bachelor when he moved here. She tried to set him up with her niece, but he wasn't interested. Anyway, Henry was drafted in 1942 and kept the apartment, but dutifully fulfilled his military obligation and was discharged as a lieutenant in 1945. 'Oh, he was so handsome in his uniform; and an officer too,' she insisted on telling me several times. He resumed his practice and continued to do very well. In 1948, he married Maria. Edith says Maria had movie star looks and is still very attractive, but and I'll quote her exactly, 'Very beautiful when he married her, still attractive and always polite, but just a little taken with herself. You know the type? A little cold, something missing.' Edith loves Henry, but Maria she could take or leave. Edith says they're very respectable and quiet people. Now, for the cleaning lady, her name is Millie Campos. Edith used her several times, but said she was too noisy. Apparently she likes to sing and play the radio loudly when she works. Millie lives over in Woodhaven, and her husband is an X-Ray technician at St. Mary's Hospital. Maria works at Sable's downtown for Lorient Cosmetics and is at least fifty years old, but she doesn't look it. Millie comes on Thursdays around 11:30 a.m., and Maria leaves for work every Thursday around noon and doesn't return home until after 10:00 p.m. Millie plays the radio very loudly after Maria leaves for work. The apartment has a front entrance and a service entrance right off the service elevator, and Millie has a key to the service entrance door. She never comes in the front door and always takes the service elevator. Henry Weiss is in Montreal on business. He told Edith on Monday he was going to Montreal. There's nothing unusual about that because he talks to Edith all the time, and every Mother's Day he sends her flowers. Mr. Zimmerman, or should I say Arthur, is a dentist. His office is in the Heights, and he works late every Monday and Wednesday. May I directly quote the lovely Edith once again, 'Mondays and Wednesdays, Arthur eats cold. Last night we had dairy, and today I felt a little tight. I called Arthur and he told me to take an Alka Selsor.' Anyway, that was around two o'clock and she was going to the drugstore and went out to get on the elevator and saw the Weiss' door was open. She thought that was strange because Henry's in Montreal, Maria's at work and Millie never goes out that door. She looked in and saw a pocketbook on the floor. It was very expensive looking, and she knew it was Maria's. She called out 'Yoo-hoo, Millie, are you there?' There was no answer, so she walked down the hallway and saw people on the floor. She went a little closer and saw the two women on the floor. She says she didn't panic and went right back to her apartment and called Tim the doorman.' (Widelsky laughed) Tim the midget doorman came upstairs, took a look in the Weiss' apartment and went to Edith's apartment and called for help. He then stood guard at the door until the police arrived. Now, Edith was concerned that the murderers could still be in the apartment so, and it's a fucking shame this is a homicide because when she was telling her story I almost wet my pants, and she told the doorman to stay in front of the door and she gave him a broom to use as protection." Widelsky closed his steno book and said, "That's the world according to Edith Zimmerman. You have to admit it; she stays on top of what goes on around here. One thing, and I didn't want to break her train of thought or insult her, but what the fuck does she mean by saying 'Arthur eats cold?'"

It was Cairn's turn to laugh, and he replied, "She means she doesn't heat up his dinner."

"Some people, huh!"

Patrolman Clay opened the apartment door and called in, "Detectives, the ME is here."

Cairn and Widelsky left Mrs. Zimmerman's apartment and went into the hallway. Standing in front of the elevator was Richard Chin, a Chinese-American doctor from the Medical Examiner's office, his assistant, Butch Jones, and Detectives Hogan and Smith from the Borough's Major Case Forensic Unit.

"Ah, the death squad is here," Widelsky said as he shook hands with everyone. "Phil you wanna give them the rundown on the scene."

"Sure, Frank. Best of my knowledge no one other than the murderer and the ambulance attendants along with the deceased and the victim, if she's not the murderer, have been in that room. There's some funny pictures, possibly nudes of one of the victims and not much else. I'm gonna notify Sergeant Kreppell and give him the names and make arrangements for the notifications. Patrolman Clay here has the crime scene log, and Frank and I are going downstairs to speak with the doorman. Murphy and Demarco are expected shortly for a canvass. Sooner you guys get started, the sooner we can get moving. Any questions?"

"Nobody smoked or used the phone inside, did they?" asked Detective Hogan.

No one answered.

"Let's see," he said suspiciously

Hogan and Smith were both dressed in blue khaki pants and were wearing white short sleeve shirts with pocket protectors loaded with pens and pencils in their left shirt pockets. Hogan was the fingerprint man, and he was busying himself with a small suitcase that contained magnifying glasses, feather dusters, and small containers of powders and various other implements of his trade. Smith was the photographer, and he had moved to the front door and was using a light meter to adjust the F-stop on his camera to begin the cycle of photography that would lead him from the front door and through the apartment to the homicide scene. Once in the room he would work his way in, methodically taking photo after photo until he had captured the death scene from every feasible angle. Hogan would follow and he, too, would methodically process every tangible object in the room for any evidence that would lead to the identity of the murderer.

Dr. Chin patiently stood by the door watching the detectives work and waiting for his cue to examine the body and start reconstructing the murder. Butch Jones remained in the lobby, sitting on the ME's gurney. He was unfolding a body bag and recounting to Clay a call he'd been on earlier in the day where they had to remove the body of a woman from an apartment where she'd been dead for a week and her cats had started eating her flesh.

Cairn and Widelsky took the elevator to the lobby in search of the doorman. The elevator door opened and they were greeted by Detectives Tony DeMarco and Gerry Murphy. Both men were smiling, and as Widelsky and Cairn exited they entered.

DeMarco said, "We'll start on the roof and work our way down. Kreppell says there are no witnesses so far, and you two haven't a clue what happened. I'll leave out the rest of what he said," DeMarco said, snickering as the elevator door closed.

"Fucking wise-asses, those two," Widelsky said to Cairn.

"You'd think they'd want a little background, no?"

"Kreppell don't like us, pure and simple," Widelsky responded. "And that's our cross to bear. What were we going to tell them anyway? We don't know shit. Let em knock on everybody's door, maybe somebody saw something. Who cares? Where's our friend from the land of Oz?"

Tim Cleary was standing in front of the Excelsior taking in the afternoon sun and trying to calm his nerves in the hot muggy afternoon air. Cairn stepped into the courtyard and called to him, "Excuse me, Tim, that's your name isn't it?"

"Yes."

"Could you come inside? We have some questions we'd like to ask you."

Tim came in the building and followed Cairn to the doorman's desk where Widelsky was standing. "Whatever you need, I'm here."

"Do you have somewhere we can talk in private?" Widelsky asked.

"Yeah, we have a lounge through that door."

Tim then led Cairn and Widelsky behind the desk and through a door into a small room. The room was furnished with a vinyl love seat, small radio, desk, two wooden chairs, floor lamp and two four drawer file cabinets.

Widelsky pulled up a wooden chair and sat down behind the desk. Cairn sat on the love seat and pulled the other wooden chair over so that it was situated between the desk and the love seat. He pointed to the chair and told Tim to sit down. Tim was sweating profusely and the presence of the two detectives had him practically hyperventilating.

Cairn looked at him, patted his hand, and said, "Tim, you might be the key to solving this case. Now, I can see that you're upset and I want you to calm down. Right now, there's nothing that would make you a suspect, but you may have seen something that could be very significant and we want to go over everything you did between the time you came to work today and the time Mrs. Zimmerman called you. Do you understand?"

"Sure I do."

"Good boy," Widelsky added.

"First things first," Cairn said as he took out his notebook. "Where do you live and how long have you worked here?"

"I live at 2810 Bailey Avenue, ten blocks from here at the bottom of Kingsbridge Road and I've worked here since June of 1953, twelve years," Tim answered as he mopped his brow, then twisted the wet handkerchief in his hands.

"How old are you? You must have started young?"

"I'm thirty-four years old. I started here when I was twenty-two. I got out of high school in '49 and tried to join the Navy, but they wouldn't take me 'cause I have the asthma. A friend of my family, guy name of Joe Dunn got me a job as an elevator operator in Huguenot City, you know, in the business district. I got in the building service union and was able to land this job in '53," he said nervously.

"Asthma, that's too bad. Detective Widelsky's a Navy man, right Frank?"

"Twelve years. That's a long time, and since you were twenty-two," Widelsky said as he leaned over in his chair and stared at Tim. "Tell me, twelve years here, did you ever fool around with any of these old dolls? You hear stories about how some of these older broads, you know, the ones with money like young guys. Maybe you were getting a little, then they turned you off. Or maybe you were screwing somebody's cleaning lady. That shit happens too. I hear a lot of stories about doormen and mailmen."

Tim squirmed in his chair and looked at Cairn. "What's he talking about? I never done nothing like that. I know all these people, I respect them."

"I'm sure you do, Tim. But we just want to cover all the bases. So I guess I can put in my book that in your twelve years here you've never had personal relations with any tenant in this building, is that correct?" Cairn said as he scribbled something in his notebook.

"Yes, never anything."

"Good boy," Widelsky cajoled. "I just wanted to make sure, and you know that we'll talk to every tenant and your co-workers just to make sure you're telling the truth, don't you?"

"You can talk to anyone, but why?"

"Basic police work, Tim, "Cairn answered. "Neither of us suspects you of anything, but it makes things easier when we ask the obvious. Understand?"

"I g-guess so," Tim stammered.

Widelsky leaned back in his chair, put his hands behind his head, and said, "Tell me everything you did today since you woke up."

"I got up at six. Showered, got dressed and had tea and an English muffin with my mother. I caught the number twenty bus at around six-forty or a quarter to seven and was here a little before seven. I unlocked the inner lobby door, put on my uniform jacket and read the paper at my desk in the lobby. It's slow in the morning. Half the people in this building are retired and don't go to business every day. The super, Mr. Morrison, is on vacation and Lunch, the porter, was working a half-day. Funny name, ain't it? He's from Alabama and says he was born at lunchtime, so his mammy named him Lunch," Tim said, laughing and with an exaggerated Negro affectation on the word "Mammy." He then continued his monologue. "Lunch's job today was to mop the hallways and lobby, then to polish the brass on the front lobby door. Maybe around eleven he left for the main office up on Riverview Avenue. Crestview Management owns the building. They're getting a new floor scraper and the salesman had to show him something on it. The mail came a couple a minutes after Lunch left and I sorted it and put it in everyone's box. Some of the tenants call downstairs and ask me to bring the mail up. Eh, maybe a few minutes after Lunch left, while I was doing the mail this woman came in the lobby. She was Puerto Rican, about thirty-five or so, I think, and pretty nice. She asked for Mrs. Weiss. I told her Mrs. Weiss hadn't gone out yet. She leaves around twelve on Thursdays. I said I'd call her, but she said she'd wait outside. Best I can remember, it was all around eleven o'clock, maybe closer to eleven-thirty, you know, people coming and going all the time, give or take a few minutes. Could I get a drink of water?"

"Sure, catch your breath, but one thing I'd like you to clarify. You said the Puerto Rican woman was very nice. What does that mean?" Cairn asked.

"Yeah, kinda hard, but nice, sexy if you like that type."

"Fine, I just wanted to know. You're doing real well."

Tim went into the bathroom and Widelsky leaned over the desk and whispered to Cairn, "Keep him talking. Don't interrupt."

Tim came back in the room. He had spilled water all over the front of his shirt and the drink hadn't reduced any of his nervousness.

"So this Puerto Rican chick comes in, and did you see the cleaning lady? Widelsky said.

"Oh yeah, she came a minute or two before the Puerto Rican woman. Then around twelve Mrs. Weiss came down. I told her about the woman and she seemed upset, so I walked her out of the building and pointed the woman out. She acted annoyed and said the woman was her husband's secretary. I went back into the building and a few minutes later Danny Monaghan came in. He lives in my building and delivers for the Associated on Kingsbridge Road. He's a real wise-ass. You guys know his father, don'tcha?"

"No, should we?" Cairn responded.

"Monaghan the Milkman, he's a real piece of work and a head case to boot. All the cops in the Summit Precinct know him. He's a cop fighter. You know what they say, 'The apple don't fall far from the tree.' This Danny's a punk," Tim said with anger.

"Whoa, slow down. You're losing us," Widelsky said. "Give us the bio on the kid's family later. What was he doing here? And what was the time, as close as possible? Please."

"Okay, he had a delivery for the Weiss'. It was maybe ten after twelve. They have a delivery entrance into a pantry in their apartment. Only their line has it. All deliveries for everyone go through the service entrance off the alleyway. Delivery guys check in with me, I send them to the entrance, and when they get there they buzz me and I hit my buzzer and let them in. Now, on the apartments with the delivery entrance I can use my key and unlock a buzzer box for those apartments if the tenants want me to and the delivery people can leave the delivery in the pantry. The Weiss' have a refrigerator in their pantry. So Mrs. Weiss always calls in her order and she doesn't have to be home to receive it. The delivery boy brings the groceries up and puts the box with the stuff that needs refrigeratin' in the refrigerator and the other stuff on the table. Then he leaves. Pretty neat, huh?"

"Pretty fucking confusing," Widelsky sighed. "Now let me get this straight. No deliveries come through the lobby, correct?"

"Yes."

"All deliveries go down the alleyway to the service entrance and you buzz them in. Right?"

"Yes, unless it's a big deal, then Lunch the porter goes down there and helps."

"Okay, but if it's just a delivery boy from the market, he comes here and tells you he has a delivery and you send him around the alleyway and buzz him in the service entrance. Why can't he just go up the elevator in the lobby?" Widelsky asked.

"Because that's only for tenants and guests."

"And why does the cleaning lady go in that way?"

"Because she has a key to the pantry door and she always goes that way," Tim answered, as if Widelsky and Cairn should have known that fact.

"Fine, now the Weiss apartment and all the other ones on that line have two entrances, correct?"

"Yes."

"And they have a service entrance into their pantry that is near the service elevator and you can buzz someone into the apartment through that service door from the lobby?"

"Exactly, we have a special panel on the wall behind my desk. I unlock it and open the door. There's an intercom and two buttons. The first button is for the intercom and the second is for the door buzzer. In front of the service door there's an intercom and one button. The delivery boy pushes the intercom and tells me he's there. I then buzz him in. Just like that," Tim said confidently, as if he was explaining a very simple task to a dull child.

Cairn sat up and said, "You mean you can buzz someone into an apartment from down here?"

"No, not the apartment, just the pantry, there's a second door that leads from the pantry to the apartment. That's a regular steel door with a heavy duty lock."

"Gotcha," Widelsky said. "What about the apartments that don't have a pantry?"

"We put it here in the lounge, or if it ain't big, behind the desk. If it's furniture or something, then you have to make arrangements for the super to go in the apartment."

"And they gotta use the service entrance and elevator just to come to the lobby?"

"Of course, this is a classy building."

"Fucking confusing," Widelsky said with a shake of his head.

"You work here, it makes sense."

"Okay, finish the story."

"Where was I?"

"You were telling us about Danny Monaghan," Cairn stated.

"Right, Danny comes by little past twelve, like ten after, like I said before, and calls into the lobby that he has a delivery. I tell him okay and he goes around to the service entrance and I buzz him in and then to the apartment and I buzz him in again."

"Hold up," ordered Widelsky. "How do you know when he leaves?"

"You don't," Tim answered. "But what's he going to do in the pantry?"

"What happened next?"

"I went outside to stretch my legs. After about ten minutes or so Mrs. Tollner came out. She was going for a walk, but we stopped and talked a bit, and while we were talking I saw Millie, Mrs. Weiss' cleaning lady, coming down the block carrying a bundle from the Chinese laundry. She must have gone back out to run an errand. She asked me to buzz her in and I told her come through the lobby, but she waved me off. That's the last time I saw her alive. Maybe it's twelve-thirty or a little later, around that time when I saw her. I don't think fifteen more minutes passed before Mrs. Weiss came back. I was still in front of the building and she looked terrible. I asked her what was wrong and she said it was one of her migraines. I offered to call her doctor, but she said she just wanted to go upstairs. So I took her to the elevator and went upstairs with her. She got off and I went back downstairs and went to the bathroom and took a dump. I then got ready to go to lunch. I took off my jacket and hat, combed my hair and washed my face, locked the inner lobby door and left. When I was leaving the apartment, I saw Danny Monaghan on his delivery bike come from the direction of the alleyway. Maybe it was one o'clock by then."

"Is that significant?" Cairn queried. "Do you think Monaghan's involved?"

"I couldn't say, but it just seemed odd. He should have finished his delivery long before that. Don't you think?"

"We don't think, until we have something to think about," Widelsky replied.

Cairn added in," You don't like Monaghan, do you?"

139

"Please, don't put words in my mouth. I'm just telling you what I saw. And please, I don't want no trouble with the Milkman," Tim said nervously.

"Don't worry," Cairn said. "Now what happened next?"

"I went over to Chock Full O'Nuts on Monmouth Road and had lunch."

"Anyone see you?"

"Yeah, Sandi the waitress. I go there three times a week, at least. I had a cream cheese on date nut loaf, a whole-wheat donut and a cup of coffee. I came back here and I found the inner door propped open. Happens all the time, people are having a delivery or bringing some things in and I'm not here, so they use their key, then they prop open the door."

"This is a building with doormen, but they're not always on duty?" Cairn asked.

"Yeah, when I started they had coverage twenty-four hours a day, every day. Now it's seven to midnight Monday through Friday and ten to six on Saturday and no one on Sunday. You should have seen the lobby before they put in that inner door and glass wall. It was beautiful. I don't get a relief for lunch, so I just put up a sign and lock the grate over the mail slots. Since Crestview bought the building everything's going downhill, and now we have a murder. I just hope the murderer didn't come in while I was at lunch."

"What next?" Widelsky said wearily.

"I started to do the word jumble in the newspaper and maybe it's a little past two and I hear Mrs. Zimmerman screaming over the intercom to come upstairs right away. I ran to the elevator and when I got upstairs she's in the hallway crying. I go in the apartment and look in the bedroom and saw what I saw. I went right to Mrs. Zimmerman's apartment and called the police. I knew not to use the phone in the apartment. Saw that on *The Naked City*."

"Two more things: Do you know where Mr. Weiss has his office and where does the Monaghan kid work?" Cairn asked.

Tim got up and went over to one of the file cabinets. He opened a top drawer and took out a file with Henry's name and apartment number on it. He opened the folder and handed it to Cairn. He then turned to them both and said, "Monaghan works at the Associated Market between Jersey and Crestwood Avenues on Kingsbridge Road. But please, leave me out of it."

"One last thing," Cairn asked as he was looking at his notes. "How good are you on all these times?"

"Like I said, everyone's coming and going, around eleven, around twelve, twelve-thirty, one o'clock. I can't be exact, just approximately, I guess?"

Cairn copied the information for Henry's office into his notes and asked

Tim if he'd wait in the lobby, as he had to make several phone calls. Tim was only too happy to oblige and quickly left the office.

Cairn turned to Widelsky and said, "What about the grocery boy?"

"Let's find out about the secretary, first."

Chapter Nineteen

Cairn turned to Widelsky and said, "What do you think?"

"I think we have to pin him down on his times a little better. We got the secretary between eleven and eleven-thirty, there's something going on there. We have the delivery boy at around noon, then we have the cleaning lady and then we have the Weiss lady and we finish it with the delivery boy seen in the area within minutes after the Weiss woman went upstairs."

"Sounds great if we're looking at the delivery boy, but what if it happened after the doorman goes to lunch?"

"I agree, that's makes much more sense, particularly if there's something going on with the husband and the secretary, you know?"

"All right, let me call the great Kreppell."

"Fine, you enjoy your chat with the good sergeant while I tour the lobby," Widelsky said as he exited the room and went out to the doorman's desk.

Tim was standing at the desk looking off into space when Widelsky came up behind him and locked the back of Tim's neck in his right hand. "Listen, Munchkin, I find out you ain't been straight up with us I'll pop your fucking head like a pimple. Got it?" he said cruelly as he released his hold on the smaller man's neck. Tim looked at Widelsky and started to cry.

"What the fuck didja do that for?" he whined. "I told you everything. These people here are good to me. I love Mr. Weiss. He's always been good to me. Why wouldn't I tell the truth?"

"No reason not to. Just that my partner can be a little soft and I don't want you to forget who're dealing with."

"I know, but you're not nice."

"I'm not paid to be nice. I'm paid to get results and I don't want to find out later on that you forgot to tell us something. You sure on all your times?" Widelsky asked in a slightly milder tone.

"Yeah, I'm sure," Tim, replied a little more confidently.

"Make sure you are, "Widelsky said as he walked back into the lounge area where Cairn was just getting off the phone.

"Fucking Kreppell, something is awfully fishy."

"What now?"

"Murphy and Demarco had Hogan process the cleaning lady's pocketbook and then they got all of her pedigree information and called Kreppell with it. He notified the police chaplain that works at St. Mary's and had him break the news to the dead woman's husband. The Weiss lady is in Borough Med. and Russo and Stanton are standing by in case she comes to and they can get a statement or if it's just for a moment before she dies, a dying declaration," Cairn said in disbelief.

"Why'd he do that?"

"I don't know, but it seems like we're not the lead team in this investigation. I told him we were going to the law office to look for the secretary and he told me okay, but he said to call him when that's done before we do anything else. He didn't even ask about the crime scene. Let's go back upstairs and see what's shaking."

"I'm sure Holmes and Watson already have this solved," Widelsky said sarcastically referring to the two Forensic Detectives, Hogan and Smith.

Detective Hogan had spread a large piece of brown butcher's paper wrap on the dining room table in Henry and Maria's dining room. He carried out the three pictures of Maria that Danny had left behind. The ME had to break one of Millie's joints on the hand holding a picture to release it. He told Hogan and Smith that she had probably suffered a cadaveric spasm at the time of death and that caused her arms and the joints in her hands to automatically lock. Hogan had told patrolman Clay to close the apartment door and had let him come to the doorway to observe the detectives at work and watch the ME perform his preliminary examination of the body.

When Smith had photographed the scene he was the first to observe that Millie's left hand was locked on the picture of Maria. "Could rigor mortis have already set in?" Dr. Chin carefully placed his hand under Millie's blouse and placed it under her armpit. "No, he answered the body is still warm. I don't think she's dead more than a few hours."

Patrolman Clay wanted to laugh when he heard the doctor speak. Dr. Chin may have been Chinese but he spoke with the unmistakable accent of someone who had grown up in the Upper Borough.

"Why so stiff? I've seen suicides where the gun is locked in the hand after some poor bastard shot himself in the mouth, but that's different than this," Smith said.

"Cadaveric spasms are the result of a major shock to the central nervous system. Possibly the force of the blow and the point of the ashtray, if in fact that's the murder weapon, damaged both sides of the brain and caused her death almost instantaneously," Dr. Chin conjectured. "I'll find out more at the autopsy, but she's dead and what you see is what you get."

Two of the pictures had gotten a good deal of blood on their bottom portions and Hogan laid them all out on the paper to dry a little before he packaged them up. Clay had gone over to view them and he remarked, "My God, she's beautiful. I wonder who she is?"

Hogan laughed and said, "Take a look around the living room. See those pictures in the frames? That's her."

Clay walked down the steps into the living room and went over to the fireplace and looked at two black and white photographs on the mantle. "You're right. It's her. What a knockout."

Smith came out of the bedroom and looked at the pictures and then at the ones on the mantle. "She's a beauty. Wonder what happened?"

Hogan responded, "Maybe she caught the cleaning lady going through her stuff and they had an argument and she hit her with the ashtray. I packaged that up and there's a nice visible blood print on it, should be the murderer's."

"Hey kid," Smith said to Clay. "Don't listen to him, it's never that easy."

Clay was still admiring Maria's pictures on the mantlepiece when Widelsky and Cairn came back into the apartment.

"Hogan what the fuck's going on here?" Widelsky snarled.

"Why did DeMarco and Murphy have you process the victim's personals?" Cairn chimed in.

"Because that's what Kreppell wanted, or so said Murphy. What's the big deal anyway?"

"Just seems Kreppell's acting like the lead on this except he ain't left the office."

"So what, you wanna know what we got or you wanna argue about the sergeant?" Smith said as he came to Hogan's side.

"Whaddya got?" Widelsky said as he frowned and took his steno pad out.

"We got a clean crime scene and I don't like that," said Hogan. "There's a blood print on the ashtray and my preliminary visual is that it's a good one, but that's it. The woodwork around the two closets is painted in high gloss enamel. Great for picking up latent prints, and guess what? Somebody wiped it clean, same thing with the doorknob leading from the pantry into the apartment. Clean as can be. There's a bucket and a damp mop and rag in the pantry and the kitchen's spotless. My guess there is the cleaning lady worked up the kitchen and got it spic and span. But who cleans the woodwork in the bedroom?"

"Nothing on the bureaus?" Cairn asked.

"Plenty on the husband's dresser, but the top of the wife's bureau is clean. Bathroom's clean, too. Everybody leans against the woodwork around a door one time or another. That should never be clean."

"You have some pictures that were there, don't you?" Widelsky asked.

"We do. Three of them, and two are fairly wet with blood. They're what you called a matte finish and that type of paper is very absorbent. Someone with greasy hands or very sweaty hands could leave a very nice impression. Only problem is how many people have handled the pictures? They're at least twenty-five years old and everybody from the original processor and fifty other's could have touched them. That could cause a lot of overlays."

"Who're the pictures of, anyway?" Cairn asked.

"Come over here," Smith directed as he led Cairn and Widelsky to the dining room. "Attractive, isn't she?"

"Very," Cairn said.

Widelsky said nothing initially, but he couldn't take his eyes off the photographs. Finally, he said, "She ain't bad, but who is she?"

Smith then said, "Follow me." And he led them into the living room and brought them to the fireplace. Cairn and Widelsky looked up at the framed photographs of Maria and Henry. Widelsky said, "Okay, she came home, caught the cleaning lady going through her stuff and killed her. Case closed. She was so fucking upset at what she did she fainted and now she's in a coma. Case adjudicated by death."

"Pretty much how I figured it out too," said a smiling Hogan.

"Guess I'm wrong, then" Widelsky retorted.

"Anything else we should know," asked Cairn.

Smith turned and looked at Hogan, then called out to the ME, "Hey, Doc, can you come here a minute?"

Doctor Chin came out of the bedroom. He had on green rubber gloves that went up to his elbows. He looked at Cairn and Widelsky and said, "Phil, Frank, what did you two find out so far?"

Cairn answered, "There's been a lot of activity today. Mr. Weiss is in Montreal. His secretary was waiting downstairs for Mrs. Weiss at about eleven-thirty this morning. She wasn't pleased to see her. At eleven forty-five or thereabouts the cleaning lady made an appearance and at around noon the delivery boy showed up. The cleaning lady went out and came back. Mrs. Weiss came back a little while later and the doorman saw the delivery boy nearby shortly after Mrs. Weiss returned and he was going for lunch. When the doorman came back from lunch an hour later he found the lobby doors propped open and shortly after that the neighbor saw the front door open, looked in and the rest is history. I may be off on some of my times but that's the case in a nutshell, so far."

Chin smiled. "I'm not going to be of much help right now. She's been dead a couple of hours. It could have been twelve-thirty or it could have been two o'clock. There's no way I can pinpoint it beyond that. The cause of death, and I'm just surmising at this point, appears to be from a blow to the head. I'll have a preliminary report tomorrow. If you find out anything of interest let me know."

Hogan said to Cairn and Widelsky, "There's a lot more I plan on doing before I'm done. I'll process the ashtray later, and I'm taking the box the delivery boy brought the groceries in. I'll get his prints. When you track down Mr. Weiss make arrangements with him to come in so we can take his prints for elimination. I want him to view the pictures too, but I'm not going to process these three photographs until we take one on one shots of them. The way I figure it, these are part of a set. Look at them. In the first picture the robe or cover whatever it is covers her breasts. In the next one we see some cleavage and then in the third one the breasts are bare. There's probably more, and I wonder what the final one is?"

"Did you look for any others?" Cairn asked.

"I looked very carefully. Nothing. There's a photo album in one of her bottom bureau drawers, but it's just old family pictures. No nudies, and that's what I think these were."

"Could it be an extortion?" Smith said.

"Too fucking easy if it is," said Widelsky.

"We can't dismiss the probable," a smiling Cairn added.

"Fine, let's go find the secretary and the delivery boy. Sooner they're in or out the easier this will be," Widelsky said.

DeMarco and Murphy came into the apartment and Widelsky said, "Phil, look, it's Kreppell's trusted gumshoes."

"What do you mean by that?" DeMarco barked.

"What do I mean?" a visibly angry Widelsky replied. "Next time you get assigned to work with us, give us a heads up about what the boss told you to do."

Murphy looked at Widelsky with utter contempt and said, "I think you're the gumshoe or maybe shoofly would be more apropos. Whatever, we're just following orders and for the record, nobody in this building heard or saw anything today. I'll file my report tonight."

Widelsky looked at Murphy and DeMarco, then turned to Cairn and said, "C'mon, Phil, I get tired hanging around minor leaguers."

Cairn gave Widelsky the address for Henry's law office, and as they were driving down Lincoln Boulevard, he said, "What the fuck was that 'Shoofly' remark about?"

They drove past Loew's Grand Palace. The movie marquee advertised that The Sound of Music was playing and Widelsky said, "I took the kids and Theresa to see that last week. I didn't want to go, but I'd promised. It was pretty good. Long but pretty good."

Cairn laughed. "I won't tell anybody, I promise."

"Fuck off, asshole."

Sophie was seated in the balcony in Loew's Grand Palace. The theatre was cool and cavernous. The ceiling had small little blue lights that twinkled like stars and as she curled up in her seat and watched Julie Andrews dance across the screen singing and laughing, she wished that Joey was with her and that they could stay there frozen in time, far away from all life's disappointments.

147

Chapter Twenty

The two detectives were standing in front of suite 610 and Cairn was reading off the names that were stenciled on the door. "Is it a law firm or just a bunch of shysters renting office space?"

"What's it matter, they're all fucking shysters."

"Just asking," Cairn said as he opened the door to the office.

A young woman with dark hair and a bright smile was sitting behind the reception desk, and behind her was a switchboard mounted on the wall. It was obvious she was the receptionist and switchboard operator. "Hi, can I help you?" she inquired in a very friendly tone.

Cairn opened his badge case and showed her his detective shield and identification card.

"Hi, I'm Detective Cairn and this is my partner Detective Widelsky. We're wondering if we could speak with Mr. Weiss' secretary."

"Oh, I'm sorry. Mr. Weiss is in Montreal on business and his secretary is with him."

"Was she in today?" Widelsky asked.

"Was who in?"

"Weiss' secretary."

"No, Sophie went with him to Montreal and they're not coming in until tomorrow. Least, that's what they told me Monday when they left," she said with a shrug of her shoulders. A light on the switchboard lit up and there was a shrill ring. The girl looked at the two detectives and as she was swiveling toward the switchboard said, "Excuse me, call coming in." With one hand she slipped the phone headset off her shoulder and up to her right ear and with the other hand she pulled out a plug from the switchboard and inserted it into the hole where a bright red light was blinking. "Mr. Futerman's office," she said. "May I help you?"

She was just as friendly over the phone as she was when you came into the reception area, Cairn thought. She was cute and he liked her. The two detectives stood there while the girl answered the call and relayed it to Mr. Futerman's secretary.

"Is this a law firm or just a group of lawyers sharing office space?" asked Widelsky.

"You'll want to talk with Mr. Futerman's secretary," the girl said, still as friendly as ever. She turned back to the switchboard and pulled a plug and inserted it into another hole, then spoke to someone on the other end. "Hi, Ruthie, it's Janet. There are two detectives here asking about Sophie. Could you talk to them?" She then turned to Cairn and Widelsky and said, "Go straight down that hallway and turn right and Ruthie will meet you. She's Mr. Futerman's secretary."

Cairn smiled and thanked her. "You've been very helpful. What's your name?"

"Janet Abonita."

"Abonita," Cairn repeated. "Very pretty, but unusual, I don't think I ever heard that name before?"

"When my grandfather came through Ellis Island they mixed up the letters somewhere."

"Guess so," Cairn said as he and Widelsky started down the hallway. They turned the corner and were met by an older woman. She had a full face, red curly hair and very white skin speckled all over with reddish brown freckles. She had on a green and orange silk print dress that highlighted the red hair and freckles, and her legs looked like they were built to rest under an upright piano. She was wearing heavy black-framed eyeglasses with thick lenses. Cairn's immediate impression of her was that she was born an old maid and had done everything possible to make that eventuality a success.

"Gentlemen, I'm Miss Goolnick, Mr. Futerman's secretary and office manager. Janet told me you were inquiring about Mr. Weiss and his secretary?"

"Is there someplace we can talk in private?" Cairn asked, aware that there were other offices off the hallway where they were standing and opposite the offices were alcoves for the secretaries, one of whom had stopped whatever it was she was doing and was staring at the three of them.

"Yes, we can use the conference room," Miss Goolnick said as she started down the hallway. "Please, follow me."

The room wasn't big enough for the table that occupied it, and when you pulled out a chair to sit down it hit the wall. The scars from the chairs banging against the walls, the lack of any decorations and the clear need for a paint job clearly indicated that whatever work was accomplished in the conference room succeeded out of necessity, and there was no need for ambiance or comfort for Mr. Futerman, his associates or their clients.

Miss Goolnick sat at the head of the table at the far end of the room. "Well, gentlemen, we don't see too many detectives around here often. Mr. DeGiacomo has a busy criminal practice, and once every two years it seems the police stop by looking for someone, but that's the extent of it. What can I do to help you?"

Cairn smiled and said, "There's been an unfortunate incident at Mr. Weiss' apartment. His cleaning lady was murdered there today."

Miss Goolnick instinctively raised her hand to her mouth and uttered, "Oh, dear Lord, that's so frightening. Did they catch anyone?"

Widelsky leaned over the table and rubbed his hands together and looked at Miss Goolnick for a few seconds before he spoke. "The cleaning lady was murdered and Mrs. Weiss was found in the same room unconscious. She could be the murderer, then again, Sophie, that's the secretary, right? She was at the building this morning looking for Mrs. Weiss. That's a long way from Montreal. So we need your help."

When Widelsky mentioned Mrs. Weiss, Miss Goolnick's hand went to her mouth and she bit on her knuckle. While he was still speaking she said, "Dear me, poor Henry, we'll have to call him right away. I hope we can still catch him?"

She started to get up, but Cairn stood up first and very calmly said, "Please, Miss Goolnick, before we call anyone I'd like to ask you a few questions. We want to notify Mr. Weiss too, but there's a few things we'd like to know first and maybe you can help us."

She sat back down and rested her arms on the table and clasped her hands. "I believe they're flying out tonight from Montreal and it's almost five, so I should call soon."

"We have a few minutes, there's nothing anyone can do right now, anyway," Widelsky said.

Cairn sat back in his chair and rested his arm on the back of the chair next to him. He gave Miss Goolnick a warm smile, the one he always used on witnesses to put them at ease, and said, "Could you gives us a little background on Mr. Weiss and Sophie?"

Miss Goolnick pursed her lips and said, "What is it you're getting at?"

"I don't know, I was hoping you could tell us something about them. Mrs. Weiss too, if you know anything? This is a homicide investigation and we do have an obligation to learn as much about everyone involved or associated with the victim as possible."

"Well," she sighed and said defensively. "Henry's in Montreal, how could he be involved?"

"It's his apartment and his wife may have been a victim too," Cairn said reassuringly, realizing Miss Goolnick's response indicated she would protect Henry if need be.

"I've known Henry Weiss for almost thirty years. He was fresh out of law school when he started in the district attorney's office, right here in the Upper Borough. He was only there three months and he was assigned to the trial bureau. Mr. Futerman was his boss and I was Futerman's secretary."

"And?" Widelsky said as he waved his hand as if he was attempting to coax some further information from Miss Goolnick.

"Henry stayed there only two years. He was very popular. And a good prosecutor. Mr. Futerman was very impressed. He always said Henry had potential."

Neither of the detectives responded to her silence, and after an awkward pause Miss Goolnick started speaking again. "Some men are born to be prosecutors. Henry wasn't one of them. He seemed as comfortable around shady characters, and please believe me, you came across plenty of them in the Upper Borough courthouse in 1936 as you did honest, hardworking people."

"You said Henry had potential. What do you mean by that?" Widelsky asked.

"He was a very good lawyer, but sending people to jail wasn't his cup of tea. As soon as he made some connections and figured out how the system worked he left the office and went into private practice. By the start of the war he was strictly dealing in real estate. I said before and I'll say it again, some men are born prosecutors. I've seen many of them leave the office and go into private practice and return a year or a year and a half later because they couldn't function on the other side. It's not the money. It's in their blood. Henry was a good time Charlie. Funny, always joking and very handsome. His taste in women was from hunger," she said as she waved her hand under her throat and showed a mild look of disgust. "But to each his own, I say."

"Do you know Mrs. Weiss?" Cairn asked.

"I've been in her company many times. She's very attractive but a little aloof. Maybe she's shy, who knows?" she said with indifference but telling them more than they'd asked.

"And Sophie, his secretary, what about her?"

"You know he hired her almost ten years ago. I think it will be ten years this fall. He's very fond of her, and she's more than competent," she said with a look of disapproval.

"Are they very close, Sophie and Mr. Weiss?" Widelsky said suspiciously.

"I don't know and I don't really care. I've known Henry a long time and I like him very much, but his personal life is none of my business. We bill him for his office space and services every month, and he pays on time. That's all I know," she said testily.

"Just out of curiosity," Cairn asked. "Is this a law firm or a group of attorneys working out of rented space?"

"When Mr. Futerman retired from the district attorney's office in 1948 I retired with him. He leased this space with his brother and they opened a small firm. That lasted a year. They couldn't work together and Mr. Futerman kept the lease and started renting space and leasing the reception, mailroom and library services to his tenants. Henry was his first tenant. He came here in 1950. Mr. Futerman has limited his practice now and is semi-retired. He teaches a course at Jesuit Law School and I look after things here at the office. It's a very nice arrangement."

"Look, lady," Widelsky said harshly, convinced in his mind that she wasn't telling them everything she knew.

"Miss Goolnick to you, young man," she shot back.

"Sorry, Miss Goolnick," he answered, half smiling. "What you tell us is confidential and I respect the fact that you're trying to protect people's privacy, but it would be very helpful if you could answer two questions and then we'll be outta your hair."

"What is it you want to know that I haven't already told you?"

"Look, I can tell by your facial expressions that you don't like Mrs. Weiss, or Mr. Weiss' secretary. All I want to know is, do you know much at all about his wife, and is he fooling around with the secretary? It's all strictly confidential."

"I don't know Mrs. Weiss that well, and my opinion of her is none of your business. I know Sophie and she's been very open over the years with the other girls in the office about her relationship with Henry. Not with me, but with the other girls. Sometimes you can hear them going at it in his office. I think she makes these horrid noises on purpose just to upset me. And she does. Everyone here knows. I try to ignore it, and Mr. Futerman refuses to deal with it," she answered with a little emotion.

"You complained to your boss about them?"

"Yes, everyone thinks I'm a prude and an old maid, but I find it very uncomfortable to hear that screeching and squealing going on in there. And Henry can be such a little boy at times. You know, everyone hears it and he'll pass by my desk later on and stop and chat for a few minutes and act like there's nothing going on. It's all very childish and entirely inappropriate. I told Mr. Futerman, and his response was that President Johnson was known for having sex on his office desk with some of his secretaries. Really," she gushed with disdain. "I think all the men around here are a little jealous. Rutting pigs, they're no better than rutting pigs or dogs in heat. Is there anything else? Or did you find out what you suspected?" she asked as she got up from her chair.

"Thank you, you've been very helpful," Cairn responded. "Do you have a phone number for Mr. Weiss in Montreal? It would be better if we called him than you."

"Yes, I'll get it for you. You can use the phone in Mr. Futerman's office. He's gone for the day" she said as she walked out of the room.

As they were following her, Widelsky said, "Do you have Sophie's full name and address, and was she here today?"

"No, she wasn't here today, and I'll give you her address."

She led them to Futerman's office and Cairn picked up the phone and called Kreppell. Miss Goolnick went to her desk in the hallway opposite the office and Widelsky sat down on Futerman's couch.

"Hey, Goosch, is that you?" Cairn asked the party on the other end of the phone. "Yeah, we're working that homicide on Lincoln Boulevard, so how'ya doing? Shit, been at least six months. What happened, you got transferred from Summit? Naw, we're temporarily at the Boulevard. It sucks. No room, yeah, I hear you. Do me a favor, put me through to Kreppell, please," Cairn said as he ended what sounded like a one-way conversation. While he was waiting for the connection to Kreppell, he said to Widelsky, "That was Eddie Goosch, same deep bass voice. Christ, he must be sixty."

"He shoulda retired ten years ago," Widelsky dryly answered.

"Hello, Sarge, it's me, Phil. We just finished at Weiss' law office."

"Find out anything?"

"A little. Mr. Weiss and the secretary are more than employer and employee and his office couch is the love nest."

"Who told you that?"

"The major domo. Old doll named Ruth Goolnick, Miss Goolnick to you, young man," he chided. "She's been with Futerman since the thirties in the DA's office, and Mr. Weiss had a cup of coffee back then working for Futerman that lasted almost two years. Miss Goolnick said he didn't have it in him to be a prosecutor. She called him a good time Charlie, and I think she's sweet on him, maybe in a sisterly way. She don't like the secretary, and has no opinion on the wife."

"All that time and that's all you got," Kreppell said critically.

"Tough dealing with old maids. She's getting us Weiss' hotel number in Montreal and the secretary's address and phone number."

While Cairn was talking to Kreppell, Widelsky got up and left the room. He went to Miss Goolnick's desk and she gave him the phone number for the Ritz Carlton in Montreal. It was after five o'clock and the office was empty. Widelsky thought about it for a minute and he said to Miss Goolnick, "You know what, why don't you call? You can tell him what's going on, then put me on the phone."

"You'd rather I deliver the bad news, Detective?" she said sarcastically.

"You've known him for thirty years, might make things a little easier. That's all."

Cairn hung up the phone and went out into the hallway. Widelsky was sitting on the edge of Miss Goolnick's desk and she was sitting in her chair writing information on a slip of paper.

"He's already checked out and Sophie wasn't on the register as a guest," she announced to the two detectives.

"That's not good," Widelsky said, then clapping his hands together said to Cairn, "What did our sergeant have to report?"

"I gave him what we got and he reminded me that it's past five o'clock and we haven't done anything all day."

"You are too sensitive." Widelsky laughed. "Fact is, we haven't done shit. Oh, excuse me, ma'am," he blurted as soon as he realized what he had just said and saw the indignant and disapproving look Miss Goolnick gave him.

"You figure the secretary was in the same room with him?" Widelsky asked Cairn.

"She went to Montreal with him, I know that," Miss Goolnick interjected.

"Makes sense," Cairn replied.

"Will you need anything else?" Miss Goolnick asked.

"No, I think we're fine and thank you for all of your help."

She fixed them closely with her eyes, and said, "Confidential, everything I told you is confidential."

"Simply, background, that's all we wanted," Cairn said with his hand over his heart.

They were going down in the elevator and Widelsky asked Cairn, "Kreppell have anything else?"

"Plenty, I didn't want to say anything in front of the lady."

"So give it up."

"Mrs. Weiss had an aneurysm and she's in a coma. They rushed her up to surgery and she's still with us, but no idea now if she'll pull through or not. They're holding the apartment as a crime scene, and as soon as Mr. Weiss gets home they'll send him over to the Boulevard. Kreppell told us it'll be a long night. Mrs. Weiss had a picture of a kid in his communion outfit in her pocketbook and Kreppell thought that was odd since the Weiss' are Jewish, for whatever that's worth."

"How's he know they're Jewish? Maybe the husband is and the wife isn't."

"We're playing a thousand fucking clues here, Frank. There was blood on Mrs. Weiss' fingers and they took a swab in the hospital. Hogan and Smith are still processing the apartment and Chin the Chinaman gave Kreppell a preliminary on the cleaning lady, and said she died from a blunt trauma wound to the brain. He's performing the autopsy now, but he likes to prognosticate too. Him and Kreppell are a great pair. Kreppell's giving me the autopsy report before it's performed and all from the comfort of his desk. What an asshole."

They stopped on the sidewalk in front of the building and lit up cigarettes. Widelsky was leaning on the fender of the unmarked car and said, "What next?"

"He wants us to interview the kid, then the secretary and get it all done tonight. He said Hogan and Smith would have a preliminary report ready by nine tomorrow morning, along with the Chinaman. Unless the kid or the secretary gives it up tonight, he doesn't want to interview the husband until after we've gone over everything."

"Okay, sounds good. It's five-thirty, you wanna eat first? Katz's is two blocks away, great pastrami," Widelsky said as he licked his lips.

"Yeah, sounds good, I'm hungry, but there's something going on with

Kreppell. He finished by saying he'd like us to get this finished by Tuesday. And when I asked him what the hurry was, his exact words were, 'I hate changing horses mid-stream.' Sounds like we're going someplace, doesn't it?"

"Maybe Inspector Greason is going to be Deputy Chief Greason and we're gonna collect the other half of our reward," Widelsky said with a smile as he pointed his finger to his head. "C'mon, let's go eat, I'm tired."

"I hear yuh," Cairn cracked as he went around to the driver's side and got in the unmarked car.

Chapter Twenty-One

As soon as the detectives left, Miss Goolnick telephoned Lee Futerman. "Lee, it's Ruthie," she said when he answered the phone.

"Yes, Ruth, what is it?"

"Two detectives were just here. There was a homicide at Henry's apartment today. His cleaning lady was murdered and Maria was taken to the hospital. They don't know if she's the murderer," she said breathlessly.

"Maria," he said with surprise. "That's preposterous. Why did they take her to the hospital?"

"She was in a coma, they didn't elaborate but they were very interested in Sophie. I told the detectives that Sophie was with Henry in Montreal, but they said she was at Henry's apartment this morning. I told you something was going on. I bet Henry's the father of that child and everything has finally come to a head. If you ask me, Sophie has a hand in this, and I wouldn't be surprised," she said vindictively.

"Ruthie, slow down. Do you know if anyone from the office was notified?"

"They never mentioned the district attorney. They made that comment about Maria possibly being a murderer, but I think that was just to get my attention. They wanted to know everything I knew about Henry and Sophie."

"And you told them what?"

"I told them that it's common knowledge that they're having an affair and have been for sometime. I wasn't comfortable but you know they'll start asking the other girls. I have always had a spot in my heart for Henry Weiss,

ANTHONY D. MURPHY

but he's his own worst enemy. He married that stuck-up beauty queen and he runs around with this little slut. That's what happens when you have no taste in women."

"I guess you're right in a way," he lamented.

"You bet I am," she said. "I'll do anything to protect Henry, and I believe in my heart he has nothing to do with any of this."

"Well, I'm going to call Frank Duffy at home. He's a pretty good guy and I'm sure he's already assigned one of his ADA's to the case. Does Henry know anything about this?"

"No, he checked out of the hotel, and I assume he's on the way home. I know they're arriving home tonight because he called yesterday morning and asked me to have the car service pick him up at eight o'clock. I have the flight number."

"Did you tell the detectives you knew when he was coming in?"

"Of course not. I figured I would call you and we could, or you, or somebody could meet Henry and tell him what's happened."

"You're a good old girl Ruthie. Verify Henry's flight and call the car service and have them pick me up on the way to the airport. I'll break the news. One more thing, could you pick up a court of milk on the way home and drop it off in my apartment before you go upstairs? If I've already left, give a cup to Booty."

"Half a cup, that cat is getting a little plump," she said with a laugh.

"Almost as plump as you," he said, chuckling. She didn't respond, and he said, "Okay, I'll fill you in on everything when I get back from the airport. Put the teapot on around ten and if I'm not home by eleven go to bed."

Miss Goolnick sat back in her chair and shook her head. *Poor Henry*, she thought. Ruth Goolnick was ten years older than Henry, but from the first time she met him she'd had a crush on him and the crush lasted thirty years. Henry never gave her a second look but he always treated her with deference and she was grateful for the attention even if it was only brotherly and not anything more. Lee Futerman, like Ruth Goolnick, had never married. He and Ruth were the closest of friends, but that relationship, once intimate for a few years, had grown platonic and over the decades they had established a bond so close that they could have been husband and wife, and to Ruthie's dismay, they should have been. Lee owned a two family house on Spencer Avenue in Riverview. He lived in the downstairs apartment and Ruth lived upstairs. Henry's behavior with Sophie over the years had been an issue of great pain and concern to her. She couldn't share her feelings about Henry with anyone

else and not look like a silly old fool, and certainly that applied to Lee Futerman.
There had been some gossip in the office about Ruth and Lee over the years,
but the two of them were so stodgy that such talk rarely raised an eyebrow.
Ruth Goolnick had been satisfied to see Henry every day and talk with him.
She didn't like Maria, but had to accept her because she was Henry's wife.
Sophie was an entirely different matter. Sophie had made a fool out of Henry,
and their sexual shenanigans in the office were a total outrage, and there
wasn't a day when Ruth didn't wish some untoward and horrid accident would
befall Sophie and expunge her completely from Henry's life. The little bit of
information she gleaned from the detectives today gave her hope, and if there
was any way Ruth could separate Sophie and Henry, she would.

Chapter Twenty-Two

Sophie walked out of Loew's Grand Palace a little past five o'clock in the afternoon. It was hotter out than it had been earlier in the day, and after spending the whole afternoon in an air-conditioned movie theater the hot humid air wrapped around her like a blanket and she immediately started to perspire. She had seen *The Sound of Music* in its entirety, slept through *Robin and the Seven Hoods*, then sat through half of *The Sound of Music* again. She knew her aunt Lucy and Joey would be anxious for her return, and she decided to give them a call and have them meet her at the China Palace on Broadway. It was too hot to cook, and eating dinner out would be a nice welcome home for everyone, she thought. She walked across Lincoln Boulevard and went into Karl's to buy some chocolate for Joey. Karl's was one of the best ice cream parlors and candy stores in the Upper Borough. Joey loved their chocolate, and every year for Easter she bought his chocolate bunny rabbit there and all the other candy for his basket. She went into the store and went over to the phone booth. She dialed her home number, and her Aunt Lucy answered.

"Tia, it's me."

"Sophie, where are you? We were worried. You said you'd be home at three."

"I know, but I had some things to do. How about we go for Chinese food?"

"No, no, RayRay called. He wants us to meet him over at Clam Island. Your cousin Freddy is with him and Lisa and the two girls are going too."

"What's the occasion?"

"Freddy and RayRay sold the car service. They met with the lawyers today and got paid off. They want to celebrate," Aunt Lucy said excitedly.

"What time? I have to change."

"We have time, he said seven-thirty. Freddy will pick us up. It's going to be fun, and Joey's all excited because he hasn't seen his cousins in weeks."

"Do me a favor, please? In my closet I have a pair of pink linen pants with a matching pink and white top. Iron them for me?"

"Sure, I'll do it right now. I already gave Joey a bath and he's dressed nice," she replied happily.

"I should be home in twenty minutes."

Sophie bought some chocolate, then hurried out of the store and up the block to the bus stop. She didn't know if it would be quicker to walk down Monmouth Road to where it met Kingsbridge Road and go to the bus stop for the number twenty bus or to wait on the boulevard for the number one bus. Each would bring her to Broadway but the twenty was a faster route and she weighed that against the five minutes it would take her to walk to the number twenty bus stop and the added strain of carrying the shopping bag with the glove and swimsuits she'd bought for Joey that morning. The decision was made for her when she saw the number one bus approaching. She got out her fare and boarded the bus. The bus wasn't crowded, and she took a seat by the window that faced the east side of Lincoln Boulevard. She opened the window and leaned her face into the opening. The air was warm, but it was still refreshing as the bus moved up the road at a fast rate. The bus came to a stop at a stand just past the intersection of Kingsbridge Road and Lincoln Boulevard. It was half a block down from Henry's building and where she'd encountered Maria earlier in the day.

She was looking out the window, thinking back on the day's unpleasantness when she felt someone staring at her. She focused her eyes and there was a small, slightly pudgy man in green pants and a white short sleeve shirt looking at her. His hair was plastered over his head and he was boyish looking, but clearly an adult. She made eye contact with him and he turned his head and started walking toward Kingsbridge Road. He was familiar, and she recalled that he was the doorman from Henry's building. She couldn't understand why he was staring at her. *God maybe he likes me?* she thought. *That's what I attract, that's what I'll find after I dump this no good, rotten bastard I love*, she said to herself. The bus started up again and she turned her head from the window. She didn't want to look at Henry's building. *I'm done with him,* she resolved.

Ray Cruz was Sophie's younger brother and Freddy was their cousin. As kids, Freddy always called him RayRay and the name stuck. Aunt Lucy had never married, but she had been, in one way or another, a mother to them all. Lucy, Sophie's mother Elena and Freddy's mother Olga were all sisters. Lucy was the only one still alive. Sophie's mother had died from cancer of the pancreas and Freddy's mother, an enormous woman, had died from diabetes. RayRay went to work for General Motors immediately after he left the service and he was now a supervisor. He and Freddy, who also owned a bar a couple of blocks from the Municipal Stadium, owned a car service in the Upper Borough. RayRay and Freddy had never done well in school, but they always worked and hustled. RayRay owned a house in the suburbs and considered it a matter of great pride that he, a Puerto Rican from the Upper Borough, owned his own home. Freddy had bought a house in Riverview and, like his cousin, considered his address a sign of status and a refutation of the libel that Puerto Ricans were lazy. They were both close to Sophie and Joey, and along with Aunt Lucy formed the core of a solid and caring family. Lisa was RayRay's wife, and she and RayRay were the parents of two daughters. One was six; a year younger than Joey and the other was four. Going out to dinner on Clam Island was a family tradition with RayRay and Freddy and Sophie could think of no more cheerful end to what had been an otherwise dreadful and melancholy day.

Chapter Twenty-Three

The waitress set the food down in front of the two detectives. They had each ordered pastrami sandwiches on rye bread with horseradish and mustard dressing. Cairn was munching on a fresh cucumber pickle and nursing a long neck bottle of Schlitz beer. Widelsky had already consumed four pickles and was on his second beer when Sally, the waitress, brought them their sandwiches. Cairn watched in silent amusement as Widelsky's broad hand enveloped one half of the sandwich and stuffed it into the wide opening of his mouth. The half sandwich was gone in two bites, followed by a long gulp of beer. Widelsky wiped his mouth and looked at the other half of his sandwich for a minute. He didn't say anything and Cairn imagined that the half chewed bolus of meat and bread was slowly making its way through Widelsky's stomach much as a small pig would when swallowed whole by a python. Widelsky let out a large belch and smiled.

"Best fucking pastrami in the world. Katz's makes the best fucking pastrami," he said with satisfaction and enthusiasm. Widelsky picked up the other half of his sandwich and waved it under his nose. He breathed deeply and said, "Oh, the mustard and horseradish are what make this food so good." He then took two huge bites and the sandwich was gone and he was wiping his mouth with a paper napkin. He finished his beer and let out another belch and said, "C'mon, hurry up. We ain't got all day."

"Pardon me. I have to chew my food first."

"What's that mean?"

"Nothing, I can't eat as fast as you. That's all," Cairn said as he was finishing the first half of his sandwich.

"I'm going outside for a smoke and some fresh air. Pay the bill and I'll square up with you later," he said as he got up from the table.

Cairn's seat was facing the window and he took his time finishing his meal. Widelsky stood outside and smoked. He took long powerful drags on his cigarette, and as Cairn studied him he shook his head and thought to himself how it seemed everything Widelsky did that was corporal in any way was done with brutish and predatory efficiency. There was nothing subtle about Frank Widelsky and, he thought, how do they live with him at home?

Cairn paid the bill. Katz knew Widelsky and Cairn were detectives and he gave them the police discount-half price. Cairn left a fifty-cent tip for Sally and went outside.

"Okay, partner, where to?"

"Let's hit the Associated Market first. See if the kid is there. If not, we'll go over to his house. What do you think?"

"Sounds good to me," Cairn answered as he started up the car and pulled away from the curb.

They made no conversation as the car traveled up Lincoln Boulevard thirty or so blocks until they reached Kingsbridge Road. Cairn made a left turn and went west on Kingsbridge Road. There were no available parking spaces in front of the market, and he parked the car in front of a fire hydrant. The two detectives went into the market. There were four registers on the right and a small office on the left. Straight ahead was the meat section and by the display case was a small man in a gray-colored linen jacket talking to an overweight man wearing a bloodstained apron. Only two of the cashier lanes were operating, and Widelsky said to the cashiers, "Where's the manager?"

One of the cashiers pointed to the two men talking in front of the meat section. "Little guy with the white hair, Mr. Kimmel."

Cairn and Widelsky approached the two men and Cairn said to the man in the gray linen coat, "Excuse me are you Mr. Kimmel?"

"Yes, what can I do for you?"

"I'm Detective Cairn from Borough Major Case and we're investigating a homicide. This is my partner Detective Widelsky. Do you have somewhere in private we can speak?"

"Yes, in my office," the man responded as he turned and walked toward the entrance to the store.

Cairn and Widelsky followed him, and Cairn thought to himself how much he loved delivering the line that they were investigating a homicide. There was something about that word that gave civilians a tweak, particularly when he said, "Is there someplace private we can speak?" It made their hearts jump and blood run a little faster. It also gave Cairn and Widelsky an edge in every interview. Being a cop always gave you leverage, but being a detective working homicide carried a mystique the popular culture reinforced and made just about everyone but the guilty want to cooperate with them.

The office was up a half flight of stairs, and there was a window that looked out over the entire store. The window looked like a mirror from the outside and store management could use it as a vantage point to watch everyone in the store without them knowing about it. Widelsky looked out the window and asked, "Catch many shoplifters?"

"A few a week, not as many that steal, but enough."

"How about the employees, they steal?"

"If they do and I catch them, they're gone. No second chances, and I tell everybody else in the business," he answered with a slap of his hands to emphasize the finality of those decisions.

"I guess you have to be tough in this business," Cairn opined.

"Tough, you're not tough, you're out of business. This is a nickel and dime operation. All the groceries on sale in this week's flier are at cost or pennies below. You know how many shoppers come in here and only buy the bargains?" he asked rhetorically. "Let me tell you, too many. But that's how you have to operate. I don't give green stamps or plaid stamps or whatever it is the chains give away. I give good service and quality meat and produce, and I make a few dollars, so it's not so bad, you know."

Widelsky yawned and Cairn spoke. "The reason we're here is there was a homicide at the apartment of one of your customers today."

"Who?"

"Mrs. Weiss," Widelsky said sharply.

"Someone murdered Mrs. Weiss?" Kimmel said as he craned his head toward Cairn.

"No, not Mrs. Weiss, but her cleaning woman was murdered and Mrs. Weiss was taken to the hospital in a coma."

Kimmel sat back in his chair and frowned. "What does this have to do with me?"

"You made a delivery there today?" Widelsky asked.

"Yes, Danny took an order from Mrs. Weiss this morning. He had to pick up some shrimp next door at the fish market, too."

Cairn had out his notebook and asked, "What time?"

"Let me think," Kimmel said, then left the office and came back with a clipboard with a stack of papers clipped to it. He flipped to the first page and said, "Danny left with that order around noon. He was gone for almost an hour and I remember we took in three more deliveries soon after he left."

"You said he was gone for almost an hour, is that typical?"

"No, but when he came back I asked him where he was and he said he'd stopped for lunch. In fairness to the boy that happens all the time. You leave with a delivery and stop to fool around with your friends or get something to eat. I give 'em a hard time when they get back, but it never happens when we're busy. If it does, they're fired."

"You know this Weiss woman? I hear she's good looking?" Widelsky asked.

"What do I know from good looking? Ninety percent of my customers are women. Good looking, ugly, fat, skinny, young and old. I care? There's only two types I like; the ones who pay their bills and the ones who don't complain. The rest you can keep."

"Which one was Mrs. Weiss?"

"Lovely woman, her husband's my lawyer for the building and the other three stores in it. She didn't come in the store much, neither did Henry. She called in the order every week. Always pays on time and never complains, they're very good people."

"Is the delivery boy here?" Cairn asked.

"No, I let him go at five-thirty. I don't take deliveries after five."

"You said he was gone for almost an hour on that delivery. Did you notice if he acted differently today or anything unusual about him?"

"Nothing, same kid as always, bit of a wiseass, but a good worker when you get on his tail. You don't suspect him, do you?"

"The timing is very good," Widelsky said with a glower. "We'd like to talk with him, and it's important you tell us what you know about him and any complaints about him you have from customers."

Kimmel sat back down. He was upset and Widelsky made him uncomfortable. He looked at Cairn when he gave his answer. "He's been with me since January. He started in the West Kingsbridge store and he was back and forth from this store to that store until I fired my produce manager last month. Walter Brown is my new produce manger, but he used to be the stock boy and delivery boy. Danny now has that job, but it's part time. I've never had a complaint about him from anyone. And he's never missed a day of work either, very reliable."

"That's fine," Cairn said reassuringly. "But it so happens he took a delivery around the time we think the homicide occurred. Maybe he saw something. Do you have his address?"

"Yes, right here in the file," Kimmel said as he bent down and opened a drawer. He went to a folder, opened it and handed a sheet of paper to Cairn. Cairn read the sheet and copied down Danny Monaghan's address.

"He was gone for almost an hour on that delivery, but nothing else. Am I correct?" Widelsky said as he pointed his finger at Kimmel.

"What can I tell you? This is a busy place, who pays attention to a kid?" Kimmel said indifferently.

"Well, if you think of anything or if your employees know of anything, please give us a call," Cairn said. He wrote his name and a phone number for the Major Case Squad on a piece of paper and handed it to Kimmel. "You can reach us at that number."

The two detectives left the market and got into the unmarked car.

"Whaddya think?" Widelsky asked.

"He pays attention to business. Everything else is gray with that guy. We gotta put a little pressure on this kid. Either he's involved or not, but the faster we get an answer the sooner we can eliminate him or concentrate on him. Follow?"

"Yeah, I think it's the secretary and the husband, but if it turns out there's a sexual assault or money missing, I'll take the kid."

Cairn pulled out from the curb and they headed west on Kingsbridge Road toward Bailey Avenue.

Chapter Twenty-Four

"Hi, Mom," Danny said as he walked into the kitchen.

"Hi honey," she replied. "Did you have a good day? Were the big tippers taking care of you?" she asked sweetly.

"Dead day, it was a dead day. I had six deliveries today. Kimmel had me stocking shelves all afternoon. I got so much work done he don't need me tomorrow morning. Instead of going in at nine, he told me to come in at noon. What a cheap Jew, works me like a dog, then steals three hours from me the next day," Danny said with disgust.

"Danny, you sound like an idiot when you talk like that," his mother said with anger. "You sound like your father. Be happy you have that job and stop complaining."

"Yeah, yeah," he replied. "What's for dinner?"

"I made fried chicken and potato salad. I'm going out to dinner at the China Palace with Father Dunphy and the other girls from the altar society. You can wait for your father or eat now. If you eat now, don't eat all the drumsticks. There are only six of them and I don't want to listen to him later on. Do you hear me?" she said with a frown.

"I'll wait til he comes home. If he comes home," Danny answered.

"What time you leaving?" he asked.

"I'm meeting Margie Kennedy in front of her house at seven, so I'll leave about ten of," she said.

"Okay, I'm gonna take a shower now, then lay down for a while. If Dad ain't home by seven, I'm eating without him," Danny responded.

"Don't be too long in the bathroom and don't steam it up. Please. I have to fix my hair before I go," she said with irritation.

"I won't, I won't," he moaned as he went down the hallway to his bedroom.

Danny found the conversation with his mother painful. *There she was going off with Father Dunphy and her altar society friends and here I am waiting for the police to show up and arrest me for murder*, he thought. His father was supposed to be the big villain in the neighborhood, and in one fateful afternoon he had caused more harm than his father had in a lifetime. Mr. Monaghan had been arrested for assaulting people on numerous occasions, but the charges never stuck and he always beat the rap. Mike Monaghan never acted too concerned when he got into trouble, "Don't worry, Mary, it's all bullshit. I'll beat the rap, I always do. It was just a misunderstanding," he would say to his wife with no more concern than he would if he were talking about spilling a cup of coffee on the floor. Everyone knew the story about Monaghan throwing the nigger off the roof years ago on his milk route when he was a teenager, but that was a nigger trying to rob him, so it didn't really count, Danny figured. His case was different and unforgivable; he killed an innocent old lady. He couldn't understand why Mrs. Weiss hadn't called the police. Why the police hadn't come to the store looking for him. *She must have recognized me*, he thought. Still, maybe she didn't and with each passing hour he prayed that somehow she never made the connection. All afternoon while he was stocking shelves in the store he was looking over his shoulder for the police. He had thought about running away, but he had no money and nowhere to go. The only thing that would accomplish, he thought, was to prove he was guilty. He was determined to play dumb and deny everything.

Danny went into the bathroom and turned on the shower. He sat on the toilet bowl and had his fourth watery bowel movement of the day. He was a nervous wreck, and it took all of his strength to keep from breaking out in tears and telling his mother everything. He had no idea what compelled him to steal the rest of Maria's pictures, and all day long he pondered what to do with them. Even if Mrs. Weiss didn't recognize him the police would, at some point, learn about the delivery and want to speak with him. He kept rehearsing in his head the dumb look he would give them. He wanted to seem concerned, but at the same time offer a response of disinterest. I'll just keep telling them, "I don't know, I don't know," he told himself.

He took a quick shower and opened the window wide when he was done to let the steam out. He went into his bedroom and fell onto the bed. He put the pillow over his eyes and drifted off to sleep, exhausted with worry and guilt.

Mary Monaghan stood in front of the bathroom mirror and combed her hair. She put on a fresh coat of lipstick and rolled her lips together to insure the lipstick was evenly applied and none had reached beyond the crescent of her lips. She adjusted her collar, stepped back and turned in front of the mirror. She was wearing a light blue dress with short sleeves and a white collar. The dress came with a white belt that she had cinched tightly around her waist. The outfit was finished off with sheer nylons and white flat shoes that came to a point. She was pleased with her appearance and she knew that Father Dunphy would appreciate how she looked.

Father Dunphy was the monsignor of St. John's parish. He was the head of the altar society and was something of an activist on the part of some of the hard luck women in the parish whose husbands smacked them around, drank away their paychecks, or committed any of a litany of offenses that demeaned their marriage vows and debased their families. It wasn't an uncommon sight to see Father Dunphy march into one of the local gin mills and upbraid a man in front of friends and strangers for not meeting his familial responsibilities. Nor was it uncommon to see him on a Friday evening at the foot of the elevated train exit at 231St Street and Broadway waiting for some wayward husband to fall off the train and escort him home before any more of the weekly pay envelope was spent against the interests of the family. The priest was a tough man, but he wasn't a fighter, and in those cases where the husband was likely to take insult and put up a fight, the priest would call on Captain Walsh from the Summit Avenue precinct and have a radio car conveniently park nearby as a reminder that anything less than subordination to the priest's exhortations would most likely result in a drubbing from the police and a night in jail. Father Dunphy never expected his interventions to turn coal into diamonds, but as his reputation grew and the term being "Dunphied" gained a place in the local lexicon as a sobriquet for personal failure, there was a slight increase in the number of men who took the pledge and stayed on the wagon, or as a smaller victory, did their drinking at home and turned over the majority of their wages to their wives. Father Dunphy was always eager to assist, but would never do so without first being petitioned by the aggrieved spouse. He felt his role as a pastoral minister necessitated a full understanding of the problems in the home before he could intervene, and any action without the wife's compliance could cause more harm than good.

Mary Monaghan knew she was the one woman in all of St. John's parish he most wanted to help. She had been working in the rectory for the last five years, and over that time she and the priest had formed a strong bond. He had told her on dozens of occasions that the best thing she could do was divorce Mike Monaghan. "Divorce him and let me work on the annulment," Dunphy would plead. The priest had even had Captain Walsh talk with her, but her answer was always the same, "I married the man and I've had two children by him, and until my Danny is grown and on his own, I can't leave him."

The altar society met for dinner once a month. It was always a nice evening, and the group switched back and forth between Fontella's Restaurant and The China Palace. Father Dunphy always bought a round of drinks before dinner and the evening usually passed in happy conversation and conviviality among all the members. Mary always sat next to the priest, and in her mind she pretended they were a husband and wife entertaining friends for dinner. She was his favorite, and she often wondered if his fantasies were the same as hers?

Mary finished primping in the bathroom and looked into Danny's bedroom before she left. He was lying down with the pillow over his head and appeared to be fast asleep. She went over and lifted the pillow and gave him a kiss on the forehead. He didn't respond, and she looked at him for a moment. It seemed to her that he was all she had. There was no one in the world she loved more than Danny. There was nothing, she believed, she wouldn't do to protect him. *But how do I keep him from becoming what his father is?* she thought. Each year as he grew and matured she could see her husband's influences. Calling Kimmel a cheap Jew and his constant comments about spics and niggers were all reminiscent of the type of coarse nonsense her husband regularly spewed when he was in a mood to converse with them. Only last week his father had regaled them at the dinner table with a story about when he was in the Army and stationed in Louisiana. One time when he and his friends got a pass they went into the local town and bought a couple of bottles of liquor. They all got good and drunk, then drove over to the colored section for some fun. Without directly saying it, he alluded to a visit they made to a whorehouse, he called it a recreation stop. That was enough to bring color to Mary's face, but then the story became even more degrading when he laughed with delight over the memory of driving back to the base and coming upon an old colored man walking up the road. They slowed their Jeep down and extended a piece of wooden board from the open panel of the jeep and bowled the old man over. Mike called it "Nigger Knocking," and he was spitting his food in bursts of laughter as he told Danny the story. Danny laughed almost as hard as his father and Mary cried herself to sleep that night. Father Dunphy had pulled strings to get Danny into Cathedral Prep, and even though Mary never believed he had a vocation or would ever become a priest, she did pray that somehow the school would be a positive presence in his life and give him some of the character she thought he was lacking. She watched her son sleep for a few more moments, then left the bedroom and blessed herself. *Dear Lord*, she prayed, *he is my son and I love him with all my heart, please watch over him and protect him from sin.*

It was a quarter to seven and she took her pocketbook from her bedroom and made her way down the hallway to the front door of the apartment. She was almost at the door when the doorbell rang. It couldn't have been her husband because the door was unlocked. She went up to the door and pulled back the peephole. Outside were two men. One was tall and was standing behind a shorter and more heavily built man. The shorter man was wearing a straw porkpie hat with a feather in it. He flashed a detective's badge and said, "Police."

Mary opened the door and let the two detectives in.

"Is something wrong?" she said calmly. Mary Monaghan was no stranger to the police, and their presence in her home normally meant that Mike had been arrested for beating someone up.

"Do you have a son Danny who works at the Associated Market?" Cairn asked.

Mary's hand immediately went to her chest and she quickly said, "Yes, why is there a problem?" She felt her blood pressure rising and her face became flushed.

"We'd like to speak with him, if you don't mind," Cairn replied.

"He's in his room, but what's this about?" she questioned.

Widelsky always favored the figurative punch to the solar plexus when dealing with people and he said, "I don't think it's anything, but there was a homicide today in an apartment your son made a delivery to and we want to talk to him."

"I wouldn't call a homicide just anything," she said nervously. "My husband should be home soon, maybe we should wait until he gets here," she added.

"Unless your husband made the delivery with your son, we don't want to speak with him," Widelsky responded with an edge to his voice.

"Please, Mrs. Monaghan, this is routine, don't overreact," Cairn said with a smile.

Mary went down the hallway and called to Danny. "Danny, Danny I need to speak with you," she said.

Danny came out of his room and saw the two detectives at the end of the hallway by the front door. He knew right away who they were and he felt his stomach turn into a knot. He was starting to sweat and he said, "I gotta take a leak, Ma, give me a minute."

Danny went into the bathroom and peed. He flushed the toilet and washed his face. He took several deep breaths and dried his face with the hand towel and went out to meet his fate.

He started back down the hallway and saw his mother standing there. The two detectives weren't in sight, but his mother was looking into the kitchen and he surmised that's where they were. "Yeah, what do you want?" he asked.

She led him into the kitchen and said, "Danny this is Detective Cairn and Detective Widelsky. They want to ask you some questions about a delivery you made today."

"Sure, go ahead," he replied.

Cairn leaned over the kitchen table and fixed Danny with his eyes. He smiled and spoke softly, with an easy cadence. "I want you to listen carefully to me son," he said. "There was a murder today in an apartment building on Lincoln Boulevard. It was in an apartment where you made a delivery. We don't know who the murderer is, and we're not at a point where we even have a suspect. The most important thing for you to do is to tell us everything you did today. Can you do that?" Cairn said as he leaned back and looked to Mary and smiled. Cairn didn't know if Danny was involved or not, and his greatest interest at that point was to read the boy's body language, especially, his reaction to the word murder.

Danny didn't flinch, and true to his plan to act dumb he let his lower jaw hang a bit and stared blankly back at Cairn and then to his mother. He shook his head several times and looked to his mother and said, "I only had one delivery on Lincoln Boulevard and that was to Mrs. Weiss' apartment today, but I saw her going down to the subway when I was crossing the street with her delivery."

"Well, that's fine, Danny, just tell the men what you know," she said as she put her hands on his shoulders.

Widelsky took off his hat, rubbed his head and said, "Listen kid, start with what you did when you went to work today."

Danny avoided Widelsky's eyes and looked at Cairn and said in a monotone voice, "I went to work at nine and Kimmel had me sweep the sidewalk in front of the store. After that I mopped the aisles, then he told me to bring up the cereals and box them out. I brought up five cases of cereal from the basement and went to the front office to get a new blade for my box cutter. The phone rang, I answered it, and it was Mrs. Weiss. She's the one who lives on Lincoln

Boulevard and the only delivery I had there today. I took her order, then went next door to the fish store and ordered shrimp for her. Benny the fish man told me to come back in about an hour. I went back to the store, stocked the cereal and filled her order. I took her order, picked up the shrimp and made the delivery." He stopped speaking and looked at Cairn and Widelsky.

Neither detective immediately responded. Cairn was busy noting something in his notebook and Widelsky just sat there stone faced studying Danny.

The silence only lasted for several seconds, then Mary spoke to the two detectives. "Is there anything else you need to know?"

Cairn looked up from his notebook and looked at Danny, ignoring Mrs. Monaghan, and said, "Do you remember what time it was when you took Mrs. Weiss' phone call?"

Danny looked at the ceiling for a moment, and said, "Maybe around eleven."

"Good, good," Cairn said. "That would mean you left for the delivery sometime around noon, if I followed what you said before?"

"Yeah, probably around lunchtime," Danny responded.

"Is lunchtime noon to you?" Cairn asked.

"Yeah, twelve o'clock is lunchtime in school," Danny answered.

"Fine," Cairn said. "If you left at noon, how long did it take you to make the delivery?"

Danny looked at his fingers, then said, "You go up two blocks to Lincoln Boulevard, wait for the light, go up one block to the building. Stop in and get Cleary to buzz you in the service entrance. Wait for the elevator and go upstairs and put the cold stuff in the refrigerator. Then, if there's no other deliveries, you're back to the store. Maybe twenty minutes, something like that," he said confidently.

Cairn made a few more notes in his notebook, then looked aat Danny. Just as he was about to speak, the front door to the apartment opened and Mike Monaghan walked in. Monaghan looked at the two detectives sitting in his kitchen and said to his wife, "What are they doing here?"

Mary looked at him nervously and said, "They're detectives and—"

But before she could finish her husband interrupted her and said, "I know they're cops, I want to know what they're doing in my kitchen. Did Danny do something?"

"No, Danny didn't do anything," she scoffed. "The police are investigating a murder that happened in a building where Danny made a delivery and they're

174

just asking him some questions. Maybe he saw something. That's all," she said as she looked at Cairn.

"Excuse me, Mr. Monaghan," Cairn said. "I'm Detective Cairn and this is my partner Detective Widelsky." Cairn stood up to shake Monaghan's hand, but Monaghan ignored Cairn's extended hand and Cairn sat back down. Widelsky frowned at Monaghan over the obvious slight to Cairn's friendly gesture and said to Cairn, "C'mon, Phil, let's pick up where you left off."

Cairn looked at his notes for a moment and felt the hard stare of Mike Monaghan on him. There was a tense feeling in the room, and Widelsky focused all of his attention on Mike Monaghan. Monaghan ignored Widelsky and Widelsky instinctively knew that Mike Monaghan wasn't the type of man who was easily intimidated or uncomfortable in the presence of the police. He and Cairn were the enemy and he expected a problem as Cairn continued his interview.

Cairn smiled at Danny and said, "As I was about to say before, you said the delivery took no more than twenty minutes. Correct?"

"No, I said it takes about twenty minutes to do that delivery," Danny answered.

"Fine, twenty minutes. That would mean that if you left at noon you would have been back to the store around twenty or twenty-five minutes after noon. Am I right?" Cairn said as he nodded his head.

"Yeah, I guess so," Danny said nonchalantly as he looked over his shoulder at his father.

"Good," Cairn said, smiling. "When you went into Mrs. Weiss' apartment did you see the cleaning lady?"

"I didn't know she had one. I didn't see anybody. I told you before; when I was crossing Lincoln Boulevard I saw Mrs. Weiss and another woman going down to the subway. They looked like they were talking, but that was just for a second and then, you know, I went across the street," he answered.

Cairn looked at Widelsky, then back at his notes, then said, "Frank, anything else?"

"Twenty, twenty-five minutes that's what he said, right?" he responded to Cairn, then looked back at Mike Monaghan. Widelsky and Cairn were practiced interviewers and one of their favorite techniques was to nail down a suspect in an obvious lie. In this case it was Danny's claim that the delivery only took twenty minutes when they knew Cleary the doorman saw Danny by the building at around one o'clock. The boy had left off about a half an hour from his story, and Widelsky waited for Cairn to change the interview to an

ANTHONY D. MURPHY

interrogation. His immediate concern, however, was on Mike Monaghan because he was certain that as soon as the questioning got a little heated the boy's father was going to erupt. Monaghan was about six feet, two inches tall. He wasn't broad like Widelsky, but his whole body appeared to be tightly wrapped in lean straps of hardened sinewy muscle. His short-sleeved work shirt clung to his body and the dark blue of the shirt was bleached with rings of salty sweat stains. He had big hands and wrists, and Widelsky imagined they'd meted out plenty of punishment over the years. His ears stuck out from his head and his tanned and deeply lined face and thick short-cropped head of salt and pepper hair gave him a menacing look. Widelsky didn't believe for a moment that this was a man who could be bullied or easily beaten.

Cairn looked up at Danny again and said, "Now let me get this straight. You've never been in the apartment except to go in through the service entrance and drop off the groceries. Correct?"

"No, I never said that," Danny quickly responded. "I been in the apartment the first time I made a delivery there. I been to some other apartments, but the first time I took a delivery to Mrs. Weiss was a couple of weeks ago. Nobody in the store told me about only taking her order through the service door. I got to the building and Cleary wasn't anywhere to be found, so I grabbed the boxes and went right to the regular elevator. It's much quicker," he said.

"And then what?" Widelsky snapped.

"I rang the doorbell, she lets me in and gives me a lecture about using the service entrance. I told her I didn't know and that was that. But I was in the apartment," Danny said with a shrug of his shoulders.

Widelsky gave Cairn an annoyed look and was about to say something when Cairn raised his hand slightly and said, "One moment, Frank. Now Danny maybe I went too fast and we lost our way here. How many times have you been to that building since you went to work for Mr. Kimmel?"

"I don't know the number, but I been there plenty of times," he answered.

"How many times to Mrs. Weiss' apartment?" Cairn asked.

"Three, four times most," he responded.

"First time you went in the front door. What about the other times?" Cairn asked.

"After the first time I always went in the service entrance like she told me," Danny said with a smirk.

"And today you went there and went in the service entrance and didn't see anyone in the apartment, Correct?" Cairn said as he looked at his notes.

"Yeah, except I wasn't in the apartment. I was just in that little entrance room," Danny said.

176

"And the delivery time was eh, twenty, twenty-five minutes, if I remember you telling us?" Cairn said almost as an after thought.

"From the store to that building and back, yeah, about that," Danny replied.

"Fine. Now today you said you left the store at around noon, or lunchtime as you call it, to make the delivery. So, according to your statement you should have returned to the store at around twelve-thirty the latest? And you've told us that several times. But I have one little problem with that," Cairn said as he put his notebook down and pointed his pen at Danny. "Would you like to guess, or should I give you the answer?"

Mary Monaghan tightened her grip on Danny's shoulders, and before he could answer Mike Monaghan said, "Whoa, pal, if you're accusing the kid of something get to the fucking point or leave."

Widelsky stood up, turned to Mike Monaghan, and said, "Your son's accusing himself. Why don't you let my partner finish?"

Monaghan took a pack of Lucky Strikes from his tee shirt pocket, took out a cigarette and lit one. No one spoke, and he said to Danny, "Did you kill someone today?"

Danny looked at his father with a stunned face, and said, "No, Pop, I didn't do nothing but work."

Monaghan looked at Cairn and said, "What's the punch line, big guy?"

"Mr. Kimmel says your son didn't return to the store until one o'clock and Cleary the doorman says he saw him riding his delivery bike past the building at around one o'clock. It seems we're missing a half hour or so of your son's time."

Before anyone else could react, Danny laughed and said, "I had lunch. When I left the store I picked up the shrimp, then stopped at Moe's candy store and bought the newspaper. I put a dime in the cigar box with the coins in it and took out my nickel change. I even yelled into Moe and told him 'Thanks for the half dollar.' You can ask him. Then I went up to Lincoln Boulevard and stopped at Joe the Greek's hot dog wagon and bought two hot dogs with sauerkraut, onions and mustard. I also got a Dr. Brown's cream soda. I put the food in the basket and made the delivery. When I came back downstairs, I got the bag with the food from my bike and went to the back of the alleyway. There's a low brick wall there that separates the building from a hilly lot that goes down to Valentine Avenue. The wall is under a tree and I ate my food and read the paper. When I was done, I went back to work. I do that all the time."

Cairn's jaw tightened, and he said, "Why did you first say it took you twenty minutes to make the delivery?"

"I thought you just wanted to know how long it takes me to go from the Associated to the Excelsior with a delivery and back. You know, I was speaking in general. You can ask Joe the Greek; he knows me and he'll tell you I was at his stand. I don't know nuthin' else. If I did, I'd tell you," Danny said in a whining and defensive tone.

Widelsky rubbed his forehead and said, "How did you recognize Mrs. Weiss?"

"I seen her a couple of times. She's kinda classy, and after that first time I saw her again in the lobby and she was nice to me. She looks like she's rich, I guess she's easy to remember," he answered in an innocent and honest way.

"And the lady with her at the subway. Do you remember her?" Cairn asked.

"No, just they were talking. I think Mrs. Weiss had on a yellow dress. I just remember the other one was a lady, not much more," Danny answered.

"That's fine, Danny," Mary Monaghan interjected. She looked at her husband and nodded her head toward the door. Mike Monaghan turned to the two detectives and said, "I think he's answered all of your questions. I'd like you to leave my house now."

Widelsky stood up, put on his jacket and said to Cairn, "I guess we're done for now. But," and he looked Mike Monaghan straight in the eye, "I find his prints anywhere except that pantry by the service entrance and we won't be so polite. Right, Phil?"

Mary Monaghan stepped back and put her finger up to Widelsky's face, and said, "You've got one helluva nerve accusing my son of anything. Was something stolen? You can search his room right now. I don't care. My son's done nothing and all you've done is waste our time."

Mike Monaghan went over to the front door and opened it. "Gentlemen," he said, "this fishing expedition is over." He then took his wallet from his back pocket, opened it and took out a worn business card. He handed the card to Widelsky and said, "This is my lawyer's business card, Patrick V. Lenihan 360 west 231st Street. You want to speak to my son again; you speak to Mr. Lenihan first."

Widelsky took the card, put it in his pocket and walked out the door without saying anything. Cairn followed, and before he stepped through the doorway, said, "Thanks for your time. I'm sure we'll be talking again."

Mike Monaghan closed the door and said to his wife, "Fucking assholes. Mary, don't ever let the fucking police through the door, ever. They're assholes, and they play those silly fucking games. You're not careful and next thing you know you're fucking framed and in jail because they're too fucking lazy and stupid to catch who really did it." He went over to the sink and washed his hands.

She went over to Danny who was still sitting down and said, "Honey, are you okay?"

"Yeah, I'm fine, but those guys are crazy. First I thought they were nice guys, but then it sounded like they thought I did something wrong," he said with great concern.

"Fucking cops are losers, Danny. They don't care about us. Motherfuckers always got their hands out looking for something for nothing. They steal, it's okay. They tune somebody up, it's sport, I do it and I'm a fucking thug. Pieces of shit all of them," he said angrily.

It was ten minutes after seven, and Mary said, "I was supposed to go my monthly altar society dinner, but I think I'll skip it. I'm too upset."

"Naw, Ma, go. Don't stay on account of me," Danny said. "I'm fine. I didn't do nothing."

"We got dinner?" Mike asked.

"Yes, I made chicken and potato salad," Mary answered.

"Well, don't stay home on my account. I'm eating and taking a shower, then I'm going to the race track with Vince and the boys," Mike said to Mary with an apparent lack of interest in how she felt.

Mary put the chicken and potato salad on the table, and plates and dinnerware, and said, "Well, if no one wants me around, I'll go where I'm wanted."

Mike Monaghan sat down and started eating and offered no response. Danny went over, hugged his mother and said, "C'mon, Mom, no point staying home when we're going out."

"All right," she said. "I'm going. Put the dishes in the sink, and what you don't eat put in the refrigerator." She picked up her pocketbook and went out the door. The two detectives and their subtle insinuation that Danny was lying left her with a sick stomach and she was happy to be on her way to see Father Dunphy. *If Danny's done anything wrong,* she thought, *Father Dunphy will know what to do.*

Widelsky and Cairn were sitting in the unmarked car in front of Danny's apartment building. Widelsky said to Cairn, "That didn't go very well, did it?"

"No, it didn't. I think the kid knows something. He was just a little too cute with that bullshit about the deliveries, just a little too dumb. Pulling teeth, it's like pulling teeth," Cairn replied.

"I think so too, but maybe we should stop at Summit Avenue and see if anyone in the squad knows anything about the old man and the kid," Widelsky added. "Fucking kid's father is a little scary. Now I know why the doorman's afraid of him. I'd shoot a guy like that before I'd fight with him," Widelsky said with a chuckle. "Guys like that always rip your clothes."

"Yeah, he looked pretty mean. But there's something sneaky about the kid. And shit, we gave up the doorman," Cairn said laughing.

Chapter Twenty-Five

Mike and Danny Monaghan sat at opposite sides of the kitchen table. Mary had laid out the platter of fried chicken and the potato salad before she left to go to her altar society supper. Danny had taken a drumstick, a thigh piece and a small helping of potato salad, and spent more time moving the food around his plate than he did eating it. Mike loaded up his plate, and as he ate his dinner he kept his eyes focused on Danny for much of the meal. Danny's table manners weren't much better than his father's, and dinner, when they were together, was a race to see who could shovel as much food on his plate as quickly as possible, eat it and go for seconds before the other cleaned his dish. Danny's lack of appetite didn't go unnoticed, and Mike knew that something was troubling the boy.

Mike saw that Danny was ill at ease with the two detectives, and when he first walked into the apartment and saw them there he thought they were following up on an incident that had happened to a girl who was at a drinking party with Danny and his friends the week before. When he learned they were there to investigate a murder and listened to them interview Danny, he knew one thing for certain the detectives didn't know, and that was that Danny was hiding something. Ever since he was a small child Danny had a strong habit of giving evasive and vague answers when he was questioned about some misdeed he had committed. His responses to Cairn's questions alarmed Mike, and as he ate his dinner he tried to figure in his mind what tactic he could take to find out what Danny didn't want the police to know.

"You know," he said to Danny in between sucking the meat off a drumstick. "I thought those cops were here for something else."

"What?"

"You know Jimmy Carroll?"

"No."

"He's a sandhog, crazy bastard. Pretty tough, but he drinks too much. Anyway, his sister Claire is married to Joe Breen and they have a couple of girls. One of em is named Mary. You know her?" Mike asked as he picked another drumstick off the platter and stuck the whole head of it in his mouth and wrestled the meat off with his teeth and tongue while he waited for Danny to answer.

"Yeah, Hand—" he was about to say, caught himself, cleared his throat and said, "Mary Breen, she hangs out with us. Why?"

"Jimmy says there was a little party last Friday night to say goodbye to one of your friends and something happened."

"Remember last Friday when you came home and you walked in the door and me and Little Danny were standing in the hallway and Mommy was saying the rosary?"

"Yeah."

"We were leaving for our party," Danny said as he hung his head. "I know I'm not old enough to drink, but Fagan was going into the Navy and we got some beer and screwdriver mix and had a little celebration up in the 212 Lot."

"Sounds like more than a celebration. Something happened to Mary Breen, and her mother went to the cops and complained, that's what her uncle Jimmy told me." He picked up another drumstick from the platter and pointed it at Danny. "Tell me what happened."

"Russian Annie and Mary drank all the screwdriver mix and got drunk. Annie puked all over Fagan and Mary fell asleep. Some of the other girls were laughing at her, but that's all I know." He paused, then asked incredulously, "Her mother went to the cops 'cause she got drunk?"

"Lot more happened, or so I'm told."

Danny looked at his father, shook his head, and said, "I was with Linda Kelly that night. We just started going together. We had quarts of beer, and maybe she had a couple of cups of beer, but she don't drink much and her parents are very strict, so she can't drink even if she wanted. She has to be home by eleven and we left the 212 Lot at about ten. I went with her and we sat on her porch until she had to go in. Everyone said the party was a blast, but I wasn't there all night. You can ask Linda, I swear. After, I left her I came home. Ask Mommy, she was surprised I was home so early."

Mike listened carefully to everything Danny said and couldn't help but feel alarmed over the contrast between this conversation and the interview with the cops. There was no doubt in his mind that Danny was telling the truth about the party. His recollection was effortless and anything but vague. "Who, was there and how'd you get the liquor?"

"We call in a phony order to the Associated and Ernie takes the delivery up to the lot. We got Ray's older brother to buy the screwdriver mix and the Seagram's in the liquor store, and we bought ice and 7-Up at the gas station. We got a big cooler we found months ago and we put everything in it. We got benches and other stuff up in the lot and we sit around and shoot the bull. Ernie, Little Danny, Billy, Duffy, Ray, Fat Murphy, Denise, Linda, everybody was there."

"Who left first?"

"Me and Linda."

"Where was Annie and Mary?"

"Annie was with Fagan, I didn't see her puke on him but that's what everyone said and Mary was sleeping on a blanket, she was really drunk."

Mike rubbed his chin and said, "That's all you know? Maybe something happened after you left and you heard about it?"

"I swear. I didn't hear a thing. Maybe something happened and nobody's talking. What did you hear?"

"I heard Mary passed out, and later on somebody pulled down her pants and tried to screw her, but she woke up, and when she woke up her hair was all wet. Seems somebody pissed all over her. One of your other buddies tried to stick his thing in her mouth and maybe he jerked off on her. You know, right in her face? That's what her Uncle Jimmy told me, and that's what she told the police. That's what I thought the cops were here for tonight. You telling me you ain't a part of this, right?" his father said as he wiped his lips with the back of his hand and pushed his plate away.

"Jesus Christ, I didn't do anything, but you gotta believe me, nobody's said anything about this at all. I mean it, if I knew I'd tell you, I swear," Danny said emotionally.

"I take your word, and if the cops come around I guess this Linda girl can back you up. Annie Rink, that's Carla Rink's daughter, right?"

"Yeah, Russian Annie, we call her that 'cause her grandmother's the Ukrainian lady that lives upstairs and curses out the window and throws stuff at the super. What about her?"

"She and this Mary, they a little loose?" his father asked cautiously.

With all that had happened during the day, Danny just wanted the conversation to end, and even though he wanted to tell his father that Annie was a slut just like her mother, he simply said, "Annie's nice, but Mary's a little loose and she let's everyone feel her up. If something happened, that's why."

"Yeah, well guys your age all got one thing on your mind, if I remember," his father replied, laughing.

"Father Noone at school calls it the war of biology against theology, and he says all of us guys are on the wrong side," Danny said with a small smile.

"Let me ask you a question then."

"Sure."

"Maybe today, you got talking to that lady's cleaning girl. Maybe she offered you a little piece for a couple of bucks. I know that's how some of those colored girls make a few extra dollars," his father said nonchalantly.

Danny looked slightly confused, and without thinking, blurted out, "Mrs. Weiss' cleaning lady's an old woman, Japanese or Hawaiian or something like that. She ain't colored."

"I just wanted to be sure," his father answered as he got up from the table. "Clean up, I'm going to the race track tonight."

Danny wrapped up the remainder of the chicken and potato salad and put it in the refrigerator. He took the plates and silverware and put them in the plastic basin his mother kept in the sink. He filled the basin with soap and hot water and left the dishes there to soak. His mother would do them when she got home. The story about Hand-job Mary had caught him by surprise, and he wished that the mystery of who pissed on her and tried to screw her was the biggest problem in his life. His kitchen window looked out over the alleyway where the garbage cans were stored near the street and where the alley led to the rear of the building where there were additional apartments at ground level. Tim Cleary lived in a ground floor apartment with his mother in the back of the building, and as Danny was standing by the window he saw Cleary make his way to the garbage cans with a bag of trash. The sight of Cleary made his blood race, and he felt a sense of fear and foreboding doom. Danny hadn't seen Cleary when he left Maria's building, and it alarmed him when the detective said that Cleary had seen him near the building at one o'clock. Stopping to grab a couple of hot dogs from the Greek on his way to make the delivery was the smartest thing he'd done all day. He was sure no one had noticed him gobbling them down before he made the delivery, and if the police questioned the Greek, Danny was certain the Greek would remember Danny asking him for extra sauerkraut and onions. *Those are the little things those kinds of people remember*, he thought. He had wiped the apartment down good and he didn't believe his fingerprints would be found anywhere. *All I have to do is stick to my story; no one is going to find me out*, he thought. "Fuck you, Cleary," he silently mouthed as the doorman made his way back down the alleyway to his apartment.

Danny left the kitchen and turned down the hallway toward his bedroom. His father was coming in the other direction from the bathroom, and as they passed Mike punched Danny in the solar plexus. It was a short, hard, brutal blow and Danny crumbled to the ground clutching his mid-section and gasping for air.

Mike stepped over him and went into his bedroom. His work clothes were in a pile on the floor, and he kicked them aside and sat on the side of the bed. He could hear Danny whimpering on the floor outside the room. Mike Monaghan shook his head and yelled out, "Stop crying and act like a man." Danny didn't answer but his whimpering stopped. Mike dressed and went out into the hallway. Danny was sitting on the floor with his back up against the wall and he had his head in his hands and was breathing deeply.

"You think I'm some dumb fucking cop, Danny?" His father sneered. "You think you fooled me with that little game of cat and mouse you played with those cops?"

"I don't know what you're talking about."

"You don't?" his father growled as he kicked Danny in the back of his thigh. Danny yelped and rolled over. "I want the truth, the fucking truth, do you understand?"

"The truth about what?" Danny said as he pulled himself to his feet and faced his father.

"Sure, I'll make it easy for you. Number one, most fucking cops can't find their own shadow on a sunny day, but those two guys today didn't seem that stupid. Number two, they don't know you like I do, and I knew you were hiding something. Your mother was fooled, but she likes being fooled. I don't. Number three, and most importantly, you said to Kern, I think that's his name, that you didn't know the lady had a cleaning lady. I baited you about a colored girl and you told me the cleaning lady was old and Japanese or Hawaiian. And that makes you a fucking liar," his father said menacingly as he approached him. Mike grabbed Danny around his neck and squeezed his neck and turned his face to his. He leaned over and said very quietly, "Tell me the fucking truth or I'll beat it out of you. Your mother isn't here, and if you don't tell me everything, I'll call the fucking cops myself."

"Why are you gonna call the cops?" Danny squealed. "You hate the cops."

"I told you a hundred times, I don't like cops because you can't trust them. They're out for themselves, and they think they're better than everybody else. But I can't protect you if I don't know the whole story, and if you don't trust me enough to tell me, then I got no fucking use for you and they can throw your sorry ass in jail and let it rot."

Mike let go of Danny's neck, went into the kitchen, took a bottle of beer from the refrigerator and sat down in his chair. He pointed to the chair Danny always sat in and said, "C'mon, I gotta be someplace soon, start talking."

Danny rubbed his forehead with his hand and took a deep breath and said, "It was an accident. I been to the lady's apartment with deliveries a couple of times, just like I told the cops. First time I was there I almost saw her naked. She had on a see-through bathrobe, and in the sunlight you could see right through it. She just had on her underwear and bra. I kept thinking about her. Today when she called she gave me the order and said she'd be out all day. When I got to the apartment, the door from the pantry, that's what she calls it, to the apartment was unlocked. I opened the door and looked around. That's all I wanted to do. I was just being nosy. It's a real fancy building and the lady looks rich. I didn't mean nothing, believe me," he said as he started to cry.

"Stop bawling," his father snarled.

Danny breathed deeply again and continued. "I went in, and there's two bedrooms. One looks like an extra room and the other one must be the lady's and her husband's room. In the pantry is a washing machine and there was some dirty laundry, so I had a dirty undershirt and used that so I wouldn't leave any fingerprints around," he said, thinking it would be better to say undershirt than Maria's panties. "I figured since I was in there maybe they had some extra money and I looked in the drawers in the bedroom. In one of the lady's drawers I found some big pictures of her. They were old pictures and she was half dressed. I was looking at the pictures and didn't hear the cleaning lady come in. Next thing I know she's screaming at me. I panicked and picked up an ashtray and threw it at her. It hit her and she went down. She didn't move, and I knew she was hurt bad. Right after that I wiped everything I touched with the undershirt. The lady wasn't breathing, and I knew she was dead. I got ready to leave and I heard the front door open. I was scared and didn't know what to do so I hid in the closet. It was Mrs. Weiss, that's the lady who lives there. I know her voice. I almost pissed in my pants and I ran out of the closet and knocked her over and ran from the apartment."

Mike Monaghan's chest heaved with emotion and the veins in his neck bulged. He finished the beer he was drinking, and said, "I'd like to take this bottle and drive it right through your stupid fucking face. Cleary told the cops he saw you at one o'clock. It doesn't sound like you were in the apartment that long."

"I was in there for a while, but when I came downstairs, I ate my hot dogs at the wall in the back just like I said," Danny countered.

"What about the lady?" Mike asked. "Didn't you think she was going to call the cops, didn't you think she saw you?"

"I don't know if she did. I panicked. From the moment I threw the ashtray, I wasn't me. I was like a robot." Danny knew he was lying about eating his lunch, but he couldn't tell his father the other things he did in the apartment because if he told him his father would think he was perverted and would beat him senseless.

"You got some set of balls. You mean you just went and ate your lunch, then went back to work like nothing happened?" his father asked in disbelief.

"Basically, yeah. What else could I do?" Danny said, then started to sob and gasp. "Daddy, Daddy," he moaned. "I didn't mean to do anything. I'm so sorry, but what can I do?"

"Stop crying and keep your fucking mouth shut. This lady, her name is Weiss, you said?"

"Yeah, Maria Weiss."

"Maybe she didn't see you or maybe you knocked her out. Let's hope so."

"What am I going to do?" Danny sobbed.

"Keep your mouth shut. If the cops pick you up, you tell them to call Mr. Lenihan and me. I don't care if they beat you, nothing is going to happen if they have no evidence, and it seems so far that's the case because if they had something, or if that lady had seen you they'd have locked you up," Mike said with a sigh.

"So, you think I won't get caught?" Danny asked with some relief in his face.

"Maybe, but that's only part of it. You got to pay a price."

Danny looked at his father, the tears were rolling down his cheeks, and he said, "What price? What can I do to ever make this better? I killed someone. I can't believe I did it, I wish I was the one dead."

Mike Monaghan sniffed and took a cigarette out of his shirt pocket. He lit it and threw the burnt matchstick into the sink. He inhaled and exhaled several times, then said to Danny, "There was a kid in the neighborhood when I was growing up named Jimmy Cullen. The Cullen's lived at 2860 Bailey. He was three, four years older than me. He was a big kid with glasses. His mother kept him on a short leash and he was a real momma's boy. When he was maybe seventeen or eighteen he got caught up on the roof of his building with a thirteen-year-old girl. I don't know if they were screwing or he was molesting her. Everybody on the block knew something happened, but never exactly what. The girl was one of the Riley's from 2840, and she was a little slow. Nobody called the police, but the Rileys and the Cullens were real lace curtain Irish, thought they were a little better than everyone else, and they went to Monsignor Stanley, he was the monsignor at St. John's then, and told him what happened. Three weeks later Jimmy Cullen was in a seminary in Nova Scotia studying for the priesthood. It was an Irish order, and a year later the Cullens moved away. Someone said Jimmy ended up a missionary in Africa, and other people said he left the seminary and joined the Army and died in France during the war," Mike Monaghan said as he stood up and extinguished the lit cigarette in the water in the dish tub, then tossed the soggy stub out the window. "Cullen screwed up and Monsignor Stanley saw to it that he paid the price," Mike said with authority as he pointed his finger at his son.

Danny bristled and said accusingly, "You killed that nigger, what price did you pay?"

Mike Monaghan's face flushed, and he responded with anger in his voice, "I never killed nobody. Jesus Christ, that fucking story's been going around the neighborhood for over twenty fucking years. Let me tell you, sonny, don't believe everything you hear."

"Well, how come that's what everyone says," Danny challenged.

"All right, I was about your age and I had a milk route in East Farms in the Lower Borough. Most of my stops were five floor walkups. You go up one side and down the other. Toughest fucking job I ever had in my life carrying those baskets of milk. I go up one side of this building and go out to the roof to cross over to the other side. It was around six-thirty in the morning and the sun was just coming up. These two spooks are standing on the roof just outside the door from the stairs and they tell me to give them the milk and empty my pockets. I say 'sure,' and I put down the two baskets I'm carrying and I come up and crack the one closest to me in the jaw and he goes down like someone shot him. The other fucking asshole turns around and starts running. Now these buildings on the block I was on are attached to one another except for the spots where there's an alleyway, and this stupid fucking nigger thinks I'm chasing him, and I ain't, and he jumps the wall from that building to the next. One problem, he jumped where the alleyway was and not where the buildings were connected, and he falls five floors to the pavement and cracks his skull and dies. Cops come, everything is okey dokey and that's the end of the story. Now who the fuck did I kill?" Mike Monaghan leaned over the table and said to his son.

"People say you threw the guy off the roof."

"People say lots of things, Danny. You gotta understand lots of people are afraid of me, lots of people think I'm a tough guy, and they make that shit up or stretch the truth just to make me worse than I am. It don't mean shit. I've never told anyone I killed that spook because I didn't."

Danny sniffled and said, "Well, what about all that other stuff you do. Like all the times the cops been here and you've been arrested, and what about Russian Annie's mom, all that stuff?"

Mike sat down and lit another cigarette and said, "Fine let's talk about everything. Put it all on the table. I was eighteen all of two weeks and your mother told me she was pregnant. We got married, and two months later I was in the Army in Louisiana. Five months later your sister was born and the war ended and six months after that I got an early discharge. Three years later in 1948 you were born. Your sister hates me. That's why she's with your mother's Aunt Kit in Liverpool studying to be a nurse. She knows she wouldn't be here and you wouldn't be here if I hadn't got your mother pregnant. I am what I am. I like to drink and have a good time, and I like women," he said as he inhaled deeply, then exhaled the smoke up toward his nose.

Danny's face tightened at his father's remarks, and he started to squirm in his seat uncomfortable with his father's confession.

Mike Monaghan put the cigarette down and continued talking, "Your mother and I tried to make a go of it, but things never really worked out. It's my fault, I know, but sometimes things are what they are. All of your life I've gone to work and put money on the table. Your mother and I've fought a lot, and maybe I haven't been much of a father, but you've never gone without. That's my end of the deal. Plenty of times your mother said she was leaving, and I told her to go. She never left, pal. I live my life and she lives hers. I did a favor for a couple of guys once. A bookie named Chick Nathan from up in Riverview and another guy, Vince Lobianco. There was a guy in Huguenot City who owed them money and wouldn't pay. I got the guy to pay, and for the last fifteen years or so I got plenty of guys to pay their debts. I still go out and break my fucking back all the time tying metal, but the money ain't enough. What I do for Chick and some other people is what buys me a new car every couple of years and pays for some other things. Times I got collared by the police was for busting some welscher's head for not paying up. As for Carla, or any other women, that's none of your business. Now you know the whole story and none of it, as I see it, has anything to do with what you done today."

Danny hung his head again and said, "I'm sorry. I know most of that, and Mommy never says much about it anyway. I guess it's your business and not mine. I got bigger problems. What can I do?"

"Like I said before, Danny, you've got to pay a price. Maybe your mother's buddy Dunphy can get you in a seminary for priests or brothers, what do you think?"

"I don't wanna be a priest or a brother."

"Yeah, you didn't plan on being a murderer either, did you?"

"How's that gonna work and why?"

"Simple, it gets you away from here and out of the eyes of the police, and it's a way to make up for what you did and never let on to your mother what happened. I've caused her enough heartache. She don't need you adding to it."

"Dad, I don't know about this."

"Danny, you have no choice. I gotta go, a couple of guys are waiting for me. Stay home tonight and don't answer the door until your mother comes home. If the cops come back, call Mr. Lenihan. The number for his answering service is in the book on the telephone table."

Mike Monaghan then got up and left the kitchen without saying anything else to Danny. He went out the front door of the apartment and left his son sitting there with his head in his hands.

Mike Monaghan thought to himself that he had resolved the matter as best he could. He'd never dreamed his son would become a priest, and he had almost as little use for priests as he did cops, but he couldn't think of a better way to protect the boy, and he knew if he was left home all summer he would slip up some way and tell someone what happened. Once that occurred, it would all be over. *Let him spend a few years studying religion and pretending to be holy, shit it'll make Mary happy, maybe she'll try and become a nun.* He laughed. *That would be perfect, just fucking perfect.*

Mike Monaghan walked out of the apartment house, and as he was going down the courtyard steps to the street he could see a group of men sitting on the wall that separated the Borough expressway from Bailey Avenue. Old man Healy and Mr. Hackendorf had lawn chairs and were comfortably seated on the sidewalk facing three other men sitting on the wall. In the center of the three men on the wall was a small sized man. His outfit gave Monaghan a laugh. He had on a tee shirt and loud red and green Bermuda shorts with black shoes and knee high black socks. The little man had a can of beer in his hand and had the attention of the other five men. It was Cleary, and Mike Monaghan imagined that Cleary was holding them spellbound with his account of the murder at the building he worked at as a doorman. Mike Monaghan also imagined that Cleary didn't fail to mention that Danny made a delivery to that very apartment today, also.

Cleary's a problem, I broke his nose last year and he deserved it, but he's a funny duck and who knows if he'll try to get even with me, he thought.

Monaghan resolved to deal with Cleary before the weekend was over. His mind made up, Mike Monaghan went down the street and unlocked the driver's side door to his 1964 Turino Turquoise metallic colored Cadillac de Ville. He opened the door, and before entering, he stopped to admire the car. The lines, the fins, the long front hood and trunk gave a sleek and powerful look to the car that Monaghan relished and believed by extension personified his own image.

Chapter Twenty-Six

The Summit Place Precinct was a lopsided fortress of orange brick stuck on the steep slope of Summit Place between Heath Avenue and Kingsbridge Terrace. Cairn drove the unmarked Dodge Polara up Summit Place to the front of the precinct and parked it half in the street and half on the sidewalk. He and Widelsky entered the precinct and made their way past the raised front desk and went down the hallway to the detective squad. They turned into the office and first greeted Walt Hoppes, an older, athletic looking man, who appeared frozen in thought, with his two index fingers poised over the keys of an old manual typewriter. Hoppes looked up at the two detectives entering the office and raised his eyebrows and without further acknowledgment directed his interest back to the typewriter. Cairn looked at Hoppes and said, "Good to see you too, Walt."

Widelsky frowned, but before he could add a comment, Billy Devine walked into the office. Devine saw Cairn and Widelsky, and said in a booming voice, "Well, well, lookee here, it's Dean Martin and Stubby Kaye. What's the occasion? No homicides in the Summit? Least none I know of. You guys had one on the Boulevard today, didn't you?"

Cairn smiled. His hair was a little grayer than Dean Martin's, but he was told from time to time that he bore a resemblance to the popular entertainer and enjoyed the comparison. Widelsky neither understood nor appreciated Devine's reference to Stubby Kaye, and he gave Devine a dirty look but said nothing. Devine went over to a desk and picked a file from an in-basket and thumbed through it without saying anything further. Cairn said aloud to neither detective in particular, "Possibly a double, we're still waiting, but we're doing the preliminaries and we wanted to know if either of you know a guy name of Mike Monaghan?" After asking his question, he looked at Hoppes and Hoppes nodded his head toward Devine.

Devine tucked the file folder under his arm and started back out of the office. As he was passing Cairn, he said, "Mike Monaghan, we got some file on him. Half a drawer at least. Give me ten minutes. I have someone in the complaint room and I have to finish up."

Cairn said, "Fine, while we're waiting I'll pick your partner's brain." Hoppes looked up from his typewriter at Cairn and yawned.

Widelsky said, "We keeping you up, Walt?"

"No, I was at Dunmoor at six this morning for a nine o'clock tee off, and now I got this heavy burglary I'm working on and I'm a little tired. It's no murder, but some miscreant removed the transom from Vito's Barber Shop next to the Broadway RKO and stole approximately twenty dollars in coins and four bottles of Odell Hair Trainer. Now we have to go out and look for a kid with stiff hair and a pocket full of change," Hoppes said as he got up from his chair and walked toward the front door of the office. He turned to the two detectives and said, "The coffee's fresh. Billy made it about an hour ago. There's clean cups on the counter. Make yourselves comfortable." He gave Cairn and Widelsky a nod of his head and left the room. Cairn went and got two coffee cups and went over to the coffee urn.

"What is it with everyone?" Widelsky said. "We got the plague?"

"Who knows? I'm sure when Devine comes back we'll hear more than we want to hear. I don't see any saccharin here, do you want sugar?"

"I'm hooked on saccharin; try a half a teaspoon of sugar. Maybe that'll do."

Cairn poured them each a cup of coffee and after he sat back down, "Might as well check in with our allied supreme commander and get an update."

Cairn dialed the number for the Boulevard Precinct and was put through to Sergeant Kreppell. "Hello, Sarge, it's Phil Cairn," Cairn said cheerfully for the third time that day.

"Where are you two? Finished with the kid and the secretary, yet?"

"We're at Summit, doing a little background on the kid and his family. Tough bunch, it seems. We didn't get to the Cruz girl yet, she's next. Anything new on your end?"

"Plenty. Weiss has an attorney, Lee Futerman. That's your Miss Goolnick's boss. He's a retired bureau chief from the DA's office, and they've already been in touch. Futerman is meeting Weiss when he comes in from Montreal tonight and he'll have him in the office tomorrow at nine-thirty. Mrs. Weiss had a mild aneurysm, if there's such a thing. The doctor at Borough who operated on her told Russo it had something to do with a communicating artery, whatever that means. It was leaking, who knows? Anyway, she's going to pull through, but nobody knows what her condition will be. Now that's what I know. Who are you arresting for this?" Kreppell smugly asked.

"Got us, boss. We don't like the kid, he's a little too cute, but his old man's a real tough guy and he got in the way. Wants us to work through his lawyer and all that shit. We need some hard physical evidence."

"So who're you speaking to there?"

"Waiting for Billy Devine to give us some background. Plus, we want to see if there's anything on the secretary before we approach her."

"One more thing," Kreppell said. "The doorman called about an hour ago and said he thought he saw the secretary on the number one bus headed north on the Boulevard around five-fifteen or so. She must have been on her way home."

"Well, she wasn't at work today. You think she was checking out the building?"

"Who knows? She could have been. I'm knocking off around nine, so get back to me as soon as you're through with her and we'll plan for tomorrow morning. And tell Billy I said hello."

"Okay, talk to you later."

Widelsky was on his second cup of coffee, and said to Cairn, "I got most of the conversation and I gather the Weiss lady's alive?"

"Yeah, she's alive, Sophie Cruz was seen riding by the building on the number one bus at five-fifteen by the doorman, the DA's office is involved, and I'd say the plot thickens!"

"Kreppell still breaking balls?"

"A little, he wants to know when we're making an arrest. But, all in all, he sounded okay, and the Weiss lady's going to pull through, so maybe will get something out of her."

"What about her, what was it?"

"He said an aneurysm and something about an artery. I didn't really understand him, but I gather she'll live and our big problem will be what she remembers."

"Yeah, she's the fucking killer, and when we ask her what she remembers she'll say 'nothing' and the joke's on us," Widelsky said, then started laughing.

"What's so funny?"

"People, murder, police work, all the fucking goofballs we deal with, whatever." Widelsky sighed.

"You're right about that. Let's hope brother Devine can fill us in on the Monaghan clan. You heard the captain last month, he said every precinct needs a Billy Devine."

"Yeah, just like everybody needs an asshole," Widelsky sneered.

"Enjoying my premium Columbian coffee?" Billy Devine asked in booming voice as he strode back in the room. Devine was a robust and hearty fellow in his early fifties. He had a thick bonnet of white hair that he kept plastered in place with ample amounts of hair cream. His face was broad and blotched with eczema, his nose was riddled with spider veins, and it all was masked behind a pair of thick-rimmed black eyeglasses. He was about six feet tall and on the stocky side, but it was hard to tell what was muscle and what was flab. Whatever it was, it was solid, but there was nothing menacing about Billy Devine. As soon as he opened his mouth and started talking he became everyone's favorite uncle. He was a storyteller, a quipster, a name dropper and so full of palaver and blarney that it was difficult to take him seriously, and almost ludicrous to describe him as a hardened and experienced detective with nearly thirty years of experience. Yet, Devine had an uncanny talent for never forgetting a face, a name, what a person smoked or drank, where he lived, or who his friends and enemies were, and because of that talent he was well respected among his peers and equally respected by his superiors. He had been assigned to the Summit Place precinct for the full fifteen years he had been a detective. He had resisted and turned down opportunities for better assignments and had used his position as a union trustee to ensure that he would remain at the Summit until he was ready to retire. His partner Walt Hoppes was his direct opposite. Walt was physically tough, had a mean streak and was happiest when his mouth was shut and he was thinking about his golf game. Together they made an effective team.

"Coffee's great," Cairn said, holding up his empty cup. "I might have another, and while I'm enjoying that second cup you might give us the scoop on the Monaghans?"

"Help yourself, that percolator makes twenty-two cups," Devine said as he got a cup off the counter and handed it to Cairn. "You can pour me one too."

"Sure."

"Now that you two girls have your coffee, could we get talking?" moaned Widelsky.

"Frank, you got to stop and smell the roses, or in this case, the coffee," Devine said with a shake of his finger toward Widelsky. "Now, is it just Monaghan senior, or are you two interested in junior also?"

"Both, in a way," said Cairn. "The kid made a delivery to the apartment where the murder happened and he fits into the time frame, and his story's a little too pat, but so far, there's no evidence and there are some other people in the mix. We thought we had the kid in a lie, but he covered it smoothly and I know his alibi is going to cover."

"Phil, you're talking in riddles. Give me the Reader's Digest version."

"Okay, the kid works for the Associated Market on Kingsbridge near Jersey Avenue. Around noon he takes a delivery to the apartment where the murder occurred and, according to him, the whole business from the store to the apartment and back shouldn't take more than twenty minutes. Now the doorman sees him by the building around one, so there's forty more minutes or so unaccounted. When we challenge him on this little fact, and the challenge was very soft, just a by the way, the kid covers himself by saying he bought his lunch from a hot dog vendor before the delivery along with a newspaper and ate the meal and read the paper after the delivery. And I know the candy store owner and the hot dog vendor will confirm he bought the paper and lunch just before noon when he made the delivery. To make matters worse, the father shows up in the apartment a little after we get there and it's very clear he doesn't like cops," Cairn said to Devine as he paused to take a sip of coffee.

"Phil's putting it mildly," added Widelsky. "The old man looked like he was ready to go ten rounds with us, and he made it very clear any further contact with the kid would be through his lawyer. Problem I see is that if the kid did do it, he had no way of getting in touch with his old man, so why's the guy so fucking protective when he don't know what's going on?"

"Well, you got to know Mike Monaghan."

"That's why we're here," answered Cairn.

"Mike Monaghan was born and raised in Kingsbridge. His old man was a milkman and worked for the old Country Lane label. They were big in the Lower Borough. Monaghan's old man was one of those quiet Irishman. The type that don't say much, but you don't know if that's the case because they're deep thinkers who keep to themselves, or there's just nothing going on upstairs. He was a cold sort and that's probably half of the son's problem. The Monaghans come from the Hill section near the river and lived on Arden Avenue. Now I just happen to know about his old man because my aunt lived in the same apartment building and she knew the Monaghans quite well. I grew up across the bridge in the Wood on Island Street, just across from Blessed Sacrament Church and I have a pretty good track on Kingsbridge. Half of my family were born and raised in Kingsbridge, which is probably why I like the Summit so much. Now, when Mike Monaghan was eighteen he knocked up his girlfriend, Mary Brown. Nice Irish girl from the other side. Her old man was a subway motorman. She had three sisters and no brothers. She got pregnant, they married and two months later Mike was in the Army. That was around the winter of 1945. Mike was a high school dropout and a milkman like his old man, but he was also quite an athlete and was very well known in Kingsbridge. I wasn't in the Summit then, I was pounding a beat in La Rochelle Station, but being that my aunt lived up here and we visited regularly and there were a few gin mills I was known to take a taste in, I picked up tidbits about what was going on here and there. Mike and Mary had a little girl and a few years after he got out of the Army, I guess around 1948, they had a son, and up to this point, and listen to me because it's important," Devine said earnestly. "In 1948 he was a just another young married guy. He had a job delivering milk and he was known for playing a lot of fast pitch softball and screwing every dame he could and not much more. In 1950 they moved over to Bailey Avenue. You were there today. You see the bar and restaurant on the corner? Pete's Bridge Lounge?" Devine paused in his monologue to ask.

"Yeah, we saw it. So what?" Widelsky asked already tiring from Devine's long windedness.

"You two have never eaten there?"

"I haven't, have you Frank?"

"No and so what?"

"Famous place in the Borough, that's all," said Devine. He then took a sip of his coffee and continued talking," Pete's Bridge has one of those crazy menus that don't make sense, but makes money. Saturday through Thursday it's the same thing every lunch and dinner. Dinner starts with a wedge of lettuce, half a tomato and a green onion. Then you have a choice of a grilled rib eye steak or a pan-fried round steak with fried onions. That comes with a choice of French fries or mashed potatoes with horseradish in them and you also get some broccoli with garlic and fresh breadcrumbs. Nothing else is served and there's no menu, just a chalkboard with the prices. Now lunch is a hamburger on an English muffin and French fries, same thing Saturday through Thursday. Friday is a totally different menu. If you're having lunch, he only serves a grilled cheese, but oh what a grilled cheese. He mixes maatszorella cheese and cheddar cheese and puts it on thick eye-talian bread and it's grilled under a heavy plate so everything melts and browns the right way. That comes with potato chips and a pickle. For dinner on Friday night he only serves fried flounder with Manhattan clam chowder and fresh coleslaw. Dessert is cheesecake. Nothing else, no choices, it's really incredible. And he packs them in. Plus, on Friday and Saturday after nine he has a piano player. Great guys he gets. All Negroes from Huguenot City, can they play? He has one guy every other Saturday, name of Benny Blake who looks like Nat King Cole. He's got the hair conked and he sings just like Cole. I was there two weeks ago. My wife was at her sister's and I was working a one to nine. Me and Jimmy Hodges went for dinner and to listen to the music. Monaghan was in there with his girlfriend, Carla Rink. Carla got up and sang a number with Benny. She's got a good voice and ain't half bad looking. Too bad she's got Monaghan and Monaghan's got a wife, you know," Devine said as he stopped to finish his coffee.

"Billy, thanks for the food review and all the other bullshit, but the clock's moving," a visibly annoyed Widelsky said.

"The art to being a good detective is to be a good listener, Frank."

"What's all this got to do with a homicide?"

"Maybe nothing, but you said you wanted to know about Monaghan, didn't you?"

"Go on, Billy," Cairn interjected, trying to keep the two men from arguing.

"Where was I?" Devine said, then started speaking again. "Okay, Pete's Bridge. Story goes sometime in 1950 Pete decided to sponsor a fast pitch softball team. The league played on Tuesday nights and that was a slow night for Pete. Now Pete is Peter Lobianco, and he has a younger brother, Vince Lobianco, and they come from over Villus Avenue in the Boulevard Precinct where you two boys are working out of. Nice little Italian neighborhood. Vince had a bar and restaurant over there called the Pompeii Room, pizza, spaghetti and meatballs, that kind of food. He sponsored a softball team and had this real racehorse of a guy playing for him name of Gino Paura. Now you have to understand that Vince, in addition to being a bar and restaurant owner, is also a bookie and a loan shark, and everything else that goes with that line of work, and this thoroughbred kid Paura is his muscle man," Devine said as he got up from his chair and walked to the open window overlooking the back yard of the precinct house. Cairn and Widelsky sat looking at Devine as he continued his monologue. "This Paura kid isn't really a kid, he's about twenty-six at the time. He saw a little action in the South Pacific in the Navy at the end of the war and he knows a thing or two. Anyway, Pete's team played his brother

Vince's team once during the season and gave them a beating, and the big difference is Mike Monaghan. He can pitch fast and he can hit and he can run. Gino's Vince's boy, and for the second game he puts money on the game and bets his team and tells Gino his money's on him. Mike Monaghan pitches a gem and hits two home runs and Pete's team wins by three runs. Now Pete don't give a shit. He ain't a wise guy like his younger brother, and all he knows is that when your team wins everybody comes back to your place and they drink up a storm. So they're all in the bar, and Pete is happy because he can hear the cash register singing, the dimes going in the jukebox, and everyone is thirsty. Vince is sitting in a corner and he's fit to be tied. He ain't making money, he lost on the game and he's giving Gino a piece of his mind. Now, remember, this is the second time Vince's boys from the Pompeii Room lost to his brother Pete's boys from Pete's Bridge Lounge. Gino's had a few drinks, and he's feeling pretty low and Mike Monaghan and his team are whooping it up. So, Gino calls them a bunch of dumb Micks, one word leads to another and he's nose to nose with Monaghan. Now, everyone knows Gino's a tough guy and a wise guy in the making. They just think Monaghan's a tough kid. Monaghan tries to blow Gino off, but Gino ain't buying it and he slaps Monaghan in the face. The whole place freezes and Monaghan shocks the whole crowd by telling Gino he better apologize or he's gonna kick his Guinea ass all the way back to Stromboli, or wherever it is he's from. Gino blinks, throws a punch, and before he can land it Monaghan has given him a short chop to the mid-section and Gino doubles over. I wasn't there, but the story is legend and I've heard it the same way from ten different people who were there, and this is where Monaghan made his bones. He has Gino doubled over, and instead of walking away he gives him a left and a right to the head and breaks the guy's jaw and knocks him out. The poor bastard is on the floor, and he kicks him one in the side, then he walks over to Vince and says, 'He shouldn't have done that, it was only a softball game.' So, they drag Gino out and take him over to Borough Hospital and that was that except Vince tells Monaghan to see him the next night at the Pompeii Room. Monaghan sees Vince, Vince gives him Gino's job and Monaghan is now collecting money for Vince Lobianco and his partner Chick Nathan. Next thing, he's no longer delivering milk, but he's working in construction as a wire latherer. The rest is history. Five years ago the three of them opened a bar on west 231st near Riverview Avenue called Bongos. That's a place for ex-cons, tough guys, rogue cops and loose women. The place is jumping all day and night and that's where you'll find Mike Monaghan when he isn't working. Now can I tell you more?" a self-satisfied Devine asked.

"How come you know so much about this guy?" Cairn asked.

"We've arrested him here eight times, and he's been pinched in numerous other places, too. Assault, burglary, robbery, extortion and God knows what. Somehow he always beats the rap, and most of the time the charges have been withdrawn or the people have just disappeared or shut up. That's why if you came here today and said he was a suspect I wouldn't be surprised. His lawyer is a fella name of Pat Lenihan. He used to be one of Frank Heaton's boys before he went out on his own. Real smart cookie, and he knows everyone and all the angles. His office is over on 231st too, between Broadway and Kingsbridge Avenue. Now, Monaghan's kid has no record and the reason I know that is we just opened a case from a girl who runs around with him and his friends. Mary Breen's her name. Seems all these good boys and girls had a cocktail party in a vacant lot on Kingsbridge Road last Friday and the girl had too much to drink and some young Lothario tried to put his you know what in her you know where. Virtue had the victory and the young man failed in his attempt, but in a moment of good cheer, nonetheless, pissed all over her and possibly something worse. Nice kids, don't you think? Danny Monaghan was an organizer of this party, but the Breen girl's best friend Annie, who, by the way, is Carla Rink's daughter says that Danny was already in the wind with a young paramour before this unseemly little episode occurred. I checked the JD file and asked about him, but he's clean. Goes to Cathedral Prep downtown and his mother works for the rectory and is very close with Father Dunphy, who happens to be very close with our precinct commander Captain Walsh," Devine said, then exhaled loudly. "What else do you need to know, boys?" he asked after catching his breath.

"Well," Cairn said, "the father sounds like he's a bad egg, but he isn't in the picture. What do you know about the kid?"

"Not much more than I told you. We got six new rookies in February and a couple of them have had a few run-ins with Monaghan and his friends. One guy in particular brought us the Mary Breen case. He also brought us the additional information that Mary Breen is also the neighborhood jerk-off queen and is well known for her handiwork, pardon the pun."

"Who's that?" Asked Widelsky

"Kid name of Clay, young guy, nice looking, very observant and he's serious, but not goofy serious. He'll make a good cop someday. I know the type. Not at all intimidated or shy about sticking his head in the door and asking a question, or sharing some information. That is unless he gets Walt. You know Walt. Raises the eyebrows, then ignores you unless it's golf."

"Clay, that was the kid on our job today," said Cairn.

"Yeah, those rookies been bouncing between here and the Boulevard the last couple of weeks," said Devine.

"Anything else, pertinent you can think of?" inquired Widelsky.

"I could talk about Monaghan until the cows come home, but what you have to remember is he's an animal and a strange bird. This is a man who's tough and mean. He's a man who likes to drink and have a good time, and is something of a whoremaster to boot. But he gets up for work every day, and when the construction business is slow and he's on unemployment, he's putting up drywall with some donkey contractor that hangs out in Bongos. Every payday he puts the cash on the table and no one can say Mike Monaghan doesn't support his family or pay his bills. Now, the daughter has no use for him and she went to Liverpool to stay with her mother's family. I think she's going to nursing school there. But what you can't lose sight of is that if his kid had anything to do with this murder, Mike Monaghan will move Heaven and Earth to get him off. And that makes him a very dangerous man."

"I guess that pretty much covers it," Cairn. said.

"Hey, I'm here and I'll keep my ears open. Talk to that rookie Clay about the Monaghan kid, he may know a little more. As for me, I can talk about the father all day, but the kid's just a kid without much history."

"One more thing," Cairn said. "What about the mother? She seemed nice."

"Mary's a saint. Some Irish got that way about them. They'll stand on a sinking ship and ignore the lifeboat rather than leave one of their own behind. Maybe she thinks he'll turn over a new leaf someday. Maybe she just enjoys being able to pay all of her bills and not worry where the next nickel's coming from? Who knows? She is extremely close to Father Dunphy. I don't know what that means, but she's strange," Devine said with a shrug of his shoulders.

Devine finished and sat in his chair smiling. Cairn and Widelsky got up to leave, then Widelsky asked Devine, "One final thing, we got another party in this mystery we've got to check out. Her name is Sophie Cruz and lives over on Kingsbridge Avenue. Does her name ring a bell?"

"Let me check the Soundex cards."

Devine went into an alcove off the squad room where there was a line of file cabinets. He called out, "You got an address on Kingsbridge Avenue?"

"...3425, the Kingsbridge Gardens."

Devine came back several minutes later and said, "We don't have a thing on that name. I know the address. Two new buildings facing one another, 3425 is the smaller one, but we have nothing for that address or name. Sorry."

"Billy, you're a gentleman and a great help," Cairn said as he shook his hand.

"Any time, boys, always my pleasure, and Frank," he said looking at Widelsky, who was almost out the office door. "Be patient, the fine art of detection is in listening."

Widelsky didn't respond and waved his hand as he went out the door. Cairn followed, and neither man spoke until they were back outside of the precinct and on their way to Sophie's address.

"What a fucking gasbag that guy is," said a tired Widelsky.

"I think he's pretty entertaining."

"Entertaining, you think he's entertaining? I think he just likes to hear himself talk."

"Well, he gave us the full picture on Monaghan, didn't he?"

"More than we needed. I don't give a red rat's ass if his aunt lived in the same building as Monaghan's family or any of the other bullshit. I ain't writing a biography. Just the facts, just like *Dragnet*, that's all we need. What a fucking gasbag," Widelsky repeated several more times

The trip from the Summit Place Precinct to Sophie's building took less than five minutes, and it was after eight o'clock when the two detectives entered the lobby. The lobby door was locked and they looked at the directory and rang the buzzer for Sophie's apartment. They rang several times, but received no answer. After a few minutes the elevator opened and a teenage girl exited it and opened the lobby door. She let in Cairn and Widelsky and went on her way. The two detectives took the elevator up to the sixth floor and went to Sophie's apartment. They rang the bell repeatedly and they listened at the door, but received no response and heard no noise from inside the apartment. Sophie's apartment was off an open terrace and they decided to park behind the building and wait until she returned home. If they parked their car on the street behind the building they would be able to watch the terrace and see her enter the apartment.

At eleven-thirty she hadn't returned home, and they decided to call it a night. They had spent over three hours sitting behind her building and they had discussed what they knew about the case to exhaustion.

On the way back to the precinct, Widelsky punched the top of the dashboard with his fist and said, "What a wasted day. We've been running pillar to post trying to connect the dots and we ain't done shit. We didn't talk to the doctor at the hospital. We didn't speak with the ambulance attendants who first treated the victims. We don't even know if Mr. Weiss made it home from Montreal. Who spoke to him tonight? Oh yeah, he's coming in tomorrow with his attorney. We're supposed to be the primary detectives on this case, and I feel like we're two green dicks assigned to pick up all the loose ends. This ain't going the right way, believe me, it ain't right."

Cairn slowed the car down, turned to Widelsky, and said, "Frank, calm down. There is only so much anyone can accomplish in a day. Tomorrow we'll find out all the information on the crime scene and the exact cause of death. We'll speak with Mr. Weiss and everything will start to gel. Plus, this story will be in the morning papers, and who knows what witnesses will turn up. Go home, have a beer, give Terry a squeeze and relax, just relax."

"It should be so easy, my friend, it should be so easy," Widelsky said with defeat in his voice.

Chapter Twenty-Seven

Ruth Goolnick used her key to enter Lee Futerman's apartment. She had a quart of milk and a small box of custard filled éclairs she had picked up in Shelvyn's Bakery on Riverview Avenue. Lee heard her coming in the door and called out, "Is that you, Ruthie?"

"No, it's the old lady burglar that brings gifts."

"I'm in the kitchen."

"That's where you always are, what else is new?"

Ruth went into the kitchen and gave Lee a kiss on the top of his head. Lee had the crossword puzzle from the Sunday *Times* open on the kitchen table and said to Ruth, "Who was Polonius' daughter?"

"Ophelia, dummy."

Lee giggled, scribbled in her answer, and said, "You're an encyclopedia at times. Now I need help with this one."

"Stop, I'm not here to help you do your homework, or anything else. If you want to waste time doing crossword puzzles, you'll have to do them without my help. I brought you the milk for the cat and a little treat. Now make us a pot of coffee while I go upstairs and change, and put that silly puzzle away. We have a lot to talk about," she scolded.

Lee laughed and said, "Okay, but we have to hurry. The car service called and they're picking me up at eight-fifteen. It shouldn't take more than twenty-five minutes to reach the airport at this time of the evening."

Lee made a small pot of coffee and put out two plates and two coffee mugs.

Ruth came back downstairs and had changed from her fashionable business attire to a pair of khaki shorts and a light sleeveless blouse. She opened the pastry box and put an éclair on each of their plates. Lee poured the coffee, and as she was stirring milk into her mug, she said, "I didn't like those two detectives. Do you know anything about them?"

"I spoke with Frank Duffy, and he said they were pretty reliable and competent fellows. The Major Case squad has a good reputation, and he said they go pretty much by the book. If you got a bad feeling, it's probably because they don't have much to go on and they're pressing, not much more than that. Anyway, they didn't kill anybody."

"I know that, I'm just worried for Henry's sake. I don't know why, but he's always had a weakness for women and it'll destroy him," Ruth said with real concern.

"Henry's a big boy and it's time to pay the piper. Duffy said he spoke with the ME and it's a clear case of murder with Mrs. Campos. That's the cleaning lady. I'm going to take Henry straight to the hospital to see Maria. She's in intensive care, and God knows but she'll survive this. Then I'm going to have a heart to heart with Henry, former boss to subordinate, old friend to old friend, and lawyer to client, whatever it takes to get the truth from him. If what you believe is true, that Sophie's child is Henry's, that means that Sophie's as good a suspect as anyone, and that Henry could some way be implicated."

"Oh, bull," exclaimed Ruth. "Henry's no more capable of murder than you are. Less come to think of it."

"Why do you say that?"

"Because, well," she hesitated and then said quickly and heatedly, "I know him. He's soft. There's nothing hard about him, never was. That's why he left the prosecutor's office. He hates conflict. Did you ever hear him carry on when he has to go to court for an eviction hearing? He's never done many of those. He's the kind of lawyer who works double time to reach a resolution without using the courts. That's one of the reasons he's built up such a fine practice. He's not a fighter. He's a conciliator. People like that don't conspire to commit murder. If Maria found out Henry was the father of Sophie's child, what would she do? Nothing, that's what she'd do. That woman is a gold digger. Say what you want, but I know character."

"Eat your éclair, they're very good," Lee responded, not wanting to pursue the conversation further.

"The discussion's over?"

"We'll talk about it when I get home. After I've picked up Henry and gone to the hospital and everything else. When I get home, I'll ring your bell and come upstairs and share it all with you. No point in speculating," Lee answered as he cut his éclair and put too large a piece into his mouth.

"You're such a slob." Ruth laughed.

After they finished the coffee and éclairs, Ruth went back upstairs to her apartment. Lee put his tie and jacket back on and promptly at eight-fifteen the checker cab from All Boro Taxi was in front of his house.

Chapter Twenty-Eight

Mike Monaghan's trip to the racetrack was a profitable one. Every so often Chick Nathan and Vince Lobianco had a good tip on a race and they let Mike in on it. There was always a catch, and it was a simple one: you couldn't share the information with anyone else, and you couldn't be too greedy with your bet. The horse was Wonderluck in the sixth race. The odds were originally posted at twenty to one, but by race time they had decreased significantly to around six to one, and it was evident that there were a few more insiders than Nathan and Lobianco. Monaghan bet him at twenty dollars across the board. Wonderluck won the race and Monaghan pocketed over two hundred thirty dollars. After he cashed in his winning tickets, he bid his associates good night and headed for the parking lot. That was pin money for his upcoming four day Fourth of July trip to the shore with Carla Rink, and it temporarily put him in a better mood. He was going to stop at Bongos and have a few beers to salute his good luck at the track, but decided to go straight home and get a good night's rest instead. His work crew was starting an hour earlier the next day, and he wanted to greet the day rested and hangover free. More importantly, he needed time to think clearly about Danny's dilemma. He knew Cleary hated him and the humiliating way in which he squished his face in Pete's Bridge Lounge last year was a sure motive for revenge. Seeing Cleary earlier in the evening holding court with the old farts club reminded Monaghan of what a sneaky little gossip Cleary was and how he might, foolish as it may seem, talk Danny up as a suspect. *I've got to put a cork in his mouth*, he thought, *but hurting him will only put the cops on my doorstep again.* He exited the expressway at 230th Street, made a left turn and then a right turn onto Bailey Avenue. He drove past 2810 looking for a parking space and eventually made a U-turn and parked in an open spot in front of the playground next to PS 22 just south of the intersection of Kingsbridge Road and Bailey Avenue. He walked across the street and made his way past Pete's Bridge Lounge. The lounge had two large front windows, and as he was walking by he looked in and saw Cleary sitting at the bar. Cleary was with a couple of the younger guys from the neighborhood, guys in their early to late twenties. Monaghan felt his adrenaline surge and was tempted to go into the bar and pull Cleary outside and give him a beating. He knew, just knew, that Cleary was milking the homicide for all it was worth, and Danny had to be a part of the story. No one ever paid much attention to Tim Cleary or his opinions and this was a time when he had a story to tell and because it involved murder he could find a ready audience. Monaghan got to the front stoop of the building. He looked at his wristwatch. It was ten-thirty and it was a joke in Pete's Bridge lounge that if Tim Cleary hadn't left the bar by eleven on a work night, his mother would call the bartender and tell him to send Tim home. His impulse was to walk around to the alleyway and wait in the back hallway near the entrance to Cleary's apartment. *It wouldn't take more than a few well-placed punches and kicks to jumble Cleary's memory,* he thought.

Monaghan went down the street, past the front of the building and entered the alleyway. The alleyway was dark, and there were lights on in very few of the rooms that faced it. Most of the rooms on that side of the building were kitchens and bathrooms, with only two lines of bedrooms. He was sure no one saw him as he went to the back and entered the rear hallway. Cleary's apartment door was opposite the door to the carriage room, a room where tenants stored baby carriages and bicycles. Cleary would probably leave the bar and go up the front steps to the first courtyard and go to the entrance for the carriage room hallway. That would be more practical than walking down to the alleyway. Also, the alleyway was dark while the courtyard was well lit. Cleary could then walk through the carriage room to his apartment. While Monaghan was waiting for him he lit a cigarette. He was only several feet from Cleary's front door and could hear Mrs. Cleary's television blaring through the metal door. He listened and heard the shuffle of her feet as she walked across the bare floors of her apartment. She had a hacking cough that was from the endless Benson and Hedges cigarettes she smoked, and Monaghan could see her in a drab and faded housecoat pacing the floor with an ashtray in her hand, smoking and waiting for her Tim to come home. He waited and pondered; should he kill Cleary or not? It was a big risk, then a new thought struck him. *Why get the cops involved anymore than they are?* he thought. *Anything happens to Cleary and the heat's on me and possibly Danny. There has to be a better way.* Without further deliberation he knocked on Cleary's door. The heavy thud of his hand on the metal door in the cavernous hallway created a drum-like echo. He only had to bang twice and heard Mrs. Cleary shuffling toward the door. She opened the peephole and said without hesitation, almost as if she'd been expecting him, "What do you want, Monaghan?"

"Just a few minutes of your time, Mrs. Cleary."

She kept the peephole open for a moment and all was still. He could see her head pull away from the peephole, then a cloud of cigarette smoke streamed through it and it snapped closed. He heard her unlock the door and slowly open it. "Well, come in, but you're not welcome," she said bitterly.

Monaghan entered the apartment and closed the door behind him. He smiled and walked past Mrs. Cleary and went from the foyer to the living room and sat down. Mrs. Cleary had a ballgame on the television.

"You're a sports fan too?" he snidely inquired.

"What do you want?" Mrs. Cleary said belligerently.

"It's not what I want. It's more a case of what you want, if you get my drift?"

"Listen, Monaghan, is this some joke? I don't know what you're getting at, and if you can't spit it out, then there's the door. You've caused me enough heartache," she said. She stood defiantly in the middle of the room with a cigarette in one hand and an ashtray in the other, with her lower lip jutted out. She was a female replica of her son, but with far more fight and pluck than he'd ever demonstrated.

"Hey, I didn't tell him to bet the wrong team, then skip town without paying his dues, and there's other things, but you can ask him."

"He didn't skip town, he went on vacation," she nearly hissed.

"Vacation," he snorted. "He had his annual trip to Puerto Rico on my boss's tab. He's down there chasing…" and he caught himself for a moment, then continued. "Well, you might as well know the truth. He's down there chasing whores on somebody else's dollar and that ain't right. And that's what goes on with those vacations he takes with your friend Fogarty. And there's something else too, but I'll let it go now," he said sadly, as revealing all that he knew about Cleary would be too much for the woman.

Mrs. Cleary put her cigarette out in the ashtray and gave out with a great laugh. "Chasing whores, is that what you think?"

209

"Think! I know damn well what he does; everything, lady, everything."

"You do, don't you. You, the big strapping ladies man that's no better than a dog in heat with some woman in the laundry room two weeks ago. And your pants hanging down around your ankles like some circus clown. That must have been a sight."

Monaghan's faced reddened, and he said, "I'm not here about me, I'm here about you."

"What, are you looking to break my poor Tim's nose again?"

"Listen, he made a mistake and…" he said with an added edge in his voice, "he oughta stop looking through the peephole at little girls when he's in his skivvies. But you don't know about that, do you?" he asked.

"I don't know and I don't care. Make up what you wish, you're a no good bully," she said back, with fire in her eyes, and without acknowledging the reference to the peephole she said, "He was going to pay his debt."

"It don't work that way," Monaghan said menacingly.

"You don't scare me," she replied angrily. "You know what I dislike about you most?" Monaghan didn't answer, and she said, "It's your poor excuse for what you did to him. I don't care if it was about money or something else. I may be an old fool, but I'm not stupid. At times my son has the maturity of a child and you should know that. You're a Goddamn bully. If you had a problem with him, why didn't you come to me?"

"It didn't involve you."

"I pray every night you get yours, every night," she proudly said.

Monaghan looked at her, his face expressionless. His earlier impulse to kill Tim was diminished by Mrs. Cleary. Monaghan was not a sentimental man, but he realized that the woman hated him and no threat of harm to her son would vanquish that hate. *What can I do?* he thought. *Kill the son and the mother? Where will that leave me?* He stood up, reached into his pocket and took out his winning bankroll from the racetrack. He peeled off five twenty-dollar bills and handed them to Mrs. Cleary, and said, "You're right. I don't know what his doctor bills were for the broken nose, but he can put this toward his next vacation. Just remind him, the only people who make money from gambling are the bookies."

Mrs. Cleary gave him a puzzled look and silently accepted the money. She took the one hundred dollars and folded the bills and put them in her bathrobe. She lit another cigarette and inhaled deeply.

Monaghan left the apartment without saying anything. As he was walking through the carriage room, he intercepted Cleary.

The doorman looked at him, and though he was slightly inebriated and was walking unsteadily, he straightened up and stopped in his tracks. "Monaghan," he slurred. "Goo…good to see you," he then stammered.

"Sad Sack, your old lady's a tough old bird, you know that?" Monaghan said as he continued walking past him.

"Mom's the best," he said with relief in his voice as he went in the other direction.

Monaghan stepped back out into the courtyard. He lit another cigarette; it must have been his tenth of the night. He leaned against the stone pillar for the second flight of steps up to the main courtyard. *Those two sorry bastards*, he thought. *They don't know how close they came to getting it.* There was a cool breeze blowing in the early summer night and it had a cleansing effect on him. *No point getting my hands dirty, just yet*, he concluded.

Chapter Twenty-Nine

Tim Cleary fumbled with his key in the door lock. After several attempts he successfully inserted the key into the keyhole and unlocked the door. He opened it and stepped into his apartment. His mother was standing there in the foyer with her cigarette and ashtray.

"You're drunk," she said with disgust.

"I am not," he said with a flourish of his hand as he turned toward the bathroom.

"Go to the bathroom and wash your face, then see me in the living room," she ordered.

Tim cautiously walked to the bathroom and had to prop his two hands against the wall to stay upright while he urinated. His mother came to the bathroom door and shrieked, "Jesus Christ, you're peeing all over the floor. If you can't stand up straight, then sit down."

"Stop yelling," he cried. "It's going into the bowl, I got good aim."

"Wash your face and hands and come inside."

When Tim was finished in the bathroom, he went to the living room. The television was off and there was a glass of chocolate milk and a peanut butter sandwich on the snack tray next to Tim's chair. "Sit down and eat something."

"I'm not hungry."

"Just eat. It's already eleven o'clock, and you'll be sick for work if you don't eat something now."

Tim didn't answer and started to eat the sandwich.

While he was eating, his mother said, "You know, I don't approve of drinking on a work night. It's one thing if a man goes out on Saturday night and has a good time, but there is no excuse for doing this on a Thursday night, and there is never any excuse for not being able to stand up straight and keep control of yourself."

Tim took a drink of the chocolate milk, and said, "I know. It was just one of those nights. There was a lot of talk and the beers were going down. Ne, ne, next thing you know," he stuttered, "I'm drunk."

"You look silly. Whatever made you think plaid Bermuda shorts, black knee high socks and wingtips were fashionable?"

"I, I, bought the shorts in Furhman's Department store. Moe told me that the wingtips go with the shorts, it's what every, everyone wears to look smart."

"You're stuttering. You stutter when you drink too much. I wanted to talk to you about something important, but it can wait until morning."

"You, you look funny too," he said with a giggle.

"I don't care what I look like, and it's none of your business," she said with annoyance.

"Well, how come you can make fun of me?" he replied defiantly.

"Because I'm your mother," she snapped.

Tim took a drink of his chocolate milk and another bite of his sandwich. They sat there silently for ten more minutes, each studying the other, but reluctant to comment on what he or she observed.

Tim's feelings were hurt. His mother was all too quick to judge him, and her criticisms stung. Moe, the salesman in Furhman's, had shown him a catalog with pictures of men in shorts with high socks and wing tip shoes. It was part of the collegiate look, and it was a look he admired. *Look at you,* he thought. It seemed his mother was either dressed in a housecoat or a bathrobe. She was bony and the skin on her face, neck and arms sagged. She wore black penny loafers and her brown stockings were always rolled down like donuts just above her knees. Her hair was dirty gray, and she wore it in a braid piled on top of her head. He often wondered if she ever washed her hair. She had a face like a walnut shell, brown and wrinkled. It was severely weathered by the constant cloud of cigarette smoke her chain smoking created. Cigarettes were more vital to her than food. Ashtrays overflowing with charred cigarette butts adorned every tabletop in their apartment. Stale tobacco was the only scent he could associate with his mother. There was nothing soft or feminine about her. That's how she looked for as far back as he could remember, even when his father was still alive. She was opinionated and eccentric, but she was all he had in the world and he desperately needed her support and approval in everything he did. Tim put the empty glass on the plate and stood up. "Ma, thanks for the snack. You're right, I shouldn't have drunk so much. I'm sorry," he slurred apologetically. She didn't answer and he went off to his room.

Mrs. Cleary watched as Tim walked away. Her thoughts went to Monaghan. *What did he want tonight? I should have never taken his money. I should have thrown it at him. Why is he so mean and such a big strong man and my sweet Tim with a heart of gold a little formless pudding of a man?* She went to her bedroom and propped two pillows on the bed. She turned on her radio and put out the light. An instrumental version of Stardust was playing, and she tried not to think and just concentrate on the music, but Monaghan's remark about the peephole and little girls and Tim in his skivvies had given her a terrible shock. She'd ignored what he said, but it was discomforting. Was there something about her son she didn't know, she pondered? Finally, she convinced herself that Monaghan was lying. Had Tim done something she would have heard about it. Few things that happened in the building escaped her attention. She felt better and eventually the music faded into the night and she fell off to sleep.

Mrs. Cleary woke up at five-thirty Friday morning. She put the kettle on for tea and washed her face and brushed her teeth. At six she woke Tim up and told him to hurry and shower and dress. She left the apartment and went to the candy store next to Pete's Bridge Lounge. Mr. Sherman, the store owner, opened promptly at six every morning. He was undoing a bundle of papers and Mrs. Cleary bought two packs of Benson and Hedges cigarettes and the morning paper. Tim was already dressed when she got back to the apartment. Millie Campos' murder had made page two of the newspaper. There were two stories. One was the usual police account of a murder, and the second was a profile on Mrs. Campos and her family. Mrs. Cleary read it with great interest and relief when she saw there was no mention of the doorman and the role he had played in the discovery of the victim. The story mentioned that the murder occurred in the Weiss' apartment and said Mrs. Weiss was taken to Borough Hospital and was in intensive care, but there was no additional information about the cause of her injury. Tim read the story while his mother toasted his English muffin and brewed his tea.

"We have to talk about this," she said.

"About what?" he answered testily.

"The murder."

"Why?"

"How do you feel this morning?"

"A little fuzzy, but it'll wear off," he answered, happy that she wasn't scolding him again.

"You were quite the celebrity last night with your little murder story, weren't you?" she said sarcastically.

"What do you mean, Ma?"

"I mean you couldn't wait to put on your new outfit and get out of the house last night so you could tell everyone about the murder in the building where you work," she said as she put the English muffin in front of him.

"I told some people, but they wanted to know."

"Why would they want to know about something they wouldn't know about unless you told them?"

"Well, they saw the cops at Monaghan's."

"You can be such a fool, Timothy Cleary. No one in this building would have known about the murder unless you told them. You couldn't wait to be the big shot and tell everyone about it. I took a walk down the alleyway last night and I saw you talking to Healy and Hackendorf and the rest of them that sit outside at night. And then when they'd heard enough, you went to Pete's and repeated yourself to anyone who'd listen. Am I right?"

"Kind of, but it was really a big story."

"Big story, I bet it was, buster. Who do you think paid me a visit last night?"

"Did that cop come here, the detective that threatened me, the one I told you about?"

"No, I would have been happy if the police were here. The police can bully you, but they won't kill you. Monaghan was here," she said gravely.

"I saw him in the carriage room when I was coming home. I meant to tell you, but you were mad and I forgot. Jesus, that's right. He said you were tough or something, I don't remember, but he scared me. You know, I was walking through the carriage room and he was just there. Why was he seeing you?"

"You told me last night at dinner, the dinner you rushed through, that you told the police you saw Danny Monaghan near the building around the time they think the murder occurred, didn't you?"

"Not quite. They were pressing me for times I did things and saw things, and I just told them that around the time I was going to lunch I saw him on his bike coming from the direction of the alleyway. That's all. Why? I never accused Danny."

"Well, Monaghan came here last night, and I don't know what he came for because it didn't make much sense. I gave him a piece of my mind and he gave me a hundred dollars. He said you could use it for your next vacation. I don't think he gives a tinker's damn about breaking your nose, I think it was a threat," she said with concern.

"He threatened you?" Tim replied, visibly upset.

"It was very strange. He walked in and made himself comfortable. I'm sorry I took the money, but I did and I think his message was that you better keep your mouth shut."

"About what?"

"Did you tell anyone about Danny Monaghan making a delivery to that apartment yesterday?"

"Well, yeah. But everyone knew the cops were at Monaghan's apartment. Mrs. Healy saw them go in."

"You don't know why they were there, do you?"

"Ma, I'm not the sharpest knife in the drawer, but I'm not that dumb. Why else?"

Mrs. Clearly squeezed her right hand into a tight little ball and punched her son in the shoulder with as much force as she could muster. He pushed her away, then she said venomously, "You are an idiot! The police have been to Monaghan's apartment before and they've taken him out in handcuffs before. Maybe his son had something to do with this, or maybe he didn't, but whatever happened you're not going to be a part of it. Do you understand?"

"But I already am!" he cried.

"Those detectives are going to speak with you again, probably today. They'll want a statement and maybe the newspaper people will be around the building too. Just remember one thing, you're not the police. You're a doorman. If they ask you about Danny Monaghan and when you saw him, act unsure. Act confused. I don't want you to be a part of it," she said with insistence.

"But I am," he repeated. "I told that cop Widelsky I saw him about one o'clock. I can't lie."

"Why not?"

"Because it ain't right."

"Oh, Tim, you are such a child. You told me the whole story last night when you came home from work. I paid attention. You said Danny came with a delivery around twelve and you next saw him at one. You made him a suspect, and if the police were at his apartment questioning him last night it was because of what you told them. You made him a suspect and that has to be why his father was here last night. Do you think the police are going to look out for you because you're doing what's right?" she said with exasperation.

"I didn't think of it that way. I saw the lady who was waiting for Mrs. Weiss go by on the number one bus when I was leaving work. I called the cops last night and told them that, too. Maybe she did it?"

"I don't care who did it. I don't care about anyone else but Monaghan. Do you understand? I couldn't go on living if something happened to you," she sobbed.

"Mom, don't cry," he said as he got up and put his arms around her and gave her a hug.

"Fine," she said as she wiped the rears from her eyes. "But you can't point a finger at Monaghan, do you understand?"

"But what if he did it?"

"That's a problem for the police to solve. We can't beat Mike Monaghan, and if you hurt his son, I know he'll get you for it," she said dramatically.

"What do I tell the cops if they come by again?" he said in a panic. "What do I say? They're not stupid. They'll know I'm lying."

"You just tell them that you spent all night retracing your steps and now you're really uncertain about times. Maybe you saw him at one o'clock, or maybe it was twelve o'clock. The murder upset you so much that you're confused. Just keep saying that. Now eat your muffin and get ready to leave for work. I want you to call me every hour to let me know you're all right, do you understand?"

Tim was totally confused by all that his mother had told him and wanted to call in sick and miss the day, but he knew she wouldn't let him. Her fear of Monaghan wasn't exaggerated, and he knew his mother was right. He brushed his teeth and gave his mother a kiss goodbye. He had never thought of Danny Monaghan as a murderer, but the visit from Mike Monaghan was a sign that Danny might be involved. He left the apartment and walked to the bus stop. The bus arrived minutes later, and he took a seat in the back of the bus, and as it was slowly climbing Kingsbridge Road he recalled his mother's criticism of his clothing from the night before. *God, she's always smothering me and telling me what to do*, he thought. *That big prick Monaghan broke my nose last year and his snotty fucking son does nothing but insult me. Why the fuck was he at our house last night? I don't care what Ma says. I'm telling the cops everything*, he decided. Fuck Monaghan. "I'm tired of being a momma's boy, and I'm tired of being a nothing," he mumbled under his breath. "Tired of being a nothing."

Chapter Thirty

It was very cold and dark. Her head was on fire, but everything else was cold. She remembered hearing Rudy's voice earlier, but it was strange. He was telling her he loved her and he called her "sweetheart," but he was talking in English, a language he didn't speak. She was sure it was Rudy, but it was only his voice. She didn't know if she was asleep or awake, and the world as she recalled it seemed very distant. The cold frightened her. She was confused and the consciousness she was experiencing was nothing more than a tangle of fearful thoughts. Her world was dark and lonely. There were no light switches or heat. She saw herself turning on a faucet, but nothing came out, the faucet was dry. She suddenly felt hungry but there was no food. She was immobile, in pain and the sunlight and comfort that played such an important part of her life were gone. She wanted to talk, but she didn't know how to and it seemed as if a great weight had descended on her head and she had the sensation of fading away. Her thoughts and her realization of consciousness were fading too and she fell back into a cold tomb of silence.

The sounds of a conversation nearby gave her a start and she opened her eyes. The room was blurry and she didn't know where she was. She went to lift her arm to feel her head, but the arm was weighed down and there was a hose taped to her elbow. Something was stuck in her nose and it was uncomfortable, but she couldn't move that either. She was frightened and she felt the urine seeping through her bedclothes. There was something wrong with her eyesight. She couldn't see from her right eye. She didn't know if there was a covering over it or if she was blind. There was some sensation of light on the periphery, but that was all. Her left eye was itchy. Her vision from that eye was slightly blurred, but she could see. The room was hazy and it was hard to focus. There were two people at the front of her bed with their backs to her. They were talking and each was wearing white clothing. Suddenly, with a jolt she realized she was in a hospital room. She had no idea what had happened to her. There were machines in the room, and though she couldn't make out the conversation the two people in front of her were having, she knew they were talking about her. She let out a moan and the two people turned around. One was a woman; she was dressed in white and had a starched hat on her head. The hat looked like it had wings. The other person was a man. He had on a white cotton lab coat and a stethoscope around his neck. He smiled at her and said, "Oh, Alice, looks like our patient is awake."

The woman in white came to the side of the bed. She said, "Hello, Mrs. Weiss, how are you? I'm Alice, I'm a nurse, and I'm here to help you?"

Maria looked at her with her good eye. She was afraid to speak. In her dreams she couldn't speak and she was so frightened and confused she just blinked her eye. The man came over to the other side of the bed and shone a small penlight into Maria's left eye. He removed something from her right eye and shone the light in there. Her vision from that eye was severely limited. She could see the light, but couldn't make anything out. He said, "And I'm Dr. Snyder and I'm here to help too. Can you hear me?"

Maria blinked her eyes and said, "Yes." She felt herself urinating again, but it was the relief she felt at being able to speak. Her head was throbbing and when she had awoken she thought she couldn't speak. Her throat burned and it hurt to talk, but she went on, "What, what?" she said, then rested.

Dr. Snyder said, "Don't try to talk just listen. Can you listen? Just blink your eyes."

Maria blinked her eyes and said, "Yes, yes."

"Good," the doctor responded. "You are a very lucky woman. You have an aneurysm. It didn't rupture, but it was leaking and we had to operate. You're alive and all of your vital signs look good. There may be some aftereffects, but we'll have to be patient. The important thing is you're conscious and talking. That's very encouraging. Your husband was here last night and he'll be back this morning."

"Rudy?"

"I thought it was Henry?"

Maria said nothing, then smiled. "Yes, Henry," she whispered.

"Nurse O'Brien is going to clean you up and change your dressings. I'll be back later. Do you remember anything from yesterday?"

Maria closed her eyes and tried to collect her thoughts. She was confused, but she remembered her dreams and being in a cold dark place. She thought of a subway tunnel, then she saw a woman. The woman was angry and her face looked twisted with hate. The name Sophie occurred to her. She vaguely remembered the woman cursing at her and throwing something at her. She couldn't remember what it was, but it was significant. She didn't know why, but it was ugly and she didn't like the recollection. She tried to remember who Sophie was, but all she could see was the angry face. There was something disturbing about it and it worried her. The doctor was talking to the nurse and Maria opened her eyes and said, "Sophie, Sophie did it."

"Did what?"

"Sophie, Sophie," she repeated, then closed her eyes. Maria was conscious of the doctor and nurse being there, but she didn't have the energy to keep her eyes open any longer or to speak.

"You just rest now, Mrs. Weiss," Alice said.

"Alice, I have to make my rounds. I'll be back in about an hour. Step outside for a minute."

Alice followed him to the front desk for the Intensive Care Unit and the doctor spoke to her quietly. "You know this woman was possibly a murder victim yesterday?"

"Yes, I heard the story when I came in this morning."

"The police were waiting around all afternoon and into the evening. They're anxious to speak with her. Under no circumstances are you to let anyone other than her husband into that room to speak with her. She might be a suspect, I don't know, but our job is to get her the hell out of ICU. Once she's stable, she can deal with the police."

"Nobody but the husband, I'll put a note on the chart and one at the desk."

"Very well, I'll be back later."

The Intensive Care Unit was a series of curtained cubicles arranged around a circular nurse's station. There was one nurse for every two patients and a support staff of technicians. Nurse O'Brien and a nurse's aide went into Maria's cubicle. Maria woke up and she felt herself being bathed and changed. The sheets were removed from her bed and dry warm ones were put in their place. Some of her bandages were changed and the bed was cranked into an upright position and she was given cold water to sip through a straw. The nurses worked quietly with little conversation, but their attentions were coordinated and in a matter of minutes Maria had been bathed and massaged and her bedding replaced. Nurse O'Brien took her temperature and measured her pulse. When she was finished she said, "You just rest and maybe if you're feeling a little stronger later we can get you up and feed you some ice cream."

Maria wasn't hungry, but the thought of cold ice cream in her burning throat was pleasant. Her head was still burning and throbbing and she laid back to rest. She wanted to sleep, but her thoughts kept going back to the woman she called Sophie. Who was Sophie? When the doctor had mentioned a husband, she immediately thought of Rudy. When he said Henry, she was stunned for a moment, but then Henry's face came into her mind and she knew who he was. Rudy was so long ago and at first she wondered what had happened to him and in a flash it all came back to her. Rudy, her father, Amos, Henry, Guy, Sable's, the apartment at the Excelsior, one by one they entered her thoughts and she started to put her life in order. Still, what happened yesterday? Who was Sophie? Again, like a bright neon light blinking on and off she saw the name Sophie and the angry face and she remembered the subway. Sophie was Henry's secretary. Sophie had a terrible secret and hated her. Someone attacked her and Millie was on the floor, she recalled, and it was so vivid that she wanted to scream for help. Her breathing increased and she told herself to calm down. She was in a hospital and there were people all around. She was safe. Yesterday she'd had a terrible migraine and Sophie attacked her. She got sick and went home and found Millie on the floor. Someone came out of the closet just like the subway train came barreling out of the dark tunnel. Sophie and the subway were inextricably mixed in Maria's mind and she concluded that Sophie was the one who came out of her closet and hit her. She could see Sophie running past her. *My God!* she thought, *Millie's dead. Sophie tried to kill us both.* She was alert now, and she wanted to tell someone. She couldn't tell the nurse. There was a clock against the wall and it was eight-fifteen. It was morning because she could see the bright sunlight behind the closed blinds over the window. *If Henry was here last night, he'll be back this morning,* she thought. *I'll just wait for Henry.*

She lay there, in bed, watching the clock. At eight-thirty Henry came into the room. She didn't see him at first, but she felt his hand as it brushed against her cheek. She could detect the sweet scent of nicotine on his long fingers. She felt safe. Henry bent over and kissed her forehead and said, "Thank God, you're alive. Do you know what happened?"

"I'm confused," she said weakly.

"You should be. You've been through hell, sweetheart," he said soothingly.

"Where's Millie?"

"Not now, I'll tell you later."

"I know she's dead."

"You remember?"

"I think so," she said, with tears in her eyes.

"Do you know who did it?" he whispered.

"Sophie, I saw Sophie," she whispered back.

Henry pulled back his hand and bent over the bed. "Are you sure?"

"She followed me to the train and she was angry, very angry. I got sick and went home and found Millie." Maria closed her eyes and her breathing increased again.

"Not in the apartment?"

She didn't answer at first, then her eyes opened and she nodded her head and faintly whispered, and "Yes, in the closet. I need water."

Henry took the little water jug with the straw and placed it at her lips. She lifted her head off the pillow and sipped a little. She closed her eyes. "Let me sleep now."

Henry sat in the chair by her bed and watched her fall back to sleep. She had IV's in each arm and her head was heavily bandaged. He couldn't believe what she had said, and he had a sick feeling in his stomach. At eight forty-five he got up from his chair. He kissed her and said, "I'll be back later. I have a meeting with the police."

Maria was fast asleep and didn't acknowledge him.

Lee Futerman was in the waiting room and when Henry came out of ICU Lee said, "How is she?"

"She looks like she's been through the wringer. Her head's all bandaged, and I didn't even get to ask her how everything is, you know. She's weak."

"Does she know anything?"

"Yeah, she knows Millie's dead and she thinks Sophie's responsible."

"Sophie, she said Sophie?"

"Lee, we'll talk in the car. Let's wait until we're outside."

"Aren't you going to wait and speak with the doctor?"

"Let's go for a ride and discuss this issue. After we see the police we can come back and see Maria and Dr. Snyder."

Lee had parked his Ford Fairlane on a side street off Manor Parkway near the hospital. Once they were out of the building, Lee said, "Wow. This is some problem. Sophie had a fight with you and left Montreal a day early. She shows up at your apartment yesterday looking for Maria and Maria tells you today that Sophie did it. What do you think?"

Henry stopped to light a cigarette and said, "I can't believe it. Maybe if Maria was dead, but why Millie?"

"Maybe she meant to get Maria, but Millie got in the way."

"It doesn't add up. Maria was going to work at noon. Sophie knows on Thursdays she doesn't get home until ten or eleven and she also knew I was coming home yesterday. Why would she be in my apartment?"

"Okay, she followed Maria. Maria came home and she was following her the whole time and somehow got into the apartment and killed Millie and tried to kill Maria. I don't know. But why would Maria say it was Sophie?"

"Maria's not all there right now. I can tell. She's confused, maybe she had words with Sophie earlier in the day and that's what's on her mind. There's more to this. The real headache is what do I tell the police?"

"Tell them nothing. See what they know. You can put it on the table that you and Sophie were having an affair, but that's it, nothing else. Let's see what they have. I'm not letting anyone speak with Maria until we know what her condition is and she's able to give us a full explanation," Lee answered, now talking as an attorney and not Henry's friend.

"Fine, you're our lawyer. You call the shots, I'll listen."

"Great, it's almost nine, let's get a cup of coffee before we head over to see the police."

Chapter Thirty-One

Widelsky was the first to show up for work on Friday morning. He brewed a pot of coffee and was sitting at his desk reading the *Huguenot Times* account of Millie Campos' murder when the forensic detectives, Hogan and Smith came into the office. Hogan's left thumb was wrapped in gauze and Smith was saying as they entered the room, "Fingerprint men are supposed to have a deft touch, aren't they, Ritchie?"

"Tommy, it was freak accident, believe me," Hogan said with embarrassment.

"What happened to you?" Widelsky asked Hogan.

"You know those knives they sell at the State Fair, the ones that can cut through anything?"

"Yeah, I bought one of those last year," Smith exclaimed. "The guy putting on the demonstration cut through a block of frozen spinach. My wife and kids saw that and they had to have it. Cost me a buck ninety-nine, I think and we never used it."

"Same thing with me; we were all there and they saw the same demonstration and they had to have it. We use ours all the time. Ginny buys ice cream by the half-gallon and I keep it in the basement in a freezer. I've got five brats at home, so all the goodies get rationed. When we have ice cream for a treat, I use the knife to cut the half-gallon in half and then into five slices for each of the kids. It works great," Hogan said.

"What do you do with the other half, eat it yourself?" Widelsky said sarcastically, as he eyed Hogan's beach ball of a belly.

Hogan patted his stomach and said, "That's Budweiser, buddy, the ice cream we save for another night. Last night I'm talking and cutting the ice cream and my hand slipped and I sliced deep into my finger. I took eight stitches, can you believe that?"

"Frank, you were a butcher," Detective Smith said. "What do you think of those knives?"

"They suck, and I been to the State Fair more fucking times then I can count, and the only thing I ever bought that was worthwhile was the Belgian waffles."

"Frank, you're just no fun, no fun," Hogan said, laughing.

"Yeah, I know, but my kids are in bed by ten."

"What's that mean?"

"Hogan, you couldn't have finished up with the crime scene until after seven and by the time you got back to the office and logged everything and did a work up on some of the stuff, shit you had to be there several more hours. What time do you give your kids dessert, midnight?"

"Midnight, "Hogan scoffed. "I was home by eight o'clock."

"What happened to the evidence?" Widelsky asked with frustration.

Detective Smith chuckled and said, "Frank, in the forensics business we call it teamwork. Pearse and Rozek were working evenings. We held the scene, but shut it down for the evening and went back to the office and logged the evidence. Pearse developed all my photos and printed them and Rozek did the fingerprint work on what we have, so far. I have their reports right here," he said as he held up a brown manila envelope. "And I have one on one copies of Mrs. Weiss' prom pictures."

"Oh, Jesus Christ, I thought you just let it all sit," Widelsky said with relief.

"Whatever we uncovered yesterday was processed last night."

"Do you have anything?" Widelsky asked.

"Plenty of nothing if you want my opinion," Hogan said with a frown as he opened up the manila envelope and took out the one on one photos of Maria and a report of several pages.

"You can read it, but let me give you an overview." He put on a pair of eyeglasses and as he was about to speak Cairn came into the office.

"Good morning boys," he said gladly. "I see the great sleuth Ritchie Hogan has what appears to be several DD 4's in one hand and a large bandage in the other. What happened?"

"He's a clumsy smuck and it ain't worth listening to," Widelsky snidely said.

"Frank, you're so charming, and Phil," Hogan said as he bent his head and examined Cairn from head to toe, "is that your Sambo suit?"

"What do you mean?" Cairn said, feigning hurt feelings.

"Mint green suit, yellow shirt, yellow socks and light brown shoes, we used to call that an Uptown get-up. What're you taking numbers on the side?"

"Fuck off. You dress like a priest, Hogan. The two of you do. Black suits, white shirts and blue ties, you two look like you spend your off time in funeral parlors. Sambo suit my ass."

"I'll take Hogan's side on this argument, but let's get down to business, huh," Widelsky said.

Cairn laughed and said, "Let me in on it, please. What happened to your finger, Ritchie?"

"Jesus Christ," Widelsky grunted. "Tell him, just tell him so we can move on."

"I cut my finger with a knife when I was slicing ice cream last night. It was one of those miracle knives they were selling at the State Fair," Hogan said as he waved his bandaged thumb in the air.

"Oh, the knife with the two little prongs on the end and the super blade that never dulls?"

"Yeah, that one, why you got one?"

"Sure, my wife bought it at the fair when she went with her mother. Thing works well, but I can see where you have to be careful," Cairn responded. Smith and Hogan started to laugh after Cairn said he had one of the knives too.

"Gee, Frank, everyone has the knife but you. I wonder what that means?" Smith said.

"Fine, fine, I'm a smuck. Who cares, can we talk about the case?"

"Sure, now where was I?"

"You said you had plenty of nothing," Widelsky reminded him.

"Yeah, let me go over everything," Hogan said as he took off his eyeglasses and wiped the lenses with the wide part of his necktie. Hogan put his glasses back on and started to spread the copies of Maria's pictures on the desk. As he was doing that, Sergeant Kreppell walked into the office.

Kreppell was a compactly built man with a prematurely gray head of hair. He was wearing a brown suit and looked more like a lawyer and less like a cop than his co-workers. There was something studious about his face, and a clear and determined look in his slate blue eyes. Kreppell greeted everyone and said, "Hogan, you have some news? And what the hell did you do to your thumb? Are you going to be able to work today?"

"Yes, sir, it's nothing. I cut it with a knife and took eight stitches, but I'm right-handed so I don't see a problem."

"Great, let me grab a cup of coffee and then we'll go over the game plan for today," Kreppell said as he went into his office. He came out a moment later with his coffee cup and went over to the coffee pot and poured himself a cup.

As he was pouring his coffee Smith said, "Hey, Sarge, congratulations, I heard you're getting your bars next week. Is that true?"

"Yes, I got the word yesterday and best part is I'm staying right here," Kreppell said with a smile as he raised his coffee cup and toasted his subordinates.

"Congratulations," Cairn said.

"Ditto," Hogan said.

Widelsky said nothing.

"Okay, where are we at?"

Hogan picked up the DD 4 and started talking. "Before you came in I was telling Frank and Phil that I don't think we have much, at least much that makes sense. The bloody fingerprint on the ashtray is Maria Weiss'. There are some other partials on the ashtray, but they're heavily smudged. I covered every surface in the bedroom and came up with fifteen good lifts. I marked all the partial values, but I didn't lift them. I'll do those today. This is the breakdown on the bedroom prints, one we got one from the side of the wife's bureau and six from the woodwork around the husband's closet, and the remaining eight from the husband's bureau. I couldn't find anything but smudges or partial values with too many overlaps in the second bedroom. It looks like the room isn't used much, but is dusted every week. There was nothing in the bathroom but smudges, except for two good prints on the mirror. The tables in the hallway, living room and dining room were all freshly dusted and waxed. The cleaning lady was pretty efficient. Same thing with the kitchen, it was spotless. Now, the inside of the front door is painted in flat paint and I couldn't pick up anything but the outside, which is done in a high gloss over the metal surface, had twelve good lifts and multiple overlaps which is common for an entryway. The pantry I'll do this morning, and that may be our most important room."

"Why didn't you do that last night?" Widelsky asked.

"That was my call, Frank," Kreppell responded. "I figured Ritchie and Smitty would do a better job today. Crime scene work is not the same as running a foot race, that's all."

Kreppell looked at Hogan, and Hogan took his cue and continued with his report. "Now this is the interesting part. Rozek had the victim's prints and Mrs. Weiss' prints last night. He matched Mrs. Weiss to the bathroom mirror and the victim to the print on the side of Mrs. Weiss' bureau, that leaves fourteen unexplained prints and guess what? They're all from the same person. We have one of all five fingers of the right hand and another of the four fingers from the left hand, and that makes identification a cinch. Any bets that's Mr. Weiss?" Hogan asked.

"So, you ain't got shit, do you?" Widelsky asked.

"Not yet. We didn't do the outside of the door, and I have to see what I get out of the pantry today. Maybe Mrs. Weis is the murderer and we're looking for something that doesn't exist."

"You said yesterday that the woodwork in the bedroom was wiped clean, right?" Kreppell asked.

"The woodwork around the door as you enter the room and around Mrs. Weiss' closet along with the top of her bureau was clean. I thought it was strange, but maybe in retrospect I spoke too soon. She could be a very neat lady who doesn't touch too many things and nothing more. The fact that the place is so clean makes this job easy."

"You guys know that at some scenes you can lift a hundred prints, easy."

"What about the photographs, any prints on those?" Kreppell asked, trying to keep Hogan on track before he launched into one of his long-winded accounts of previous cases he'd worked on.

"Well, we had to make a decision last night on how to process them. Two of the three were still a little damp, with blood on some spots. We did one on one photographs of them, front and back, and later today I'm going to iodine fume them and see what comes up. Rozek wanted to spray them with Ninhydrin, which is great for bringing up old prints, but I figured we want what went on them yesterday. Problem with pictures and documents in general is that when people pick them up they all hold them in the same spot, the upper right corner and the lower left corner. I expect multiple overlays. But we'll see," Hogan said with a shrug of his shoulders.

"I thought the ME said she died almost instantly yesterday. Why so much blood?" Cairn asked no one in particular.

"Gravity," Kreppell replied. "You have a head wound, the head's loaded with blood, you make a hole, it drains out. If her heart was still pumping after she was hit, and she didn't die right away you could have had a small flood."

"I guess so."

Widelsky cleared his voice and said, "Seems to me you're making this more complicated than it is. We have the murder weapon. It has Mrs. Weiss' fingerprint on it. I assume you sent it to the lab, and we'll get a confirmation that it's the cleaning lady's blood and maybe a little trace evidence from her wound. What else do we need?"

"He's got a point," Cairn added. "There's no sign of a forced entry and no theft, at least from what I saw."

"You guys like it neat, don't you?" Kreppell said sarcastically.

"I think we look too hard sometimes, that's all," Widelsky answered. "Sometimes it just is what it is, a fucking ground ball and no bad hops."

"That's all well and good, but what about the delivery boy? What about the secretary and her ongoing affair with the husband? Don't you think we should rule all of those things out first before we put this to rest?" Kreppell said thoughtfully.

"Yeah, we have to run those leads down, but I think Frank has a point. The delivery boy was cute, but he has no record, and even though his old man's a blister we don't have any physical evidence or a witness or a motive that makes him a viable suspect. He made a delivery there that day. So what? Same thing with the secretary, she has a motive, but we need to put her in the apartment, and if she's going to kill anyone wouldn't it be Mrs. Weiss?" Cairn replied to Kreppell

"Slow down, it's nine-fifteen. Interview Weiss, then interview the secretary and check on the kid's alibis. After all that's been accomplished, we can regroup and go over this," Kreppell said with authority.

Cairn said, "That's fine, Sarge, but could Frank and me speak with you for a minute in private?"

"Sure, c'mon into the office. And Hogan, Smitty, I want you two back at that apartment, pronto. Process the pantry, then go back over every room. Hold the scene until we're through with Mr. Weiss. I want him there to confirm if anything was stolen. We can't rule out a burglary. Neither woman was sexually assaulted, but burglary is still a possibility."

"You got it, boss" Hogan answered.

Kreppell went into his office followed by Cairn and Widelsky. He sat behind his desk and pointed to the two wooden chairs in front of it. "What's up?"

"You seemed a little pissed with us yesterday," Cairn said.

"Pissed, in what way?"

"I don't know, but you didn't seem happy, and I got the feeling that something was up, that's all."

"You're right. I haven't been thrilled with either of you. In fact, let me clarify that, Phil, you I can tolerate without much complaint, but Frank you're an entirely different story," Kreppell said with a pained expression.

"Me, what did I do?" Widelsky asked with surprise.

"Since you two got here you haven't been happy. Now I know how you got here and why, and I also know where you're going," Kreppell said with a smile as he folded his hands.

"Look, Sarge, we were happy downtown. We made a good collar, got a promotion and next thing we're up here. We do our job and do it well," Widelsky said defensively.

"You're both good detectives, Frank, but I like team players. I like guys with ambition, but guys who work in the system and don't try to work it. Do you understand?"

"What do you mean work the system?" Cairn asked.

"I'll explain," Kreppell, said. "About a year and a half ago or so two very enterprising third grade detectives assigned to the Robbery Squad in Huguenot Central were on Western Avenue by the boat basin returning from an interview with a robbery victim when they saw two known criminals. Now, these two criminals were easy to spot since one of them has a clubfoot and red hair. That fellow's name was Reilly and he's a very good-looking lad. Now, he has a friend named the Mongrel whom he met while on vacation upstate. The Mongrel got his name because he's colored, Puerto Rican and Irish among other things. Ring a bell?"

"Two bad boys, those two are," Cairn answered.

"Anyway," Kreppell continued. "The Mongrel's a gorilla and Reilly is his boyfriend, and they play a version of the Murphy Game where Reilly picks up a fag and they go for a little recreation and when the mark has his pants down or Reilly's pants down, whatever the preference of the day is, the Mongrel explodes on the scene and robs the fag or extorts money from him, whatever. Sometimes for sport he beats the fag. Correct?"

"We bagged them for that twice, and both times the fucking marks failed to testify," Widelsky responded angrily.

"Nothing's perfect," Kreppell said. "Now, on this night a year and a half ago, you two saw Reilly and the Mongrel, and instead of following them you used your detective intuition and took a ride around the park near the boat basin, and behind a row of hedges you found a man with his pants around his ankles beaten to death. Numerous cigarette burns on his body, especially the genitals and several Marlboro butts with the filters chewed littering the scene. Am I correct?"

"Yeah, it was a good job, if I do say so myself," Widelsky said proudly.

"No doubt it was. But, and it's a big but, you called it in and didn't immediately share everything you knew with your superiors, am I correct again?"

"We notified Inspector Greason, who was our boss," Cairn said.

"Inspector Greason, but not the duty lieutenant for homicide; anyway, you found out from the watchman for the boat basin that the deceased was living on a boat belonging to a very influential lawyer and big time lobbyist and political heavyweight, and then you left the detectives assigned to investigate the case on their own without telling them all you knew, correct? In fact, you didn't even know who the big shot boat owner was until you told Greason."

"We told Greason," Cairn dead-panned.

"Yes, you told Greason, then you picked up Reilly and the Mongrel and found out that the Mongrel witnessed Reilly and the victim give each other blow jobs and that incensed the Mongrel so much that he killed the victim. Reilly's semen was in the victim's mouth. The Mongrel had the victim's blood on his clothes. And to make a long story short, they confessed and went to jail and no one ever knew that the victim was a lodger on the aforementioned big shot's boat. Was my source on the money?"

"I guess so, but we were concerned with sending these guys upstate to prison, Sarge. That was our interest in the case," Cairn said defensively.

"I'm sure it was, but, nonetheless, keeping the connection between the boat owner and his guest was particularly important since the boat owner thought he was just helping out an aspiring artist and had no knowledge that his guest was homosexual, and that somehow could have been scandalous. Of course, Inspector Greason, who was actually Deputy Inspector Greason, was able to control this whole shebang and make brownie points for himself and you two fine detectives. What happened? Greason moved up in rank to full inspector and the two third grade detectives became second grade detectives at the behest of and with the influence of the big shot boat owner, and this story had its happy ending. Need I say more."

"Not happy for us," Widelsky snapped.

"That's right, Frank. I forgot one thing. Some people in headquarters found all of this a little too self-serving, and Greason went to the Beach precinct in the Lower Borough and you two came to the Upper Borough. Which was fine with me, except you let us all know how unhappy you were with that outcome, especially you, Frank," Kreppell said as he pointed his finger at Widelsky.

"Man, how'd you find that all out?" Cairn asked with a laugh.

"I didn't fall off a turnip truck, guys. Soon as you were transferred up here I did my homework, and never said boo to anyone, but I'm tired of the act, and I was about to start coming down on the two of you when I got word yesterday that, along with my promotion, I'd be losing the two of you."

"Losing us, where are we going?" Widelsky asked with a mix of apprehension and excitement.

"Back to Huguenot City."

"Downtown, great, see I told you so," Widelsky said to Cairn.

"Where downtown?" Cairn asked with less enthusiasm. There was something in Kreppell's manner, something subtle that Cairn detected and made him uncomfortable.

"Well, it seems that along with your redemption was the resurrection of Anthony Greason, formerly Inspector Greason and now Deputy Chief Greason," Kreppell said coyly.

"All right, Chief Greason sounds good to me," Widelsky exclaimed. "I knew he was getting his stars."

"Yes, Chief Greason is the new commander of Internal Affairs. It seems Downtown wants to create a new initiative to combat police corruption, and Greason's been named to lead the charge. Of course, he'll need a task force of pure and unsullied investigators to aid him in this task and you two are among that elite group. Soon as this investigation is closed, you're out of here. There were plenty of rumors around here about this yesterday and some of the guys found out," Kreppell said apologetically, then sat back in his chair and took another sip of coffee. The two detectives sat there stone-faced, and before anyone else could think of something to say the phone on Kreppell's desk rang.

"Kreppell here," he said. He listened for a moment and said, "Send him in."

A dark-skinned man approached the door and knocked on it. Kreppell stood up from behind his desk and motioned the man to come in. The man was wearing blue serge pants and a yellow shirt. He had on black alligator loafers that were almost as shiny as his bald ebony head. Kreppell smiled and extended his hand and said, "I'm Sergeant Kreppell, you are?"

"Patrolman Nat McNair, Transit Police."

"Patrolman McNair, please take a seat. Detectives Cairn and Widelsky," Kreppell said as he pointed to the detectives. "What can we do for you?"

Patrolman McNair smiled and said, "Well, it's more a case of what I can do for you. I was up early this morning; it's my day off and I went out early for the paper. I was thinking it be a fine day to drive over to the track and try my luck. I picked my horses and was reading the paper when I saw a story about a murder on Lincoln Boulevard yesterday. I spoke with that woman around noon yesterday," he said with a nod of his head.

"What woman?" Widelsky questioned.

Patrolman McNair pulled a rolled up newspaper from his back pocket and opened the front section to page two. He put his finger on a line of newsprint and said, "Right there, Sarge, Maria Weiss. That woman and some little Puerto Rican honey, a…" and he took out a slip of paper from his front pocket and read from it, "Sophie Cruz, 3425 Kingsbridge Avenue, Upper Borough. That was the address she gave me. Well, this little honey and Mrs. Weiss were having a catfight at the Kingsbridge Road subway stop. Mrs. Weiss was so cool, nothing was gonna mess her hair, you know, and it's funny, but I was at the rear of the platform by the back wall stealing a smoke when I watched them go at it. Cruz was making all the noise and she was pointing her finger and cursing at the woman. She threw something at the woman, and I know it's my imagination, but shit, she threw something and the woman let it fall to the ground and when Cruz went to pick it up off the ground I thought the woman was going to kick her on to the tracks. Man, I know, you know you have that feeling that something was going to happen. I coughed and started walking to them and they stopped and the train was coming into the station. I asked what the problem was, and the woman, Weiss, said the other one was bothering her. She got on the train, and just before the train door closed, the other one, Sophie Cruz, throws something at Weiss and it was a picture. I don't know what type of picture 'cause it wasn't big, but it was definitely a picture. This morning I read the story and called my command and they ordered me over here to tell you what I saw."

"Weiss leaves on the train and Cruz stays behind, what happened next?" Cairn asked.

"I told her to calm down, and she did. I told her she could have been arrested and she was cool, got her act together and mumbling under her breath, but cool. I took her name and address and sent her on her way. Now here's the funny thing, as she's walking away I call to her and ask what the other woman's name is, and she says, and I remember this like all the dogs I've bet on that never finish, she says, 'Maria Weiss, W-E-I-S-S like in ice.' And then she left the station."

"About what time?" Widelsky asked.

"My time was eight minutes after twelve noon. Shit happens on the trains all the time, but when I saw the story today I said to myself, Nat, that little girl with the sassy mouth and the tight jeans, she may be a murderer. Man, you can't tell anymore. I have to go over to my district command and file a report on this. My captain said he'd send a copy over later. Anything else you need?" he asked as he stood up.

Widelsky and Cairn looked at one another, then to Kreppell.

Kreppell stood up and said, "That'll do for now. I want to thank you for your cooperation. This may be the break we're looking for, don't you think so? Frank," he said as he looked over at Widelsky.

Patrolman McNair stopped before he left the office, and said, "Hey, Sarge, this thing works out for you, maybe a little letter to my captain. Nothing big, but a little boost, you know. I been riding the trains rain too long. A change to plain clothes would make this brother a happy man."

He flashed a wide smile and, as he was going out the doorway, Kreppell said, "You got it, McNair, and it'll be more than a little letter. Tom Swinton is your boss, right?"

"Straight as an arrow Swinton, that's my boss," McNair said with a chuckle.

"We're old friends, I'll do what I can," Kreppell said enthusiastically.

McNair left, and Widelsky muttered under his breath, "Fucking eggplant."

"You'll fit in real well on your next assignment, Frank, real well," Kreppell said with disdain to Widelsky, then turned to Cairn and said, Still think it is what it is and Mrs. Weiss did it?"

"Sarge, I don't know what to think, especially now."

Chapter Thirty-Two

The news of their impending transfer cast Cairn into an immediate funk and elevated Widelsky into a mild state of euphoria. Widelsky acted like a death row inmate given a reprieve, while Cairn interpreted it as the summary execution of his career in the police department. Cairn was clearly in shock. His normally unruffled and relaxed demeanor was crumbling, and he sat red-faced and sweating in the chair in front of Kreppell's desk. Widelsky, for his part, was buoyant, almost giggly.

His face appeared frozen in a broad grin as he peppered Kreppell with a series of questions, "You're not putting me on, are you? This is for real, I hope? Are we getting upgraded to first grade? That's lieutenant's pay, you know?" he said to Kreppell.

"I have no idea if there's an upgrade to first grade, but I assume that some promotions will result."

Cairn frowned at Widelsky, and said to Kreppell, "With all due respect, Sarge, but just when were you going to tell us? That fucking wiseass Murphy must have known yesterday. Little prick called me a shoofly. I don't think it's fair, fair at all."

"Who gives a shit, we're outta here and on to better pastures, Phil," Widelsky said, with a wave of his hand at Kreppell.

"Better pastures, for who?" Cairn said in disbelief. "This is the end of my career, I don't know about you, but if I can get out of this I will."

"Suit yourself."

"Sarge, I'd still like the courtesy of an answer. When were you going to tell us the news? Were you going to wait until we'd worked our asses off on this case, or just until everyone else in the unit knew? You know, the last laugh's on us guys."

Kreppell folded his hands and lowered his eyes to his desk. He cleared his voice and said, "You're right. I waited around to tell the two of you last evening, but you got stuck waiting for the secretary. The guys in the squad didn't hear it from me. I had every intention of telling you right after we finished with Mr. Weiss this morning. Honest. And believe me, I didn't know what your reaction was going to be anyway. If I were a betting man I would have thought that your reaction would be the same as Frank's. You're not unhappy about this, are you Frank?"

"I've got three years to go until retirement, and I can count all the friends I have on this job on one hand. If I make first grade, I retire on a lieutenant's pension, that's right by me."

"Weiss and his attorney are here," Hogan said as he stepped into the room.

"Do me a favor, Ritchie," Kreppell said. "Get his prints, then bring him to the interview room. Call us when you're done. And one more thing, did you process the elevator yesterday?"

"No, just what I told you before. Why the elevator?"

"Why not? Maybe a print from one of the suspects will show up, and if nothing else they'll have to explain why they were there, right?"

"Yeah, but if it's the doorman his prints could be in plenty of places. Same for the delivery boy, and the elevator could have a hundred prints in it. That's a lot of work," Hogan said with a note of complaint in his voice.

"Yeah, and maybe someone who never had any business being in that building or elevator who is also a suspect in this case might have left her prints in the elevator, Ritchie. Both elevators, understand?" Kreppell scolded.

"Who you thinking of?"

"I'm thinking the secretary, but all I need you to do is process everything I told you to process. I'll get Tracy to take the elimination prints today, you just do Weiss now, then get over to the scene. The sooner we get that finished the better off we'll be."

"You got it, boss, but I have to stop at a drugstore, you know one that sells surgical supplies. I need a surgical glove for my left hand. I don't want all that black powder on my bandage."

"Fine, just get a move on. Less talk and more work, got it Ritchie?"

Widelsky got up from his chair and said, "I gotta take a piss, excuse me." He left the room.

Kreppell looked at Cairn and said, "Your partner seems pretty happy over the news, I can't say the same for you, can I?"

"Please, we're two entirely different guys," Cairn said emotionally. "Frank's a great cop, terrific instincts, hasn't missed a day of work in the six years we've worked together. You know when he called that colored cop a 'fucking eggplant' after he left the room before? Well, that's just Frank. I'm a dumb fucking Mick and DeMarco's a fucking greaseball, bosses are fucking assholes, you know?"

"I must be number one on his list?"

"Sorry, but you're missing my point. It doesn't matter what any of us are. Frank refers to himself as a dumb fuck all the time. It's just his way of dealing with people. Frank's an ambitious man. He failed the sergeant's test twice, and it's always bothered him. Come hell or high water he wants that first grade detective's shield. Me, I don't really care. Frank lives in the Pointe in the Lower Borough, just across the river from Huguenot City. He's a butcher by trade. His father and uncle own a shop over there and Frank moonlights on his off days cutting meat. He's big in the Elks; that's his life. The Pointe, the Elks, his bowling league, those are the things that matter. This job is just a paycheck, and even though he's good at it, in his heart he's still a butcher, and when he retires that's what he'll do. Why do you think he got so twisted when he came to the Upper Borough?"

"I wouldn't even hazard a guess, Phil," Kreppell answered tiredly.

"He didn't own a car. When we were in Huguenot Robbery I used to pick him up on the way in from the Beach. I live out there. If he had to go in on his own he jumped on the subway. He owns a two family brownstone with his father. His old man owns a car, and if Frank is taking the family somewhere, he drives the old man's car. When we got the transfer up here he had to buy a car. He was too far out of the way to depend on me. That's the main reason he hates the Upper Borough. He's not like other guys on the job. That's why going to Internal Affairs doesn't even bother him."

Kreppell looked at his watch and said, "That's more about Frank than I ever knew, and I'll still be the first on line to say goodbye."

"Like I said, Frank don't care if you don't like him. But this transfer means real problems for me."

"Why? You're an honest cop, and it's a job that needs honest men to enforce the rules. It protects us all."

"Sarge, you know very little about me. I'm thirty-seven years old. I've been a cop for fifteen years, almost my whole adult life. I have no kids. My wife was a stewardess for Pan Am. She owns a travel agency out at the Beach. We live in Atlantic Harbor, one block from the ocean. My sister's husband is a battalion chief with the fire department. He lives around the corner. My wife's sister is married to a sergeant in emergency services. He works in the Lower Borough and they live in the neighborhood, too. I play handball and basketball every week. I play with cops and firemen. Most of the families where I live have someone on the PD or the FD, or they work for the telephone company or in construction. These are my wife's customers. She makes almost three times what I make. If I make nine thousand this year, she'll make twenty-five. Being assigned to robbery in Huguenot City or homicide in the Upper Borough carries a little weight. People respect me. Being a fucking shoofly is the kiss of death. You put me in that job, and if I do my job it won't be a month before I'm accused of fucking over someone who's related to someone in my neck of the woods. Next thing I'm a rat, and after that my wife's business will take a hit and no one will want to know me. What do I do, move to the Pointe and join the Elks?" he said in voice oozing with self-pity.

"Phil, I think you're being overly dramatic. Do you really think this transfer will ruin your friendships and hurt you wife's business, or are you just making excuses?"

"What if it happened to you?"

"I spent two years in internal affairs when I first made sergeant. You do what you have to do. Now enough of this, lets get back to this murder."

Widelsky, who had been outside the door listening to Cairn's conversation with Kreppell, came back into the room. "Weiss is washing his hands and Hogan's packing his ditty and getting ready to go back to the crime scene. I'll give you odds of ten to one it takes him another twenty minutes to get out of the house. Forty-five minutes minimum before he's at the scene. Fucking guy is slower than shit going up an icy hill in the dead of winter. We've wasted a lot of time on bullshit this morning," he said as he gave Cairn a half smile.

"Frank's right, we are wasting time. How are we going to handle this today?"

Cairn was pouting and didn't answer Kreppell. Widelsky sat back down and picked up Cairn's notebook from off Kreppell's desk. He opened the book and took a red pen from his pocket and underlined something on the page he was looking at. He handed the open book to Kreppell and said, "That's Weiss' office. Why don't you give it a call and see if the secretary is at work?"

"Okay, what's my line?"

"Pretend you're somebody looking for a lawyer and Weiss was

recommended to you. Say you're buying an apartment building or something."

Cairn shook his head and sighed. "You'll get the switchboard operator first. Miss Abonita I recall, pretty name and a pretty girl. Make sure she puts you through to the office."

Kreppell smiled at Cairn, happy he was back in the game and dialed the phone number Widelsky had underlined. The number rang twice and a female switchboard operator with a happy and perky voice answered, "Law offices, may I help you?"

"Yes, Mr. Weiss please."

"One moment while I put you through," the operator responded.

Three rings later another female voice answered the phone, "Henry Weiss' office, can I help you?"

Kreppell could detect that slight Latin inflection Puerto Ricans spoke English with, and he knew he had Sophie Cruz on the other end of the line. "Mr. Weiss, please?"

"Mr. Weiss is unavailable right now, can I be of assistance?" Sophie asked in a professional manner.

"I'm in the process of bidding on a large commercial property, and I was referred to Mr. Weiss. I need a good real estate attorney."

"If you leave your name and number, I'll see that he gets back to you at his earliest convenience."

"I'm on a payphone now and I won't be in my office all day. Is there a good time for me to call back?"

"You can try between ten and ten-thirty, but I can't guarantee that he will be in his office. Mr. Weiss has a very busy calendar."

"Excellent. I'll call back then. Oh, and I'm speaking to whom?" Kreppell asked as an afterthought.

"Miss Cruz, I'm Mr. Weiss' secretary, and you are?"

"Tom Franks."

"I'll tell him you called and to expect a call back from you, Mr. Franks."

"Thank you, you're very helpful."

"Thank you too," Sophie cooed as she hung up the phone.

"Beats me," Kreppell said as he put the headset to the phone back in its cradle. "She's either one very tough broad, or she's got nothing to do with this murder. That didn't sound like a woman with a lot on her mind, or one who knows her boss' cleaning lady was murdered yesterday and she's one of the suspects."

"Or she is one very cool lady. The transit cop that was here this morning said she was carrying on some yesterday and had a mouth, then the doorman sees her six hours later on a bus going past the building. Then again the cop thought for a moment Mrs. Weiss was going to kick Cruz when she bent down to pick something up. Who knows?" Cairn said.

"Listen, fellas, first you have to interview her, then we'll be in a better position to offer an opinion. I'm going to have Murphy and DeMarco follow up on the kid's alibis. We can get those out of the way this morning. Before we speak with Mr. Weiss why don't one of you call the kid's attorney and make arrangements to have him come in today for his elimination prints. Also, I want the doorman's prints, too."

Widelsky picked up Cairn's notebook and said, "I'll call them." He walked out of the office.

Cairn turned to Kreppell and said, "Sarge, I know you've got some juice of your own, and maybe I don't deserve it, but I'd go back to third grade if I had to. I can't call Greason. He's Frank's guy anyway. I can't ask Frank 'cause we've been partners too long, but I just can't do that transfer. It ain't in me. You and Frank, you're better men."

"Phil, I said it before and I meant it, my problem was with Frank. I'll call Grimsley later. The captain's still got some friends downtown, and he's owed a lot of favors. If we can help you, we will, and if it works that means you're here and you're a part of the team. There's only one thing I ask of my guys, one thing, loyalty?" Kreppell said as he locked his eyes on Cairn.

"Sarge, I'll give you my blood, I mean it. Frank may never forgive me, but so be it."

"C'mon, let's go meet Mr. Weiss."

Sophie wrote the name Tom Franks on the yellow legal pad she kept next to her phone and put a question mark after the name. She got up and went over to the small refrigerator Henry kept in his office and took out a can of Tab. She opened it and drank half the can. She lit up a cigarette and looked at her watch. It was a nine-thirty and Henry wasn't at work yet. She knew he was livid with her for leaving him in Montreal, and she couldn't imagine what his mood would be over the confrontation she had with Maria yesterday. Sophie had never seen Henry angry. She had witnessed little tantrums over the years, and bouts of crankiness, but Henry always seemed too good-natured to be able to demonstrate real anger. She expected him to come into the office glowering at her and to give her the silent treatment, possibly even fire her, but she didn't expect a major scene. It just wasn't in him. He had a meeting scheduled for eleven, and there was a lot of paperwork to be completed from the Montreal trip. *Where is he? Maybe Maria killed him over Joey? Wouldn't that be tragic?* she thought.

Sophie finished her Tab and picked up the phone. *Let me call Janet*, she thought. *Maybe Henry left a message?* "Hi Janet, it's Sophie, did Mr. Weiss leave any messages?"

"No, I haven't heard from him since you went to Montreal on Tuesday."

"Okay," Sophie said and hung up the phone. *Let me ask Ruthie, she knows everything,* Sophie mused, as she left Henry's office and walked down the hallway to Ruth Goolnick's desk. Miss Goolnick was sitting at her desk reading the newspaper. She had on a light-blue A-line dress and matching shoes. Her face looked a little puffy, and Sophie wondered if she had been crying or had been up all night and was overly tired.

"Ruthie, have you heard from Henry?"

Ruthie's eyes narrowed and her lower lip trembled in anger as she spoke to Sophie, "Haven't you heard?"

"Heard what?" Sophie asked, suddenly feeling her stomach tighten.

"It's in all the morning papers. I was going to go in and tell you, but I thought you knew," she said with a snarl.

"Knew what?" Sophie said nervously.

Ruthie said nothing in response, but handed the *Huguenot Times* to Sophie. She turned to page two and pointed to the story.

Sophie read the article detailing Millie's murder. She dropped the paper on Ruthie's desk and said, "What about Maria?"

"You don't know?" Ruthie said accusingly.

"Why would I know?"

"She's in Borough in intensive care. Whoever killed Millie Campos attempted to kill Maria, too. I wonder who would do something like that?" Ruthie sneered.

Sophie didn't answer and turned and went back to her office. She went inside to Henry's office and opened his desk drawer. In a brown envelope were extra keys to the office and to Henry's apartment. She knew which keys were which because Henry had asked her to have extra sets made only a year ago. Sophie's heart was racing. She knew Ruthie hated her and that enmity, up until now, had always been a source of joy for Sophie. Ruthie would have given anything to be Henry's mistress, and every time Sophie made love to Henry in his office it always increased her pleasure to know that at that moment when she was in Henry's arms and they were grunting and heaving on Henry's couch Ruthie was sitting at her desk just outside the door and down the hall. Sophie had never felt threatened by Ruthie because she believed that Ruthie hated Maria almost as much as she hated her, and in some perverse way Henry's infidelity with Sophie gave Maria the comeuppance that Ruthie thought she deserved. It always seemed so petty and silly, everything about it, Sophie thought, until this morning when Ruthie said, "I wonder who would do that?"

Ruthie's remark suggested Sophie was the murderer. Ruthie had implied so, and Sophie accepted the implication as a direct accusation. Her concern was over any other information that Ruthie might possess, but didn't reveal that would connect Sophie to the murder at Henry's apartment. Yesterday, she had engaged in a hysterical and thoughtless encounter with Maria. Her inability to rein in her temper and her desire to hurt Maria had placed her in jeopardy. *The doorman saw me twice yesterday*, she thought. *And then that cop. He had such a nice smile and was very patient, but he saw me yelling at Maria, and worse, he saw me throw Joey's picture at her. I gave him my name and Maria's name. He has to know.* She sat at Henry's desk sobbing. *The police always want a motive*, she thought. *Being Henry's mistress is no big deal, she figured but being the mother of his child is something else. What if they find Joey's picture and the cop says that's what I threw at Maria?* she thought. Then they'll have the motive. It makes complete sense. *I went to Henry's apartment to kill his wife so I could have him to myself. The cleaning lady got in the way and I killed her, too.* "Oh, my God," she said aloud. "I just know they're going to blame me," she sobbed.

Sophie took Henry's keys and left his office. She snatched her pocketbook from under her desk and ran out to the lobby. She took the elevator down, went out to the street and started walking north on Lincoln Boulevard. *I've got to get that picture*, she repeated to herself.

The bus stop for the number one that ran up and down Lincoln Boulevard was a half a block north of the entrance to Henry's office. Sophie saw the bus coming and sprinted up the block to the bus stop on the balls of her feet, purposely keeping her sharp spiked heels from hitting the pavement and breaking. She made it just in time and she was out of breath as she boarded the bus.

The driver had a deep brogue and said to her as she dropped her fare into the change box, "Darling, no need tuh race after my bus, I woulda waited all morning for ya."

"Thank you, honey," Sophie demurely said with a weak smile as she stepped to the rear of the bus and took a seat. She got off at Kingsbridge Road and walked up the street a block to Henry's building. Her plan was to get into Henry's apartment and look for the picture she had thrown at Maria. She knew Maria had picked it up and it was probably in her pocketbook.

What do I do if someone's home? she thought. She went back down to the corner of Kingsbridge Road and Lincoln Boulevard where there was a payphone. She put in a dime and dialed Henry's number. She let it ring seven times, but no one answered. She dialed the number again, but received no answer. She went back up the street to the building and walked past it. *How do I get in without the doorman seeing me?* she thought. As Henry's secretary, one of her duties was handling his household accounts and other personal matters. Sophie paid the Associated Market bill every month, and was well aware of the system whereby the delivery boy entered the apartment through the service entrance and left the groceries in the pantry. Sometimes she even called in an order for Henry. There were four keys on the ring. She didn't know what doors they opened, but she was confident that they could get her into the building and into Henry's apartment.

The alleyway was on the north side of the building. She had never been in his apartment, but she knew they took the deliveries in that way. She quickly walked past the front entrance to the building and went down the alleyway and came to the service door. She tried one of the keys in the door, but it didn't work. She tried a second key and the door unlocked. Fifteen feet down the hallway was an elevator and next to it was a staircase. It was the service elevator and she pushed the button. She didn't know which was drumming louder, her heart or the motor to the elevator. The elevator came down to the basement and came to a stop. She got on and pressed the button for the seventh floor.

The hard click of her high heels echoed in the hallway, and when she got on the elevator she leaned her left hand against the wall and bent her right leg backward and took off her right shoe. She then put her right hand against the wall and lifted her left leg backward and took off her left shoe. The elevator floor was warm and she could feel the heat of the motor under her feet. The soles of her nylon stockings were soaked with sweat, and as she moved about the elevator she saw that her feet left moist impressions wherever they stepped. At the seventh floor the door opened and she exited the elevator. There was no sound in the hallway.

The stairs were next to the elevator and she tucked her shoes under her arm and started up to the eighth floor. She was walking tiptoe and trying to be as quiet as possible when she thought she heard the hard scratch of a wooden chair leg against tile, then the rustling of newspaper pages turning. There was someone on the eighth floor and Sophie slowly and quietly backed down the staircase. She was too frightened to wait for the elevator, and when she got to the seventh floor she turned and raced down the stairs with one hand on the banister and the other clutching her shoes and handbag. She was too scared to breathe, and several times she almost slipped on the slick marble stairs. She got back to the basement and put her shoes back on and walked up the ramp and back out the service entrance to the alleyway.

She went up to Lincoln Boulevard and turned north. Two blocks later she came to the bus stop for the number one bus. She lit a cigarette and waited. *There must have been a cop guarding the apartment*, she thought. She looked at her watch, it was just ten o'clock and she didn't know what to do. *I can't go back to work*, she thought. *Let me go home and rest. I haven't done anything but sleep with a man and have his child. They can't put me in jail for that*, she reasoned.

Chapter Thirty-Three

Cairn followed Kreppell out of his office and down the hallway. Widelsky was leaning against the wall in the hallway about ten feet from the door to the interview room and chewing on the end of a pencil stub. Kreppell had decided to try and keep Cairn in the unit, and in the first step toward the divorce between Widelsky and Cairn, he said to Widelsky, "Frank, take Russo, Slattery's in court, and go and pick up Sophie Cruz. Phil and I will handle the interview with Mr. Weiss."

"You want us to bring her back here? Might be some fireworks between her and her boyfriend they cross paths, dontcha think?" Widelsky asked, apparently undisturbed by the separation from Cairn.

"You have a point. Take her over to Summit and give me a call when you get there," Kreppell answered.

"Talk to you then," Widelsky said with a nod of his head as he went back to the squad room in search of Detective Russo.

Kreppell turned to Cairn and said, "After the introductions you can take the lead in the interview. Remember, Futerman is a retired bureau chief with the DA's office. He's wired in there and Frank Duffy's his man. He probably knows as much about this case as we do."

"That ain't much," Cairn said as they walked into the interview room.

Henry Weiss and Lee Futerman were seated at the far end of a gunship gray metal table with an inlaid black rubber surface. They were seated next to one another in matching gray metal chairs. The décor of the room was strictly government issue, with a large glass mirrored window on one wall that permitted observers from the adjacent office to look unseen at the room's occupants. Lee was wearing his trademark rumpled gray suit and black wingtips. His faded black socks reached just above his ankles and a shank of hairless shin shone dully in the artificial light of the room. The paunch below his belt was prominent, and he had all the appearances of a life long bureaucrat who had spent too much time indoors tirelessly poring over paperwork and deliberating issues that were of pressing importance at the time, but in retrospect were either unmemorable or irrelevant. The ever present cigar stump was lodged in his left hand, and upon Kreppell and Cairn's entrance into the room he stood up and extended his right hand and introduced himself, "Gentleman, I'm Lee Futerman. I'm representing Mr. And Mrs. Weiss in this matter. You are?" he asked confidently.

"Sergeant Kreppell and Detective Cairn," Kreppell responded as he took a chair alongside Cairn.

Henry leaned across the table and extended his hand to the two detectives. "Henry Weiss," he said in a friendly voice.

Henry was wearing a tan camp shirt with dark brown slacks. He looked well rested, and despite some thickening around the middle and thinning of his hair he appeared quite robust in comparison to his attorney.

Henry sat down and Lee led off the conversation. "We probably have as many questions for you as you do for us. Why don't you start and we can fill each other in. And let's be frank. I guess the first question and most important is, do you have a suspect?"

Kreppell immediately responded, "You know I was a young cop in the River Street precinct back in forty-seven when you were still in the DA's office. I collared a guy for a street robbery and Frank Duffy prosecuted the case. He was a crackerjack and you were his boss, if I recall?"

"Frank was a terrific young lawyer. The war got in his way. He had two years of law school done when he joined. You could always count on Duffy to do the right thing. Finished up right after the war and joined the office in 1946," Lee answered in a friendly manner, then changing his tack, said rather sternly, "Might I infer from your remark that you believe my connection with Duffy could interfere with this case?"

"Maybe, but have you been in touch with Mr. Duffy concerning this case?" Kreppell shot back.

"Just to ask him to ensure that everything is done by his office to assist the police with the apprehension and conviction of whomever it is who is responsible for the murder of Millie Campos and the assault on Maria Weiss," Lee flatly stated.

"Just asking; however, my information on Mrs. Weiss is she had an aneurysm. We haven't received any information concerning an assault. Perhaps, there's an update we haven't received yet," Kreppell answered.

Henry leaned forward in his chair and said to Kreppell, "I believe she has some bruises on her body."

"Let's not get ahead of ourselves, please. This investigation is in its early stages still. Detective Cairn has some questions to ask and some information to share. When he's finished, maybe we'll all know a little more." Kreppell replied.

Cairn opened up his steno notebook and turned to the first page. "Mr. Weiss, does your wife follow the same routine every day?"

"She works as a manager in the cosmetics department at Sable's Department Store, but she's an employee of Lorient Cosmetics. She works every Thursday from one to nine, and every Saturday from nine to five. Monday, Tuesday, Wednesday and Friday she works from ten to six, or sometimes nine-thirty to five-thirty, but she has one of those days off during the week and normally picks Monday or Friday as the day off," Henry replied.

"So, you're saying that Thursday and Saturday are definite work days, but the other days she has a choice?" Cairn asked.

"More or less," Henry replied.

"Does anyone else live in the apartment besides you and your wife?" Cairn asked.

"Just the two of us," Henry answered.

"Do you have any children?" Cairn asked.

Henry paused for a second, then said, "Maria and I are childless."

"What days of the week do you have the cleaning lady come in?" Cairn asked.

"Mille comes every Thursday. She's been with me since the early fifties," Henry answered.

"You or your wife ever had a problem with her?" Cairn followed.

"Wonderful woman, like a member of the family," Henry replied.

"Would your wife say the same?" Cairn asked.

"Certainly." Henry quickly answered.

"Would she say the same thing about your secretary, Sophie Cruz?" Cairn asked casually.

"Maria knows very little about Sophie. I doubt she's ever formed an opinion," Henry replied slightly defensively.

"How long has Sophie Cruz worked for you?" Cairn asked.

"A little over ten years, why?" Henry questioned.

"You don't know?" Cairn asked and then smiled.

"There's plenty I know. I asked you why?" Henry responded.

"Didn't the two of you just take a trip to Montreal this week?" Cairn asked.

"Yes, I handled several closings for Ancowitz Realty. Morris and Bert Ancowitz are two of my longstanding clients, and Sophie's my secretary and she accompanied me," Henry answered.

"Did you and Miss Cruz stay in separate rooms or the same room?" Cairn asked.

Henry slapped the palms of his hands on the tabletop and said to Cairn," What is this, a ten cent inquisition? Sophie's worked for me for ten years and I've been sleeping with her for almost as long. What's that got to do with Millie's murder or what happened to Maria?"

Lee Futerman was sitting in his chair with his hands folded over his paunch and looked like a frog asleep on rock when he suddenly interjected, "Detective, when you first came into the room I suggested and, or at least I thought, that I suggested politely that we share information and not play a cat and mouse game."

"You said, 'Let's be frank' I recall," Kreppell stated. "Who is playing cat and mouse?"

Neither Henry or Lee immediately responded, and Cairn picked up his notebook and turned the page and said, "Let me help. Did your wife know about your affair? Who is the young boy in the communion picture that was found in your wife's pocketbook yesterday? Why did Sophie Cruz leave Montreal ahead of you? Why was she at your building yesterday waiting to speak with your wife? Why was she seen on a bus passing the building last night around six o'clock? Is that frank enough?" he said caustically.

Henry put his hand to his mouth, then rubbed his jaw. Cairn's questions supported Maria's accusation of earlier that morning, and he found himself confronted with the reality that Sophie could be a murderer. Still, he didn't believe it, but he saw no point in misleading the investigation and decided to reveal all he knew. "I don't think she knew about the affair. We've had some problems in our marriage over the years and Sophie was my release, simple as that. Sophie has a child. His name is Joey and it appears I'm the father. I never contested it, but all you have to do is look at him and I can't deny it. Sophie and I had an argument up in Montreal. She wants me to leave Maria and I won't. Truth is, I'll never leave her. Maria called me when I was up there and she was very lovey-dovey over the phone and Sophie overheard what was going on and had a tantrum. She packed her bags and left Wednesday evening and took the overnight to Huguenot City. I can't tell what she did after that, but this morning when I saw Maria at the hospital she was in a bit of a daze, but she told me that yesterday she saw Sophie. Sophie followed her to the train, then when she went into the apartment and found Millie, Sophie came out of the closet. She was very weak and I couldn't get much more out of her," Henry said with a crack in his voice.

"When were you going to tell us this?" Cairn asked.

"I wanted to know what you knew. I cannot believe that Sophie did this. It makes no sense," Henry retorted.

"Fine, Sophie didn't do it. Your wife is lying. We have her bloody fingerprint on the ashtray that was used to bash in Millie Campos' skull. It's really very simple. Your wife was confronted by Sophie Cruz and found out that, not only was her husband fooling around, but was also the father of Sophie's child. She went back the apartment and killed Millie and says Sophie did it. Easy as pie, except I don't know how you plan an aneurysm?" Cairn stated with a deadpan expression on his face.

Lee Futerman popped up from the slouch position he was sitting in and said, "Detective, you're right on target. You don't plan an aneurysm, and I think the bloody fingerprint probably occurred when Mrs. Weiss walked into her bedroom and found Millie on the floor dead. The ashtray was probably by Millie's head and Mrs. Weiss picked it up, normal inquisitiveness, I'd say. I'm surprised that fingerprints from the initial officers responding weren't found too."

"That's a possibility. When can we interview Mrs. Weiss?" Cairn asked.

"Not until her condition is stabilized," Lee replied with authority.

"By the way," Henry said, "what's this about some compromising photographs of Maria that were found at the scene?"

Kreppell reached over to a manila envelope he'd placed on the tabletop. From it he withdrew six one on one copies of the photographs of Maria found at the murder scene. Three were reproductions of the front of the pictures and the other three were of the backs of the pictures. "Ever see these before?" Kreppell asked as he handed them to Henry.

Henry studied them for a long moment, then smiled as he placed the photograph of Maria baring her breasts face down on the table. "No, but it's her. You found these there?" Henry asked.

"Those are copies of the photos we found there. The actual ones are in the lab being processed for prints. It appears that these were part of a sequence of pictures, but a search of the room failed to turn up anymore. One theory was that Millie Campos had found these pictures and was using them to extort money from your wife," Kreppell answered.

"Absurd, totally absurd," Henry responded.

Cairn looked at his notes and said, "Any significance to the A.K. stamped on the backs of the photos?"

"A.K.," Henry mused and then said, "Amos Koch. Maria's employer and benefactor in Berlin."

"Then you know him?" Cairn asked.

"I know of him," Henry replied. "Maria lost her first husband and family in a fire in Berlin back in the thirties. She went to work for Koch, and after a year they moved to Paris, then Koch went home to Argentina and Maria landed a position with the British Royal Navy as a translator. She's fluent in multiple languages. She's never been very open about her relationship with Koch, and I, for that matter, never inquired much about her past. I didn't care then, if you want to know, and I don't care now. She was, and still is, a very beautiful woman and why those photographs were taken or exist is beyond me. This is the first I've ever seen of them."

"Then your not shocked?" Kreppell asked.

"Shocked, why?" Henry asked.

"Some men might react differently," Cairn said.

"Like I said, I don't know much about the relationship between Koch and Maria. You have to remember that things in Europe weren't necessarily peachy keen in the 1930s, particularly in Germany. It's all about the flesh in the end, isn't it?" Henry said philosophically. "You know, Maria's taking off her clothes for this Koch fellow, and probably was his mistress, and now we suspect my mistress of killing Millie and trying to kill Maria."

"We don't know if anyone tried to do anything to your wife, at least not yet," Kreppell corrected. "And, I must say, you don't seem that upset by all of this," Kreppell added.

"That's uncalled for, Sergeant," Lee said with indignation.

"That's okay, Lee. I'm a big boy," Henry interjected. "Sergeant, I'm a private man, and the less of my life I have to reveal the happier I am. I am devastated by Millie's death. She was a wonderful woman, and because it happened in my home I feel responsible, but I'm also relieved that my wife is alive. I don't wear my heart on my sleeve, but I assure you, I'll do whatever I have to do to cooperate. However, what took place in Europe before the war with my wife and whomever is none of my business, and, as far as I can see, none of yours."

"Of course, Mr. Weiss," Kreppell responded. "But we have to ask the questions and I can't discount the fact that somehow these pictures play a part in this crime."

"It appears you don't quite know what you have, do you?" Lee said soberly.

"That's right, so let's move along," Cairn said, and took up his notebook again and turned to a new page. "How about keys to your apartment. Any extra sets?"

"Yes, I have a full set in my desk. I had Sophie get an extra set made for me last year. Keys to the office too, now that I think of it." Henry answered.

"And the extra set is kept where?" Cairn asked.

"Top drawer of my desk on a large key ring with a green plastic tab and the word 'apartment' written on it." Henry replied.

"Just a key to the front door?" Cairn asked.

"No, a full set of keys. There's the key to the front entrance and the service entrance, that's the same key. Then there's a key for the front door to the apartment, a key for the service door to the apartment and a key for the door that leads from the pantry into the apartment. Four keys in all." Henry recited.

"Why so many keys?" Cairn asked.

"It's a pain in the ass, but there was a time when we had a door man twenty-four seven. There was no inner door to the lobby. Years ago there was no buzzer system, and anyone coming in the service entrance was let into the building by the doorman or porter, and if they were going up to the apartment to do work or make a delivery the doorman or porter would open the door to the pantry. No one ever came upstairs unannounced. Only the super could get into the apartment. It's not the building it once was," Henry said.

"How come Millie Campos had to be buzzed into the building, but had a key to the apartment?" Cairn asked.

"There's a clause in the lease that forbids a tenant making a copy of the lobby and service entrance key, and there's a second clause that forbids giving the key to anyone other than a tenant of the apartment," Henry replied.

"That doesn't make sense," Cairn said.

"Well, you have to understand the psychology of the real estate business," Henry answered.

"Meaning?" Cairn asked.

"The Ancowitz brothers used to own the Excelsior, along with two premium properties on Manor Parkway and another on Waverly. They sold those buildings between 1959 and 1961. They have a large inventory of rental housing throughout the Upper Borough, but they sold the premium ones at a time when they thought the value of those properties and the demand for that type of housing was going to decline, and they were right," Henry said with a point of his finger toward Cairn.

"And what's that got to do with needing four keys to get into your apartment?" Cairn asked.

"When the Ancowitz's sold the Excelsior, it had a doorman around the clock and two porters. You could eat off the lobby floor, and most of the residents were professionals or shop owners. But their children were moving to the northern suburbs from the Upper Borough. Neighborhoods were changing, and when you own a lot of housing stock in those changing neighborhoods you get a heads up on which direction things are going in," Henry said.

"Okay, but we're getting off track here. My question is how good is the security in the building and why do you need four keys? How does someone get upstairs to an apartment if they don't have a key and the doorman hasn't let them in?" Cairn asked.

"That's what I was getting at before," Henry replied. "The people who owned my building knew five years ago that the Upper Borough was in decline and there would be a negative return on a luxury building located on Lincoln Boulevard. That would have been hard to believe in 1941 when I moved in, but not now. They sold high. The investment company that bought it slowly started to cut corners. They reduced the doorman's hours, cut out one porter, then the second porter is part time. People want security, so they go through the charade of putting in a buzzer system and an inner door that only tenants and no one else can have a key to. When the doorman's on a break, the porter is supposed to cover, but half the time he isn't around. Eventually when everyone gets comfortable with things, the doorman will be gone. The doorman sorts our mail now, but we received a letter from management last month notifying us that they would be installing secure mailboxes. Pretty soon we'll be just another apartment building, nice but no different from all the others up and down the block," Henry said.

"So, in your estimation does that mean that your building has good security right now?" Cairn asked,

"Yes and no. If the doorman is on duty and the porter's in the building, yes, but if the doorman's not around and the porter is off at some other location the answer is no. People will buzz strangers in and leave the lobby door propped open; it happens all the time," Henry answered.

"Fine, but yesterday with the doorman on duty to get into the building without his help someone would need the key to the service entrance?" Cairn asked.

"That's right," Henry answered.

"Well, we called your office this morning just before we came in here and Miss Cruz was at her desk. My partner and another detective went down there to pick her up and they should be with her now. Does Miss Goolnick have access to your office?"

"I'm the landlord," Lee said. "We have spare keys for every office, what do you want?"

"I'd like to see if the keys to Mr. Weiss' apartment are still in his desk if that's okay with him?" Cairn replied.

"Fine with me," Henry snapped.

"I'll call now," Lee said.

Lee Futerman got up from the table and followed Cairn out of the room. They went into another office and Cairn pointed to a telephone. Lee dialed his office number, and after two rings, said, "Hello, Janet, it's Mr. Futerman. Put me through to Miss Goolnick, please." Lee held the phone close to his face and closed his eyes and yawned. His eyes blinked open and Cairn could here the somewhat shrill voice of Ruth Goolnick over the telephone as Lee pulled the receiver away from his ear. "Ruthie, it's me, Lee. I can't talk now, but did two detectives take Sophie out of the office just now for questioning?" Lee looked at Cairn and arched his eyebrows. He put his hand over the mouthpiece to the phone and said, "Sophie ran out of the office this morning after Ruthie showed her the newspaper article about the murder. Around nine-thirty or so she says. The two detectives you sent there are in my lobby now. Do you want her to get one of them so you can talk?" Lee asked.

"Yeah, tell her to get Detective Widelsky," Cairn said.

"Ruthie, get Detective Widelsky and put him on the phone," Lee said. He then handed the phone to Cairn and stepped aside. Cairn placed the phone to his ear and after a minute he heard Widelsky barking on the other end, "What the fuck is going on? Oh, excuse me, ma'am."

"Listen, Frank, get Miss Goolnick and go into Henry Weiss' office. We have his permission. In the middle drawer of his office desk should be a set of keys. You're looking for four keys on a ring with a green plastic tag that has 'apartment' written on it. I'll hold on," Cairn patiently said.

"Four keys on a ring with a green tag, hang on," Widelsky answered.

Cairn had the phone in his right hand and rested it on his left shoulder. He said to Lee, "So what if she did do it? She could have taken the keys yesterday and put them back today."

"I don't think she was in the office yesterday," Lee answered.

"Could she have come in before anyone else got there?" Cairn asked.

"That's a possibility, but if she was coming from Montreal you're cutting it close. Janet, my receptionist, is in at eight-thirty and she would have seen her. Sophie would have had to be in before eight-thirty. Find out when the train from Montreal arrived in Huguenot City?" Lee replied.

Cairn heard Widelsky's voice and put the phone to his ear. "Yeah, Frank, whaddya got?"

"No keys like you just described. There's a set of three keys on a ring with a red plastic tag but they say 'office' and not 'apartment.' Also, Miss Goolnick said Sophie was pretty upset when she saw the article, but she thought the whole business was contrived. Her words not mine," Widelsky said.

"Why's that?" Cairn asked.

"Because asking anyone if they heard from Mr. Weiss at nine-thirty is something she's never done before. Sometimes Weiss is in early and other times late. He's unpredictable, and it's something she's never done before, so Miss Goolnick thinks it's suspicious, if you get my drift," Widelsky said.

"Is Miss Goolnick there?" Cairn asked.

"No, I'm in her boss's office. She said I could use the phone in here in case I swear again and offend everyone," Widelsky said, laughing.

"Glad you're back in good spirits," Cairn responded.

"Hey, pal, we're on our way outta here, least I am," replied Widelsky.

"Yeah, but more importantly," Cairn said seriously, "why does Miss Goolnick think Sophie was acting this morning? We know she has it in for her, so how can we accept that at face value?" Cairn asked.

"I asked her that and she got a little prissy, but then she laughed and told me that she was being objective. She said that Sophie Cruz has never come looking for Henry Weiss before, why today?" Widelsky replied.

"Okay, I guess it means something. What are you and Russo going to do now?" Cairn asked.

"Look for Miss Cruz, what else?" Widelsky answered.

"Give us a call when you find her," Cairn said and then hung up the phone.

Lee was listening carefully to everything Cairn had said, and although he hadn't heard Widelsky's responses he was able to put the conversation together. "You're very perceptive, Detective. You know Miss Goolnick has no fondness for Sophie Cruz, and after only one audience with her," Lee said.

"She was pretty open about it; I'd be pretty dumb if I didn't catch on. The big thing is how accurate and objective she is about this morning's scene," Cairn said in response.

"No one knows Ruthie Goolnick like I do," Lee said. "If she says she's being objective you have to take her at her word. Also, I surmised that her suspicions were aroused because Sophie was looking for Henry this morning and I would say she's right. Henry doesn't keep normal hours. Some days he's early, some late, and sometimes he doesn't show at all. Sophie is an excellent secretary and she runs that office very well without him there. Why today?"

"You're right. Kreppell called his office just before we came to the interview room. We wanted to see if she was there and when we asked for Mr. Weiss she said he was expected after ten," Cairn said in agreement.

"Exactly," Lee said with a smile, then went on to say, "right now, and I'm speaking as a former prosecutor with decades of experience in criminal investigations, and I would urge you to put all your efforts toward tracking down Miss Sophie Cruz. It appears she's your leading suspect."

"We're trying. C'mon, let's go back to the other room," Cairn said as he made his way back to the interview room. Cairn and Lee Futerman entered the room, and Henry was sitting by himself smoking a cigarette. "Where'd Sergeant Kreppell go?" Cairn asked.

"Stepped out, said he'd be back in a minute," Henry answered.

Cairn left the two men in the room and went in search of Sergeant Kreppell.

"Henry, the keys aren't in your desk and Sophie left the office a little past nine-thirty this morning," Lee said to him.

"No kidding?" Henry asked.

"Yes, she came into the main office around nine-thirty and asked Ruthie if anyone had heard from you? Strange, isn't it? Apparently Ruthie showed her a newspaper article about the crime and she turned hysterical and left the office. Any ideas?" Lee asked.

"She can be a little high strung at times, I don't know. Why do you think it's suspicious behavior?" Henry queried.

"Ruth said Sophie has never come into the office before and asked if anyone has heard from you. Particularly at nine-thirty in the morning. It's not like you're in the office every day at eight, is it?" Lee replied.

"You have a point, and they're certain my keys to my apartment are missing?" Henry said.

"That's what the other detective told Detective Cairn. I'm sure he looked carefully," Lee said with a nod of his head.

Cairn and Kreppell came back into the room, and Kreppell said, "Detective Cairn filled me in about the keys and Miss Cruz's disappearance. We haven't finished processing your apartment, but I've been told the job should be completed by one or two this afternoon. Is there a number we could reach you at because I'd like to walk through the crime scene with you before we relinquish it? Possibly you'll see things we didn't see. Naturally, we'd like to speak with you again, and as soon as Mrs. Weiss is able to we would like to interview her."

"Why don't you give us your number and we'll call in at one o'clock and you can give us they exact time then," Lee said.

"Fine," Kreppell answered as he wrote the number to his office on a slip of paper and handed it to Lee.

"Nothing else?" Lee asked.

"Yes, just one more thing," Cairn said. "The delivery boy, he was at your apartment close to the time this happened and hasn't been ruled out as a suspect. Do you know anything about him?" Cairn asked Henry.

"I've been dealing with the Associated Market since it opened a couple of years after the war. A colored kid, Walter, was the delivery boy for years. He was an aspiring songwriter. Maria liked him and she asked me to pass a few of his songs along to a music publisher I knew. I did, but he said the stuff was junk, but who knows? I don't think Maria ever believed me. She really liked this kid. A few weeks ago they made him the produce manager, and I don't know who the delivery boy is anymore. I only know about Walter because Maria told me, and she was happy he got a better position. Why?"

"Like I said, the kid was there around the time we think this all happened. Do you always keep the door from the pantry into the apartment locked?" Cairn asked.

"I think so, but I always come in the front door and any groceries are handled by my wife. Honestly, I couldn't tell you one way other. You'd have to ask my wife," Henry answered.

"Yeah, I hope I get that chance soon," Cairn replied.

Lee walked toward the door and said, "Mr. Weiss is anxious to get back to the hospital, and I have to go to my office. We'll call at one. Are you ready, Henry?"

"Sure thing," Henry said as he stood up and shook Kreppell and Cairn's hands.

"We'll let ourselves out, I know the way, very well," Lee offered as he stuck his cigar in his mouth.

After the two lawyers left, Kreppell said to Cairn, "Learn anything?"

"Yeah, Mrs. Weiss can do no wrong."

"And?" Kreppell coached.

"The girlfriend's expendable. He feels funny about it, but I think she's expendable and he's coming round to believing she could have done it," Cairn said with conviction.

"What about real estate?" Kreppell asked.

"I think his point was there's more money in the low end than the high end. Also, security is a joke at the Excelsior." Cairn said.

"Very good, you pay attention. Now the bad news," Kreppell said with disappointment in his voice.

"Bad news?" Cairn asked.

"Smitty just called. They just got to the Excelsior and guess what? Lunch, the porter, was polishing the inside of the main elevator," Kreppell said with a frown.

"How much did he do?" Cairn asked.

"Just finishing up. That Goddamn Hogan, how many times did I tell him to put a move on? Frank was right. They got there at ten after ten. It only takes ten minutes to clean the elevator, Goddamn Ritchie Hogan and his bad thumb," Kreppell cursed.

"No freaking luck," Cairn scoffed.

"Oh, there is a little good news. The porter last cleaned the service elevator on Wednesday and there was only one delivery yesterday and that was the kid from the market for Mrs. Weiss. Smitty figures that the only people in that elevator were the kid and Millie Campos. Hogan is processing the elevator now. Maybe, we'll get lucky and find something that doesn't belong there," Kreppell said.

"Well, the kid's carrying two boxes of groceries so I don't think his prints will show up and anyway, it wouldn't mean anything," Cairn replied.

"Nor would Millie Campos, but someone else's would be a lead, maybe," Kreppell said with a shrug of his shoulders.

"You think it's the secretary, don't you?" Cairn asked.

"I don't like to speculate, but she's our best suspect, so far," Kreppell answered.

"The pictures bother me. I don't know where they fit in," Cairn remarked.

"Cruz is in the apartment and she's pissed off. She starts going through Mrs. Weiss' stuff, who knows why, but she's looking for something. I've never met her, but you can't dismiss the fact that she's the mother of Mr. Weiss' son and the Weiss' have no children of their own. She figures she has a bigger stake in him than his wife does. She finds the pictures and Millie Campos catches her in the act and she hits her with the ashtray and kills her. She tidies up, but before she can leave Maria Weiss comes home. She hides in the closet, then surprises Mrs. Weiss, knocks her down and the rest is history. Or I could be completely wrong," Kreppell said with a short laugh. "Who knows?"

"That's a neat package, but I don't think it's going to be that easy," Cairn said with a smirk.

"Phil, the sooner your partner and Russo can track this Cruz gal down and we put her to the test, the sooner we'll know."

"Frank will find her, don't worry. I can't wait to hear what she has to say," Cairn said with confidence.

"Okay, Dr. Chin is on his way and Monaghan's lawyer called back and said they'd be in at three o'clock." Kreppell said.

"Good, I'd like another shot at that little prick, even if I don't think he's involved, and if this Cruz girl did it, why would she go to work this morning? Wouldn't she blow town?" Cairn opined.

"And just where does a single mother with a seven-year-old kid go? What does she do? Pack a suitcase and take the few hundred bucks she's probably saved and hop on a bus to Canada? She can't afford to run, she has to stay and try to bluff her way through things, there's no other choice. Then again, she could be nothing more than a victim of circumstance. It's our job to get at the truth," Kreppell stated authoritatively.

Chapter Thirty-Four

The law offices of Lenihan and McKee were located on the second floor of a row of stores on West 231st Street between Broadway and Kingsbridge Avenue. The office took up a corner of the building and the windows faced 231st Street and the city steps leading up to Naples Terrace. A large picture window advertised the firm's name, *Lenihan and McKee, Attorneys at Law* in bold, oversized, gold lettering. The entrance door was at street level between Howard's candy store and The Contemporary Haberdasher's clothing store. The window on the front door advertised the firm's name in smaller print and Sophie had passed it a hundred times without giving it much thought until this morning. She didn't know what type of law Lenihan and McKee specialized in, but she knew she needed a lawyer and she didn't trust anyone she knew from her association with Henry's law practice.

Sophie opened the entrance door and found herself in a hot, dark, musty hallway. A steep set of creaky wooden steps led the way to the second floor. As she climbed the steps she had second thoughts about seeking legal help from Lenihan and McKee. If the quality of their practice was anything like the entrance to the building their office was in it was strictly second rate, she thought. At the top of the stairs were two doors. On the right was a dented and chipped green metal door with no signage and on the left was a broad oak door with Lenihan and McKee's marquee spelled out in brightly polished raised brass letters. The fancy oak door looked out of place in the seedy hallway, and Sophie thought that Lenihan and McKee would have been better off spending their money fixing up the rickety staircase. It reminded her of one of Henry's favorite lines, "New shoes won't fix a broken foot." It was usually reserved for landlords who thought superficial building repairs were all that was needed to cloak the underlying structural defects that necessitated the repairs in the first place.

She opened the office door and found herself in an air-conditioned waiting room. The waiting room was separated from a secretarial area by a half wall. The constant whirring of air conditioners caught her ear first, then the gentle punching sound of electric typewriter keys at work directed her to the secretarial area. She approached the half wall and a bony, middle aged woman with flat black dyed hair swept up in a beehive hairdo looked up from her typewriter and said, "You got an appointment, honey?"

"No, but I was hoping I could speak with someone this morning about a personal matter," Sophie shyly said.

"Civil or criminal?"

"Criminal, although I haven't done anything wrong," Sophie said more boldly.

"Of course," the woman replied sarcastically. "Mr. Lenihan just stepped out a little while ago and he should be back any minute. It's twenty-five dollars for the consultation, and if he agrees to take the case the twenty-five is credited toward your fee."

"Mr. Lenihan specializes in criminal law?"

"Mr. McKee is a former U.S. Attorney and Mr. Lenihan spent five years in Frank Heaton's office. They're both very good, if that's what you need."

"That was Frank Heaton the district attorney?"

"Yes, the one and only Frank Heaton, the famous district attorney," the woman replied tiredly as if she'd heard Frank Heaton's name one too many times and was tired of repeating it.

"Twenty-five dollars, you said?" Sophie asked as she went into her pocketbook and took out a twenty-dollar bill and five singles. She reached over the wall and extended her hand with the money to the woman. "What if I decide I don't want Mr. Lenihan to handle my case?"

"Irregardless, it's going to cost you twenty-five dollars. Time is money and Mr. Lenihan can't waste his time giving free legal advice to everyone who walks in off the street," the woman curtly replied with an emphasis on the word "irregardless."

Sophie's first instinct was to tell her that 'irregardless' wasn't a word. How many times had Henry corrected her when she used that word, she thought.

And her second instinct was to tell her the only thing flatter than her ass and chest was the cheap dye job she had done on her hair, but she held her tongue. *Five years in the district attorney's office had to count for something and the only person I would really trust for an honest referral would be Henry and that's not an option,* she thought. The woman took out a receipt and said to Sophie, "I'm Blanche, what's your name?"

"Sophie Cruz," Sophie answered. Blanche filled out a receipt for the twenty-five dollars and got up from her desk and handed it to Sophie. Sophie took it from her and said, "Thank you." She put the receipt in her pocketbook and sat down in an upholstered chair in the waiting area. Blanche went back to her desk and resumed typing.

Sophie sat in the chair and looked around the room. The walls looked freshly painted, and the wooden floor looked like it, too, had recently been scraped and lacquered. The upholstered chairs in the waiting room all matched and were very comfortable. What little she saw of the secretarial area appeared new and well kept, and it appeared that Lenihan and McKee were the operators of a prosperous law practice, and considering what the rest of the building looked like she figured Lenihan and McKee weren't the landlords and only rented space. Sophie thumbed through a copy of *LOOK* magazine and smoked a cigarette. After about fifteen minutes she heard whistling in the hallway and the scuff of shoe leather scaling the creaky staircase at a quick pace.

Pat Lenihan never entered a room quietly in his life. It wasn't an act or an affectation; it was just his natural way and this day was like every other. He was whistling the "Gypsy Rover" when he came into the building, but by the time he opened the front door to the office he was in full voice, "*Ah dee doo da dee doo da day, ah dee doo da dee dayay, he whistled and he sang til the green woods rang and he won the heart of his lay-a-ady,* oh, excuse me miss, I didn't see you sitting there," Lenihan said as he abruptly cut off his singing.

"Her name's Sophie Cruz and she'd like to speak with you about a personal matter," Blanche called out. "She fully understands what the consultation fee is about."

Pat Lenihan extended his hand and gave Sophie a broad smile. "Miss Cruz, I'm Pat Lenihan, follow me to my office. Blanche, hold all my calls while I speak with Miss Cruz," Lenihan directed.

Sophie had second doubts again. The lawyer seemed a little too bubbly, and the secretary was so disagreeable she didn't know what to expect. *Wasting twenty-five dollars might be the least of my worries today,* she thought. She stood up, shook Lenihan's hand and followed him to his office. Lenihan was a big man. Sophie estimated he was at least six foot four and looked like a football player. Lenihan was well built, with sandy blond hair that was a little long in the back. He had on a well-tailored navy blue suit and black tasseled dress shoes. Sophie wanted to ask him if he belonged to a country club and played golf? She didn't, but there was something about the way he was dressed and how he carried himself that induced Sophie to conjure up the image of Lenihan in plaid pants, a golf shirt and sweater vest with a drink in his hand in some swank barroom at the club talking about the pathetic little Puerto Rican girl who got knocked up by her boss and was now accused of murdering his maid and attempting to murder his wife.

She took a seat, and Lenihan went behind his desk and practically fell into his oversized leather chair. She wondered for a moment if he was drunk? The whistling and loud singing, the extra bounce in his step and the reckless way he treated his furniture was possibly an indication that Pat Lenihan, attorney at law, was not the type of man who paid attention to details, and under the circumstances was not what she was in the market for should she need a competent lawyer to defend her from the accusation she was certain would be directed at her. She took a deep breath and told herself to clear her mind and pay attention. Lenihan put a clean yellow legal pad in front of him and said, "Did you do it?"

"Do what?"

"Whatever it is you're accused of doing."

"I didn't do anything," Sophie exclaimed, then she started crying.

"I understand. You didn't do anything, but you're accused of doing something, correct?"

"Not quite," she replied through her stifled sobs.

"Not quite, I don't get it?"

"I think I'm going to be accused of murder, and I didn't do it. The police haven't caught up with me yet, but I know they're looking for me," she said as she took a tissue from her pocketbook and blew her nose.

"That could be a problem. Tell me the whole story?"

"I work for Henry Weiss. He's an attorney who specializes in real estate and small business partnerships. Have you heard of him?"

"Rings a bell, but I come across so many people, who knows?"

"I've worked for him for almost ten years and we have a child in common. Henry is married and has been for seventeen years."

"Ah, the plot thickens," Lenihan, said with a smirk. "Does he have any children with his wife?"

"No."

"Continue," he said as he put his hands behind his head and stretched his neck.

"We went to Montreal on a combined business and pleasure trip on Tuesday and Wednesday. We had a fight and I left and came back home on the overnight train. I got in to La Rochelle Station around six in the morning and went home. I live right around the corner from here on Kingsbridge Avenue. My mouth is dry, do you have any water?"

"Yeah, let me get you a glass," he said as he got up from his desk and left the office. He came back moments later and handed Sophie a wax paper cup filled to the brim with water.

"Thanks."

"So, that's how you found me. You live in the neighborhood?"

"Yes, my son goes to St. John's and I must have passed your door a hundred times. You know, working for a lawyer I'm the type of person who notices other law offices. Do I recognize the name? That kind of thing."

"Did you recognize my name?"

"No, I didn't, but I needed a lawyer and I didn't want to use anyone Henry knew."

"Makes sense. So your son goes to St. John's?"

"Yes, he's in the second grade. He just made his Holy Communion last month."

"I'm a graduate of old St. John's, as was my father, mother and aunts and uncles. You know how in the Godwin Terrace building they have all the graduation pictures in the hallway?"

"Oh, sure I've seen them. They go way back."

"Well, my picture and pictures of members of my family are hanging there that go all the way back to 1912. Imagine that? Did you grow up around here?"

"No, I was born in Arecibo, Puerto Rico and we moved here in 1933. I was only five. We first lived on Atlantic Street in the Lower Borough, then when I was nine we moved to Fulton Avenue over near Corinthian Park. My father worked in a razor blade factory in the Lower Borough, then got a job as the super's helper in the building we lived in on Fulton Avenue. We lived in the basement next to the boiler room, but the rent was free and he could still work the night shift in the factory. He worked so hard, God bless him, then he died of cancer in 1946, right after I finished high school," she said, and started crying again.

"You loved your father?" Lenihan asked sweetly.

"Oh, my poppy was so good, I still miss him." Sophie said, sniffling.

"That's the immigrant experience, you work hard for your family and so many die young," Lenihan sincerely said.

"Yes, I know. And now he'd be so disappointed with me."

"Please," Lenihan said. "I know you're upset, but let's get back to the problem. What is it that happened and why do you think you're going to be accused of something you didn't do?"

"Foolishly, I decided to confront Henry's wife yesterday and tell her about Joey. He's seven years old. I went to Henry's building and waited for her to come out to go to work. I spoke with the doorman, and when Maria came out I followed her to the subway station and we had an argument. I showed her Joey's Communion picture and threw it at her when she got on the train. A cop saw the whole thing and almost arrested me for disturbing the peace or something. He took my name and Maria's name. Yesterday, Maria's cleaning lady was murdered and Maria was attacked too, and she's in the hospital in intensive care. I just found about the murder this morning, but I know I'm going to be blamed, I just know," Sophie said and started crying again.

Lenihan took a clean handkerchief from his inner pocket and handed it to Sophie. "One question, and if you want my help, you have to answer it honestly."

"What?"

"Did you do it?"

"No, I didn't do nothing but sleep with her man for ten years, nothing else, so help me God, I swear on my mother's grave," Sophie said as she blessed herself and continued crying.

"All right, calm down. You're talking about the homicide of the cleaning lady that happened in an apartment building over on Lincoln Boulevard yesterday afternoon, I believe, are you not?"

"Yes, you read about it in the paper today?"

"I'm already involved in the case."

"Involved? Somebody else hired you?" Sophie asked in a relieved voice.

"I had an inquiry from someone who was questioned by the police last evening, but I have no reason to believe that person has any connection with the crime."

"Then the police got someone else?"

"The police don't have anyone. They questioned the delivery boy who made a delivery to the apartment yesterday. His father is an old client of mine and was just concerned, that's all. I wouldn't call him a suspect. All I was told is the kid delivers to the building regularly and has had no problems at work. At least that's what the father said. Whatever else I know is from the papers. The kid's father isn't the talkative type, but he said his son could fill me in."

"Why would you hire a lawyer if you weren't guilty? Do you think he did it?"

Lenihan started laughing and said, "Excuse me, but why are you here if you didn't do anything?"

"I know I'm going to get blamed for this, I just know," Sophie said angrily. "I never even been in his apartment. And how are you gonna represent two people in this case at the same time?"

"Whoa, calm down, little lady," Lenihan said. "First of all, you're right. I can't, but I can ask my partner to represent the delivery boy. He's a seventeen-year-old kid who's never been in trouble with the police. He's a decent student and plays basketball on his school team. That's all I know about him, but with what little I know I'd say he's a regular kid and not a good suspect."

"And what am I, chopped liver?"

"No, but this kid is a delivery boy. He makes deliveries of groceries to apartments. How many dead housewives or cleaning ladies have turned up lately? None," he said answering his own question. "None, that is but this poor woman yesterday. You, on the other hand, from what you've told me, are deeply involved in a relationship with Mr. Weiss, who is the employer of one victim and the husband of the other victim. Isn't that so?"

"So if he's such a good kid, why doe he need a lawyer? And how can you and your partner represent us both. Isn't that a problem, too?"

"Let me answer your first question. The cops went to his house and gave him the third degree in front of his parents and they didn't like it. And, as for the second question, this isn't a partnership. I should have clarified that before. I say McKee's my partner, but we're just sharing space. All the files are separate. Makes it easier for cross referrals, you know. People in the neighborhood think we're partners. Sounds better, that's all."

"Okay, but if the cops gave him the third degree don't that mean they got something? Isn't that what I said before?"

"No, not at all, I don't have all the facts, but I have friends in the police department and the D.A.'s office and from what I could put together this morning the police don't have much to go on and they're following up on everyone who had contact with the victims yesterday. Mrs. Weiss had a grocery delivery that should have come sometime around when the murder occurred. Naturally, they interviewed the delivery boy. Some cops have no finesse. These two detectives who interviewed him last night, I'm told, treated the kid like he was an accessory to the crime. There was no reason to act that way, but they did. This afternoon I'll get Roger to bring the kid over to the precinct so they can take his fingerprints and do a follow-up interview if needed. I'm not worried because the kid's innocent. You could be a different story?"

"Why?" Sophie asked defensively.

"Because he doesn't have the dirty laundry hanging on his clothesline like you do. Now, I'm going to give you your twenty-five dollars worth of legal opinion on your little personal problem. I spent five years in the district attorney's office. For four of those years I tried cases, and I can say with pride that I sent my fair share of criminals up the river. So be it, but those were five tough years, and would you like to know why?"

"I don't know, you worked long hours and didn't make a lot of money," Sophie weakly replied.

"The experience I picked up in the office was invaluable. But, and it's a big but, I also learned that not everything and everyone in law enforcement is on the level. Not everyone is interested in the truth," he said emphatically.

"I know, and that's why I'm so upset."

"And you should be. That doesn't mean the police and prosecutors are all corrupt. It's just that sometimes they believe all the B.S. about being the first line between civility and disorder. They really believe they wear the white hats and that creates a false concept of moral superiority. I've seen it too many times. I call it the distortion of perception. You know what that distortion is?"

"No," Sophie answered as she thought about asking for her twenty-five dollars back.

"They decide, long before they should, who is guilty. They call it gut feelings and intuition, but it's nothing more than muddled thinking. And to justify that so-called superior intuition, they lie, they distort the facts, or sometimes they omit facts altogether. Anything that distorts their perception of who is guilty is tossed aside as unimportant. Like I said, I've seen it happen too many times. Juries often aren't any better, particularly when the defendant is a minority. Same thing applies to judges. Too many are nothing more than lawyers who got tired of hustling to make a buck or guys who made a few pennies and decided it was time to go at a slower pace. Or pack a jury full of minorities and watch them let some guilty S.O.B. off the hook. I sound a little jaded, don't I?" Lenihan said, laughing.

"Cynical, but what's that got to do with me?"

"You or any suspect or target of an investigation has to be mindful that not every cop you meet is an honorable and upstanding guy. Not every prosecutor lusts for the truth and only the truth. Sometimes they just look at the fact pattern and decide who is guilty, then they go about building the case to meet the standards of their superior intuition, got it?" he said with a snap of his fingers.

"You mean they could have already decided I was guilty? That's crazy." Sophie said with disgust.

"Maybe it is, but if everything you told me was correct, you've got a problem," he said seriously, then without giving her a chance to respond, continued talking. "First off, does Henry, that's his name, right?"

"Yes, Henry Weiss and his wife is Maria Weiss."

"Okay, do Henry and Maria have any children?"

"No, the only child Henry has is Joey and I already told you that."

"Sorry, I forgot. How long have Mr. and Mrs. Weiss been married?"

"Seventeen years, like I said before."

"Yeah, you did. Good, seventeen years and no kids, and for almost ten years he's been playing around with you. And he has a child with you, right?"

"So, I told you all of that," Sophie replied tiredly.

"For more than half of his marriage he's been keeping time with you. Suddenly, you're in Montreal and his wife calls up and you fly off the handle and check out and come home. But you just don't come home and call it quits, you go over to the boyfriend's apartment and wait for his wife so you can rattle her cage by letting her in on a very choice bit of information. She's a stepmother. That's very nice. And in front of a cop you throw a picture of the stepchild at her. Did I miss anything? I was paying attention."

"What do you mean 'stepmother' are you fucking crazy!" she shouted as she stood up and turned toward the door. She looked back and added, "She didn't even know he existed until yesterday. How the fuck could you dirty my son's name by calling that bitch his stepmother?"

Lenihan burst out laughing, and said, "Leave if you want, but right now I'd say you sound like one angry woman. Maybe you are the type who could plan a murder."

Sophie stopped and the tears started flowing again. "Jesus Christ, who are you? I thought you're a lawyer, someone who helps people?"

"I am, but I can only help if the person I'm helping is honest."

"And you don't think I'm telling the truth?"

"I'm not sure. Now, if you want my help, sit down. If not, go and find yourself another lawyer. I'll keep our conversation private. You can trust me," he said sincerely.

Sophie sat back down and said, "Please believe me, I didn't do it."

"Fine, that's the premise. My retainer is five hundred dollars and I charge thirty-five dollars an hour plus expenses."

"I have some money in the bank. Did you really mean it when you said I sounded like someone who could plan a murder?"

"Yes. Anger and jealousy are two of the primary components that lead to murder. Now, if I'm a detective investigating this crime, I ask myself the question, "Why now?" Lenihan smugly said. "Don't answer," he commanded. "Why not when the kid was born or when she was pregnant? Why does she wait until the kid is seven years old to tell her about him, and why when the husband is out of town? And what was it about that phone call from the wife that pissed her off so that she left Montreal? Or is that all bullshit? Could the husband be in on it, too?"

"What are you talking about?" Sophie shrieked. "Now Henry's a part of it also?"

"You're not listening again," Lenihan commanded. "I said I was thinking as a detective. What's going through the minds of the people investigating this murder? They want to solve it. They can't solve it without suspects. You, by your own admission, and I agree with it by the way, have said you're a suspect. You may be innocent, but you're still a suspect or you wouldn't be sitting here and I would already have sent you out the door."

"So what do we do?" she said half-heartedly.

"Have you ever been in Henry's apartment?"

"No, never," she quickly replied.

"Great. I'm going to call the precinct and make arrangements to bring you over this afternoon to have your fingerprints taken for elimination purposes and we'll let them interview you. Now, I'll need to know the entire history of your relationship with Henry Weiss and everything else you can tell me about your relationship with his wife? Is that okay with you?"

"Do you want the check now?"

"We can wait until next week. Are you ready to meet the police today?"

"Are you ready to defend me?"

"Miss Cruz, right now I'm the best friend you have in world. I'm your friend and hired gun, and I'm going to do everything in my power to make certain that no one abuses you or blames you for something you didn't do. I'm good at it, believe me I am," he said confidently and forcefully.

"I do," she said with relief in her voice.

"Hey, it's almost lunchtime. How about we go across the street to Erlich's, just for a light lunch, on me, of course, and you can tell me your life story. How's that sound?"

"So that's what the twenty-five dollars was for?" she replied with subdued laughter.

"C'mon, it's good to see you laughing," Lenihan said as he got up from his chair and led her out of the office.

Chapter Thirty-Five

Sophie's head was swirling as she followed Lenihan out of his office. There was something larger than life about him, but she didn't know if that was going to work for her or against her. He was animated and seemed somewhat mercurial and was nothing like Henry. Henry's legal demeanor was always reserved and conciliatory. He was never aggressive or impatient. Henry refrained from offering his personal opinions on any issue when the discussion was related to business, and he limited his interaction with clients to purely accomplishing what he was hired to do: buy the property or business or sell the property or business. Henry's understated way of conducting business had served him well and his practice prospered. From Sophie's perspective, Henry was the perfect lawyer. He didn't make mistakes, and his clients could thoroughly rely on him to protect their interests. Her immediate impression of Lenihan, after spending twenty minutes in his company was decidedly different. Lenihan was outspoken and opinionated. He acted like a man who enjoyed a good fight and wouldn't be reticent to throw the first punch. Being a suspect in a murder case, and Sophie was certain that's what the police considered her, was not the same as being the seller of a property. Henry's smooth and low key approach to prickly clients and complicated business deals was not necessarily the correct approach when dealing with heavy-handed policemen and predatory prosecutors. *I'm innocent*, she thought, *and I need someone with enough ego, brains and confidence to protect me.* Pat Lenihan, she decided, was that man.

Lenihan stopped by his secretary's desk and said, "Blanche, did Roger get back?"

Blanche looked up from the magazine she was reading and said, "He's in his office, just came back five minutes ago.

Lenihan turned to Sophie and said, "Give me a minute. I have to talk to Roger about that other fellow."

Blanche smiled at Sophie and said, "You decided to hire Mr. Lenihan?"

"Yes."

"Did he discuss a retainer with you?"

"Yes, he told me it would be five hundred dollars, thirty-five an hour plus expenses. I offered to write him a check, but he said to wait until next week."

"Yeah, he hates to ask for money, and five hundred is a lot of money, but you can write the check, now, if you don't mind."

"I know it's a lot of money, but I'm hoping this can all be cleared up and you'll be returning some of that five hundred," Sophie said as she opened her pocketbook and took out her checkbook. While she was writing the check, Lenihan came back into the secretarial area. "Oh, oh, I see the treasurer has got her hooks into you," he said laughing.

Sophie said nothing, and Blanche sarcastically remarked, "I'd rather be the treasurer than the woman from the collection agency chasing down all the deadbeats you gave a pass to, present company excluded," she said with a nod of her head toward Sophie.

Sophie handed Blanche the check and said, "I work for a lawyer, real estate. At every closing one of the first checks I collect is my boss's fee. Sometimes he tells me I'm too pushy, but before every closing he says, 'Sophie, did you figure out the fee?' and I say to myself, yeah, I'm too pushy."

"You're okay, honey," Blanche replied, and for the first time that morning Sophie felt that there was someone else who understood her.

"All right, let's go to lunch. Blanche, please call Sergeant Kreppell. I gave you his number this morning. Tell him that Roger will be in with the Monaghan boy at three this afternoon and I'll be over with Miss Cruz at one-thirty. If one-thirty is no good, he'll have to wait until Monday to speak with her. That ought to fry his ass," Lenihan said, laughing in an exaggerated voice.

It was eleven forty-five in the morning and Ted Kreppell was seated at his desk. He had a scratch pad in front of him and was recording notes from the morning's business. He had spoken with Futerman at eleven-thirty, and Futerman had informed him that Henry had to be at the hospital at two p.m.

and could they move up the walk through the murder scene. Kreppell told him it was no problem, as the borough command had dispatched two more forensic detectives to the scene over an hour ago and was informed that the crime scene could be released as early as twelve-thirty. He didn't believe it would take more than fifteen minutes for Henry to determine what was out of place and he was certain that they could finish up in plenty of time for Henry to get back to the hospital by two. Kreppell's greater interest was Maria's condition and when she would be available for an interview. Futerman told him that her condition had been downgraded from critical to guarded and that she was undergoing several procedures this morning and the earliest they could interview her would probably be Wednesday or Thursday of the following week. Kreppell was frustrated by the unavailability of Maria and couldn't help but wonder if this was a tactic engineered by Henry and Futerman to protect Maria and/or Sophie Cruz. He was also annoyed at Futerman's reference to "several procedures" and would have been more comfortable if the lawyer had spelled out exactly what was wrong with the woman. He sensed that Futerman wanted to stall certain areas of the investigation, and in other areas had used his influence with the district attorney's office to expedite matters. The appearance of two more forensic detectives at the Excelsior at ten-thirty this morning to assist Hogan and Smith proved that theory, he thought, but he couldn't understand what Futerman's ultimate goal was. If he had to guess, Futerman's primary goal was to protect Henry and Maria, with an emphasis on Maria. Kreppell knew that his role was to facilitate the investigation and not to take an active lead and push his subordinates out of the way. It was an impulse he often had to resist. Kreppell prided himself on his objectivity and his sense of fairness, and recognized that if he allowed himself to become too active a participant in an investigation he risked losing his objectivity and his ability to insure that every lead and possible motive and suspect were thoroughly examined before being removed from the equation. With that in mind he went over to the chalkboard he kept in his office and under the heading "Suspects" where he had placed the names Sophie Cruz and Maria Weiss he added the names Tim Cleary and Danny Monaghan. Cairn's passing comment about the nude photographs of Maria Weiss and how they didn't fit into Sophie Cruz committing a murder sparked by jealousy and envy troubled him and left open the question that there was some sexual connection between Maria and another man. *Could that other man be the doorman or the delivery boy*, he pondered? Cairn's description of the doorman leaned toward exclusion, but the delivery boy was another possibility and he resolved to sit in on the interview with Danny Monaghan that afternoon and to personally speak with the doorman, if for no other reason than to get a feel for what type of man he was. Kreppell finished adding Monaghan's name to the list on the board when the phone rang.

"Sergeant Kreppell."

"Hello, Sergeant, this is Blanche O'Connor from Patrick Lenihan's office," Blanche dryly recited.

"Yes, what can I do for you?"

"Mr. Lenihan asked me to call and tell you that he would be available to bring Sophie Cruz in today for an interview, if you're interested?"

"Sophie Cruz?" Kreppell repeated. "Why do I want to see her?"

"He said he can bring her in at one-thirty this afternoon," Blanche said, without answering Kreppell's question.

"Why does Mr. Lenihan think we're looking for her, and isn't he coming in with Danny Monaghan at three?"

"Don't know, and another lawyer, Mr. McKee, will be in with the Monaghan kid at three."

Kreppell felt himself getting angry with Blanche. Her diffidence was annoying, and he said, "Did Mr. Lenihan tell you anything about Miss Cruz?"

"She's a client, do you want to see her at one-thirty or not? I have a lot of work to do, I'm the secretary and Lenihan's the lawyer."

"One-thirty it is," Kreppell said, and abruptly hung up the phone. *It has got to be Sophie Cruz*, he thought, as he went back to the chalkboard and wrote one-thirty next to her name. Kreppell was wiping the chalk dust off his hands with his handkerchief when Dr. Chin walked into his office.

"Ted, putting notes on the board for your students?"

"Richard," Kreppell warmly said as he greeted the medical examiner. "What have you got for me?"

"A preliminary and not much more."

"Does that mean there's a surprise here?"

"No, not at all, just waiting on the toxicology results."

"So it's your original assessment?"

"Yes, death by blunt trauma. I'd say the assailant is anywhere from five feet two to six feet. Probably right-handed and struck the victim in the vicinity of the head near the left temporal lobe with enough force to snap the brain against the opposite side of the skull, then back again, causing injury to the tissue of the left temporal lobe and the brain stem to snap. Freakish, but that's what happened, and I expect nothing from toxicology," the doctor said as he handed Kreppell his one page report. "My preliminary findings are there, and when the final report is done, I'll send you a copy."

"Any ideas on how powerful the assailant had to be? You know, man, woman, that type of thing?"

"The ashtray weighs three pounds and has pointed corners. Honestly, a healthy adult, man or woman is capable of inflicting the wound. Mrs. Campos' bone density is not good, and though she had excess body fat, there was very little muscle and her neck was quite thin. I'd say she couldn't take a punch," the doctor said with no more emotion than if he was talking about a piece of bruised fruit.

"You really think an average sized woman could inflict that much damage?" Kreppell said, pressing him.

Doctor Chin laughed and said, "You have male and female suspects?"

"Yes, and my most likely suspects are either Mrs. Weiss or Mr. Weiss' secretary, and I've never met either of them, so I couldn't begin to tell you if they're big and strong or small and weak."

"You're leaving out an important factor. If I were to match the strength of your average forty-year-old woman against that of an average man her age, the man would be stronger. No argument. However, this is a murder and murders many times are crimes of passion. Heightened anxiety, increased levels of adrenalin resulting in increased strength. I have no problem admitting that a five foot two female weighing one hundred and ten pounds and in high heels could strike the victim with enough force to cause the injuries that were incurred."

Kreppell frowned and read the one page report doctor Chin had given him. "All it says is blunt trauma to the head, preliminary cause of death. That's it?"

"Ted," Chin said with condescension. "Mrs. Campos' death was caused by blunt trauma. There is bruising to the brain on the opposite side from where she was initially struck and there is damage to the brain at the point of impact and damage to the brain stem. In this case those are the injuries resulting in death from blunt trauma. And before you ask, there are no signs of a sexual assault of any kind. I've done my part, the rest is up to you." He stuck out his hand and shook Kreppell's hand. "Until we meet again, and as an occupational hazard that should be quite soon."

Doctor Chin left Kreppell standing in the middle of his office. Kreppell placed the pathologist's one page report on his desk and put his suit jacket on. He took a set of car keys from a hook on the wall, closed his office door and went outside to the driveway of the precinct where his car was parked. *Be patient*, he reminded himself, *just be patient and it will all come together. It usually does*, he thought.

Lenihan and Sophie were seated in rear dining area of Erlich's Restaurant. Lenihan had ordered bratwurst and potato salad for the two of them and tall mugs of Lowenbrau beer. Sophie was admiring the collection of fancy German beer steins that were ubiquitous throughout the bar and dining area. She had never eaten bratwurst before, but Lenihan persuaded her to try it and promised that she'd be back there to dine again.

"So, you graduated high school and went to work at Metropolitan Life as a clerk. How'd you become a legal secretary?" Lenihan asked with genuine interest.

"I started school a year later than other kids. Guess it had to do with coming from the Island, but I was nineteen when I got out of high school. My father was sick with cancer and I couldn't go on to further my education, so I got a job. After my father died I worked and stayed at home with my mother and my younger brother Ray. He's two years younger than me. When Ray went into the Army after high school, my mother came down with pancreatic cancer and died in 1950. It was really sad. I was only twenty-two and there was a little insurance money so I used some of that to pay my way through secretarial school. I went to the Stanhope School at night. It took me three years, but in 1953 I graduated and got a job with the law firm of Rose and Smart," she said as she paused and took a sip from the large mug of beer Lenihan had ordered for her.

"I'm impressed, I love people who aren't satisfied and move on."

"I got my job with Rose and Smart and was assigned to the steno pool. I worked mostly for a couple of associates who did work for the partners in the real estate end of the business. It's where I learned a lot."

"How did you end up with Weiss?"

"Well, I was at the firm for over two years, and a couple of girls had gotten better jobs in the firm, and I was still stuck in the steno pool. The office manager was a Mrs. Buckley. Real old bitch, pardon my French," she said apologetically.

"That's okay, I've heard worse."

"Mrs. Buckley didn't like me. I think it was partly because I was Puerto Rican, but also because of my bad skin," she said as she leaned her face toward Lenihan and pointed at the numerous pockmarks. "She used to ask me if I could do something about my complexion, then she'd complain that my skirts were too tight. Shit like that. I really hated her, but it was my first job as a secretary and I didn't want to blow it."

"So when did Henry Weiss come into the picture?"

"I did a lot of work with this one associate, Burton Hecht. Great guy," she said fondly, and smiled. "Burton was a real pisser, always kidding around, and lots of times when he was doing a closing he'd like to have me there with him to help. These weren't little deals, but pretty big real estate transactions. Henry was representing a client who was selling a shopping center to one of our clients that Burton was representing. It was a big deal, and I spent a lot of time working on it. When we were almost done, Burton and the client left the room and I was alone with Henry. His client had already left. Henry complimented me on my work and asked me how long I had been with Rose and Smart and other things about my work. He then asked me what I earned, and when I asked him why, he told me that he wouldn't be able to offer me a job unless he knew what I was earning so he could offer me more money."

"Just like that, he offered you a job?" Lenihan interjected.

"Yeah, just like that. He told me his secretary was pregnant and was leaving him in two weeks, and he hadn't found someone satisfactory. He offered me five dollars more a week and an annual bonus. He didn't say how much, but there'd be a bonus. When I found out it would be just him and me and no Mrs. Buckley's around to make me miserable I accepted his offer, gave my two weeks notice and that's how we ended up together."

The waitress came with their order and as was placing it in front of them. Lenihan said, "When did everything else happen?"

Sophie waited until the dishes were placed on the table and the waitress had left. Then, in a softer voice, she said, "What do you mean by 'everything else?'"

"The affair, how long after you went to work for Henry did you become more than his secretary?" Lenihan asked as he placed his napkin in his lap and picked up his utensils.

He cut his food into small pieces and was careful not to overload his fork when he pushed small measures of the food onto it. He lifted the fork gracefully to his mouth and slipped it in, then chewed the food quietly. After each bite he wiped his lips with the corner of his napkin and placed it back on his lap. He paused between forkfuls to focus his attention on Sophie and she found it hard to believe that this man with the booming voice and the big body whom she would have expected to tear into his food with the same energy he expended getting into a chair or climbing a flight of stairs sat at the dining table and exhibited such delicate table manners.

Sophie didn't immediately respond to his question about when the affair began. Dining with Lenihan suddenly made her self conscious of her own manners. Sophie had a terrible habit of speaking with food in her mouth and eating her food quickly. She didn't know what Lenihan's initial impression of her was, but if it was negative she didn't want a display of bad manners to add to his impression. She found him mesmerizing and wanted him to like her.

"Try the bratwurst," Lenihan said enthusiastically. "You'll love it."

Sophie cut off a small section of the grilled sausage and put it in her mouth. The sausage was pungent and flavorful. After she swallowed, she smiled and said, "It's delicious. You know, I've heard the word, but had no idea what it was. I thought it was like liverwurst. I hate liver."

"Makes two of us. You should have the sauerbraten here, it's the best."

"I've passed this place so many times. I thought it was just a bar, I didn't ever really pay much attention to it."

"They do a great bar business, but the restaurant is excellent too; best German food in the Upper Borough. Now, you haven't answered my question?" he said as he continued eating.

Sophie put down her fork and waited until she had finished chewing a piece of food, and said, "I started working for him in September of 1955. We're still in the same office on Lincoln Boulevard, down by the courthouse. It's nice."

"I'm sure it is. Is it a single practice or does he have partners?"

"Single practice, but he's in with a group of attorneys. They all rent space and office support from this one attorney who has a long-term lease on half the floor. Lee Futerman, you ever hear of him?"

"Lee Futerman, holy smokes!" Lenihan exclaimed. "Who doesn't know him? He was a professor of mine at Jesuit. I had him for criminal procedure law. Great guy, helped me land my job with the district attorney's office. Lee's a heavyweight. He' a former bureau chief in the office and something of a political force in the Democratic Party here."

"He's a very good friend of Henry's."

"Jesus Christ, that's why Duffy's interested in this case."

"Who's Duffy?"

"Big shot bureau chief and number two man in the office, and a protégé of Futerman's. Futerman probably called him yesterday about the murder and I bet the D.A.'s keeping a close watch on this case."

"That's good then, isn't it?"

"Don't know yet. My guess is Futerman wants to protect your boss and his wife."

"Small world, isn't it?" Sophie said with a sigh.

"It is, and that can be good. Lee Futerman is a standup guy. I have a lot of respect for him, and even though he'll do what he can to protect Henry, he's not the type to help railroad a suspect," Lenihan said with conviction.

"You know him well?"

"Yes, I'm something of a party hack myself. In a good way, I might add. You know, seventy percent of my law practice is spent on criminal and family matters, but seventy percent of my income comes from personal injury and negligence cases. You don't do well in that area unless you've made the right connections," Lenihan said instructively.

"You mean you fix cases?"

"No, I'm honest, at least as honest as a good lawyer can be, and in the real world you've got to have connections. Judges don't throw cases, but they can make favorable rulings, or at the very least, reasonable rulings, and good rulings make insurance companies and the like eager to reach fair settlements. Criminal is an entirely different beast," Lenihan stated as he called for the waitress and asked for another beer. "So, you know Lee Futerman?"

"Yeah, his secretary hates me, but he's all right. Friendly, but kind of impersonal, if you know what I mean?"

"Why does his secretary hate you?"

"I think she's always had a thing for Henry. He used to work for Futerman in the D.A.'s office back in the thirties and she knows we've been having this affair forever, you know?"

"How long exactly were you working for Henry before the affair began?"

"About three months. Like I said before, I went to work for him in September of 1955. He had a very busy office and we were together a lot. We got along so well. We both liked to work, and after a couple of weeks I had his business down pretty good. You know, I got to know the clients and Henry's mood and how he worked. Henry was very friendly and warm. He'd take me to lunch, or if we worked late, to dinner. I had a boyfriend, but I was living at home with my aunt, and I was pretty free. It was nice, he made me feel important and he complimented me a lot," she said happily.

"What about his wife?"

"I knew he had one, she'd call regularly, but she wasn't very friendly, and he didn't talk much about her. I knew they had no kids, but he didn't talk too much about his personal life and I didn't ask. I was just happy he was so nice to me and I was making more money, and it only took me twenty minutes to get to work."

Lenihan had only eaten half of his meal and had pushed his plate away. He was on his second beer and he waited quietly as Sophie ate. She saw that he hadn't eaten his entire plate of food and feeling self-conscious she pushed her plate away too. "It was delicious, but too much for me," she said as she wiped her mouth with her napkin and dropped it haphazardly over her plate.

"You ready for coffee?"

"That would be nice."

"Good, now continue with this most compelling story,"

Sophie sat back, took a deep breath and said, "We really got along good together, and two weeks before Christmas, on payday, he paid me every other Thursday, I got a hundred dollar bonus in my pay. It was a hundred dollar bill, and I was amazed. I'd never had a hundred dollar bill. Tens, twenties, but never a hundred. That was my bonus, and he told me how great it was that I had come to work for him. The title company on the next floor, we used them all the time, was having a Christmas party and Henry and I were invited. We went to the party and had a good time. Lots to drink and eat and we got a little tipsy. When I drink I get a little touchy, you know, I'm everybody's friend and I was clinging to Henry a little, but he didn't seem to care," she said, then stopped to light a cigarette. Lenihan waved to the waitress and held up two of his fingers and she understood the signal for two coffees and brought them over promptly.

"We were having fun, and Henry asked me if I wanted to go out for dinner. He said his wife was working late, I said sure, and we left. We were giggling about something when we got down to the office to get our coats and I just impulsively kissed him on the lips, quick you know, and thanked him for the bonus. He kissed me back and we were all over one another and that's how it began," she said with a shrug of her shoulders.

"Office Christmas parties are notorious for little affairs. So that's excusable, things happen. When did it become serious?"

"Well, we never made it to dinner. Henry put me in a cab and sent me home. Next morning I felt a little funny, but I was embarrassed, but not embarrassed. It was like it was meant to happen. I come in at eight-thirty like I always do and Henry's already there and on my desk is a cup of coffee and a jelly donut. He comes over to me and says, and I remember it exactly, 'Last night was nice, you can't explain it, but sometimes people find one another,' and he goes back into his office. I followed him in and said, 'I feel the same way,' and suddenly we were kissing again and making love on the couch in his office. Just like the night before."

"And I imagine that became a regular routine?" Lenihan stated as much as asked.

279

"Worse, it not only became a regular thing, but I met Maria the following week and it became a contest."

"Contest?"

"The next week we had our office holiday party. Back then, most of the lawyers were Jewish. Most of the help too, so no one was talking about Christmas the way we would, or the girls at my old job at Rose and Smart or Metropolitan would, you know, shopping and gift giving and cooking, all that stuff. At Henry's half of them were going to Miami or Puerto Rico for the Christmas holidays. A couple of the secretaries were ticked off because their bosses were going away, but they had to come in and work, and when you work for just one attorney, and he's away, there isn't much work. Anyway, Henry was going to Vegas with Maria and was giving me the week after Christmas, when he'd be away, off. I was happy and I guess madly in love with him. It sounds silly, but I was. He was really nice, and we had the holiday party and some of the wives showed up. I didn't realize they were coming and I almost panicked. I didn't want to meet his wife. Mr. Futerman ran the party and had it catered. A bar was set up and a table with little sandwiches and hors d'oeuvres. Mr. Futerman gave a champagne toast and wished everyone the season's greetings and a happy New Year. We were standing around eating and drinking and this drop dead gorgeous woman in a green dress comes in the door. Mr. Futerman rushes over and gives her a big hug, and she's really cool. She gives him her cheek to kiss. You know, she ain't gonna kiss him, the little frog," Sophie said with a sneer.

"Stop, let me guess. The gorgeous woman is Maria Weiss?"

"Who else?" Sophie replied with dejection. "All the lawyers are going to her like she's some fucking queen, excuse my French, but she just pisses me off," Sophie said apologetically.

Lenihan put his finger to his lips and said, "You have some mouth, we're in a nice place. If you're going to curse, whisper, please."

"I'm sorry," she whispered.

Lenihan laughed and said, "That's okay. You can speak up, just whisper when you curse."

Sophie giggled and resumed talking. "Henry was standing next to me and Maria came over to us. Henry introduced me, and Maria said, 'So you're the new girl? I need to speak with you.' And I said, 'Nice to meet you and what is it you wanted to speak to me about?' And then I got this cold feeling. I'm thinking, shit, she knows all about us and I was ready to run out of the party and never come back. Anyway, I don't remember everything she said, but she complained to me about her grocery orders. One of my jobs was to call in their weekly grocery order and she tells me that sometimes they send regular milk instead of skim milk, and either I'm getting it wrong or the store is, but get it right from now on. Can you believe that? Like I was her personal slave, the bitch," Sophie said in a soft voice.

"She wasn't happy to make your acquaintance?"

"I didn't exist, and she walked away after giving me my orders. I don't think the other woman liked her much, but all the men talked to her and, you know, I could see she loved the attention. Also, and it was odd I thought, but like I said, before Henry and most of the other the other lawyers were Jewish and she has around her neck, a gold chain, not a choker, but a little longer than a choker and on it was a gold cross. You couldn't miss it, and I thought to myself that she wore that for a purpose. She wanted them to know she wasn't one of them," Sophie said as she tapped a long ash off the end of her cigarette, then stubbed it out in the saucer of her coffee cup.

"Maria, what was she Italian?"

"No, she was, eh, European. You know, from Europe."

Lenihan laughed and said, "Italy's in Europe. I just thought of the name Maria as a common Italian name and was wondering what nationality she was since it's obvious from your story she isn't Jewish. Then again, Marie would be Italian and Maria Spanish."

"Oh, no, she's from Germany, but I think she's Czechoslovakian or something. Whatever, she came here after the war. And she speaks all these languages. You know, that's what I was getting at before. She's very, what would you say, eh," and she paused and Lenihan answered the question for her.

"She very sophisticated?"

"Yeah, if you like that brand," Sophie said with disdain.

Lenihan didn't respond and took the interview in a different direction, "Did Henry leave with her?"

"Of course he did. They stayed for about an hour and left. He said goodnight to me and she said goodnight to most of the people, but I was ignored."

"Did you mention any of this to Henry the next day?"

"No, the next day was Christmas Eve and I worked a half a day. Henry sent me home early and told me not to come back until after New Year's. He never mentioned her, and as far as I was concerned I was gonna do what I felt like. I felt sorry for him. You know the expression; 'Beauty's only skin deep?' Well, that fitted her to a tee."

"How long did the affair go on before you had your son?"

"About two and a half years. I had a boyfriend, Carl. I was going out with him before I met Henry. It was crazy, you know. I loved Carl, but there was something about Henry. My periods were always regular. I could pick the day and I was always careful. Carl was away in the National Guard and I slipped, you know, miscalculated, and I got pregnant. I counted back on the calendar and I knew it had to be Henry because Carl had been away a month."

"It didn't bother you, two-timing your boyfriend?"

"No, because Henry was two-timing Maria. We never talked about Maria or Carl, but it was like a secret thing, we had each other. It was special. When Carl found out I was pregnant he wanted to marry me. He had a business installing blinds and drapes. A small shop, and he did all right, but he wasn't the kind of guy who really minded your business, you know, he didn't ask how many months was I pregnant or information like that. He could never believe I was fooling around with someone else, it would have killed his machismo, and probably Henry."

"So how did you fool him?"

"I didn't. I just refused to marry him. I said it was my responsibility to be careful and I wasn't ready to marry. His name went on Joey's birth certificate, then I think he figured things out and got a new girlfriend," she said sadly.

"Sorry you didn't marry Carl?"

"No, not at all. It was a relief. If I had married him I would have had five kids and not been able to work. You know, I'd be home cooking and cleaning and waiting on him all the time. He was that type."

"So what did Henry think about the pregnancy?"

"Not much. I didn't tell him until I was five months, I didn't show much. He asked if Carl and I were going to marry, and I said, 'No.' Henry has a habit of avoiding uncomfortable situations. You know, just act like nothing happened and keep doing what you're doing," she said with resignation.

"I had an uncle who showed up drunk at every family affair. You'd see a couple of raised eyebrows among my grandparents and aunts and uncles, but no one ever said boo, it's the old line about ignoring an elephant in the room."

"That's Henry. I was pregnant and he didn't ever want to think he could be the father, so he just ignored the situation. Two years after Joey was born we had a fight and I told him the truth. He was pretty angry, something you don't ever see from him, but he calmed down and he's helped me ever since, you know, he moved me to the new building and pays the rent and other bills. Like I told you earlier, he wants Joey to go to a private school in Riverview. He's been pretty good, I think."

"Sure, he sounds like a prince. It's a good thing you didn't get pregnant again," Lenihan said sarcastically.

"I'm not stupid, I made him wear a raincoat after that, you know. Of course, I'm the one who goes to the drugstore and buys them," she said with a shake of her head.

"He has no children with his wife. You'd think he knew something about birth control?"

"I never got into that with him but I think the bitch can't have kids."

"Maybe he didn't want children, why do you think it's her?"

"She's a bitch. Take for instance the way she treats him. Henry likes a good time, who doesn't? He'd go out to dinner every night, if she would. Loves to go to ball games and shows he's a doer. Maria, all she does is break his balls, and the last two years she's been miserable," Sophie said quickly. She was in such a rush to press her case that the complaints came tumbling off her lips in a disjointed harangue that offered far more insight into Sophie's personality than it did Maria's.

"Wait a minute, you said before that he never talked about his wife?"

"Yeah, early on, but I've been with him for nearly ten years. He talks plenty now. You know how many times he's had tickets for a play and she's called him at work and said she had a headache or something and didn't want to go?" Sophie stated. "At least five times," she said, answering her own question. "And, c'mon, who doesn't like to go out and eat? I hate cooking. He likes a nice restaurant and a good meal, she wants to stay home and eat salad and poached fish or cottage cheese," she said as she puckered her mouth and made a face.

"They're not compatible? Is that what Henry's led you to believe?"

"Oil and vinegar."

"Tell me, how many times have you met Maria, you know, actually been in her company with Henry?"

"She's been to some of the holiday parties and to the office once in a blue moon. But she don't talk to me at all, and even when she calls she never makes any small talk, basically "Hello, it's Mrs. Weiss, put Henry on the phone," and nothing else."

"All right, you and Henry have been engaged in this affair for almost ten years. You have a child in common and it seems that things have been working fine for all this time. What happened in Montreal that pushed you over the edge?"

"We've never gone on that many trips together, me and Henry. I was looking forward to being with him, and on Monday I asked if he'd pick me up on the way to La Rochelle Station. You know, we could go in a taxi together. He told me 'No,' and said I should take a taxi myself and meet him there. Now, I knew he didn't want to go with me because he wanted to take Maria to work. I took a taxi and the traffic was so bad I got out two blocks before the station. I was carrying my bag and Henry saw me and got out of his cab. I told him I took the subway just to make him feel bad. He can be so dumb, he believed me. Now if I took the subway why would I be up on the street? But I said that just to make him feel bad and gave him a big hug and he sort of pushed me away. I knew something was going on."

"What happened next?"

"We had breakfast, but he was quiet. I got it out of him that he gave Maria a ride to her job and it hurt because, even though the trip was business, he was going to be mine for two days, but I could see that any chance to be with her was more important than being with me. I just felt it," she said emotionally, as tears formed in her eyes again. "That night we went out to dinner and when we went to bed he didn't want to do nothing. That's not like him. I didn't say boo because, to tell you the truth, and I don't know why I'm telling you all of this when it's so personal, but I was just happy to be in bed next to him. To know that the next morning when we woke up we'd be next to one another. Something she gets to do every day, but don't give a shit about, I know, believe me."

"Telling me how you feel, deep down is very important," Lenihan said in a soothing and encouraging way.

"Wednesday was all work in the morning; Henry, these Canadian lawyers, different properties changing hands and Mr. Ankowitz, he can be a real pill at times. We finished late in the day and were back in our room at the Ritz. We had a quickie, that's what he likes, and we were planning on going some place nice and romantic for dinner when the bitch called."

"Maria called?"

"Yeah, and I could see it on his face. I don't know what she was telling him, but he was on the phone with her and it was like I didn't exist. I knew right then and there that she knew about us and was going to use her power over him to end it all, I just knew," she said as her voice grew louder.

"Calm down," Lenihan said soothingly. "What power?"

"She's like some sacred being to him. It's more than her good looks. It's like she's something he has, but can never possess. Maria's his, but only on her terms. Like I said before, he always wants to do things, go to dinner, shows, good stuff, and she's always putting him off at the last minute. They'll be in a restaurant and she won't eat her order, claim its garbage, or he'll make plans to meet and she'll come late. I know. He tells me, but it don't matter. She say's "jump" and he says "how high?" Sophie said, her voice dripping with contempt.

"Good for you, you had enough and left. Now tell me exactly what you did from the time you left Montreal until this morning when you found out about the murder?"

"I have to pee," Sophie said as she stepped out of the booth. "I'll be right back."

Lenihan watched her walk to the bathroom. She had her back to him and he admired the sensual sashay she affected when she walked. Sophie was no more than five feet four or so he thought, but in a pair of spiked heels she appeared much taller and there was a certain equine grace to her. Earthiness was the word that came to mind, and from the neck down, or from behind, or at a distance she was a woman he'd hungrily give a second or third look too. Up close, the acne scarred skin was a detraction, but after being in her company for a while that faded and he found her immensely attractive. Although he'd never met Henry Weiss, he could understand the attraction to Sophie. Lenihan chided himself for thinking about Sophie in that way. She was a client, but nevertheless he found her appealing.

He imagined that under the right circumstances she would be an easy woman to bed. The clothes would peel off quickly and she would present herself playfully and aroused. A woman like Sophie treats sex as recreation, he figured and even though she may have limited her favors to one man, those favors were awarded freely. *The Sophie's of the world don't interpret sex as some long drawn out quasi-religious ritual*, he thought, *they accept it for what it is, a normal expression of human emotion and more importantly, a necessary one. What was unnecessary was her overt hatred of Maria. No matter how much she hates Maria I have to insist that she bury her feelings or she'll end up convincing the police she's guilty,* he thought as she made her way back to the table. He suddenly felt self-conscious. *I shouldn't stare*, he told himself, but as she was approaching their booth he couldn't help but stare at her legs.

After she sat back down, he redirected his attention to the conversation and said, "You took the train from Montreal to Huguenot City. What time did you arrive in La Rochelle Station?"

"Around six in the morning, maybe twenty to the hour. I don't remember exactly. It was early."

"How'd you get home, and did you go directly home?"

"Of course, I took the subway. It's easier than going upstairs with your bags and looking for a cab. Cheaper too."

"What next?"

"I got home and my Aunt Lucy was there. She was happy to see me. I woke Joey up and we had French toast and I took him to school. I then went over to Monmouth Road and bought him a baseball glove and bathing cap for camp. I had a cup of coffee from a coffee shop and drank that in St. Jerome's Park. Then I got the idea to confront Maria."

"Just tell me everything exactly as it happened?"

"I went over to her apartment house and saw the doorman. He said she goes to work around noon on Thursdays, so I waited outside. The doorman was a creepy little guy. You know, I didn't like the way he stared at me. It's funny, but some men, men you find attractive, can look at you that way and it's a compliment. Other men, the creepy ones, they look at you like that and it makes you sick."

"Stick to the story."

"Well, maybe it's the doorman."

"That's for the police to find out."

"I waited out in front and smoked a couple of cigarettes and finally she came out. The creepy little guy was with her and she sees me and says something like, 'What do you want?' or something snotty. And I just started talking. I don't even remember what I said, but I followed her to the subway and right down to the platform and showed her Joey's picture and told her about me and Henry. I was pissed," then she whispered, "Fucking pissed."

"Was anyone else on the platform with you two?"

"I didn't see anyone, but after I gave her the picture, she dropped it, and I was cursing and saying stupid shit, this cop comes out of nowhere. He broke it up and she got on the train. I threw the picture in just as the doors were closing and that's the last I saw of her, I swear," she said dramatically as she put her right hand over her breast.

"Then what?"

"The cop took my name and told me he could have arrested me for disturbing the peace and asked me Maria's name, and I left."

"Did you get his name? Do you remember what time it was when this all happened?"

"No, but he was a Ni…" and she caught herself and said, "he was a Negro, you know, a colored man. Real black skin, but friendly."

"What's that mean? The darker the skin the friendlier the officer?"

"No, I was just describing him. He was a colored man, his skin was very dark and he was friendly. Why are you being mean?"

"I don't want you to sound prejudiced, that's all. Negroes, Jews, and any other group, you have to be careful how you speak about them. Don't paint yourself in a corner."

"Prejudiced," she shot back at him. "I'm a fucking Spic as far as plenty of people are concerned, and that includes Jews and you know who. I never heard of no fucking Puerto Rican double ACP, did you?"

"Cool down and stop cursing, I'm making a point. Let's get back on track. What time was it about when this happened?"

"It was around noon. She left on the subway train and I went to the movies," she said petulantly, obviously tiring of Lenihan's questions.

"What theatre, what movie?" Lenihan said in a sharper tone.

"Loew's Grand Palace, I saw *The Sound of Music* and *Robin and the Seven Hoods*. I came in and *The Sound of Music* was already playing. I slept through *Robin and the Seven Hoods*, I don't like Sinatra, and I saw the beginning part of *The Sound of Music*, then left around five-thirty or so. I went to Karl's and bought some chocolate for Joey, then called my aunt. I wanted to go out for Chinese, but she told me my brother Ray and cousin Freddy wanted to go to Clam Island. They finally sold their car service. I went home on the one bus and my cousin Freddy picked us up around seven-thirty and we went to dinner at Nicky's Seafood, then we went to Freddy's house for coffee and got home around midnight, and I went to work today to face the music. You know, with Henry and the scene with Maria. Then Ruth Goolnick, that's Futerman's secretary, she hates me too, she told me about the murder and—"

Lenihan interrupted her and said, "Let me stop you there. Up until you went to work this morning you knew nothing about the murder, correct?"

"Nothing, I swear."

"Did you keep your half of the ticket stub for the movie yesterday?"

"No, I threw it away."

"What did the ticket seller look like, can you describe her?"

"No, I think it was a woman."

"Did you go to the candy counter and buy something?"

"No, I bought a box of Night and Day licorice candy from the candy machine."

"Is there anyone who could place you in the movie theatre yesterday, or in Karl's, or the bus going home?"

"Yeah, when I was going home on the bus we were stopped by Kingsbridge

Road and I saw that creepy little doorman. He didn't have his jacket on, but he was staring at me," she said with some relief in her voice, happy to answer one of his questions in the affirmative.

"That was between five-thirty and six, you said?"

"Approximately, I'm always bad about time."

"It's something," he answered. "Now did you tell your aunt or brother or anyone about the scene with Maria?"

"No, never. They hate Henry. They know he's Joey's father and he pays my bills, or most of them, but they don't want me to have anything to do with him. It's a sore subject, and my brother's angry I still work for him. I tell Ray to mind his own business and we don't talk about it, but I would never bring Henry or Maria up with my family. Like you said before, it's the elephant in the room," she said, laughing. "That's all that happened yesterday. I've never been in Henry's apartment. I just came to you today because the doorman saw me, then the cop, and I don't want to get sucked into this. I just want to be done with him. I'm okay don't you think?"

"Yes and no," Lenihan replied. "First of all, your behavior is suspicious, and I'll tell you why. What you did was stupid and cruel. And, I'm being honest, because an hour ago you gave me a five hundred dollar retainer. I hope that by next week I can return a good portion of that to you, but I owe you the truth."

"What do you mean stupid and cruel?"

"Listen, please listen to me. I told Blanche to tell them one-thirty and it's getting late. You started an affair with a married man and ended up with his child. You hate his wife, you haven't said one nice thing about her, but let's be frank, you don't even know her. Henry's been married to her for seventeen years. He didn't stay with her because he couldn't afford to divorce her, he's got money and it hasn't bothered him to pay your rent and extra freight. Didn't you tell me when we were crossing the street that he wanted to send your son to an expensive private school?" Lenihan didn't wait for her answer and put his fingers to his lips and said, "Shh. Just listen. You hate Maria because Henry loves her and won't give her up. Simple as that and for my money that's your business. You can hate whomever you please. But Maria's not the bad guy. How she treats her husband is her business and not your business. He hasn't left her yet, and I doubt he will. Now, she may have treated you poorly and that's a negative reflection on her, but who says she has to be a nice person? Nobody! She's his wife and you're his mistress. You lose. Now why did I say stupid? It appears to me that in Montreal you finally came to your senses and realized Henry Weiss is a first class bum and heel. Selfish prick, if you'll pardon my French this time. From your description it sounds like everything has to be his way, and not his wife's. And here you are fifteen years younger than he is, give or take a year, and he's making time with you all these years and letting you ruin your life for his pleasure. Stupid, and I'll tell you why. You should have left Montreal and found my office yesterday and we should have begun a first class paternity suit against this heel and bled him dry so that your son would get everything he deserves. Now, for cruel, you were cruel because you blamed all of your boyfriend's shortcomings on his wife and complicated the matter by shoving a picture of his illegitimate son in her face at a time and place that was inappropriate and unexpected," he said with a good deal of emotion. Sophie was shocked by Lenihan's sharp upbraiding of her and started to cry and went to step out of the booth. He leaned over with his oversized hand and gently took her hand. "Sophie, please. I really like you, and I want to help, but I can't unless you understand the truth. We're due at the precinct in a half an hour. You and I both know they'll want to question you and we also know that if you refuse to answer their questions or act dumb about everything that'll make you that much more of a suspect. The murder and assault, I guess Mrs. Weiss was assaulted, took place in that apartment. An apartment you were never in. Logically, it can't be you, and I believe you. The police need to believe you too, and that means Maria Weiss can't be the enemy. You need to tell the story of your affair with Henry and what you did yesterday with as little emotion as possible. You love Henry, you were angry and confronted his wife out of spite, you feel sorry for what you did, and so on, but you cannot, simply cannot, express the venom for her that you expressed to me today. If you do, you'll make yourself a suspect. Do you understand? Remember what I told you in my office? I'm your best friend, your protector, but I can't succeed unless you do what I tell you."

Sophie wiped her eyes and smiled at Lenihan. His rebuke hurt her feelings, but she knew he was right. At that moment there was nothing more she wanted than his respect, and she quietly answered him, "Yes, I understand."

Lenihan smiled and reached across the table and patted her hand. "Good, now this morning was the first you heard about the murder, correct?"

"Yes, Henry hadn't come into work and I went to the outer office and asked Ruthie if she'd heard from him. Ruthie showed me the newspaper story and said something, I don't even remember but it was like I already knew. I ran back to my office and started crying. I don't know why, but I knew Maria had Joey's picture and with the doorman and the cop I just was going to be a suspect. That's why I came to you," she said and almost started hyperventilating. She was going to tell Lenihan about going to Henry's apartment that morning, but decided not to. She found his criticisms cutting and to admit that she was so stupid that she actually contemplated entering a murder scene to recover the picture would have cast her as a complete idiot. She didn't want him to have any lower an opinion of her than she expected he'd already formed, and she decided to say nothing. *After all,* she thought, *no one saw me and there's no need for anyone to be the wiser.*

Lenihan paid the check and said, "It's one o'clock. Let's check with Blanche and make sure were on for one-thirty and take a drive by Loew's Grand Palace. I'll get out and ask the ticket booth clerk if she was working yesterday. That way you can take a look and be able to describe her to the cops if they ask. I want to cover all the bases. And, Sophie, I was tough on you for a reason. You take your lumps from me and when the police question you it'll be a cakewalk. Remember, you answer each question. Don't volunteer information and don't call anyone names. There's no crime in being in love with someone and hoping someday they'll love you back. Hey, maybe they have some evidence and know who did it and this was all a silly exercise," he said cheerfully.

"I hope so, but what about Henry?"

"Sophie, if I wasn't a happily married man I'd ask you for a date myself. Don't sell yourself short. There are plenty of good guys out there, ones without wives. When we get done with Henry and you see him for what he really is you'll only be too happy to take him to the cleaners. And believe me, you'll find someone else and maybe a little happiness, too," he said with encouragement as they left the restaurant.

Chapter Thirty-Six

Kreppell pulled up to the front of the Excelsior. Hogan had the forensic bureau station wagon parked in front of a fire hydrant and there were no other available spaces. He was tempted to double park the unmarked police car, but that constant habit he had to always try and do the right thing won over and he drove a block past the building and found a legal parking space. Since his days as a rookie when his first partner was an old timer who believed that in between every run it was proper etiquette to stop at a grocery store or bar and grab a cold beer, Kreppell was contemptuous of fellow cops who believed laws were for everyone else. That attitude had made him something of a pariah when he first made sergeant and though he tried, with little or no success, to impart those values to his subordinates, he remained steadfast in his determination to not abuse his position or take liberties with the law. Captain Grimsley, his boss, had once told him after Kreppell had complained at length about how accepted police courtesies and petty abuses were nothing more than veiled acts of corruption that "Values are like religion. Something you should practice but not preach." Grimsley's message was simple and direct: worry about number one. Grimsley was a tough, straightforward taskmaster who wanted his unit to succeed and was willing to let the ends justify the means if it meant success. "If they have to cheat to get the job done and they get caught, that's their fault for being sloppy or stupid," he would lecture. Grimsley wasn't one of the boys and didn't have much of a heart. Kreppell was an outsider, but he was competent and judicious and would never embarrass his boss, and because of that Grimsley collected every favor he was owed to ensure that Kreppell would remain in the homicide unit as a lieutenant after his promotion.

It was a hot muggy day, just like the day before, and Kreppell loosened his tie and undid the top button of his shirt. All the possibilities surrounding the investigation were swirling through his mind and he hoped that Hogan or Henry Weiss or some unknown witness would come across the smoking gun they needed to wrap the investigation up. Cairn and Widelsky's upcoming transfer, picking their replacements and whether he could keep Cairn in the unit or not along with his promotion to lieutenant were all matters that would be easier to handle if this investigation were closed. The day's newspaper stories about the homicide were brief, but he expected interest to build as the case went on. Millie Campos' husband was a deacon in St. Elizabeth's Church in the northwest section of the Upper Borough, and Grimsley had already fielded an inquiry from the Archdiocese about the progress of the investigation. Lee Futerman was a heavyweight and used to be one of the In Crowd. His clout and interests couldn't be ignored either. It wouldn't be long before a call was made to police headquarters downtown and some chief with a bug up his ass was riding Grimsley over the lack of progress in the case. Grimsley was a survivor, and Kreppell knew that no matter how much Grimsley liked him or depended on him, he was expendable. As Kreppell was approaching the building, he saw Hogan coming out of the courtyard carrying the square leather book bag that contained all of his evidence recovery tools. Hogan smiled and waved to Kreppell with his bad hand with the bandaged thumb. The bandage was covered in black fingerprint powder and Kreppell wondered what had happened to the surgical glove he was going to buy to protect the thumb?

"Hey, Sarge," Hogan called out, "I think I got something."

Kreppell increased his stride, anxious to hear what Hogan had found and intent on not sharing the information with the neighborhood. Kreppell put his finger to his lips to quiet Hogan, but the garrulous detective ignored him and shouted out, "You were right. I got a couple of hits from the service elevator."

"Hogan, pipe down," Kreppell ordered. "No need to let the world in on what you found. Some busybody overhears you and she tells someone else and then some bored reporter gets a lead and it's in the newspaper."

"This ain't no big case, and I ain't seen a reporter all day."

"Whatever, what did you find?"

"The service elevator was cleaned Wednesday afternoon. They keep a log of all deliveries and there were none between the time it was cleaned and the murder was reported except for Weiss' delivery, none after the murder either.

Lunch, the porter, is a pretty efficient cleaner and the walls were sparkling clean except for three very nice impressions. One is a small hand on the right wall and a little above it is a slightly larger hand. On the left wall is the impression of three fingers, I think the pinkie, ring and middle fingers and I think they're from the same person as the bigger hand on the other wall. Now there are overlays on the basement elevator button and the button for the eighth floor, but a clear impression, like it was rolled, you know, on the button for the seventh floor. The elevator buttons have the floor number in black and white under a clear plastic covering. That's great for getting prints. Now the way I figure is the overlays are the delivery boy and Millie Campos', just like the small handprint on the right wall is Millie Campos'. But who is the slightly larger print on both walls and the seventh floor button?" Hogan asked with a big grin on his face.

"Maybe it's Lunch the porter's prints?"

"No way, he's got a hand could palm two basketballs. I think it's a woman's hand or an older kid's."

"What about the pantry?"

"Tracy and Collins are doing that. Prints and smudges all over that room. Mr. Weiss and his lawyer are here. They went up with Cairn to the apartment."

"Already? They're here early," Kreppell, said with annoyance. "Where are you going now?"

"Back to my office. I'm gonna sort all these prints out and get ready to do the eliminations. Tomorrow's a duty day, but I hope to have all my comparisons done today and most of my reports filed."

"I'll have Frank or Phil take care of Sophie Cruz and the Monaghan kid, and I'll get them over to you as soon as I can. Get a move on what you have now, okay?"

"Sure, Smitty and I are gonna grab a quick bite, then I'll get to it."

"See you later," Kreppell called out as he headed into the building.

Kreppell walked into the lobby of the Excelsior and met up with Lee Futerman, who was engaged in a conversation with Tim Cleary. "Counselor," Kreppell said solicitously. "You're early."

"Sergeant," Futerman politely responded. "Henry was anxious to get back to his apartment. He's upstairs with Detective Cairn. I didn't want to intrude, and Mr. Cleary was filling me in on all the unfortunate excitement that occurred on his watch yesterday," Futerman added as he gave Tim a pat on the back. "Mr. Cleary's quick response may have saved Mrs. Weiss' life."

"Thank you, I was just doing my job."

"Mr. Cleary, Tim is your first name, isn't it?"

"Yes, Tim Cleary."

"I'm Sergeant Kreppell. Detectives Cairn and Widelsky told me you were very helpful yesterday."

"I tried my best, sir."

"I'm sure you did, but could we have a word in private?" Kreppell demanded, rather than asked.

"Yeah, we have an office over here."

"You'll excuse us counselor, won't you?" Kreppell asked as he followed Tim to the small office behind the reception desk.

"Of course, Sergeant, Mr. Cleary already gave me a full report on his actions yesterday and I thought it rather comprehensive. I imagine you're somewhat confused over whether it's the secretary or the delivery boy, but I'd pay close attention to our doorman here. Henry tells me he's a fine young man. Once Henry's finished, we're going over to the hospital to visit Mrs. Weiss," Futerman said with the utmost casualness.

Kreppell found Futerman annoying, and the remark about Sophie Cruz or Danny Monaghan being the murderer was smarmy. It seemed that Futerman's only objective was to keep Maria Weiss out of the investigation. Kreppell walked into the small office and closed the door behind him. He sat down behind the desk and said to Tim, "Who is that man?"

"Who, Le, Le, Lee?"

"Yeah, that old fart we were just talking to."

"I thought you knew him. He's Mr. Weiss' friend. I think he's a lawyer and you, you called him counselor. So, you must know him?"

"Yes, he is a lawyer and a very good one. Why would Mr. Weiss need a lawyer?"

"Got me, but I didn't do nothing wrong," Tim said with a pained scowl on his face.

Kreppell could understand why Widelsky didn't like Tim Cleary. He was defensive by nature and easily scared. A good defense attorney would render him useless and unbelievable on the stand. "So you told him everything you told the detectives yesterday?"

"Yeah, same story," Tim answered. He started to fidget with his hands and found it hard to make eye contact with Kreppell. Kreppell had developed a slow and easy cadence in interviews over the years with witnesses and suspects, and he always waited a few seconds after someone spoke to ask the next question. Many times the interviewee found the pause unnerving and started talking again just to fill the void. It was a common tactic in the business, and Tim Cleary fell into Kreppell's trap immediately after Kreppell failed to respond with another question. Tim took a quick peek at Kreppell's blank face and said, "I didn't accuse nobody. I just told him about the Puerto Rican chick and Danny."

"Who's Danny?"

"Danny Monaghan, the delivery boy for the Associated. He came around twelve, and then I must have seen him close to one o'clock coming from the alleyway area. I told those detectives yesterday. I just told that to Lee, but it's old news."

Kreppell let a few seconds pass, and said, "I heard. Tell me about Mrs. Weiss; is she nice, you know, pretty, friendly, a pain in the ass? You see her every day."

"She's nice, real classy woman. You see her dressed up and she looks like something out of one of those movies from the 1940s," Tim said with a little more enthusiasm than he had shown so far in his conversation with Kreppell.

"This is 1965, she dresses like it's still the forties?" Kreppell asked in a way that made it sound as if Tim had been ridiculing Maria.

"No, don't get me wrong, she's always in style. Shoes and bag and the times she wears a hat, everything matches. I just meant she's classy, like a movie star or something. She goes for walks and wears sneakers and a sweatshirt and a scarf and sunglasses and she don't look like nothing. Then the next day she'll be going to work and everything about her will be just perfect. Ain't no lady in the building can keep up with her," he said with an approving shake of his head.

"Sounds like you fancy the lady a little," Kreppell teased.

"No, she ain't my type. She's kinda a blonde and I like the Spanish girls, and she's too old for me anyway," Tim offered off with a wave of his hand.

"Pardon me," Kreppell said. "I didn't know you were such a connoisseur of women. Classy and movie star like isn't enough for you."

Tim bowed his head and sheepishly said, "Aw c'mon. Lady like that wouldn't give me a second look anyway."

"That's more like it. Now you said she was too old for you. Is she old looking?"

"She's fifty, but if you saw her you'd never know it. I just said she was too old for me because I found out yesterday how old she was, but she don't look it at all, not at all."

"That's all I've heard since the murder yesterday is how good looking this woman is. I was interested in what you thought, that's all," Kreppell said in a very friendly way.

"She's got great legs and always wears high heels when she goes to work. I hold the door for her and follow her right outside and watch her go across the street. You should see what lives here. Bunch of old bags, real yentas, you know. But, what the heck, it's Lincoln Boulevard," Tim replied with a short laugh.

Kreppell laughed along with him and said, "She got a nice ass, Mrs. Weiss has?"

"Nice ass, legs and tits. She's got it all, and in the warm weather she always keeps a button open on her dress so you can see the cleavage. I think she's a tease, but you stand here all day and see what I see and you'd pay a lot of attention to her too," Tim said in a knowing way growing more comfortable with Kreppell as the conversation continued. At first he had expected Kreppell to belittle him and bully him like Widelsky had. Kreppell's interest in Maria and Tim's opinion of her made him feel important, and even though this was the first time he had ever spoken about Maria Weiss in such a revealing manner to anyone except Lunch and it made him feel much more like a man than the invisible cog who opened doors and sorted mail and performed other menial tasks without ever attracting much attention or recognition from the majority of people he came into contact with every day.

"My wife used to be like that til she had kids. Now she's as fat as a house," Kreppell lied.

"That's what Lunch says. Mrs. Weiss looks so good 'cause she ain't never had no kids. Lunch says kids ruin a woman's figure."

"Is Mrs. Weiss nice to you? She ever flirt with you or tease you?"

"She's always very nice to me, but she treats me like I'm a little kid."

"So, she would be shocked if she heard you talking about her this way, wouldn't she be? You know, nice ass, tits?" Kreppell said with a strong edge of criticism.

Tim blushed and his voice went up a pitch, "We were just talking, you know, man to man. Mr. Weiss is so nice to me, pl- pl-please," he stammered. "We were just talking."

"My lips are sealed," Kreppell said as he put his fingers to his lips. "By the way, do they make you wear that heavy doorman's coat all summer long?" he said changing the subject.

"After May 1st I can wear a short sleeve shirt and a bow tie or the coat. It's my choice. I always wear the green pants and hat. I'm only wearing the coat yesterday and today because all my short sleeve shirts are in the Chinks and I got home too late to pick them up. Up until last year we had to wear white gloves, too. Like the traffic cops wear," Tim replied, obviously relieved that the discussion about Maria had ended. Tim then walked over to the desk and opened a drawer on the lower left side and pulled out a small cardboard box. He opened the box and inside were several pairs of white cotton gloves. "The company used to buy these by the dozen until we got a new manager. He said it was a waste of money and that was that. Mr. Spinelli was the old manager. He was a retired military guy and what a ball buster. He left and the new guy, Mr. Ferrara, could care less. I'm always neat and clean anyway, but do you know how fast those gloves get dirty?"

"I can imagine," Kreppell replied.

The door to the room opened and Cairn and Widelsky walked in. Widelsky ignored Kreppell, and turned to Tim and said, "My friend the munchkin. We gotta take a ride over to the precinct so I can get your prints. Just routine, of course, unless that is, you told the sergeant something you didn't tell me," he said to Tim as he put his hand on Tim's shoulder and gave it a hard squeeze. Widelsky's mere presence accelerated the doorman's blood pressure.

His face reddened, and when Widelsky squeezed his shoulder he felt a chill go down his spine. He looked to Kreppell and said weakly, "Whenever, you're ready. If, I'm finished here?"

"We're finished, for now."

"Mr. Weiss is outside, he'd like to talk with you for a moment," Cairn said as he pointed to the lobby. Tim grabbed his hat, put it on his head, and without looking at either Kreppell or Widelsky he quickly slipped out of the room.

"Boy, you love to give it to that guy Frank, why?"

"Phil, we got four suspects. Delivery boy, doorman, secretary and Mrs. Weiss and I'm fucking with each and everyone of them until I know which direction to go in," Widelsky said with determination.

"I thought you had your mind made up this morning that it was Mrs. Weiss?" Kreppell asked sarcastically.

"I did, but then I thought about Colonel Mustard in the library," Widelsky quickly and impudently retorted. "Sarge, we're like two prom queens picking out shoes when we work a case. If there are six suspects, we'll end up looking for number seven before we make any real moves. This is still very preliminary," Cairn said in an attempt to reduce the friction between Kreppell and Widelsky.

"My apologies, I think I underestimated you two."

"No offense taken. If Frank had a personality things would be different."
Cairn chuckled.

"Fuck off," Widelsky said to Cairn as much as to Kreppell. "You learn
anything from that little geek?"

"Yes, he has a very keen eye for Mrs. Weiss, nice ass, legs, tits, outfits,
etc.," Kreppell replied. "Maybe you two should spend a little more time with
him, particularly if we don't get anywhere with Sophie Cruz."

"Definitely, I still think there's an angle on those girlie shots of Mrs. Weiss
we may have missed. Maybe the munchkin's been in her apartment before and
has rummaged through her things. You never know," Widelsky said.

"We got the call over the radio. How'd she turn up?" Cairn asked, changing
the subject to Sophie Cruz.

"With a lawyer and guess what? Same guy who was going to represent
Danny Monaghan."

"Lenihan, Russo gave me the low down on him," Widelsky added.

"Yes, Lenihan, I hear he's pretty sharp, but we'll see."

"Fucking lawyers, they all think their sharp. You ever meet one who
didn't?"

"On that we agree Frank," Kreppell assented. "Now, you boys have a very
busy afternoon ahead of you. Hogan says he recovered some good prints from
the service elevator, so we'll see. Phil, did Henry Weiss uncover anything of
interest in his apartment?"

"Not a thing. Her jewelry is still there, and he had three hundred in tens and
twenties in his drawer along with some watches and rings. Her other picture
album is in her drawer and he has absolutely nothing to add about those semi-
nudes, nor much interest in them. I don't think he'll be much help. I asked again
about what his wife said she saw in the room, you know the reference to the
secretary and his reply was, "Maybe she was hallucinating.""

"We released the apartment to him?"

"The apartment, but not the pantry. They should be done there in another
hour. After that it's his, and that was at the district attorney's recommendation.
I don't see the hurry."

"Forces greater than us are at work," Kreppell said with a frown. "Let's
get back to the precinct. I'll give the doorman a lift. He's not as easy to read
as he appears. It takes nothing to rattle him, but I have a feeling there's another
side to him that's a little bolder. You never know, he could be the one."

Neither of the two detectives responded to Kreppell's remark, and the
three men left the office and went back into the lobby. Henry and Futerman

were gone and Tim Cleary was standing obediently by the lobby door with his hat in hand waiting for further directions. "C'mon with me, young man," Kreppell instructed as he went out to the courtyard. Tim followed a half step behind as they walked up Lincoln Boulevard to where Kreppell had parked his unmarked police car.

Sergeant Kreppell confused Tim Cleary. He wasn't overtly threatening like Widelsky was nor did he appear as easygoing as Cairn. He was suspicious of Cairn and afraid of Widelsky, but that was fine because they were detectives and that's how detectives make people feel, he thought. Kreppell was different. He didn't possess that aura the other men gave off. There was nothing hard-bitten or cynical about his approach, and when you first met him you would have thought he was a teacher or an accountant rather than a detective sergeant. Tim wasn't certain if Kreppell was just friendly and pleasant or cleverly manipulative, and he regretted being so open with Kreppell about Maria. His stomach was churning as he replayed in his mind the remarks he had made about Maria. He would have given anything to take back what he said. His mother, despite having an opinion on everyone and everything, and skin thick enough to not care what people thought about her, had cautioned him throughout his life to be mindful of what he said about others. "Keep your opinions to yourself, and if you can't say something nice, don't say anything at all," was one of her regular harangues. Kreppell had gotten him to open up much too easily, and Tim told himself that he should have taken his mother's advice and behaved like the dumb doorman he was and volunteered no information except for what was already known by everyone.

They reached the car, and Kreppell unlocked the front passenger's door and opened it for Tim. They were on their way to the precinct and Kreppell casually said, "Tell me, Tim, are you married?"

"No, never met anyone I wanted to marry. I live with my mom, right down on Bailey Avenue."

"No girlfriends?"

"No," he answered without elaboration.

"I thought you said before that you liked Spanish girls?"

"I know a couple of girls I visit in Puerto Rico every October."

"That's a long way to go for a date," Kreppell said. "How long have you been going to Puerto Rico?"

"I been going there for years. I used to go to Cuba, but Castro screwed that up, screwed it up big time."

"Cuba, what's so great about Cuba?"

299

"You can have a lot of fun in Cuba, all you needed was money. You didn't have to be rich, either."

"I'm surprised a young guy like you is a world traveler," Kreppell said as if he was really impressed.

"I'm not the world traveler. I go with Fogarty; he was in the Merchant Marine years ago and went everywhere. He's working downtown at the Lancashire Hotel as a doorman. That's how I got in the union. Fogarty and my mother are old friends, and he took me on my first trip to Cuba. We've been going away every year since. My mom don't know, but I met a lot of nice girls on those vacations, if you know what I mean?"

"Gotcha," Kreppell said knowingly. "I guess that's why you said you liked Spanish girls when we were talking about Mrs. Weiss. The woman who said she was Mr. Weiss' secretary. I guess she was your type, huh?" Kreppell said suggestively.

"I didn't pay her no mind," Tim replied cautiously. He was determined not to get back to Maria Weiss.

"Nevertheless, you're pretty familiar with Mrs. Weiss' physical attributes aren't you?" Kreppell said, knowing the subject unnerved Tim.

"I see her all the time, that's all, and I never think of her in that way, you kn-know."

"You're a funny guy, you know that?"

"What do you mean by that?"

"She's got nice legs, likes to show the cleavage, nice tits, but I never think of her that way. Who do you think you're kidding, buddy?" Kreppell said angrily as he brought his right arm back and drove an open backhand into Tim's chest.

"Ow," Tim shrieked. "Why'd you do that?"

"Because I hate liars. One moment you're a choir boy next moment you're a real cunt hound. Make up your mind before I let Widelsky eat you for lunch."

They drove in silence the rest of the way, and when they arrived at the precinct Kreppell brought Tim to his office and asked him to sit down. "Tim, according to my detectives you suggested that the Monaghan kid may be involved in Millie Campos' murder. How do I know you're not covering for something you did?"

"I didn't do nothing, I told you that before. Maybe I said some things about Mrs. Weiss I shouldn't have, but that don't mean a thing. Monaghan's a punk and so is his old man. I don't want to point fingers and I ain't told nobody, but I'll tell you," Tim said in a lowered voice. "I think Danny did it.'

"Did what?"

"Killed Millie."

"Tim, see that blackboard against the wall?" Kreppell directed. "Your name is on there too, how come?"

Cleary jumped out of his chair and went over to the board and said, "Yesterday I was doing my job. I helped Mrs. Weiss, and when Mrs. Zimmerman called I did everything I should have done and I was honest with everybody, too fucking honest."

"Too honest, why, because we talked about Mrs. Weiss' ass?"

"Yeah," he whimpered. "I let you trick me into thinking you was a regular guy and we were just talking silly shit about women. I was stupid, but that don't make me a murderer, and if you think I am, then maybe you should be the doorman and I should be the cop," he said with bitterness. "You know what?" he said angrily. "You're all the same, nothing but bullies.'

"Bullies, I'm not a bully. I'm just a cop doing his job."

"Then do your job and leave me alone," Cleary said, fighting back the urge to cry.

"What makes you so sure Danny Monaghan is the murderer? What proof do you have?"

"Last night when I was out his old man went to my apartment and threatened my mother."

"What did he say?"

"He asked her about my nose. He broke it on me last year. He gave her a hundred dollars and said he was sorry for doing it."

"Why didn't you tell someone about this earlier?"

"My mom don't want me to talk about it. She made me promise."

"What was the exact threat?"

"He gave her the hundred dollars, but she thinks it was money for me to keep my mouth shut about Danny, you know?"

"Is there something else about Danny you didn't tell us?"

Cleary paused, took a deep breath and tried to regain his composure. He wanted to act mature and composed and after several seconds he said in an even voice, "No, I told the cops everything like I said. But they went to Danny's house last night, and I know they told them about what I said and that's why Monaghan threatened my mom."

"Tim, you're not making much sense. Did Monaghan talk about this murder or what you saw or said to the detectives?"

"No, my mom said he said he was sorry about my nose and gave her the money. She thinks that meant I should keep my mouth shut or I'll get hurt. He's a real bad guy, you know?"

"I don't know. Why'd he break your nose?"

"I owed this bookie he collects for three hundred dollars I lost betting on the Yankees in the World Series. Instead of paying off, I went on my vacation to Puerto Rico with Fogarty. I came home and was gonna pay when he broke my nose. He said he had to teach me a lesson. Slammed it right into the bar in Pete's Bridge Lounge, the big prick," Tim said with a look of pitched anger as he thought back to that humiliating moment months ago.

"Is that your motive for picking out Danny Monaghan as a suspect?"

"I ain't picking no one out, I saw what I saw and told the truth," Cleary said defiantly.

"I don't know, you take off ten minutes here and add fifteen minutes there and you get a suspect. Maybe when you went upstairs with Mrs. Weiss you were thinking about her nice ass and cleavage and all that good stuff you can only get once a year in Puerto Rico, and you did something you shouldn't have done, lover boy," Kreppell said accusingly.

Tim Cleary started to breathe heavily. His attempts to control his emotions were all in vain and he felt as if he was going to faint. "I swear on my father's grave, I ain't done nothing. You were the one who asked me if Mrs. Weiss was attractive. I just answered your question, I only look, I don't touch, I swear," he said as he started blubbering. "I ain't no suspect, you gotta take my name off your list, you gotta," he whimpered.

Kreppell went to his doorway and called down the hall, "Widelsky, get down here."

Widelsky walked into Kreppell's office followed by Cairn. "What's the problem," he asked abrasively.

"Take his prints, please."

Widelsky motioned with his head for Cleary to follow him. Cleary gave Kreppell a sheepish look and left the office. Kreppell turned to Cairn and said, "I don't like that little shit. I think he's a perv. You know the type, lives with mom, the only sex he has is with himself or a prostitute. He has a very keen eye for Mrs. Weiss, and he let me know he thinks she's got a nice ass and legs. I don't know what he's capable of, but I don't think the Monaghan kid has the same interest in Mrs. Weiss that he has. He told me he has his suspicions about Monaghan, then gave me some cock and bull story about Monaghan's father visiting his mother last night and giving her a hundred dollars as payment for breaking his nose last year. Something's not right with that guy, and after we get through with this Cruz woman I want you and Frank to bring him back in and give him the third degree."

"You and Frank are starting to sound the same," Cairn said with levity.

"I did admit earlier that I may have underestimated Frank."

"About the Monaghan kid," Cairn said. "I spoke with that young cop, Clay, the one Devine told me about. He was on the crime scene yesterday. He says that Monaghan and his friends aren't a bad lot. Typical teenagers, they have a little hideout in a vacant lot on West Kingsbridge Road next to number 212. It's an old building foundation and Clay said that in the far right corner they have a little clubhouse or hangout. You know, chairs and benches and a cooler buried in the ground. Maybe if this kid's involved and he stole those other pictures we think exist, he would have hid them there. We should take a look, I think it's worth a shot."

"What do you mean a cooler?"

"You know an ice chest. They keep in the ground and put their beer in it to keep cold, I guess."

"Okay, innovative teens, I like that. Send Russo and Slattery to take a look. Cruz should be here soon. I want to move this thing along," Kreppell said as he buttoned the top button on his shirt and tightened his tie.

"I'll tell them now."

Widelsky squeezed a glob of black gooey ink on the hard pad. He spread it over the pad with a small roller. He put the roller down and took Tim Cleary's sweaty hand and felt it with the pads of his fingers. "Take a paper towel and wipe your hands dry. What the fuck are you sweating for? You said you didn't do nothing. What's the big fucking deal? Something you haven't told me?"

"I'm just nervous. Sergeant Kreppell, he got real nasty with me for no reason."

"Yeah, Kreppell's a real prick." Widelsky laughed. "Give me your right hand." Tim stuck out his right hand and Widelsky carefully inked his fingers. When he finished taking Tim Cleary's prints, Widelsky pointed to a sink in the corner of the room and said, "Munchkin, go over there and scrub your hands. There's a can of Borax there. Scrub your hands good 'cause I want you to sign these cards, and I don't want any stains. I like things neat. When you're done, you can go back to work. Of course, I might want to talk to you again, so keep the lights on."

Cleary didn't reply and went over to the sink and washed his hands just as Widelsky had instructed. When he was finished he was drying them and Cairn came into the room with Sophie Cruz. Cairn smiled and said to Widelsky, "Frank, allow me to introduce you to Miss Cruz. Her attorney's down the hall with Kreppell, and he said to please refrain from asking Miss Cruz any questions about this investigation until he's present. Pedigree information and nothing more, got it?"

"Pleased to meet you, miss," Widelsky said with his best poker face.

Sophie was standing in the doorway to the room where they took the fingerprints and mug shots, and she looked past Widelsky to Tim Cleary who was standing by the sink drying his hands. Tim was staring at her and she recalled the way he'd ogled her the previous day. "What are you looking at, you little creep?"

Cleary averted his eyes from her and said quietly, "Nothing, I wasn't looking at you."

"Yeah, you were, you fucking pervert."

"Munchkin, you're having one tough day," Widelsky laughed, then said, "Okay, miss, you're next. Cleary, beat it."

Cleary left the office, and as he walked by Sophie he gave her a dirty look. She stared angrily at him and muttered under her breath, "Pervert."

Chapter Thirty-Seven

It was a different doctor this time that examined her. He identified himself, but she'd already forgotten his name. He was alone, and after introducing himself he removed the bandage from her right eye and shone a flashlight into it. He moved the light back and forth, then did the same thing with her left eye. A second man came into the room, but he wasn't introduced. She didn't know who he was, but she knew he was a doctor and he was there for her. He bent over and looked in her eyes, too, with a flashlight. He then felt around her right eye and said, "Can you feel my fingers pressing against your skin?"

She felt a slight sensation, but the skin around her right eye felt numb and she whispered, "A little, very little." He said nothing else to her and stepped back, then she heard the two men talking quietly. They had moved toward the door to the room and the only two words she could distinguish were, "Rectus and oblique." The conversation grew fainter and dissolved as she fell back into a deep sleep.

She didn't know how long she had slept, and when she awoke Henry was sitting by the bed. He was stroking her hand and she started to cry. She covered his hand with her hand and said, "I'm sorry."

Henry bent over and kissed her hand and said, "No, you have nothing to be sorry for. I'm the one who's sorry, and I promise, if you'll forgive me, I'll make it up to you."

"I'm not the same anymore," she cried. "I think I'm going blind.'

"No, I spoke with the doctors, you're going to be fine. It's not that bad. Dr.

Snyder said the aneurysm was leaking and had affected some of the muscles that control your right eye. That's why you're having problems seeing with that eye, and your face might be a little numb on that side too. But it will improve, just rest. It could have been much worse," he said reassuringly.

"Are you sure?"

"Yes, I'm sure. It might take a couple of months, but you're going to be as good as new," he said as he gently squeezed her hand.

She smiled and said, "Thank you."

"This might be a bad time, but this morning you told me that you saw Sophie yesterday. Where was it you saw her?"

Maria pulled her hand from his and leaned her head toward him, and said, "I know about your son."

Henry took a deep breath and ran his hands over the top of his head. He got up from the chair and walked to the window and hid his face from her. He didn't say anything.

Maria watched him turn away and said, "Henry, Sophie was in the apartment. I saw her. I won't lie."

He turned and said in hushed, but urgent tone, "Are you sure? Are you certain? She'll go to jail for this and the boy's life will be ruined."

"What about Millie?"

"I know, you're right, but I have to be sure."

"Do you love her?" Maria asked as she closed her eyes and put her bed back on her pillow.

"No, and I can't explain the relationship either. I'm to blame, and I fear my actions have caused so much harm, so much harm."

"What are you going to do?"

"Lee told the police you wouldn't be available for an interview until next week. But we're faced with a terrible choice."

Maria put her fingers to her temples, shook her head ever so slightly, then said, "Henry, I'm so tired. I don't want to think, but it happened and she was there. Just tell the truth"

"I told the police this morning, but I said you were confused. I'm afraid they're going to arrest her now."

"I'm not confused, she was there."

"What happens to her son if she's arrested?"

"Your son Henry, he's your son, too."

"I really don't know what to do," he said as he sat down beside her again.

Maria's hand found his and she said, "Do what's right, Henry. For once do what's right. Maybe Gloria can help?"

"She's outside in the waiting room. What could she do?"

"Tell her I'm too tired to see anyone. Go somewhere and tell her everything, I know you trust her," Maria said in a stronger voice. She lifted her hand up and shooed him away. "Go, do it. I have to sleep."

Henry bent over, kissed her head and quietly left the room. Maria closed her eyes and thought of Joey's communion picture. He was a handsome boy. *In time he'll come to love us*, she thought. In time, then she drifted off to sleep again.

Chapter Thirty-Eight

Futerman was sitting with Gloria in the waiting room. She was wearing an intricately patterned green and gold light cotton caftan that flowed almost to her ankles. Gloria had put on weight, and the bold design of the robe she wore made her look even heavier than she was. Her breasts swung freely like pendulums beneath the thin fabric and when she raised her arm to make a point in conversation the fabric clung to her and Futerman could clearly see the outline of her breasts and that she wasn't wearing a bra. He recalled Henry saying recently that Gloria had become something of an "earth mother" and was taking guitar lessons, studying African culture and other pursuits he defined as "on the cultural fringe." Henry always talked much more about Gloria than he did Maria and his conversation about her usually focused on her "latest cause." In Henry's own words Gloria was "a little offbeat," but she was his sister and it was always very clear that Henry cared for and respected her deeply. Futerman had last seen Gloria at her younger son's Bar Mitzvah three years ago. He recalled how happy she was at the time and was surprised at how she had changed. She had always been lean and lithe and to his taste, very sexy. Beneath the noisy opinions and rapacious appetite for spirited arguments on social issues was a feline quality he'd found graceful, attractive and intimidating. Her husband Joel, always studious and measured in everything he did, was her alter ego and the balm that quelled whatever Gloria upset. The supple Gloria of his recollection was now bordering on the leviathan and he thought it remarkable that her weight gain could so distort his perception of her.

Similarly, her ubiquitous passion for social activism now seemed obsessive, and Futerman found it disturbing that after he confided in her that the police had intimated that Maria was a potential murder suspect, she dismissed that as unimportant, along with Maria's aneurysm and instead changed the subject completely and went into a long diatribe about a recent magazine article she'd read that applauded Castro's ambitious plans for eradicating illiteracy in Cuba. Futerman wanted to interrupt her and ask her why she bothered to come to the hospital. It was always obvious that she and Maria tolerated one another, at best, and since she wasn't too interested in Maria, what was she there for?

That question was immediately answered when Henry walked back into the waiting room. "Henry," she said in a firm voice, "you're coming home with me. I cannot believe that you didn't stay with us last night. I know," she said looking at Futerman, "that you and Lee are good friends, but at a time like this you should be with family."

"Gloria," he said, as he spread his hands open and made a pushing motion toward the floor. "I was a little upset last evening when Lee met me at the airport and filled me in on all that's gone on. The last thing I needed was to get you all wound up. Tonight I'm going back to my apartment. The police are through and I need a good night's rest."

"Oh, please," she exclaimed haughtily. "You're going to sleep in the same room where someone was murdered? The blood on the floor probably hasn't been cleaned up. "It's just ridiculous," she said with a wave of her hand. "Simply ridiculous."

"Gloria, it would be very helpful if you'd just listen for a change. I need you right now, I really do. Maria and I both need you."

"Maria, how is she? I told Lee she can't be that bad. I mean if she was conscious yesterday it must have been a little bleed," Gloria stated answering her own question.

"She's very weak and needs some rest now. There's a problem with her eyesight, but the doctor said that in time it can be corrected."

"Did you tell her I was here?"

"Yes, and she said thank you for coming, but she isn't up to company right now."

Gloria looked at Lee, frowned, then said to Henry, "Would you like me to send my girl Imelda over to your apartment to clean up?" Imelda was a cleaning woman Gloria employed to clean her house once a week and Futerman deemed it ironic that Gloria, who was so very much a champion of the underclass, so determined to prove she was devoid of any prejudices, referred to the woman who cleaned her house as "my girl."

"No, I've already spoken with the landlord and they're sending a cleaning company over tomorrow to clean the apartment. If they can't get the bloodstains out of the carpet, Maria can pick out a new one when she comes home," he said, indicating the conversation was closed on that subject.

"Fine, but you should stay with us. We gave Marshall the third floor and converted his old room into a guest room. Toby, Marshall and Joel would love to have you. We could have a scrabble contest," she joked.

"I'll see," Henry said tiredly. "More importantly we have to talk about something," he said turning his head to Futerman. "I'll need your input too, Lee."

Gloria sensed his seriousness and said, "You know I'm here for you, Henry."

"I know. Let's get out of here."

Futerman watched the sister and brother as they walked in front of him down the hallway to the elevator. The caftan Gloria was wearing fell in a gentle swirl and the vibrant mix of green and gold in the fabric unfavorably accented the generous beam of her buttocks. Futerman had never noticed before, but Gloria had big feet, too. Futerman found it hard to believe that he had once secretly fantasized about a relationship with Gloria. Maria was a pleasant fantasy of his too, but she treated him like a pet rather than a man. She would occasionally dote on him and make a fuss but it was all very playful and no different than he'd seen her act with other men. Gloria was another story. She was smart, and she appreciated his mind. Futerman knew that one of the reasons Gloria loved to argue with him was that he was informed on so many different and disparate issues. Furthermore, he treated her as an equal and was never dismissive of her point of view no matter how radical the subject. Gloria could be intense, and he could think of any number of occasions when she'd lean toward him, cigarette in hand, and look into his eyes with such conviction that you'd think she was looking into his soul, and she'd deliver what she thought was the consummate and decisive line of reasoning that would seal the argument in her favor, then pull her head back in triumph and say, "And what do you have to say now?" Futerman for his part, so many times, would quickly respond and trump her with some other fact she didn't know, or hadn't considered, then purposely and smugly sit back, arch his eyebrows and say, "It's a good thing for our young women in high school that they only let you teach geometry!" Then they would both burst with laughter. At moments like that he thought there was a bond between them that transcended their difference in age and taste and appearance and made them a perfect match.

He recalled one time when they were at an Upper Borough Democratic Party dinner dance and he and Ruth Goolnick were seated with Henry and Maria, Gloria and her husband, Henry's brother Steven and his wife and Henry's good friends Jack and Bobbi Stern. In between the music and dinner, Gloria and Futerman found plenty of time to discuss politics, and halfway through the dinner they were engaged in a heated exchange over school busing. Gloria was a proponent and Futerman thought the whole business entirely too divisive and, therefore, not worthwhile. Henry and Maria were seated between them and as if on cue, after Futerman had articulated a point quite well and taken the upper hand in the discussion, and Gloria was forming her retort, the band came back from a break and started playing.

Before Gloria could speak, Maria said ever so sweetly, "Lee, they're playing *Stardust*, please dance with me?" She then took Futerman's hand, led him to the dance floor and left Gloria sitting in her chair looking dumbfounded and speechless. Futerman was an excellent dancer, and although Ruth was his regular escort at most social functions, she never danced. Futerman loved to dance and Maria was an excellent dancer, too. Together they glided across the floor, and Futerman was content to hold her at arm's length and admire her lovely face. Maria was fond of Futerman, and as they danced she managed to survey the room and identify all the people Futerman disliked and point out some flaw in their dress or manners for Futerman's amusement. It was a happy three minutes, he recalled, and as the band finished the song they segued from *Stardust* into *The Way You Look Tonight* and Maria kept on dancing and Futerman was happy to indulge her. They were only moments into the second song when Gloria and Joel came onto the floor and Gloria took Futerman from Maria and handed over her husband.

"You can't have him all to yourself, Maria," she said as she led Futerman away.

Maria, never losing a step, happily replied, "Lee, you are popular tonight," and then smiling at Joel she added, "Joel, let's dance. Now you'll get a chance to hear the music."

They drifted off, and Gloria glared at Futerman and said, "How could you go off with her right in the middle of our conversation?"

It all seemed so innocuous at the time, he remembered, but there was fire in her eyes and she was genuinely upset. Maria could do that to other women and Gloria's animus for her, like Ruthie and Sophie's, was real and much deeper than the cattiness and petty jealousies that often occurred among women. Maria kept her opinions to herself and though she was exceptionally adept at passing pithy and accurately sharp observations about the foibles of others; it was a talent she kept in reserve and never overworked, and when she did employ it, she did so to amuse or enhance the importance of her listener rather than herself. Other women, in his opinion, quite simply didn't threaten her. He adored her as many other men did, but there was no expectation that she would ever think of him in a similar fashion. Gloria was an entirely different kind of woman. She was blood and bone, fire and fury, and many times he'd imagined what it would have been like to share his life with a woman like her.

They all stopped to wait for the elevator. Gloria's back was to him, and as he stared at the floor he felt a sudden feeling of shame over his present opinion of her and how radically it had changed between today and when he'd last seen her several years ago. Lee Futerman had never thought of himself as a shallow man; however, the new Gloria, as he had currently labeled her in his mind, was no longer attractive to him, and he found an embarrassing satisfaction in the knowledge that his feelings for her had been far more superficial than he realized. The shame he felt was the same shame he felt about Ruth Goolnick. His own physical inadequacies he could excuse. He couldn't excuse them in a woman, and just as he'd been happy that the brief affair with Ruth Goolnick had cooled into a life long friendship, he too, now felt the same way about Gloria. It wasn't Gloria's soul that had changed, just her appearance, and Futerman succumbed to his own vanity and, uncontrollably, he recognized that no matter how sharp her mind was, no matter how much passion and emotion he imagined she could bring to a relationship, the new Gloria in her garish outfit looked and sounded like an overstuffed loudmouth. The fire and fury had been reduced to noise, and the woman he'd once lusted after had grown frowsy and asexual.

Henry held the elevator door for Gloria and Futerman. He stepped in after them and said, "We can go downstairs to the cafeteria, have a cup of coffee and Danish or something and talk this over."

"Sure, Henry, that's what I need, a Danish," Gloria deadpanned as she patted her backside. "Lee, I stopped smoking two years ago and put on forty fucking pounds. I never ate sweets until then. I stopped smoking because I knew it was unhealthy, but Drake's Cakes and macaroons are worse. Just look at me."

Futerman smiled and said, "A sweet tooth can kill you. Is it just sweets, or did you find yourself eating more in general after you quit?"

"In general, my appetite blossomed and me with it. I've thought about starting smoking again, I mean it. When I smoked, I was never very hungry.

Cigarettes and coffee were what I lived on all day. No breakfast and a little lunch and dinner. I didn't put on a pound in twenty years, even after my kids were born."

The elevator reached the first floor, they got off and Henry led the way to the cafeteria. They found a table off to the rear of the room amid a group of empty tables and Henry went and purchased three coffees.

He came back to the table, sat down and, in a serious voice, he said, "Gloria, Lee already knows most of what I'm going to tell you and some of it may be a little disturbing, but here it is."

"My God, Henry, you're being so dramatic," she exclaimed. "Did you kill someone?"

"No, of course not, it's a very messy personal situation I'm in, and because of it I feel partly responsible for Millie's murder."

Gloria pushed her container of coffee aside, extended her arms across the table and took Henry's hands in hers. "Responsible for what?"

Henry hung his head and took a deep breath. He freed his hands from Gloria's and said, "You know, things haven't been all peaches and cream between Maria and me."

"What else is new?"

"I've been having an affair with my secretary for almost as long as she's worked for me, and it's been a very intense relationship at times, especially lately."

"Oh, my God," she said with surprise. "Sophie, oh, you poor dear. Henry, listen to me, Joel, Steven, even Muriel, we've all believed for years that you and Maria weren't going to make it. I've tried to be nice to her, but she's a tough woman to get along with. I can understand you turning to someone else, but Sophie?"

Henry bristled at Gloria's statement, and said, "Gloria, yeah, maybe Maria can be a problem, but so can I, and quite honestly, you've never bent over backward to get along with her either. But this isn't about how you or Muriel, or anyone else, for that matter, gets along with Maria. It's about me."

"Don't get mad, Henry," she said soothingly. "I'll keep my comments to myself. Well, at least until you're done," she said cautiously.

"Fine, if it was just about an affair it wouldn't be a big thing, but Sophie and I also have a child, a seven-year-old boy."

Gloria's jaw dropped, and she grabbed Futerman's hand, "Lee, my God, did you know about this?"

"Not until last night. Let him finish," Futerman said as he gently withdrew his hand from Gloria's hand.

Henry resumed speaking and said in a monotone voice, "Tuesday, Sophie accompanied me on a trip to Montreal. It was business related and a little vacation, too. Lately, she's been loading up on Maria to me all the time. You know, she's a bitch, she's cold, she doesn't love me, stuff like that, and it's all drawn from conversations we have about Maria from time to time. I really don't talk much about Maria to her, and once in a while I'll complain, but most of it's a figment of her imagination, or an exaggeration about something I said. I don't like to argue, and I let it go. I pay Sophie's rent and I give her money for childcare, but over the last year she's come to the conclusion that I'm going to leave Maria and marry her."

"Well, Henry," Gloria interrupted, "If you're screwing the woman regularly and you don't do anything to discourage her contempt for your wife, what did you expect? Tell me about your son."

"The boy is seven. I didn't know until he was about two that I was the father. The affair started shortly after Sophie came to work for me. It was all really innocent. Holiday party, too much to drink and one thing led to another and we ended up on my office couch. She had a boyfriend and I had a wife and it was this little illicit romance between us. You know, just recreational, no ties to bind us that sort of thing. Out of the blue she tells me I'm the father. I hit the roof but what could I do?" he quietly implored.

"How do you know you're the father? Did you have a blood test?"

"I didn't, but Carlos or Carl, he used both names, was away on National Guard duty for six weeks the year she got pregnant and it coincided with her getting pregnant. He offered to marry her, and I believe he thought he was the father. It's his name on the birth certificate, but I think he did the arithmetic and backtracked the birth date and came to the conclusion he wasn't the father. Anyway, they broke up and that was that."

"So, what makes you so sure you're the father?"

"All you have to do is look at the boy, Gloria. He's me and I understand he's a wonderful kid."

"Wonderful kid, what's his name? Have you spent time with him?"

"No, he's been in the office several times with Sophie, but I'm Mr. Weiss to him, nothing more."

"Henry, listen to yourself. You haven't said his name once," she said with disappointment.

"His name is Joey."

Gloria took a sip of her coffee and said to Futerman, "Lee, I have a nephew I've never met. My two sons have another cousin and I have a brother, a brother I adore but a man who cannot make a commitment. Do you agree?"

Futerman smiled and said, "A question I'll reserve decision on, if you please."

She turned to Henry and said, "Honestly, I think you have to face up to reality and stop trying to keep everyone at arm's length. You say you love your wife, but you manage to have a ten-year affair with your secretary and a love child to boot. How could you keep all of that a secret from Maria all these years? Does she know, or does she not care, not care to know, or not care about you?"

Henry cleared his throat and replied, "Gloria, it was, like I said before, all very innocent. I don't love Sophie. I care for her, but, and it's embarrassing to be talking to my sister about something as personal as this, but it was just sex. You know, on the office couch a little something to jazz up the afternoon. After everything that's happened I'm sick and disgusted with myself. I really am, but I can't undo the harm that Sophie's done."

"What do you mean Sophie? What about you?"

Henry nodded to Futerman and said, "Lee, fill her in, I'm tired of talking about it."

Futerman shifted his chair toward Gloria and said, "Henry's right, it's better I tell the story. When Henry and Sophie were in Montreal on Wednesday, Henry received a call from Maria. Basically, Maria made an overture of sorts to Henry that I would interpret as a good faith effort to repair a relationship that was off track. Would you agree with that, Henry?"

Henry nodded his head, but didn't speak.

"Sophie, being an astute woman, recognized that Henry was never going to leave Maria and that the relationship with Henry was going nowhere. She was angry, and I don't blame her," he said with disdain as he gave Henry a disapproving look. "But, that being said, she's not Mrs. Weiss and appropriately she told Henry, in so many words that they were through and packed her bags and came back to Huguenot City. Now, if that were the extent of the story and she did nothing more than find a good lawyer and sue to have Henry Weiss legally recognized as her son's father, I'd say good for her and too bad for Henry. And I mean it," he said with a shake of his head as he looked at Henry with disapproval once again. "However, Miss Cruz didn't use her head. She lost it. She came home from Montreal and yesterday morning parked herself in front of Henry's apartment house and waited for Maria to come out. She spoke with the doorman and found out what time Maria left for work and around noon when Maria left the building Miss Cruz confronted her. She revealed that she was Henry's mistress and that they had a son. While they were on the subway platform she took a picture of her son from her pocketbook and gave it to Maria. This was witnessed by a police officer, and from what little information the police gave us; Miss Cruz was angry, loud and confrontational. The train came. Maria boarded the train and the police officer escorted Miss Cruz from the station. Have I left anything out, Henry?"

"No, so far so good."

"Maria knows. How did she take that?"

"I'll answer that," Henry said with a deep sigh. "Maria has been suffering from severe migraines lately. A precursor I'm sure to the aneurysm she suffered yesterday. She got on the subway, but Sophie didn't. I don't know exactly what happened next, but about a half hour later Maria made it back to our apartment and found Millie dead. What's crazy is Millie had an old photo of Maria, partially nude, in her hand and there were a few others on the floor next to her body. Maria apparently saw Millie and these photos. They're photos she never showed me but they must have been in her dresser. As best as I can put it together and I don't think the police are doing any better is that Maria saw Millie and the photos and went into shock and had the aneurysm. Just before she lost consciousness she saw someone come out of the closet and that person hit her in the chest and ran out of the apartment," he said shaking his head in disbelief.

"Did she recognize the intruder?" Gloria asked anxiously.

"Oh, she recognized the intruder all right. She told me it was Sophie and she's not backing down."

Gloria gasped and said, "Oh, shit. Give me a cigarette, please." She put her hand to her forehead and said, "Two fucking years and forty pounds, screw it, give me a cigarette, Henry."

Henry took a cigarette from the pack in his shirt pocket, lit it and handed it to his sister.

"Are you sure she said it was Sophie? How'd Sophie get in the apartment and how could she know Maria was going back home if she got on a train going downtown?" she said in between puffs of her cigarette.

Futerman didn't wait for Henry to answer and started speaking. "The officer sent Sophie on her way. Maria must have gotten off her train at some point and taken a train back or maybe the next stop and walked back. We'll have to ask her. Henry keeps a set of keys to the apartment in his desk drawer. The police checked for them this morning and they're gone. I surmise, and it's much more than an assumption, but I believe Sophie had the keys and was intent on confronting Maria in her apartment and harming her. Henry doesn't like that theory but I think it's a good one," he said as he gave Henry, yet, another disapproving look. "Now Sophie may have had the keys, but she didn't figure out how to get around the doorman and she had to wait outside. I believe that after the confrontation on the subway she somehow managed to get into the building, and you can go through the service entrance for which there was a key on the ring and get into Henry's apartment. Maybe she wanted to destroy Maria's things, who knows? All very clever and consistent with her anger toward Maria, which Henry cannot deny. Can you?"

"She's got a temper, I never thought of her as malicious, but there's a temper and the blowout in Montreal was very ugly. She called me a fucking Jew and a Kike and other hideous things. It was a side of her I'd never seen before, and it sickened me, sickened me," he said sadly.

"Do you really think she did it?"

"Gloria, I don't know, I don't know, but there's one little twist, right, Lee?"

"What? You mean Maria's fingerprint?' Futerman said with annoyance.

"The police have a fingerprint?" Gloria asked, then added," Lee, you did say upstairs, earlier, that the police had her on the suspect list, didn't you? I thought you were speaking in general."

"Maria's bloody fingerprint was found on the murder weapon, an ashtray from her dresser. Now my source in the DA's office told me the ME's report will show that Millie died from one very violent blow to her head from that ashtray. There is no way the murderer is going to leave a bloody fingerprint on the murder weapon where there is no evidence of repeatedly striking the victim with the murder weapon. Take it from an old prosecutor," Futerman said firmly, "Maria walked in and found Millie on the floor dead. She touched Millie and picked up the ashtray and put two and two together. I call that normal inquisitiveness."

"So you think the shock from finding Millie dead was enough to trigger the aneurysm?"

"Certainly, and if that wasn't enough, the added shock of seeing someone emerge from a closet surely set it off."

Gloria was dumbstruck. The cigarette was gone in four drags and she asked Henry for another. He lit another cigarette and handed it to her. The three of them sat silently for several moments, then Gloria said, "What about these pictures of Maria you mentioned?"

"Well, there are four, I think four, maybe three, do you recall Lee?"

"Three or four, what's it matter?"

"There are these pictures of Maria with her breasts exposed, one all the way, and the others partially. Artsy type nudes, eight by tens on good paper, they must have been taken twenty years ago, and guess who the photographer was?"

"Oh, that man she worked for, I bet," Gloria said. "That's odd, you know. Joel is writing a paper; actually, it might be a new course he'll teach on the economics of war. He was telling me about it a couple of weeks ago and asked me if I remembered that time at your apartment at the dinner party when Maria brought out her family album. Remember the fight we had?"

"I'll never forget it. It's come up a time or two, and not happily."

Gloria said to Lee, "Muriel asked Maria if she had any pictures of her family. They're all dead. Died in a fire, real tragedy, and Maria took out an album, I made some crack about her father and then it got real icy."

"Let me clarify that, sis," Henry said. "I recall you called her father a Nazi."

"I merely asked a question. Anyway, she told us about this man she worked for after her first husband and family died. He was from Argentina and exported beef to Europe. I got the idea that Maria was his mistress, but I didn't want to push the subject too far. It was an ugly night."

"Very ugly, Gloria was demonstrating what a fine prosecutor she would have made."

"The man, the man from Argentina, I bet he took the pictures. What was his name? Joel wanted to know because he was going to research his company, you know, how wealthy did they get selling beef to the French and Germans and English during the first war."

"His name was Amos Koch and that's the initials on the back of the pictures."

"Wow, how does that all fit into the puzzle?"

"It doesn't," Futerman quickly answered. "It's all ancillary. Every indication I have is that Sophie Cruz had a motive to harm Maria. Her confrontation with Maria yesterday, witnessed you'll recall by a police officer, is proof of her intent. Only two people have access to Henry's office and his extra keys, and they're Henry and Sophie Cruz. The keys are missing. I believe Sophie had the keys and went to the apartment intending to vent her anger by destroying Maria's property. She got caught by Millie Campos and killed her, maybe not intentionally, but in her fury she grabbed the ashtray off the dresser and hit her with it. Before she could clean up the mess, Maria came home. She hid in the closet, then panicked and fled from the apartment. Just that simple," he said decisively.

"Why not kill Maria, too?"

"She's not a murderer," Lee said dramatically. "There's no well thought out plan here. This is a hot-tempered, impulsive woman. She loves Henry and hates Maria. She hates Maria because Henry loves Maria and not her. The confrontation, the picture of the boy, the yelling and cursing, that's all uncontrolled anger. Maria got on the train. She's gone. Sophie Cruz is still pissed. She has the keys to the apartment, so she figures, what the hell, I'll rip all of her dresses apart, write Fuck You on the mirror, stupid, impulsive behavior. Then the one thing she forgot about was the cleaning lady. She was probably going through Maria's dresser, and think about it, those pictures might have given her a little pause. The police think there are several missing, and it's a series of photos that end with the subject completely nude. Maybe Sophie found them and decided she could use them to sway Henry. We're dealing with a woman whose capacity for rational thought is overwrought with emotion. She's gawking at the pictures, dreaming of how they will somehow change Henry's feelings and Millie walks in. It's all very elementary, as Holmes would say, very elementary," Futerman said with satisfaction.

"You're one helluva lawyer, Lee. You made the case for me," Gloria said, complimenting him.

"I still don't like it," Henry added. "It's likely, but I hope not, or if it is the case, I hope and pray the police find some good evidence."

"You don't believe Maria?"

"Gloria, she had an aneurysm. Apparently, it didn't burst, but it was leaking and that's pretty serious. The doctors are amazed she can even talk today, no less remember what happened yesterday. I know Maria's not the murderer, but Sophie hit her with some pretty shocking news and maybe that's what's on her mind. Could have been anyone coming out of the closet. She just recalls Sophie because of the scene they had and the proximity in time between the scene and the attack," he said with conviction.

Futerman rubbed his forehead and said, "Henry, Henry, you always look for the good in others. A trait I admire, but an Achilles heel nonetheless."

"That's what I love about my brother, Lee. He wants everyone to be happy. The only problem is that he causes more problems than he solves."

"You're right," Henry agreed.

"So how did Maria take the revelation that you have a son?"

"That's why we're sitting here discussing this. She was pretty sanguine about it, taking into account all that happened. She believes Sophie's a murderer, and that I have a responsibility to own up to being the boy's father.

She told me I have to do what's right and she asked me to come to you for some input."

"Me, she told you to ask me?" Gloria said incredulously.

"It's no secret you and Maria don't get along. You both try, but I can always feel the discord. Still, Maria does admire you, believe it or not, and she has often remarked that you're one of the few people she knows who has any real principles."

"You could have told me that, you know. It might have made things better," Gloria replied self-consciously.

"Not my place to do that. What's important is that Maria respects you, and while there are few things she would ever agree with you on, she does believe you're a good person and I think that says something," he said strongly.

Gloria didn't immediately reply, and again they sat in silence for a few moments, then she said, "Maria was talking about your son, wasn't she? What do you do if Sophie gets arrested and goes to jail?"

"I think so. She didn't seem too upset, but with Millie's death this all seems less important, you know."

"I think Lee painted a pretty bleak picture for Sophie, and I think you've got to listen to your wife. She said you have to do what's right, and I believe she's right. You have a son, he deserves to have a father, and if that boy's mother goes to jail, then who is there but you?"

"He's got Sophie's aunt and Sophie's brother. That's his family. He doesn't know me from a hole in the wall. I'm Mr. Weiss, his mother's boss. The kid's only seven," he said with desperation. "I'm fifty three years old, do you think Maria and I are ready to become parents. Parents of a kid who would surely hate us; hate us both. If anything happens to Sophie, the boy will have to go with her family. I'll recognize him as my son and pay all the bills, shit, right now I'd pay Sophie's bills and Millie's, everyone's, if it were only that easy," he said with greater despair in his voice.

Gloria reached over and took his hands again. "Henry, he's a Weiss too, your son, my nephew, Steven's nephew. We have a stake in him too. Maria told you to come to me and that's why. What I'm about to say may sound hypocritical, but I don't care. I've met Sophie. I know her type, Henry. You live in different worlds. Simple as all that, your son deserves all that you have to offer. That's more than money. Get joint custody, do what you have to do."

Henry laughed sarcastically and said, "Sounds great, doesn't it, Lee. I'll just snap my fingers and the kid will love me. Gloria, that boy adores his mother. My wife is going to supply the police with the information they'll need to put Sophie in jail. I don't think anything's going to work out here."

Gloria's face flushed and her jaws tightened, "Henry Weiss, you're a weak man. I said it before and I'll reiterate it, you can't make a commitment. That's why your choice in women has always been so pathetic. Maria's a beauty, but cold and aloof. Sophie's an easy lay on the office couch and a couple of extra bucks kept her quiet for a long time. Now you have a son and you don't want him because it might be painful to create a relationship. You're selfish. All that easy-going, hale well good fellow bullshit is a cover for selfishness. You love Maria because she's selfish too. She had an epiphany yesterday, granted, a painful one, but she saw the light. The time is right for you to do so too, don't you think so, Lee?"

"Yes and no. Henry is right. If Sophie goes to jail the boy is going to be destroyed, and I don't believe there's a Chinaman's chance of Henry and Maria taking Sophie's place. But Henry also has a moral obligation to be a father to the boy and that does mean something more than money. It's one for Solomon."

"You're both full of shit," she exclaimed. "Do you know how many girls I've taught over the years that come from broken homes and fractured families? Goodness knows a child needs a stable family. If Sophie goes to jail, you'll have to save that child. To do otherwise would be criminal. I'm going back upstairs and I'll wait to speak with Maria. I have nothing else to say," she said as she got up from the table, obviously in a huff, and marched out of the cafeteria.

"That wasn't very helpful," Henry said to Futerman.

"No, it wasn't," Futerman replied in agreement.

"Do you really think she did it?"

"Henry, my dear, dear friend, based on what I know, yes. I pray things will change, but if they don't, you're going to have to deal with a very thorny problem. The Cruz family will hate you and not want that boy anywhere near you. And your sister is on target, as she often is. You have a moral responsibility to do what's in that child's best interest, and that may very well be leaving him with Sophie's family, but I can see that Maria and Gloria won't find that too acceptable."

"Maria said to do the right thing, I don't interpret that as moving the kid in with me, do you?"

"At least it means owning up that you're the father and after that forming some bond."

"Damn it, I should have never listened to Maria and told Gloria. You know she's already made up her mind that Joey is a Weiss. She'll work on Maria.

God, poor Millie, it's all my fault, what a jerk I am," he said full of self pity.

Futerman stood up and said, "I agree. I need to go back to my office. I'll call Duffy when I get back and see if the cops got anywhere with Sophie. Are you going home, or to Gloria's house tonight?"

"I'll go to Gloria's. If I go home she'll only harangue me over the phone, and at this point Joel might supply some assistance. Christ, I never wanted kids. Lee, I never had the patience, and the way things are I'm not ready to be a father now."

Chapter Thirty-Nine

The armchair was made of walnut. The back was curved and the chair was on a swivel and you could turn from side to side or tilt backward and forward. Each armrest was padded and covered with a dark brown leather saddle, and on the seat of the chair was a bold purple pillow with "Boss K" embroidered across the center of the pillow in gold silk stitching. The embroidered pillow was a gift from two former detectives who had since been promoted to sergeant. They were the last subordinates Kreppell could recall who regularly called him "Boss." The rules forbade familiarity of address among the ranks, and although the rule was broadly broached, Kreppell rarely encountered a subordinate who didn't address him as "Sarge" or "Sergeant." The title of "Boss" when proffered by a subordinate was a sign of respect to Kreppell, and it was an honor he rarely received. Too often, he felt his subordinates tolerated him, and although he was awarded the nominal respect his rank deserved it was perfunctory and paid to the rank and not the man. Kreppell was, by nature and choice, a company man. His superiors valued him because they knew he was dedicated to the department and would always err in its favor. For that very same reason the men he was chosen to supervise and lead kept him at arm's length because they knew he would never give them the benefit of the doubt. It was a concession he had become accustomed to, and it rarely bothered him except for those times when he lamented the reality that so few of the men he worked with were like he was. Swinton and Klass, the two detectives who had given him the seat cushion upon their promotion to sergeant, were very much cut from the same pattern as Kreppell. They were solid family men and good students. They were moderate drinkers and evidenced few of the vices that were so common among members of the force. Klass and Swinton, like Kreppell, hoped some day to be chiefs. Kreppell found his world populated by subordinates who spent far more time figuring out what they had to do or who they had to impress in order to increase their detective grade rather than opening up a book and studying for a promotional exam. Cairn and Widelsky, especially Widelsky, were prime examples of that type of detective and it was the reason why Kreppell gave them both such a hard time. He couldn't imagine Widelsky calling him Boss. Kreppell had no interest in looking the other way when subordinates fumbled. There were no allowances in his world for rule breakers and marginal employees. He remembered a revered detective lieutenant from Huguenot City, who, over the years, had covered up and cleaned up scores of messes created by detectives under his command. One time he tried to write off with a written reprimand two detectives who had been caught in a bar cocktailing when they were supposed to be staking out an address for a wanted felon. They missed the felon and he was caught later committing a burglary. The lieutenant found himself back in uniform in the Lower Borough going around the clock. Fortunately, he had his twenty years in and retired. Kreppell remembered his retirement party when a hundred detectives stood shoulder to shoulder and chanted, "John the Boss, John the Boss," when the lieutenant was escorted into the reception hall. It sent a shudder down his spine and the power from the respect in that reception hall from all those men for that one man was overwhelming. Kreppell, like so many men, craved that respect, yet, he knew when it came his time to retire it would be a small affair without any fanfare and he'd take his plaque and fade away.

He had once expressed his admiration for "John the Boss" to Captain Grimsley and was stunned by Grimsley's dismissal of the man as a phony and a do nothing. "Oh, I love fellows like him. They don't need the rules, the rules and policies and procedures don't matter. All they care about is cultivating the admiration of the men they're supposed to lead. And how do they lead? They let everyone run amok!" He remembered Grimsley sneering. "So a hundred cops, half of em screw-ups, no doubt, showed up and clapped and cheered for their fallen hero," Grimsley went on. "And not a one of 'em could save the man's job, could they?" Grimsley asked him, and Kreppell recalled saying, "Yeah, but the respect they felt for him was enormous."

And Grimsley laughed and replied, "So what? Didn't save his job, did it?"

Kreppell remembered they went back and forth for a good fifteen minutes until Grimsley ran out of patience and ended the conversation with a little speech that burned its way into Kreppell's memory and guided him through his own career. "The only respect that matters is self respect; when you look in the mirror each morning, that's who counts. When you look the other way because that's the easy way you don't earn shit, my friend. We're all subordinate to the rules, and your friend "John the Boss" forgot that and he got the boot, and all I can say is good riddance. There are too many bosses like that on this job. They're all whores, and they make it doubly hard for guys who want to do the job the right way to succeed. Fuck him and everyone like him."

Kreppell was standing behind his chair, admiring the pillow, lost in thought thinking about all he'd learned from Grimsley over the years and how contradictory the man could be, when Cairn knocked on the door. "Sarge, Widelsky's printing Sophie Cruz. What room do you want to use for the interrogation? I got her lawyer cooling his heels out at the front desk."

"Use room two, and the lawyer can take a seat in here with me until we're ready, and have Teague take the prints over to Hogan's office. Last time I saw him he was reading a newspaper," Kreppell said sourly. There were two chairs in front of Kreppell's desk. He had picked them up in a second hand furniture store on Beechwood Avenue. They were very simple chairs and Kreppell considered them an integral part of his management style. They were straight-backed hard wood chairs with narrow seats and no armrests. It was impossible to sit in one of the chairs for more than two minutes without feeling some discomfort. Kreppell believed the chairs gave him an advantage with every visitor. While he was comfortably seated in his own chair, the visitor could never get comfortable. The narrow seat and straight hard back forced the person sitting in the chair to sit ramrod straight. You couldn't slouch or lean, and even crossing your legs was uncomfortable due to the narrow hard seat. It was a simple dynamic created by Kreppell to give him an advantage over every visitor whether that visitor was a superior, subordinate, or, in this case, Miss Sophie Cruz's defense attorney. Cairn showed Lenihan into the office. Kreppell was impressed by Lenihan's appearance. Lenihan's suit was expertly tailored and the white starched shirt with just a half inch of cuff extending beyond the suit jacket sleeve and the fine silk blue and red regimental striped tie gave the tall man a commanding presence Kreppell expected a few minutes in one of the guest chairs would diminish. Lenihan looked at the two chairs and without hesitation took one of them in his big left hand and turned it around. He pushed the chair up close to Kreppell's desk and straddled it, simultaneously sticking out his right hand to shake Kreppell's extended hand.

"Pat Lenihan, and you're Ted Kreppell, right?" Lenihan said with a friendly smile. Lenihan's left arm was leaning over the back rail of the chair, and before Kreppell could answer the first question, Lenihan's left hand came of the chair and he pointed his finger at Kreppell and said, "You're very well thought of in my circle, and that's a good thing."

Lenihan's approach rattled Kreppell, and he found himself slowly inching his chair backward, subconsciously trying to put some distance between himself and his guest. Kreppell didn't immediately answer, and he broke eye contact with Lenihan and tilted his chair backward and finally said, "Thank you. I've heard good things about you too, and I hope we'll both feel that way when today is through."

"My client is ready to cooperate, and since she hasn't done anything criminal, I'm not saying she hasn't done anything stupid, mind you," Lenihan said in his familiar and friendly manner. "But I hope she can clear a few things up, then you and your men can get about doing some real police work. I was an assistant in Frank Heaton's office for five years before I went into private practice, you know, so I do have some insight into this kind of thing from both ends of the stick," he said smugly as he pulled the second chair over and leaned his right arm on it.

Kreppell nodded his head, got up from behind his desk and said, "I'm sure you do. Why don't we go down to the interview room. Miss Cruz should be there shortly."

"Interview room?" Lenihan chuckled. "I thought they were interrogation rooms?"

"We use them for both."

Lenihan got up from the chair, turned it back around and set it in its proper place. "You know the city should spring for a few bucks and buy you some better furniture. Last time I sat in a chair like that was outside the principal's office when I was in the fifth grade."

"It's not our job to make people comfortable," Kreppell answered as he led Lenihan down the hallway.

Interview room two had a mirror on one wall that permitted viewers from interview room one (the room adjacent) to look into the room unseen. There was also a hidden microphone that was connected to a speaker in interview room one. The two rooms were constructed so that viewers in interview room one could watch and listen, unseen and unheard, to an interview-taking place in room two. Kreppell had initially planned on sitting in on Sophie Cruz's interrogation, but after meeting Lenihan he decided to view it through the one-way mirror. Kreppell was unsure of what to expect from Widelsky, and he imagined that Lenihan was going to do everything he could to dominate the interrogation, much the same way Kreppell felt he had taken control in his office. He was happy to get Lenihan out of the office, and happier that the lawyer hadn't seen the Boss K seat cushion as he was certain it would have prompted the lawyer to offer some snide remark. Kreppell wasn't easily intimidated, but he he'd formed an immediate dislike for Lenihan and didn't want that negative emotion to affect the examination of Sophie Cruz.

Kreppell let Lenihan into the interview room. Lenihan looked at the mirror on the wall, fixed the knot in his tie and pushed his hair back. "Sergeant," he said authoritatively. "If you're recording this interrogation, that's improper without my consent. You can watch," he said pointing to the mirror. "But are you making a recording?"

"No, Mr. Lenihan, we're not recording anything, and I wouldn't concern myself about anyone watching from the other room."

"What about identification? You know, you bring in a witness to view Miss Cruz, I'm entitled to notice about that, too."

"I'm not sure what you're entitled to under the circumstances since Miss Cruz hasn't been charged with anything, but to put you at ease, if anyone happens to be listening in on the interview" Kreppell said, stressing the word interview. "It'll be me, and possibly an assistant district attorney assigned to this investigation."

"Very well, I'll take you at your word," Lenihan said curtly as he pulled up a chair and sat with his back to the mirror. Kreppell nodded his head and walked away without responding.

Widelsky opened the door to the interview room and held it for Sophie. She went in, and Widelsky said, "We'll get started in a few," and disappeared from the doorway.

Lenihan popped up from his chair like a giant Jack in the Box and reached for Sophie with his left hand. He took her by the elbow and sat her in the chair next to him. He examined both her hands and said, "Terrible experience isn't it, having your fingerprints taken? Did you wash all of the ink off?"

"Yes, and that creepy little doorman was down there right before me," she said as she puckered her lips and made a face.

"They're taking elimination prints of everyone who was in the apartment, that's all."

"I wasn't in the apartment," she said indignantly.

"I know, they don't, but I do, so don't sweat it," he said as he squeezed her hand

"What's the big mirror for?"

"They do line-ups in here. The witnesses stand on the other side and the bad guys can't see them."

"You mean someone can watch us now and we wouldn't know?"

"Yes and so what? Forget about who's watching; just listen to what these detectives are going to ask you. You tell the story like you told it to me. They don't have a thing, so don't worry."

Sophie squeezed Lenihan's hand and said, "You give me strength, thanks, you really do."

"Good, that's the way to feel. These guys start getting a little nasty, you let me handle it."

"Got it, coach," she said with a little laugh.

Cairn and Widelsky entered the room together. "Mr. Lenihan," Cairn said. "This is my partner Detective Widelsky. Miss Cruz has already been introduced to us both."

Lenihan didn't stand or extend a handshake. He eyed Widelsky for a moment and said, "Nice to meet you, pal. If the sarge is on the other side of the glass, give him a wave for me, will you?" He then reached back and knocked on the mirror with the knuckles of his right hand. Widelsky sat at the head of the table and said, "Nice to meet you too. Let's get started."

Sophie gave Lenihan an admiring smile. She was impressed by the way Lenihan addressed Widelsky. It was clear that her attorney wasn't at all intimidated by the two detectives, and that gave her added confidence that she'd made a good choice in picking a lawyer on short notice. Cairn was seated across the table from Sophie and Lenihan. He opened his notebook and asked Sophie for her full name, address, date of birth, place of birth, marital status and if she had any children? As she answered each question, he recorded the information into his notebook. When he was finished, he smiled and said, "I want to thank you for coming in for this interview. You know that we're investigating a homicide and serious assault that occurred in the apartment of your employer yesterday, don't you?"

Sophie glanced at Lenihan, and he said, "Relax, answer the questions."

"Yes, I learned about the murder this morning."

"Miss Cruz, how long have you been employed by Mr. Weiss?"

"Almost ten years, eh, ten years this coming September."

"Long time, good boss, Mr. Weiss, is he a good boss?"

"Yes, he's a good boss."

"Do you know his wife?"

"Yes, I know her, not well, but she's his wife, so I know her, you know, more like I know who she is, not like she's a friend or something," Sophie said defensively.

Cairn made eye contact with Widelsky, and Widelsky asked the next question. "Miss Cruz, you have a child, don't you?"

"Yes, my son Joey, he's seven years old. Why?"

"When Detective Cairn asked you your marital status before you answered single, correct?"

"Yeah, I'm single, Joey was born out of wedlock. That's what they call it, don't they?"

Widelsky paused, then said, "Just made his first Holy Communion didn't he?"

Lenihan patted Sophie's hand and interjected, "Detective, what's your point? Miss Cruz had a child out of wedlock. It happens. Are you trying to shame her?"

"Last thing on my mind," Widelsky said with a look of surprise on his face. "I was trying, eh, perhaps not too effectively, to getting around to who the boy's father is, that's all. I don't mean no disrespect, miss."

"None taken," Lenihan conceded.

"Good, now about your son. Henry Weiss is his father?"

"Yes," Sophie whispered.

Cairn asked the next question and said, "Are you uncomfortable talking about this, you know, about your son?"

"Of course, I know what happened yesterday but it's only because Henry's Joey's father that I'm here."

"Right, and according to what we've learned Mrs. Weiss didn't know anything about the existence of your son or who his father is until yesterday around noon, and she found that out from you and at the time you were quite upset. Weren't you?"

Sophie turned to Lenihan again and said, "Tell him the story."

Sophie took a deep breath, then said, "I made a big mistake starting a relationship with Henry. I thought he was going to leave his wife and marry me someday, but I learned different. Yesterday, I was pissed, I ain't gonna deny it. I went to Henry's apartment to talk to Maria, that's his wife. The creepy little doorman," and she stopped talking when Widelsky issued a muffled laugh.

"Something funny, Detective?" Lenihan said with annoyance as he gave Widelsky a dirty look.

"No, it's just that the doorman can't get a break, I find it funny, excuse me."

"Sophie, what happened next?"

"Well, the doorman told me she was coming down at noon and I waited. When she came down I followed her to the subway, and while she was waiting for the train I told her everything. I even threw a picture of Joey at her. That cop must have told you. And then I left and went to the movies and I didn't know nothing until I went to work this morning. I swear that's everything," she said as she made a sign of the cross and kissed the two fingers she made the sign with.

Widelsky smiled and said in a harsh accusing tone, "Now, did you just happen to have your son's communion picture in your pocketbook and this happened, you know, spontaneously, or did you plan this whole little scene? Which was it?"

Sophie's cheeks reddened and her lips narrowed. She glared at Widelsky and responded, "I just got the proofs from his communion two weeks ago. I carry lots of pictures of Joey all the time. He's my world, the only fucking thing I ever got from Henry that means a thing. I didn't plan nothing, you wanna see a picture of my son? I got ten, fifteen right here in my bag." Sophie unzipped her pocketbook and started combing through it. Lenihan grabbed her gently by the wrist and said, "Whoa, calm down. You gave Mrs. Weiss a picture of your son. That's no crime, why are you getting upset?"

Sophie pushed his hand away and pulled her wallet and then a packet of photos and a small photo album from her pocketbook and pushed them toward Widelsky. She let go of the bag, let it fall to the table, rubbed her temples with her fingers and said through half clenched teeth, "I'm not upset. I'm still pissed off. This is all about Henry being Joey's father. If telling his wife he's got a kid is a crime then I'm a criminal, if not, I'm leaving."

Cairn gathered the album and the packet of pictures and Sophie's wallet and was about to hand them back to her when he felt Widelsky step on the top of his foot. That was a signal the two detectives had used between them for years as a sign that the one doing the stepping had just observed something and needed to take the lead. Cairn placed Sophie's property back on the table and said, "Don't be so defensive."

Widelsky said, "Do you have a copy of the picture you gave to Mrs. Weiss?"

She reached over and took the envelope that contained Joey's communion pictures from Cairn and opened it. Widelsky increased the pressure on Cairn's foot. Cairn knew that Widelsky must have observed something, but for the life of him he didn't know what. He put his hands behind his neck and stretched his neck to the left and right while carefully scanning the table in front of him. Then he saw it. At the open mouth of Sophie's handbag was a key ring with a green tag. He couldn't make out the writing on the tag, but Widelsky was closer and had a better view, and Cairn knew from the pressure of Widelsky's foot that the tag must have the word, "Apartment" written on it. Sophie withdrew a picture of her son from the envelope and handed it to Widelsky. He admired the picture for a moment and showed it to Cairn.

"He's a good looking boy."

"Looks like a ballplayer," Cairn added as he handed the picture back to Sophie, then her wallet and the small photo album. Sophie pushed everything back into the pocketbook and seemed completely unaware of the two detectives' observation.

Widelsky yawned and said to Lenihan, "Mr. Lenihan, we could do this dance all day, or just get down to brass tacks. We have a murder and Miss Cruz is a potential suspect based on her relationship with Mr. Weiss, you'd agree, wouldn't you?"

"No, not at all. Henry Weiss is the father of her child. That's it, and yesterday she had the misfortune of coincidence to approach Mrs. Weiss and reveal that uncomfortable fact, right, Sophie?"

"Yes."

"So, Miss Cruz, you didn't enter Henry Weiss' apartment yesterday and kill Millie Campos and attack Maria Weiss?" Widelsky bluntly asked.

"No, after I left the subway I went to Loew's Grand Palace and saw *The Sound of Music* and *Robin and the Seven Hoods*. I left the movie around five-thirty and went home. The doorman saw me on the number one bus. Last night I went with my brother and his family, and my aunt and my cousin to Clam Island for a family party. I didn't do nothing, and didn't know anything until this morning. Just like I said," she answered with indignation.

"You've never been in Mr. Weiss' apartment?"

"Never, not yesterday, never. I have never been in the building except yesterday when I was in the lobby and spoke with Creepy the doorman."

"Phil, anything else you can think of?" Widelsky asked.

"No, that covers it all for now."

"Mr. Lenihan, I'd like to take a short statement from Miss Cruz based on what she told us. There isn't much to her story, but if she's telling the truth, and she says she is, we'd like it on paper."

"Under the circumstances that would be fair. Next time you want to ask her any questions the district attorney will be doing it for you at a grand jury.

Today was your one bite of the apple," Lenihan said as he winked his eye at Sophie.

There was a typewriter in the room and a stack of paper and carbon. Cairn threaded three sheets of paper with two sheets of carbon in between them into the typewriter. Widelsky took Cairn's notes and repeated many of the questions Sophie had already answered. The questioning was much more orderly this time and followed the chronology of how Sophie had spent the previous day.

Kreppell watched and listened from the adjacent room. He was incredulous at the sloppy manner in which Cairn and Widelsky had handled the interview. *All softballs*, he thought. *This is our main suspect and these two fuckheads are all over the page. What about Montreal?* he thought. *Or what about Maria Weiss' allegation that she saw Sophie in her bedroom and Sophie attacked her?* By the time they were taking the statement Kreppell was about to explode into the room and throw the two detectives out and take over himself. He knew that he couldn't because Lenihan would have taken his client and left, and there'd be nothing to work from. He resolved that as soon as the statement was completed he'd throw Widelsky and Cairn off the case and bid them farewell to their new assignment in Internal Affairs. "Fucking Cairn, guy's a zero," he repeated to himself. "To think I was going to fight to keep him in the squad," he muttered to himself.

Danny Monaghan was sitting in the office of the Associated Market. It was two-fifteen and his father had told him Mr. McKee was going to handle the case instead of Lenihan. He would pick him up at a quarter to three and take him to the precinct. His father had told him not to worry. Mr. McKee would be there the whole time while they took his prints and questioned him. His father was very calm and told him to keep the story simple, just as he had the night before. Danny was replaying the story in his head when the office phone rang. It was Ernie Lombardi, his friend and counterpart from the Associated Market at West Kingsbridge Road.

"Hey, Danny, good thing I got you. Manager Gail went on her break. I'm not supposed to use the phone, but listen to this."

"Make it quick, old man Kimmel don't want me on the phone, too. And I gotta go soon."

"I was coming back from a delivery up on Kingsbridge Terrace and I see a cop car, you know, detectives, parked on the sidewalk by 212 Lot," Ernie said in a low voice.

"So what?" Danny asked indifferently as he felt his insides tightening up with the image of the detectives looking for the pictures of Maria he had hidden behind the rotted tree at the far end of the lot.

"So what?" Ernie bellowed. "Something's up. Right? I went up to the roof of 212 to look down into the lot and I see these two dicks, one guy's got no jacket on, but you can see the shoulder holster and the gun, clear as day, and they're over at The Spot."

"The Spot, doing what?"

"One guy climbed the wall and got the Playboys from the Library. He looked at them, then showed them to the other guy and then they tossed them. Next they went for The Coffin. They took it out of the ground and threw away the blanket, you know, and then they carried The Coffin from the lot and put it in the back seat of the cop car and drove off. What do you think about that?"

"Got me, maybe that shit with Hand-job Mary. My old man said she told her mother that someone jerked off in her face or something and her mother called the cops."

"I thought that too, but that's a week ago. What about you? You know, the cops being at your house last night?" Ernie said suspiciously.

"What the fuck you talking about?"

"C'mon, you know, everybody knows. Fucking Cleary was blabbing all over the neighborhood last night about the murder. He told Mr. Mulvey that you delivered groceries to the apartment where the murder occurred."

"Yeah, I did, and the fucking cops were at my house asking all sorts of questions. You know why? Because that fucking shit face Cleary is giving me a bad rap. I'm in and out of there in two minutes and the fucking cops are giving me the third degree last night. Good thing my old man came home and gave them the heave ho."

"Yeah, I hear you. Fucking Cleary, he's such a gasbag. He told old man Mulvey, old man Mulvey told his wife and you know old lady Mulvey's the queen of the crossing guards, so she calls my old lady to fill her in. Cleary said you were seen leaving the building around the time the murder happened. And then you didn't come out last night, so what's the fucking scoop?" Ernie said, laughing. "You ain't murdering them old bitches for cheap tipping, are you, Deadly Dan," he chirped.

"Ernie you're a fucking wiseass, you know that? Listen to this? I got this big order for this Mrs. Weiss; I even had to go to the fish store for her. I get the order and I get a newspaper and a pack of butts, then I get two dogs with the works and a soda from the hot dog guy on Kingsbridge Road so's I can have my lunch after I make the delivery. You know old man Kimmel don't let you eat when you want to. Anyway, I make the delivery lickety-split and I go back downstairs to the back of the alleyway and sit on the wall and eat my dogs, have a smoke and read the sports pages. When I'm done I go back to work. That's when asshole Cleary seen me. Fucking Kimmel broke my balls for returning late, but that shit happens all the time. I just tell him I stopped for a bite to eat. Next fucking thing you know the cops are at my door and I'm getting roasted. Now I gotta go and have my fingerprints taken for elimination, they say. Fucking crazy, and Cleary's gonna get his ass kicked by me when this is done. Do you believe it?"

"Yeah, life's a bitch," Ernie said in sympathy. "My mother said Cleary's a gossip and should have his mouth washed with soap. Hey, the other reason I called was we're going to the movies tonight to see *Goldfinger*. You coming?"

"*Goldfinger?* We already saw that."

"Yeah, but it's playing at the Dale with *from Russia with Love*. James Bondo all the way, you know."

"Okay, what time?"

"Seven on the dot, on the corner."

"I'll be there. What do you think those cops wanted in the lot?"

"I think they were there to steal our cooler. The guy with the shoulder holster wiped it down with the blanket. I think it's his now, you know. Hand-job Mary probably told them about our place and they figured they'd fuck with us. That's all."

"Yeah, you're probably right."

"Talk to you later."

Danny put the phone back down on the receiver. His hands were sweating. He didn't believe the cops were there because of Mary Breen's complaint, but why were they there, and did they know something else, he wondered? *All I can do is pray*, he told himself, *just pray. I never meant to hurt anyone, not a soul*, he thought.

Sophie's statement was two-pages long. Cairn made three sets, one original and two carbon copies. Cairn separated the three sets and threw the carbon paper into the wastepaper basket. He handed the original to Sophie and one of the copies to Lenihan. "Why don't you read it over, and if you want to make any changes we'll make them. Once you're satisfied you can sign the original and the two copies. That okay by you, Mr. Lenihan?"

"Let us read it over?"

"Sure."

Cairn excused himself and left the room. Widelsky sat in his chair patiently staring at the ceiling and attempting to act as disinterested and bored as possible.

Cairn stepped into interview room one and said to Kreppell, "I think we caught her in a little lie."

Kreppell was leaning against the wall and said, "What type of God awful softball interrogation was that?"

"You didn't see what we saw, Sarge."

"What do you mean by that?"

"Sarge, Frank and I got a little routine we do with suspects sometimes. We start off taking turns asking questions. Nothing tough, but we mix it up just to see how the suspect responds. Frank got her riled pretty easy over her kid and she starts with the pictures and the attitude. You saw that, didn't you?"

"Yes, and at that point I thought you were doing all right, and then it went downhill."

"That's what you think, but Sophie's back was to you. She got pissed and unzipped the top of that big pocketbook and started pulling crap out. Well, old eagle eye Widelsky sees a key ring in her bag with a green tab and the he can make out the word 'Apartment' on it. He steps on my foot, we have a signal system, and I don't know what the hell he heard or saw, but I figure it's something he saw so I do the stretch routine. She's so hopped up about her kid she can't see that the keys are almost coming out of the bag. So, Frank being the cagey guy he is, softens up the questions and I played along. That fucking asshole she got for a lawyer don't pick up on nothing. He thinks the hardball is when we ask her if she did it, you know. Next thing she's telling us she ain't never been in his apartment and was only in the building to talk to the doorman. Now she's going to sign her statement, then we'll give them the old "by the way" and ask why she had Weiss' keys. Then it should get interesting."

"So what if he says, 'no more questions' and they leave?"

"That's when I tell them that you're sending a stenographer and an assistant DA to Borough Medical Center to take Mrs. Weiss' statement about Sophie being in her bedroom yesterday. Then we'll give them a few minutes to sort things out alone. I think he bought her story hook line and sinker, that's why he's such a smart ass, you know?"

"All right, but let's get them to sign that statement first. I'm going to check and see if Russo and Slattery found anything in that vacant lot, and I'll give

Hogan a call and see if he got started yet or if he's still flapping his gums."

Cairn went back into the interview room and sat down. Widelsky was handing Sophie the copies of the statement, and as she signed each one, he then signed them and handed them to Cairn for his signature also. After all three sets were signed, Widelsky placed them in a folder. Lenihan stood up and took Sophie by the elbow. "Gentlemen, it's been a pleasure and we'll take our leave. Good luck, and I do hope you find the guilty party. Do not contact Miss Cruz concerning this case. Here's my card. If you have any questions, call me."

"Sure thing Mr. Lenihan," Widelsky replied. "Just one little thing, I'd like to ask before you leave."

Lenihan looked at his watch and said, "Make it quick, I believe my partner will be here shortly with young Monaghan. I wouldn't want you two to keep him waiting."

Chapter Forty

Widelsky picked Lenihan's business card up off the table, held it up to the light, and without looking at Sophie or Lenihan said, "This morning I was in Henry Weiss' office with Ruth Goolnick. I was looking for a set of keys to Mr. Weiss' apartment: key ring, four keys and a green tab with the word "Apartment" written on it. Me and Miss Goolnick searched, but we came up empty."

The color drained from Sophie's face and her breathing increased. Lenihan was uncertain where Widelsky was going, but he sensed it wasn't good for his client, and he said sharply, "Listen here, Detective, if you've got something to say, spit it out."

Widelsky dropped the business card on the table and said, "Why don't we all take a seat again. Miss Cruz, is there any reason why the keys to Mr. Weiss' apartment are in your pocketbook?"

"What are you talking about?" Lenihan said with anger. "Sophie, don't answer that question. Detective, make your point, she's not talking."

"Mr. Lenihan, the keys to Mr. Weiss' apartment are in her bag. Would you please ask her to give them to me?"

"What makes you think that?"

"I saw them. Detective Cairn did too. Right, Phil?"

"And how would you know?"

"Mr. Lenihan, you want to play games, we'll play games. You know and we know that if we see something in plain view, we don't need a search

337

warrant. Phil and I both saw the keys. They are exactly what Mr. Weiss described they were. You want, we'll detain her and keep the pocketbook and get a search warrant. It's no big deal, but she ain't going nowhere until we look in that pocketbook. It's your call." Cairn eased back down in his chair and the two detectives sat poker-faced, staring at Lenihan.

Lenihan's face was red, his lower jaw was extended and he was tapping his left foot at a steady pace. His face relaxed, and he forced a smile and said to Sophie, "Is there a set of keys in your pocketbook that matches the keys the detective described?"

Sophie gave Widelsky a defiant look and said, "I don't know."

"C'mon, quit the horse crap, miss. I saw them."

"Detective," Lenihan said tiredly, "I'll not ask you again to refrain from questioning my client. Sophie, take a look in your bag. If they're there, put them on the table."

Sophie took the strap to her pocketbook off her shoulder and unzipped the top. The color had come back to her face, and she said as she moved her right hand through the bag. "If there's keys in here like that Henry must have put them there, or maybe I did by mistake up in Montreal when I was getting my stuff together to leave. I was in a hurry, you know?"

Lenihan's chin sunk to his chest, and he said in a slow and correcting tone, "Sophie, just shut up. Please."

Sophie ignored his remark and kept probing into the pocketbook until she withdrew the ring of keys. "These what you saw?" she said as she handed them to Widelsky. "I haven't the foggiest idea how they got there," she added contemptuously.

Lenihan immediately interjected, "Okay, so she has keys to Mr. Weiss' apartment, if that's what they are, so what?"

"You don't think that's in conflict with her story?" Cairn replied, holding up the folder they had placed Sophie's statement in.

"Not at all," Lenihan remonstrated. "Miss Cruz must have accidentally placed them in her bag up in Montreal, as she alluded to a moment ago."

"Yeah, we didn't talk about Montreal today, did we? Miss Cruz took a powder up there and came back to Huguenot City a day ahead of time, didn't she, Phil?"

"Yes, Frank, there was a phone call Mr. Weiss received from his wife. Mr. Weiss said it really pissed Miss Cruz off. I recall him telling us earlier this morning, Frank."

"Right, didn't he also tell us that his wife said it was Sophie Cruz she saw in her apartment yesterday when she discovered Millie Campos' dead body?" Widelsky said as he stared directly at Sophie.

"Well, Frank, I think that's hearsay. Right, counselor?" Cairn said in a taunting voice.

Lenihan slammed his hand on the table and said, "This interrogation is over, either place my client under arrest or we're leaving. Do you read me?"

Widelsky's revelation of Maria's accusation had left Sophie momentarily breathless and in shock. Lenihan's outburst of anger caught her attention, and she said, "Maria's a fucking liar. I was never in that apartment I didn't do nothing, nothing, do you hear me, nothing!" She put her hand on the chair and started sobbing.

Lenihan moved closer to her and put his hand on her shoulder. "Calm down, I'll straighten everything out, just calm down," he said soothingly.

Cairn adjusted the knot on his tie and craned his neck, and turned it from side to side. He stood up and said, "Frank, why don't we give them a few minutes alone."

Widelsky got up and the two detectives walked out of the room.

"You wait here. I'll go and see if Kreppell sent anyone over to the hospital. I don't think we have enough to arrest her, and I think that hot shot lawyer wants to get her out of the building."

"They're gonna take a hike, what can we do?" Widelsky said with a shrug of his shoulders. "We have to talk to the D.A. She's lying, and she ain't very good at it, except when she lies to her lawyer."

Sophie had gotten control of herself again and Lenihan said to her, "Listen, we can walk right out that door, but that doesn't mean you're not going to end up getting arrested. I told you this morning in my office and I think I stressed it when we were having lunch that the most important thing was for you to tell me the truth. Don't answer now. I don't believe those keys somehow ended up in your bag. I think you're holding back, and what I want to do is go back to my office with you and go back over your story."

Sophie sniffled, stood up and adjusted the strap of her pocketbook to fit over her shoulder. She didn't say anything, but gave Lenihan a wan smile. "Keep your mouth shut," Lenihan directed and opened the door to the room.

Widelsky was standing outside. "Going somewhere?"

"We're leaving. If you have plans to arrest Miss Cruz you can call my office. If the office is closed, the calls are forwarded to my answering service and they'll get in touch with me."

Widelsky was flustered; he didn't want to let her leave. Lenihan was intent on leaving the precinct with Sophie. The story she told them was weak, but the possession of the keys to Henry's apartment wasn't sufficient to warrant an arrest. He decided to act aloof and replied, "Whatever, I'm sure we'll be in touch soon."

Lenihan took Sophie by the arm and escorted her down the hallway and out of the precinct. They made it out to the street and walked down the block to where Lenihan's car was parked. Lenihan unlocked the front passenger's door to his car. He put his hand on the handle, but hesitated in opening the door. He focused his eyes on Sophie and said, "You have two choices. One is you tell me everything, even if it means you committed a murder. The other choice is you grab a cab and go home. Find yourself another lawyer. I'll have Blanche return your check. Maybe I'm the wrong guy to handle your problem, which is it?"

Sophie couldn't make eye contact with him. She took his hand off the door handle and opened the door herself. She got into the car and closed the door. Lenihan walked around and got inside on the driver's side. Neither of them spoke and they drove in silence back to 231st Street. He let her off by his office and said, "I have to find a parking space. You go upstairs and I'll be back in a few minutes."

Mike Monaghan was sitting on a bar stool in Erlich's Tavern. He was at the front of the bar and had a clear view out the front window. The tavern was on the opposite side of the street from Lenihan's law office. He saw Lenihan pull up with Sophie and he saw her get out and go into the street entrance door that led to his office. Lenihan pulled away from the curb and Monaghan's line of sight. All the parking spaces were taken on 231st Street and Monaghan figured that Lenihan would look for a space on Kingsbridge Avenue and walk back to the office. Eddie the bartender put a fresh Pilsner glass of beer in front of Monaghan and took two dimes from the pile of change in front of Monaghan's coaster. Monaghan was staring out the window and without looking he reached back and took the full beer glass in his hand. Eddie the bartender was watching him and looked past Monaghan out into the street to see what it was that had captured his patron's attention so completely. "What are you looking at that I can't see?"

"Nothing, I just don't feel like looking at you."

The bartender offered no response and instead went to the other end of the bar and joined in on a conversation two other customers were having.

Monaghan had no idea who Sophie was, but he knew she was the client Lenihan took on this morning that precipitated Lenihan's referral of Danny to Roger McKee. *McKee may be a good lawyer,* he thought, *but Lenihan's my man, and after all the money I've given him, and all the referrals I've made to him, he treats me like this. I should kick his fucking ass, is what I should do,* he thought further.

Lenihan found a parking space on Kingsbridge Avenue near Naples Terrace. He walked up Naples Terrace and down the City steps to 231st Street. Monaghan saw him coming down the steps and was going to confront Lenihan. He thought about it for a moment, then returned to his barstool. He didn't know how Danny's second interview with the detectives was going to turn out, and he subdued his urge to strike out at Lenihan and reserved it for another time. *I may still need him,* he thought.

Roger McKee and Danny had been sitting on a wooden bench in the precinct lobby for fifteen minutes. Danny was getting antsy and said, "What do you think the hold up is for, Mr. McKee?"

"They're probably busy doing something else, Danny, be patient. Remember, be polite and make eye contact. Tell your story the same way you told me, and if they ask you to be exact on your times, tell them you can't. You don't wear a watch and everything is about or approximate. Soon as you get very specific, they start to trip you up and that happens to the innocent almost as often as it does to the guilty."

"Don't worry, I got no story to get tripped up."

"That's the spirit," McKee replied as he turned the page of his newspaper and resumed reading.

Kreppell hung up the phone and smiled. Cairn and Widelsky were seated like two mannequins in the chairs in front of Kreppell's desk. Kreppell rested his elbows on the padded armrests of his chair and his smile effused into a broad grin and said, "Things are breaking our way. Duffy said he'd have an ADA and a stenographer at Borough Med in forty-five minutes. Futerman agreed to the interview. For what it's worth, Mrs. Weiss is in pretty good shape. This aneurysm or whatever it was isn't all that bad. She has some numbness around the face and trouble with her vision in one eye, but her memory's fine."

"What changed Futerman's mind?" Widelsky asked.

"Duffy told Futerman about Weiss' keys in Cruz's pocketbook."

"What about the kid?"

"I'll have Slattery roll his prints, then Slattery and Russo will go to the hospital and hook up with the assistant from Duffy's office. I want you two to head down to Lenihan's office and start a tail on Cruz; she must be there. I'll talk to the kid's lawyer."

"You gonna call us over the air once you get a confirmation from Borough Med?"

"No, find a phone booth near Lenihan's office and call in. We have plenty of time, no need to rush things. Duffy may want to get an arrest warrant and then pinch her, you never know."

Slattery stuck his head in the door and said, "Sarge, Hogan's on line two, he has some news. Sounds like the Spic chick's been a bad girl."

Kreppell lifted the telephone receiver off the hook, "Ritchie, news?"

"Sarge," Hogan said excitedly. "I got a hit. Right side of the elevator, the big print is Sophie Cruz's. Almost as good as the print Frank took."

"Hold on," then he put his hand over the mouthpiece and said to Cairn and Widelsky. "Hogan got a hit on Cruz's print from the service elevator. She's our girl for sure. You two head out now. Don't grab her, not yet." Cairn and Widelsky shook hands and headed out of the office.

Kreppell took his hand off the mouthpiece to the phone and said, "Ritchie, you sure?"

"Sure as shit I'm sure. It's a great print and the smaller one is Millie Campos'. When you look at the photo of the two prints, it appears that Cruz was right behind Millie Campos, you know? Maybe she took her to the apartment by force. Hey, it's just a theory."

"Whatever. What's important is you have the print. What else did you get?"

"Nothing else. The partial prints on the left wall were smeared and I couldn't pick up more than five, six points. I need a minimum of eight for a match. Same thing with the elevator buttons."

"How many points on Cruz's print?"

"At least twenty, I'm still making the match. By the time I'm done, I'll have them and no one's gonna be able to dispute that. Shit, it's so good they'll accuse us of manufacturing it."

"All right, Ritchie, get back to work. And good work by the way, good work," Kreppell said sincerely before he hung up the phone.

Kreppell was relieved. He was also quite pleased with himself for having ordered Hogan to process the service elevator. Sophie's prints in the elevator didn't put her in the apartment, but the fingerprints along with Weiss' keys in her pocketbook and Maria Weiss' expected statement that she saw Sophie in the apartment and was struck in the chest by her was more than enough to prove the case against her. Why she murdered Millie Campos was unimportant as far as Kreppell was concerned. "Motive is the one thing you don't have to prove if you have the evidence," he could recall Grimsley telling him any number of times. Kreppell picked up the phone again to call his boss and was interrupted by Slattery. "Sarge, that lawyer's still waiting out front with the kid. What do you want to do?"

Kreppell hung up the phone and said, "Bring them in here and don't go anywhere just yet."

"You got it," Slattery called over his shoulder as he walked away.

Kreppell decided to wait until after he'd spoken with Danny Monaghan and his attorney before calling Captain Grimsley. It occurred to him how uncertain police work could be when you were pressed for time and had few leads to follow. *This time yesterday,* he thought, *there were two suspects, the delivery boy and the secretary. The doorman was adamant that the delivery boy was involved and the boy's father had unwittingly added to that cloud of suspicion. Now, it all was so irrelevant,* he thought. Kreppell was tempted for a moment to have Slattery print the boy and send him and his attorney on their way without any further discussion, but that was what a slacker would do and decided to conduct a brief interview with the boy and his lawyer. He'd add a short report for the file, then close Monaghan out as a suspect and direct all of the detectives' efforts toward locking up the case against Sophie.

Slattery appeared at the doorway with McKee and Monaghan. "Sarge, Mr. McKee and his client, I'll be in the squad room if you need me."

Kreppell stood up, reached across his desk and shook Roger McKee's hand, then extended his hand to Danny Monaghan. "I'm Sergeant Kreppell. The two detectives who caught this case are out of the office. Please, take a seat."

Roger McKee pointed to the chair on his right, and said to Danny, "Daniel, sit down. Sergeant, I'm representing Daniel on this matter and we're prepared for him to have his fingerprints taken and to answer any questions you or your detectives may have relative to this case."

Kreppell immediately liked McKee. Unlike Lenihan, he was subdued and deferential. He didn't detect that air of arrogance he sensed in Lenihan. McKee was as well dressed as Lenihan was, but he was a smaller man and lacked that bullyboy persona and exaggerated familiarity that Lenihan had. He was wearing a tan seersucker suit with cordovan penny loafers and a white button-down collared shirt with a striped brown and gold tie. He looked to be in his late thirties or early forties. His hair was thick and white, with traces of blonde and his skin was ruddy but firm. He had that certain genteel Irish look you found in bishops and some police chiefs. It was the look of a man who controlled his appetites and temper, and chose his sins carefully. McKee seemed as comfortable and relaxed in the hardback chair as Kreppell did in his chair. Kreppell considered the murder investigation closed and in an instant of magnanimity he was about to dismiss McKee and his client and tell them the culprit had been apprehended, but he caught himself and decided to go through the motions, if for no other reason than to justify the tactics of Widelsky and Cairn and make McKee earn his fee. Kreppell pushed his chair back and stood up. He went around his desk and said, "Daniel, why don't you come with me. I'll have Detective Slattery take your prints, then we can get started."

Kreppell smiled at Danny and chuckled to himself over the ordinariness of the boy's appearance. Danny was dressed in blue dungarees with a green polo shirt and black low cut Converse sneakers. He looked liked a thousand other teenage boys, and there was nothing about his appearance or mannerism that hinted in any way he was a murderer. Danny stood up from his chair and smiled at Kreppell and said, "Yes sir."

Kreppell pointed to the door, and as they went out, he called out, "Slattery, we're ready."

They were halfway down the hallway when Slattery intercepted them. "He ready for his prints, Sarge?"

"Yes. When you're done bring him back to the squad room." He then said to Danny in an avuncular way, "Detective Slattery will take your fingerprints. This is an ordinary process for elimination purposes for people who were at the crime scene. Stay cool."

Danny lowered his head and glanced up at Kreppell nervously and said, "Thank you, sir."

"No problem."

When he walked back into his office, McKee was still sitting in the same pose he'd left him in, upright and calm. Kreppell took his seat again and said, "We've had a breakthrough in this case, so I don't know if it's practical or necessary to conduct the interview today. There are still a few issues my investigators have with your client's story."

"Well, I'm aware of that," McKee said gravely. "The boy is not involved. I can assure you of that, but there is a problem with his family which may have colored your detectives' impression of Daniel."

Kreppell laughed and said, "Could that be his father or Tim Cleary?"
McKee laughed too and replied, "Both."

"I've met Cleary, and I've heard about Mike Monaghan. What's your point, or is it a question?"

"There's no question, but there is a very serious point to be made and one I'm more comfortable making without having the boy present."

"I'm all ears."

"Well, the boy is going into his senior year at Cathedral Prep. That's a Catholic prep school for young men contemplating entering the priesthood. I don't believe Daniel is a candidate for the priesthood, but he isn't a bad boy. His mother is a wonderful woman and very active in the church. They're good people. The father is another story. He's something of a nightmare, and I can't for the life of me understand why his wife has hung in this long, but she has. Mike Monaghan is a criminal. He goes to work every day, but he's a thug. Mr. Lenihan has represented him in numerous cases and in this particular matter I don't want the son to pay for the sins of the father. I don't know much about Tim Cleary, but I do know that sometime last year he had his face pushed in by Mike Monaghan. It appears Mr. Cleary was late paying a gambling debt and Mr. Monaghan, among his many criminal endeavors, collects money for a local bookie. The incident happened in full view of a barroom full of people in Pete's Bridge Lounge. Did you know about that?"

"I heard, what else?" Kreppell asked casually.

"Daniel heard from one of his friends that last night that Cleary was the talk of the neighborhood. He and Daniel live in the same building. He told the neighbors who were out for some evening fresh air and later on all the patrons in Pete's Lounge about the murder and Daniel's possible connection. I feel very strongly, that while Cleary may have a legitimate grudge against Mike Monaghan, he is trying to get even by implicating Daniel in this crime. Aside from that, this appears to be a matter of strange coincidences."

"How's that?" Kreppell asked.

"Don't you think it is rather unusual that Cleary and Monaghan live in the same building, and Monaghan and the secretary of a victim's husband, Miss Cruz is her name I believe, I contacted the same lawyer?" McKee replied.

"I know all that, but strange coincidences do occur and I choose to let the story play out. Now, as for your client," Kreppell paused, then leaned forward in his chair. "I'd agree with your suspicion about Cleary's motives except the boy's time pattern, you know, making the delivery and then being seen roughly forty-five minutes to an hour later leaving the area of the building is suspicious you must admit?"

"Certainly, but those time patterns, as you call them, could be exaggerated by five or ten minutes and in this case, like any other criminal matter, five or ten minutes can make a world off difference. I already spoke with Mr. Kimmel, he's Daniel's boss at the Associated, and he said he wasn't sure about how long Daniel was gone except he returned sometime around one and that it wasn't unusual for Daniel to stop and get lunch after making a delivery. No one was wearing a stopwatch and recording times. That's all. I find his conduct very innocent, but then, again, I'm his lawyer."

"Honestly, I agree too. Wrong place at the wrong time, and my detectives did take quite a dislike to Mr. Monaghan."

"Monaghan doesn't like cops. It's one of his many character deficiencies. But he's a tough man, and he pays his bills, and who am I to judge anyone," McKee said with a wave of his hands.

Kreppell slowly nodded his head in agreement and said, "We're not going to interview the boy today. No point right now. If his prints don't appear anywhere in that apartment except the room where he delivered the groceries, I'd say we have no other interest in him. That's not a guarantee, but right now it's the best I can offer."

McKee stood up and picked up his briefcase. He extended his hand to Kreppell and gave him a firm handshake. "Sergeant, under the circumstances I wouldn't expect it any other way." He then placed the briefcase on the chair and opened it. He withdrew one of his business cards and gave it to Kreppell. "If you need to speak with Daniel just give me a call. I've taken up enough of your time. When you're done with Daniel send him outside, I'll be waiting in front of the precinct." Without waiting for a response from Kreppell, he picked up his briefcase and left the office.

Kreppell went to the forensic office. When he got there, Slattery had already taken Danny's fingerprints and Danny was washing his hands. Kreppell said, "Kid, your lawyer's waiting in front of the building for you. If we need you, we'll give him a call, but I wouldn't lose any sleep over it. Slattery, soon as you're cleaned up, get Russo and head over to Borough."

"Russo already made the call, and the ADA's going to wait for us. I'll be done in five minutes."

"Great, and when you get the statement, give me a call."

Danny listened intently to the exchange between the sergeant and the detective. He surmised that they were not interested in him and had identified another suspect. It gave him an eerie feeling. He felt a strong pang of guilt, and at the same time a great feeling of relief. He hurried out of the office and practically jogged out of the building. McKee was waiting patiently on the sidewalk with his briefcase sitting on the sidewalk between his legs and a copy of the *Huguenot Times* folded neatly in his right hand opened to the sports section. He was reading and didn't notice Danny until Danny said, "Hello, Mr. McKee, I'm done."

McKee put the paper under his arm and said, "I told you this would be a piece of cake. They were just acting on that silly doorman's information. They've got nothing on you and no interest in you. So don't worry. Got it?"

"Yes sir," Danny said with relief.

"You need a ride back to work or a ride home?"

"You can take me back to work if it's no trouble?"

"Okay," McKee replied, then led the way to his car. Danny followed slightly behind and counted his blessings. It never occurred to him that someone else was going to take the blame for what he did.

Chapter Forty-One

Sophie was sitting alone in Lenihan's office. The blinds were partially drawn to keep out the afternoon sun, and strips of sun and shadow lined the floor and walls. The room was cool, but she was sweating and uncomfortable. Lenihan had barely spoken to her since they left the precinct. He had driven the whole way with both of his big hands gripping the steering wheel. Along the way he had mumbled a few indistinguishable remarks to himself and Sophie found his presence frightening. He had ordered her to take a seat in his office and left the room without further comment. She must have been alone in the room for at least fifteen minutes and she started crying again.

Her mood went from anger to hopelessness, and as her initial sniffles turned into gasps and great heaving sighs Lenihan strutted into the room and roared, "Please, shut up and stop wailing. It's getting so every time you turn the faucet on I expect to see a neon sign over your head blinking- Guilty, Guilty, Guilty."

Sophie forced herself to stop crying and said, "I'm sorry. What do you expect me to do?"

Lenihan stood over her, gave her a searing look, then said mockingly, "Oh, perhaps you could tell the truth. As far as I'm concerned you have a problem with your emotions and a problem with the truth. That cock and bull story about your boyfriend's keys mysteriously appearing in your pocketbook was pure cellophane. Now tell me the truth or get out."

Sophie coiled back and said meekly, "Please sit down and listen without yelling." She wanted to leave, but didn't have the strength to, and she knew she couldn't bear going through the whole story again with another lawyer. Lenihan took up his seat behind his desk and rested his chin on his closed fists. "I'm waiting."

"I swear that everything I told you about yesterday was true."

"Fine, what didn't you tell me?"

"This morning when I went to work I was prepared for the worst, you know? I was afraid Henry was going to fire me and God knows what else. I got to work about eight-thirty, maybe a little later. My paycheck was in the mail from the accountant and I had an office check to replenish the petty cash for two hundred dollars. I went to the bank, it opens at nine, and waited outside until it opened. I was the first customer. I cashed everything and went back to the office. Henry wasn't there yet, and I was nervous. You know, what did Maria say to him, it had to be crazy in his house with all that shit I told her? Then a man called, Tom something or other, he wanted to speak with Henry and said someone had recommended him. I told him to call back later. I had a can of Tab, then I went and asked Ruthie, maybe around nine-thirty, if anyone had heard from Henry? I don't ever do that, but with what happened I wasn't thinking right. Ruthie, that's Futerman's secretary, Ruth Goolnick, was real nasty. She said, 'Don't you know what happened?' or something like that. I said, 'No.' And then she showed me the newspaper article about the murder and told me that Maria was in intensive care and was also attacked. I couldn't believe it, would you?"

"Why wouldn't I believe it, it happened?"

"I mean, who could believe that would happen in Henry's building? Anyway, I thought about yesterday and my throwing Joey's picture at Maria and I got crazy. Ruthie said she was in a coma or something, right? I thought that she didn't have a chance to tell Henry about us or knowing about Joey or anything. I just had to get Joey's picture. What if Henry found the picture in her bag, or if the cops found it and showed it to him; I was dead? I wasn't thinking, I took his keys from the desk and went to his apartment. The bus driver would remember me get on this morning from the office because I was running and he told me he would have waited. He was Irish, you could tell by his accent," she said breathlessly. Relaying the story to Lenihan took an effort, and she was winded from her non-stop monologue.

Lenihan continued to stare at her and said nothing.

She caught her breath and continued. "I got off the bus at Kingsbridge Road and went to a phone booth. I dialed Henry's apartment twice and let the phone ring. No one answered. I wanted that picture, I knew the cops would blame me and I thought that was the evidence they'd use. I knew about the service entrance because of all the grocery orders I'd called in, and I went to the alleyway, past the entrance to the building. I went in and no one saw me, I'm positive. I got on the elevator, the service one, and got off at the seventh floor. Henry lives on the eighth. I had my heels off, and when I got off the elevator I heard noise on the eighth floor, maybe a chair scraping and I got scared so I ran down the stairs and out of the building, then I came to your office. Swear to God," she said as she wiped her face with a tissue she'd taken from her pocketbook.

"And that happened this morning?"

"Yes, after nine-thirty."

"And you're sure no one saw you this morning go into that building or get on the elevator?"

"I'm positive."

"That's too bad, the murder happened yesterday. If someone saw you there today that would support your story about taking the keys this morning."

"You still don't believe me, do you?"

"Doesn't matter anymore what I believe. Right now you are in a big kettle of hot water and the cops are ready to turn up the flame. I suspect Mrs. Weiss is going to give them a statement, and by sundown there will be an arrest warrant for murder with your name on it," he said unsympathetically.

"Oh, my God, Oh, my God," Sophie whimpered.

"You're going to need more than prayers. I just don't know, yet, how we're going to win this. First off, I've got to get you out of town for the weekend or you'll end up spending it in jail."

Sophie hung her head and rubbed her brow. "Where can I go, and what about Joey?"

"Your aunt is at your apartment, isn't she?"

"Yes."

"So, your son will be taken care of for the short term. I'm concerned about you," he said with a little more warmth.

Sophie looked at him with surprise. "Coulda fooled me."

"I can be concerned and very pissed off at the same time. You made me look like a jerk with those cops. That's not the end of the world, but I like the upper hand. As soon as Roger gets back I'll see what he's found out and we can plan from there. Is there anywhere you can go this weekend where the cops will have a hard time tracking you down?"

"No, my brother went upstate to Mohican Lake with his wife and kids today, and my cousin Freddy has a place in Riverview and he's in the phone book. Henry knows them both, so I can't go to their places. My aunt has a little apartment on Kingsbridge Terrace near Kingsbridge Road, but Henry knows her address, too. He got her the apartment and did Ray and Freddy's closings."

"You could book a hotel room in Huguenot City. How much money do you have?"

"My paycheck and the two hundred dollars for petty cash. I forgot to put that in the safe this morning."

"Good, you have enough. Call your aunt and tell her you can't come home. Tell the whole story if you must, but not where you're going. I have a man who'll take you downtown. Go out for dinner, catch a movie, whatever, but it'll beat spending a weekend in the women's house of detention."

"Jesus Christ, You really think they're going to arrest me?"

"Without a doubt, if they get you Monday we can have a bail hearing. Your brother and cousin own houses, how much have you got in the bank?"

"Seven thousand dollars. I save most of my paychecks, Henry pays for a lot of things," she said wistfully and the pain of losing Henry was so evident in her voice.

"You should make bail, I can't see a judge setting no bail. The seven thousand will initially go toward your bail, but eventually you'll be paying legal bills from that sum. This isn't going to be cheap."

"Mr. Lenihan, I can't go to jail, I can't," she sobbed.

"Call your aunt. You can use my phone. I'll be in the outer office, I have some other business to attend to," he said as he got up from the desk and left the room.

Sophie sat there crying silently for several more minutes. She knew she was innocent, but it didn't seem to matter. Lenihan's remark that he had some other business to attend to wounded her terribly. *Here she was facing ruin, and he was just another guy making a buck*, she thought. He'd already spent her seven thousand in savings and was appropriating her brother and cousin's property for bail security. It all seemed so mercenary, but she knew she'd do everything he told her to and she'd beg her family to help her because the alternative was unacceptable.

Cairn and Widelsky had parked the unmarked car on 231st St in front of the Army Navy clothing store. They were across the street and several doorways east of Lenihan's office. "If we sit here he might make us," Widelsky said.

"Okay, let's go up the street. You wanna stop in that gin mill there, Erlich's, catch a pop?"

"Not now, I think there's a pizza place up a little further. Let's get a slice, we can still watch the office from there."

"A slice sounds right by me."

The two detectives walked up the block. Monaghan was still perched on the bar stool watching Lenihan's office. He watched Cairn and Widelsky walk by. He did a double take, then felt a cold rush in his stomach. He lit a cigarette and took a long drag, then finished the full glass of beer Eddie the bartender had just placed in front of him. *What the fuck are those two doing here?* he thought. *It can't be Danny. He's with McKee,* he reasoned, then the thought occurred that Danny had panicked and failed to make the appointment. He told himself to stay calm and got off the stool and moved closer to the front window.

Widelsky and Cairn went into Sam's Pizzeria. Widelsky ordered them each two slices and cokes. He stood by the front counter and kept a close watch on Lenihan's office. It was evident by the design of the building that there was only one-way in and out. Sophie had to be in the office and while they waited, Widelsky enjoyed the pizza. Cairn went to the rear of the pizza shop and found the payphone. It was next to the jukebox and several feet from one of four tables. At the table closest to the phone were three teenage boys. They were sitting there over cokes singing the song *You Belong to Me.* It was a fair rendition of a remake of the Jo Stafford hit that was made by a group called the Duprees in the early '60s. Cairn admired the group's talents for a few moments, and said, "That's real nice boys, now pipe down while I make this call." They ignored him and kept on singing. Cairn moved his jacket back and exposed the thirty-eight chief's special in the black holster on his hip and said harshly, "Hey, did you hear me the first time?"

Two of the three teens saw the gun and understood who Cairn was. All three got up and sang a little louder as they exited the pizzeria.

Cairn laughed to himself and dialed Kreppell's number. "Sarge, we're on 231st Street by Godwin Terrace across from Lenihan's office. We're having a couple of slices and keeping an eye on his store. You want the number so you can call us back?"

"Yeah, give me the number, but if you see her put a tail on her. I don't want to lose her. Oh, and by the way, the delivery boy's story about buying the newspaper, cigarettes and hot dogs all held up. Murphy and DeMarco just got back. No one's sure about the time, everything is around noon, but the candy store and the hot dog vendor all back up the kid's story."

"How about the kid, did he come in?"

"Yeah, but all we did was print him, no point in wasting time that way right now."

"Waste of time now, for sure," Cairn said. He then gave him the number and Kreppell repeated it back to him and hung the phone up. Cairn went back to the front counter and ate his pizza. Widelsky had already finished his and was standing outside in front of the pizza parlor.

Monaghan was anxious and the feeling disturbed him. He was the type of man who worried about few things, if any at all. He took life day by day and was confident he could handle anything that got in his way. Over the years of his association with Vince Lobianco and Chick Nathan he'd done far worse than rough up a few free loaders who were late with their payments. Hijacking, burglary even an arson once, he'd done them all, everything but murder, he thought, and he'd never lost a minute's sleep over anything, even all the times he'd been pinched by the cops. But this was different. Mike Monaghan never acknowledged Father's Day and it was for a very good reason—he never considered himself much of a parent. Still, Danny was his son, and in his own way he loved him and the thought of his son facing the disgrace of a homicide charge for murdering an old woman and going to prison or worse, getting the gas chamber or electric chair was too chilling a scenario to contend with, and for the first time in his life he was truly frightened.

The payphone in the pizzeria rang. Cairn held his hand up to the man behind the counter and said, "I think that's for me." Cairn went to the payphone and picked it up "Pizza place," he said. "See the pyramids across the Nile," came the reply in three-part harmony. Cairn laughed and hung up the phone. "Freaking wiseasses," he said. He went back to the counter and the pizza man said in broken English, "For you? Phona wasa for you?"

"Wrong number."

He waited by the counter another five minutes and the phone rang again. He went over and picked it up, and this time it was Kreppell. "Phil, that you?"

"Yeah, Sarge."

"She gave us a statement. Signed, sworn and delivered. Very short and not much on the facts, but she's adamant that it was the Cruz woman in her bedroom and the Cruz woman who knocked her down."

"Good enough for me. You want us to pick her up, or are we getting a warrant?"

"Make a summary arrest, we have enough. I'll call Lenihan's office and give him the bad news. Maybe he'll make it easy for us. So standby and I'll call back."

Kreppell dialed the number for Lenihan's office. Blanche answered the phone, "Lenihan and McKee, law offices," she flatly drawled.

"Mr. Lenihan, please?"

"May I ask who is calling?"

"Sergeant Ted Kreppell, Borough Major Case squad."

"He's on another line, may I put you on hold?"

Lenihan was sitting in Roger McKee's office talking on the telephone with McKee. McKee had gone home after dropping Danny Monaghan off at his job. Blanche went to the door and said, "Pat, excuse me. Sergeant Kreppell's on the other line."

Lenihan shook his hand and said, "Tell him to hold on. Roger, I have that sergeant on the other line. I'll call you back." Lenihan left McKee's office and went out to the secretarial area. Blanche pointed to the phone on the desk next to hers and said, "Line three."

Lenihan looked at the blinking light on the phone and said, "I wonder what new surprise this clown has for me now?" He picked up the phone and in a clearly irritated voice he said, "Yes, Sergeant Kreppell, what now?"

"Is Miss Cruz, still with you?"

"No, she went away for the weekend. I told her to call me first thing Monday morning, in case you needed her. Why?"

"Bad news for her. We have her fingerprints in the elevator, and Mrs. Weiss gave us a sworn statement putting Miss Cruz at the murder scene."

"Has the court issued a warrant?"

"Not yet, I thought you could bring her in and get it over with."

"I would if I knew where she was, but I don't. I'll bring her in Monday, that's the best I can do, Sergeant, anything else?"

"In the meantime we'll be looking for her."

"You do that," Lenihan said with scorn as he hung up the phone. "Blanche, is Fritz on the way?"

Blanche got up from her desk and walked into Roger McKee's office. She separated two slats of the Venetian blinds and looked out the window toward Broadway. Parked in the bus stop in front of Gibbon's Bar was a white Plymouth Valiant with the motor running and a plume of white smoke billowing out of the tailpipe. "He's in front of Gibbon's."

Sophie was still sitting in her chair. Her head was back and she was staring at the ceiling. Lenihan closed the door to his office and said, "Did you get a hold of your aunt?"

"Yes, I told her I had to go back to Montreal and I'd call her tomorrow."

"You didn't tell her what's going on?"

"I'll tell her tomorrow, when I have more time. She'll get hysterical, and I need more time. Maybe I'll call my cousin Freddy and have him tell her."

"Fine, my Uncle Fritz is parked down the block in a white Plymouth Valiant, right in front of Gibbon's Bar. He'll take you down to the city. He'll wait for you. Buy two changes of clothes for the weekend. He has a little suitcase in the car. Then you can pack the new clothes in the suitcase and he'll take you over to the Mayflower Hotel. They have plenty of vacancies. Check in and lay low for the weekend. Call me at eight o'clock Monday morning from the hotel and we'll take it from there. Do you understand?"

"I just want to go home and see my baby," Sophie softly sobbed.

"I know this is difficult. I'm trying to help you. The Mayflower's a nice hotel. Use the petty cash money. I need the weekend to think this out, and I don't want to risk having you picked up and thrown in jail," he said with real concern.

"Okay," Sophie replied as she stood up. "You do believe me, tell me you believe me?"

"Sophie, what I believe is unimportant. Under the circumstances it is best I don't know. Hurry, Fritz will make sure you get where you're going," he answered as he held open the door to his office and pointed to the front door of the office.

Sophie said goodbye to Blanche and left.

Kreppell had already called Cairn back at the pizzeria. Cairn and Widelsky had left the pizza parlor. Cairn was across the street sitting in the unmarked police car. Widelsky was standing in the candy store two doors from Lenihan's office. Cairn saw her first and honked his car horn. Widelsky stepped out of the candy store onto the sidewalk. Sophie had just passed the store. The high heels, the tight red skirt and the sheer white blouse passed him in a blur. He increased his pace and said, "Excuse me, Miss Cruz."

Sophie looked back over her shoulder and saw Widelsky. His arm was reaching for her and she started to run. She hadn't taken more than two steps when her heel caught a small crack in the sidewalk and she pitched forward and fell to her knees. The heel broke off her shoe and she attempted to get up and run, but Widelsky was there to intercept her, and before she could take another step he had her in his grasp. "Hold on, honey."

Sophie started screaming, "Oh, my God, let me go, let me go.'

Cairn had made a quick U-turn and the unmarked police car was now

355

double parked parallel to Widelsky and Sophie on the sidewalk. The red gumball was affixed to the roof of the car by a magnet and was rotating and making a whizzing mechanical noise. Cairn jumped out of the car to assist Widelsky and was almost struck by a Plymouth Valiant that pulled away from the curb at a high rate of speed. Sophie was fighting and screaming. Widelsky had her arms pinned behind her back and Cairn expertly snapped the handcuffs on her.

"C'mon, miss," Cairn said. "No use fighting, c'mon."

Sophie gave up and let her body go limp. She hung her head down and her hair fell over her face. She kept repeating, "Oh, my God, oh, my God." The heel on her right shoe had come off and she limped with her left foot and hopped on her right foot as the two detectives escorted her to the police car. Her stockings were torn and her left knee was bleeding. Widelsky opened the rear door and put his hand on her head and guided her into the seat. He then got in next to her and Cairn went around and got in the driver's side and they made another U-turn and drove off, east on 231St Street.

Monaghan had left Erlich's as soon as he saw Sophie leave Lenihan's office. He witnessed the arrest and was on the opposite side of the street when Widelsky grabbed her. As the unmarked car made the U-turn and drove past him he caught a quick glimpse of Sophie's tortured face as she looked out the window of the police car.

Lenihan and Blanche had watched the entire scene from the office window. Lenihan saw Monaghan and said to Blanche, "Just what I fucking need now, that lunatic to start breaking my balls. Call Kreppell and find out when they'll hold her arraignment."

Monaghan crossed the street and picked up Sophie's heel from the sidewalk. He went up the street and turned into the doorway to Lenihan's office and went upstairs. He walked in and Lenihan and Blanche were standing by Blanche's desk. Blanche was on the telephone and Lenihan put his finger to his lips to tell Monaghan to be quiet. He then waved his hand and went to his office. Monaghan followed him, and when they were inside the office Lenihan said without enthusiasm, "Mike, what can I do for you? I guess you saw the show?"

Monaghan tossed the heel to Sophie's shoe onto Lenihan's desk. "That the woman you dumped Danny for?"

"Unfortunately."

"Those were the same two detectives who were at my apartment last night. What gives? And where's Roger."

"The police have no interest in your son. That woman was just arrested for the murder they questioned Danny about yesterday."

Monaghan absorbed the information for a moment, kept his poker face, then said, "Strange, you get two clients for the same murder, isn't it?"

"Maybe, but she lives around the corner on Kingsbridge Avenue and passes my office all the time. Who knows? After I spoke with her today I asked Roger to handle the matter with your son. It was pretty clear Danny didn't need an attorney. Tell you what, we won't even bill you for the service."

"I'll pay, that's not my complaint. I just thought that I had hired you, that's all."

"Mike," Lenihan said plaintively. "The girl came in with a long cock and bull story. She's guilty and the police have plenty of evidence. I'm a defense attorney. Danny's situation was a waste of time and this girl needed me. Please, no hard feelings."

"All right, those cops coming on like gangbusters last night didn't mean anything after all. Is that what you're telling me?"

"Exactly, they were feeling around in the dark."

"That's okay, I guess you got your plate full. Sorry for the intrusion," he said, then turned and walked out the door.

Lenihan buzzed Blanche over the intercom and said, "You get a hold of Kreppell?"

"Yes sir, the arraignment will be after seven in Criminal Part II.'

"Great," he moaned. "I'll be there all night, all night!"

Chapter Forty-Two

Monaghan had a sour taste in his mouth and his stomach was gurgling. He was belching gas and a few times he thought he was going to vomit. It was an unusual ailment for him and as he entered the lobby and crossed to his side of the building he detected the heavy scent of oil based paint and felt even sicker. He instinctively knew the point of origin was his own apartment. Mary Monaghan didn't sit still when she was worried over something. If there was a family problem that she couldn't resolve she immersed herself in physical activity to make the time pass. In times of great stress, and there had been many over the course of their troubled marriage, Mary had sought solace in a gallon of paint and a new color for one of the rooms in their apartment.

The apartment door was partially open. Mary was on her hands and knees rolling up the old linen sheets she used as drop cloths. The cool mint tone that had once been the color of choice for the long hallway that led from the entranceway and foyer of the apartment to the living room and back bedroom was now a bright lemony yellow. The woodwork was painted in white enamel and was slowly drying to a hard sheen. Monaghan stopped short of the doorway and sniffed in disgust. "Jesus Christ, Mary, you painted the hallway last year. That shit stinks, fucking stinks."

"I opened all the windows. The smell will be gone by morning. I talked to Danny before. Thank God," she said as she blessed herself. "He said the police weren't even interested in him. They took his fingerprints and sent him on his way."

"I know. I just saw Lenihan."

"He said McKee went with him. What happened to Lenihan?"

"McKee has the case. They just arrested some woman for the murder; she's Lenihan's client, now."

Mary Monaghan closed her hands over her heart, raised her head upward and exclaimed thankfully, "Oh, dear God in Heaven, all day I prayed and prayed. Does Danny know?"

"No, what the fuck, he had his mother with a paintbrush in one hand and her rosary beads in the other praying for him all day, what does he care?"

"Don't be so crude. Do you know the woman?"

"No, why would I know her?"

"I don't know, I just thought you might have learned something from Lenihan. I know you were worried."

"If he didn't do anything, why should I worry? I gotta lie down for a while. What's for dinner?"

Mary frowned. She'd been dismissed and knew there was no point in continuing the conversation. "Tuna and chowder, are you leaving for the shore tonight?"

"No, first thing tomorrow morning, I'm going out later. Did you clean my softball pants?"

"Yes, I packed your bag. Why don't you take Danny with you?"

"That's all right, he's gotta work tomorrow."

"I'll call you for dinner after he gets home."

"I'm not that hungry. Eat without me."

Monaghan walked past his wife and went into their bedroom. He closed the door and stripped down to his shorts and sat on the bed. He lit a cigarette and looked out the window at the brick wall of the neighboring apartment building. There was a slight breeze blowing from the west and the acrid smell from the empty garbage cans in the alleyway two floors below the apartment wafted into the room and combined with the smell of the paint and the cigarette smoke. It was an unpleasant odor. Monaghan flicked his cigarette out the window. He sat there staring out the window.

Soon the bricks faded to a blur and he saw Sophie's tortured face.

The hopelessness of the expression on her face haunted him. He had only caught a glimpse of her, but he could visualize the tears and the streaked makeup. It was the face of a sad clown, and he felt guilty.

Mary Monaghan said a silent rosary as she finished cleaning the paintbrushes. She placed them in an empty coffee can half filled with turpentine and set it in a box on the fire escape outside the kitchen window. She couldn't wait for Danny to come home and for her husband to go out. She despised his crudeness and the off-handed way he talked about the woman who'd been arrested for the murder. *How could one man be so uncaring?* she thought.

As she was setting the table Danny came home. He gave his mother a hug and a kiss. "Hey, Mom, I love you," he said affectionately.

Mary was surprised by his behavior and she hugged him back and brushed the hair away from his forehead. She smiled at him and said softly, "I prayed for you all day. I knew you didn't do anything, but I prayed just the same. Wash up and we'll have dinner."

"Yeah, it was a piece of cake, Mom, you know? The sergeant was a nice guy, and he told me not to worry. Those guys last night were real assholes."

"Watch your mouth," she scolded. "You're not too old to have your mouth washed out with soap."

Danny laughed and went down the hallway. He looked into his parent's bedroom and saw his father sitting on the bed looking out the window. He went into the room and Mike Monaghan coughed, then cleared his throat. "Come over here."

Danny went before the window and looked at his father.

"The cops busted some broad for the murder an hour ago."

"You're kidding."

"I don't kid."

"What are we gonna do?" Danny whispered conspiratorially.

"Nothing, keep your fucking trap shut. I don't want to talk about it anymore. Got it? It's over."

Danny closed his eyes and bit his lower lip. Nothing would chase the sense of dread that came over him. The joy he'd felt when Kreppell had sent him on his way was nothing more than a brief deception of conscience. The police had arrested someone for something he'd done, and no matter his sense of guilt; his father had ordained what the response would be. "It's over." And there was nothing he could do.

Mike Monaghan lit another cigarette and looked past Danny to the brick wall that was twenty feet across the alleyway. Danny waited for him to say something else, but there was nothing there but stony silence; all that had to be said was said.

Danny left the room and went to the bathroom. "Hey, Mom," he called out. "I'm gonna take a quick shower; we're going to the movies tonight"

"That's wonderful, honey," she cooed. "I'll get dinner ready. Do you want your sandwich on toast?"

"Yeah, but don't burn it."

Mike Monaghan listened to the conversation between mother and son. The relief in Mary's voice was evident. In her world all was well. The police had arrested the murderer and they had no interest in her son. Mary always believed what she wanted to believe, and Mike had a sudden urge to tell her the truth. He despised her constant praying and reliance on an unseen God that demanded thanks and praise for every benefit, but was never responsible for all that went wrong. She was childish. It was that childishness twenty odd years ago that led to her pregnancy and their marriage. Mary had seen something in Mike Monaghan he knew didn't exist. She foolishly gave herself freely to him, and he indulged himself over and over again. In the park, on the roof, in the basement stairwell to her building, almost anywhere he chose. And on the evening of the day he returned home from basic training there was a knock on his apartment door. His father answered the door and there was Mary Brown with a suitcase and a face full of tears. Monaghan senior looked at the girl and called out to his son, "Mike, in the kitchen." He left Mary standing at the door and told his son, "Your girl is at the door. She's come with a suitcase and I expect you're to blame."

Two weeks later they were married and Mary moved into the Monaghan apartment. Seven months later Kathleen was born. It was an unsteady union from the start, and by the time Danny was born the marriage had settled into a compromise; Mike paid the bills and Mary prayed for his soul. Her piety was suffocating, and the revelation that Danny, her son, her pride and joy, had committed a murder would have tested her faith to the very core. He wanted to tell her the truth. He didn't know if the impulse to do so was borne out of mean spiritedness or a simple attempt to temper her air of moral superiority, but he had to make a conscious effort to keep himself from sharing Danny's sin with her. *Not now,* he thought, *there's too much at stake.*

Chapter Forty-Three

Monaghan found a parking space three blocks down the street from Bongo's. It was almost ten at night, but he felt good. He'd slept a good four hours and when he awoke he felt like himself again. He'd taken a shower and put on a pair of dress slacks and a short sleeve shirt Mary had ironed for him.

The crowd in Bongo's was two deep at the bar. There were as many women in the bar as there were men. Most of the men were married. A few of the women were too, but there wasn't a married couple present in the bar together. "Crazy" by Patsy Cline was blaring over the jukebox and a few couples were dancing closely in the open area between the bar and the front door. Monaghan walked the length of the bar and greeted most of the regulars with a quick nod of the head and the slightest hint of a smile. A few of the women gave him big hellos and he responded with affectionate slaps to their hips and a friendly, "Hey sweetheart, what's cooking?" His tour of the bar was a practiced ritual he conducted every Friday and Saturday night. Mike Monaghan enjoyed his reputation as a tough guy, but he also had the business sense to know that people loved a tough guy who treated them like friends.

At the rear of the bar was another open area. There was a pool table, an electronic shuffleboard machine and six square tables with two chairs for each table. The tables had red laminate tops and silver aluminum stands. The chairs were black wooden frames with red vinyl padded seats. All the tables were empty except for the last one next to the kitchen and office.

Vince LoBianco was sitting alone nursing a scotch on the rocks. Monaghan saw him and immediately went over and sat down.

"Vin, don't we count the dimes and quarters on Monday?"

"Yeah, I was just getting a feel for what goes in all these machines."

Monaghan looked at LoBianco suspiciously and waved his index finger at him. "Vin, you ain't ever been in here on a Friday night and those fuckers are bursting with change every Monday, so what gives?"

"Maybe I just wanted to check out the broads. See what it is that gets you so hot and bothered."

"Nothing here but a bunch of hard broads that'd rather get drunk than laid, that's the truth."

"Okay, you got me. My brother Pete come by today and told me last night that little fuck that welched on the series and went to Puerto Rico instead was in his place last night."

"Cleary, Sad Sack Cleary the doorman. So what?"

"He was tossin' your kid's name around. There was a murder up on Lincoln Boulevard?"

"Yeah, Danny made a delivery there. Fucking cops were at my house last night. Two pricks, Karn or Kern and some Polish guy, Delsky or something like that, why?"

"Pete got the feeling that your kid did something."

"Pete's wrong, thanks for asking, but he's wrong."

"You sure?"

"Yeah, I'm sure. They locked some broad up today."

"Oh, good, I was just worried, that's all."

"I was too, you know? Half those fuckers couldn't find their shadows on a sunny day. That fucking Cleary pointed them at Danny. He's a little cocksucker, but they got somebody else, so I'll let it ride for now."

LoBianco laughed. "Pete had me worried. Shit, I come down here with a plan to get your kid out of the country."

Monaghan laughed and replied, "Out of the country. Uncle Vin to the rescue. What were you gonna do? Ship him back to Sicily in a wine barrel?"

"No," LoBianco whispered. "We got friends in Canada. Good friends. I done this before."

"Done what? What the fuck you getting at?" Monaghan sarcastically challenged.

LoBianco bristled, and with added authority, he said, "Don't forget your place, Mike. Don't forget, you sit at my table."

Monaghan realized that LoBianco was angry. "Vin, I don't mean nothing. It's been a bad day. You thought I was in trouble and you came here to help me. I appreciate that I just didn't know what you were getting at. You know, how you get someone outta the country? Don't take no offense, I mean it."

LoBianco relaxed and sipped his scotch. "What, you think I'm just some dumb fucking guinea? You stupid Mick. If your kid had done it, I woulda had him in Canada, and in a day he'd have papers and a new name. Next stop woulda been Costa Rica. He'd learn Spanish, but he wouldn't be rotting in jail."

Monaghan shook his head and said sorrowfully, "Vin, you think my kid's a murderer. I might be no good, but my kid?"

"Mike, I don't judge people. Kids do stupid things; they get caught up in the wrong things sometimes. Nothing surprises me. Ain't no saints in my world. Anyway, I wanted to help, nothing else."

"Vin, you might be the only real friend I got. Thanks."

LoBianco stood up and finished his drink. He pointed to a sultry looking brunette who was sitting on the edge of the shuffleboard machine with her legs crossed at the ankles. Her head was cocked to the side and she was pouting and staring at Monaghan. She was lazily swinging her legs back and forth, and when LoBianco pointed to her she smiled, arched her back and puffed out her chest. He caught Monaghan's eye and said, "Tell your girlfriend to get her ass off the shuffleboard machine, she's costing us money."

"She's pissed at me. We were s'posed to go down the shore tonight." Monaghan got up and waved Carla Rink over to the table. "Carla, c'mon over and give Vince a kiss."

Carla took her time walking to Monaghan's table. She gave LoBianco a hard look, put her hands on her hips, pursed her lips and suggestively said, "Vinny, if I give you a kiss, will you take me to the shore?"

LoBianco ignored her and said to Monaghan, "I'll be in Monday night around six." He then put his hand on Carla's waist and eased her out of the way and left the bar without any further comment.

Carla was still pouting and remarked to Monaghan, "He has no personality."

"Yeah, he don't like you, so what?"

"Well, I don't like him. Buy me a drink."

Monaghan escorted Carla over to the bar. It was crowded at the end of the bar, but two of the men standing there made room for them. Monaghan put a twenty-dollar bill on the bar and told the bartender, "Teddy, get me a scotch and water, Carla a gin and tonic and a round for everyone else."

"You got it Mike." Teddy winked.

Whenever Monaghan came in on a weekend night he told the bartender to buy everyone a drink. Monaghan always put up a twenty and expected five dollars change whatever the cost of buying the bar. *After all, he owned a third of the place and his generosity was good for business,* he thought. Teddy the bartender served them first, and Monaghan lifted his glass and toasted Carla, "To the girl who loves me even though she hates me."

Carla didn't answer him. She frowned and took a sip of her drink. "We have to talk."

"Ain't that what we're doing?"

"No I mean about us, something came up."

"You ain't pregnant?"

"No!"

"So what gives?"

"Eddie called yesterday. He wants us to get back."

"Racing Eddie Rink wants back in. I thought when he got outta jail and found out about you that was it?"

"Well, the auto body business is going good. He owns it now, and he stopped drinking a year ago. He's been outta jail over four years now, you know?"

"Yeah, I know. But how long is he gonna keep his head outta the bottle? How long fore he crashes another one of those hot rods and kills somebody else?"

"I seen you get behind the wheel plenty times when you were drunk," Carla said defensively.

"You're so right, but I didn't think I was entering the Indy 500. You can drive drunk no problem so long as you keep one eye closed and drive slow. Eddie kept both eyes closed and tried to go a hundred miles an hour. That was his problem," Monaghan said derisively.

"He says he's changed. Annie's been going to see him a lot lately. The body shop is doing real well, and he's concerned about her. I am too."

"The apple don't fall far from the tree."

"What's that mean?"

"You think you can just change? You know, move back in with Eddie and suddenly you're Donna Reed?"

"Listen, if Annie's been acting like me, it's my fault. I know that."

"So you're gonna change overnight?"

"I don't know. I was fine until Eddie went to jail. I was only seventeen when Annie was born. She was only seven when he went away. Those were tough years."

"What, when he went to jail, or when you two were first married?"

"Both. I really loved him, but he was crazy."

"Just like me, huh?"

"No different. He was wild, and all he wanted to do was drink and screw around with cars. He ain't like that no more. Annie wants to move in with him down in the Lower Borough. He told me we could start all over and the past would be the past." Carla played with the drink glass for a moment and continued talking. "I been thinking about it a lot, and today when you didn't call I got real upset. My bag was packed and I was ready to go to the shore. Annie went to Eddie's for the weekend. I was thinking about me and him, and then you and me." She finished the drink and pushed the empty glass to the edge of the bar. Teddy the bartender took the glass and refilled it with gin and tonic.

Monaghan was sucking on an ice cube. He spit the ice cube back in his drink glass and yawned with indifference.

"I think about us all the time. I don't ever think about Eddie but it's Eddie who's thinking of me. I'm only thirty-three. I could still have kids. I could change, but I don't know if I should because of how I feel."

She took a big gulp of her drink and was about to start talking again when Monaghan interrupted her, "Land the plane, Carla, land the plane."

Carla could see he was growing impatient, and found the nerve to ask the one question she'd never asked Monaghan before. "Would you leave your wife?"

"Honey, I left my wife a long time ago. That box of Trojans in the glove compartment ain't for her."

"I mean, would you move out?"

"No," he answered coldly and abruptly.

She bowed her head and let her hair fall in front of her face. She then flipped her head backward and brushed her hair back with her hands. "Maybe Annie should go live with her father?"

"He didn't expect an answer right away, did he?"

"No, I told him I didn't know how I felt. I'll talk to him Monday. I don't know," she said sadly.

Monaghan laughed. "C'mon, cheer up. Tell you what? We go to the shore tonight like I promised."

Carla smiled and asked, "You meant that about staying with your wife, didn't you?"

"Until death do us apart. No point in ruining more than one woman's life."

"I think I'm gonna go back to Eddie," she said seriously.

"Fine, but are we going to the shore or not?"

Carla laughed and finished her drink. "I told him I'd call him Monday, this is Friday."

Monaghan pushed the five-dollar bill to the lip of the bar and said to the bartender, "Teddy, we're heading down the shore. Around two put the cash in the drop safe. Just leave twenty-five in the till."

"Have fun," Teddy replied.

Monaghan and Carla wove their way through the crowd and exited the busy bar. "We got a long walk to the car. I got here late and all the spaces were taken."

"I'll wait here. I hate walking in heels."

"But you look good in 'em," he playfully replied as he turned and went down the street at a fast pace.

Chapter Forty-Four

The movie let out a little before midnight and the gang was going to Lord's Soda Fountain on Broadway by 231st Street Linda told Danny she had to be home by a quarter past twelve, and Danny said goodnight to the rest of their friends and he and Linda started home together.

Linda was talkative and she had Danny by the hand. He couldn't get over her boldness. He had known her since the third grade when they sat next to one another in class. When she was in the eighth grade Danny nicknamed her T-shirt Kelly because she was still wearing tee shirts and not a bra like the rest of the girls. Linda was a good student and athlete, and she played on her school basketball team and tennis team. Two years ago she beat out all of the boys in a free throw contest run by the Park's Department at the neighborhood playground, and as a practical joke Danny glued two M&M candies to the chest of the figurine atop the trophy awarded to Linda. When the playground director reached into the box with the trophies to make the award and saw what had happened to Linda's trophy he was enraged and threatened to ban Danny and the rest of the boys from the park for the remainder of the summer.

Linda laughed and picked the M&Ms off the trophy and said to Danny, "I thought these fell out of your underwear?"

Everyone laughed, even the playground director, and the incident was forgotten. Somewhere between her second and third year of high school Linda changed. She was more involved in school and sports and had a part time job. She didn't come around much anymore, and it wasn't until April when she started dating Joe Fagan that she was back with the crowd. It was a different Linda; the braces were gone, her body had filled out some and her hair was longer and blonder than Danny remembered. She seemed very sure of herself, and although Danny hadn't seen her since the previous Friday when he took her home from Joe Fagan's going away party, it was evident that the slight necking they'd engaged in was enough for her to assume they were going out together. Danny was intrigued by Linda and was glad to accept her assumption, particularly so in light of the murder. He needed someone to be in his life, someone worthy besides his mother to care about him, and Linda was the perfect candidate. She was clearly ahead of the other girls, and the only thing that troubled him was why she was interested in him.

Danny had had girlfriends since the sixth grade and it seemed every relationship was mired in discord. Girls liked him, but as soon as they started going steady they became angry with him. He was "too cocky" or "too bossy," or he was "always putting me down" and other petty complaints that eventually grew too tiresome to deal with. Ernie Lombardi was the self ordained expert on women, and his favorite expression "if she's a broad she's a bitch" was based on his belief that most girls would eventually metamorphose into carbon copies of his mother, whom he often referred to as the Dreaded Helen Lombardi. Mrs. Lombardi was a crossing guard and took great delight in scolding every child who made his or her way through her intersection without coming to a complete stop and waiting for her to direct safe passage across the street. She was the Nazi, Tugboat Anne and Ernie's favorite, the Dreaded One. Ernie, for all of his toughness, never took exception to the unpleasant sobriquets offered to describe his mother. Secretly, he enjoyed her reputation and assumed, quite naturally, that most of the mothers in Kingsbridge were similar to his own in disposition and temper. Danny and Ernie and the guys had spent countless hours discussing girls, and Ernie's observations always made the most sense. Ernie had a profile for most of the girls in the neighborhood. Who was "too bitchy" or another favorite, "If the old lady's a hag, what's the daughter going to look like when she gets older?" and a host of other sayings that neatly categorized their distaff counterparts and portended a lifetime of misery for anyone who didn't have the sense to find a suitable mate someplace other than Kingsbridge. Danny always agreed with Ernie on this issue, though he was beginning to believe Linda was unique and wouldn't fall into any of Ernie's simplistic generalizations about the local girls.

"How come you gotta be home by twelve-fifteen? If you're fifteen minutes late, is it a big deal? Your mother thinks you're gonna turn into a pumpkin?" Danny asked sarcastically.

"Probably not, but I'm never late."

"You never tested your mother?"

"Why would I do that? My parents won't go to bed until I'm home. Why would I keep them up?"

"Would they punish you?"

"I don't know? Why should I upset them?" Linda said with annoyance.

"I mean, we went to the movies and everyone's going for a soda at Lord's, it's no big deal, like I said. That's all, no big deal."

She let go of his hand. "Hey, don't let me keep you from your friends. You want to go with them, go."

Linda started walking ahead of Danny and he caught up with her and took hold of her hand. "C'mon, I was just asking a question. You know, it wasn't like I was saying you were a goody goody or something."

"Goody, goody," she laughed. "You don't know what I am. Oh, maybe you do. What was it Joey was calling me, Saint Linda?"

"How'd you know?"

"Billy Shaw told Denise, and she told me. He said I was Saint Linda because I wouldn't French kiss. God," she said with disgust, "I didn't even want to kiss him."

Danny remembered the previous Friday when he and Linda were making out. She French kissed. He remembered Joey Fagan saying what a prude Linda was, and how stuck up she was and grew curious at her obvious contempt for her former boyfriend.

"I thought you two were a big item?"

"Please, his mother and my mother are friends. Joey and I are both change of life babies. My mother was forty-three when I was born, and Mrs. Fagan was forty-four when Joey was born. My brother Bill is seventeen years older than I am, and my other brother Eddie is fifteen years older. Joey's two sisters are even older than that. The only reason I went out with him was because my mother asked me to and would I go to his prom with him. The prom was in May and we started dating in April. I knew he was going into the Navy as soon as he graduated, so I did my mother a favor. She and Mrs. Fagan are best friends."

"So how come he broke up with you?"

"I wanted that to happen. That way my mother wouldn't feel bad about it and Mrs. Fagan wouldn't bother her. Mrs. Fagan's had Joey and me married for ten years now. She always talks about it."

"I get it. Man, you really are a goody goody," Danny said teasingly. "You went out with a guy just to make your mother happy?"

"My parents have always been very good to me. They're really nice, maybe because they're older, I don't know. It didn't hurt, but Joey Fagan is so obnoxious. I told my mother, and she said, 'Just be nice and go to the prom with him.' We went out together maybe five times. He tried to kiss me a couple of times, but I'd turn my head. His big fat tongue would be sticking out, ugh!" she cried.

Joey Fagan was a good friend of Danny's, and he found it surprising how Linda talked about him and how much she didn't like him. Still, Joey was a friend and Danny didn't understand what she found so objectionable. "Joey ain't a bad guy; he's pretty funny."

"Funny to you, but to me he's a dope. Did you ever listen to him talk? Everything is either 'copasetic' or 'boss,' and every third word is either 'basically' or 'like.' Sometimes we'd be talking and that's all I'd hear, plus his plans to join the Navy and then when that's over he'll become a fireman like his father."

"He knows what he wants to do in life, what's wrong with that?" Danny asked seriously.

"Nothing, but I'd think in 1965 you'd have bigger plans than joining the Navy and becoming a fireman. Standing in front of the firehouse waiting for the bell to ring, that's some life." Linda stopped and smiled at Danny, and said, "What are your plans? I know you're not going to become a priest, even though you're going to Cathedral Prep?"

"No, I'm not going to become a priest, and I sure as shit ain't gonna join the Navy."

"You're smart, aren't you planning on college?"

"Yeah, I am. I have to declare my vocation this September when I go back to school. Every year they make the senior class do that. There are thirty of us in the senior year. Forty started when we were freshman, and I think there's only two guys who want to be priests. But I have to do my ecumenical service before Christmas."

"What's that?"

"Every student has to do forty hours of church related service. I gotta go see Father Dunphy when school starts, you know, plan stuff."

"Like what?"

"You know, helping old people or serving mass and doing good deeds. Just like the priests do," he said, laughing. "It's really stupid. We go to school for free and out of forty of us they get two possible priests."

"So, what about college?" Linda asked.

"I wanna go, just where and how much. My grades ain't too bad. I'd like to play basketball, but no one from Cathedral, least none I know of, ever got a scholarship to college for basketball. What about you?" he asked, tired of talking about his future when he had no idea of what he wanted to do or where he wanted to go in life.

"I'm going to Villanova. I'm applying early, and I might have a chance to play tennis, and I expect some type of scholarship. When I'm done college I plan on going to law school." she said confidently.

Suddenly, Linda's confidence irked him. She seemed very mature, and he felt small and childish. Danny could be very brazen in such situations, and he blurted out, "You got a high opinion of yourself. Villanova, college tennis, scholarship, law school, you should be with one of those guys from the Jesuit Prep."

Linda squeezed his hand, lifted her chin, and in a show of pride said, "I was ranked number three in the city for girl's varsity tennis this year. That's pretty good, and if I improve I'll get some offers. Not as many as they give boys, it's really so unfair."

Danny felt humbled. He had no idea that Linda was such a good tennis player. "Ranked third, that's great. I'm sorry. I guess I gotta learn to stop teasing you," he said apologetically.

Linda smiled and sidled up next to him as they walked along. "I must be crazy, but I've never minded your teasing me. There's something cute about it."

"Hey, I'm ranked number one around here for teasing and sounding people out. I'm only kidding with you."

"You've been teasing me since the third grade, and I've had a crush on you since the third grade."

Danny put his arm around her shoulders. "Yeah, we used to walk home from school all the time. Remember, you could run faster than most of the boys."

"Run faster, I could play basketball better than most of them too."

"When did you start playing tennis?"

"When I was in the sixth grade my father took me up to the Riverview Tennis club. I took lessons for three years, and when I was a freshman I made the team at St. Ursula's."

"Geez, I never knew that. You know, after the fifth grade they separated all of us. All the girls went to the building on Kingsbridge Avenue and we stayed behind. I knew you could play basketball, but it wasn't until Fagan told me you played tennis that I even knew and he never said nothing 'bout you being ranked in the city."

"Never said nothing," she mocked.

"Oh, pardon me, 'Never said anything.' What're you gonna be an English teacher someday?"

"I said I wanted to be a lawyer. Our English teacher this year was Mr. Cosgrove. He was an incredible teacher. Very demanding, and God forbid if you said, "You know," or "like" he'd read you the riot act. At the beginning of the year he had some girls in tears. 'No, I don't know,' he'd say viciously. He'd have a field day with you."

"What was his problem?"

"None at all, he just didn't care for it when his students spoke poor English. 'You know' and 'like', or Joey's favorite, 'basically,' are bad habits. Some people curse all the time and don't even know they're doing it. Mr. Cosgrove called them empty fillers used by people with empty heads who were too careless to form concrete thoughts."

"You're getting too deep for me, Linda," Danny moaned.

"Danny, there is nothing wrong with trying to improve yourself. Some people think I'm stuck up because I talk this way, or get picky over how someone speaks. But think about it. Really think," she said seriously. "Why bother going to school and studying and getting an education if you're going to talk like an uneducated dope? If I had a tape recorder and you heard yourself talk you'd understand what I'm saying."

"Tape recorder!" he protested. "I wouldn't want anyone taping me. God, I say some pretty stupid things, I wouldn't ever want them repeated."

"Case closed," she said with a laugh. "You proved Mr. Cosgrove's point."

"I meant more about the things I say than how I say 'em."

"It's the same thing. If you are more careful about how you speak, you would be less likely to say some of the dumb things you say."

"Now I'm dumb?"

"No, I know you have a lot of potential, and I want to see you improve. Danny, I like you, I like you a lot," she implored.

Danny found all of this very boring, and at the same time complimentary. Linda's feelings were strong, and he couldn't ever remember having a conversation like this with anyone else, particularly someone his own age. More importantly, he knew she was right. If he had learned anything after eight years of Catholic grammar school and three years of high school was good grammar. He was mindful of his faults, and often made them on purpose, as if speaking well was a sign of weakness rather than strength. Everyone else spoke like he did, and what was a conversation among friends if it wasn't littered with endless profanities? It wasn't until this evening that he had ever given the subject any thought. He didn't understand how she could exhibit so much disgust for Joe Fagan when he was no better. Danny wanted to change the subject, but didn't want to sound uninterested, and he said, "I know you're right, but we get into bad habits and they're hard to break."

"Mr. Cosgrove says that knowing is half the battle."

They were approaching Bailey Park. Just before the playground area was a large blacktopped yard with basketball courts and a softball diamond cut out in white paint. There was a hole in the fence that led to the ball field, and on the other side of the field there was a set of steps that led up to Heath Avenue. Danny and Linda stepped through the hole and walked across the field. Danny hadn't responded to Linda's last remark and they walked together silently; when they got to the steps Linda stopped and put her arms around his waist. Danny leaned against the railing to the steps and realized that Linda was controlling everything. It was Linda who stopped, and Linda who put her arms around him.

She was staring straight at him and said, "Don't you like me?"

"Yeah, I do. Just you're different from some of the other girls."

"That's good or bad?"

"It ain't, oh, excuse me, professor," he teased. "It isn't either. You seem to be way ahead of most of the people around here. You know where you're going and what you're doing."

"I think I do, maybe it'll all turn out differently." Linda then leaned into him and kissed him. Her tongue was in his mouth and as he was responding he put his hands up to hold her against him. His left hand came to rest on her breast. He didn't intend for that to happen and was about to pull it away, in fact, he expected her to pull it away and scold him as that was what most girls in the neighborhood did, but she just kept kissing him. Her legs were straddled over his left leg and she was gently rubbing herself against him. Danny was totally surprised. It wasn't only Fagan's reference to Linda as a prude that came to mind, but his own impression of her as being very proper. He was stroking her breast now, and she pulled away and started tonguing his ear. She was wearing a midriff top and the bottom of the top stopped two inches short from the waistband of her shorts. Danny slipped his hand under her top and reached up to feel her breast. Again he expected her to protest and pull his hand away, but she didn't. He popped her breast out from her bra cup and massaged it with his fingertips. The only other exposed breast he'd ever felt was Hand-job Mary's, and all the time he was feeling her breast she'd been pulling his hand away. This was different. Linda put her tongue back in his mouth and Danny felt himself growing excited. This was as unexpected as the day he'd seen Maria in her underwear beneath the see-through nightgown. He kept massaging her and kissing her, but he didn't know what to do next.

Linda stopped kissing him and pulled away. She gently pushed his arm down, then reached under her top and adjusted her bra. She leaned over and kissed him again, and said, "Do you want to go to the beach on Sunday? I could pack a nice lunch?'

"Just the two of us?"

"Why? We need someone else?"

"No, that'd be great. What time?"

"Ten o'clock. I'll go to the eight at St. Peter's; it's closer to us than St. John's."

They had started walking up the steps, and Danny said, "You know, it's probably past twelve-fifteen. You're gonna be in trouble?"

"No, I told my mother I'd be home by twelve-thirty."

"You said twelve-fifteen before," Danny argued.

"I just said that so we could be alone," she replied, smiling.

Danny's head was swimming and he laughed. "What are you doing tomorrow?"

"My brother's having a barbecue and I have to go, but I'll meet you at the bus stop at ten on Sunday morning."

He was standing on Linda's porch and could see the shadow of her mother through the curtains. Linda put her arms on his shoulders and gave him a short kiss on the lips. "See you Sunday."

Danny stood on the porch and watched her go inside. He was excited and confused.

Through the curtained covered glass panels of Linda's front door Danny could see the silhouette of her mother in the hallway. Linda stopped on the stairs, leaned over, then went up the stairs. The downstairs lights went out and the shadows and silhouettes vanished. Danny stood for a moment looking at Linda's darkened house, then went across the street. Diagonally across from Linda's house was the rear entrance to the 212 Lot. Danny approached the path to the lot and looked back to Linda's house. The light in an upstairs bedroom was on, but the shade was pulled and no one was by the window. He hastened his steps and entered the lot. It was a warm night, but there was a stand of trees at the rear of the lot and the oxygen pouring from the trees filled the air, and it felt ten degrees cooler. The air smelled fresher, and Danny felt invigorated.

Linda's amazing, he thought. Her response to him had him dizzy. He hadn't seen her since last Friday. When he came out of the apartment house earlier in the evening, she was standing with his friends on the corner. She was wearing white shorts and sneakers and a red midriff top. She was tanned, and the color of her skin against her blonde hair reminded him of pictures of surfer girls you'd find on a Beach Boys record album. He said hello to everybody, and she came over to him and took his hand. He knew at that moment the night would be special.

The lot was silent, and as he made his way to the old tree where he'd hidden Maria's pictures he felt a sudden release from the pain and guilt of Millie Campos' death. Somehow, and for some extraordinary and inexplicable reason, he had absolved himself of any guilt for what had happened. It was he rationalized, a sad accident. Millie had startled him and caught him in an embarrassing moment and he'd reacted unconsciously. He had never meant for it to happen. The few intimate minutes he had spent with Linda were sexually intense, and she had aroused in him the same feelings he had experienced that morning with Maria. Although he knew the experience with Maria was an accident, it had still created sensations he didn't know existed. Those sensations were so strong, he told himself, that he had no choice but to relieve the sexual tension by masturbating in Maria's bedroom. She was, indirectly, to blame and Millie just happened to come along at the wrong moment. It was nothing more than that and he couldn't blame himself for what had happened. Linda was the answer to Maria, and her presence washed over him and released the pale of gloom that had so absorbed him. His father was right, he thought. *Forget it and keep your mouth shut.* They had arrested a woman, but she didn't do it, and there was no reason to worry. *She'll get off,* he said to himself. *She'll get off.*

The bag was there, behind the tree, untouched and just as he had left it. His initial plan was to burn the pictures, but he decided that the flame of the burning pictures might attract attention and there was no way he could guarantee that he'd completely burn the evidence. He took the pictures from the bag and looked at them. Maria's image was beautiful, and he grew sexually excited. He held the full frontal nude of her in his hand and thought of Maria and of his hand on Linda's exposed breast. Mechanically and without any real conscious thought, he undid his pants and let them fall to his ankles. He fantasized that he was with Maria and then Linda, and he furiously stroked himself as he focused on the dim image of the naked woman in the photograph. It was only several seconds before he spent himself all over the picture and let it drop to the ground. In the weak moonlight he saw the splotched semen stains on the picture and stood there breathing deeply as the cool night air caressed his exposed genitals. He waited until his erection subsided, and when he was content and his breathing had returned to normal, he pulled his pants up and took the other full frontal nude picture of Maria and hid it under his shirt. He then took the remaining pictures and tore them into small pieces and carefully placed them back into the paper bag. He left the lot on the Kingsbridge Road side and walked down the street to the bottom of the hill.

The bag with the torn pictures was under his arm. He walked past the front of his building to the alleyway. He went into the alleyway and stopped in front of a line of bent and rusted metal garbage cans. He lifted the lid off one can and removed an oily bag of garbage. He placed his bag in the can and put the other garbage bag on top of it. He closed the lid and went upstairs to his apartment.

He entered the apartment and saw the flickering gray blue light of the television in the living room. His mother called out, "Danny, is that you?"

"Yeah, it's me."

"*Arsenic and Old Lace* is on. It's almost over. It's so funny, come and watch the end with me. I love Cary Grant."

Danny walked down the hallway to the living room. "Ma, the paint stinks."

"Oh stop, you sound like your father. Come and watch the movie. I'll make us a sandwich at the next commercial break."

"Okay, I'm gonna put on my shorts."

"How was your movie?"

"James Bond, what do you think?"

His mother didn't answer, and he went into his bedroom. He opened the closet door and took off his dungarees and hung them on the hook on the back of the door. He pulled out the bottom of his shirt and slid Maria's photo out. He didn't look at it, and quickly put it face down on the shelf in his closet. On one side of the shelf was a stack of board games. He hadn't played most of the games in years, but they sat there untouched, collecting dust. He surveyed the stack and lifted the box that said Clue and withdrew the game box for Sorry that was underneath it. He opened the box and inside was a game board, dice, game cards and six plastic colored pieces. He emptied out the box and put Maria's picture in face down. He put the game board back in on top of the picture, then followed with the game cards, dice and plastic game pieces. He put the box back in the middle of the stack and closed the closet door. He couldn't explain to himself why he kept that one picture, nor could he explain why Linda Kelly was so attracted to him. He only knew that hidden forces and intense, uncontrollable sexual desires consumed him. These were feelings he had never known. He couldn't articulate what they were, but in his mind he saw them as adult influences. What sex really was compared to what he and most of his friends had thought it was? Hand-job Mary had been nothing more than a release for teenage lust. In her company there was little satisfaction and much shame. He felt no shame over the things he had done in Maria's apartment. Wearing her panties and going through her personal things was too exciting to feel shame over. He was still overwhelmed by Linda's apparent promiscuousness. He was certain that this evening's exchange was a prelude to greater things. He could still feel her straddling him and rubbing against him. The soft scent of her perfume was on his shirt, and he had a sudden impulse to masturbate again. His penis felt thick and warm, and as he was about to reach into his shorts and extract it his mother walked into the bedroom.

"Do you want a spiced ham sandwich?"

She startled him, and he gave her a blank look, then said, "Sure, not too much mustard."

She went down the hallway. He picked up a dirty sock from the floor and placed it over his swollen penis. He shut off the bedroom light and closed his eyes and imagined himself in Maria's bedroom with Linda. He was wearing Maria's panties and Linda was wearing the see through nightgown. His fantasy was like a slide show and scenes of himself with Maria and Linda sped through his mind until he exploded into the sock. He felt cleansed and calmed. He let the sock fall to the floor. He picked up his dirty socks and underwear and went to the bathroom and placed them into the clothes hamper. He went to the living room and sat on the couch.

His mother followed and placed a plate of sandwiches and a pitcher of iced tea on the coffee table. He picked up a half of a sandwich and started to eat.

His mother was sitting next to him. She put her arm around his shoulder and said, "I love you, you're such a good boy. Do you know that? How happy you make me?"

"Aw, c'mon, Mom, I'm too old for that bull," he answered half-heartedly.

"Danny, no matter how old you are, no matter how big you get, you'll always be my baby."

Chapter Forty-Five

Maria sat upright in bed. Two pillows were propped behind the small of her back for support. She wasn't the least bit lightheaded or weak, and all she wanted to do was go home. It was Monday and she had been in the hospital for four days. The man in front of her was a new doctor. His name was Marble, Roland or Randall Marble, and he had a British accent.

His accent brought back memories of her years in London during the war. She was sharing a flat with a co-worker. A bright happy girl named Penny Sheets. Penny was dating a British lieutenant from the Tank Corps. His name was James Bowen and she called him Jamey. Dr. Marble sounded like Jamey. There was a smooth, soft cadence to his speech and she could hear that same quality in Dr. Marble's voice. She remembered the damp scent of his woolen uniform and the gaunt look of his face. He was handsome, but in a frail way, and there was something sad about him, sad and unspoken that made you want to hold him close and comfort him. He had deep brown eyes and a shy smile that projected kindness. He was underweight, as many of his countrymen were at that time. *It was so obvious, the difference between the American servicemen and the British servicemen*, she thought. The Americans were well fed. They were healthy looking with well-trimmed bodies and mouths brimming with teeth. The British soldiers and workingmen were thin, with bad teeth, or so it seemed for so many of them. She came home from work one evening and found Penny sobbing on her bed, "Jamey, my Jamey has left me for Africa. What will I do?" she wailed.

Maria comforted her and promised, "He'll be back, I know he will, he'll be back."

England in 1943 and 1944 saw wave after wave of American servicemen encamped throughout the country. They were brash and cocky. Disrespectful of authority and an insult at times and at other times a relief to the common British stoicism the war had engendered. Bowen wasn't gone more than a week and Penny, now recovered from the pain of his departure, found herself a new beau. He was an American officer. Another lieutenant, but this one was special. He didn't wear a worn, damp woolen uniform. He didn't smell from body odor, and his dress shirt didn't look like it needed a fresh washing and ironing. His uniform was tailored and his hair was neatly clipped and his mood was gay and cheerful. Joe Listerneck was his name, and he hailed from Milwaukee, Wisconsin. His father owned a car dealership, and Joe was the service manger. His father had sent him off to automotive school instead of college and his mechanical skills had landed him in the Combat Engineers. Joe had a friend, another officer, and he thought that friend would match up well with Maria. Unlike Penny, Maria didn't need a man in her life. She cultivated suitors, but they were for her benefit. Maria had no time for love. Rudy had satisfied that urge and Koch had poisoned any future needs.

The Americans were different. Their enlisted men and officers had more money than their British counterparts and they were eager to spend it before they were sent to battle on the European mainland. Joe Listerneck had befriended Henry Weiss on the troop ship across the Atlantic. They were both excellent poker players and had enjoyed a profitable cruise on their way to war. It was Joe's steadfast belief that fortune had awarded them more than their fair share of winning pots and they had a duty to spend that money well. Henry wasn't interested in blind dates, but, as a favor, or so he thought, to his friend, he agreed to join Joe, Penny and Maria for dinner.

Maria recalled the first time she met Henry. Somehow, this new doctor, a tall man with a beard and long fingers that were probing the right side of her face and describing what muscles and nerves were hidden under her skin and what he was going to prescribe to make them all work again so that the vision in her right eye would be fully restored, refreshed her recollection with the simple sound of his voice and she saw in her mind the surprised looked on Henry's face when Joe Listerneck first introduced them.

Henry was standing on the sidewalk in front of their flat. She never found out why he hadn't accompanied Joe upstairs when he came to call, but there he was, she remembered, quietly and with perfect posture standing, almost at attention, on the sidewalk and when he saw Maria follow Penny and Joe out of the building a charming smile broke across his face, and he approached her and gently touched her hand, and said, "I've never been on a blind date before and I must admit this is a most unexpected pleasure. I'm Henry Weiss and it is my pleasure." He was tall and reasonably handsome, and like Joe, was wearing a carefully tailored uniform. He was mature looking, and didn't at all resemble the hordes of teenage American soldiers that had become, for many, the bane of England. Henry was polite and polished. He had good manners and exuded confidence, but wasn't over talkative. He didn't exhibit, what she found to be a very American characteristic, the need to dominate his company. He could dance and tell a story, but he was better at listening than he was at talking, and Maria regretted not having told him more about herself. Maria immediately liked him and though they only dated several times before he, like Bowen, was dispatched to Northern Africa, she determined in her mind that if she ever fell in love again, it would be with Henry Weiss.

Dr. Marble had finished his examination, and with it his recitation of how he was going to treat her. Maria sat in the bed, wrapped in a pink quilted satin bathrobe feigning her utmost attention to him, aware of the words he was saying, but without any comprehension for what they meant. The doctor waited patiently for a response and finally Maria acknowledged him and said, "Thank you."

Dr. Marble was certain that Maria hadn't heard a word he'd said. "You said 'thank you' but did you follow everything?"

"Some of it. I'm sorry, but I'm still a little foggy." Her thoughts of London and Henry and the war were erased, but now she found herself fixated on Dr. Marble's tie. It was a shiny blue tie with a big silver fish painted on it for decoration. The fish had a green eye that appeared to be looking up at the knot of cloth above it. The knot was tight and dirty. The patina of dirt and body oil on the knot made Maria queasy, and she recalled how Penny always complained that her Jamey smelled of body odor and his clothes were in need of a good cleaning. *Are all Englishmen dirty*, she thought *or just ones that sound alike?* Dr. Marble's white shirt was more gray than white, and he had on black pants fastened with a brown belt. She couldn't see his shoes, but she was certain, they too, were scuffed and worn.

"As I was saying, a Miss Barry will be here this afternoon. She'll put you through the first stage of exercises and we'll build on that."

"Yes, we will," a smiling Maria, said. Dr. Marble and his mumbo jumbo about her eye didn't interest her. Suddenly she wanted to see his shoes and was tempted to ask him to show her them. She didn't understand where this silliness was coming from, but it made her feel good. She didn't feel weak anymore, and the fact that her mind was entertaining a variety of thoughts released some of the heaviness of heart that had been with her since she regained consciousness.

"Good," he said as he scratched his beard. "I'll check in on Wednesday. Dr. Snyder hopes to send you home on Friday."

"Oh, that would make me very happy," she said enthusiastically.

"I'm sure it would."

With that, the doctor was gone and Maria laughed, content in seeing that his shoes were brown, scuffed and worn. *He's an unmade bed*, she thought. Dr. Snyder had said Dr. Marble was a leader in rehabilitative medicine, and Maria felt a pang of envy. *How remarkable, how rewarding it must be to live your life consumed with a vocation and to have no vanity,* she thought.

She was hungry. Breakfast normally came at eight and it was almost eight-thirty. She felt strong and was going to get out of bed and walk to the nurse's station to inquire about her morning meal when an orderly came into her room carrying a tray.

"Good morning, ma'am," he beamed. "The doctor called ahead this morning and asked us to hold up on your meal until he was finished his examination. Nice man, your oatmeal's hot. You know, he don't call, you eating cold mush and drinking warm orange juice."

Maria was sitting up in bed when Henry walked into her room. She had a small container of orange juice in her hand and was sipping the juice through a straw. She withdrew the straw from her mouth and picked up a napkin from the tray beside her bed and wiped her mouth. She subconsciously fixed her hair and gave Henry a big smile. The smile was unexpected and seemed out of place with all that had happened. "Henry, the food here is awful. I'll go down a dress size if I'm here much longer."

Henry went up to the side of the bed, bent over and kissed Maria on the forehead. He brushed her hair with the back of his hand and returned her smile. "Honey, you don't need to go down a dress size, you're perfect the way you are."

"That's my Henry, never a bad word."

"So, how do you feel?"

"I feel much better today. Last night was the first night I really slept. The right side of my face is still stiff, up here under my eye," she said as she touched the area around her right cheekbone with her fingers. "My vision is still blurry in the right eye. Dr. Snyder called in Dr. Marble. He's another specialist. You just missed him. I think he's English. He's an unmade bed, but he sounds very confident, and Dr. Snyder said he's very aggressive. We'll see," she said with a yawn.

"That's good, what's he going to do?"

"Some woman is coming this afternoon. I'm to start a program of exercises; it all sounds tiring, but what can I do?" She sighed as she let her head sink back into the pillow.

The vibrancy Henry had noticed when he first came into her room was gone. It seemed in a matter of seconds she had changed and the energy her smile had conveyed vanished and was replaced by a pall of fatigue.

"You okay?"

"I don't know, suddenly I felt dizzy," she replied weakly.

"I can come back later. Maybe I should speak with Dr. Snyder?"

"No," Maria said as she smoothed the bedcovers with her hands. "Dr. Snyder told me it's going to be awhile until I'm out of the woods. I'll be here at least until Friday. God, I hate this bed; I'm a prisoner."

"You looked so good when I first walked in."

"I was happy to see you."

"I was happy to see you, too."

"I'm tired, but I can listen."

Henry fidgeted with his hands and frowned. "Listen to what?"

"Henry," she snapped with a little more energy. "We have a lot to talk about. You managed to avoid the subject Saturday and Sunday, and I was too weak anyway, to pay attention. I still fell pretty weak, but I want to know what's going on. Everything. Gloria's coming today, so she'll tell me what you won't, but I'd rather hear it from you."

There was a hard look on Maria's face, and even though her color was bad and she looked sickly, Henry felt the strength of her feelings. She wanted to talk about the murder and Sophie and Joey and all that had happened. He wanted to avoid the subject, but eventually he knew he couldn't avoid it. He frowned again and rubbed his hands. He pulled the chair close to her bed and sat down next to her. "Maria, I'm ashamed of myself. I'm to blame for all of this. I'm sick over it, but you must understand that it's you I love. There's no point in talking about any of this until you understand how I feel about you, and how I feel things will never be the same between us."

Maria let out a small cough. A little dribble of spit seeped from her mouth, and Henry dabbed at it with her napkin. She pushed his hand away. "Henry,

I'm not some doddering old woman. I coughed. I was going to clean my lips. I don't need you to be my nursemaid."

Maria's little outburst surprised him, and once again he was confused over how sick and weak she really was. Snapping at him for wiping her face was vintage Maria, and he didn't know if that was a good sign or a bad sign. "Damn," he said with visible annoyance. "I was trying to be helpful."

The smile was gone from Maria's face. Her head was resting on her pillow and she leaned toward Henry and said, "I'm listening."

Henry immediately understood that she was in no mood for sympathy or coddling. "All right, the police arrested Sophie Friday night."

"Yes, Gloria told me that yesterday. You didn't, but she did."

"I was waiting until you felt a little better. This is very stressful, and I'm concerned about you. It's also very hard on me. I just told you how I feel."

"Henry, you didn't kill Millie Campos. I didn't kill Millie Campos. Sophie Cruz did."

"Yes, but if I hadn't been involved with Sophie this would never have happened."

"But you were, and we can't change that. Isn't there a saying, 'The future will soon be yesterday' or something like that?"

"I don't know, maybe something like that, but I feel what I feel, Maria."

"Yes, you do, I do, we all do," she said as she put her hand on her forehead. "Henry, what I'm saying is that each day goes quickly. Tomorrow will be here and gone before we know it. What do our lives really mean?"

Henry didn't answer her question. He got up from the chair and walked to the window. He separated the closed blinds with his fingers and looked out at the street below. Maria sat a little higher against her pillow and cleared her voice. "Henry, we're selfish people, you and I. It's what's been at the heart of our problems. I don't fault you for what you did. I don't, and I don't expect you to fault me for the way I've treated you. I understand now things I didn't understand before. I want my life and your life, our lives to have meaning."

Henry withdrew his fingers from between the slats on the blind and looked at Maria. "What are you saying?"

"Henry, do you love Sophie? Do you love her more than you love me?"

"I, I don't love Sophie, I mean not in the way I love you, it's different, I can't explain it," he replied uncertainly.

"You do or you don't, Henry?"

"Why, why, is it that simple?"

"Oh, it's not simple at all, but the woman was your lover, wasn't she?"

"Not in that way; it's too hard to explain."

"Oh, listen to yourself. This is what I'm saying. I know you love me, and given the choice she's out in the cold. I already knew that, I always knew that from the moment I suspected something was going on. But, Henry, you had to have feelings for her, you must have them now. You mean to say you don't?"

"I do. I care for her, but I'm ashamed to admit it to you. I feel so disloyal, sneaky, oh, I don't know," he said with self-disgust.

"Henry, I would think you cared for her, and I'm not as hurt as you think. I said we were selfish people and I meant it. I also said we have to look to today and tomorrow and not yesterday."

Henry bent over and kissed Maria on the lips. The kiss was gentle, and he lingered for a moment and sat back up. "Sweetheart, this is one of the most awkward conversations I've ever had. Are you telling me that this is water under the bridge? This isn't going to affect our marriage?"

"I'm telling you I love you. Yes, I'm not happy, but I take some of the blame. I know you. I know you feel ashamed. That's enough. I can't spend my life dredging up the past, warring over past sins. It's wasteful and tiresome."

"Okay," he said somewhat relieved. "There are still so many issues."

"Yes, and they are issues we must face together. Gloria suggested we hire Boyce Fortescue."

Henry backed up and his face twisted. "Fortesuce, why him, you're divorcing me?"

"My goodness," she laughed. "You have to gain custody of your son. My God, what do you think I've been saying? Don't you comprehend?"

"Who'd want Fortescue?"

"He's on the board at the university. Gloria and Joel both know him. Lee also recommended him."

"Lee, he never said anything to me."

"Gloria called him yesterday. Lee thinks Boyce Fortescue would be perfect. You know, custody determination is a big part of the divorce process, and Boyce Fortescue is one of the best around."

"Also one of the most flamboyant and expensive."

"Henry," she said with annoyance. "I think this is going to be a high profile case that'll be in the news. Lee thinks this is a juicy story that's not going away. What's his name? Lenihan? Sophie's lawyer, is that his name?"

"Yes, what about him?"

"He already got it into the papers about my pictures. How did that happen?"

"The police executed a search warrant on Sophie's apartment on Friday night. They came up dry, but he got notice of the warrant and what they were looking for. He's grasping at straws."

"Fine, fine, Gloria showed me the article yesterday, and I know this is going to get ugly."

"Well, I wish she hadn't. It pisses me off that Gloria's doing an end run around me. I was going to tell you everything, but I wanted to wait until you got a little stronger, that's all."

"Henry, I'm not dying. I'm sick, but I'll get better. Stop babying me. I lie in this bed all day and night; what do you think goes on in my head?"

"I'm not babying you; I don't see any need to upset you right now. The innuendo in that news story was nasty, and I'd like to punch that Lenihan in the nose."

"Please, listen to yourself? Gloria spoke to Lee yesterday and Lee is concerned that Lenihan is going to try and smear me so he can create some doubt. He said he was going to talk to you about it today. Boyce Fortescue is a very effective at getting favorable press. Lee thinks we can start custody proceedings right away. Also, we're going to have to buy a house if we're going to raise your son. Gloria said there are several very nice homes in her neighborhood in Riverview. They're a little pricey, but I've got about $80,000 in the bank and with that I could buy two houses and pay Fortescue's bill."

Henry closed his eyes ands slowly shook his head. Maria's revelation that she had $80,000 in the bank, that she wanted to buy a house and, most importantly, was determined to have Henry gain custody of Joey was overwhelming. He felt helpless. His adultery and the consequences it created, namely Millie's murder and Joey's existence was a living nightmare. He was trapped. He swallowed a mouthful of air and blurted out, "...$80,000. Where'd the hell did you get that kind of money?"

Maria laughed. "I earned it."

Henry's face flushed. "That's a lot of money, that's all. This is all going so fast. Millie's not even buried. I offered to pay for the funeral, but her family turned me down. I spoke with her oldest daughter, Jenny, and she was very cold. I asked her about the funeral. She said they were waking her for three days. She's to be buried tomorrow, but Jenny said there was a television crew in front of the funeral home on Saturday and some newspaper people called several times. She wants her mother's wake and funeral to be dignified. Bottom line was I could come to the funeral home before the regular viewing hours to pay my respects. That really hurt. Weddings, the births of her grandchildren, I was always very generous, and to listen to the phone conversation it was plain that they're mad at me, at us. Christ, that's where my mind is at right now. You start talking about Fortescue, and houses and custody fights and it's all beyond me. You're moving too fast, and I understand how you feel, but maybe you and my sister should slow down and just let this play out. I don't think it's going to help anyone to go rushing into anything, not just yet."

"Henry, grow up," Maria whispered. "Everything is going very fast. Our lives are racing by and we've accomplished nothing. It's all just transient," she lamented.

"What the hell are you talking about?" he whispered back.

"We have no roots, Henry. We have so much to offer, and we keep it to ourselves. You have a son. Gloria's right. She said he's just as much your son as he is Sophie's. My God, don't you understand what an opportunity this is?"

"It's an opportunity for disaster, is what it is! You think we can just tear that boy away from his mother?"

"She'll be in jail and he won't be there with her."

"He'll want to be with his family, Sophie's family," Henry said strongly.

"Christ, Henry," Maria hissed as she sat up in the bed. "You're his father. You're his family too. If you can't face reality, than maybe we should separate. I thought you were a man, now I'm not so sure," she said with disgust as she turned away from him and pulled the bedcovers up to her chin.

Henry stood there stunned. Maria had her back to him, and he could hear her heavy breathing. He didn't know if she was crying, and he wanted to touch her and tell her he was sorry. "Honey, please just give it a couple of days. I need you and I love you, I really do," he pleaded.

Maria didn't look at him. She wiggled in the bed and he could see her hand smoothing her hair. "You make the decision, Henry. I'm leaving it up to you. Leave me alone now, please? I need some rest."

Henry went over to the bed and reached out and touched her shoulder. She didn't move or react at all. "Okay, give me a few days, that's all I ask. Just a few days, I'll be back this evening." He gently lifted his hand from her shoulder and left the room.

Maria heard him leave and sat back up. She picked up the orange juice container and sucked the last ounce of warm juice up through the straw. She took a mirror from the drawer in the small bureau beside her bed and examined her face. She'd aged, she thought. She could see the wrinkles around her eyes and the many traces of gray in her honey blonde hair. "I'm still far better looking than that slut Sophie," she said aloud. *I wonder if Joseph knows any*

Spanish. If he does, it's probably a bastardized version. I'll have him speaking like a Spaniard in six months, she thought. *Maybe I'll teach him French, too.* She put the mirror down and lay back on her pillow. "Poor Henry, poor, poor Henry." She laughed.

Chapter Forty-Six

Futerman was on the telephone. Henry didn't bother to stop at Ruth Goolnick's desk, but went directly into Futerman's office and took a seat in one of the two chairs across the desk from Futerman. Lee looked up at him and smiled and continued his conversation, apparently unconcerned by Henry's presence. Henry sat there stewing and staring at his friend and lawyer. Whatever the conversation, Lee Futerman was listening and except for an occasional "Yes," or "I know, I know," he didn't have much to say.

Finally, after what seemed an hour, but wasn't more than five minutes, Lee closed the conversation and Henry heard for the second time that morning a name too disconcerting to repeat. "Okay, Boyce, it was good talking to you and I'll call you soon," Lee said before he hung up the telephone.

Lee placed the phone in its cradle and sat back in his chair. He took out a handkerchief from his pocket and heartily blew his nose into it. He wiped his nose with the handkerchief and folded it over and placed it back into his pocket. Henry sat there mutely staring and Futerman bent forward and solemnly said, "Do you know what that was about?"

"You bet your ass I do," Henry angrily replied.

"Maria said this was what you wanted. I had every intention of talking to you first, but believe it or not, it was Fortescue who called me just now. Totally unrelated to your problem, but I answered his question, then told him what was going on. Please, no matter what Maria or Gloria said I was going to follow your lead."

"Sure you were, until Fortescue just happened to call, then all bets were off."

"Henry, please," Futerman said contritely. "I had him on the phone and gave him a quick one, two, three about the situation. I was feeling him out. It goes no further than that phone call unless you say otherwise."

"Otherwise? Maria gave me an ultimatum a little while ago. This is lunacy."

"What are you talking about?"

"Maria wants me to gain custody of my son. She wants us to raise him. Suddenly we're going to be Ozzie and Harriet. This is dreamland, a bizarre dreamland!"

"Henry, I know you're under a lot of pressure, but you have to face reality. If it were up to you you'd meet your financial obligations and leave the child with Sophie's family. Morally, that might be wrong and may not be in the child's best interests, but I think that's where your heart is on this issue, isn't it?"

"Certainly it is. And why is it morally wrong and not in the kid's best interests?"

"A child is entitled to carry his father's name.'

"No problem, change the birth certificate, now he's Joseph Weiss," Henry said petulantly.

"Henry, it goes deeper than that. A boy wants to identify with his parent, and no child, I don't care what his background is, wants to be denied his birthright. You're that boy's father."

"An accident of biology; what other connection is there between us?"

Futerman took out his handkerchief again and went through the ritual of blowing his nose. "Pardon me, but I feel a cold coming on."

"Yeah, you're a real Beau Brummell with that rag in your hand."

Futerman ignored Henry's remark and said, "Henry, Sophie Cruz is going to jail. The big question isn't when, but for how long? Anyway you shake it, she's going to jail."

"That's a tragedy and I feel terrible, but that boy doesn't know me and what court would separate him from the rest of his family and put him with us? It's cruel, downright cruel. What, the kid gets stuck with a father who's never acknowledged him, but kept his mother as a mistress? And worse, his father's real wife will be the primary reason why the boy's mother went to jail. How long before that festering little fact explodes in our faces? Of course," he said sarcastically, "we'll be a happy little family and when he's fourteen or so he'll put a knife through each of our hearts just the way we did it to him and his mother."

"Boy, you have done one hell of a job convincing yourself that this is all wrong, haven't you?"

"C'mon, give me some credit here, Lee. I'm right. I'm one hundred percent right."

"Henry, the kid is only seven. He lives in a happy little world with his mother and the rest of her family. Daddy's probably some vague heroic figure she tells him stories about. That's easy to do with a seven-year-old but it doesn't work as well on ten year olds, and less so with teenagers. Who are Sophie's family?"

"She has her Aunt Lucy and her brother Ray. He has two little girls, a nice wife, and a cousin Freddy who is something of a ladies man. The brother owns a neat little house. I did the closing. The boy should go with him. God, he's going to be brokenhearted if Sophie goes to jail. He'll need family, not strangers."

"Henry, that's the point. Family!" Futerman said emphatically. "You're family too. Some of the points that you made I brought up to Boyce before. I was as certain as you were, and although I didn't voice that opinion to Maria or Gloria, I felt the same way. Yes, there is a moral issue, but my feelings concerned the immediate effect this whole event will have on the boy."

"Thanks for that, but what's changed your mind?"

"I spoke with Duffy first thing this morning. He says the case against Sophie is airtight. He was concerned with the way Lenihan played it to the newspapers. She isn't going down without a fight, but in the end, she's done."

"We were talking about the kid."

"Yes, we were. Boyce made two very cogent points to me. First of all, you are the boy's father. Sophie has already conceded that and it will be part of her defense. If she goes to jail it puts you next in line. Her family can contest it, but the court will side with you. Now, I, like you, wondered about the boy's emotional stability. Boyce said, and believe me he has a lot of experience in this field, that Sophie going to jail will have the same emotional effect on this kid as if she had died. My immediate response was that if that's the case wouldn't the kid be better off with family? Her family, people who know and love him."

"That's exactly what I've been saying, Lee."

"Right, but Boyce's second point is very interesting. Sophie isn't dead. She's going to jail for murder. Most families move to a certain rhythm. Sophie's brother has kids, right?"

"Yes, two little girls, both younger than the boy."

"Good, why don't we start calling him by his name?"

"Joey, okay."

"Your perspective is Joey would fare better with his aunt and uncle and cousins than he would be with two strangers, namely you and Maria?"

391

"Without a doubt," Henry scoffed.

"Joey is going to have a reaction to the loss of his mother. He'll not take it lightly, and he'll either become withdrawn or act out emotionally. That's going to disrupt the rhythm of that household. When they all sit down to dinner it will be mommy, daddy, their two daughters and the cousin. Take it to the bank. They may be good people and try not to favor their children over him, but subconsciously they will and he'll be attuned to it. And when that happens, trouble will start. See where I'm going?"

"No, I don't. It all sounds like a lotta claptrap, psychiatric voodoo and nothing more. Is this what Fortescue was telling you?"

"Basically, yes. I'm paraphrasing what he said, but the gist of it was that while initially Joey would be in more comfortable surroundings and in all likelihood would receive a lot of love and comfort from Sophie's family, that attention would be short lived. Kind of like a honeymoon, but honeymoon's end and the normal routines of everyday life take over. That's when the concentration of attention reverts back to Sophie's brother's children and away from Joey. Bear in mind that the aunt is an in-law. Joey's her husband's nephew and he's not her blood."

"Do you really believe all that?"

"Yes. Unless they are very exceptional people they are going to favor their own two kids. That doesn't make them criminals. It's human nature. Particularly if Joey misbehaves, which would not be out of character for a small boy who has had the center of his universe wrested away from him and sent to jail."

"So how does my taking him in make things any better?"

"First of all, you are taking him in because you want him. You are saying, 'Joseph, I'm your father. I will care for you while your mother's away.' Secondly, there are no other children from your marriage. No other children in the home for him to compete with. Furthermore, Maria said you are buying a house and I would imagine that a home in Riverview, enrollment in a quality private school and the association with your family, your brother the doctor, your sister the teacher and her husband the college professor and the association with your nieces and nephews, all of whom are older than Joey, but good kids and in a perfect position to act as surrogate big brothers and sisters creates a formidable family atmosphere that would over time nurture the boy and put him in the best position to successfully deal with the loss of his mother. Henry, time heals all wounds, and while it may be a little harder on him at the outset it will become much easier in the end"

"Quite a sales pitch, Lee. Is this what Fortescue thinks, also?"

"Yes, but he explained it better than I did. He talks fast and, actually, said quite a bit more, but basically that's his read. Now, the greater issue is how you feel about all of this."

"Lee, Sophie and her brother and aunt and cousin are very close. She's told me on any number of occasions that Ray is like a father to Joey."

"Maybe that was a dig at you?"

"Sometimes yes, but they're really very close. I can't imagine them ever treating Joey poorly."

"Boyce's point is that they would never set out to treat him badly. If they're good people, and I'm sure they are, they would probably make every effort to make the child as comfortable as possible. Joey's the one who is going to feel like an outsider and subconsciously, if not consciously, they will probably, in time, treat him like one."

"But I don't want to raise a child. God, I don't want a house. Fucking Maria tells me this morning she has eighty grand in the bank. She'll buy the house and pay for the lawyer. Where'd that come from?"

"What does she do with her paycheck?"

"Damned if I know. I guess she puts it in the bank every week."

"Well, you've been married for what is it, eighteen years?"

"Seventeen years."

"What's it matter? She wants to buy you a house and make a home for your son."

"You don't think that's a little bizarre? She wants to raise my bastard?"

"Henry, Maria's a survivor. She's seen a lot in her life. Gloria told me that Maria said she felt bad for Sophie. She never liked her, but she feels for her. She sees Joey as an orphan. You know, Maria lost most of her family when she was young. Maybe there's a lot of empathy for Joey, and I think there's that natural longing a woman has to love and raise a child."

"Lee, it doesn't make any sense to me at all. Especially since Sophie almost killed her, too."

"Henry, she had an aneurysm. That thing was leaking and whether or not she had a confrontation with Sophie she was going to fall ill. Stop making excuses. If you don't want the boy, say so and we'll end the discussion. It's your life."

"My God, I can't believe you. You think I have a responsibility to raise him, don't you?"

"Henry, I'm a flawed man. I know it and I regret that I never married and had children. I spent too much time with my nose in a law book chasing crooks and playing politics. You're ten years younger than I am. Take a chance, listen to Maria, she's right."

Henry ran his fingers through his thinning hair, then brought them down with an angry slap on his thighs. "Okay, you win, Maria wins, everybody knows better than I do. What's the game plan?"

"Boyce suspects Sophie will bring a paternity suit against you. So he said to sit tight for a week." "You think so?" Henry asked.

"She has no choice," Futerman replied.

"I would think that would establish a motive for what she did," Henry opined.

"Her goose is cooked, Henry. She has to bloody as many noses as possible, and you and Maria are number one. Believe me, this will be ugly," Futerman said knowingly.

"Okay, then what?"

"If she doesn't bring a paternity suit, Boyce will, and one way or the other you'll be recognized as his legal father. After she's indicted, Boyce will commence the custody suit. She can't fight two battles at once. She'll be knee deep defending the criminal charges and there'll be no energy or time to fight a custody battle."

"God, that's pretty calculating."

"I said he's the best."

"What happens to Joey in the meantime?"

"Sophie's bail hearing is tomorrow. Duffy's asking for no bail, but he'll settle for $50,000. Whether she can post it is another story. I figure they won't schedule a grand jury until Maria's out of the hospital and has a clean bill of health. Maybe the end of next week they'll put it in the grand jury and you'll see a trial in September. Two day trial, and she's off to jail, but all things considered the court will expedite the custody proceedings and you'll have custody just in time for the start of the school year."

"You've got it all nailed down, don't you?"

"It's not very complicated. Gloria told me there were some very nice houses for sale in her neighborhood. If I were you I'd start looking. Private school is another consideration, and I'd start looking at schools too."

"I'm not looking at anything. Maria and Gloria can do all that."

"Henry, out of all this tragedy, maybe there'll come some good?"

"Lee, take off the rose-colored glasses, it's unbecoming. I don't have the time or temperament to be a parent. You know, last Tuesday Maria gave me a kiss goodbye before she got out of the cab and when she called the next day I told myself it was a whole new beginning. That wonderful feeling lasted all of ten seconds, then Sophie started in on me. It's over. I'll own a house and my wife will be busy playing mother to my son. I'll be out in the cold again, my friend. Out in the cold again," he said softly as he dragged himself out of the chair and slowly walked from the office.

Futerman shrugged his shoulders and frowned. He wanted to yell at Henry, he wanted to curse him out and tell him what a fool he was, but he remained silent. *I wouldn't mind having his problems,* he thought. *I wouldn't mind having them at all.*

Chapter Forty-Seven

The squad room was empty except for Widelsky. He was sitting at his desk typing out the final page of his report on the Millie Campos murder investigation. There had been a homicide and two attempted homicides over the weekend in the Upper Borough and all of the other detectives were out on the road engaged in follow-up investigations. Widelsky was happy for the time alone. Cairn had gotten word from Kreppell that he was staying on in the unit. It was Widelsky's last day in Borough Homicide, and tomorrow he would begin a new chapter in Internal Affairs. He would miss Cairn, but the reassignment was such a relief that he convinced himself Cairn's loss was a minor upset and something he would get over. Phil could get tiresome and anyway, he thought, breaking in a new partner would be a pleasant diversion from the humdrum of police work.

Kreppell was in his office. He was half-heartedly reviewing the incidents from the weekend. The homicide and the two attempts all stemmed from domestic disputes. The murder was a sorry case. An elderly man with a history of alcoholism had been thrown down a flight of stairs by his drunken son and died from a broken neck. The son confessed and the detectives investigating the case were busy getting statements from neighbors about all of the previous disputes and suspected abuses that had occurred. The other two cases involved alcohol, too. In one, a husband came home drunk and stabbed his wife five times because she didn't answer the door fast enough. The other case was a laugher and in that one a wife, quite sober, walked into a neighborhood tavern and fired several shots at her drunken husband and his girlfriend. She wasn't much of a shot and neither the philandering mate nor his girlfriend was hit, but the wife's intentions were quite clear and the case was initially being carried as an attempted murder. Kreppell was certain the DA would plead that one out as a disorderly conduct.

Kreppell had a difficult time reading the cases. He'd read a paragraph, then pause and think back to his own situation at home. That morning at breakfast he'd had an argument with his wife. She didn't want to go to his promotion ceremony on Tuesday. She told him her depression was coming back and she didn't think she'd be up to it. He told her it was okay and whatever she decided would be fine with him. When he left the house she was in the kitchen cleaning the dishes, and when he said goodbye she had that far away look that normally meant something bad was going to happen. He read the cases and stopped to think about his wife. He called his house several times, but there was no answer.

Widelsky had stopped in the office earlier and advised Kreppell that once he was finished with his report he would be cleaning out his locker and desk and be on his way. Kreppell had told him fine and thanked him for the solid work he did on the Millie Campos murder.

It was ten-thirty Monday morning, the day before his promotion to lieutenant, and Ted Kreppell recognized that he was alone in the world, again. Kreppell didn't succumb to melancholy very often, but when he did, his sense of self-pity was excessive and was usually exhausted over half a bottle of scotch at the end of the bar in Gordon's Steakhouse in the small suburban city of Washburn where he lived with his wife Alice and his daughter Audrey.

Kreppell was in the mood for a drink, but it was Monday and tomorrow was his promotion and there was a lot of work to do. *I can wait until Friday to tie one on*, he thought. *Maybe by then, I won't want to.* He was in a mild daze when the phone on his desk rang. He sprang to attention and answered the phone, "Kreppell, Borough Major Case."

"Ted, it's Tommy Hanrahan up in Washburn."

"Hi, Tommy, how are you?"

"Listen, buddy, I got bad news," Hanrahan said apologetically.

"Is it Alice?"

"Yeah, she's three sheets to the wind. She parked her car in a fire lane, then came into the store and shoplifted a dress. It's really sad," he said sympathetically. "The sale's clerk and one of my store detectives saw her in plain view. She tried on the dress, then went back out to the rack and stuffed it into a shopping bag she was carrying."

"How drunk is she?"

"She's got a good load on. Unsteady on her feet, slurring her words, a little combative."

"I knew it, I knew it this morning," Kreppell lamented.

"Yeah, well this is the third time in two years we got her here in Macy's. Worst is she don't have the keys to the car. We're not pressing charges, but you got to get her outta here before she gets going. Last time she bit Pearl and I had no choice. I don't want that to happen again," Hanrahan said nervously.

"Okay, hold tight. I got an extra set of keys to her car. I can be there in twenty, twenty-five minutes. Can you hold on that long?"

"I'll be waiting," Hanrahan replied.

Kreppell walked out to the squad room. Widelsky was the only one there. It killed him to do it, but he had no choice. "Frank, I need a favor, about an hour of your time. Do you mind?"

"No, no problem, I was just taking off 'cause there was no reason to hang around and I got some time coming to me. But sure, what do you need?" Widelsky said suspiciously.

"We have to take a ride up to Washburn. I'll tell you in the car."

"Sure thing," Widelsky said as he got up from the chair and put his sports coat on.

"We're leaving the city, and it isn't official business, so we'll take my private car. I'm out on the Boulevard. I'll tell the desk officer to log me out for an hour," Kreppell said as he left Widelsky standing in the squad room.

"Yeah, I gotta hit the head before we go anyway," Widelsky replied.

Kreppell drove a 1957 Ford Fairlane 500. He was as fastidious about the car as he was about his own appearance. The car was black with a gold chrome stripe across each side, and it was polished to a high sheen. The interior was all black, with black leather seats and trim. The windows were rolled down and Kreppell was behind the wheel waiting for Widelsky. Widelsky admired the lines on the car, then opened the door and got in.

"This is one beautiful car, 1957, right?"

"Yes, I garage it and wash it every week and wax it once a month. It's my baby."

"Hey, cars last a lot longer when you give them some attention."

"Cars and dogs, they're a lot easier to keep than people," Kreppell said with some hint of regret.

"Yeah, you got a point, Sarge," Widelsky replied, without adding anything else. Widelsky felt a little nervous. Kreppell obviously was dealing with a personal problem, and as a last resort he had asked him for help. Widelsky wanted to know as little about Kreppell's problem as possible, and unless Kreppell brought it up he wasn't going to broach the subject. They drove for about five minutes in silence. They were on the parkway headed for Washburn. Kreppell uttered a small laugh, then said, "Want to know where we're going?"

"Sure."

"I live up in Washburn. Nice little city. Actually, it's more like a town than a city."

"I been up there. They got a mall with a Macy's. My wife drug me up there."

"One of the first malls built in this state. Did you know that?" Kreppell asked.

"I know it's a new idea. Pretty nifty if you ask me; it could be raining out and you're inside dry as a bone."

"That's the concept. Anyway," and Kreppell paused for a moment, "my wife likes the Macy's there. A friend of mine was a detective sergeant in Washburn. He retired when the mall opened and is the security chief for that Macy's store. Nice job, pays almost as much as he was making with the PD. Add that to his pension and he's doing well."

"Ain't bad, but it seems like you always need a hook to land those jobs, you know?"

"Yeah, I'd go along with that."

"So, we going to visit this friend of yours?"

"In a way, but I have a personal problem and I just ask that you try and keep it to yourself. I know I'm the one asking the favor, and I don't mean to put you on the spot, but it's personal," Kreppell said with embarrassment.

"What's this about?" Widelsky asked uncomfortably.

"My wife has a little drinking problem. She suffers from depression, started ten years ago. Our second child died at eight months from meningitis. Goddamn doctors let him come home from the hospital too soon."

"Sorry to hear that."

"Alice never recovered. In and out of depression, then she started drinking. Not too often, but every once in a while, and over the last two years it's become a real headache."

Widelsky sensed that Kreppell wanted to tell him more and his discomfort grew. Widelsky had been indifferent toward Kreppell as he had been with most of the men he worked with. Even his relationship with Cairn was largely superficial, and he liked it that way. He didn't have many problems in his own life, but those he did he kept to himself. He kept silent and after another thirty seconds or so Kreppell started talking again.

"My girl Audrey is eighteen. She'll turn nineteen in October. She just finished her first year at Penn State. Came home a week and a half ago, and I don't think she and her mother said much more than "hi" and "goodbye" to one another. Friday, Audrey left for her job as a camp counselor at a sleep away camp up in the mountains. Camp Hiawatha, seems like every other camp is called Hiawatha, you know?"

"Yeah, it does," Widelsky answered disinterestedly.

"It's a pity, but Audrey was eight when little Teddy died, and something in my wife died with him. After that she and Audrey were always at odds, and now it's just cold between them. I'm close to her, but not my wife. Alice knows it, and she broods about it, but she doesn't do anything to make it better. So go figure, Audrey leaves for camp with not much more than a quick goodbye to her mother and two days later Alice falls into the bottle again."

"Did something happen to your wife?"

"She got pinched shoplifting in Macy's. Hanrahan's my buddy, and he won't hold her on the charge, but I have to get her out of there, and she can be a handful at times. Also, her car is in a fire zone and they can't find her keys. I don't mean to put you on the spot, but I have to get her and the car home and get her out of there as quickly as possible before this gets worse."

"How could it get worse?"

"Last year she did the same thing, and bit one of the store detectives. It was a woman, and she made a stink and Tommy tried but he couldn't get a hold of me and they ended up arresting Alice. I worked it all out later, but it made the local paper. Audrey was a senior in high school and the story in the paper killed her. Like I said before, Washburn is more like a town than a city."

"Sounds like you got your hands full. Your wife got any family could help. You know, talk to her, maybe?"

"Plenty of family, but what can they really do? Her father owns a big hardware store there, and her two brothers run it now. Her mother practically raised Audrey. Alice never stopped going to school. Finished college, graduate school, then her Ph.D., she's a helluva lot smarter than me."

"Ph.D.?" a clearly impressed Widelsky said.

"Oh, she's smart. She's a specialist in education for children with developmental problems. Autistic kids, mental retardation, anything you'd qualify as abnormal. She's very dedicated, and that's what keeps her going."

"Sounds confusing for a woman to be so educated and have a drinking problem."

"Oh, it's probably a lot more common than you think. My problem is she won't go for help, and her family wants to help, but she's as cold to them as she is to me. They're good people. Audrey's very close to Alice's mom and that's important for her."

"Family always helps. You come from Washburn?"

"No, I was raised in Pennsylvania, a small town called Gerberich near Lebanon, Pennsylvania."

"Your family still there?"

"Haven't any."

"They're all dead?"

"Don't know," Kreppell said as he turned to look at Widelsky. "I was raised in an orphanage. The Emil Dreiser Lutheran Home for Orphans to be exact."

Kreppell made that statement with pride in his voice and Widelsky was not only surprised, but he felt an unusual pang of sympathy for the man. Widelsky lived in a neighborhood where he estimated there were close to forty relatives belonging to his and his wife's families. The thought of growing up as an orphan without family was disturbing to him. "What happened to your parents?"

"Don't know. I was a foundling."

"Abandoned?"

"Yes, I was a couple days old, and I was left in the Reading Railroad terminal in Philadelphia, Pennsylvania."

"That's tough."

"September 6, 1923. And you know what? I had a name."

"Oh, they knew who your parents were?"

"No luck there, but my mother, I guess it was my mother, pinned a note on my blanket and the note said, "Baby Theodore Kreppell. Imagine that?"

"Was that her name?"

"Don't know, I think it was a made up name, but who knows where she got it from? The record keeping wasn't that great back then, and somehow I ended up in the Emil Dreiser Lutheran home for Orphans in Gerberich, Pennsylvania."

"Jesus," Widelsky said with interest. "Were you ever adopted?"

"No, not too many adoptions in those days. Stayed there until I was seventeen and out of high school and I joined the Army. Never went back."

"It was tough, the orphanage?"

"Not tough, just wasn't much about it I liked. We were never mistreated, but there just wasn't much there. It was a fucking orphanage," he said, laughing.

"Many kids, I mean orphans?"

"Forty or so. It wasn't a bad place, and the people who ran it were okay. There was a small factory where we made wooden chairs, Shaker chairs and a nice sized truck farm. Grew all of our own vegetables and plenty more for a roadside stand. Funny thing, I knew a lot about woodworking and plenty about gardening, and I haven't gone near any of it since the day I left the orphanage."

"What was it, child labor?"

"Oh, no, not at all. It was a very well disciplined operation. Mr. And Mrs. Gardenhire ran the place and Mr. Gardenhire employed a couple of men in the factory. As kids and teenagers we did chores. Bundling and sorting wood when we were younger, and wood shop type stuff by the time we got to high school. It was educational. We started in the gardens very young. When we went to the public school for high school, our girls were sought after, at least the pretty ones were."

"Cause they were good looking or good workers?"

"Both; it wasn't bad for a local boy to hook up with a pretty girl from the orphanage. You knew you were getting a hard worker and there wasn't any family to deal with. No in-laws, you know?"

Kreppell turned off the parkway at the Washburn exit and made his way to Broad Street.

"What about the boys, weren't they hard workers, too?"

"Different story, weren't too many families wanted their daughter dating an orphan, much less marrying one. And for that matter most of our girls wanted to move away too. Living in an orphanage had a stigma to it and moving away was like washing the stink of that stigma off."

"I don't know, I got more family than I can handle."

"That's why you feel the way about the department that you do," Kreppell said knowingly.

"What do you mean?" Widelsky asked earnestly, as if some secret about him had been revealed.

"You've got family and friends outside of the department. Being a cop isn't what you're all about. That's good, it keeps things in perspective."

They were driving down a broad tree lined street heading toward Washburn's business district.

"So how'd you end up in Washburn?"

"Easy. I joined the Army right out of high school, and after basic training in 1941 I was sent to the Army base on Mudd Island which, you know, is located where?"

"Washburn."

"Right. I was a cook, and I stayed there until I was shipped over to Europe after D Day in 1944. Went all across Europe and heard the bombs and shells burst, but never saw a moment of battle. And guess what? That was fine with me."

"You met your wife while you were stationed on Mudd Island?"

"Yeah, I met her, and to make a long story short, I think the fact that I was an orphan played into the picture. In retrospect, I look at her education and what she does with disabled kids and I think she saw me in the same light," he said dejectedly.

Widelsky, who had started the trip determined to ignore Kreppell, found himself thoroughly engrossed in Kreppell's story. They were nearing the new mall, and as Kreppell pulled into the parking lot Widelsky asked him, "You think she felt sorry for you?"

"No, not sorry, not in a way you would pity someone, more she just wanted to love me. I don't know, but it's something like that," Kreppell said, suddenly feeling self conscious about revealing so much of himself to someone he didn't particularly care for.

Widelsky pressed on as Kreppell pulled the car into a parking space by an entrance that said Employees Only. "When did you get married?"

"...1944, she was in her last year of college. We got married and I went overseas. When I came back I started college at the Jesuit University and two months into my first semester in the spring of 1946 she told me she was pregnant. I took the police test and became a cop. She had the baby, kept on going to school and you already know the rest," Kreppell said with a smile as he exited the car. "And now you get to meet her. She can be very nasty when she drinks. We'll go in and get her, then I'll take her to her car and you can follow me home in my car. Shouldn't be more than ten minutes. And please, if she insults you, just ignore it and don't take it personal. Anything she says is meant for me," Kreppell said dourly.

"You lead, I'll follow."

They went through the Employees Only door and up a flight of stairs to another door. That door was locked, but there was a bell and Kreppell rang the bell. A moment later a blonde-haired woman in black pants and a black short-sleeved blouse with a thick silver chain and medallion hanging around her neck opened the door. "Hey, Pearl, how'ya doing?" Kreppell said engagingly.

"Hi, Ted, she's really pissed off, but she ain't biting today," Pearl said with a smirk as she turned around and led them down a narrow well lit hallway. They came to a door at the end of the hallway and went in. It was a small with bright neon ceiling lights. Standing against a door at the opposite end of the room was a man that Widelsky thought for a moment was Captain Grimsley. He had to take a second look before he realized it wasn't Grimsley.

"Teddy," the man said in a friendly tone. "Good thing you got here. She was mouthing off something terrible before, but she's calmed down quite a bit. She doesn't like Pearl."

"Tom," Kreppell said seriously. "I apologize, really, for all your trouble. I'll have her out of your hair in a minute."

"I hate to rush you, but the mall manger is raising the roof over the car parked in the fire lane. He already complained to the store manager. You know how it is?"

"Tom, believe me, I appreciate this. Oh, this is Frank Widelsky. He's one of my guys and he was nice enough to come up here and help me," Kreppell said as he introduced Widelsky to Tom Hanrahan.

"Pleased to meet you, Frank," Hanrahan said as he walked across the room and shook Widelsky's hand. Widelsky was amazed by the resemblance between Hanrahan and Grimsley. Hanrahan, like Grimsley, wasn't more than 5'10" or 5'11," but he looked much taller. The long neck and the hawkish nose and bony hands and thin wiry build fit the footprint of Grimsley to a tee. The dark suit and narrow dark tie was as much a uniform as it was a style of dress, and Widelsky was certain that Hanrahan carried himself with the same no nonsense demeanor that Grimsley was so well known for. Kreppell waited for the two men to shake hands, then said, "Tom, is she in there?"

"Yes, and all alone."

"Let me go in and get her."

Kreppell went into the room and Widelsky and Hanrahan waited outside.

"You work with Teddy very long, Frank?"

"Little over a year, but I'm going to Internal Affairs tomorrow. At the request of my old boss," Widelsky answered.

"Good man Ted Kreppell," Hanrahan said flatly. "That Goddamn woman will be the death of him," he added disgustedly. Widelsky didn't answer and stood there silently.

The door opened and Kreppell walked out. A short, slightly overweight woman followed him out of the room. She had dull brown hair, and her eyes were red from crying. Her head was bobbing up and down and she repeatedly licked her lips. She was wearing a pink housedress and white sandals, and there was nothing remarkable about her appearance at all that would make one take notice. Compared to her always immaculately and tastefully dressed husband, Mrs. Theodore Kreppell looked like one of the shopping bag ladies wandering the streets in downtown Huguenot City.

She stopped short and looked at Widelsky. "Teddy, who's this?" she asked.

"Alice," Kreppell said firmly. "He works with me, but you can meet him some other time. Come along, we have to move your car right away."

"You can't, I lost the keys," she slurred.

"I have an extra set, let's go, please."

"I want to go with your friend Frank. He looks very tough. I like tough men. I like Tom too," she cooed.

"Fine, honey, but for now let's get to the car." He ushered her to the doorway and nodded his head for Widelsky to follow. He extended his arm and threw a set of keys to Widelsky. "Just wait by my car and when I come by you can follow me. It's a canary yellow Cadillac. You can't miss it."

Alice Kreppell pulled back from her husband and leaned toward Widelsky. "Canary yellow, I paid for it myself. If it was up to Cheapo, I'd walk." She giggled, then gave her husband a cockeyed salute and almost stumbled backward as her hand slapped against her forehead.

Kreppell grabbed her arm to steady her. "Alice, be careful," he said.

She shook of his grip and said with a sneer, "Sergeant Cheapo doesn't like it when I call him that. Do you Cheapo?"

Kreppell blushed, pulled on his wife's arm and made his way through the door. Widelsky followed them down the hallway. When they got to the door they had originally came through Kreppell turned right and went down another hallway. Hanrahan followed him. Widelsky went through the door and walked down the stairs into the garage and went to Kreppell's black Fairlane. He got in the car and started it up. He reflected on all that he had witnessed about Kreppell and blessed himself. "Thank God," he said, "this is my last day in this unit."

Two minutes later Kreppell pulled up and honked the horn to his wife's car. He made a motion with his hand for Widelsky to follow him. Widelsky pulled out of the parking space and followed Kreppell out of the parking garage.

They entered a large commercial strip with two-way traffic. Widelsky was two car lengths behind Kreppell, but it was easy to follow the big canary yellow Cadillac. They were headed to the south side of Washburn, and as the traffic lessened Kreppell picked up speed. He was in the left lane and Widelsky had to press a little harder on the accelerator to keep up with him.

Alice Kreppell was seated in the front passenger seat next to her husband. He was driving too fast, but he didn't care. She knew that all he wanted to do was get her home and out of his sight. "You don't love me. You could care less about me, Teddy, isn't that so?" she demanded.

Kreppell didn't acknowledge her and kept on driving.

"You and Audrey, you're both the same. Cold and selfish, I know," she went on to say, knowing full well that nothing she could do or say would garner a response from him. That was how he handled her. He would ignore her until she sobered up, then he would act as if nothing happened. "I wonder what that blockhead you brought with you today thinks about us, Teddy?" she said mockingly.

Kreppell wouldn't even look at her. He scanned the rear view mirror and saw that Widelsky was keeping up. *Another mile*, he thought, *and we'll be at the house. I'll bring her in and leave her. I won't need his help, he's seen enough.*

"Teddy," Alice whined, "talk to me, talk to me. I'm so sorry, so sorry for what I did. I only want the best for us, but I fall apart, please talk to me. I'll apologize to your friend, I'm sorry, sorry," she said, crying.

Kreppell stared straight ahead. The driver's side window was open several inches and his left arm was resting against the window and his fingers were drumming the roof of the car. His right hand was wrapped tightly around the steering wheel and barely moved as he pursued a straight course down the thoroughfare.

Alice had put a cigarette in her mouth and was waiting for the cigarette lighter to heat up and pop out of the dashboard. She put her hand on his right leg and said, "Please just talk to me. That's our problem, we don't communicate," she slurred. He kept driving, and it was as if he was deaf and couldn't hear a word she said. The lighter popped and she withdrew it. The coil of metal inside the lighter glowed hot orange and in a moment of anger at his silence she stabbed at his right hand with the lighter. It was unexpected and he jerked the wheel away from her burning touch and yelled, "Christ."

It was nearing midday and the sun shone hard and bright against his windshield. Widelsky was squinting and his eyes were burning from the hot sun and he wished he hadn't left his sunglasses on his desk. He heard a siren, then saw the rotating gumball light on the roof of a squad car racing toward them. The police car was in the opposite left lane and just as it was about to pass Kreppell Widelsky instinctively swerved to the right and rode his brake until his car skidded into the road curbing and stopped. The sudden stop caused his head to snap back and he immediately felt pain in his neck and head, but the pain was nothing compared to the shock of what he had just witnessed. *If it was intentional, the timing couldn't have been better*, he thought. The speeding police car was approaching Kreppell's car and it appeared they would pass one another when suddenly Kreppell's canary yellow Cadillac pulled into the path of the oncoming car. The collision was head on and the violence of it was like nothing Widelsky had ever witnessed in his life. He didn't understand how he had managed to avoid the accident. He reacted before his mind could consciously process what was about to and actually did happen.

Traffic stopped, people screamed and Widelsky's head was aching. He sat frozen behind the wheel of Kreppell's 1957 Ford Fairlane 500. The carnage was instant and devastating. Alice Kreppell was thrown from the car and her body lay still in the street. A man came over to him and asked him if he was hurt. He ignored his inquisitor and pulled the rear view mirror down a few inches and inspected his face. There was no blood. He could move his neck and back. He felt a surge of adrenalin and the aching feeling lessened. "I'll be fine," he told himself. He got out of the car and walked toward Alice Kreppell. There was a crowd milling and the distant sound of sirens nearing the scene. He identified himself as a police officer, pushed his way past the onlookers and bent down and touched her neck. He felt her carotid artery, but there was no pulse, no life. She was dead. He didn't dare approach the two crashed automobiles. Kreppell and the police officer were dead, too. Each man's face was pressed against the windshield of his car. They looked like two limp andirons supporting a smoking and twisted knot of torn sheet metal. The steam from the cars' ruptured radiators hissed and spurted. Antifreeze and transmission fluid flowed freely into the street. Widelsky walked back to Kreppell's car and rested his foot on the rear bumper. He lit a cigarette and watched the responding police cars and ambulances pull up.

Within minutes half of the Washburn P.D. must have arrived at the accident scene. An officer canvassing the crowd asked him if he had witnessed the accident.

Widelsky identified himself and his relationship to Kreppell. The officer left and came back with his captain. Widelsky was directed to report to the Washburn P.D. headquarters.

Widelsky would never know if Alice Kreppell had caused the accident or Ted Kreppell had condemned them to death. What he did know is that there was nothing in the roadway that would have caused Kreppell to lose control of the steering wheel. He decided that he would tell the police that on the trip up from Huguenot City Kreppell had had a sneezing fit. "Allergies," he claimed and possibly that had happened again and that was how he lost control of the car. It wasn't very original, but cleverness was a trait he disparaged.

Chapter Forty-Eight

Widelsky decided that before subjecting himself to an interview with the Washburn Police he would notify his command. He was looking for a payphone when he saw one on the corner in front of the Parkway Diner. He pulled into the diner parking lot and exited his car and walked over to the phone booth on the corner of Rose Avenue and Parkway Drive. He put a dime into the phone and dialed the number for the Upper Borough commander's office.

"Borough Command," a tinny female voice answered.

"This is Detective Widelsky from Borough Major Case. I need to speak with someone from Chief Keegan's office. One of our sergeants was just killed in a car accident in Washburn."

"Yes, we know. The chief is on the line now with Washburn. Where are you?"

"I'm in Washburn, I was in a car following the sergeant. I'm supposed to go to the local PD, but I wanted to report in first. I'm on a payphone and—"

"Hold on," the female interrupted.

Widelsky stopped talking. He could hear voices in the background, then the gruff voice of Chief Keegan filled the earpiece, "Who the hell is this?"

"Detective Frank Widelsky, Borough Major Case, Chief," Widelsky replied just as gruffly.

"What's going on? How are you involved in this?" the chief demanded.

"I was working a half shift. Had some time coming to me and Sergeant Kreppell asked me to do him a favor and drive up to Washburn with him. It's a long story, Chief, and I'm outta change. Can I give you this number and you can call me back?" Widelsky asked, knowing that in another minute or so his three minutes would be up and if he didn't put a nickel in the coin box the call would end.

"No," the chief replied. "Where are you right now?"

"I'm in a phone booth in front of the Parkway Diner in Washburn, on Rose Avenue."

"Okay, I know the place. Go inside and get a table and have a cup of coffee or something. We'll be there in twenty minutes," the chief directed. Before Widelsky had a chance to respond Chief Keegan hung up the phone.

The phone booth was hot and stuffy, and Widelsky was dripping with sweat. He wiped his brow with the sleeve of his sports jacket and made his way up the steps of the diner. The diner was cold and he could taste the air conditioning in the air. It was a nice sensation. The cashier's booth was immediately adjacent to the front door. The cashier looked at Widelsky and said, "You want a table, or do you want to sit at the counter?"

"Table, I'm expecting company."

"Take your pick, plenty of empties," she said in a friendly voice.

Widelsky turned left and headed toward a large dining room that looked out over the parking lot. He stopped by the end of the service counter and stared at the desserts that were lined up on shelves behind the counter. Chocolate cakes, éclairs and several cream pies were attractively displayed and Widelsky felt a pang of hunger followed by a stronger pang of guilt. It bothered him that he was thinking about enjoying a plate of dessert when a colleague had just met his death in a terrible accident not more than a half hour ago. It disturbed him even more that he was calculating in his mind how he could discreetly find out if Kreppell's survivors would put the Ford Fairlane up for sale.

Widelsky picked out a booth in the far corner of the room and took a seat. A waitress came by and he ordered a cup of coffee and a piece of banana cream pie. The Ford was in plain view from the diner window. The waitress brought his order and in five forkfuls the pie was gone. He pushed the plate away and sipped the piping hot coffee. He closed his eyes, shook his head and whispered to himself, "What a fucking phony I am. Tough guy, I'm a real fucking tough guy. What a joke."

He was ashamed of himself. Kreppell's death had left him stunned, but he felt no emotional connection. He was hungry. He entertained the thought of getting the dead man's car at a bargain. He was concerned that Kreppell hadn't made a notation in the daily attendance log crediting him with the use of four hours comp time and he would end up being accused of leaving the city without permission. These issues were of greater concern to him than the end of Kreppell's life, and as Widelsky recognized how venial and petty they were his self disgust grew. Introspection was a foreign art to him. He lit a cigarette, leaned his chin on his hand and focused his attention on Kreppell's gleaming black Ford Fairlane. "Fuck it," he mumbled to himself. "I didn't do anything wrong."

The waitress came over and refilled his coffee cup. "You want anything else?" she asked.

"Not now, I'm expecting someone, thanks," Widelsky, responded indifferently.

The diner was filling up for lunchtime and it seemed everyone was talking about the accident. Widelsky overheard snippets of conversation and learned that the dead Washburn officer was the Washburn mayor's nephew. He heard one waitress tell another that the officer was "a great kid, but a real hot dog." No one was talking about Kreppell or his wife, and while he strained his ears to pick up every bit of conversation the consensus among the diners he could hear was that it was just a terrible accident and nothing more. He was hoping the Washburn Police would see it the same way.

One more cup of coffee later and he saw Captain Grimsley, Chief Keegan and an unknown police lieutenant in uniform standing by the cashier's counter. He got out of the booth and walked toward the front of the diner. Grimsley spied him and motioned with his hand for Widelsky to go back to his table. Widelsky obeyed and no sooner had he sat down then he was standing up again to greet his bosses.

"Sit down and don't make a show of it," Chief Keegan quietly ordered.

"Frank," Captain Grimsley said with surprising familiarity. "This is Chief Keegan and Lieutenant Mikulik. The lieutenant is from the Standards and Legal Division."

"Chief, Lieutenant." Widelsky nodded respectfully.

Keegan was a solid man, built somewhat like Widelsky, but with a hard square face instead of Widelsky's round broad face. He and Grimsley were contemporaries. They had joined the department in the 1920s, and although they were considered dinosaurs by many, they were responsible for introducing a number of innovative and modern programs into the department during the last decade. They were serious men, and their loyalty to the reputation and integrity of the Huguenot City Police Department went unquestioned.

411

The waitress came over to the table and the chief ordered coffee for the three of them. No one spoke until she was out of earshot, and Keegan broke the ice and said to Widelsky accusingly, "Jesus Christ, I hope you got a good explanation for this. The chief of police up here in Washburn thinks Kreppell crashed his car on purpose, and the dead cop is the mayor's nephew."

Widelsky was about to respond when Grimsley interrupted him. "Frank, how many years until you can claim your pension"

"About three, sir."

"Make sure you tell the truth, or Lieutenant Mikulik will have the separation papers filed so fast you won't know what happened, and the only pension you'll be eligible for is the one from the next job you get."

Grimsley's threat embarrassed Lieutenant Mikulik, and he avoided making eye contact with Widelsky when Widelsky glanced at him after Grimsley had said his name.

"Captain, I got nothing to hide," Widelsky said defensively.

"Didn't think you did, but we can't waste time here worrying about how all this might reflect on you. So, just tell us the story, but leave off the gratuitous grace notes."

Widelsky didn't understand the reference to "gratuitous grace notes," but he knew enough not to be cute with his superiors and with uncharacteristic meekness, he said, "Captain, Chief, believe me this is a crazy story, but I was just doing the man a favor, just a favor."

The waitress arrived with the coffee. "Anything else?" she asked.

"Just the check when you get a chance," Grimsley replied.

Keegan pushed his coffee away. He had no intention of tasting it. He clapped his hands together softly and looked at Widelsky harshly. "What happened?"

"Today was my last day in Major Case. I start tomorrow with Chief Greason in IAD. Some new anti-corruption group, and I was cleaning out my desk and finishing my report on the Campos homicide from last week." Widelsky paused and looked at Grimsley. Keegan took advantage of the pause and interjected, "Deputy Chief Greason, not chief, please."

Widelsky sensed that Greason wasn't a popular name, and he nodded his head and resumed talking. "Earlier I had asked the sergeant if I could take some time and knock off early. I figured I had nothing to do since all my reports were done and there was no point hanging around. Plus, I had a lotta hours on the books I knew I couldn't take with me so, like I said, I figured I 'd use them."

"There's nothing in the attendance log," Grimsley said.

"Well, I asked and Sergeant Kreppell said, 'Okay.'"

"Did you put the request in writing?"

"Only if it's for a whole day, otherwise it's a verbal thing and the sergeant would note it in the log and take the time off your total. We do it all the time."

"Whatever, he didn't. What happened next?" Grimsley asked.

"I was getting ready to take off. All the other guys in the squad were out on the road. We had a busy weekend. Sergeant Kreppell came into the squad room and asked if I could do him a favor and take a ride up to Washburn with him. He said it was personal. I said, 'No problem.' I was only taking some time 'cause I had it on the books and there was nothing left for me to do hanging around the squad with my transfer coming the next day and all that. So I went."

"Did the sergeant notify the lieutenant on the desk?" Mikulik asked

"He said he was going out to the desk to tell them to take him off the clock, but I don't know who he talked to. I had to run to the john and he said to meet him outside where his private car was parked. I went outside and we drove up to Washburn in his Ford Fairlane. That car right there," Widelsky said as he pointed toward the window at Kreppell's car parked in the lot.

"Very clean car," Keegan remarked.

"We drove up here, and during the ride he told me about his wife. Matter of fact, he told me about himself and it was kinda sad, you know?"

"Sad," Grimsley inquired.

"Yeah, very sad. He was such a squared away boss. Break your balls in a minute, but like I'd tell my partner Phil, 'He's a boss, that's what he's supposed to do,' but his life had a lot of heartache."

"How's that?" Grimsley said with annoyance.

"He was an orphan. Grew up in an orphanage in Pennsylvania. Abandoned at birth, then he had a son died from meningitis ten years ago and his wife never got over it and started drinking. His daughter's in college, but she don't say five words to the wife. He told me all of this on the way up here and I felt bad for the guy. To work with him you'd think every duck was in a row and life was neat as a pin. God, you find out the guy's life is miserable. Least that's the impression I got." Widelsky stopped for a moment and took a sip of coffee.

"You're on target there, Frank," Grimsley said in agreement.

"He tells me this story, then he tells me his wife got a load on and got picked up for shoplifting in Macy's, and it's happened before. The security boss is a friend of his, a retired Washburn detective boss. Sergeant Kreppell said we'd get the wife, drive her car home and then go back to Huguenot City."

"What was the story when you got to Macy's?" Keegan asked.

"Sad. Mrs. Kreppell was three sheets to the wind, and she'd parked her car in a fire zone. The guy in charge of security was a real gentleman, but you know he just wanted her out of there. It was the third time they'd nabbed her, and last time out she bit one of his store detectives. Tom Hanrahan was his name, and he told me that him and the Sarge were good friends. The Sarge went into another room and came out with his wife. She looked like shit. Looked like she just fell out of bed, but wasn't all there. She gave me a queer look, and on the way out the Sarge tells me they'll be in a yellow Caddy and she starts calling him 'Sergeant Cheapo' and I don't know, she wasn't nice."

"Jesus," Grimsley moaned. "Teddy was my boy. The best, that guy, the very best and he ended up with that woman. What then?"

"He took his wife to get her car and I went to his car," he said, pointing to the Ford Fairlane. "Minute or so later he came by in the yellow Caddy and I followed him."

"Where were you going?" Keegan politely asked.

"I was following him to his house. He was gonna drop her off, then come back to the city with me."

"Was he upset?" Grimsley queried.

"I think he was. It began when he had to ask me the favor. He was a good boss," Widelsky said defensively. "But I wasn't one of his favorites. I don't blame him, I bitched too much about getting transferred up from Huguenot City, you know, downtown, and he didn't much care for that. I got under his skin."

"Lot of people did," Grimsley said smiling. "What happened next?"

"I followed him. He was in the left lane, going kinda fast. Maybe he had a car and a half-length on me or two, but you couldn't miss that Caddy, canary yellow. We're going down the street and I hear a siren, then I see a radio car coming at us from the opposite direction. Next thing, bang," Widelsky said as he clapped his hands. "The two cars crash."

"How'd you miss hitting one of the cars?" Keegan asked.

Widelsky leaned forward and frowned. "Got me, Chief, I musta seen it happening before I knew what was going on and I instinctively pulled to the right."

"Did you see anything happening in Kreppell's car? Was his wife attacking him or something like that?" Grimsley asked suggesting in his tone that what he said was what happened.

"Too much sun, Kreppell had a sneezing fit in the car on the way up to Washburn, maybe that happened again and he lost control of the car," Widelsky weakly replied.

414

"Frank, I thought you were a big time detective," Grimsley said with a short laugh. "That's the best you can do?"

Widelsky sat back and uttered a muffled laugh. "Truth is, I didn't see a thing, but if it was the wife grabbing the steering wheel the car should have pulled to the right. Figure, she's sitting on the right side. It's awfully hard to lean over and push the wheel to the left. She has no leverage and it would be easy for him to hold the wheel tight. Plus, she was pretty tipsy. No way she's strong enough to push that wheel and drive the car into the oncoming car at the angle they hit, no way," he said emphatically.

"Very good, Frank," Grimsley commented. "What do you think happened?"

"Kreppell did it. It's a murder suicide," he whispered. "No other explanation."

"What about the sneezing fit?" Keegan asked.

"I made that up."

"I think you're wrong, Frank," Grimsley said somberly. "Teddy had his problems, but he wasn't suicidal. Something happened in that car, something you didn't see. Let's keep your opinion to yourself, okay?"

"Sure, Cap," Widelsky, answered.

Keegan looked at Lieutenant Mikulik and said, "Marty, go with Frank up to the Washburn P.D. and sit in on the interview if you can. Frank," he said, pointing his index finger in Widelsky's direction, "tell them you saw nothing. You were driving along and it just happened. Mention the sneezing fit, but play dumb. Make sure you let them know that both you and the sergeant were off-duty and this was done on your own time. Also, you didn't know his wife had been pinched for shop lifting until you got to Macy's. All you knew was she was drunk. Got it?"

"Yes, sir," Widelsky answered.

Keegan turned to Grimsley and said, "Okay, Bobby, we'll go back in your car. Marty can follow Frank to Washburn, then bring him back."

The waitress saw the four men standing up and came over with the check. Keegan took it from her and scanned it quickly. "Frank, nothing affects your appetite, I see."

Widelsky dipped his chin down and didn't respond. The chief took out a wad of bills from his front pants pocket. He pushed several back and extracted a five-dollar bill and laid it on the table with the check. "Next time it's on you, big guy."

They left the diner by the side door that led to the parking lot. Widelsky started up Kreppell's Ford and was about to put it into drive when Grimsley pulled up alongside of him in his unmarked police car. "Frank, one more thing, the chief appreciates your cooperation. Your transfer to IAD is cancelled. You'll be staying in Major Case with me."

Widelsky couldn't disguise his body language and his face dropped at the disappointing order Grimsley had just issued. Keegan leaned over and added in, "Frank, Greason's an asshole. That new initiative is nothing more than a dog and pony show for the mayor's election campaign next year. Soon as it's over, Greason will move on and you guys will be left out in the cold. No good assignments, no friends. I did you a favor, smile."

Chapter Forty-Nine

A couple of noisy teens were splashing about in a rowboat in the middle of Dutchman's Lake. The lake was more a pond than a lake, but the Parks Department called it a lake, and to the youth of the Upper Borough that's just what it was. Widelsky was sitting alone on a park bench along the path that circled the lake. It was about 5:30 in the evening and the sun was still high in the late June sky. The sun was warm and it felt good. He wanted to take off his sport's jacket, but he was wearing his shoulder holster and didn't want to attract any attention. He loosened his tie and watched the kids in the rowboat with envy. *Ah, to be young again*, he thought.

A car door opened, then slammed shut. Widelsky looked over his shoulder and saw Cairn approaching. Cairn was carrying a green metal cooler in his left hand.

"Frankie boy," Cairn said affectionately as he held up the cooler. "Cold beer, Doctor Cairn's on the case."

"What're you so happy about?" Widelsky almost snarled.

Cairn rocked his head back in mock indignation, and said, "Frank, you got a fucking heart in there after all?"

"Quit fucking around, Phil."

"I'm not fucking around, I'm being serious."

"You think Kreppell's death is funny?"

"Of course not, it's a fucking tragedy and I know you're upset. I was just trying to cheer you up. Why are you being so touchy?" he asked sincerely.

"You're right," Widelsky said contritely. "It's just this was such a fucking queer day. I got up today. I went to the bakery. I picked up a coffee cake and came into work. Last day in the Upper Borough, last day with my friend and partner, I was happy, but sad. You know?"

Cairn opened up the cooler and took out two cans of beer. He took out a can opener from his coat pocket and popped open the two cans.

Widelsky smiled and said, "Schlitz, my favorite."

Cairn laughed. "Hey, I wanted to cheer you up." He handed Widelsky a can, then with the other can in his hand he held it up and tapped Widelsky's hand. "To life, partner, to life."

Widelsky nodded his head in agreement and took a long drink of the cold beer. "Ah, that hit the spot." He sighed.

"That it did," Cairn answered.

"Anyway," Widelsky continued. "I thought we'd have a little coffee and cake this morning. I'd finish my report and be on my way. I felt funny about you not coming with me, but what the hell, that's life."

"You gonna tell me the whole story?" Cairn asked.

"Grimsley didn't tell you guys everything?"

"Sanitized version. He left you out of the story. I found out from that young cop Clay. He was on the desk this afternoon. He was the reserve driver and he asked me how you were."

"What did Grimsley tell you?" a perplexed Widelsky asked.

"We were out on the road. Nobody knew about Kreppell, then around two-thirty we get a radio call to 10-2 to the office. I was with my new partner, Slattery. Thank God that only lasted a day. He has six kids and he's been married nine years. He drives a limo on the side for some car service. He can't stay awake. Don't talk, don't eat lunch, don't spend money. I can tell he's the type that if it ain't for free he don't want it."

"He never impressed me much. I think his wife's related to somebody with juice. So what about Grimsley?"

"Yeah, what about Grimsley. Queer fucking duck, Captain Grimsley is. He gets us all in the squad room. Called in the evening guys early and tells us about Kreppell dying in a car crash up in Washburn. He says there's a lot of speculation about what happened, but he don't want anyone saying anything until we know. And he was very firm about that. He gets that cold look in his eyes. Murphy, he's got balls. He asks the captain very politely but ballsy nonetheless, 'Hey, cap. You have to tell us a little more. It isn't fair to say speculation without tipping your hand. What if the press starts hanging around?

I could say the wrong thing.' Grimsley got pissed off and says, 'You keep you're mouth shut.' Murphy says defiantly, 'He was our boss. You can't trust us?' Grimsley got red in the face and said, 'They think his wife caused the accident on purpose. This is a hot potato. Do you understand now? No one says anything' and Grimsley left the squad room and went to Kreppell's office. Can you believe that?"

"So when did you learn I was up there?"

"The box with your stuff was still on your desk. I wasn't going near Grimsley, so I went out to the front desk to find out if the desk lieutenant knew anything. He was in the shitter, so I asked the rookie. He tells me you were up in Washburn with Kreppell and you were still up there. That's why I waited around outside by your car for you. Grimsley didn't say anything, but I knew for sure he was hiding something."

"You're a good detective, Phil, but it isn't much of a mystery."

"Frank, have another beer and fill in the blanks," Cairn said as he reached into the cooler and took out two more cans of beer.

"We had our coffee and cake this morning, and you guys all hit the road. I asked the sergeant for some comp time and he told me no problem. I finished up my report and cleaned out my desk. I'm ready to clean out my locker and leave and Kreppell comes into the squad room. He looked a little upset. He asked me to go with him to Washburn on a personal emergency. What could I do? Say no? We ain't friends, but the Campos murder ended up well and he changed his opinion of us for the better, so why leave on a bad note I thought? I went with him. We went up in his car, Ford Fairlane, beautiful car. On the way up he starts making small talk and lets on about why we're going there, and I know it's personal and I'm trying to ignore him. I don't mind helping a guy," Widelsky said with a frown, then grimaced. "But I didn't want to hear all the details because it wasn't going to be anything pleasant. You know?"

"That don't sound like Kreppell," Cairn replied.

"Exactly, "Widelsky agreed. "I knew it was something really bad or he would've never asked me in the first place. Well, one thing leads to another and he's telling me his life story, and it was a fucking sad tale," he said, shaking his head.

"Kreppell, Mr. Squareroot, all the angles always figured out," Cairn declared.

"Not the case," Widelsky said as he crushed the empty can of beer and tossed it into a nearby trash basket. "Mr. Squareroot was nothing but troubles. His wife's a Ph.D., but she's a drunk and don't get along with the daughter.

He lost his son ten years ago to meningitis. Poor bastard's got no family of his own. He was abandoned as an infant and grew up in an orphanage."

"You got to be kidding?" Cairn said incredulously.

"I wish I was. The drive to Washburn's no more than fifteen or twenty minutes, but on the ride up I find out this guy's life is a living hell. We're going up there because his wife got picked up shoplifting in Macy's. Now, the store dick is his buddy. A retired Washburn detective sergeant, but he's got to get her out of there quick before she starts acting up and they got to arrest her. That's the only reason he asked me. Nobody else in the office." Widelsky pointed to the cooler and Cairn took out another beer and opened it for him.

"Jesus, Frank, he never let on at work. I mean he could bust them, but I always assumed he was one of those guys with a neat little house and everything perfectly planned, control freak."

"A fucking charade. We get to Macy's and the security guy, eh, eh, Hanrahan was his name. Nice guy, but looked just like Grimsley. He was upset and just wanted her out of there. They had her in another room and Kreppell goes in and then comes out with her. She looked like shit. Dumpy and wearing a potato sack or something close to it. Nothing to write home about, and she was bombed. She looks at me and says something about liking tough looking men, or something stupid like that. Anyway, he tells me to wait in his car and he'd come by in hers. He says it's a big yellow Caddy. She then pipes up again and says she paid for the car herself and if it was up to Sergeant Cheapo, that's what she called him, Sergeant Cheapo, she'd walk. He turned red and grabbed her arm and we left and I went down to the garage. I waited for them, and he comes by in the big yellow Caddy. I'm following him home and he's driving fast. We were on Commerce Avenue. It's a big four-lane road going through the business district on the south side of Washburn. I'm following him and I hear a siren and see a squad car coming in the opposite direction and then Phil, I swear I saw it happening and instinctively I moved my car to the right before I knew what I was doing. And then, as Kreppell's car and the squad car are almost passing, Kreppell drives right into the front of the squad car. It was fucking horrible. The wife got thrown from the car and Kreppell and the cop were DOA." Widelsky took a small sip of beer and lit a cigarette.

"Lucky you got out of the way," Cairn offered, then fixed his eyes on Widelsky, silently urging him to continue with his story.

"Lucky for me. It was a mess. I found a Washburn cop and gave him a heads up and he got a captain and they directed me to their station. On the way I thought it might be a good idea to notify the command. I stopped at the

Parkway Diner and called the chief's office. Keegan got on the line and told me to sit tight until he got there. I went inside and had a cup of coffee and about a half hour later Keegan, Grimsley and a Lieutenant Mikulik showed up. Mikulik's a lawyer from the Standards Bureau. Grimsley gives me the third degree like I did something, can you fucking believe that?" Widelsky said angrily.

"Sure," Cairn replied. "Kreppell was his boy. Handpicked and groomed by that old bastard."

"Just what Grimsley said. Kreppell was his boy. I got upset, but I told them the story and they calmed down. Bottom line was they sent me to Washburn with Mikulik and told me to tell them as little as possible. Just before we left the diner parking lot, Keegan tells me my transfer's been canceled and I'll be staying in the Upper Borough. Unfucking believable," Widelsky moaned as he put his hands up in the air."

"That's the part I left out," Cairn said. "Just before Grimsley left, he called me into Kreppell's office. He said that you were staying in the squad and we'd still be partners. I just said, 'Okay' and left."

"Well, Keegan said Greason was an asshole or something like that. Him and Grimsley left and Mikulik and I went up to the Washburn P.D. They didn't even know I was coming. Fucking place was in an uproar. They had it in their minds that Alice Kreppell was crazy. Pure and simple, she was crazy and the only way the accident could have happened was she caused it. And they were fucking pissed at the ex-cop, Hanrahan. Shit, he was one of them, but all these guys are walking about badmouthing him and tying to figure out if there was some charge they could hit him with. Fucking screwballs. They were blaming him for calling Kreppell and not just having her locked up. Mrs. Kreppell was well known in Washburn, and even though her family has a big lumberyard and hardware store up there they didn't care. She was a frequent customer of the Washburn P.D., and Hanrahan should have known better. I waited around for two hours before I told my story. Fucking farmers weren't even interested in me. They could have cared less about the Kreppell's too. All they cared about was their cop."

"What did you tell them?" Cairn asked.

"I didn't see a thing. We were driving down Commerce Avenue and next thing I see the two cars crashing. I was two car lengths behind and swerved out of the way at the last second. I said it was very sunny and I wasn't concentrating on Kreppell's car and they bought it and sent me on my way."

"So what really happened?" Cairn asked very seriously.

"Kreppell did it. He committed suicide and killed his wife and that cop. She was too drunk and too soft looking to be able to grab the wheel of the car and push it away from her. That's what she would have had to do to force the car to the left. Maybe if she was pulling to the right, but not the left. The swerve was to sharp, and it would have needed a very strong pull to the left. Kreppell was the only one who could have done it. It's fucking pathetic. Mr. Squareroot must have snapped."

"Christ, how bad could it have been?" Cairn asked.

"Phil, I don't know, but just from the little I got from him it was pretty bad, and remember he came to work every day and never let on. Tough boss, but he kept the squad running smoothly. Not too many dropped balls on his watch. You know, I feel bad for him."

"I don't believe it. Not too many people kill themselves. Kreppell was a hard guy. I betcha she did something in that car. Maybe she made a move for his gun or something and he pulled away too quickly?" Cairn guessed.

"I don't think so, but enough of that shit," Widelsky snapped as he got up and stretched. "Hey, I'm going home it's been a long day."

"You wanna stop at Grogans for one more?" Cairn asked.

"Naw, this ain't a day for drinking. If I really start, I won't want to stop."

Cairn picked up his cooler and the two men started back to the parking lot

"Hey," Widelsky asked, "any news on the Campos case. Kreppell had said this morning we might be in the Grand Jury by Thursday."

"Yeah, an assistant from Duffy's office called this afternoon. They have a bail hearing tomorrow morning and he's lining it up for next Tuesday, week from tomorrow."

"He's moving fast.'

"You saw all that crap Lenihan got in the papers over the weekend, didn't you?"

"Sure, real cheesy. He got the story in about the Weiss lady's pictures. Cheesecake prints he called them."

Cairn laughed. "Yeah, cheesecake and pinups. It's gonna get ugly, and too bad we didn't find anything in the girlfriend's apartment."

"Hey, it's in Duffy's court now. We gave him enough. You can't have everything."

They had reached the parking lot. Cairn stopped by his car and said sincerely, "Frank, it's been a tough day, but I am happy you're staying in the unit."

"Whatever," Widelsky said indifferently.

Chapter Fifty

The accident received heavy coverage on the evening news, and when Widelsky returned home from work he found his wife sitting on the front stoop to their building nervously smoking a cigarette, anxiously waiting to hear the first hand account of Kreppell's death. Although he hadn't spoken with any reporters, he was part of the story. Alice Kreppell's shoplifting arrest and the part Hanrahan played in letting her go were given major air time on the local radio and television stations, and the conspiracy theories were flourishing. Widelsky was identified several times by reporters as the "other police officer" that accompanied Kreppell to Macy's and assisted in engineering Alice's release. The Washburn police were demanding a grand jury investigation into the matter, and the subject of their scorn was retired Detective Sergeant Hanrahan. The Washburn police had concluded that Alice Kreppell intentionally caused the accident, and in doing so murdered her husband and a young police officer. How they had reached that uncertain conclusion Widelsky didn't know. Widelsky's wife was flushed with worry when he first saw her, but after a careful recounting of the story and his insistence that he had done nothing wrong, nor was in any trouble did she calm down.

The next morning Widelsky got up an hour earlier than he normally did and left for work before his wife could resuscitate the conversation about Kreppell from the night before. It seemed to him that for fifteen hours straight all he did was talk about and think about Ted Kreppell. On his way to work he stopped by a newsstand and bought a copy of the *Huguenot Times* and the *Huguenot*

Daily News. Each paper dedicated front-page coverage to the gruesome accident. The *Huguenot Daily News* displayed a full front-page photograph of the car wreck while the *Huguenot Times*, the more staid of the two, presented a bold headline and a photograph of the Washburn mayor weeping at the scene of the accident. Widelsky bought the papers, but didn't bother to read the stories. He knew what really happened and didn't have the stomach to digest all the journalistic embellishments and conjecture that would wrestle a week's worth of newspaper print from what he reluctantly decided was a cowardly and desperate act by Kreppell, but what the newspapermen would portray as a choice between murder and tragedy. If it were murder, Alice Kreppell would bear the blame, and if it was tragedy, no satisfactory answer existed to close the story.

None of the other detectives had arrived in the office, yet, and it was as quiet as a chapel in the squad room. He had made the morning coffee and was waiting for the little red light on the urn to brighten and tell him the coffee was ready. Grimsley was in Kreppell's office, but Widelsky hadn't bothered to stop by and wish him "good morning." The windows to the squad room faced west, and in the morning the room was always dark and cool. Widelsky liked it that way, and he liked being alone and in quiet. He wasn't in a hurry. The sweet aroma of the brewing coffee was a soothing tonic. *Coffee smells better than it tastes and strawberries look better than they taste, and Kreppell wasn't who I thought he was*, he glumly pondered.

Just then one of his co-workers came into the room. It was Detective Gerry Murphy. He paused before speaking, then said with contempt, "Oh, look who's here."

Widelsky was caught by surprise and uttered a grunting, "What?"

"You got that box you were stuffing your shit into yesterday?" Murphy demanded.

"What box, what's your problem?" a puzzled Widelsky retorted.

"My problem, no problem," Murphy said as he pressed the tips of his fingers against his chest. "That is if getting transferred to Internal Affairs downtown isn't a problem. You know, that new special unit, the one you were going to, you remember, don't you?" he dead-panned.

Widelsky absorbed what Murphy said and didn't respond. He went over to his desk, reached under it and took out a large cardboard box. He walked over to Murphy's desk and dropped the box on it, then went over to the coffee urn. He expected the red light to come on any second, and with his back to Murphy he said, "Listen, whatever happened has nothing to do with me. I'm just a foot soldier here, same as you, sonny. You got a beef, take it down the hall." The red light came on and he poured himself a cup of coffee and went back to his desk.

Murphy was carelessly tossing his personal effects into the box. "Sure, Frank, nothing to do with you except somehow I gotta take your spot in that new shitass squad. How'd that happen?"

"I told you, take it down the hall," Widelsky said coldly.

"Yeah, that's right; it's got nothing to do with you. Keep your nose clean, tough guy," Murphy sneered. "Never know when I'll be watching." He then picked up the box he had haphazardly packed and left the squad room without saying anything more.

Widelsky watched him leave. He wasn't angry. *Poor bastard*, he thought, *he's got a right to be pissed*. It was quiet again in the squad room and he closed his eyes and wrapped his fingers around the warm coffee cup. Whatever peace he had shared with himself in the office was gone. Murphy had startled him, and their brief encounter reminded him of how unpleasant his job had become and how inadequate it made him feel. He was a poor communicator, particularly when the moment demanded an honest response and the response was personal. As a detective, he had fashioned an abrupt and caustic demeanor in order to mask how deeply the daily drain of police work affected him. A hesitant "I'm sorry for your troubles" was all he could muster to offer comfort to a victim, and even that was grudgingly and self-consciously admitted. There was no joy in police work, no real satisfaction and little actual accomplishment. He never understood how the penalty of imprisonment mitigated the pain and suffering that victims endured. His job was to investigate crimes and arrest the guilty. It was simple work when reduced to that equation, but there was no equity there in his eyes. The dead, the beaten and the pillaged were dead, beaten, pillaged and nothing more. A jail sentence, even a long one was the cold coinage of retribution for the crime committed, and often the exchange was at a discount for the accused. The punishment was never enough. Restitution as a species didn't exist in the realm of criminal justice. He released his grip on the coffee cup and thought about his father's butcher shop. It was Frank Widelsky's sanctuary.

He had worked all day Saturday in his father's butcher shop. The coldness of the meat locker and the woody smell of the sawdust on the tile floor with the radio on and the ball game being played out through the colorful descriptions of the announcer was a scene he would never tire of, and a world in which he was better suited to live. There was something clean and precise about the work that would never compare to police work. The feel of a sharp steel blade surgically separating a wall of hard glossy fat from a strip of well-marbled meat was a sensation he enjoyed. Laying that trimmed piece of meat over a brown sheet of butcher paper and folding the paper over the meat into a neat package, then handing it over the counter to a smiling customer was a transaction of a type he would never experience in police work. So many of the men he worked with loved police work because they found it unpredictable and exciting. Widelsky saw no excitement in the game and everything about police work was, to him, predictable. A crime was crime, some were more brutal, terrible than others, but at the end of the day it was all the same sorry menu of human behavior that had to be contained. Widelsky knew his role and, more importantly, he harbored no conviction that he was a part of a noble enterprise; police were a necessary evil. Police did the bully work. Intimidation and enforcement were the muscle the police used to keep order, and Widelsky knew he was good at it. He could knock a man senseless with one punch. A hard slap or a firm squeeze to the back of the neck was usually enough to gain compliance, and the exercise of that force, although confined to the workplace, was second nature to him. It was his dark side, his grubby underbelly. It was something his wife had never seen and the customers in his father's shop would never see. *Three more years*, he thought. *Three more years and then I'm free*. He hated wishing his life away, but at that moment he was.

He heard voices in the hallway, then the sound of Tony DeMarco's booming voice broke the silence in the squad room. "Hey Cheech," he said smiling. "What'd you do to Murphy? I was on the phone with him last night for a fucking hour. He never liked you, now he wants to kill you," he added with a loud laugh.

DeMarco was older than Widelsky. He was in his late forties and had joined the department before the war. Murphy and he had been partners for four years. The older man had taken the brash young detective under his wing and treated him with as much concern and nurturing as a father would a son. DeMarco surprised Widelsky when he addressed him as "Cheech." For DeMarco that was a term of endearment, and based on Murphy's reaction to the transfer he had expected DeMarco to treat him coldly. Particularly since DeMarco had never been very friendly to him or Cairn.

"Tony," Widelsky sadly said. "I told the kid I got nothing to do with that. I'm not happy about it either. You know?"

"Best thing coulda happened to him," DeMarco replied.

"Why?"

"Hey, he's only thirty, that fucking smartass kid's really bright. Sergeant's test is in November. Way I figure this will give him the motivation he needs to hit the books and ace that thing, and if he tries, he will," DeMarco proudly stated.

"Thirty? I knew he was young, but Christ how long has he been a detective?" Widelsky asked.

"Four years, and all of them with me. He's only got eight years on the job and he didn't take the last sergeant's exam," DeMarco answered.

"Liked detective work, I guess?" Widelsky offered.

"He did, but I'm gone in three months. My wife's driving out to Vegas with my boys in August. We already signed a contract on the house, and my brother-in-law got me lined up for a bartending job in one of the casinos. That's why I'm happy the kid got the boot. He ain't gonna like being a gumshoe, and I know he'll hit the books."

"That's a big move," Widelsky replied.

"What, being a gumshoe?"

"No, Vegas."

"It is, it is."

"How old are your boys?"

"My twins are in high school. But they're twins and they got each other, so they don't mind moving, and the little guy's in grammar school. I probably woulda had kids sooner," he scoffed, "but the fucking war got in the way. I was getting married in forty-two, but I got drafted instead."

"What does your brother-in-law do?" Widelsky asked.

"He's a cop in Vegas, he's got an in with the union, and I don't gotta worry about getting a job. One will be waiting for me. I coulda worked security, but I'm sick of this shit."

"Three months, pretty nice," Widelsky said.

"Me and the old lady, we ain't never lived in a house before. Apartments all our lives, it's gonna be nice," DeMarco said as he walked over to Widelsky's desk and picked up the copy of the *Huguenot Daily News*. "Some shock, huh?" he said pointing to the graphic picture of the accident on the paper's front page.

"Please, I'm tired of thinking about it." Widelsky said with disgust.

"Yeah, I hear you, Cheech, I hear you," DeMarco said as he walked back to his desk with Widelsky's paper under his arm.

Cairn walked into the office, and Slattery and Russo were right behind him.

"Morning, guys," Cairn chirped. "Any word on the funeral arrangements, yet?"

No one answered. "Okay, you're a happy group. I was just asking," he said defensively.

"Funeral's a private affair, family only," said a dour Captain Grimsley as he walked into the squad room. All of the detectives nervously jumped to their feet and directed their attention to the captain. Murphy's unexpected transfer had them rattled, and no one wanted to displease the captain and risk a similar fate.

"Nothing?" Russo asked incredulously.

"Unfortunately, Teddy had only a daughter and it's his wife's family that's arranging things. With all the bad news and speculation that's in the papers and on the television it stands to reason they want to address this as privately as possible," he said without any trace of emotion or feeling. "Widelsky and Cairn, see me in the office," he demanded and then left.

The two detectives looked at one another, then dutifully followed the captain down the hall to Kreppell's office.

Grimsley was sitting in Kreppell's chair. The purple cushion with the gold K embroidered on it was sitting atop a box that Widelsky assumed contained the late sergeant's personal property. It was as if Kreppell never existed, he thought. Everything was the same as it was and had been, except Kreppell was no longer a part of it. Grimsley was temporarily taking Kreppell's place, and in time another boss would be installed to run the unit and Kreppell would be a fading memory, a reference point in conversation, perhaps, but nothing more.

Widelsky and Cairn took their places in the two hard backed wooden chairs facing the supervisor's desk and waited for the captain to address them. Grimsley was busy looking over an empty manila folder that had a long series of notes scribbled on the inside cover. He put the folder down and looked up and smiled. Grimsley didn't smile too often, it was said around the office, and even though the two men had rarely been in his company to know if that was true or not they knew of his reputation and the appearance of the smile put them at ease. Grimsley looked at each man, then fixed his eyes on Widelsky and said, "Well, Frank, how are you holding up?"

"Captain," Widelsky said earnestly, "I'm fine except I didn't like hearing my name on the news last night, got the wife a little crazy."

"Press was calling the chief all afternoon. Mikulik handled it. Identified you and gave them the basics. You and Teddy were off-duty, and based on our investigation you were along for the ride, nothing to worry about," Grimsley said reassuringly. "You're all right?"

"Yeah, I'm fine," said Widelsky nonchalantly.

"Good, let's get down to business," Grimsley said, changing the subject and opening the manila folder. "Teddy had a habit, a good one I might add, of enumerating any problems he had with a case on the inside of the file folder. The only report I've seen so far is yours, Frank," he said as he lifted Frank's typewritten report with his left hand, then dropped it back on the desk.

"I've got most of mine done," Cairn said.

"Fine, that isn't my point," Grimsley corrected, intimating that he didn't care to be interrupted. "Teddy made it a habit as soon as an investigation began to list any questions or thoughts he had inside the case file folder." He opened the manila folder he'd been holding before and pointed to the scrawled notes Kreppell had apparently entered.

"I suspect he asked you boys these questions, and I'm just wondering what the answers are?" Grimsley said.

"Can I get my notebook?" Cairn asked.

"If it will help," the captain replied.

Cairn got up and left the room. Grimsley smiled at Widelsky and said, "I overheard Murphy's outburst before."

Widelsky shrugged his shoulders and replied, "He's pissed at me, story of my life."

"Moved too fast he did, between you and me," Grimsley said, pointing his finger at Widelsky. "Keegan's wife's sister's daughter is married to Murphy. Got the connection?"

"Well, kept secret I guess, but it explains how he got a gold shield in four years. This is a special unit, how'd he get past doing a stint in a precinct squad?" Widelsky asked.

"Keegan's wife's sister's daughter," Grimsley said, laughing.

"I gotcha," Widelsky answered, then asked, "The chief made this move?"

"Sergeant's test is coming up and the chief can't take it for him."

"That's what DeMarco said," Widelsky said, realizing DeMarco was only repeating what he'd probably been told by Murphy.

While Widelsky was talking, Cairn returned.

"Question number one," Grimsley said directing his attention to Cairn. Miss Cruz said that on Friday she boarded a bus in front of her office building and got off at Kingsbridge Road."

"Yes," Cairn answered. "She said the driver was an Irishman, called her sweetheart or darling. Slattery and I tracked him down yesterday. Bernie Mulhroe, been driving the 1 bus for twenty years. It's one of the busiest routes in the borough. He holds the bus for everybody and calls all the girls darling, sweetheart or honey."

"That's nice, but did he remember her from Friday?" Grimsley questioned.

"Yes and no," Cairn replied. "He remembers her running for the bus and thinks it was the morning, but he doesn't remember where she got on or got off."

"Good, now we had a fixed post at the crime scene from Thursday to Friday," Grimsley said as he held the manila folder in one hand and put his finger on a section of the notes Kreppell had written on the inside jacket cover. "Miss Cruz said she was in the building, but heard a noise and that spooked her. She also said that before coming to the building she called the apartment from a phone booth on Kingsbridge Road."

Cairn turned a page in his notebook and answered, "Two problems here, sir. If you use a payphone and call a number and no one answers the phone company can't trace the call. They don't have anything in place to trace local usage from payphones where there's no answer. You put your dime in and if you don't get an answer you get the dime back. Phone company don't care."

"Makes sense," Grimsley remarked.

"Now, about the crime scene post, there's a little hitch," Cairn said with a grimace.

"What's that?" Grimsley said immediately annoyed by Cairn's reference to a "hitch."

"The Weiss' have a neighbor, a Mrs. Zimmerman. Frank made her acquaintance," Cairn said smiling.

"Real headache, major busybody," Widelsky said, with a shake of his head.

"Go on," Grimsley directed Cairn.

"We set the post up in the hallway outside of the Weiss apartment. That was how the sergeant wanted it. Mrs. Zimmerman felt bad for the cop posted there and insisted the cop on the post watch the Weiss' door from her foyer."

"Could you see everything?" Grimsley asked.

"No problem with a line of sight, but there may have been a few distractions, the biggest being Mrs. Zimmerman," Cairn said apologetically.

"I'm getting the picture," Grimsley said.

"She put the officer in a comfortable chair, turned on the radio, made coffee, coffee cake, and talked and talked and talked. The cop on the post Friday morning was a rookie, Desi Clay. I spoke to him yesterday afternoon. He said Friday morning he was sitting in Ms. Zimmerman's foyer and he didn't hear a thing."

Grimsley got red in the face. "Jesus Christ, did you check his memo book?"

"I'm not a boss sir," Cairn said defensively. "Slattery and me came in an

430

hour early yesterday. Russo caught that homicide with the kid pushing his old man down the stairs. We were going to do a canvass of the building in the morning before people went to work. The sergeant was already here and called me in and gave me a checklist of things he wanted done on this Campos case. What you're asking me about is the things Sergeant Kreppell told me to do yesterday. Why would I check his memo book?"

"You're right." Grimsley sighed. "I'll check the book myself just to see if the sergeant in charge of the platoon stopped by the crime scene to check on the officer and sign his book. They call that supervision. Of course, I don't know which delinquency is greater, willfully letting the officer neglect his post, or not checking up on him in the first place."

Widelsky and Cairn sat silently while Grimsley stared at the ceiling for several moments.

"All right," Grimsley continued. "With respect to the crime scene, it is my understanding that there are two entrances to this apartment?"

"Yes sir," Cairn answered. "There is an entrance off the pantry into the kitchen, but that door is locked with a deadbolt from the inside of the apartment."

"Fine, but if the officers assigned to the crime scene post were sitting inside this woman's apartment, albeit the door was open, and they had a clear sight line I can surmise that there was enough noise and interference that the officer might not have heard, or in this case didn't hear the phone ring inside of the Weiss apartment, or anything else for that matter?" he said sharply.

"Yes," Cairn said.

"So we can neither prove nor disprove Miss Cruz's statement that she went to Weiss' building on Friday morning and called him from a phone booth?"

"None of it except the bus driver's vague recollection of her boarding the bus, which is no big deal because we know she was at work that morning and what time she left. Also, that's the bus she takes to and from work every day," Cairn responded.

"We can safely say that this young officer, Clay was his name?"

"Yes, Desi Clay," Cairn answered.

"Desi Clay did not hear a phone ringing in Mr. Weiss' apartment on Friday morning?" Grimsley asked.

"Under the circumstances, no he didn't," Cairn said in agreement.

"Have him file a report and answer those questions. No need to include he was sitting in this woman's apartment having tea and cakes," Grimsley ordered. "I don't want to complicate things, particularly in light of all the press her lawyer got in the papers over the weekend," he added.

"I cut all those articles out, they're in my case file," Cairn said.

"Does he know something we don't?" Grimsley asked.

Widelsky laughed. "Good God, he didn't know shit from shinola last Friday. That girl had him going one way, and when we pulled the rug out from under her that blowhard got all tongue tied. It was beautiful, right Phil?"

"So he's getting even with us?" Grimsley asked skeptically.

"I don't know what he's up to. I think he's throwing as much mud against the wall as he can hoping something will stick," Cairn said.

"To what end?" Grimsley asked.

"Confuse a potential jury? What else? According to Lenihan, we're a bunch of keystone cops who ain't got a clue about anything. Where does he come off with that crap?" Cairn said, with growing agitation.

"Phil," Widelsky interjected, "guy's a lawyer, what do you expect? And the one's who worked in the DA's office once are the worst. You know what happens? When they're on our side we're all pals. They love us. Soon as the old lady starts squawking she wants a house or a summer place, or the kids gotta go to college they turn in their badge and go into private practice. That's this Lenihan. Treats us like piss, and why? Because he don't care about the truth, it don't matter. They lie and lie and lie, all they care about is winning a reputation so they can keep Mr. Green coming in the door. That's why I don't read the papers."

Grimsley cleared his throat and rapped his knuckles on the desk. "Frank, Phil, that's all well and good. Everything you both said, but you sound like two whining schoolgirls. We all understand that Lenihan's role is to protect his client. At least I think we do, don't we?"

Widelsky lowered his head and mumbled, "Yes."

"Good." Grimsley said. "Now, as I was saying, what's his motive and does he have something?"

"I don't think he has anything. He called Weiss an adulterer, but it's his client Weiss was involved with. He said Mrs. Weiss was the murderer because she was involved with pornography. That was crazy. We find a few dirty pictures taken of the woman years ago and she's a murderer? C'mon," Cairn said incredulously.

"Sex sells," Grimsley said knowingly. "Sex catches people's interest, and the newspapers don't let go of the story that easily. What's very tricky here is how he was able to get into the story the relationship between Frank Duffy, Lee Futerman and Henry Weiss? Start to put it all together and the story has legs."

"You mean the deck is stacked against Sophie Cruz?" Widelsky asked.

"He doesn't have to say that," Grimsley said emphatically. "He has several motives. First, he wants to get the story as much play as possible. Ted's accident didn't help. He gets it into the paper and into the headlines, and sex is what sells. You just said it, both of you: adultery, pornography, murder and a relationship, a very strong one at that, between the district attorney's office and the lawyer representing the interests of Henry Weiss. Secondly, all he needs is reasonable doubt. There was a small item in yesterday's *Times* quoting Millie Campos' daughter claiming that Millie didn't like Maria Weiss. She thought she was very haughty. That was the word, haughty. It isn't much, but how much does the defense need to plant a seed of doubt. Remember, it wasn't Sophie Cruz who posed in the nude. It was Maria Weiss. All he needs is a reasonable doubt."

"Maybe," Cairn said. "But what's with the Campos family? You think they'd be happy we got the murderer?"

"Millie Campos didn't like Maria Weiss. Sophie Cruz didn't like Maria Weiss. Get the point, Phil?" Widelsky scolded. "They ain't happy campers. They think their mother was a saint and can't imagine anyone would hurt her. It's all the Weiss' fault. Right, Cap?"

"Very good, Frank," Grimsley said in agreement.

"So what can we do?" Cairn asked.

Grimsley picked up the manila folder, studied it, then said, "Well, we can't control what already happened, and we can't let Mr. Lenihan get under our skin. Whatever he's doing, he's doing to trouble the district attorney at this point and not us. All we can do is properly cover the bases. Now, the Friday morning business is all accounted for. You had no luck with the search warrant?"

Widelsky shook his head and spoke. "No, we went with Russo and Smitty. She has a very nice apartment. It was clean. Her taste in furniture's a little loud. Pink rug in her bedroom and a red bedspread with red velvet lampshades on the lamps and stuffed animals all over the bed. Right Phil?" Widelsky said.

"The linoleum in the kitchen was red and orange and yellow. Oversized flowers, the place was hard on your eyes, but it was spic and span clean," Cairn said with an intonation that a clean apartment wasn't what they expected to find.

Widelsky picked up the conversation where he had left off. "We did a systematic search. Phil and I did a room, then Russo and Smitty did the same room again. We didn't miss anything. There was a photo album in her dresser drawer that had a few snapshots of her and Weiss somewhere, but that was it. We didn't find a thing. If there were more nudes and Mrs. Weiss said there are, they ain't in Sophie Cruz's apartment."

"She had plenty of time to dump them and probably did," Grimsley conceded. "The photos of her and Weiss, did you take them?"

"Yeah, but that was it," Cairn replied.

"Now, Teddy has two other notes here about the delivery boy and the doorman. The delivery boy is Monaghan and the doorman is Cleary?"

"Yes, that's right, Captain," Cairn answered.

"He says here in his notes," and Grimsley showed the notations to the two detectives. "Live at same address, strange coincidence? Monaghan—much ado about nothing. Cleary—little pervert, tried too hard to point the finger. Did we make a mistake?"

"Any ideas?" Grimsley asked as he took the folder back and placed it on the desk.

"We didn't like Monaghan, but the sergeant said we were biased because of the run in with the old man. He coulda been right," Cairn said. "And we felt sorry for the doorman, but the sergeant was convinced he was a pervert. That was the word he used several times. And they do live in the same apartment building on Bailey Avenue, but like the Sarge said, 'strange coincidence.'"

"Is there anything on either of them?"

"Not a thing," Widelsky answered. "I said this last Friday, sometimes we try too hard. It's her, plain and simple."

"Good, good," Grimsley said with some satisfaction. "Get all your reports in by tonight. It's in the district attorney's hands now. We're covered. Good job, boys, good job."

Widelsky and Cairn stood up and left the office. They went down the hall silently, and when they were out of earshot Widelsky stopped and said to Cairn, "Listen to this, Murphy, that little stuck-up shit, he's Keegan's nephew through marriage, phony fucking hotshot. How's that for a rabbi?"

"Pretty good if you ask me," Cairn replied. "Why'd he get transferred?"

"Think about it. The storyline is the chief wants him to study for the sergeant's exam and do well. You know, he won't like his new assignment so he'll work harder. That was DeMarco's line, but I know he's friendly with the chief, they play handball at the Y together. You know what it is?" Widelsky challenged.

"What?" Cairn asked.

"He's setting the kid up for a first grade shield. I know it. Don't you see? First grade makes lieutenant's pay. If you're a first grader and you make sergeant you keep the higher rate of pay. The chief is setting the kid up. He's taking care of his own. Greason promised me he'd make it up to us, and I know this new detail was the real thing. When Keegan told me yesterday it was a dead end and a bullshit assignment I knew, I just knew he was stringing me along."

"You really think so?" Cairn asked suspiciously.

"What are you, a fucking blockhead?" Widelsky said angrily. "What was that Q and A with Grimsley about? More bullshit! He's looking over Kreppell's notes and going over the case with us like we're a real team. I'm Frank, you're Phil, and we're all old pals. Last time he was here he walked right by us as if we didn't exist. Three more years, Phil, three more years until I can retire. I'm wishing my life away."

"C'mon," Cairn protested. "The captain's just following up."

"Widelsky laughed. "Phil, you're too fucking innocent about some things. That was all a game with Grimsley. The only concern he has about this case is that nothing happens to make him look bad. As soon as he found out the cop at the crime scene didn't hear a phone ringing in Weiss' apartment, that was it. He don't give a red rat's ass if Sophie Cruz was telling the truth or not. Don't muck up what we already proved. Simple as that, my friend, simple as that," Widelsky said with self-satisfaction.

"And, so what?" Cairn challenged. "What's your point?"

"My point," Widelsky said mocking Cairn's tone. "My point is that not one of these mother fuckers we work with is on the level. Murphy knew his transfer was coming and he knows there's something in it for him. We got snookered. When DeMarco, a guy who normally don't have the time of day for you or for me starts calling me "Cheech" like we're pals and saying how he wants to see his buddy study and get ahead a light should go off in my head. It's all for show. We lost out and I can live with that, but these guys, these friends of Kreppell's, they act like the guy died twenty years ago instead of twenty hours ago."

"C'mon, you're being too hard. We deal with death all the time. The guys are upset the boss died, they just don't all show it. Shit, Frank," Cairn said, giving him a serious look, "you're about the coldest guy I've met at times, now you're all busted up over a man who didn't even like you?"

"Hold on," Widelsky said. "I'm not busted up, I'm just pissed off. Kreppell was a good cop, he did his job and he wanted his unit to do well. Whether I like this job or not, I feel the same way. It's my way. I'm just saying all these phonies around here only think of themselves. Yesterday, in that diner in Washburn, Grimsley starts out giving me the third degree. He says, 'Don't give me any gratuitous grace notes,' or something like that. What the fuck is a 'gratuitous grace note?'"

"Got me," Cairn replied.

"Me too, but he talks funny a lot of times. Anyway, him and Keegan, they were all but holding their noses when they figured out how crazy Kreppell and his wife were. I told them it was Kreppell crashed the car and not his old lady."

Cairn lowered his eyes and shook his head. "Frank, Kreppell was Grimsley's main man. You're just guessing. Anything coulda happened inside that car."

"Yeah, whatever, but the noise they got from Washburn shook 'em up. All of a sudden, just like that," he said snapping his fingers for emphasis, "Kreppell became a potential embarrassment and they wanted to put as much distance between him and them as possible. And the timing was right, so Keegan used Kreppell's death as an excuse to pull me from that unit. I betcha Greason took your spot and gave it to another one of his guys, and Keegan pulled me at the last moment so he could slip that sneaky little nephew of his in."

"Okay, maybe you're right," Cairn said in agreement. "We can't do nothing about it."

"No, we can't. Like I said, we got snookered."

Cairn didn't initially reply, then as they started toward the squad room, he said, "You think Kreppell had second thoughts about Sophie Cruz, you know, whether she was guilty or not?"

"She's guilty. That's why that asshole Lenihan's feeding the newspapers all that garbage. He's making it sticky for the D.A. I'll buy you dinner if she goes to trial."

"You think they'll give her a plea?"

"I'm sure that's what he's looking for. You think Weiss and his wife want to testify? Weiss knows he'll have to answer all the questions about the mistress and the illegitimate kid. Worse, his wife will have to testify about those pictures of her half naked we found at the murder scene?"

Cairn snickered, "Oh, man, Lenihan could have a field day with those mug shots."

Widelsky extended his chin and scratched his neck. "Phil, she'll take a lesser plea and everyone will be happy."

"We're forgetting the victim's family, Frank. What are they going to say?'

"Victims don't count. You think the D.A. is going to decide how to handle a case based on what the victim's family thinks?"

"I guess so. Let me read the carbons from your report. No use repeating what you wrote," Cairn said, changing the subject.

"I covered everything we did Thursday and Friday. You write up what you did yesterday and we should have it all covered. I gotta hit the john," Widelsky said as he walked up the hallway to the bathroom.

Chapter Fifty-One

The clock on the wall read ten-fifteen. Lenihan tried not to look at it, convinced that if he did so the hands wouldn't move at all. Time spent waiting was time wasted, and when he had to wait for someone he didn't have the discipline to do anything else. He couldn't enjoy the newspaper or catch up on some reading for a case, or even for pleasure. He hated jails and detention centers. They were the worst. The employees were no different than the inmates in his estimation; they were all doing time one-way or the other, and since time was the only commodity to be spent it was spent freely.

Lenihan had arrived at nine-thirty. Normally, he never waited more than fifteen or twenty minutes to see a client, but today there was a delay and he nervously bided his time while the knot of anxiety that tied up his insides grew tighter with each passing minute. He'd briefly scanned the articles about Kreppell's death and thought through the dead man's involvement in the investigation. He concluded that Kreppell's death provided no advantage for his client and. while unfortunate. was of little concern to him other than as an item of curiosity falling into the category of, "Goodness I was with him only Friday and to think?"

The waiting room was drab and friendless. The walls were made of pea-colored concrete blocks and the height from the cement floor to the unpainted cement ceiling was at least sixteen feet, and the room resembled an oversized bunker. Six rows of metal folding chairs faced a desk where a dull looking uniformed jailor sat staring at a copy of the Reader's Digest. Lenihan wondered if the man could read because in the forty-five minutes he'd been sitting there he didn't believe the man had turned a page in the magazine. The desktop was home to a large logbook and a black telephone. Those two items, the magazine and the jailor's elbows formed a still life picture for Lenihan of how despairing an environment jails and courtrooms were. No one looks attractive in a jailhouse waiting room, he thought; same thing for the hallways outside the criminal parts of a courthouse. His eyes went back to the clock, then to the telephone on the desk. When will it ring and will it be for me? he wondered. There were seven other people waiting with him in the room, and four of them were already there when he arrived. He believed he was the only attorney and hoped that he would be given the courtesy of going to the head of the line. Sometimes the courtesy was extended and sometimes it wasn't.

The jailor looked to be in his early forties, but he carried himself with defeat. Lenihan's father would have described the man as a "gin face." It was a term offered without condescension or contempt, a neater way of calling someone a drunk. Lenihan thought he read people well. Many drunks got up every morning and went to work. Life for them was a struggle measured out between drinks. "When is it time for the next drink?" That was how an alcoholic functioned. The jailor had all the characteristics: the wandering vacant stare, no visible musculature and a slight trembling of the hands, poor hygiene and unkempt clothing, all telltales that progressed with the severity of the condition. The jailor looked up from his desk and fixed his eyes for a moment on Lenihan, almost as if he intuitively knew he was under examination. He picked up the *Reader's Digest* and opened a drawer in his desk and put it away. He took out a folded newspaper and a thermos, and poured himself a drink. Lenihan suspected it was a thermos of coffee laced with whiskey. Suddenly, as if on cue to break the monotony, the black phone on the jailor's desk rang. He reached for the phone with one hand and with the other he pulled a sheet of paper from underneath the large binder and picked up a pen. He offered no greeting and after several seconds he then uttered a quiet, "Fine," and hung up the phone. He paused and looked at the sheet of paper for a moment, then carefully wrote something on it. When he was finished writing, he looked at the sheet of paper for another moment, then, appearing satisfied with his work, he lifted his head and looked out at the seven people sitting in the room, and without a trace of a smile, a frown or any animation at all said, "Mr. Robert Cardullo."

"That's me," said a casually dressed older man seated two chairs away from Lenihan. The man quickly walked to the jailor's desk and the jailor pointed to the door to his left, "Wait there."

The jailor then looked at his sheet of paper again and said, "Mr. Patrick Lenihan."

Lenihan promptly stood up, but before he could say anything the jailor pointed to Cardullo and said, "Follow him."

Lenihan had been through this drill many times. Not more than a minute passed when the door opened and a female jailor greeted them. "Good morning, gentleman. Sorry for the delay, but we had a little cat fight up in ward three this morning while the ladies were going to breakfast. We got us some very testy ladies in this place, and for my money we oughta go back to feeding them in the cells like we used to when Johnny Mac was running the jails," she said cheerfully.

"Johnny Mac," Lenihan said wistfully. "We should bring back the trolleys too."

She raised her eyebrows, uncertain over how to interpret Lenihan's remark. She didn't know if it was a wisecrack about her age, or just an innocuous response and, not wanting to reveal her perplexity, she simply replied, "Follow me."

Two long hallways and an elevator ride brought them to the visitor's room. They stopped at a security desk and Lenihan had to open his briefcase and allow a jailor to inspect it. The inspection was perfunctory. After the inspection he was told to take a seat at table six. He followed the instructions and moments later a red light flashed on over the steel door that separated the visitor's room from the secured area of the detention center. One of the two male jailors who were stationed in the visitor's room went over to a heavily barred security door and inserted an oversized key into a brass-plated keyhole in the wall next to the door. A bell rang and the door slowly opened. A dark-skinned and chunky female jailor escorted Sophie Cruz into the visitor's room and handed her over to the male jailor.

Lenihan hadn't seen her since her arraignment in court that past Friday and was shocked by the change in her appearance. She was wearing a baggy pair of blue dungarees and an even baggier white sweatshirt. Four days in jail had cost her five pounds she couldn't afford to lose and left her looking malnourished and weak. Her hair was pulled back into a tight ponytail and held in place by a thick rubber band. She was wearing no makeup, her face was gaunt and her eyes looked like two sunken black holes. She was ugly and pathetic looking. Her attractiveness was largely contrived, Lenihan realized. Blush, eye shadow, lipstick, hair falling over her cheeks, tight skirts and pants, high heels, sheer blouses or clinging sweaters and a practiced sway when she

440

walked were what comprised Sophie's attractiveness. *What did Weiss see in her?* Lenihan thought. *What had he seen?*

Lenihan was already seated at table six. Sophie was placed at the opposite end of the table. The table was five feet long and a wooden divider eight inches high ran across the middle of the table and separated them. Sophie sat down and glared at Lenihan. Neither of them spoke, and it was an awkward moment. "Do you have a cigarette?" Sophie asked.

"Sure," Lenihan replied as he took out a pack of Marlboro's he had specifically bought for her and peeled off the cellophane wrapping and extracted a cigarette from the box and lit it. He looked to the jailor seated several feet behind Sophie and asked, "May I?"

The jailor nodded his head and Lenihan reached over the divider and handed Sophie the lit cigarette. She smoked the cigarette and continued glaring at him. Finally, after she'd drawn the burning tobacco down to the filter and dropped it into the metal ashtray that was fastened to the table, she remarked, "Long time no see."

Lenihan smiled and said, "A matter of opinion."

Sophie didn't argue the point. "Can I have another cigarette, please?" she said politely.

Lenihan repeated the ritual of lighting the cigarette and obtaining the jailor's approval. Sophie smoked in silence again and Lenihan watched her. The tension between them was unsettling, and he thought it odd that he had only known Sophie for four days and this was only the third time he'd been in her company, yet he felt an intimacy that went well beyond the extent of their acquaintance. He couldn't put his finger on it, but there was something childish and innocent about Sophie Cruz that appealed to him, appealed to his better nature, his urge to protect the weak and the powerless. He didn't know her very well, and he was certain she was guilty, but he didn't think she was evil, mean, or possessed any other miserable qualities that were so common with the criminal classes. She was a poor slob and he wanted to help her, it was as simple as that.

When she was finished smoking, she cleared her throat and said, "Am I getting out today?"

"Yes, we have a hearing at 2:30, but it's just a formality. The DA asked for no bail, but under the circumstances that's entirely unreasonable. Your brother and cousin will be there with the bail bondsman. The judge should set it at $25,000. That's twenty-five hundred cash to you, a sizeable sum for most folks."

"I know," she said quickly, then asked tentatively. "Ray's putting up the cash?"

"His house," Lenihan answered. "You'll have to work out the details with him later."

"Isn't that big of him, the little bastard," she sneered.

Lenihan smirked, then made an apologetic facial gesture by drawing back his chin, and said with a soft laugh, "You stole my line. I had the pleasure of meeting with him and your cousin yesterday. A fine way to start the week," he said sarcastically. "He questioned my competence and implied that I was out to make a quick buck and didn't give a damn about you. I didn't take too much offense, you know? Family members can get a little crazy when things like what happened to you happen. Nonetheless, he didn't balk about making the bail arrangements. Why are you mad at him?"

"He showed up yesterday. First thing he does is call me a "fucking whore. And he spit at me and said 'puta, puta'," she said scornfully. "Now he wants to make my bail. Fuck him, puta, I'm a fucking puta?"

Lenihan shrugged his shoulders. "Yeah, he was hot, but he'll calm down. There was a lot in the papers over the weekend, and I guess it got to him."

"He was away until late Sunday, what papers did he see? I'm the one in jail. I'm the one who got arrested for murder, something I didn't do," she said as she pulled her head back and coughed. "I'm getting a cold in this Goddamn place. One of the girls I got friendly with, Vicky, I think she's Irish, well, she has red hair, you know. She says this place is a fucking trashcan and they got to keep it filled and we're the trash they fill it with. Now I'm a piece of trash and my brother, someone I always looked after and helped, he calls me a 'puta', what a bastard."

Sophie was angry, and Lenihan was surprised by her venomous tone. Her eyes were dry and there were no tears. It was a far cry from Friday when it seemed she was in a constant state of histrionics. She was angry, and there was something hard about her manner that he hadn't seen before. *Maybe she's not so innocent*, he thought, questioning his prior feelings about her. Lenihan rolled his eyes and let out a low whistle. "You feel better, got it off your chest?" he asked sympathetically.

"No," she snapped, "I don't feel better. This girl Vicky, she's in for forging checks. I know her type, always out for a good time, knows all the angles. She got comfortable collecting welfare and doing a little check forgery, shoplifting. Anyway, she's been around, and I told her my story and she didn't buy it. Nobody believes me, and now I'm doubting it too."

"Listen," Lenihan said sternly, "you don't make friends here. You can't trust anyone in here. Not the inmates and not the jailors. Don't tell your story to anyone. Understand?"

"Why, we were just talking?" she said defensively, wondering to herself if he knew what he was talking about or was just a big bullshit artist?

"Trust me, I don't have a lot of time, I have a conference on another matter at 11:30. I wanted to prep you for the hearing, but you sound all right. I didn't want you in court crying and protesting. It's important to establish your behavior as we go through this. Quiet and dignified is what I want the prosecutors to see every time they're in your company," Lenihan said instructively.

"I can do that, but what's going to happen?"

"You're going to be free on bail this afternoon. You get out, go home, and see your son, clean your house and we plan for the next step. Nice and easy does it," he said reassuringly.

"Then what?"

Lenihan looked at his watch and made a sour expression. "It all depends."

"My aunt came yesterday. She couldn't get a sitter for Joey on Saturday, and she was only allowed to drop off some clothes for me, and there's no visitors allowed on Sunday. After I left you Friday night I didn't see anyone I knew until yesterday," she said sadly.

"Sophie," Lenihan said firmly, "I'm not your friend, and I'm not family. I'm your attorney. I don't make social visits."

Sophie laughed. "I wasn't talking about you. I meant my family. It was a long weekend, you know? Me and my jailhouse girlfriends."

Lenihan's face softened, and he took a small breath and moved his head back and forth several times, not making eye contact with her, and said, "Hey, I know it's not easy, but you have to face reality. You're in a tough spot and it doesn't look good."

"I'm all confused," she said nervously. "You say it's tough, my aunt tells me there's all this shit in the papers about Maria and nude pictures and I'm thinking maybe there's something to this, you know, maybe Maria did it, and then my aunt tells me the cops were in my apartment looking for these pictures and I'm thinking where the hell is Lenihan."

"It is confusing," Lenihan said calmly.

"So what the hell do you know?" Sophie screeched with agitation. "You're acting like we lost the case."

"We didn't lose anything, yet, but there isn't much good news. There were some pictures of Maria Weiss at the murder scene. Eight by tens of her half nude, taken, I bet, thirty years ago. I didn't know about the pictures until I learned about the search warrant for them. The DA's office is giving up some information because they think this is a slam-dunk."

"Do you have something on Maria?" Sophie said hopefully.

Lenihan looked at his watch again and said, "Quickly, listen. I was here early, but there was a delay and I haven't much time, but when I found out the cops were executing a search warrant on your apartment and they were looking for photographs, nude photographs mind you, of Maria Weiss that were stolen from her apartment, that was an opportunity to get some unflattering information about the Weiss' into the public domain."

Sophie grew excited and clapped her hands together, "Maybe she caught Millie going through her things and killed her, then blamed me. Maybe Millie was blackmailing her. That makes more sense than me killing Millie. Doesn't it?"

"No, it doesn't," Lenihan, said somberly.

"Why not?" Sophie responded angrily.

"Because none of it ties in to her having the aneurysm. More so, she just found out her husband is the father of a seven-year-old and has been having an affair with his secretary for what, ten years? I think in that scenario he's the likely candidate for blackmail."

"Maybe she killed her before she found that out."

"No good, we have the doorman who saw Millie after Mrs. Weiss left the building."

Sophie sighed and her face lost what little color it had. "Then what was this stuff you got into the paper?"

"Noise, interference, intrigue and anything else that will keep this in the public eye and make it more than it is," Lenihan said smugly.

Sophie quietly replied, "What's that gonna do for me?"

Lenihan stood up and gripped his briefcase with both hands. He took out the pack of Marlboros from his pocket and called out to the guard. "Can you check these for her? I'm going to leave them."

The guard didn't move from his high stool, but called back, "I saw you open them, you can give them to her."

Lenihan tossed the cigarettes across the divider. Sophie caught the pack, pursed her lips, then said, "You didn't answer my question. What's all that shit about Maria gonna do for me?"

Lenihan looked at his watch again, then sighed. He laid the briefcase back on the table and sat down. "John Malfetano is going to be appointed a federal judge in three weeks, did you know that?"

"Malfetano, who? The DA?" Sophie replied indifferently.

"Yes, our district attorney. And that's important. Do you know why?"

"No," she said tiredly, "but I'm sure you do."

"Listen, because I don't have time to repeat myself or play fifty questions. Frank Duffy is Malfetano's heir apparent, the next in line. Now, Duffy's been a loyal soldier and he's a good prosecutor and administrator, that I know, but he's no John Malfetano, which is to say he's no politician. Duffy has all the appeal of lukewarm glass of beer. The governor will appoint Duffy to finish out Malfetano's term, which is up this year, and that means Duffy will have to run for office. The Republican Party and Liberal Party will join forces and nominate Stephen Brooks and Duffy will have the fight of his life. Duffy's a Democrat and needs the minority vote to win. That means the colored vote and the growing Puerto Rican vote. It's summer, and even though he wants to put your case into the grand jury next week, or the week after, he won't get a trial date until late September or early October, and I can prevent him from scheduling it for after the election. Now, and this is where it gets interesting," Lenihan said as he stood up again and leaned toward the divider and fixed his eyes intently on Sophie's eyes." Duffy doesn't want to alienate the people he expects to automatically vote for him. Weiss and Mrs. Weiss are white, upper middle class people. They live on Lincoln Boulevard in a ritzy apartment. They have a woman come in and clean their house and wash their dirty clothes. Colored women and Puerto Rican women do work like that; clean the shit out of other people's toilet bowls and pick up after their messes. Better yet, Mr. Weiss is involved in a love triangle with his wife and secretary and has a bastard son to boot," Lenihan said spiritedly.

Sophie winced at the reference to "bastard son," but said nothing and kept her attention focused on Lenihan's every word.

"What's the point?" he said with exaggeration. "Poor Sophie Cruz is a misguided girl, a minority, a poor Puerto Rican girl trying to improve her life, a life waylaid by the conniving machinations of her lecherous boss. And who is that boss? A well-heeled, well-connected attorney with a wife who poses nude and a close friend and associate named Lee Futerman, who is also a close friend and associate of Frank Duffy the democratic candidate for district attorney. And that's the point which I'm sure the newspapers will work to death. Sex and lies always sell," Lenihan said confidently.

"How does that prove my innocence?" Sophie said with annoyance and not at all appreciative of his describing her as "poor and misguided."

"With what we know, I can't prove your innocence. Maybe after the grand jury something will come out, but I'm going in another direction with this. We'll talk about it," Lenihan said less confidently.

"Talk, talk, talk, that's all you do is fucking talk," Sophie practically snarled. "How does that prove my innocence?" she pleaded.

Lenihan leaned his elbows on the table and folded his hands as if he were about to pray. He dug the tips of his thumbs into his forehead and the expression on his face bordered on contempt. "Maybe I talk, talk, talk in the vain hope that you'll listen to me."

"I'm listening," she said with dejection.

Lenihan's expression grew brighter, and he said, "What you need to understand is that if we turn up the heat and make it politically uncomfortable for Duffy to bring you to trial for murder he might be willing to make a deal. Millie Campos' family has stated in the papers that they believe their mother's death is some sort of freak accident. They're not looking for the proverbial pound of flesh, and the last thing Henry Weiss wants is to have his personal life played out in the newspapers. I'm sure his wife feels the same way. Duffy has a long road to hoe, as they say, and he'll need every vote. Stevie Brook's a great lawyer and has a lot of charisma. That's what Malfetano had and that's what made Heaton great. Duffy ain't got it, and that's why I'm certain he'd be willing to let this case sit through the summer, sit quietly and then after Labor Day take a plea for a lesser count. Three or four years and you're free. Maybe you could even get some time off for good behavior; now we're talking two and a half years. What's two and a half years when you're facing twenty-five to life?"

Sophie was rocked by Lenihan's plan. She gasped for breath and weakly stated, "But I'm innocent."

Lenihan didn't answer her at first. He stretched his long arms out and let out a loud yawn. She didn't know if he was feigning indifference, or just being rude, but his admission that they should be planning to strike a deal had turned a bad dream into a screaming nightmare. They sat there staring at one another, then Lenihan stood up and picked up his briefcase. He was confused. Was she tough? Was she soft? Was she a murderer? He didn't know and it didn't matter. A plea for a lesser crime and fewer years in jail was the best she could hope for. Sophie sat still in her chair waiting for him to answer her. Finally, before he turned to leave, he said, "It's not a matter of guilt or innocence at this point. Give it some thought. I'll see you this afternoon. Remember, quiet and dignified. Don't speak until spoken to, and when you're addressed keep your answers specific and to the question. Chances are you won't be asked to say much more than state your name. Remain calm and composed."

"Calm and composed, you can count on me," she replied without emotion.

He was walking away when suddenly he spun around and walked back to the table. "Christ, one other thing I forgot to tell you," he said as he gently tapped himself on the head.

Sophie ignored him.

"It might help, but it is a little disturbing," he said cheerfully as he sat back down in the chair, acting as if he'd just arrived and had nowhere to go. "You remember Sergeant Kreppell, the detective boss?"

Sophie perked up at the mention of Kreppell's name, shifted sideways in her chair and lifted her legs and shook her feet. "See those, the sneakers I'm wearing?"

"Yeah," Lenihan replied, surprised once more at the mercurial shifts in her demeanor.

"Didn't you notice I was wearing them in court when I was arraigned on Friday night?"

"No, I didn't."

"Well, when that fat head detective was arresting me he scared me and I started to run and my high heel broke and I fell down," she said angrily.

"Right, right," Lenihan said in agreement. "I was looking from my window."

"You bastard," she blurted out. "You saw that and didn't do anything?"

"Hey, it was over in seconds. I called the precinct and got the particulars. I was at the arraignment, wasn't I?"

Sophie shook her head with disgust. "You're something. Some fucking lawyer you are. That sergeant sent one of his men out and bought me a pair of sneakers because he felt sorry for me when he saw me hopping around on one leg. And they're Keds, not Skippy's," she said impressively, suspecting Lenihan didn't know Skippy's from Skippy peanut butter. "He also sent me to the emergency room to have the cut on my leg cleaned and bandaged. He was nice to me, all things considered. So what about him?"

"I thought he was a prick," Lenihan crankily replied. "But, unfortunately, none of that matters. He was killed in a car crash up in Washburn yesterday. He was in a car with his wife and they crashed into a police car speeding to a call in the opposite direction," Lenihan said dryly as he stood up and picked up his briefcase.

Sophie gasped and started to cry, "Oh, the poor man. Jesus, he was a nice guy. I feel bad."

Lenihan adjusted his wristwatch and stared at it intently. "It's a little past eleven. I have to go. They think it might have been a murder suicide. Seems the sergeant and his wife had some difficulties. Nice to know you can shed a tear for the guy who was so eager to put you behind bars. The cops already did their damage, and I don't think his being out of the picture will help you any," he stated coldly.

"I don't care about the cops. Maria Weiss put me behind bars." She sniffled. "I feel bad about that man, that's all. He was nice to me. He didn't treat me like shit. There's nothing wrong with that, is there?" she hissed.

"Whatever," Lenihan said as he hurriedly walked away, intent on getting to his next appointment.

Sophie waited for the jailor to come over and escort her back to her cellblock. She was now crying freely and asked him to give her a moment to compose herself. She didn't want the other women in her section to see her crying. The jailor was considerate and asked her if she wanted to sit and have another cigarette. She thanked him, he lit her cigarette, and she leaned against the table and tried to process everything that Lenihan had told her. She couldn't believe that he was suggesting that she was guilty and they should try to work a deal. Nor could she believe how callous he acted about Sergeant Kreppell's death. The news shocked her, but he delivered it as an afterthought. It wasn't going to help her, so in Lenihan's opinion it had no relevance, period. *That's the kind of man he is*, she sadly lamented. *He's my lawyer and pretends to have a heart, but he's a cold bastard. I'm nothing more than a paycheck*, she thought bitterly. Four days in lockup and the universal sentiment from every girl she'd talked to was that the first thing a lawyer wants to find out when he meets a client is where Mr. Green's coming from. Sophie made the mistake of telling Lenihan she had seven thousand dollars in the bank. That took care of Mr. Green. Lenihan wouldn't get all of it, but he'd collect a nice fee for saving her from a life sentence for murder. It was simple and direct, and she knew he was right. All Maria had to testify to was the encounter with Sophie at the subway station, then her claim that when she returned home she found her housekeeper dead and was attacked by Sophie and collapsed into a coma. The fingerprints in the elevator, her affair with Henry and the child it produced would provide a jury with all the evidence they needed to put her away forever. She dropped her cigarette into the ashtray and signaled to the jailor that she was finished. There were no more tears left. *I'm too emotional*, she told herself.

"Your lawyer got you a little upset, miss?" the jailor said as he walked her to the security door.

Sophie wiped a few lingering tears from her face and said, "He's all right. Thanks for letting me have the extra smoke."

He placed the brass key in the keyhole, a light when on and the distinct whirring sound of a hydraulic motor slowly turning increased as the heavy metal door slid open. A female jailor was waiting on the other side of the door. She took custody of Sophie, searched her, then led her down the corridor back to her cellblock.

Chapter Fifty-Two

The plan was to meet at the Oyster House for lunch at noon. It was Maria's first week back at work and six weeks since Millie's murder. Boyce Fortescue had suggested meeting for lunch rather than meeting in his office. He had assured Maria that everything was moving smoothly, there were only a few minor issues to discuss and he thought that lunch in the Club Room at the Oyster House would be a better venue than his office was to conduct business. Henry had acquiesced to Maria's demand that he recognize his son and win custody of him if Sophie went to jail, and partial custody if she didn't. It was that or risk losing Maria, and he gave in to her without a fight. Maria thought Fortescue was charming and Henry had the distinct feeling that Fortescue felt the same way about her. When the meeting was first proposed Henry told Maria he had a conflict and her response was that Boyce didn't think it was necessary for both of them to be present. Maria agreed with Boyce and the discussion was over. Henry tolerated Fortescue, and while he was told that his work was first rate he found his personality irritably pretentious.

The Oyster house was an old Huguenot City landmark. It was two blocks from City Hall and had been in business for over fifty years. The main dining room was a cavernous hall bustling with activity. At lunch and dinner the room was usually packed and the combination of shouting waiters, clattering trays and the heavy scent of frying fish and tangy seafood stews gave the room a hearty ambience that stimulated the weakest appetites and challenged the strongest. The Club Room at the Oyster House was added on in 1960. It was

450

a concession to fine dining and good manners, and everything the Oyster House wasn't. The room was well appointed in soft pastels with a marble floor, green plants in gleaming brass buckets, small tables covered in white linen, upholstered chairs and leather bound menus. By contrast, the dining room for the Oyster house was rustic, with rough wooden floors strewn in a quarter inch of saw dust and hard lacquered tables with paper menus that doubled as placemats. You went to the Oyster House to eat, and you went to the Club Room to dine.

Henry was fifteen minutes late, but he wasn't hurrying. The lobby was crowded with diners waiting for a table in the big dining room. Henry would have been glad to wait, but it was the wrong room. He turned left and went up the steps to the Club Room. Two large French doors with leaded lites of glass opened up into a small reception room with a bar and a piano tucked into the corner. A young woman in a long shapeless black gown was playing the piano. Her playing was mechanical. A thick music book was propped up on the piano and the pianist was bent over the keyboard studying the book as she played. Henry suspected she was a music student from the nearby Academy of Arts and Music, and her familiarity with the subject matter she was playing was quite recent. There was no emotion to the music, no rhythm or feeling, and Henry, who had an encyclopedic knowledge of American popular music and could normally name a song after hearing two notes, had to listen carefully to the woman's performance as he attempted to identify the song. She stopped playing momentarily and turned a page in the book and a new melody was in the air. He tried not to listen to the song she was playing and replayed over in his mind the few notes of the previous melody. He was standing still surveying the room. He wasn't impressed with the Club Room. It tried too hard to be sophisticated and, like the piano player, was soulless. He saw Maria and Fortescue. Fortescue was talking and Maria appeared to be listening intently. They didn't see Henry and he turned and went down the hallway to the bathroom.

He was standing in front of the mirror combing his hair and it came to him that the song he had heard when he first came into the bar was "That Old Feeling." He repeated the opening line to the song to himself and his thoughts turned to Sophie. It was only six weeks since he had last seen her, but it seemed like six years. He had already gone through three office temporaries and finally hired a secretary two weeks ago, but he was on the verge of firing her too. The new woman was competent when given direction and Henry found himself each evening writing out a list of what had to be done the following day and leaving it on her desk so that when she arrived at work in the morning she would have a head start in organizing her work. He didn't know if she was a slow learner, or if her push me I'm coming attitude was a personality flaw beyond correction.

He missed Sophie. Moreover, he missed the sex, and in that regard, although things had improved with Maria, it wasn't the same as with Sophie. What he had craved for so long had finally arrived and now he was disappointed. The second honeymoon began two weeks ago, and with each encounter he found their lovemaking wanting. In the past Maria had been very passive up until the point he had excited her sufficiently to garner a pleasurable response. Now she wanted to be massaged and caressed, and she wasn't shy about giving him instructions on what to do. This was foreign to him, and it made sex more of a chore then a treat. Sex with Sophie was fast and fun, and at times totally unexpected. Sophie never said, "No, be careful," or "That hurts don't be so rough," or "You have a hangnail, go trim it right now." Between them nothing ever interrupted the act, no directions were given, nor complaints registered. They simply did it, and now that she was gone he realized what an integral part of his life Sophie had been.

Henry straightened his tie and washed his hands. Satisfied with his appearance, he left the bathroom and headed for his table. *Things will never be the same*, he thought. *Never.*

They didn't see him approaching. Fortescue and Maria were busy eating their salads.

"Hello, enjoying the food, I see," Henry, said cheerfully as he pulled out a chair and sat down.

Fortescue immediately stood up and said, "Henry, a pleasure. Don't be offended we started without you, but Maria insisted."

Henry laughed and reached over and patted his wife's hand. "No, I did. I knew I'd probably be late."

"We ordered already, dear," Maria said, smiling.

Henry saw that Fortescue and Maria were each drinking mineral water with a twist of lemon in it. There was a half filled bottle of imported water on the table. He didn't see any wine glasses and asked, "Did you order wine?"

Fortescue lifted his water glass and said, "I don't drink. I find alcohol neither uplifting nor refining. Of course, that's my opinion."

Fortescue spoke with an air of superiority and the confidence of a man who enjoyed candor and didn't at all mind being rude or offensive, and if his intent was to insult Henry, it had its effect. Henry curtly replied, "I didn't ask for your opinion. I asked if you had ordered wine?"

Fortescue was about to answer when the waiter leaned slightly between the two of them and handed a menu to Henry. "Would you care for something from the bar, sir?" he asked politely.

Maria started laughing, then Fortescue started to laugh and said smugly, "How apropos."

Henry looked at them and laughed too. The irony posed by the waiter's question was obvious and the timing was such that whatever tension had occurred between Henry and Fortescue quickly dissipated. The waiter ignored their laughter and waited patiently for Henry's reply. Maria put her hand on Henry's shoulder and said to the waiter, "My husband would love a scotch and water in a tall glass with plenty of ice."

It was exactly what he wanted her to do. He marveled at how easily she could read his mood and take over a moment. The slight accent in her voice, the soothing and lighthearted way she addressed the waiter and indirectly Fortescue's intimation that drinking alcohol was unacceptable momentarily put him at ease. She had been the first to laugh, and that was all that was needed to erase what was an awkward and potentially unfriendly exchange. He smiled at Maria, and she in turn winked at him. Henry lowered his eyes to his menu and opened it. Maria moved a piece of lettuce on her plate and said to Fortescue, "You were so right about the house dressing. It's delicious."

That started Fortescue off on a monologue about salad dressings. Henry ignored him and kept his eyes on the menu. He imagined Sophie in the same situation. She would have instantly taken offense to Fortescue's opinion and an argument would have followed and the lunch ruined. Maria was so much smoother, so much more sophisticated. There was no contretemps, no uneasiness. Fortescue's opinion was insignificant, and she dismissed it without hesitation, then engaged him in conversation on another subject as if nothing had happened at all. He lowered the menu and stole a peek at Maria. She was leaning forward, just slightly, with her full attention on Fortescue as he enthusiastically recited the merits of using olive oil instead of vegetable oil when mixing an Italian dressing. The table wasn't very wide, and Maria was sitting opposite Fortescue. Her chair was pulled up close to the table and Henry noticed the draped edge of the tablecloth by her lap shift and it appeared that she was extending her right leg out to stretch it. Henry suspected her foot was brushing the calf of Fortescue's leg. Henry was sure that to Fortescue it appeared casually accidental and not intentional. Maria didn't flirt, that was something Sophie would do. It was calculated innocence and he'd seen her do it to Futerman a dozen times. The toe of her shoe would nestle his pants leg or if they were sitting side by side she might lay her leg up against his. It was never more than a long moment, but always long enough to create that fleeting second of tension and physical contact. Henry knew, of course, that it was just Maria playacting. Henry had met few women in his life that could compete with Maria in attracting a man's attention and holding it for as long as she wanted. She had Fortescue's attention now and she enjoyed it.

Fortescue was Henry's age, but he had a reputation for dating much younger women. Maria was past that mark, but Fortescue didn't seem to notice. He completely ignored Henry and his eyes never deviated from Maria's direction. Henry looked at Maria and wondered to himself what it was she possessed that so deeply attracted men? She was aging and the natural effects of time were undeniable. He had first noticed it in the hospital. Finely etched lines around her eyes were visible and it appeared that for every strand of honey blonde hair there were two strands of gray. The gray was gone now, rinsed out in the beauty parlor, but the wrinkles, though faint, were there and would only grow deeper with time. The effects of the aneurysm were minimal. The eyesight in her right eye was weakened and the facial muscles around the right eye were frozen, but Maria had said that wasn't so bad since it would reduce wrinkling. Other than that she was the same. Maria was, he reflected, much more than a physical attraction. What had not changed with age was her charm, or, more precisely, her ability to be charming when it served her purposes. It was a gift more than a developed art and her subtle exercise of grace and deliberate insouciance however insincere was captivating. He wasn't listening to their conversation. It was innocuous and silly, and at that moment he felt himself sinking into despair. His mood suddenly changed and he didn't know why. Maria had fooled him. She fooled everyone, and he asked himself, *What's her motive? Why would she want to be the mother to my son? Why does she suddenly care for me after so many years of neglect?* These were serious questions. Important questions, and as the thoughts raced through his mind he felt the urge to slam the table with his fists and demand an answer. He wanted to interrupt her and Fortescue and commence an interrogation, and it was for Sophie, for Sophie's sake, that he wanted to do it. For six weeks he had felt nothing but shame and guilt. Maria had carefully manipulated him into accepting the premise that it would be the honorable thing to fight for Joey. *Why?* he asked himself. *It was Sophie he should be fighting for. It was Sophie who had kept his empty marriage alive for ten years, it was Sophie who had nurtured him and loved him in spite of his own selfishness.* But he was emotionally bankrupt and too much a coward to speak out. He was responsible for Millie's murder. He had manipulated Sophie, used her, and finally driven her to murder. He didn't believe she had done anything deliberately, but the facts were evident, and his punishment, his sentence, was to go along with his wife, a woman he only moments ago realized he could live without, and become a family to the child he had so willfully denied. He was checkmated.

Henry laid down his menu and motioned to the waiter who was standing silently only a few feet from their table. The waiter approached and leaned forward deferentially toward Henry and took out his order pad, "Sir, you are ready?"

"Yes," Henry replied. "I'll have the crab cakes and the pan seared potatoes"

The waiter made a quick note on his pad, then asked, "Perhaps you would enjoy an appetizer, salad?"

"No, what I ordered will be fine and another drink, too."

"Scotch and water, tall glass, plenty of ice, right away sir, right away."

"You know what?" Henry said decisively to the waiter. "Just bring me the drink and forget the crab cakes. When you bring their meal, bring along some of those pumpernickel rolls and a little butter."

"Henry," Maria said with embarrassment, "you're not eating."

"No, I'm not really hungry. The rolls will do fine," he answered without emotion.

Fortescue gave Maria a sly grin, then said, "I guess we should get down to business, shouldn't we?"

"That's why we're here," Henry said cheerfully as he lifted his drink glass to Fortescue and Maria.

"And just where are we?" Maria asked seriously.

"Where we want to be, not the winner's circle yet, but everything's on schedule," Fortescue answered.

Henry made a sour face, put his drink down, and said, "Winner's circle, this is a contest?"

Fortescue sat upright in his chair and looked at Henry coldly. "Henry," he said as he straightened the lapels on his suit jacket. "You retained me. My objective is to address the client's concerns and achieve a favorable outcome. I view favorable outcomes on the same par with winning. Perhaps my use of the term "winner's circle" was a touch cheeky, but my intent is to serve your purpose. The last thing I wish is to offend anyone."

"Henry," Maria scolded, "you owe Boyce an apology."

"Not at all," Fortescue said, interrupting Maria. He raised his hands and rubbed his palms together. The sleeves of his well-tailored suit folded, exposing hard white starched French cuffs held together with gold nugget cuff links. He was male model handsome, and every detail of his wardrobe, like his demeanor, expressed confidence. "Maria," he said warmly as he turned his attention to Henry, "no need for an apology. This is a subject that invites discord. Marital Law and Domestic Relations is what I practice. Has a benevolent ring to it, don't you think?" He didn't wait for an answer, but went on. "A euphemism of sorts for what is as close to a blood sport as I can think of. Theoretically, the law should aid people in settling their differences, apportioning wealth and fixing responsibility for paternity and child-care and maintenance. That and nothing more, and it should be that easy," he said, laughing.

Maria raised her eyebrows and remarked, "Is anything to do with the law easy?" She saw that Henry was upset, and she didn't know what to do. She couldn't change the subject, and it was obvious that Henry had challenged Fortescue, and he wasn't a man who let a challenge pass. He had taken the case as a favor, and she didn't imagine, despite his excessive politeness at the moment, that he would tolerate much more of Henry's rudeness. She wished she hadn't scolded Henry, and she knew it would only make matters worse. Henry was brooding, and although she didn't find anything offensive in what Fortescue had said, she could see by the expression on Henry's face that he was spoiling for an argument. She wasn't surprised and had half expected him to revolt at some point in time. There was nothing she could do and she decided to stay quiet.

Henry sat stone-faced, holding his empty drink glass, staring at Fortescue with obvious contempt.

"Henry," Fortescue said in a friendly voice, as he pointed a well-manicured finger at him, "I have no opinion regarding your conduct with Sophie Cruz. Adultery, children out of wedlock, physical abuse, mental cruelty, those are matters I deal with regularly. I don't judge my clients or their behavior, and I'm rarely if ever shocked by anything they tell me about themselves. I have an open mind and a wonderful ability to remain disinterested in morality. I'm in the trenches every day. Your situation is a simple one and I expect a full resolution to your satisfaction. That is what you hired me to do, isn't it?" he said with a smile, then wiped it away with his napkin.

Henry let his body relax and the tightness in his face softened. Fortescue was a hired gun, he told himself, and he had no argument with him. It was his decision to go ahead and no one else's. He realized he couldn't turn back now and replied in a far more civil tone, "Boyce, I see no winners here. The full resolution you speak of is an accommodation, a moral accommodation I have to make in order to repair all the harm that's been done. To be frank, this has been a very difficult and emotional decision and one I've gone back and forth on hundreds of times over the past weeks. I'm exercised, and I didn't mean to snap at you. You're correct. I, I mean, we, hired you to do a job. If I get a little hot under the collar, you have to bear with me. It's not personal."

Fortescue waved his hand at Henry, and said, "Henry, I don't have the time or the temperament to get emotionally involved with my clients. You hired me to get custody of your son and that's what we'll do. How you feel has no relevance for me. It doesn't resonate with me. That's why I'm successful. I don't lose sight of where I'm going. And as a postscript, I think your course of action, and I mean that regarding each of you, is honorable and appropriate."

Maria, who now wished she had a glass of wine to calm her jangled nerves, smiled with relief and said, "Boyce, that was very well said. Thank you."

Henry had nothing more to say and was relieved when the waiter arrived with the lunch. Fortescue and Maria had each ordered Dover sole with asparagus. The portions weren't very large, but the presentation of the food was done elegantly and the aroma from the fish and buttered asparagus awakened his appetite. Henry looked at their plates hungrily. The waiter placed a basket of assorted rolls on the table and put a plate with three pumpernickel rolls and pats of butter in front of Henry. "I'll be back with your drink in a minute, sir" he whispered as he slipped away.

Henry methodically cut open two of the rolls and buttered them. Fortescue and Maria busied themselves with their meals and the table was silent for several minutes while the three of them ate.

Fortescue and Maria were slow eaters. Henry ate the three rolls quickly and had to refrain from reaching for the basket and buttering another roll. He felt foolish. In a moment of petulance he had impulsively denied himself lunch as a way of registering his pique with Fortescue and Maria over this entire business and, despite his claim he wasn't hungry, he was stuffing himself with bread. He regained his composure, pushed his plate away from him and folded his hands on the table. His sins were now virtues and there was nothing left for him to say. He opened his hands, allowing his body language to preface his surrender, and said, "We haven't done anything yet, have we?"

Fortescue put down his fork. His lunch was only half-eaten, but he was through with it. He dropped his napkin over the plate and pulled his chair back several inches from the edge of the table. "Let's put it into perspective. We're reacting to whatever it is Mr. Lenihan does, at least now we are."

At the mention of Lenihan's name, Maria made a face. "Lenihan," she said with contempt. "He's despicable."

Fortescue laughed. He drew his chair in close again, reached over the table and tapped his finger in front of Maria's plate. "Now, now," he gently scolded. "Remember what I said? You can't be thin skinned. It's his sworn duty to defend his client as best he can."

"Dragging Maria through the mud is justifiable?" Henry said with annoyance.

"The case is a loser. He's trying to make some noise. Deflect the attention from his client," Fortescue replied.

"For goodness sake," Maria said. "That was a model's portfolio. Those photographs were art pictures. There was nothing salacious or pornographic about them. You know," she said raising her voice and pointing her finger around the dining room, "Europeans don't harbor the same puritanical notions about the human body that many Americans do. I'm proud of those pictures, and I think it's a travesty that someone can do what he's doing, and it's accepted behavior because he's duty bound to protect his client. What? At my expense," she closed with a huff.

"Maria," Fortescue said gently, "you're his only hope. Let's take this step by step and examine it. She's guilty, and I don't see how a jury couldn't convict. But I don't believe Lenihan is hoping to influence that oddball potential juror. No, I think he's hoping to spook the newly appointed district attorney. Malfetano's gone. He's on the bench and out of the picture. The governor did what was expected and appointed Duffy. Right now, his legacy as a district attorney may not last longer than four months. He has to run for office, and do so on short notice. Add to that the troubling factor that Duffy is not a household name. Regardless of his long years of service and his excellent track record as a prosecutor he's been kept in the shadows as has just about everyone in that office except the reigning district attorney." Fortescue paused and took a sip of his mineral water. It was evident to Henry that the trial lawyer in him was just getting warmed up, and they were in for a long dissertation on the upcoming election and how Lenihan would be outsmarted. Henry said nothing and waited for him to continue.

Maria was frowning and interjected, "You're going to tell me the same thing Henry's been saying, I know it."

"Wait until I'm finished," Fortescue humorously admonished. "You have to pay attention to the timing, and you have to respect Lenihan's familiarity with politics. The weekend after the homicide he was able to sully your reputations in the local papers, and even on the local television news. I think at that point he was just acting on instinct, but those pictures were a Godsend and he made the most of them. Less than two weeks later Sophie Cruz was indicted for murder, and once again he was in the news and the pictures were used to provide a motive for someone other than Sophie Cruz killing Millie Campos. And that someone was you, Maria." Fortescue said dramatically.

"Despicable, unquestionably despicable," Maria uttered under her breath.

"Despicable and untrue, but he's not worried about the truth. He needs a cause. Three weeks ago he filed the paternity suit. Something I hoped he would do because it is the necessary preface to our action to secure custody of the boy. He drops that bombshell, totally expected I would like to note for the record, and he's in the papers again. Now things are picking up steam and we have a small but vocal faction of Puerto Rican activists from the fourth ward Democratic Club taking issue with Frank Duffy and the manner in which the district attorney has handled this case. Both city papers have not shied away from writing about the relationship between Frank Duffy and Lee Futerman, and the relationship between you and Lee Futerman. Throw in adultery, sex and a bastard child and you've got a story people will read. Note also, as I said before, no one knows Frank Duffy. John Malfetano was a master politician. He always took the credit, and when there was a screw-up, he was always out front taking the blame, but somehow the mud managed to land squarely on the offending subordinate. And if one didn't exist, he created one. He was the best at that type of thing." Fortescue paused again and took another sip of mineral water.

Henry rubbed his jaw, then said, "Master politician, why the hell would he bury himself on the bench?"

"We have a popular governor and two popular senators. He's biding time waiting for an opening, and he grew tired of playing district attorney. Who really remembers district attorneys? Whatever the party, they run on the same platform, law and order, good government, reform politics. It's a tried and true platform, and the only platform. Name recognition is what carries the day, and why incumbents win election after election. Stephen Brooks is well known in Huguenot City. He was a councilman for ten years and ran a close race for mayor. He has the Republican and Liberal parties behind him, and just who exactly is Frank Duffy? His best ally is John Malfetano, but judges can't campaign. Duffy has an uphill battle and needs all the friends he can get and can't take the minority vote for granted. Democrats may not vote Republican, but they'll vote for a Liberal. It is in Duffy's best interest to let Sophie Cruz plead to a lesser charge and get her out of the picture long before Election Day. Democrats have a wide edge on registered voters, but that's no guarantee, and he's been training for this job for twenty years and isn't going to let a highly publicized murder case deny him what he believes is his for the taking. That's what I think."

"Sounds very calculated," Maria said coldly.

"Calculating, but I agree," Henry said with the secret hope that it would happen and Sophie would be spared.

"However it turns out, whether she goes to jail or goes free, you'll have custody. Partial if she's free, and full if she's in jail," Fortescue said confidently.

"You're confident of that?" Maria asked.

"The paternity suit was the key. Lenihan must have kept some very late hours to get all of his filings in as quickly as he did, but the favor was for us. He managed to get Carlos Gomes to submit to a blood test, furnish his military records and sign an affidavit declaring that he had mistakenly believed he was the father and allowed his name to go on the birth certificate. All of that saves us quite a lot of leg work and negates having to file for an order of filiation."

"Who is Carlos Gomes?" Maria questioned.

Henry's face reddened and he looked to Fortescue. Fortescue said, "Henry can answer that."

"He was Sophie's old boyfriend. When he found out she was pregnant he assumed he was the father. By the time the kid was born he did the arithmetic and it didn't work out. He's a solid guy. He let his name go on the birth certificate and offered to marry her but she turned him down."

Maria nodded her head, but didn't offer any response. Fortescue took another sip of his mineral water and resumed speaking. "Mr. Gomes may have been a solid guy, but his blood test came back improbable and that, along with the other proof he produced, rules him out."

"Who would contest that?" Maria asked with slight bewilderment.

"We're dealing with the Family Court. It's a relatively new court, and the very reason for its being is to protect the family and hold it together. Particular interest is there for children. The court is not going to remove Carlos Gomes as the legal father in place of Henry without certainty that Henry is, in fact, the father. Henry says he's the father, Sophie says he's the father and we have five years of solid financial records to demonstrate that Henry has met his obligation to provide for his child. If the blood test shows probability, which I'm sure it will, the court will recognize Henry as the father and the only effort made by us was Henry's blood test."

"What's the timetable then?" Henry asked.

"Once your paternity is legally established, we petition the court for custody," Fortescue answered.

"That should upset Mr. Lenihan's apple cart," Maria said with sharp satisfaction.

Fortescue offered a sly smile and gently clapped his hands together. "He'll never see it coming. Mr. Lenihan is predictable and shortsighted. Recall, I said he was up on the local politics. That doesn't make him smart. Information is knowledge, but it's no indication of intelligence. Duffy is vulnerable, Lenihan saw that and has made every effort to attack that vulnerability and that helps your case," Fortescue said with a little too much smugness. He leaned in Henry's direction and said, "Do you think Sophie Cruz expects that you'll attempt to win custody of your son? Better yet, you would readily admit paternity without any argument?"

Henry shook his head and answered, "No."

"Precisely. I don't know her, but what I've learned from you and what's been in the papers Mr. Lenihan was convinced the paternity suit would be the extra leverage he would need to paint you as a total skunk. You'd deny it, initially, and he could run to the papers again and get another week's worth of story lines. That's all he wants. Keep it fresh and hope Duffy weakens."

"And?" Maria asked. She found Fortescue too long-winded and circuitous in his explanations. He lacked Henry's directness and she was annoyed. Particularly because Fortescue assigned no guilt or blame to anyone.

"And," Fortescue replied flippantly. "And what? Lenihan is defending a criminal case. The paternity suit is his idea because he has insisted on telling anyone who'll listen that Henry is a scoundrel. He has totally misrepresented the two of you and done it with such fervor that he believes it too. It is eminently clear that all of his efforts are directed at getting the district attorney to plea bargain this case. Paternity and child custody are not his bailiwick, and I do not suppose that he has thought this through, or, for that matter, really cares."

"Maybe he'll try to make that an issue in the papers? Twist the story to make it sound as if we're stealing her child," Henry said.

"Henry," Fortescue said as he raised his to index fingers in the air for emphasis, "remember, you have financially provided for that boy from the time you learned you were the father. There are two components to this argument.

ANTHONY D. MURPHY

Firstly, a parent cannot dodge his or her obligation to provide for the well being of his or her issue. That means food, clothing, health care and education. Secondly, a parent has a right, both natural and legal, to share in the child's rearing and development. That's all we're asking for. You've met the first obligation, and now you want to share in what is your legal right. What argument can they make? I'm prepared to allege that it was Sophie Cruz who wanted to keep your paternity secret. It was Sophie Cruz who wanted a child because she wanted a meal ticket to a better life and didn't care how she got it. Our response overwhelms their complaint. Every penny she has will be spent in her criminal defense, and there won't be a cent left over to wage a custody battle. And when the smoke clears there'll be no Patrick Lenihan at her side ready to wage the next battle."

"Do you really think it will be that easy?" Henry asked skeptically.

"The only wrinkle I can portend is that the court will appoint a legal guardian for the child. It will be the guardian's role to insure that the resolution that's arrived at is the one that is in the child's best interests. That may stretch things out some, but we welcome that and encourage it," Fortescue answered.

"Provided Sophie goes to jail?' Maria asked.

"I think that's a given, but even if she were to go free you would still have a right to partial custody. The fact that you're buying a house in Riverview, you're prepared to pay for private education in one of the more prestigious schools in the city, a school that has already agreed to blindly admit the child, and you're prepared to hire a respected child psychologist to provide family counseling for both of you and the child are all indicators of your good faith and fitness as custodians or partial custodians for the child. The court is guided by reason and law. The law is on your side, and there is nothing unreasonable in your intentions. This isn't a proposition. It's reality. It's only a matter of time before it's a fait accompli."

"You're very confident," Maria said in a complimentary voice.

"Thank you," Fortescue replied. "But this is a fairly simple matter, emotionally nerve wracking for you, but an exercise without challenge for me."

"Fine," Henry added. "But if she doesn't go to jail I think I'll be paying the bills and not much more."

"Then it's up to you. The court should allow for liberal visitation rights and a say so in the child's development. She may resist, but you have your right as a parent. I don't think she'll have much fight left after I'm through with her." Fortescue said soberly.

Henry nodded his head in disagreement, "You don't know Sophie. I don't have the stomach for that fight. Do you, Maria?"

Maria didn't want to hear it. Henry had said, "You don't know Sophie" with a mix of dread and pride, and she wondered as she had these past six weeks if he knew, really knew, who he loved or how to love. *Perhaps he loves us both, and his only way of dealing with us was the arrangement that existed before Millie's murder,* she thought. Whatever his feelings were, she didn't want to hear that Sophie would go free. Henry was correct. If Sophie went free, they would meet their financial obligations and that would be the extent of it.

Maria hadn't answered, and Henry said testily, "Do you, Maria, do you have the stomach?"

Maria merely sighed and replied, "I'll do my part."

"Good, very good," Fortescue said. "How about a little coffee and some fruit or dessert?"

Maria gave him a puzzled look. "Is that it?" she asked.

"That's why I suggested lunch. This was mainly a rehash of what we know, and a confirmation for what we're going to do. Otherwise we're reacting to what happens and I expect everything to happen quickly. So far, things have gone according to the timetable I predicted. I'm sure Duffy will decide what to do soon. No matter what, as soon as the court confers paternity we'll make the move for custody."

"Don't you think we should wait?" Henry asked.

"No, that would be a mistake, and I don't make mistakes," Fortescue said with annoyance. "If you don't want to go through with it, just say so."

"Fine, fine," Henry said wearily. "What you think is best."

Fortescue broke into a wide grin, "Leave it to me, things will work out just as we planned."

Maria looked at the two men and said, "I've heard enough. I have to go back to work. Henry, you'll walk me back?"

Henry stood up and said, "Boyce, thanks for lunch and the update. Maria, when you're ready." He went to pull her chair out, but Fortescue was already there.

"Maria," Fortescue said as he pulled her chair out and guided her elbow with his hand as she stood up, "it is always a pleasure."

Maria's face softened and she smiled. "Boyce, there's a bit of the rascal in you," she teased. "I don't know if that's good or bad."

"For my sake I hope it's good," he answered.

Henry and Maria said their final goodbyes and left the restaurant. They went down the stairs and out onto the street. Henry stopped and lit a cigarette, and Maria asked him, "Did we set a date for the closing?"

"Next Thursday. I can't believe I'm leaving the Excelsior. Based on what Fortescue said, this could be premature. What if Sophie doesn't go to jail?"

"Henry, stop wishing for that. She's a murderer and she will go to jail. I can't believe you men. You're all so shallow," she said with disgust.

"About what?" Henry asked.

"About your ambitions," she answered sharply. "To think a man would let a murderer go free to win an election, how pitiable."

"No one is letting anyone go free. The smart money says that Duffy will cut her some slack to get her out of the way. That's life in the real world, Maria," Henry retorted knowingly.

"Real world," she said sarcastically. "Henry Weiss, you don't know what the real world is. You think you know, just like that popinjay Boyce Fortescue thinks that he knows."

Henry was in no mood to argue and he didn't answer her. Suddenly she sounded like the old Maria, and it made him happy.

They walked on for another block, and Maria said to him, "Are you going home or back to your office?"

"Back to the office. Mrs. Langdon will have ten messages and twenty questions for me, and who knows what else?"

"Don't forget, Gloria invited us to dinner tonight."

"Yes, I'll be there by six-thirty."

Maria took his hand, reached up and kissed him on the cheek. "I can make my way back to work. Go back to the office, I love you."

She went up the street, and Henry waited for the green light and crossed at the corner in the direction of the subway.

What's going on with her? he thought. *What's going on?*

Chapter Fifty-Three

Maria was emotionally exhausted. She went through the revolving door into Sable's and it took all of her energy to move the door. Henry was wavering. She could sense it, and Boyce Fortescue wasn't an asset. He had seen to that at lunch and she was convinced that Henry was looking for an opportunity to resurrect the argument that fighting for custody of Joey was wrong and not in their or the child's best interests. Boyce was narcissistic and overbearing, and she regretted having put as much faith in Gloria's opinion as she had in choosing him. She caught her reflection in one of the many-mirrored columns on the sale's floor and realized she was talking to herself. She let out a nervous giggle and said, "I should have kicked him a little harder." It was right after the comment about not drinking when Boyce went into a long spiel about salad dressings that she saw Henry's eyes half close. She had stretched out her leg and given Boyce a little nudge hoping to shut him up but it was to no avail and, in retrospect, she wished she had dug the heel of her shoe into his shin. Henry had it right all along she thought. "We don't need a headliner for this," he had told her.

Henry, in his heart of hearts, had no desire to be a father to his son. She and Gloria and Futerman, to a lesser extent, had made the argument that being a father to Joey, a flesh and blood father, was what he was morally bound to do should Sophie go to jail. He gave in quickly and went long with them, but Maria knew that just under the surface his inclination was to resist and resist forcefully. She had trapped him at a weak moment, at a time when he was

465

preoccupied with Millie's murder and Sophie's arrest. Henry's initial reaction to all that had happened had been one of total shock. She saw it in his face that morning in the hospital when she had just come out of the coma. Henry was reeling, confused and drowning in his own guilt. She wasn't angry with him, nor did she make a display of forgiving him. She simply stated that they had both failed one another and, in doing so, had failed others. He was grateful to be forgiven and thankful that she was willing to share his guilt. She had left him no choice, and despite his weak protests he went along with her and agreed to fight for his son. But that was six weeks ago, and she was startled at how the mere passage of six weeks had dulled the impact of all that had happened to them. In the past two weeks they had gone to a ballgame and a show and had eaten out several times. Life as Henry had known it and enjoyed it was returning, and as the normal rhythms of daily life returned to where they had been before Millie's murder, she feared he would capitulate to his own selfish weaknesses and agree to provide financial support for his son, but nothing more. It wasn't in Henry's nature to argue. He would rather buy his way out of a fight than bloody his nose or someone else's. She knew him well, and what worried her most was that Henry had no tolerance for conflict. Waging a custody battle he was sure to win, with the prize being the new responsibility of raising an eight-year-old was an empty victory for him. He didn't want to be burdened with a child. He didn't want to move from his beloved apartment, and each step in the process that brought them closer to becoming parents to an eight-year-old boy and setting up household in a house in Riverview further removed Henry from the life and world he was comfortable in and increased the likelihood of his abandoning them all.

Maria felt vulnerable, and for the first time in their long union she was unsure if she had the power to control him. She admitted to herself that the stresses in their marriage were primarily of her own doing. She enjoyed being angry with him over the slightest offenses and, if anything, brooding over his shortcomings was a pleasant diversion and made it easier to deal with all the disappointment she felt over how poorly she had managed her own life. Most importantly, she had purposely kept him at a distance and, in doing so, had fueled his obsession with her. Sophie had been a mild diversion. She wasn't sure if that was still the case, and she didn't want to give him the slightest opportunity to turn on her or to find fault with her. Things had to happen quickly, and the idea of Sophie accepting a reduced sentence and going to jail without the delay of a trial was an idea she embraced. *After all*, she thought, *with Sophie away in prison, who would be left to fight?*

The lunchtime flurry of activity in Sable's was quieting down, and the number of employees in the store would soon exceed the number of shoppers. At the Lorient counter two of Maria's sale's clerks were busy with customers. Maria went behind the counter and checked the sale's log.

Karen, one of her clerks, gave her a perky smile and said, "I put the June sale's report on your desk. Guy dropped it off while you were out."

"He didn't stay?" Maria said with disappointment.

"No," Karen replied. "He said he'd call you this afternoon."

"Very well," Maria answered. "It's on the desk?"

"Yes, in a white envelope."

"I'll be in the office if you need me," she said as she walked away.

The office space Sable's provided for vendors and department managers was Spartan in contrast to the spacious offices the store manager and on site senior executives occupied on the top floor of the store, but Maria was always happy to steal away to the small room at the rear of the second floor sale's floor to catch up on paperwork, or find a few minutes to enjoy a quiet cup of tea.

Maria plugged in the hot pot and filled it to the brim with cold water and put a tea bag into her teacup. She unconsciously smoothed her skirt, sat down at the desk and opened the white envelope with the June sale's report. She scanned it quickly, then put it down and opened the middle drawer to her desk. Inside of the drawer was an empty picture frame for a five by seven inch picture. She took the frame out and put it on her desk. She opened her pocketbook, took out another envelope, and from it extracted a photograph, then went about setting it in the picture frame. She set the frame on the desk and wiped it clean with a tissue. It was the Holy Communion photograph of Joey that Sophie had thrown at her that day on the subway platform. There was something about the little boy's face that excited her. Henry was there in the boy's face, but that wasn't what excited her. *After all*, she mused, *he was the father*. It was eerie and exciting to her because the face she saw, the innocent but intriguing resemblance she saw was Rudy's. Of course, it was coincidental and nothing more, but it was real. She opened up the envelope that had contained Joey's picture and took out a second photograph. That one was of Rudy. It was a closeup of him in his gymnastics outfit, and she placed it next to the framed photograph of Joey. The water in the pot started to boil and she removed the plug from the wall plate and poured the boiling water into the teacup.

She put a saucer on top of the teacup to let it steep and placed it to the side of her desk. She leaned over the desk and stared at the two photographs. The physical resemblance between the two was general and not specific. They each had strong masculine noses, dark thick hair, unblemished skin and deep open eyes expressively capped by two tails of perfectly formed black eyebrows. They were handsome to a fault, each of them, but that wasn't the resemblance that moved her. It was the simplicity of their facial expressions. Each face was honest and sincere, or so she thought, and though Rudy was lost forever, she hoped to recapture his spirit and the comfort of his company in Henry's child. From the first moment she saw the photograph of Joey she recognized Rudy's ghost. Perhaps it was simply her imagination, or a subconscious desire to find some connection to a place in time or a face in time, she playfully thought, that resonated so emotionally with her. Whatever the cause, her feelings were real, and she longed to meet the little boy and take him into her life.

She removed the saucer from the teacup, lifted the soggy tea bag from the water and disposed of it in the wastebasket. She sipped the hot tea, all the while admiring the two photographs on her desk. *There had been so much she and Rudy had planned to do together*, she thought. *So much that had never happened*. Joey was a second chance for her, an opportunity for redemption and the challenge to pour her heart and soul into another's life without any expectation of reward. It wasn't love she was seeking. She readily acknowledged she didn't need to be loved, what she needed was to love someone else and to love that someone else unconditionally. Inexplicably, the mere image of a child captured by a photographer's magic had awakened feelings she didn't know existed, and she longed for this new union with all the hesitancy and nervousness of an expectant mother.

She didn't want anyone else to see the framed photograph of Joey, at least not now with all the uncertainty over whether Sophie would go to jail and Henry would obtain custody of the child. Nor did she want to hide it away in her locker where it wouldn't be accessible if she wanted to take a quick peek and dream about their future. Reluctantly, she took the photograph out of the frame and placed it along with Rudy's photograph back in the envelope and into her pocketbook. She went to her locker, opened it and put her pocketbook inside for safekeeping. Every time she looked at Joey's photograph it left her feeling hopeful and happy. She hadn't felt like that since her days with Rudy, and she made a vow to herself that she would do all that she had to do to make this dream happen.

She was determined to move into the new house before Labor Day. They had already hired a painting contractor and a landscaper. Henry didn't know it, but she had also bought the furniture for Joey's bedroom, a bed and bureau with a matching desk, bookcase and chair. She had picked out a creamy yellow paint for the walls in the child's bedroom. It was soothing and warm, and she found a matching wallpaper border festooned with balls, bats and racquets that would line the wall of the bedroom and add a boyish brightness to the room. It seemed she spent much of her time thinking of things she could do to help him settle in to his new environment. She wanted his room to be cozy and to be a safe place for him. It would all fall into place. She was confident that Sophie would go to jail and Henry would be granted sole custody of the child. Once that happened, the most important issue, the only issue, she thought, would be the child's well being. Somehow she would obtain photographs of Sophie and Sophie and Joey and put them in frames on his bureau and bookcase. She would assure the child that his mother loved him; every night as she sat by his bed and read him a story she would have him kiss his mother's picture and say a prayer for her before he went to sleep. She even practiced what she would tell him, "Joseph," that was how she would address him. "Joseph, you know I'm not your mother and I can never take her place. I'm your friend. Your best friend, and you can tell me anything because I will always be here for you." And then she would bend over and kiss his forehead and tuck him in. She knew he would cry and be angry with her, but she would meet the challenge with grace and patience. She would tell him that God had put her there to help him suffer through the terrible loss of the world he had known. He could blame his mother or Henry, or both of them, but she would do everything in her power to keep him from blaming her. No matter how much Sophie would try to poison him and make him hate her she would wear him down. She had no idea what visitation rights prisoners were permitted, but she would ensure that he saw his natural mother as often as allowed or he wanted because she knew that to win his heart she had to be his ally. His would be a reluctant heart and it would be a painful start, but for her this was a challenge unlike any she had met in her life and she was determined to succeed.

Chapter Fifty-Four

Lenihan angrily slammed the phone down on its hook and called out, "Blanche did the mail come?"

"Not yet, probably around 10:30," she replied.

"Get Eddie Simon for me if you can," he yelled back.

Blanche didn't answer him. Three minutes later his phone rang and he heard Blanche's throaty voice call out, "Pick it up, it's Simon."

"Eddie," Lenihan said with a trace of despair in his voice, "what are you doing to me?"

"What're you talking about?" A suddenly confused Eddie Simon replied.

"I just got off the phone with Dennis Broderick from the *Huguenot Daily News*. It seems he had a long chat yesterday with Ray Cruz, and Ray Cruz told him that you had discovered a cover-up in the DA's office. He also said that your investigation pointed toward Danny Monaghan as a strong suspect."

Eddie Simon let out a deep breath and said, "Holy shit, that is not what my report says."

Lenihan calmed down slightly and said, "That's my other problem. How in God's name can you give Ray Cruz the report before you touched base with me?"

Eddie Simon coldly answered, "Because he's the client. He hired me. Granted, he did so on your recommendation, but he's the guy who hired me and he's the guy who paid me."

"Do you have a copy of your report for me?" Lenihan demanded.

"Yes. I was going to mail it to you today. I thought Ray Cruz would have called you and gone over the details, but I guess he didn't?" Eddie Simon answered.

"No, I haven't heard from him, and right now that's fine because when I do speak with him it always ends up that I'm to blame and I missed something. According to that snoop from the newspaper, that's the case."

"He's way off base," Eddie Simon said reassuringly. "I found out one thing new, and that was about the older Monaghan. On the night of the murder he paid a visit to Cleary's apartment and had a conversation with Cleary's mother. Cleary is the doorman, the one who pointed the finger at Danny Monaghan. According to Cleary, Monaghan gave Mrs. Cleary a hundred dollars, which was an apology of sorts for breaking her son's nose last year. Cleary claims that it was Monaghan's way of telling him to shut up about what he saw that day. You know? Cleary said he saw the kid leaving the alleyway ten minutes after Mrs. Weiss went into the apartment building and a good thirty-five minutes or so after he made the delivery to her apartment."

Lenihan was silent for a moment, then replied, "What exactly is in the report you gave Ray Cruz?"

"Tell you what," Eddie Simon answered. "I'll drop by in an hour. Are you free?"

"Yes, I'll be waiting," said Lenihan curtly, and without saying anything else he hung up the phone.

"Motherfucker," he said out loud as he spun out of his chair and went over to a brown wooden file cabinet and opened a drawer. He took out a file folder and brought it back over to his desk. He sat down, opened the folder and took out the folio that contained copies of the police reports and a list of who had been subpoenaed for the Grand Jury. No matter how many times he reviewed the material he came away defeated and convinced that Sophie was destined for a long prison term. The list of witnesses included everyone involved with the case but the doorman. Timothy Cleary hadn't been called to testify, and that meant the prosecution wasn't going to use him as a witness at the trial.

Gordon Alpert was the ADA who presented the case at the Grand Jury. Lenihan didn't know him personally, but his reputation was first rate, and it was obvious from the police reports that every aspect of Henry Weiss' relationship with Sophie Cruz had been revealed. There were no secrets. Maria Weiss' pictures and the bastard son were all on the table. The grand jurors may have come away not liking the Weiss', but they probably disliked Sophie Cruz even more. That was how he interpreted the Grand Jury's subsequent indictment of Sophie Cruz for felony murder, burglary and assault. The omission of Cleary avoided any suspicion of Danny Monaghan, and Gordon Alpert had done exactly what he would have done if he were prosecuting the case. Alpert was tailoring the prosecution's case so that Sophie's guilt would be undeniable. The indictment made it obvious to Lenihan that Alpert had made little effort to prove that Sophie's mental state that morning was one of premeditated murder. If she were intending to murder someone, it would have been Maria Weiss, he thought and the felony murder charge was predicated on the burglary charge, but on that account, too, Lenihan felt Alpert had included the charge without proving it. If Alpert followed the chronology of the police reports, he started with Henry Weiss, and after Henry it was a simple sequence that began with the transit policeman encountering an angry Sophie arguing with Maria on a subway platform, followed by Edith Zimmerman finding a dead Millie and an unconscious Maria in Maria's apartment. Maria's testimony described the confrontation with Sophie on the subway, finding Millie dead, when in a sickened state she returned to her apartment and her identification of Sophie coming out of the closet and knocking her to the floor. It didn't necessitate any imagination. *In fact*, he thought, *this one was a ground ball*. It was a neat little soap opera begging for a villain, and who better than the scorned mistress to fill that role. Sophie was a woman bent on revenge. And as events unfolded on the day of the murder, Sophie played an active part in every scene. The medical examiner determined that the cause of death was from a blow to the head and the murder weapon was the ashtray that had been on Maria's bureau. Detective Hogan found Sophie's fingerprints in the elevator. Maria would have testified that when she entered the bedroom and found Millie on the floor she handled the ashtray. Hogan had her prints, but her story made sense. Detective Widelsky surely testified at length about Sophie's adamant denial, backed up by her sworn statement taken in her attorney's presence that she had never been in the building. Hogan had already contradicted that point, and it was all downhill from there. Lenihan cringed at the thought of how the actual Grand Jury minutes would read, but he was certain that when the time for the trial came and he would have his opportunity to read them they would be even more damning than he was imagining now. "We're fucked," he said to himself in a loud and tired voice.

"And you've got no one to blame but yourself," an angry Roger McKee said as he entered Lenihan's office. "I just got off the phone with some clown from the *News*."

"Yeah, I already know," said Lenihan, cutting off McKee.

"Do you understand what this means?" McKee queried.

"It means nothing," Lenihan said dismissively. "Read the police reports!"

"You are incredibly unprofessional. Do you know that?" McKee said. "I foolishly, and I repeat, foolishly allowed you to pass off that Monaghan kid to me. Without getting into the ethics of the matter, it would suffice to say that you owed it to Monaghan's father, a former client, to represent his son. But that would have gotten in the way of taking on a client whose case appeared a little more interesting, wouldn't it have?" McKee said as he waved his hand in disgust at Lenihan.

Lenihan laughed and replied, "What's gotten into you?"

"Ethics, my friend, ethics, legally, we're not partners and we follow the rules to a degree, but those are our two names on the window, and it would be reasonable to expect that the two of us wouldn't be representing potential defendants in the same case. You're an impulsive man. That woman gave you her sob story, you fell for it and conveniently got me to take the Monaghan kid off your hands. The reporter who called gave me a line about Monaghan's father threatening a witness in this investigation and the witness's mother on the evening of the murder. Probably a few hours after the detectives had grilled his kid, and now Ray Cruz is claiming that Monaghan's a good suspect and this reporter is running with the story."

"Ray Cruz gave that story to the paper, but Eddie Simon just told me that he's got it all wrong," Lenihan said in a soft voice, hoping to calm McKee down. McKee's ruddy face was a shade redder and Lenihan could never recall seeing the man angry. "The Cruz's are clutching at straws. Read the police reports, see for yourself," Lenihan said as he reached down to the floor and picked up the folder.

"Jesus Christ," McKee snarled. "That's what I meant when I said you have no grasp of ethics. You hired a private detective to dig up dirt on my client. A client who was once your client, but you peddled off on me and I foolishly picked up. You came in that day, and I remember exactly what you said to me. 'Roger, you won't believe it. I've got another poor soul the police are grilling over that homicide on Lincoln Boulevard.' And I told you to refer her to someone else. Right?" McKee challenged.

"But who knew?" Lenihan countered.

"Who knew? You did. You said it was the same B.S. the Monaghan kid was dealing with, and I reluctantly agreed to help you out. Five hours later your girl is under arrest for murder. Please, you fooled me and now we're on opposite sides of the fence. You're the enemy right now. I told the reporter I had no comment, and it was a shame to smear the names of innocent people in a pathetic attempt to exonerate the guilty. So the answer is twofold: Firstly, it would be improper of me to read the reports you were given. Secondly, it would be improper to even discuss this case with you. Kathleen will be coming in every day from now on, and it won't be necessary for Blanche to take any of my calls. As far as this case is concerned, I have nothing to say to you. There will be no conversation. I tried to reach out to Monaghan, and I'm sure I'll be hearing from him. For your sake, I hope I get to him before he gets to you."

"Roger," Lenihan responded, "you're making too much of this. I'll call Monaghan and straighten this out. Ray Cruz grossly misrepresented Simon's report."

"Until they discharge me, and that couldn't happen sooner, the Monaghans are my clients and I would appreciate it if you have no contact with them. Understand?" McKee said threateningly.

"Whatever, Roger, Roger whatever," Lenihan said with a wave of his hand.

Roger McKee stepped out of Lenihan's doorway and walked away. Lenihan leaned back in his chair and sighed. "Fucking Monaghan, now all I need is that crazy bastard coming after me."

Chapter Fifty-Five

Eddie Simon let out a yawn as he crossed the threshold into Lenihan's office. "Patty boy," he said cheerfully, "smile, we're only here for a visit and then we're gone."

Lenihan didn't respond. He extended his right arm and motioned with his index finger toward the envelope Simon held under his arm.

Simon took the envelope in his left hand and dropped it on Lenihan's desk. He then started backing out of the office. "It's all there. You got any questions, give me a holler."

Lenihan blinked, then called out, "Wait a minute. Take a seat. You're not getting off the hook that easy."

Simon laughed and approached the chairs in front of Lenihan's desk, pulled one back and sat down. "Jesus," he sighed. "You're awfully effing serious."

Lenihan picked up the envelope Simon had dropped on his desk and weighed it in his hand. "Not much here. What is it, two or three type written pages, double spaced?"

"It's three and there isn't much there, not much at all."

"So where did Broderick get his story from?" Lenihan asked.

"Ray Cruz may have embellished the storyline some, whatever, it's understandable given the circumstances," Simon casually replied.

Lenihan gave Simon a disapproving look and turned his head away. "Understandable, what in God's name does that mean?"

"Ray Cruz is a very nice guy. Hard worker, good family man, and smart enough to know his sister did it, and loyal enough to do whatever he can to get her off the hook. What do you expect him to do?" Simon said earnestly.

Lenihan got up from behind his desk and walked to the window. He stared at Simon for a moment and said, "Don't you wear socks?"

Simon was wearing a blue short sleeved oxford shirt with a button down collar, tan chinos and penny loafers and no socks. He was tall and thin with reddish blonde hair. His face was creased and lined from too much sun, and though he was in his early forties there was boyishness to his face and build that made him appear years younger. He laughed at Lenihan's question and replied, "Not in the summer, if I can help it. It's the casual look. It relaxes people. Gets them to open up to me, you know what I mean?"

Lenihan smiled and shook his head again. He liked Eddie Simon. They had first met ten years earlier when Simon was an investigator with the State Police Bureau of Criminal Identification. Simon was assigned to a squad investigating auto thefts, and much of the work was in Huguenot City. Lenihan was a prosecutor then, and had worked several cases with Simon and was impressed with his thoroughness and overall professionalism; something he too often found lacking with some Huguenot City detectives. Simon had only completed thirteen years when he unexpectedly quit and went into business for himself. Everyone told him he was crazy, but in a year he had easily doubled his salary and was turning work away. He was honest, confident and smart, and he never milked a case or a client, and if there was nothing there he let you know right away.

"So, that's the secret," Lenihan said jokingly.

"I dress for success."

Lenihan's smiled faded. He looked down at the floor, then raised his eyes and said to Simon. "I think I got a big problem here. Right now I have the *Huguenot Daily News* pointing a finger at my former client and the reporter running with the story is a guy I thought I had in my pocket. My associate Roger McKee is ready to move out, and my plan to get my client off the murder hook with a manslaughter, or if she's really lucky, a negligent homicide, is about to be derailed and I'm going to end up going to trial and losing. This isn't good and you are definitely not helping me."

Eddie Simon sat up in his chair and shrugged his shoulders. "I think you're overstating the case. First of all, what I found out, and what's recorded in the report Ray Cruz gave to Broderick," he said as he pointed to the envelope on Lenihan's desk, "is not the whole story, and I know Ray Cruz took some liberties with the facts, but what's it prove?"

"Nothing," Lenihan countered. "Except Sophie might believe there's a chance she can beat the charge and I don't think she can."

"I came up empty, except for that bit about Monaghan visiting Cleary's mother the night of the murder."

"How'd you get that out of Cleary and the cops didn't?" an impressed Lenihan asked.

"Cleary told Sergeant Kreppell, but I guess Kreppell never passed it on, or if he did, no one paid much attention to it since they figured they had Sophie Cruz in the bag and the case was closed."

"Ah," Lenihan sighed. "That's good. Very good, you know? I just wish it wasn't Monaghan."

"You think Monaghan is involved?" Simon asked.

"Well, isn't it odd that the doorman makes a claim it took Danny Monaghan at least a half hour to forty-five minutes to complete the delivery, then that night after the detectives were at his apartment questioning Danny, Mike Monaghan went and threatened Mrs. Cleary? My problem is I agreed to represent Danny, then pawned him off on Roger."

"I don't follow you?" Simon said.

"I'm just thinking out loud. I have an ethical and possibly a legal problem here. I'm not the attorney of record for Danny Monaghan. Mike Monaghan called me and asked me to represent the kid in any further dealings with the police. I got a very brief sketch of the incident from Mike and it was much less than what was reported in the papers, but I never spoke to the kid, and right after I met with Sophie Cruz I asked Roger to represent Monaghan. Basically, Mike told me his kid was a good boy; played basketball on the school team, went to church, had a girlfriend, was popular, stuff like that and I had no reason to doubt him. Now, I wasn't very up front with Roger, but since Monaghan didn't tell me anything that wasn't already public knowledge, what was my obligation? That's why your angle is so disturbing. If the kid's a good suspect and the cops suppressed that, then it looks good for Sophie, and that's good for her, but then I have to deal with Monaghan and that may not be good for me," Lenihan concluded with a perplexed look on his face. "Also," he added. "I was very quick to dismiss any idea of the kid being involved. Maybe your little discovery changes things."

"Jesus Christ," Eddie Simon exclaimed. "You're going too fast for me. What are you getting at?"

Lenihan placed a pencil in his mouth and bit down on it. He broke the pencil in half and spit the smaller end from is mouth into the wastepaper basket, pointed the remaining end at Eddie Simon and said, "Why would Monaghan go and threaten Mrs. Cleary if he wasn't worried about something?"

"Who said he threatened her?"

"You did," Lenihan replied.

"No, all I said was that Monaghan visited her that night. Now, there's more to the story, and at Ray Cruz's direction I put it into two reports. Report number one is what he gave Broderick. That's what I meant about him taking liberties with the facts. Think about one thing for me, please?" Simon asked.

"What?"

"You told me that a year ago or so Monaghan broke Cleary's nose because he was late paying off a bet to Chick Nathan, right?"

"So I'm told," Lenihan answered. "Story goes he walked into Pete's Bridge Lounge and smashed Cleary's face against the bar."

Simon gave Lenihan a knowing smile and shook his head in disbelief. "You may know Monaghan, but I know something about Chick Nathan and his pal Vince LoBianco, and what I know is those guys are all about the money and nothing else."

"Right, and Monaghan does their dirty work, and Cleary was several weeks late, so Monaghan lowered the boom."

"Pat," Simon said condescendingly. "Why? Why does he slam this guy's face into the bar in front of several witnesses? Why does he do it to a guy who is not only defenseless, but lives in the same building he lives in? And why does he do that when the people he works for would be just as happy to collect fifteen bucks a week in interest from Cleary until he could pay the three hundred off? That's the way they work. Monaghan's an intimidator and a collector. There's no real interest in busting people up. It's just the threat they want to communicate."

"He's a bully, I don't know?" Lenihan shrugged.

"Look, Monaghan did visit Mrs. Cleary. I never said he threatened her, and according to her son Monaghan gave her a hundred bucks and that was to cover his medical bills from the beating, but he made no overt threat. Mrs. Cleary interpreted it as a threat, but Cleary told me that if I asked her she'd deny the whole thing. Now what's not in the report and what is of interest and shoots down your theory is what else I learned, and that's in report number two," Simon said smugly.

Lenihan frowned. "I don't want to tangle with Mike Monaghan but that story in the paper did it for me. I only want to capitalize on it for Sophie's sake."

"You'll have to be careful," Simon warned. "No matter what Sophie Cruz says, her brother thinks she did it. He told me she can be a little crazy at times and just go off and does things impulsively. I say that because this case doesn't make a lot of sense. I checked out Danny Monaghan's story about buying lunch and the paper before he made the delivery. Everything checked out. He's never had a problem at the supermarket, and no one has ever complained about him. He's never been arrested, same for Cleary. He's at that building for more than ten years and no complaints."

"There's always a first time," Lenihan replied.

"Be patient," Simon admonished. "Forget about the Monaghan kid, that's a dead end."

"You have something on Cleary? Is that what's in report number two?" Lenihan asked.

"Not really, but he's interesting. I went over to the Excelsior, but he didn't want to talk to me. He was nervous, but I was able to get him to go to dinner with me."

"You love to work a free meal into the case, don't you?" Lenihan chided.

"Drinks, a meal, those things put people at ease, just like wearing no socks," Simon said reproving Lenihan. "We met at Pete's Bridge Lounge and in less than twenty minutes I had his life story. More than I wanted to know, but all I needed to know.'

"What about Cleary don't you like?" Lenihan asked.

Simon took a deep breath and then laughed. "He's an engaging little fellow, this guy Cleary. Here's the long and short of it: he lives with his mother, who's a cranky old hag. She has something to say about everyone and spends most of her time in front of their apartment house watching the world go by. If it's above sixty degrees and daylight, she's out there. The Monaghan kid's a bit of a wiseass and likes to tease Cleary. Nonetheless, he's not fond of him, but he realizes he's just a kid. The day of the homicide the kid made his delivery and Cleary saw him leave the alleyway about forty minutes later. Cleary's observation about the kid and his reporting it to the police was nothing more than a reiteration of what he saw that day. Plain and simple and not made up, since the kid admits he ate his lunch and read a newspaper at the back of the alleyway after he'd made the delivery. Now think about it? What did he do to piss this guy Monaghan off?"

"I guess Monaghan thought he was getting even for the beating," Lenihan answered.

"Wrong," Simon said with a wave of his finger. "Cleary seemed like a pretty up front guy to me, and his version of things came across as unrehearsed. The cops were a little rough, and he told them the truth as he knew it. That night he goes out for a few beers and everyone wants to hear the story from him since he works at the building. He held court in the bar, Pete's Bridge Lounge, of course, and at around eleven or so when he's going home he encounters Monaghan coming from his apartment. He almost shits in his pants because he knows the detectives were at Monaghan's apartment and he's the guy who pointed a finger at Monaghan's kid."

"Exactly," Lenihan interrupted. "Monaghan threatened Cleary's mother."

"Yes and no, but mainly no," Simon replied. "I challenged Cleary myself and told him his story didn't make sense, particularly the bit about Monaghan breaking his nose over the unpaid debt and for the same reason I told you. Chick Nathan and Vince LoBianco do a very brisk loan sharking business, and it's done small scale. Two-bit bettors like Cleary bring in a lot of cash. Figure the Vig for a gambler's ten percent. You bet fifty and lose you pay fifty. You bet fifty and win and you collect forty-five. That's how it works. Smart bookies lay off what they can't even out and live off the vigorish. Cleary's three hundred dollar bet only amounts to thirty dollars after all is said and done, but if he's paying interest until the bet is squared that's fifteen or twenty bucks a week. He's not going anywhere. Why beat him up?"

"Like I said, Monaghan's a bully, I don't know?" answered Lenihan.

"That's what Cleary initially said, but he drank a few more beers and I got it out of him," Simon said smugly.

"Got what?"

"The truth."

"Really?" Lenihan said scornfully.

"Happens," Simon said in agreement, then resumed the account of his dinner with Tim Cleary. "A couple of weeks before he got his nose broken Cleary was home alone on a Saturday afternoon. Mom was out shopping and junior had just stepped out of the shower when he heard some commotion outside his apartment door. Now," Simon said instructively, "the Cleary's live on the ground floor of the building. Their apartment is in the back, just off a carriage room where tenants keep baby carriages and bicycles. The carriage room is a frequent hangout for some of the neighborhood kids and that upsets Mrs. Cleary, and according to her son she isn't shy about grabbing a broom and taking a few swipes at any noisy kids she finds in there. Now, on this day he hears some noise and looks through the peephole, but since his front door isn't square with the door to the carriage room he only gets an angle view and doesn't see anything, but hears what he calls 'loud screeching.' So he opens his door to take a better look and sees two teenage girls hitting each other with what looked like pillows, but were probably mattresses from baby carriages. He steps out from his doorway and yells at these two girls and tells them to knock it off. Problem is he's in his boxer shorts and the two girls start screaming. They call him a pervert and accuse him of exposing himself. He runs back into his apartment and they run away. End of story, right?" Simon asked Lenihan.

"Of course not," Lenihan dryly replied.

"Correct, you are," Simon said laughing. "An hour later Cleary receives an angry phone call from an angry mother. She accuses him of exposing himself to her daughter. This he vociferously denies, but she gives him hell over the phone and threatens to kick his ass. That night he's in Pete's Bridge Lounge and so is this woman. Pete's Bridge Lounge is a Saturday night hot spot. They have a piano player and draw a nice crowd. He's having a beer at the bar and this woman comes over and says, 'I know who you are, you little pervert and I'm going to kick your fucking ass. I seen the way you're always looking at me, but it don't work that way with my little girl.' With that said she slaps him in the face. He's in shock and calls her a 'fucking skank and says she and her daughter ain't worth looking at in the first place' and pushes her out of the way and leaves the bar. Five days later he leaves for his annual trip to Puerto Rico. So what do you think?" Simon asked Lenihan.

Lenihan gave him a knowing nod of the head and said, "The woman is Monaghan's girlfriend."

"And you win a cigar," Simon said, laughing. "Carla Rink is the woman, and she just so happens to be Mike Monaghan's girlfriend. Monaghan is married, but that doesn't seem to mean much, and Cleary tells me that Monaghan's been with this woman for a while, did you know that?"

"Yes," Lenihan said. "It's a pity. Mrs. Monaghan is a lovely woman. Works in the rectory and is very active with the church. I think it was a shotgun marriage, but God only knows why she stays with him."

"Lower-middle class bondage," Simon retorted.

"What?" Lenihan said.

"She can't afford to leave him. Too many, way too many marriages like that. He works, he pays the bills, there's food on the table, what's she to do?" Simon asked rhetorically.

"I guess you're right. He probably ignores her, and maybe she likes it that way."

"Some women enjoy the suffering, don't forget that either," Simon added.

"Okay," Lenihan said. "What else happened?"

"Well, it falls into place. Cleary loses his bet on the World Series and is out three hundred dollars. He gets in this jam with Monaghan's girlfriend and wants to avoid Monaghan for as long as he can, so he takes his trip without paying off his debt. He comes home and a week or so later Monaghan catches up with him and gives him the business. Cleary knows it was about the girlfriend more than the bet. Monaghan don't care because the girlfriend was probably riding him hard the whole time and he did what he had to do, and doing it in front of witnesses would insure the story, heavily embellished, would get back to her. Nobody in the bar takes much notice because the girlfriend has been telling people Cleary's a pervert, not to say she has a sterling reputation. Cleary tells his mother it was over the bet and she in turn spends the last year persecuting Mrs. Monaghan every time she sees her because Timmy was out a hundred bucks in doctor bills. Get it now?" Simon said, acting very pleased with his reconstruction of events.

Lenihan laughed mildly and said, "It makes more sense than anything else I've heard. However, could Cleary have a little problem keeping his dick in his pants? Maybe Monaghan's girlfriend was on to something? Maybe Cleary was snooping around the Weiss' apartment, who knows, sniffing underwear or something and he got caught. It's a possibility."

Simon held his fingers to his nose and said, "That stinks, please."

"Why?"

"What are you saying? Cleary's suddenly a pervert when there's absolutely no record of this ever happening before and he's already thirty-four years or so of age?" Simon said incredulously.

"There's always a first time," Lenihan said defensively

"He's too old to be a dickie waver and still have a clean record. He's lived in Huguenot City all of his life, and except for this annual jaunt he makes to Puerto Rico, he's never been anywhere."

"I said, there's always a first time," Lenihan reiterated.

"Yes, but you don't know very much about the human psyche. You don't wake up one day in your thirties and start waving your pecker around. Taking into account Cleary's age, you would have to figure that if he was a pervert and doing this type of thing he would have been doing it for twenty years. Now, his record is clean. I called my friend Billy Devine up at the Summit Avenue precinct and he told me there's nothing on Cleary in the books and he checked the Lincoln Blvd. precinct too, and they had nothing. He also asked around with some of the sectors boys, but he came up empty handed. Now, you know

Devine, he ain't much of a detective, but he's a hell of a gossip, and if there's something juicy to be known, he knows it. Cleary's clean and I believe him," Simon said adamantly.

Lenihan laughed. "Monaghan didn't."

"Did he really care?"

"I don't know." Lenihan shrugged.

"I don't either, but I bet this Carla's a bit of a handful. I'm told she's a real piece of ass and I'm sure that Monaghan gets plenty of it, but there's no such thing as a free lunch and I'm sure getting tough with Cleary wasn't too difficult a price for Monaghan to pay to keep his girlfriend happy."

Lenihan didn't immediately reply and leaned back in his chair and closed his eyes. For a moment Simon wondered if he'd put the man to sleep as Lenihan's breathing grew slightly heavier. At least two minutes had passed when Lenihan leaned forward and with some enthusiasm exclaimed, "It makes sense. Everything you said makes sense, except why you put it into two reports?"

"Ray Cruz picked up from you very quickly," Simon said smiling.

"How did he manage that?" Lenihan asked.

"He knew you were baiting the district attorney through those stories you kept getting into the papers and decided to do the same thing. I gave him a verbal and he asked me to type it up in two parts. Part one he gave to Broderick at the *News* and I'm sure part two will follow next week. He's keeping the flame alive. Remember, he thinks she's guilty too, and is hoping you can work a deal. Get it?"

Lenihan tapped his fingers on his desk and then asked, "Any suggestions?"

"I would do everything I could to implicate the police in some sort of cover-up. You know, they jumped on Sophie Cruz and failed to investigate other suspects. They were lazy, sloppy, whatever. That's what I'd do. Of course, there's still Monaghan."

"Fuck him," Lenihan said bitterly. "He panicked and that tells me he isn't as tough as I thought."

"How do you figure that?" Simon asked.

"His attitude has always been 'screw them, let them prove it.' And I have to admit I was impressed with just how hard a man he was, but in this case the cops came to his house inquiring about his kid and he cracked. Going to Cleary's mother and giving her a hundred bucks was a clear attempt to buy her goodwill. When it hit home, he got spooked and that means he'll stay as far away from this as he can."

"Why wouldn't he? I got some other background on him, and as I put it together he's a hustler. He works steady, has a piece of that bar Bongos and does the strong arm for LoBianco and Nathan. Why would he want to call attention to himself? Unless he's the vengeful type and can't help himself, you know?" Simon said with just a hint of mischief in his voice.

"Screw you," Lenihan said dismissively. "He's a cold fish and a hard man, but he isn't stupid. He'll ride this out and I'll hear from him eventually, but part of this is his own doing, and I believe he knows it."

"So, you're going to accuse the police of incompetence and the DA of a cover-up?" Simon asked with renewed enthusiasm.

"I'll nuance it some. I don't want to point the finger at Monaghan's kid, but I like the idea of accusing the DA of greasing the skids. The trick is to put another pea under Frank Duffy's mattress without implicating Danny Monaghan, but," he said and then paused for a moment, "I don't see how the business about Cleary helps Sophie. That seems to take the heat off Monaghan," he said with perplexity.

"He's waiting for the cops to exonerate Monaghan, then he drops the Cleary bomb," Simon said, laughing. "You know, you could learn a thing or two from Ray Cruz. He's a sharp cookie."

"I could learn a thing or two from a lot of people," Lenihan replied in agreement. "Thanks, you did well."

"I wish you the best," Simon said as stood up and prepared to leave.

Lenihan didn't bother standing, but gave Simon a big smile and said, "Speaking of the best, you're one of them. Although, using that windbag Devine as an information source does indicate your judgment isn't perfect."

Simon laughed and left the office without further comment.

After he heard the door to the outer office close, Lenihan called out to Blanche, "Blanche, would you please get Broderick on the phone for me?"

"Sophie Cruz called while you were in with Mr. Simon. She said you didn't call her back yesterday and she has to talk to you," Blanche replied.

"Fine, "Lenihan answered. "After you get Broderick, call Sophie up and see if she can come in before noon."

"She sounded very upset," Blanche said from his doorway as she gave him a sour look. "If she comes in and starts blubbering and screeching, I'm taking a walk. I felt sorry for her at first, but not anymore. She's trying you out for her Oscar performance, but if I was on her jury I'd vote guilty in a heartbeat."

"Thanks," Lenihan said sarcastically. "Just make the calls, please."

Chapter Fifty-Six

Blanche couldn't get through to Dennis Broderick at the *Huguenot Daily News*. Twice she was put on hold and hung up after waiting five minutes. The third time she called she was put on hold again, then after a minute the line went dead. Lenihan had the number for the city editor's desk and got through. A secretary answered, and after Lenihan identified himself and the reason for his call she advised him that the editor and Broderick were both unavailable and someone would get back to him.

That was half an hour ago and he was still waiting. "Blanche," he called out impatiently. "Do we have another number for Broderick?"

"I thought Broderick was your man," Blanche said mockingly from her desk in the outer office. "I've only got the number you gave me a few weeks ago."

"My man, who said he was my man!" Lenihan shouted back.

"Isn't that what you told Eddie Simon," she answered.

"Who told to listen in on my conversations?" he replied.

"You talk so loud sometimes, I can't help but listen," she dryly retorted.

"Well, then," he said with exasperation. "From now on you can escort all visitors into my office and close the door. That way I'll have some privacy."

"Whatever you say," she answered lazily, then asked, "How come he hasn't called back?"

"No reason to," Lenihan said as he stood in the doorway to his office and stretched his hands above the frame. "Right now he thinks he knows more about this case than I do and until he thinks differently he hasn't the time of day for me. If Ray Cruz called him up, he'd be on the phone in a heartbeat."

"I thought you knew him, you know, well enough to get him when you want."

"We started out around the same time. He was a beat reporter and I was a green prosecutor. Nice guy, give you a plug in a story when he could but not more than that. We know each other, but that's about it, and if there isn't something in it for him, then who am I?" Lenihan said with shake of his head. "When's Sophie coming in?"

Blanche looked at her watch. "Guess it depends on the outfit, maybe another ten minutes, maybe an hour."

"Women are so catty," Lenihan said with a scowl.

Blanche sneered. "Catty, not at all. She's just cheap and I don't like her. Who killed that poor Millie Campos after all?"

"Like I said, catty, and don't be so quick to judge," Lenihan said curtly as he retreated back into his office.

He read and re-read Simon's report and Broderick's piece in the newspaper, but found little advantage for his defense in the revelation that Mike Monaghan had coincidentally attempted to repair his relationship with the Cleary's on the same day his son had been indirectly fingered as a suspect by Tim Cleary. It was nothing more than another irritation for Frank Duffy to suffer in his quest for election. Blanche's assessment of Sophie was a clear harbinger of how the average Huguenot City juror would preemptively judge Sophie Cruz, and Lenihan was confidant the district attorney's office would clear this latest hurdle without much concern or effort. There was a knock on his door and Blanche interrupted his reading, "Miss Cruz is here," she said coldly. "Shall I show her in?"

"Yes, Mrs. O'Connor, please do," he unctuously replied.

"Mrs. O'Connor," Blanche answered sourly, with a slight look of bewilderment on her face. Lenihan stared at her impassively but didn't reply. Blanche held his stare for several seconds, then in her smoky voice said to Sophie, "Go on in."

"What's her problem?" was all she said as she came into his office and dropped a shopping bag in one of the two chairs in front of his desk and sat in the other. She was well tanned and conservatively dressed in beige slacks with a blue short sleeved blouse and brown loafers. It reminded him of how his wife often dressed, and Blanche's snide remark, "Guess it depends on the outfit," repeated itself in his mind and he despaired at how cruel women could be to one another. Sophie had lost weight and her eyes appeared slightly sunken, with some bluing of the skin under her eye sockets evident beneath her deep tan. He gave her his warmest smile and said, "Pay her no mind."

"She thinks I'm guilty. I can tell. She won't look at me," she tiredly replied.

"I wouldn't say that," he said unconvincingly. "Blanche isn't strong in the personality department."

"That's for sure," Sophie answered.

"You look worn out. Are you getting enough sleep?" Lenihan asked.

"No, not much, I lay down, but every ten minutes I'm up and smoking a cigarette. You know, pacing the floor and wishing I could wake up from all of this."

Lenihan shook his head sympathetically. "It's written all over your face." He then picked up a copy of the *Huguenot Daily News* from his desk and said, "I guess you've seen this morning's paper?"

Sophie appeared nonplused and replied, "Ray's all excited, but I think it was a waste of money."

Lenihan was surprised by Sophie's reaction and sat still in his chair with a puzzled look on his face. She leaned forward, sucked in her lips, then let them out and slowly said, "Waste of fucking money. Pardon my French, but that's how I feel."

"Why?" he finally asked.

"Because it don't mean anything. Ray wants to run the show. He thinks he can do a better job than you can. Eddie Simon found out something that made the cops look bad, but it won't help me. I know that. Ray doesn't. He thinks this is all going to blow up in the district attorney's face. You know, Monaghan's a suspect and the police didn't bother investigating it. That's what Ray thinks, but I know he doesn't think Monaghan killed that woman. He still thinks I did it. And Eddie Simon found out all about the doorman. I knew he was a pervert soon as I saw him at the police station," she added, with emphasis, before continuing. "But being a pervert doesn't make him a suspect either. All it does is explain why Monaghan's father did what he did. It looks good in the paper today, but as soon as the police talk to Cleary it will be cleared up. That's why it's a waste of money."

"I'm sure Mr. Duffy has everyone running around in circles today."

"So what, they're gonna find out everything and say it's no big deal. Ray's talking to that newspaperman like he's in on it," she said angrily. "They're on the phone yesterday, back and forth, like two schemers. Even Eddie Simon told him it didn't look good, but he won't listen."

"You're right to a point," Lenihan said soberly. "But I have a good idea what your brother is up to, and it was the same thing I was trying to do. But you don't want to go there, so maybe it is a waste of money. But I'm at my wits end on how to defend you."

"No, I'm not right, up to a point I'm completely right because you're wrong, Ray's wrong and the district attorney is wrong," she said loudly as she took the shopping bag from the chair and reached into it. She pulled out a long grey legal envelope and flung it onto Lenihan's desk. "Read that, Mr. Lenihan and then tell me I'm wrong!"

Lenihan picked up the envelope, carefully holding it at the edges as if he was unsure he wanted to touch it or not. He turned it around and read the return address printed in the upper left corner of the envelope. "Fortescue Wilcox Bram," he said as he held the envelope upside down and let the contents fall out. "Someone's divorcing you?" he asked without looking at the papers he had just removed form the envelope.

"I've never been married. Try again or better yet, read the petition," she said sharply.

He followed her direction and picked up the packet. It was ten pages long and stapled to a grey backing. As he started to read, he repeated aloud some of the words on the pages. Sophie sat silently with tears welling in her eyes. "Petitioner Henry Weiss, minor child Joseph Weiss...a.k.a. Joseph Gomes, .a.k.a. Joseph Cruz...respondent Sophie Cruz...joint custody..."

He didn't read every page, but as he scanned it she read his every twitch and facial movement, and before he finished reading the complete document, she impatiently said, "He's taking me to court. He wants joint custody of my son. On the last page he asks for full custody in the event of my death or other incapacitation."

Lenihan put the document down and exclaimed, "Jesus Christ, he wants custody. Why?"

Sophie was crying, and she offered a weak laugh followed by several gasps and sniffling attempts to regain her composure. Lenihan blushed and said, "Jesus Christ, the paternity suit. What is he doing? Getting even with you for that?"

Sophie caught her breath and said plaintively, "Listen to me, please. This is Maria's doing. She wants to punish me, and she's going to do this by taking my son from me. Incapacitation is another way of saying I'm going to jail."

"This is unexpected," Lenihan said distractedly as he scanned the pages of the petition again, ignoring Sophie's last remark.

She was fumbling with a package of cigarettes, trying to peel off the cellophane wrapper when she suddenly threw the pack at his head. "Didn't you hear me?" she shrieked. "Dead or incapacitated," she repeated slowly and loudly.

The flat side of the cigarette pack slapped weakly across his face and fell to the desk. He was stunned, but only momentarily, and without uttering a response he calmly removed the cellophane wrapping and handed the pack back to Sophie. She was more stunned by her action than he was, and once again the uncontrollable river of tears poured down her cheeks and she took the pack and placed it back into her handbag, all the while sniffling and choking back her tears.

Lenihan folded his hands together and bowed his head, and, as if he were reciting a prayer, he said, "Sophie, Sophie, I can't help you. I want to, but I can't."

She stuck out her chin and started to speak, but he raised his hand to quiet her and kept on talking. "Sophie, it's over. You're going to go to the bathroom and wash up and compose yourself. Then you're going to sit down and listen to me. And then and only then, after I've had my say will you have a chance to say anything." He stood up, came around his desk and very gently placed his hand on her elbow and assisted her to her feet. He took a Kleenex from the box on his desk and wiped away a stream of tears from her right cheek and with warmth and tenderness in his voice said, "Right out the door, to the right is the bathroom. Wash your face up and calm down. Please, I care about you, believe me, I really do."

Sophie took the Kleenex from his hand and wiped the other side of her face and pushed his hand away from her. "I don't want your sympathy, and I'm tired of being treated like some kind of fool who doesn't understand what's at risk. I'll wash up after we're through," she said abrasively and defiantly as she made her way back to the chair she'd been sitting in and sat back down.

"Fine," Lenihan said coldly as he went back behind his desk. He sat down and picked up the legal brief she'd given to him, and said, "Boyce Fortescue is a very able attorney. He is one of the leading attorneys in this state when it comes to divorce and custody matters. I'm not in his league, and this has nothing to do with your pending trial for murder." He handed it back to her. "I don't do that. As a matter of fact, I owe you an apology. I should have never taken you on and I've mishandled this case. I thought you were guilty, or if you were innocent the police had more than enough evidence to prove you were guilty." He paused, waiting for a reaction from her, but she sat mute and rigid, giving him all her attention. "I thought the best avenue to follow would be to throw as many question marks into the mix as possible with the hope that the district attorney might feel some discomfort with the case and give us a deal. That hope was greatly advanced when John Malfetano stepped down as district attorney and his hand-picked successor Frank Duffy was awarded the interim position. Duffy's been hunkering for that job since he joined the office. I thought we had a shot, and with a tight race between Duffy and Brooks I knew that every reference to this case we could get into the paper was a thorn in his side. Frank Duffy and Henry Weiss are both closely connected to Lee Futerman. Duffy and Weiss may not be close, but Futerman was the link I needed to plant the seed that this was something of a railroad job. Eddie Simon's lead on Monaghan isn't a waste of money," he said with insistence.

"Please," she answered with annoyance.

"Please?" he replied raising his voice. "Monaghan's a tough man. Something spooked him and he went to Mrs. Cleary to make nice. That meant it wasn't beyond him to suspect his son did something. I agree that the cops can explain it all away, but it has value in the news. More than I initially thought this morning. But everything I've tried to do and what your brother is trying to do has only one goal, and that goal is to force Duffy to make this case go away and give you a deal. But," he said as he rose from his desk and leaned over and looked at her harshly, "you're innocent, so why bother."

"I am innocent, you son of a bitch," she said, with spittle spraying from her lips.

"Well, I'm going to give you back every penny you paid me, and I'll also pay Simon's fee since I recommended him. The judge and trial date was supposed to be assigned next Tuesday, but I'll contact Joe Daley, that's Duffy's number two man, and tell him we need an extension since you'll be acquiring new counsel. That will only make Mr. Duffy very happy since he can push the trial past election day and get this out of the papers. I'll have Blanche write you a check and you can send me Simon's bill. Thank you," he said firmly as he made his way to the door to show her out.

"I'm not going anywhere," she said defiantly.

"I can't help you," he replied just as defiantly.

Sophie looked at her wristwatch. "It's ten to one. Today is the last day of day camp for Joey. I don't know why they always finish on a Wednesday, but they do," she said casually as if the tension between them had faded away.

"I don't care," Lenihan said with his hand on the doorknob.

"Well, you should. The camp puts on a little play for the parents on the last day, then they give some awards and serve hot dogs and ice cream. It's very nice and I have to be there by one-thirty, so we have time," she said calmly and business-like.

Lenihan was incensed, and glared at her, but he could see she wasn't moving. She had the same hard determined look on her face he'd seen at the city jail when he met her several days after her arraignment. "Okay," he said as he went back behind his desk and sat down. "What is it you want to say?"

"I told you before, and I'll tell you again," she said as she stood up and leaned toward him. "I'm innocent, and I just want you to understand that. I'm innocent, why would I want to make a deal for something I didn't do."

"Fine," he nearly shouted. "Fine, but will you please listen to what I've been saying, what I've been trying to tell you since we first met?"

"Yes," she said demurely.

"You're obsessed with the word innocent. In the court of public opinion you're guilty. And you were right about my secretary. She thinks you're guilty, and that's based on having met you and read the newspaper stories. I've never said a thing to her about the case."

"Oh, that's terrific," she scoffed. "You decide what to do because of what your secretary thinks."

"The court of public opinion is what I said. Can't you comprehend reality?" he asked.

"Reality! I'm living in the freaking Twilight Zone," she said with a mocking laugh.

"We could go to trial and you could be acquitted and most of the half-baked people out there who pass for good upstanding citizens would say you're still guilty. That's reality, and the sooner you open your eyes the better off you'll be," he said with exasperation.

"So what do you know that I don't know?" she asked.

"I have spent a lot of time reviewing the police reports and considering the severity of the indictment against you. Based on my experience, this business about a deal, the district attorney offering you a deal is probably a moot point. I don't think it's going to happen."

She laughed sarcastically. "I don't want a deal. I want my day in court."

"Exactly," he said in agreement. "You deserve your day in court, and you deserve the best representation you can get."

"So," she said in a quaking voice, "why are you dropping me?"

"Because I haven't served you well. We blew it the first day, and that puts me at a disadvantage. They, the police and the district attorney, have an edge on me."

"You're afraid?" she cried incredulously.

"Hear me out, then you can decide."

"You're afraid?" she repeated.

"Yes, I am, and here's why."

"You don't care about my case, you're worried about yourself, you big phony," she said tauntingly.

Lenihan leaned back in his chair and reached for the ashtray on the corner of his desk. He pushed it toward her and said, "Relax, light up a cigarette and take a few drags." Sophie obeyed, and while she was searching in her pocketbook for her cigarettes Lenihan resumed talking. "Sophie, the man prosecuting this case is a barracuda. He's a courtroom assassin and he enjoys that role. His name is Gordon Alpert, and I know enough about him to know that in order for you to have a chance you need someone as tough and relentless as he is. I compromised myself that first day at the precinct when I brought you in. Alpert will not hesitate to put every salacious aspect of your relationship with Henry out there for the jury to consider. You regularly had sex on his office couch, didn't you?" he asked.

Sophie nodded her head, but said nothing.

"It will all be up for grabs, and when he's finished you'll be nothing more than a grasping little tart who went off the deep end when her sugar daddy closed the door in her face. That's what he's going to do, and Henry will sit in the witness box like a big stooge and you," he said angrily, pointing his finger at her, "you will be the manipulator, the one in control. You will be the author of this entire sad and seamy tragic little tale!"

Sophie looked at him with horror and the color drained from her face. "You think?" she asked with embarrassment. "Why?" she added, once again on the verge of tears. "I didn't seduce him, you know, he was a part of it," she said defensively.

"Sophie," Lenihan said shaking his head. "This is a man's world. If a woman lifts her skirt and a man drops his drawers to oblige her, who's at fault?"

"Why's anyone at fault?" she asked.

"Because society says that boys and girls shouldn't play like that if they aren't married. We're talking convention here, not what people really do," he lectured.

"So, I'm to blame," she said, pointing a finger at herself.

"Yes, you seduced him. He was having problems in his marriage going back to when he first hired you. You Sophie, you scheming little hussy, you figured that out and took advantage of him. You literally or figuratively lifted your skirt and he, being a weak and simple-minded man, as all men are considered to be when it comes to women and sex, did what comes naturally."

"That's bullshit, pure bullshit," Sophie said with disgust.

"In 1936 my uncle was working at Emerald Foods in the lower borough. He worked in the same department, doing roughly the same work as my aunt did. They weren't married at the time, but that's where they met. Anyway, my uncle was making twenty-one dollars a week, but my aunt made only twelve dollars for virtually the same job," he exclaimed raising, his voice a tone. "It's man's world. Back then and now it hasn't changed much. Society is tilted toward men, and women do their damned best to make it work that way. Don't you see?" he implored.

"This is so tiring," she whined.

"Frustrating, isn't it?"

"No, it's stupid, just Goddamn stupid."

"Is this too difficult for you?" Lenihan said sarcastically.

"No, how come you think you know what's going to happen if I go on trial?"

"Because I was a prosecutor too, and it is exactly what I would do if I was trying this case. Believe me, when I was done every member of the jury would believe you purposely had Henry's baby and did so just to blackmail him and," he paused and stood up and leaned over the desk and pointed his two index fingers at her, "the rent receipts and every other dime he spent on you would prove my case."

"What about Maria and those pictures?" Sophie asked as she lit a cigarette from the lit end of the one she was smoking.

"Meaningless," he said with a flourish as he waved his hands in the air. "I saw the pictures along with the crime scene photographs. Alpert was snickering when he showed them to me. They're nothing more than standard nudie shots."

"You saw the pictures?" Sophie said with mild astonishment.

"Discovery, we're entitled to everything before trial."

"You didn't tell me," she said with disappointment in her voice.

"You'll get to see them in time. Satisfying your curiosity isn't at the head of my list."

Sophie blushed. "I really do hate her. Are they embarrassing?"

"They are what they are, and I doubt they will even be a topic. Forget about them, forget about Maria."

"Why?" she asked insolently.

"Because your hatred for her is so strong I can taste it. This isn't about

Maria Weiss. It is about Sophie Cruz, and the sooner that sinks in the sooner we can decide what to do."

She gave him a bored look and tapped her watch with her finger, "I have to get going."

"We have a decision to make," Lenihan said with frustration in his voice.

Sophie took several breaths and looked at Lenihan. "Decision!" she said angrily. "You think this is about me, about me and Henry when it's about my son."

"Sophie," he said with just as much anger in his voice, "I've heard it all. I want to call somebody. He's excellent and just the man you'll need for this fight. Save the story for him, please."

She glanced at her watch and put here fingers to her lips, and in doing so asked for his attention and silence. "You have to understand my situation," she pleaded. "When Joey was big enough to climb out of his crib he used to come into my bed every night. In the morning he would always wake up first. He would tickle me and kiss me singing 'time to get up, Mommy, time to get up.' When he got a little older he'd sleep through the night, but then on Saturdays and Sundays when I stayed in bed a little longer he'd come in and get in with me. Sometimes we'd wrestle or have tickle contests. He was so lovable," she sighed. "But," she said sadly, "by the time he was four he started asking about his 'Poppy' and I would make up stories. Every week I'd make up a new one and that worked for a while, then if I changed the story he would correct me. Pretty soon it got serious, you know," she said as she paused and smiled at him, hoping to see some expression of sympathy or understanding from him as he sat across from her looking as bored as she had only moments ago when he was talking. "It wasn't a game anymore, and for the last two years I've told him the same story. He thinks his father is away in the Army. He turned eight a few weeks ago and that isn't working anymore and he wants to know if he has a father. That's why I was so hard on Henry the last couple of years. I couldn't go on lying to my son, and now he's old enough to catch me at it."

"So, you've never told him the truth?" Lenihan asked.

"No, I've lied and lied and lied. I was happy living with Joey. I didn't need a man there. Believe me. I only wanted Henry, you know, full time because his son wants a father. All of his friends have fathers. Why does he have to feel different?"

"I thought you loved Henry?"

"I do, I did," she said, throwing her hands in the air. "What's it matter. Don't you see? That's why I did what I did. It was for Joey, not for me. I saw that things between us would only get worse as he got older. That's why I got so angry that day in Montreal. I realized that Maria would never let him go, and he wasn't man enough to leave her."

"Or he didn't love you," Lenihan challenged.

"You don't have to rub it in my face," she answered as she looked away from him and blew her nose into the shredded strands of Kleenex that were crumpled in her hand.

"It doesn't matter, Sophie," Lenihan said with annoyance. "From the beginning I've told you that your motive is immaterial to your defense. And just to set the record straight, that fatal Friday when I took you on we went to lunch at Erlich's. Do you remember?"

"Yes," she said. "You were very nice."

"Well, I recall you telling me about the trip to Montreal with Henry. Do you remember that?"

"Of course I do," she said with surprise. "We've gone over that twenty times."

"We have, but I recall you telling me that when you two went to bed you just went to sleep. There was no fooling around, so to speak."

"Yes, that's right. Well, that night, but the next day, you know, we did it," she said, still puzzled by what he was driving at.

"You said that you were happy just to wake up next to him."

"So what if I did?" she replied.

"Two minutes ago you said you were only pursuing Henry because of your son. You said you were happy with the arrangement. So which is it?"

"What?" she said defensively.

"Sophie, Sophie," he sighed. "You don't get it. You can't get it because you're ruled by emotion. Two months ago you were happy just to wake up next to the man. Two minutes ago you were happy in your little apartment with your son. You didn't need a man there. You can't have it both ways."

"Now I'm a liar," she said indignantly.

"No, not a liar, not at all, you're simply too emotional. You'll have to testify in this trial. You'll have to tell your story, and there isn't much there, save for your emotions, that can exculpate you. There's no existent proof that can exonerate you, is there?" he asked.

"I'm a liar."

"Not a liar, Sophie, but you react emotionally to every challenge. When you testify under direct examination, it should be okay. You tell your story and you do your best to convince the jury that you're innocent and to a large degree a victim."

"Yes, I'm a victim and I'm happy you finally said it."

"One problem," he said sourly. "One little problem. The prosecutor gets to cross-examine you and it isn't going to be pretty. You cannot, and I say that emphatically and sincerely, you cannot control your emotions. You fly off the handle, burst into tears, throw things and do ten other things I can't think of at the moment that broadcast an innate inability to control your temper. Didn't you hit me with the cigarettes before?" he asked.

She hung her head and whimpered, "I'm sorry."

"The prosecutor is going to pick and prod. Remember, he asks the questions and you have to answer. You don't ask, and if you don't answer the question he appeals to the court and you're directed to answer. However, if you don't directly answer the question, but go off on a tangent and offer additional information that can harm you, neither the prosecutor nor the court will stop you. Nothing favors the witness, nothing. My assessment is that when Gordon Alpert finishes with his cross-examination you'll be spilling tears and sitting in a puddle of your own urine. And I don't say that cruelly, but it's what I can see happening."

Sophie held her breath for a moment, then gushed, "Whose side are you on?"

"Yours," he said emotionally. "I want you to speak with Leo Sheridan. He's a good man and tougher than I am, and I'll admit it. Right now he's the only chance you have of beating this charge. Otherwise it's a one way bus ride to Deerpoint."

"Deerpoint?" she questioned.

"That's the women's maximum security prison, and where you're likely to end up barring a miracle."

"I never heard of it," she said with a quiver in her voice. Lenihan had mentioned prison any number of times, but it was always in the abstract and his giving the prison a name sent her into a panic. "I never heard of it," she repeated shrilly.

"Leo Sheridan is your best bet," Lenihan said reassuringly. "I'm going to call him this afternoon, right after you leave and ask him to take you on."

"Deerpoint," Sophie said, ignoring Lenihan's reference to Leo Sheridan. "Deerpoint, where is it? I never heard of it."

"Let's forget about Deerpoint for the moment," Lenihan said confidently. "I want you to meet with Leo. I think you'll like him."

Sophie interrupted Lenihan and said excitedly, "Let's not forget about Deerpoint. You brought it up. Why would I go there? Why would you say that?"

"I brought it up because I am trying to impress upon you just how precarious and serious your situation is. You are on the precipice and about to tumble down a hole too deep to crawl out of. You're on your way to prison," he said emphatically.

"Where's Deerpoint?" she asked again.

"What does it matter?" he replied angrily.

"Where is it, just tell me where it is?" she pleaded

"...83 miles north and 67 miles west, and no shortcuts in between," he answered.

Sophie had her cigarettes in her hand, but then threw the pack back into her bag. The color was coming back into her face and she had sunk into the chair. Her posture was gone and she looked as lifeless as a dishrag. "We talked about jail, but I never thought of prison. All I could think of was that horrible Huguenot City jail I was in. I was there four days and that was horrible."

"Sophie, forgive me for being harsh," he said sorrowfully. "Forgive me, but we have to face facts. The cards are stacked against you, and from where I sit it looks like a twenty to twenty-five year stretch in Deerpoint. I wish I could tell you different, but if I did I'd be lying. Can we talk about Leo? I think he'll give you a chance, I really do."

Sophie looked at her watch and stood up. She reached over the desk and stuck her fingers in the Kleenex box and took out a wad of tissues. "I have to go. I don't want to be late. I'm meeting my aunt and I don't want her to worry."

"Sophie, what do you want to do?"

"It's too much, too much, and I can't think right now. Maybe next week, maybe tomorrow, I don't really know. I have to go see my baby. That's what's important to me. I have to go see my baby," she mumbled as she picked up her handbag and turned for the door.

"Can I call your brother Ray?" Lenihan asked.

Sophie didn't answer. She had moved from his office and was making her way quickly to the front door. Lenihan was in pursuit. "Sophie, I need an answer," he pleaded. She ignored him and was out the door, and he could hear her rapid steps down the stairs and a second later the bang of the street level door as it slammed closed.

Blanche's desk was empty. Roger McKee's part-time secretary, Kathleen Drew, was seated at her desk. She gave Lenihan a reassuring smile and said, "Blanche told me to tell you she had a headache and was going home."

"I'd like to do the same," Lenihan said with a shrug of his shoulders. "I'd like to do the same."

Chapter Fifty-Seven

The district attorney's office for Huguenot City was located in the Upper Borough. Mayor Cornelius Cody had engineered the erection of the new courthouse and adjoining legal services office building to the Upper Borough in 1923. That was two years after Frank Heaton had won the first of nine consecutive elections as Huguenot City district attorney. Mayor Cody, a well liked and powerful Republican politician, was prescient enough to know that the handsome young district attorney whose offices were directly opposite City Hall at Government Square was too ambitious and smart to go unnoticed by the local powerbrokers and would eventually become a force to be reckoned with in Huguenot City. His relocation to the Upper Borough was nothing more than an attempt to give the mayor some additional time to run out his own career before his party faltered and Heaton and the Democrats took over. Frank Heaton was thirty-one years old when he won his first election, and by the time he was halfway through his second term in office he knew that there was no other role for him in life than that of district attorney. Heaton was more than handsome, ambitious and smart. He was shrewd, vindictive, generous and wholly amoral in the wielding of his power when necessary to advance his own interests. His public persona was that of a crime fighter and champion of law and order. His private one was that of an unforgiving potentate who expected more than he received and never forgot a slight. He was, in the simplest of terms, a masterful politician, and nine victories at the polls, the last of which was achieved while he was dying from esophageal cancer, was all the testimony that was needed to affirm his success. Mayor Cody may have misjudged where Heaton's ambition would take him, but his instincts about the man were certain.

Upon winning his third term as district attorney, Frank Heaton accepted the honor of permitting the Huguenot City Ladies Art Committee to commission Robert Bench, a well known portraitist, to capture the district attorney's royal visage with oil and canvass. The portrait was a remarkable likeness, and upon completion was affixed to a wall in the main conference room of the district attorney's office. Heaton's successor, John Malfetano, had removed the portrait shortly after taking office and had it hung in the lobby of the legal services building. His reasoning at the time was that he thought the painting should be hung where the public could enjoy it, although anyone who knew Malfetano knew he couldn't bear competing with the legend of his predecessor, and the removal of the portrait from the conference room was the first of many steps to remind his subordinates that Heaton was dead and he was the new boss.

It was John Malfetano who made Frank Duffy his second in command, and it was John Malfetano who groomed Frank Duffy as his hand-picked successor, but it was Frank Heaton who had given Duffy his start, and out of respect for Heaton's memory Duffy's first official act as district attorney was to return the portrait to the conference room where Heaton had originally had it placed. Joe Daley, the recently appointed deputy district attorney to Frank Duffy, sat alone in the conference room. The first time he had ever been in the conference room was his initial employment interview. He recalled sitting there, alone, for a half hour with little to do but study Heaton's portrait. The interview was unpleasant. Heaton was accompanied by a young prosecutor named Frank Duffy. Heaton introduced Duffy, then took a long look at Daley's resume and tossed it on the table. "You've got the job," he said sourly, then as he stood up and prepared to leave the room, he said, "Mr. Duffy will explain the facts of life to you. Say hello to your mother for me." Without another word Heaton was gone and Daley sat embarrassed and red-faced over the way his uncle had treated him. Daley knew that it was only because he was the son of Frank Heaton's favorite sister that he was hired. He knew that his lackluster law school grades, equally lackluster college transcript, and his 4F military classification that had allowed him to stay in school and avoid the war qualified him as everything Heaton didn't look for when hiring new prosecutors. Duffy was a gentleman and made no mention of Heaton's rudeness or Daley's substandard resume. Daley was a new hire and Duffy spent the better part of two hours discussing how the office worked and taking Daley on a tour of the district attorney's offices and the adjoining courthouse. Daley was never introduced as Heaton's nephew and, at the conclusion of the day, Duffy mentioned that it might be a good thing not to let on the familial connection with Heaton. Daley did just that and for five years spent his time shuttling between Motions and Appeals and a satellite office in the Lower Borough. He might as well have been stuffed in a closet, and it wasn't until Frank Heaton died and John Malfetano took over that his career as a prosecutor really began.

It was Frank Duffy who provided Daley with his first assignment in the trial bureau, and whether it was done out of sympathy for how Heaton had treated his nephew, or perhaps because Duffy saw quality where Heaton had seen inferiority mattered not a bit to Daley. It was an opportunity, and he made the most of it. Three years later he was promoted to deputy trial chief, and three years later he was made the trial bureau chief. His greatest moment of success arrived just several weeks ago when Frank Duffy had appointed him as his deputy district attorney.

The past was the past, he thought, and in some small way he was content with the memory of how his uncle had hired him, then made him invisible. Whatever he had achieved he had done on his own, and if there was any lingering bitterness it surfaced when Daley was appointed to the number two position in the district attorney's office and both the *Huguenot Daily News* and the *Huguenot Times* dedicated several stories to the familial connection between Daley and Heaton and the close relationship between Duffy and Heaton. There was nothing he could do to distance himself from his legendary uncle, and if the press declared the late Frank Heaton as a posthumous powerbroker still calling the shots, then it was so, he reasoned, even if it wasn't true. What was important and pressing was how he was handling the upcoming prosecution of Sophie Cruz and how he was going to explain this morning's revelation in the *Huguenot Daily News* that the father of one of the initial suspects had allegedly threatened the mother of one of the state's witnesses. He had told Duffy it was horseshit and just another cheap ploy by Lenihan to derail the case.

Duffy's response, "If you believe that you're a horse's ass," was uttered with glaring contempt, and when Daley tried to respond he was quickly quieted with a wave of Duffy's hand and the added threat, "If this isn't straightened out today somebody's going to pay."

The timing couldn't have been worse. Gordon Alpert, Daley's favored gunslinger of a prosecutor, was away on vacation. Alpert was obviously the target of Duffy's rage, and while Daley felt Duffy was being unfair, he was reluctant to defend his protégé. *I'll take care of this myself,* he thought at the time, *and by day's end it'll be water under the bridge.* It was several minutes past three in the afternoon and he knew no more than he had known at nine in the morning when Duffy had first confronted him, and as he awaited his audience with his boss the only defense he could think of was to blame the detectives for initially bumbling the investigation. It wasn't a question of being nervous or fearful of telling his boss that the police had made little headway determining the truth of the *Huguenot Daily News* story so much as it was watching the slow disintegration of Frank Duffy's granite character as it buckled and cracked over any reference to the Huguenot City district attorney's office that wasn't positive.

Daley heard the sound of muffled voices, then the door to the conference room opened. He expected to see Duffy and was surprised when Rick Kopek entered the room alone. Kopek had joined Duffy's office as a special advisor upon Duffy's appointment as district attorney. Kopek's background was in labor relations, and over the course of a very successful career he had represented almost every labor union in the Huguenot City metropolitan area. The skills he had honed at the bargaining table were just as sharp when it came to politics, and it was considered a coup for Frank Duffy when he was able to persuade Kopek to take a hiatus from his practice and join his campaign. Daley was jealous of Kopek. Being the number two man wasn't turning out the way he had thought it would. His contact with Duffy was limited to a five or ten minute meeting every morning, and the fraternity he had always felt for his boss was waning in the wake of Duffy's undisguised and raw ambition to win the election. Kopek was always at his side, and if the news wasn't good then it was Daley's fault.

Daley didn't bother to stand when Kopek came into the room. He pushed his eyeglasses to the tip of his nose and said, "Where's Frank?"

Kopek had a file folder in his left hand. He sat down at a chair positioned directly across from Daley and replied, "The district attorney is busy."

Kopek's terse answer took Daley by surprise. "My secretary said he wanted to meet with me at three. I guess he wanted the update, not that there's much to tell right now," he said almost apologetically.

"I'm standing in for him," Kopek said coldly.

Daley gave a nervous laugh and then said, "Isn't that my job?"

Kopek ignored him and said, "The district attorney would like to know what you've found out about Monaghan and the story in this morning's paper?"

Kopek intimidated him. He didn't know why, but he wanted to please the man, while at the same time he wanted to reach across the table choke him. His anger got the best of him and he said, "He's Frank, Frank Duffy. You keep calling him the district attorney like he's the fucking Pope or something. I've known the man for fifteen years, and he's Frank. So let's cut out all the formalities and do what we have to do, please!"

Daley's outburst had no discernible effect on Kopek, and he calmly replied, "I gather you haven't found anything out yet, have you?"

The man was cold, and his icy reserve was overwhelming. Daley nodded his head negatively and said, "The cops have screwed this whole thing up. I spoke with Captain Grimsley this morning and he assured me that we'd have it all cleared up by this afternoon. That was at a little after nine this morning. I spoke with him again around eleven, but at that point his men had come up zero on Monaghan and Cleary. They did speak with Mrs. Cleary, but she was uncooperative and said the whole story was bullshit."

"They can't find Monaghan or Cleary?" Kopek asked.

"Cleary has the day off, and his mother didn't know where he went. She's lying, I'm sure, and no one was home in the Monaghan house."

"It's a little late in the game for this, don't you think so?" Kopek asked.

"What's it matter what I think. This is just another slice of baloney that creep Lenihan's thrown out to make us look bad," Daley said defensively.

Kopek sighed. "That's helpful."

Daley's cheeks reddened and he testily replied, "Maybe not today, but by tomorrow I'm sure this will all be explained. It's another bullshit story in the paper. What's the big deal anyway? Gordon's going to make mincemeat out of Lenihan's defense. For the life of me I can't understand why this case gets under Frank's skin so."

Kopek looked down at the folder he had laid on the table. He fingered the corner of it abstractedly, and after giving a moment's reflection to Daley's complaint, said, "Nothing's that simple, my friend. Your job was to manage this case, and I don't think things are going well. If it was, we wouldn't have seen today's headline because that aspect of the investigation would have been fully vetted."

Daley looked across the table at his uncle's portrait hanging on the wall. If he was looking for support, it wasn't there. All he saw was his uncle's icon, frozen in time, regal in appearance and disdainful of failure. Daley knew he had failed. Duffy's absence was all the proof he needed. Kopek sat still, confident and patient. Daley was unsure of what Kopek wanted, but he was resolute in affirming that the screw up was the fault of the Huguenot City P.D. and not the D.A.'s office. "Listen," he said angrily. "I'm not happy either. Just before I came upstairs I put in a call to the police commissioner. He wasn't available, but when I'm done I'll call again. I'm letting him know personally how pissed off I am, and we are over this."

"That doesn't solve the problem, though, does it?" Kopek asked.

"What can we do? By Friday I'm sure this will be water under the bridge," Daley said in a more relaxed tone.

"Joe," Kopek said somewhat solemnly, "we did a survey last week of two hundred registered Democrats. We canvassed voters in the Upper Borough, Lower Borough and Huguenot City. It was a fair representation of the city. What do you think we found out?"

"What was the survey about?" Daley asked sullenly, expecting further insinuations from Kopek that he was not competent.

"Two questions were asked. The first question was a simple one: Do you know who Frank Duffy is, and do you know who Stephen Brooks is? The second question was: if you know either man, how do you know of him? We wanted a cross section of two hundred registered voters, and we wanted to know if they recognized either of the candidates, and if they did, to what context. Plus, we only surveyed registered Democrats because they constitute our voting base."

"It's about five to three in our favor, isn't it?" Daley asked, comfortable in his knowledge of the edge Democrats held in the voting balance of Huguenot City.

"Brooks is running as a Liberal and as a Republican. The Liberal line appeals to Democrats and can occasion broad crossovers, so the five to three edge doesn't mean much in this race," Kopek corrected.

"So what were the results?"

"One hundred and eighty-one of the people surveyed knew Stephen Brooks. They either knew him as a former councilman, or as a candidate for district attorney, or both, and some also identified him as a reformer. So, among the one hundred and eighty-one potential voters we had a little over ninety percent who knew Brooks. Pretty good, don't you think?" Kopek asked.

Daley shook his head and then said, "What about Frank?"

"One hundred and four people knew Frank Duffy, and while each and every one of them knew him as the district attorney, eighty percent of the one hundred and four identified their recognition of Frank Duffy through articles appearing in the *Huguenot Daily News* and the *Huguenot Times* relating to the Millie Campos murder case. What do you make of that?"

Daley perked up and smiled. "Looks like this case is helping, Frank. According to that survey nobody would know him if it weren't for all that crap in the papers."

"Ninety percent know Stephen Brooks and fifty-two percent know Frank Duffy, but eighty percent of that fifty-two percent know him primarily through negative references in the newspapers and you think that's a positive?" Kopek said sarcastically.

"We had a terrible murder, and it was solved quickly by the police. We have an easy case to prosecute despite the bullshit that's been put in the papers and you think it's mostly negative?" Daley asked with some confusion.

"I'm not talking about the merits of the case, I'm talking about the references to Frank Duffy and they have been in the negative and have followed a theme that paints all of city government, and particularly the district attorney's office as one big club, one close-knit fraternity where everybody takes care of everybody else. That's what the core of Brooks' campaign will be about, and he has already and will now, especially after this morning's headline, exploit that. I can hear the litany of charges now—cronyism, fraternalism, nepotism and anything else that suggests corruption. Isn't the mayor forging a new anti-corruption program? And he doesn't run until 1966! Maybe it's all a little more than the 'bullshit' you seem so insistent on saying it is," Kopek said condescendingly.

Daley was rattled by Kopek's cold and superior demeanor. "So what do we do?" he asked. "Hang the police out to dry? Accuse Gordon Alpert of doing a bad job building the case and reassign him? What's the damage control if it is as bad as you say?"

"It's bad, Joe, and some tough decisions have been made."

Daley bristled and his cheeks reddened. It seemed to him that Kopek was setting him up for a fall, and he immediately expected that Gordon Alpert was going to be the scapegoat. "Well, if you're going to try and make Gordon the scapegoat for this, then you'd better pay some attention to the police, especially that son of a bitch Grimsley. I last heard from him at eleven, and since then I've called five times and he isn't in."

"Grimsley was at a luncheon this afternoon."

"Fine way to run a department," Daley scoffed. "The wheels are coming off the car and he's out to lunch."

"Well, it was the semi-annual Huguenot City Investigators luncheon. Grimsley's the past president, and the Investigators Association is made up of cops and just about everyone else in the security industry. It's a big association.

and Frank Duffy was the guest speaker. It appears they will endorse him for district attorney after their executive board meeting next week. That's a big endorsement, and that's where Duffy was, and that's where Grimsley was, and that's where the police commissioner was. The last thing we want to do, Joe, is piss off the police."

"You're going to blame this on Gordon Alpert?" Daley said angrily.

"Let me ask you a question?" Kopek said. "Is Gordon Alpert handling this prosecution without any assistance?"

"No, of course not," Daley said. "Bill Sullivan is assisting, and I also assigned one of our junior prosecutors, Helen Thames. She's been with us a year and a half. She finished law school two years ago and we picked her up right after she was admitted to the bar. Frank's made an effort to hire a few women."

"Does Miss Thames have any input?" Kopek asked.

"She's wet behind the ears. She's basically an observer, and if something has to be referenced or researched she'd be the one to do it," Daley said blandly, unsure of where Kopek was heading.

"Then if Miss Thames had said to Mr. Alpert seven weeks ago that she believed they should have insisted that the police thoroughly investigate the delivery boy instead of the cursory investigation that was conducted, Alpert would have taken her advice?" Kopek asked.

"I don't know what Miss Thames may have or may have not suggested. I have complete confidence in Gordon Alpert to prosecute a case, especially, this one."

"You don't know what Miss Thames suggested or why, do you?" Kopek asked mildly, not wanting his questioning of Daley to sound like an examination of a witness.

Daley's cheeks grew red again, and he replied with annoyance, "Listen, this isn't labor negotiations. Gordon's running the prosecution of Sophie Cruz. I trust him completely and I don't assign him assistants so they can report back to me any disagreements they may have with Gordon over case management."

"Joe, you were the trial bureau chief. Your job was to oversee the management of every case brought up for trial. Gordon Alpert dropped the ball, and you failed to recover the fumble. Excuse the weak sports metaphor, but had Gordon Alpert not been satisfied with what the police initially gave him and instead probed a little deeper, as his young assistant Helen Thames asked, we would have avoided today's embarrassment, along with some of the other nonsense that's surfaced this summer."

"Helen Thames was there to learn. Gordon Alpert has been my best prosecutor. I'll take his intuition and instincts over that of some green newcomer any day," Daley said defensively.

"Too bad she was right and he was wrong," Kopek replied back sourly.

The desire to physically assault Kopek was growing stronger by the moment. Daley had experienced a series of emotions throughout this conversation and felt as if Kopek was purposely baiting him to do or say something he would regret. He tried his best to contain his emotions, and in a defeated voice he asked, "What do you want from me? I feel like some school kid that's been brought into the principal's office, but I can't believe that I'm here only for a scolding. Would the district attorney feel better if I reassigned Gordon from the case?"

Kopek covered his right hand with his left hand. The two hands were spread over a white envelope that he had taken from the folder he brought into the room. He lifted his left hand and rubbed it over his mouth, then said gravely, "The district attorney already made a decision. It isn't one he wanted to make, but he has no other choice." Kopek took the envelope in his right hand and handed it across the table to Daley. "Effective noon today, your service with the Huguenot City District Attorney's Office was terminated."

Daley gasped and his face whitened. He stared wide-eyed at Kopek and started to laugh. "Fifteen years I've been here, fifteen years I've been as a loyal as they come. Christ, my uncle was the district attorney for thirty-five years. That doesn't count for something? This is how you treat me? Frank Duffy did this to me? I can't believe it, I just can't believe it!"

He went to get up from his chair, and Kopek motioned with his opens hands for Daley to sit down.

"Joe, the district attorney acknowledges everything you said. He appreciates both your loyalty and the connection to your uncle. This was the hardest decision he has ever had to make, and he did it reluctantly, but it was, in the end, his decision, not mine, nor anyone else's. There is a little more for you to consider."

Daley sneered and said, "Enough, I don't want to hear about how bad he feels. The prick did it to me. That's all that matters."

Kopek nodded his head. "Yes, the prick did it to you. He also secured a position for you as a supervising administrative law judge with the state Worker's Compensation Board. That will commence October 5th. Here's the deal, your time in service entitles you to accrued leave and severance which amounts to three month's salary. You get six weeks off, then you start your new job, which is at the same pay grade you made as a trial bureau chief. My arithmetic tells me you got a paid six week vacation and a six week bonus on top. You take a shot for this, but you get a soft landing in the end. Is it really that bad?"

"You think a new job's going to make a difference. I've been fired and I'm humiliated. And," he said as his voice went up several registers, "I've lost my job, a job I loved in a place where I belonged. You think some new post as an administrative judge is going to buy me off?"

Kopek was only half listening to Daley. He had promised Duffy that he would go easy on Daley and let him down gently. He had tried reasoning with the man, but the more they talked the more he grew to dislike him. *He's hopeless and hasn't a clue*, Kopek thought.

"Joe," he said earnestly, "you're one hundred percent on the money about the scapegoat business. It's you, plain and simple, but you've got to look at the bigger picture."

"Bullshit," Daley said with contempt.

Kopek couldn't help but laugh. "You love to say everything is bullshit, but that doesn't change the facts. Gordon Alpert's your, what do you call him?" Kopek asked.

"Gunslinger," Daley said sheepishly. It was how he often referred to Alpert, but in the context of his conversation with Kopek the term sounded juvenile.

"Right, gunslinger," answered Kopek. "What's that imply?"

"It's a little silly, but this is the banter in the office. It wasn't for public consumption."

"It's indicative of your attitude toward him and your trust in him. He was your killer. Your top guy, and you trusted him implicitly and because of that you provided no oversight. Helen Thames told me that during the six weeks she was assigned to Alpert she couldn't recall even one occasion when there was a discussion of the case between you and the prosecution team. Is that right?"

"I spoke to him a few times about it," Daley answered.

"The procedure is for the trial bureau chief to sit with the prosecution team before and after the grand jury to review the case. Isn't it?"

"Yes, but it was Gordon, there were a lot of other things going on and," Daley paused and sighed. "You're right, I should have been more attentive, but I don't believe it should cost me my job."

"Joe," Kopek said sympathetically, "I mentioned, before that we conducted a survey and that Brooks was known to almost forty percent more voters than Duffy was."

"Yes, but the election campaign hasn't even begun in earnest," Daley answered.

"Joe, the facts are the facts. Frank Duffy has no more than a fifty-fifty chance of winning this election. Stephen Brooks is known to more people. He has more money, and he's younger and better looking than Frank, although I think Frank is a handsome man. Those things count. Now you're pissed off because you've been fired, and I can understand that, but tell me, how many times has somebody tried to lure you away from the district attorney's office with the offer of a better job? Tell me, please, how many times?"

"Never," Daley answered. "What's that mean?"

"It means that if Frank Duffy isn't successful on the first Tuesday in November, he is going to have to start thinking about his future on the first Wednesday in November because on the first day of 1966 he's going to be unemployed. Did you ever think of that?"

"The D.A.'s been a Democrat since my uncle first won in 1921."

"Duffy's got no more than a fifty percent chance of winning, and that means that quite a few people in this office may be unemployed come January. You could have been one of them, and with that said I don't think you've been treated unfairly. It took a lot of doing to get you that slot with the state. You're still in the pension system, and you'll never have to worry about the outcome of an election. Not a bad price to pay when you take it all into account."

"I can't imagine for the life of me that Frank could lose. It's unimaginable. We always win," an incredulous Daley answered.

"Times are changing, Joe," Kopek said. "That's why I came on board. I'll do everything I can to get us a victory. If you want to help, take the heat. If the newspapers ask for an interview, show some humility and take the blame. It'll make a difference."

The natural color had come back to Daley's face. He stood up and placed the termination letter in his coat pocket. "Is Frank available?" he asked Kopek.

Kopek smiled and said, "The district attorney isn't, but he said to tell you that he'll catch up with you after the election. Your secretary and Bill Sullivan are waiting for you in your office. Go through your files and take whatever personal effects you have. Accounting will have your check brought over before five." Kopek then reached over the table with an extended hand, and said, "Joe, I wish you the best. You're going to like the compensation board. They get some very entertaining cases, and you get to be a judge."

Daley shook Kopek's hand very quickly, and without saying another word slowly walked from then room.

Kopek waited several minutes until he was joined in the conference room by Frank Duffy.

"How did it go?" an apprehensive Frank Duffy asked.

"Exactly the way you said it would," Kopek replied.

"He never saw it coming, I knew he wouldn't," Duffy said regretfully.

"I took the long route, but I think I prevailed in the end. He understands what's at stake and that story today helped us usher him out the door.'

"Great timing is what that story was," a grinning Duffy said. "I gave the poor bastard the job just so I could fire him, but this made it easy. It was a rotten thing to do, but politics is war and every war has it casualties," Duffy said with no indication that he felt any sympathy or guilt over Daley's demise.

"It's a smart move. The papers and Brooks have tied you, Frank Heaton and Joe Daley up into one ball of nepotism. You not only fired Joe Daley, but you also fired Frank Heaton," Kopek replied.

"If I could only get rid of Futerman and his buddy Weiss that easily," Duffy lamented.

"Once we put this case to bed we will," Kopek assured him. "Have you heard from Grimsley?"

"No, but I put the press conference off until eight tonight. That leaves enough time for the late night news and the morning papers to get the story out. I'm going to pummel Daley and take a few shots at myself for being sentimental at having appointed him in the first place. I think that will put some distance between me and Heaton's memory and all that trash Brooks is throwing my way," Duffy said confidently.

"How do you plan on handling any questions about the police investigation, or lack of one, into Monaghan's conduct if Grimsley can't come across with an explanation?" Kopek asked.

"If he doesn't nail this thing down I'm going to remind the press that I'm the chief law enforcement officer in Huguenot City. Then I'm going to announce the formation of a special unit to reopen the case and conduct a full investigation. I'll also reconvene the grand jury."

"You're leaving the Huguenot City P.D. out of this?" a concerned Kopek asked.

"No, I'm going to ask the police commissioner to assign Captain Grimsley to my office and to let him pick the personnel. I'll take responsibility for the final outcome, but I'll let everyone know that Grimsley and the police department can handle this. You have to remember that Kreppell's suicide derailed this investigation to a large degree. Daley and Alpert were down right incompetent, and their inability to probe a little deeper and ask more questions is at the heart of the breakdown. We give the P.D. a pass and take some heat, but correct it before any real injustice is done. How's that sound?"

"It won't make the case go away," Kopek said with a troubled look on his face.

"No, it won't. And if there is some merit to the story and Monaghan is a suspect, we have no option but to follow it to the end. Maybe Sophie Cruz is innocent?"

Kopek shook is head and frowned. "Do you believe that?"

Duffy smiled and replied, "No, not at all. I'm pretty sure that the police will have an answer for Monaghan's behavior and that we'll be back on track with Miss Cruz as our killer."

Kopek frowned again. "Still won't make the case go away, will it?"

Duffy pointed to Frank Heaton's portrait. "The old man taught me a lot. He was never the type to explain why he did what he did, but if you were observant you learned. Frank Heaton hated criticism. He was terribly thin-skinned and honest about it. If a case or an incident was going to put him in a bad light he made it disappear. I believe Grimsley will deliver a suitable excuse for Monaghan's visit to Mrs. Cleary, and I'll have it in time for the press conference. If it goes that way, then tomorrow we will contact Mr. Lenihan, and in the interests of justice we will offer Miss Cruz an opportunity to plead to a lesser offense. She takes some jail time, and the whole shebang is sealed and delivered before Labor Day."

Kopek snapped his fingers. "Just like that?"

The smile had left Duffy's face and he narrowed his eyes, and with great sincerity said, "Whatever it takes, whatever it takes."

Chapter Fifty-Eight

"I'm starved," Cairn said as he waited at the traffic light under the el.

"Me too," a bored Widelsky yawned.

"We'll take one more pass by Bongos and if he ain't there we stop and get a slice or something," Cairn said in reply as the light turned green and he steered the car through the intersection and up 231st Street.

"We can stop at the pizza place we ate in the day we nabbed the Cruz girl," Widelsky said, suddenly perking up.

"That's what gets me," Cairn said. "Remember that day, the way she ran when she saw you walking toward her?"

"Right, tell me she wasn't fucking guilty," Widelsky said, laughing. "Now we gotta play cat and mouse with this asshole Monaghan. I wished we had found the munchkin first, you know? Least we'd know what we're driving at."

"We'll know soon," Cairn answered. He drove on for two more blocks, then said, "There's his turquoise Caddy, parked right out in front."

"Good," Widelsky said sourly. "He can tell us to go fuck ourselves and we can be on our way."

"Betcha he don't," Cairn said.

"Why?" Widelsky answered as Cairn made a U-turn and pulled up to an open space two storefronts west of Bongos.

"Two slices and a coke say's he makes nice with us," Cairn said cheerfully.

"You're on, but I'm gonna win. The guy's a prick," Widelsky answered knowingly.

The two detectives walked through the front door of the bar. It was their third trip to Bongos in search of Monaghan that day. The first time was about ten in the morning and there were two customers, the second trip was a little after noon and there were five customers. On this visit most of the stools were occupied, and Cairn said to his partner, "This place is a fucking gold mine. It's not even three-thirty on a Wednesday and he's got a full house." Cairn found an open stool, leaned over the bar and called to the bartender, "Any luck?"

The bartender pointed to the rear of the bar and said, "He's in the Jungle."

"Jungle?" Cairn queried, not understanding the bartender's reference.

"Out back," the bartender said as he motioned again to the rear of the bar.

"Follow me," Widelsky said as he pointed to the wall above the open door at the back of the bar.

Cairn had to focus his eyes to the clash of light and darkness at the rear of the bar. A door was open and the backdrop of bold sunlight was blinding as it illuminated the opening to a rear patio. Just above the door was a weakly lit red sign that said exit, and above that in crude bamboo stick lettering was a sign that said "The Jungle."

"I get it," Cairn sarcastically.

The two detectives stepped through the doorway onto the rear patio.

"It's a fucking playground for grownups," Widelsky sneered.

"No different than what you got at that Elks club or whatever it is you belong to," Cairn said sarcastically.

The backyard of Bongo's was deeper than the building itself. To the left as you came though the door was an outdoor bar with a thatched awning above it and images of monkeys and coconuts painted on the wall behind the bar. Strings of lights ran overhead from the rear of the building to the wooden fence that separated the property from the property behind it. Five round tables with umbrellas and chairs were on the patio, and at the far right as you came out the rear door was a horseshoe pit. Two men were playing horseshoes, and at the sound of Widelsky's voice one of the men turned and casually said, "Give me a minute."

It was Monaghan. The man he was playing against had just thrown his second shoe as the detectives had stepped through the door into the yard. The man's toss landed on top of two other shoes that were inches from the stake. Monaghan was holding a horseshoe with the fingertips of his right hand. He swung his arm back gently, and without stopping reversed direction and brought it forward without any apparent change in speed until his hand passed his hip and he let the shoe fly from his fingers in a high arch. It was a graceful toss and the shoe held the same position for the few seconds it was aloft until it fell with precision around its target. "Son of a bitch," Monaghan's opponent muttered with disgust as he walked away from the pit. "That's the last time I ever bet you double or nothing."

The man went back into the bar without saying anything else or acknowledging Cairn or Widelsky.

"You guys want a beer?" Monaghan asked.

Cairn looked up at the bright August sky. The sun was too bright for him and he closed his eyes, but let his face bask for a few moments, then lowered his head said, "That's what sunny afternoons are made for, right, Frank, cold beer and refreshing conversation."

Widelsky didn't answer, and Monaghan went over to the rear door and called in to the bartender, "Petey, bring me a pitcher and three glasses."

Monaghan walked past the two detectives to one of the tables, opened the umbrella and sat down. Cairn and Widelsky followed, and as Cairn was sitting down he gave Monaghan the once over and said, "Day off today?"

Monaghan wasn't in work clothes. He was wearing chinos, a short sleeve shirt and moccasins, and seemed very relaxed and at ease in the company of the two detectives.

"I take a few days off here and there," he replied. "I understand you two have been looking for me."

"All day, all over the city," Widelsky said in unfriendly tone.

"You got me now," Monaghan said as the man he'd been playing horseshoes with came out of the bar carrying a pitcher of beer and three beer mugs. He put the pitcher and beer mugs down on the table. "That's on me, gentlemen," he said very respectfully. Without waiting for a response he went back into the bar. Monaghan called out as he was going through the doorway, "Jimmy, triple or nothing later."

Jimmy didn't answer, and Monaghan poured them each a beer. Widelsky pushed his mug toward the middle of the table. Monaghan ignored Widelsky's gesture and said, "At a buck a game, I can afford triple or nothing."

"Thanks for the beer," Widelsky said in a serious and unfriendly manner. "There's a few things we gotta clear up, my friend."

"Ask away," Monaghan said nonchalantly.

Cairn sat there placidly sipping his beer. Of the two detectives he was not only calmer and more patient than Widelsky, but he was not easily intimidated or threatened. Widelsky, despite his brawn and demonstrated fearlessness, was much quicker to feel threatened and to strike first. Widelsky found

Monaghan threatening. He wouldn't say so, but then he didn't have to because his face and body language always betrayed his true feelings. Widelsky's face was pulled tight, his eyes had narrowed and the furrows on his brow grew deeper as his breathing became heavier. He was preparing for a fight, but it was evident to Cairn that fighting was the last thing on Monaghan's agenda. The target of their inquiry sat there just as placidly as Cairn sat. He sipped at his beer, lit a cigarette and acted as if they were old friends doing nothing more than killing time over a few beers. Monaghan was in no hurry to answer questions, nor did he appear as if he was hiding something. He was completely relaxed, and it was his ease and relaxation, so contradictory to his demeanor when they had last encountered him at his apartment on the night he interrupted their questioning of his son, that had Widelsky out of sorts. Widelsky was the wrong man to conduct the interview, and Cairn gently stepped on his foot and said, "Frank, the beer's good."

Widelsky felt the pressure of Cairn's foot over his and reluctantly reached for his beer and took a sip. Cairn put his beer down and said to Monaghan, "Did you see today's *News*?"

"Yeah, Cleary showed me the paper this morning."

Widelsky's head jerked back when Monaghan mentioned Cleary's name and said, "Was that supposed to be funny?"

Before Monaghan could answer, Cairn asked, "You saw him today?"

"I was with him a good part of the day, and if you couldn't find me I guess you didn't find him either."

"You knew we were looking for you?" Widelsky skeptically asked...

Monaghan laughed. "I know now, and to tell the truth I figured this morning you guys would be on the lookout for us. As a matter of fact, I told Sad Sack to make sure he tells you the truth, not his version, but the truth."

"Slow down," Cairn cautioned as he pulled his notebook from his jacket and opened it to a clean page. "Excuse me, but why don't you start from scratch with this," he said to Monaghan while he once again stepped on Widelsky's foot.

"Sure," Monaghan said confidently. "But why don't you tell me what Mrs. Cleary told you."

"What's that matter?" Widelsky said belligerently.

"Well, if you couldn't find me, I know you didn't find Sad Sack, so that leaves his mother, and I bet you talked to her."

"Tell you what," Cairn said in a friendly and encouraging way. "I'll tell you everything we learned today and then you can fill in the gaps. How's that sound?"

Monaghan stubbed out his cigarette and poured another glass of beer. "Spill the beans," he said.

"We spoke with Mrs. Cleary this morning. She said nothing ever happened, and her son has a habit of making up stories to make him look important. She told us that through the peephole, then she told us not to bother her anymore. That's everything we learned today except we've been to four construction sites where your local told us to go to find you and we came up empty every time. So fill us in, please."

"There ain't much to tell," Monaghan said, "but this is the whole kit and caboodle. Today is the fifth annual Eddie Lutz Clambake. Lutz was a fireman and a bartender over at Hogan's on the Crescent. Six years ago today he went down to the cellar in Hogan's to tap a keg and had a heart attack. They found him dead and colder than a keg of beer on the basement floor. Lutz ran the Riverview Ravens football club. That's a pretty well known sandlot club. Lutz was a good coach and he had a good following at Hogan's."

"I heard of them," Widelsky said, suddenly sounding more interested in Monaghan's story and less belligerent toward him.

"Good teams, always," Monaghan said in reply to Widelsky "So, a year later a bunch of his friends put together this clambake. They hold it out at the Fish Trolley on Clam Island. They have a horseshoe contest, fishing contest and a rowing regatta. They get over a hundred guys every year. Whatever they make they donate to the football club. It isn't much, but it's in Lutz's name and that counts for something."

"Today was the clambake and you and Cleary went," Cairn said.

"Me, Cleary and a lot of other guys. I didn't go with that little prick," Monaghan corrected.

"I know," Cairn answered, "but that's where you were for most of the day."

"Right," Monaghan said.

"Cleary showed you the story in the paper," Widelsky asked suspiciously.

Monaghan laughed. "Not exactly, my friend. Jimmy Murphy, the guy I was just tossing shoes with, he showed it to me and I saw Cleary getting off the bus and I called him over. Make a long story short, he owned up to it. Said he was interviewed by some private dick the girl that got arrested hired. He ends up telling the guy that I went to see his mother the night of the murder and gave her a hundred bucks for breaking his nose last year."

"That was over a debt he owed to a third party, if I'm correct," Cairn said knowingly.

Monaghan frowned, then smiled and said with annoyance, "That's a fucking Billy Devine story if I ever heard one. Sad Sack didn't get his nose busted because of a debt he owed; you can take that to the bank." He then reached into his shirt pocket for his cigarettes and as he lit one up he never took his eyes off Cairn.

"Did I hit a sore spot?" Cairn said apologetically.

"No, but you're going in the wrong direction."

"Didja break his fucking nose or not?" Widelsky interjected.

"I guess I did," Monaghan said blandly.

"And you didn't do that while working as the muscle for Vince LoBianco and Chick Nathan?" Widelsky asked.

Monaghan took a deep drag on his cigarette and said, "No."

"No, what?" Cairn replied.

"I broke his fucking nose because two weeks before that he fucked up big time."

"Right," Widelsky said with annoyance. "He skipped town for a trip to Puerto Rico and didn't pay up on the World Series. We know that and we don't care. So cut the shit and tell us the truth. Why did you visit his mother that night and give her money?"

Monaghan laughed and poured himself another beer. Cairn saw that he was enjoying the back and forth with Widelsky, but he also saw that it was getting out of hand and for the third time he stepped on Widelsky's foot. "Why don't you tell us why you broke his nose," Cairn asked.

"First of all, I don't know anything about gambling debts and LoBianco and Nathan. Is that understood?" Monaghan asked the two detectives.

"Fine," Cairn answered.

"I have a very good friend. Her name is Carla Rink, and she has a daughter who's about my son Danny's age. Carla's mother lives in my building, and Carla's daughter gets babysitting jobs here and there."

"Carla," Widelsky interrupted, "she's your girlfriend."

"Fucking Billy Devine," Monaghan swore with disgust. He gave Widelsky a hard look and said, "Let me tell the story. Forget what that bullshit artist told you because most of the time he's wrong."

"Frank," Cairn said with annoyance, "let the man tell us his story."

Monaghan looked at the two detectives, and seeing he had their attention resumed talking. "Carla's daughter and another girl were putting a carriage away in the carriage room in my building. Now you two were there today visiting Mrs. Cleary, so you know what I'm talking about. Annie and this other girl are making noise, or doing whatever, and they realize that the peephole to Cleary's door is open and someone's watching them. They say something fresh and the door opens and it's Cleary with his pecker in his hand. They scream and run away. Annie tells her mom and Carla goes to Cleary's apartment and bangs on the door but no one answers. So happens later that night she catches him in Pete's Lounge and calls him out. He tells her she's a fucking skank and a liar, and he leaves. I caught up with him two weeks later and I slapped him on the back of his head. His head hit the bar and his nose got bloody. That's all I know. Don't ask me about LoBianco and collecting money or any of that other shit because it ain't got nothing to do with why I smacked Cleary."

Widelsky was still skeptical and he said, "Did he bet on the World Series, did he run off to Puerto Rico?"

"He told his mother he lost three hundred on the World Series and that's why I broke his nose. He also told her that he needed the money for his vacation and that's why he ran off without paying up. So what fucking happens is that his mother's been breaking my wife's chops ever since about the broken nose and the medical bills. I tell my wife to mind her own business, but she's been on my case because the old bag embarrasses her whenever she can."

Widelsky was exasperated, "Between you and me, I don't fucking care, just tell me one thing. Did he lose money on the World Series?"

Monaghan started laughing at Widelsky and after a few moments said, "He dropped three hundred on the series, but don't ask me anything more. I broke his fucking nose because he was waving his dick at my girlfriend's daughter." He then motioned to Cairn with his hand and said, "Give me a piece of paper and your pen."

Cairn ripped a sheet out of the notebook and handed the sheet of paper and his pen to Monaghan. Monaghan bent over and in neat block letters wrote out Carla's name, address and phone number. He then handed the sheet of paper and pen back to Cairn. "That's Carla's address and phone number. Interview her. I'm not making this shit up."

"Let me get this straight," a calmer Widelsky asked. "You're not admitting to being a collector for LoBianco and Nathan, but you're admitting that you did break his nose and it was because he's a dickie waver and you also know that he lost money on the World Series and did run off to Puerto Rico without making good on his bet."

"I am," Monaghan answered.

"So why would you pick that night to give Mrs. Cleary a hundred bucks?" Cairn answered.

"Because Mrs. Cleary has it in for me. She thinks I'm a big bully who beat her little baby up over a gambling debt, and that's not true, but I come home and you two guys are in my kitchen sweating my kid over a murder and it turns out that Cleary's the one pointing a finger at him."

"And?" Cairn asked.

"And I didn't know if my kid did something or not. I put the squeeze on him after you left that night, but he swore he didn't do anything. So I figured I better shortcut the Cleary's just in case things got out of hand," Monaghan said with conviction.

Widelsky laughed and took a long drink of beer. He finished and wiped his lips with the back of his hand and said, "Cleary will back this up?"

"I told the little prick to tell you the truth. I'm sure he will," Monaghan replied with some menace in his voice.

"That's good," Cairn interjected. "Where can we find him right now?"

"The bus from the clambake ought to be pouring all of those drunks off at Pete's Lounge about four o'clock I'd guess," Monaghan said with amusement.

"Pete's Lounge?" Cairn asked.

"Where else," a relaxed and smiling Monaghan answered.

"Thanks for your time," Cairn said as he and Widelsky stood up. "You may have to repeat this if the DA reconvenes the grand jury."

"Just let me know," Monaghan replied agreeably.

Chapter Fifty-Nine

"Told you he'd cooperate," Cairn said smugly as he pulled the police car into traffic and up 231st Street toward Bailey Avenue.

"I owe you lunch," Widelsky answered.

"You're not surprised?" Cairn asked with some disappointment.

"I was wrong, but he made sense and," Widelsky said pausing for effect, "I still think he's a prick."

Cairn frowned and said, "I can't mention him without you reminding me he's a prick."

"Fact's a fucking fact, the way I see it, Phil," Widelsky replied, then asked, "Why do you want to be so chummy with that prick?"

"Who says I'm being chummy? Didja ever hear that old saying, 'you get more with honey than vinegar?'"

"Whatever," Widelsky said with a shrug as Cairn turned the car onto Bailey Avenue. They traveled the next three blocks in silence until they pulled up across the street from Pete's Bridge Lounge. Cairn made a U-turn and doubled-parked in front of the bar.

There was no sign of a bus in front of the bar, or a crowd of drunks standing outside, but the scene inside the bar was quite different. Cairn opened the door, and as he and Widelsky walked in they saw that the bar was packed and there was some commotion going on at the other end. Above the din of voices and laughter was the unmistakable brogue of the bartender pleading, "Come now, Mrs. Cleary, be a nice girl and let go of the broom. You've done as much damage to the boy's face as the big fellow did last year."

519

Widelsky, with Cairn on his heals, pushed into the crowd and saw the cowering figure of Tim Cleary laying across the seat of a dining booth with blood seeping from his nose. Standing in front of Cleary was Tommy the bartender with his two hands wrapped around a heavy broomstick holding back a little sprite of a woman with her stockings rolled like donuts at her knees and a green and red housecoat twisted up several inches above her knees as she struggled to wrest the broom from Tommy's fat hands as she simultaneously tried to kick at him while she wailed, "Let go you Goddamn oaf, let go and let me take care of my own problems."

It appeared that Mrs. Cleary had assaulted her son, and the only person in the crowded bar who saw fit to intervene was the bartender. Widelsky moved quickly, and with one arm he swept Mrs. Cleary into the air and with the other took control of the broomstick. She was momentarily silenced, and he quickly moved to his left and ushered her out the side door of the bar to the street. He placed her on the sidewalk and was met with a kick to his left calf.

"Who do you think you are?" an enraged Mrs. Cleary shrieked.

Before Widelsky could answer her Cairn came out of the bar with Tim Cleary in tow. Cairn looked at Mrs. Cleary and Widelsky, and with his hand on Tim Cleary's shoulder directed him toward the police car.

"Tim, Tim," Mrs. Cleary called with authority. "Get over here right now. You're going home."

Tim didn't answer his mother, and Cairn opened the car door and guided an unsteady Cleary into the rear seat. Mrs. Cleary went to grab the broom from Widelsky's hand, but he brushed her arm away, then broke the broom over his left knee and took the two broken pieces and threw them into the gutter. "You'll have to go find yourself a new broom to ride, Mom," he sneered.

"You son of a bitch," she said with contempt. "Give me my son, let him go. I don't want you talking to him, do you hear. He's simple, a simple simpleton."

Cairn was already in the car with Tim Cleary. Widelsky ignored Mrs. Cleary and opened the passenger's side door to the front seat and got in. Mrs. Cleary followed him to the curb and stopped. She had her hands on her hips and said, "You big fathead, I said to let him go."

Widelsky laughed at her and said, "You don't like it, call the cops."

Cairn drove off, and said, "Summit, or all the way back to our place? Where do you want to take him?"

Widelsky looked over his shoulder into the rear of the car. Tim Cleary was slumped in the seat behind Cairn. He was holding a blood stained bar rag to his nose. The bleeding had stopped, but there was visible swelling to the left side of his face under his eye. He was sunburnt and the expression on his face was a combination of sullenness, moroseness and disinterest in the two detectives in the front seat of the car.

"He's drunk, beat up and pissed off. You're a little pissed, ain't you, Munchkin?" Widelsky asked Cleary.

Cleary refused to answer as he closed his eyes and repeatedly dabbed at his nose with the dirty bar rag.

"Let's stop at the diner and get some coffee," Widelsky said. "Then we can go over to Dutchman's Park and give the little man some fresh air."

Cairn raised his neck and looked at the rear view mirror. "Is he awake?" he asked as he focused his attention back to operating the police car.

"He's awake, but if he don't become more cooperative I'll toss the little shit into the lake," Widelsky said maliciously.

"We'll get him a little fresh air and see if he can perk up. Otherwise we have to bring him back to the stationhouse and sit with him until he's ready to talk. Grimsley won't be happy unless we can fill in all the blanks," Cairn said as he doubleparked the car in front of Eddie's diner.

Widelsky opened the car door and said, "You think he drinks tea or coffee?"

"Black and sweet is what he gets," Cairn replied.

Ten minutes later they were seated at a picnic table under an enormous chestnut tree. Cleary was ignoring the two detectives. His hands were cupped around the cardboard coffee container Widelsky had handed him. His head was bobbing up and down and his eyes were fixed on the container he held in his hands.

The two detectives stared at him for several minutes, then Widelsky lost his patience. "All right, asshole," he snarled as he got up from the bench and snatched the coffee container from Cleary's grip.

Cleary's mouth opened wide, his head fell back and he mumbled, "What?"

"Wake up or I'm gonna toss you into the fucking lake and let you sink," Widelsky said as he grabbed the smaller man by the arm and yanked him to his feet. Widelsky started walking Cleary down the hill to the lake.

As they picked up speed, Cleary became more alert and shouted, "Stop, stop, please stop."

They weren't alone in the park, and several women at a picnic table twenty feet from theirs took notice and as one woman called to the children playing nearby, her companion called out to Widelsky, "Hey, leave that man alone or I'll call the police."

Widelsky stopped and pushed Cleary to the ground and called back to the woman, "I am the police. Mind your own business."

The woman said something back, but Widelsky had already turned his back to her and was barking at Cleary, who was now sitting on the ground, awake and sulking. "Listen, you little cocksucker, I'll beat the piss out of you right here. Do you understand me? Now get the fuck up and walk back up the hill."

Cleary gave him a defiant stare, then stumbled to his feet. Widelsky gave him a gentle shove from behind and Cleary started a sluggish climb up the hill and back to the picnic table where a visibly amused Phil Cairn sat quietly drinking his coffee.

"Now you've roused the natives," Cairn said.

Widelsky didn't look at Cairn and concentrated his energy and interest on getting Cleary seated back on the bench.

"That's what we need right now, a couple of busybodies," Widelsky said as he finally got Cleary seated on the bench. Once seated Cleary appeared somewhat more alert and took the plastic top off his coffee container. He stuck his finger in the coffee and then took it out and placed it in his mouth. Satisfied with the taste, he picked up the container and took a drink.

Cairn was calm, and with some empathy said, "Hasn't been a good day, has it, Tim?"

Cleary shook his head to the left and right several times and looked at Widelsky. "Why are you such a prick?" he asked sadly.

"That must be the word of the day," Cairn wryly remarked.

"I'm a prick because it's the only way I can get things done sometimes, Munchkin," Widelsky answered, while ignoring Cairn's remark.

"My name isn't Munchkin, fathead," a defiant Cleary retorted.

"Fair enough," Widelsky said contritely, showing a sudden softening to his abrasive demeanor. "You're Mr. Cleary and I'm Detective Widelsky from now on."

"How's that, Mr. Cleary?" Cairn interjected.

"Call me Tim, that's all I'm asking," Cleary replied grudgingly.

"Good, that's good, Tim," Cairn said approvingly. "Now that we cleared that up, why don't you tell me how that story got into the *Huguenot Daily News* this morning?"

"What story?" Cleary said fuzzily

"Jesus Christ," Widelsky sighed, "the story about Mike Monaghan going to your apartment and giving your mother a hundred dollars."

"It's all a bunch of bullshit," Cleary answered indifferently.

"Not true," Cairn asked.

Cleary hiccupped and then tiredly said, "It's a long story."

"You wanna go back down the hill again? This time I'll go all the way and let you drown," Widelsky said impatiently.

Cleary's shoulders jerked at the raised sound of Widelsky's voice and put up his right hand and said defensively, "Please, I'm gonna tell you. I'm just tired, that's all. It's been a lo-lo-long day."

"You ain't going anywhere until you tell us, so start talking," Widelsky ordered.

Cleary let his chin fall to his chest and stuttering again, said, "Ye-ye-yes, I know."

Cairn smiled at him and said, "Tim, tell us everything that happened that night. Exactly as you remember it, can you do that?"

"What night?" a confused Cleary answered.

"The fucking night Monaghan threatened your old lady," Widelsky growled.

Cleary's shoulders jerked once again in response to Widelsky's harsh tone. "Nobody threatened my mother. Monaghan gave her a hundred dollars for breaking my nose."

"Just out of the blue," Cairn asked.

"No," Cleary said.

"No, what," Cairn asked.

Cleary smiled. "He didn't want me talking bad about his kid. You know, with the murder and all. He was a little scared of me."

"You gotta do better," Widelsky ordered.

"He broke my nose last year. Smashed it into the bar in Pete's," Cleary said sadly.

"And," Cairn said, leading him.

"My mother was pissed off about it. I was too, but what could I do? It cost me almost a hundred bucks for the emergency room, the doctor and the ambulance."

"You needed an ambulance?" Cairn asked.

"He did it, and I was bleeding bad. Not like today," he said as he put his hand to his nose. "I went home and my mother called the ambulance. All year she's been after Mrs. Monaghan for the money."

"And out of the blue Monaghan picks the day of the murder to give your mother the hundred dollars," Cairn inquired.

"Well, you guys were at his apartment earlier and it had to be about his kid, that's why. He was afraid I could hurt him, and he figured if he gave my mother the money she'd make me shut up. Th-th-that's what I think," he stuttered.

"Why'd he break your nose," Widelsky asked.

Cleary hung his head and looked at the picnic table top. "I lost money on the World Series and was late paying up," he said unconvincingly.

"No other reason?" Cairn said suspiciously.

Cleary kept his eyes focused on the picnic table top, then said, "There was something else, but it ain't true."

"Spit it out," Widelsky said impatiently.

Cleary appeared to be sobering up by the minute. "He accused me of exposing myself to his girlfriend's daughter. I didn't do it. It was a misunderstanding, but his girlfriend gave me a hard time and I ca-ca-called her a skank, and when he caught up with me in the bar he smashed my head and whispered in my ear that I was a 'pervert.' Everyone in the bar thought it was about the World Series because they knew I lost money and the Milkman's the collector, but I kn-kn-knew what it was for."

"Did you tell your mother what it was about?" Cairn asked.

"No, I said it was about the bet."

"Well, if your mother was badgering Monaghan's wife, weren't you afraid Monaghan would tell your mother what it was really over," Cairn asked as a follow-up.

No, he ain't that way. He did what he did, and it was over. It was just with me pointing my finger at his kid that got him worried, so he went and saw my mother that night and gave her the money."

"Did he tell your mother to tell you to keep your mouth shut," Widelsky asked.

"No, he'd never do that. He's like ice, that guy. He just made some small talk, that's what she said, and gave her the money, but she got the message."

"I guess you did to," Cairn said.

"Wh-wh-what do you mean?" Cleary asked in reply.

"You didn't tell us anything. How come you told the private investigator about it?" Cairn asked.

Cleary laughed. "I told the sergeant. What was his name? You know, the one that died."

"Kreppell," Widelsky almost shouted with annoyance.

"Yeah, Kreppell, I told him the next day. That fucking Monaghan don't scare me," Cleary said as he subconsciously rubbed his nose.

Widelsky looked at Cairn and said, "That son-of-a-bitch, he never said shit to us."

Cairn smiled, closed his eyes for a moment, and said, "Think of how that

Friday went. Everything happened too fast. I'm sure if he hadn't of died we would have followed this all up. What gets me is how come you didn't tell the district attorney about this when you were interviewed for the grand jury?"

Cleary waved his right hand at Cairn in disgust. "The DA asked me three questions, and they were all about the girl that got arrested, didn't have the time of day for me," he said as an afterthought. "The investigator that girl hired, what's her name, Sophie Cruz?"

"Yes, Sophie Cruz," Cairn answered.

"He was real smart. He told me the story about the Milkman breaking my nose for being late to pay on the bet wasn't the truth. I couldn't bullshit him, and we were having dinner and a few beers and I told him everything."

"Let me get this straight," Cairn said. "Monaghan broke your nose last year because he accused you of exposing yourself to his girlfriend's daughter. So you never lost money on the World Series?"

Cleary sighed and took a deep breath. He was still drunk and tired, and the effort to pay attention to Cairn and Widelsky's questions was taxing all of his energy. He folded his arms on the table and placed his head down. Widelsky was about to slam the table with his hand, but Cairn reached over and stopped him. "Give him a minute," Cairn said.

After several minutes Cleary raised his head and looked at Cairn.

"I lost three hundred dollars on the World Series. Fifteen dollars was the extra Vig for every week I was late paying. It cost me three hundred and sixty dollars when I finally paid everything up. Eddie Simon, that was the investigator Sophie Cruz hired, he figured that out, you know, he knew how it works. That's why he knew the story about Monaghan beating me up because I was late paying wasn't true. Carla Rink is Monaghan's girlfriend. Her daughter was in the carriage room outside my apartment one afternoon and was with some other girl. My mother was out shopping and these girls were making a lot of noise. I looked through the peephole and they saw me and started calling me names. I opened the door to tell them to get the hell out of there. I was in my boxers and they screamed and ran away. I swear that's all that happened."

"And this Carla Rink, what happened between you and her?" Cairn asked.

"A little while after that happened she came to the apartment and started banging on the door. I wouldn't open up, but later on I saw her in Pete's. She started calling me names and I called her a skank and a bitch and I left. I was away for a week after that, and when I got home Monaghan caught up with me and smashed my face into the bar."

Cairn nodded his head and said, "Let me get this straight, Monaghan broke your nose because of this business with his girlfriend and her daughter."

"Yeah," Cleary answered.

"Monaghan does, however, collect money for Chick Nathan and Vince LoBianco?" Cairn then asked.

"He collects for Chick Nathan. I heard of LoBianco, he's Pete's brother, but I don't know about him," Cleary answered nervously.

"Okay, it doesn't really matter who he collects for. I just wanted to know if he did that," Cairn said calmly. "What's really important is that we know why he broke your nose and we know why he gave your mother the money."

"It was his way of telling me to keep my mouth shut," Cleary added.

"What about the other people in the bar? You know, the people who were there when he hit you? What did he say to them?" Widelsky asked.

Cleary laughed loudly, then sniffed his nose several times, and still laughing, said, "The Milkman don't care what people think about him. Nobody's gonna say boo to him. He don't give a fuck, period."

Cairn looked at Widelsky and then said to Cleary, "What happened between you and Monaghan today at the clambake?"

"Nothing," Cleary said as he shrugged his shoulders and nodded his head slowly.

"He didn't talk to you at all?" Widelsky asked.

"He told me to tell the truth if I talked to the cops. That's all. He don't talk to me much anyway."

"Are you working tomorrow?" Cairn asked.

"Yeah, I am."

"We'll be by in the morning. We'll have to bring you in and take a statement. We'd do it tonight, but under the circumstances I rather do this tomorrow after you've had a good night's rest," Cairn said as he stood up.

"I, I, I don't know if I can get off from work," a stuttering Cleary answered as Widelsky motioned with his hand for him to stand up.

"We'll work it out, don't you worry about a thing," Cairn said reassuringly. "Where do you want us to drop you off?"

"Home is fine," Cleary answered.

"Mom's not gonna be a problem?" Widelsky asked.

"Mom's always a problem," he said with self pity evident in his voice.

Chapter Sixty

"I understand," Rick Kopek said impatiently as he tapped the receiver of the telephone gently against his ear. "That's fine, Captain, I'll speak with the district attorney, and if he has any further questions I won't hesitate to call." Kopek paused and rolled his eyes up to the ceiling, then said, "No, no, the district attorney is fully satisfied with your end of the investigation. It's how things played out on our end that has him roiled. Thank you for all your effort today," he said in conclusion as he lowered the receiver and placed it back on its cradle

Frank Duffy was sitting in a chair in the corner of Kopek's office, and as Kopek hung up the phone Duffy wiped his brow with a dramatic flourish, and said, "Whew, you let him off the hook. I could see the way your head was bobbing on that call that the good captain had his dander up and was on the defense, wasn't he?"

"Defense!" Kopek said with exaggeration. "There's a man who doesn't take well to criticism."

"No, he doesn't," Duffy said in agreement.

"Has an air about him, not snooty, but odd. I can't exactly categorize him," Kopek said as he looked at the notes he'd scribbled on a yellow legal pad while talking to Captain Grimsley.

"'Odd' is the perfect description," Duffy answered. "Grimsley is a Clam Islander. His family goes way back. When you first come over the bridge, just to the right, is the Dutch Reformed Church. The building must be a hundred and fifty years old and next to it is a cemetery. There are a number of headstones in that cemetery bearing the Grimsley name. Last year the *Times* did a little piece on his mother. She's a music teacher, and at eighty-five is still teaching. The family owns either the land the Fish Trolley is on, or the lot where the Clam House is. I always get it confused, but he's got money, and the Clam Islanders, well," Duffy paused and smiled, "it's not that they think they're better than the rest of us, just different. I can't explain it any other way," he finished, laughing.

"Different or not, we have to deal with him," Kopek replied.

"So, why is he on the defensive?" Duffy asked.

"The police were advised the day following the homicide that Monaghan had approached Mrs. Cleary."

"What?" a suddenly agitated Duffy said in response.

"It's a convoluted story, but according to Grimsley, Cleary told Sergeant Kreppell that Monaghan had paid a visit to his mother on the night of the murder and given her a hundred dollars. The money was to cover the medical bills Cleary experienced as a result of Monaghan breaking his nose," Kopek said in a monotone voice as he lifted his eyes from his notes and looked intently at Duffy.

"Kreppell's dead," Duffy said with annoyance.

"This is where it gets convoluted. The detectives interviewed Mrs. Cleary, Monaghan and Cleary today, and in that order. Mrs. Cleary denies the newspaper story and stated her son likes to make stories up. Monaghan contradicts her and says the story is true and goes on to claim that he did break Cleary's nose and that the reason therefore had nothing to do with gambling, and that he went to Mrs. Cleary because he knew she had it out for him and thought by buying her off she would keep her son from making trouble for his son. Do you follow?" a slightly confused Kopek asked.

Duffy rubbed his chin, then said, "I gather this is a long story."

"Grimsley will be here first thing tomorrow morning with all the reports. What I got from him over the phone was basic, but it supports everything you planned to do. That's the way I see it."

Duffy shook his head. "Rick, tell me what he told you. Then let me decide if it supports my actions or not. If Cleary told the police about Monaghan, how can I in good conscience fire Daly? Or for that matter prosecute Sophie Cruz?"

"I thought you gave Daley the job just so you could fire him?" Kopek replied testily.

Duffy twisted his lips in a scowl and said, "I did, but I never knew how I was going to pull it off. It just made good sense from a tactical point, and Daley is such a boob at times that I was certain he would stumble, and I was counting on this case to provide the opportunity. And it did, or so I thought," he said with no conviction

"Okay, okay," Kopek said calmly. "Here's the fact pattern. Sometime last October Monaghan broke Cleary's nose. He slammed it into the bar in Pete's Bridge Lounge. Everyone who saw it or heard about it thought it was over Cleary not paying off a World Series bet he lost. The aggravating factor was he skipped town for a vacation in Puerto Rico without paying the bet. Monaghan collects the debts for a local gambler. But," he said with emphasis, "Monaghan told the detectives today that it was common knowledge that Cleary lost money, but that wasn't why Cleary got a beating. Monaghan denied any association with gamblers and instead related that Cleary had exposed his genitals to a couple of teenage girls. One of those girls was the daughter of a woman that Monaghan describes as a good friend, but the police and Cleary allege is his girlfriend. This disgusting episode happened near Cleary's apartment, and when Cleary was called on the carpet by the girl's mother he called her some choice names and went on his way. When Monaghan caught up with Cleary he assaulted him. Cleary, who was also interviewed by the police today, confirmed the story, but claimed the part concerning the public lewdness was a misinterpretation of events."

"I don't like this," Duffy said, interrupting Kopek.

Kopek raised his left hand chin high, rolled his fingers into a fist, extended his index finger and said reassuringly, "I don't think it's that bad, but let me finish. Cleary told his mother that Monaghan broke his nose because he was late paying the debt. Mrs. Cleary, who by all accounts, again according to Grimsley is hard as nails, made it her business to constantly harangue Monaghan's wife over the beating and the cost of the medical bills. I don't know what state Monaghan's marriage is in, but he has a wife and a girlfriend and it didn't bother him a whit that Mrs. Cleary was harassing his wife over something he did to avenge a wrong done to his girlfriend. That is until the murder and the indication by Cleary that Monaghan's son, who had made a delivery to the apartment where the murder took place, was seen leaving the alleyway of the building shortly after Mrs. Weiss came home, long after his arrival to make the delivery."

"Yes, he was on the short list of suspects, but they cleared that up, at least I thought they did," Duffy added.

"And the detectives went to his apartment that night and questioned. Monaghan, who, by his own words, and again I'm repeating what Grimsley told me, said he didn't believe the kid had done anything, but he did know that the Cleary's could make trouble for him, so he went and saw Mrs. Cleary and gave her a half baked apology and paid her a hundred dollars, which is the sum she had been seeking from Mrs. Monaghan. All of which Cleary told Kreppell the next day, and which Kreppell took to the grave without telling anyone else," Kopek said as he neatly placed the yellow pages to his legal pad in place and put the pad back into his leather portfolio.

"So how does that keep Daly on the hook?" Duffy asked.

"Grimsley stressed the point that when the police feel they have sufficient proof they'll make an arrest. There is a good faith expectation that the district attorney will scrutinize every step of the police investigation and when necessary request further interviews, investigation and so forth. In this instance the district attorney, i.e. Gordon Alpert, accepted the police case without exception. For example, they didn't see a need to investigate Daniel Monaghan any further than the original interview conducted by detectives. Nor did Alpert feel it necessary to probe Cleary over what he had observed. Cleary's grand jury testimony is limited to what time Sophie Cruz came to the Excelsior and that she asked for Mrs. Weiss and waited for her to leave the building. When the detectives grilled Cleary today he told them that the district attorney never asked him about Monaghan, and the interview before the grand jury was limited to the questions he testified to. Think about it. Cleary readily told the police everything he knew, including the business about Monaghan visiting his mother."

"Right, I went over the Grand Jury testimony earlier this afternoon," Duffy said defensively. "The D.A.'s office is to blame."

"That's what you want, isn't it?" a perplexed Kopek replied.

Duffy shook his head and chuckled. "It is what I need, but Grimsley's position is tiresome, and what we get from the police all too often."

"They're cops, not brain surgeons," Kopek answered.

"No fooling," Duffy complained. "And he is right, but it wouldn't hurt if the cops were a little more attentive to cleaning up their own messes before they hand them off to us."

"So, how are you going to play it?" Kopek asked.

"Close to the vest," Duffy said as he got up and closed the office door. "My position will be that the prosecution team had ample opportunity to examine Cleary and Monaghan and failed to do so. The police investigation is still ongoing, but after carefully reviewing the facts I'm confidant that nothing has been uncovered that would diminish or dissolve the weight of incriminating evidence against Sophie Cruz. However, there are a number of issues that have been aired in the press this summer, and though they are nothing more than harmless distractions, they would not exist had the assistant district attorneys charged with handling this case under the supervision of Joseph Daley performed their duties up to the expectations and standards demanded of the Huguenot City District Attorney's Office. What do you think?"

"That's the high dudgeon approach," Kopek remarked positively.

"The press will be far more interested probing my sacking of Frank Heaton's nephew than they will be in pursuing this new, but relatively weak twist in the Millie Campos murder investigation. Heaton's still an icon and this is gossip, juicy gossip."

"What if Daley squawks, claims he's being made the scapegoat?" Kopek asked.

Duffy smiled. "You gave him his walking papers, but just for added insurance Bill Sullivan had a little conversation with Joe when he was cleaning out his office, and the sum and substance of the conversation was that the administrative judge's position was contingent upon Joe playing ball with us."

"That's a threat, couple that with his sacking and maybe," Kopek paused and frowned, "just maybe he can't control himself and starts wailing like a stuck pig that he's being made the fall guy. I detected that potential in him in our little interview today. He could be mercurial, no?" Kopek asked.

Duffy waved his hand in dismissal at Kopek's theory. "Wife, kids, house and a sizeable mortgage, that's what hangs in the balance, Rick." Duffy was standing in the middle of the room and suddenly he was Frank Duffy the prosecutor, and Kopek was the jury. His feet were spread apart and his hands were on his hips. He slowly rocked back and forth on the balls of his feet and repeated to Kopek slowly, "Wife, kids, house, mortgage, he has to account for all of that. No matter how badly he wants to hurt me, he can't. Joe Daley needs a job. You were smart. You went into private practice and found your niche. You don't live on a paycheck, do you?"

Kopek nodded his head in agreement. "I've done well, if that's your point."

"Of course it is. I'm not very far from where Daley is. This," he said pointing to the office walls, "is provided by the taxpayers. They cover the overhead, and every two weeks we get a paycheck. This hallowed institution is the means to a solid middle class existence. That's why our brighter men, for the most part, get their experience and move on. I didn't, Joe didn't, and others like us didn't. Bottom line is, Joe Daley needs that paycheck. He has a wife, kids, a house and a mortgage, and Bill Sullivan in a very blunt, purposely blunt manner, reminded Joe of that. So, in answer to your question, I'm not worried. Joe Daley may never talk to me again, but he won't squawk."

"A question of economics and nothing else," Kopek asked.

"Nothing else," Duffy answered with confidence. "I'm not so confidant that the press won't give me a hard time over Joe getting canned, but I'll take that risk. That's why it is so important we close the door on this case and get Sophie Cruz to plead out to a lesser offense."

"I agree," Kopek said.

"We give it our best shot," Duffy answered confidently.

"One last question," Kopek said as he sat back in his chair and loosened his neck tie. "How did you mange to line up another job for Daley so quickly, and what made you so confident he'd screw up. This has really worked out when you think about it."

"Honestly, I hadn't a clue. The plan was to make him a fall guy somehow, but whether he would screw up or not was another story. If he didn't, I would have stuck with him through the election and lived with the results. Before I gave him the spot, I discussed this with Andy Quinn and—"

Kopek's head went back and his face reddened as he interrupted Duffy. and said, "Andy Quinn, that son of a bitch, just because he's the party chairman he thinks he can do anything he wants. That son of a bitch, he never said a damn thing to me about this."

"That was before you got here," Duffy responded. somewhat taken back by Kopek's angry reaction to Andy Quinn's name.

"I took this position as a favor to the party. No, let me correct that. I did it out of duty to the party. Quinn thought you needed a guiding hand. I thought so too. and agreed, but, Christ, you'd think he'd tell me he was providing guidance of his own and you were following it."

"Listen," Duffy said seriously, "this type of thing isn't really my cup of tea, and I told Andy that, but he was insistent. 'This is politics,' he would say and he was right. You say the same thing. If anyone would screw up it would be Daley. I knew that, and I didn't want to hurt Joe, but then Andy promised he'd find another spot for him and I figured why not? I never thought Joe would accommodate us, but he did, and as far as the old boy network and Frank Heaton and all that baggage is concerned, Andy was right. I fire Joe Daley and, in essence, I douse that theory and get on with the race. Tomorrow morning Bill Sullivan is going to put it to Pat Lenihan. Sophie Cruz can roll the dice and go for twenty-five to life, or she can take a plea to a reckless assault and burglary and get three to five. I'm betting she pleads and this goes away. That's it in a nutshell."

Kopek stood up, walked over, shook Duffy's hand and patted him on the back. "I didn't know if you had the balls for this," he said enthusiastically. "But I know now you do, and I'll work my tail off to see you win this damn election and beat that prissy liberal gadfly Brooks."

"We'll see," Duffy said warily.

"Why don't you freshen up a bit? I'll see who is here from the press, then we can get that out of the way," Kopek said, all business-like. Then he laughed as he was going out the door, and said, "And then I'll ring my buddy Quinn and wring his balls for not keeping me in the loop."

"Be nice," Duffy called out. "Quinn's the reason I got this shot in the first place."

Kopek stuck his head in the door and answered, "Bullshit, you're the reason you got this shot. It was you and nobody but you, and come election day it's going to be you."

Chapter Sixty-One

The heat in the elevator was stifling. The back of his shirt was soaked with sweat and his sleeves were wrinkled and creased from the humidity in the air. Walking to Sophie's apartment from his office had been a bad idea. It was only six blocks, but Lenihan realized he should have driven. Three blocks uphill and another three blocks downhill on a hot humid August afternoon was a marathon for him. The elevator door opened and he stepped out to the eighth floor hallway. He unbuckled his belt and tucked his shirt into his pants and tried to neaten himself up. The waistband to his suit pants was soaked with sweat too, and he felt like a wet dishrag. There were six apartments on each floor. Sophie's apartment was the last one on the south side of the building, and there was an open terrace leading to her entrance. It was a nice touch, Lenihan thought as he opened the door and felt a hot, but nonetheless refreshing breeze sweeping across the exposed walkway. Her living room windows were open and the Venetian blinds were pulled up halfway. Thin sheer drapes fluttered softly from the breeze, and he was tempted to lean his head inside the window and say hello. He checked his impulse and rang the doorbell; this was no time to act folksy. Seconds later a very distraught looking Sophie Cruz opened the door.

She didn't say hello. She stood behind the door, slowly pulled it opened and looked past Lenihan.

He entered her apartment and said, "Hello, Sophie, how are you?"

Sophie let the door slam and went past him into her living room. The windows on both sides of the room were open, and despite the humidity and heat the room was considerably cooler than it was out on the street. Sophie set herself down in a black vinyl recliner. Her hair was damp and she was clad in a white terrycloth robe. She had tucked one leg up under her thigh and the robe was open and exposed her bare thighs. Lenihan was certain that she had no other clothing on. He sat down on couch and repeated his initial greeting, "Sophie, how are you?"

She gave him a halfhearted smile and said brusquely, "Not good."

Lenihan assessed her physical appearance again and couldn't help but appreciate the shapeliness of her legs. He tried to flush those thoughts from his mind, but since he first met her there was a sexual appeal she radiated that overcame him. His thoughts were uninvited guests and momentary for the most part, yet always there. She shifted uncomfortably in her chair, readjusted her robe and covered her thighs. When she did that she released her hand from the upper edges of her robe and a good portion of her two breasts fell forward and slipped out of the robe. Sophie seemed unaware and nonchalantly sat back and covered up. Lenihan took a deep breath and said, "Did I get you out of the tub?"

"I was soaking when you called. Lucy took Joey to the zoo and I took a cool bath. I don't know why I answered the phone, but I did. I guess I knew you'd call. You said a half an hour, so I soaked a little longer. When I heard the bell ring I didn't have time to dry. You got here fast."

"You must have been enjoying your bath. I called over an hour ago. but what the heck. I'm almost as wet as you. I walked and it's a steam bath out there."

"This apartment always stays cool. It's nice to have windows on both sides, the whole building is concrete and that keeps it cool too," she said pleasantly.

Lenihan's eyes were on Sophie's legs. They were tan and sleek, and she had slim feet with perfectly proportioned toes. The toe nails were painted bright red, and while he was nodding his head in agreement to her description of her apartment and why it was cool, he seriously entertained the thought that she was coming on to him and was waiting for him to initiate some further action. He was tempted to get up and move across the room to her when he felt his cheeks flush with embarrassment at the absurdity of what he was thinking. He stretched his legs and replied, "This looks like a nice building. It's clean and well maintained."

"I saw the news last night," she said with despair in her voice.

Lenihan knew the small talk was over and replied cautiously, "I have some news."

Sophie showed no interest in his last remark, and said, "Why is that Duffy so mean and arrogant? He said my name, and it sounded so cruel. And the way he said there was, what?" She paused to think, then said quickly, "Yes, 'the weight of evidence is overwhelming' that's what he said. So fucking mean and serious, you know?"

Lenihan loosened his tie, and said, "He's scared. He wants to win this election at all costs. That's my news."

Again Sophie ignored his remark, and said, "What's winning got to do with me. Who am I? I'm a nobody."

"No, you're not. You and this case have been in the papers too much this summer, and he wants you gone."

"Yeah, gone to jail. What's that place, Deerpoint? That's where he wants me, the bastard."

Lenihan sighed, then smiled. "He wants to be the elected district attorney. That's the only thing he wants. You wanted to be Mrs. Henry Weiss, didn't you?"

"Fuck him," she spat out.

"Sure, you feel that way now, but two months ago that was what you wanted and you did what you did and now look where you are."

"I didn't do a damn thing but act stupid. I didn't kill that woman," she hissed.

"Am I wrong? Answer me? Did you or did you not want to be Henry's wife?"

"I did, once," she answered meekly.

"And you would have moved Heaven and Earth to make it happen, wouldn't you?"

"I don't know about that, but I tried. Look where it got me."

"He feels the same way about becoming the elected district attorney. Bill Sullivan called me this morning."

"Who is Bill Sullivan?"

"One of Duffy's bureau chiefs, and he made an offer."

Sophie frowned, but said nothing in reply.

"You plead guilty to assault and burglary. Three to five years in Pinewood, which amounts to no more than two and a half years and you're a free woman." He didn't know what to expect and gave her his best poker face.

Sophie crossed her ankles and looked at her feet. "Why would I plead guilty to something I didn't do?"

"Two and a half years is ten percent of twenty-five years," he said solemnly.

"That makes me only ten per cent guilty," she answered haughtily.

"It reduces your sentence, that is, if you go to trial and are found guilty, by twenty-two and a half years."

"What if I'm innocent?"

"Leo Sheridan agreed to be my co-counsel for the trial. We'll split the fee. Leo's as tough as they come, and if that's the way you want to go, then we'll do it. I have to give Sullivan an answer by tomorrow morning. He gave me a 10:00 o'clock deadline. So give it some thought." Lenihan stood up and smiled. "I have nothing else to say, Sophie. It's your call. Frank Duffy had a moment of weakness. This case should be nothing more than a minor irritation to him, but he's treating it as something bigger and you are the beneficiary. His offer is good news."

She started to cry. Lenihan felt useless and reached over and touched her on the shoulder. "Sophie, it stinks. If I thought you had a chance I'd urge you to go to trial. I don't. Leo thinks our only hope is in picking the right jury. He's good at that, one of the best, but it is still a longshot. Give it some thought. Let me know in the morning. You have any questions this afternoon or tonight call me." He took a card from his wallet and handed it to her. "My home phone number's on the back. I don't care if it's four in the morning, If you have a question or want to talk about it some more, call," he said reassuringly.

She took the card from him and said, "Don't go. Wait. Sit, please, sit for a minute."

He sensed that she was breaking and sat back down on the couch.

"What happens to my son?" she pleaded.

"Small world, Leo knows Fortescue. They both serve on the board of The Bishop's House."

"Bishop's House?" she repeated.

"It's a home for unwed mothers. Leo's a do gooder. He's involved with all sorts of charities. Fortescue's a society fat cat and it looks good for him to be involved. He's also very good at raising money."

She had dried her tears. "How does any of that help me?"

"Yesterday Leo called Fortescue. It was after I had spoken with you and I had my copy of the papers that were served for the custody suit. I remembered that Leo knew the man and asked him to make an inquiry on your behalf."

"Okay, what do they want?"

"I don't know. Leo said that Fortescue was very pleasant, but his answer was that Mr. and Mrs. Weiss were prepared emotionally and financially to do everything they could to ensure the well being of your son and to unite him with his father."

"What the hell does that mean?" she said with anger.

"Whatever they want it to mean," he answered coldly.

Sophie let her head fall back against the back of the chair several times and breathlessly uttered, "Unbelievable, this is unbelievable." She sat back up and looked at Lenihan intently and said, "Is that near Washburn?"

"It's in Lichenville, right over the line from Washburn."

"How far is that from here," Sophie asked?

"Twenty, twenty-five minutes by car depending on the traffic; a good hour if you take the bus to Monmouth and Western and grab the train up to Lichenville. The train lets you off two blocks from the prison," Lenihan said with the knowledge of someone who had made the trip before.

"What's it like?" Sophie asked.

"What? You mean Pinewood?" he asked.

"What else?" she replied sarcastically.

"There are three prisons for women in this state. The maximum security prison is in Deerpoint, you don't want to go there. Then there's Fulton up in Wellington. That's the oldest one in the state and originally held everyone before they built Deerpoint. You don't want to go to Fulton either; although it's a lot closer to Huguenot City than Deerpoint is."

Sophie interrupted him and in an annoyed tone she said, "I asked about Pinewood. I didn't ask about anything else."

"Just giving you the lay of the land," he answered without showing the slightest reaction to her edginess. "Pinewood is a prison, but it is what they now call minimum security. Instead of cells you're placed in a locked room with a glass window so that the guards can see in. It's very different, and while you're locked up they don't want you to think you're a prisoner."

"Is it like that rotten Huguenot City jail I was in?"

Lenihan made a face and shook his head back and forth. "No, no," he said with reassurance. "Compared to those other places it's a hotel."

Sophie bit her lip and stretched her legs out. The recliner opened up, the back of the chair tipped slightly and she stared at the ceiling for a minute, then said, "You know what I was thinking about in the tub all morning?"

"No, I haven't a clue," he said.

"My things, what do I do with all of my things?"

Lenihan looked around the room and said, "You mean clothes, furniture, that stuff."

She was still staring at the ceiling, and without averting her gaze, said, "The apartment, clothes, furniture, pictures, everything. Going to jail is like dying. Maybe I'm selfish, but I love Joey. He's my whole world, but I know that there will be people to take care of him. Shit, even if it's Henry and the bitch I know now that they'll do what they're supposed to do. You know," she said as she looked at him and then laughed self-consciously, "Henry wouldn't take me to court if he didn't mean to be a father to his son. He broke my heart, but it's my own fault."

Lenihan didn't answer and she weakly waved her hand at him and went on, "I know what you think of him, but believe me, he has a heart of gold. That's his biggest problem. I'm soaking and crying about myself and my baby, but my baby's going to be okay. You know? And suddenly all I can think of is my stuff and what am I going to do with it. I'm sick," and she started to cry. "I love this apartment. This is my home. How can I leave it, and who'll take care of these things? I'm being selfish, I know, but when you're faced with what I'm faced with your mind goes crazy and you really don't know what to do."

Lenihan clasped his hands together and said with a hint of enthusiasm, "Sophie, you're not being selfish. Not at all, you're thinking reasonably. What do you do with a lifetime's accumulation of personal belongings?" He winked at her, then said, "I thought about this too."

"You did?" she said with surprise.

"Hear me out," he said carefully. "What if you took the deal and kept the apartment. We get your aunt to move in here while you're away. Your legal fees are a couple of hundred bucks, and that leaves more than enough to cover the rent for two years. I don't know if your aunt has a lease where she is, but if she can get out of her apartment then she can kick in a little too. You've got enough room. And that way nothing would be disturbed and when your free you can come back home. It also keeps some continuity with your son's life. He still has his room, and no matter how this custody issue ends up Henry can't keep your son from visiting your side of the family and we can twist his arm and make him the party responsible for insuring that your son regularly visits you."

Sophie had an agonized look on her face. She sighed and twisted her fingers in her hair. "I can't risk going to jail for twenty-five years. Joey would be a man by the time I got out. But I didn't kill anyone," she whimpered.

"I believe you, honestly I do," Lenihan replied. "It's your call."

"If I do take this deal, how long before I go to jail?"

"They'll want you to plea out before Labor Day. That means next week, and if we're lucky you might get another week before you begin the sentence. More importantly, I think Leo can work with Fortescue on this."

Sophie took a deep breath and covered her eyes with her hands. She cradled her head in her hands, and with her eyes streaming tears said in a very soft voice, "What do I tell my son?"

"As much of the truth as you think he can understand," Lenihan said bluntly. "At his age that may not be much, but I would put the ball in Henry's court. I suspect Fortescue will have that covered."

"I don't understand," she replied.

"I'm certain Fortescue has a lot of experience in this area. He probably has a couple of very good child psychologists that he deals with regularly, and I imagine that Henry and his wife and Joey will all go through some counseling to make this easier. You don't think that one morning you would just pack Joey's bags and send him off with Henry do you?"

"I don't know what to think, and if I do this I'll be in jail, so how the hell can I help," she said, visibly annoyed.

"This is where Leo comes in. If you decide to take the deal I'll see that Leo gets through to Fortescue with some demands. For instance, there's no need for Joey to immediately go with Henry. He could stay here with your aunt and get to meet Henry and his wife slowly. That's where we demand some type of counseling and you make some ground rules. How often does he visit with you, how does he get there, who takes him, who pays for it, that type of thing."

"I want him to go to church every week. He just made his Holy Communion in May. I don't want him becoming a Jew."

Lenihan stood up. "Let me get going. I have to call Leo, then I've got to call the district attorney. Are you sure about this?"

Sophie stood up too. She took Lenihan's left hand in her two hands and squeezed his hand. "I've been taking baths two three times a day for the last week. I thought about killing myself. Cutting my wrists, crazy thoughts, and I realized that if I do that I lose. I'm not giving up. I'll go to jail because I have no choice, but when it's over I'm putting my life back together. I love my son. That's all I can say."

Lenihan felt his eyes tearing up. He covered Sophie's hands with his right hand and pulled her closed to him. "I never believed you until today. I wish I'd done a better job, I do, and I'm sorry. Sorry for you, sorry for your son, sorry for all your pain. Maybe it was the kid, or the doorman or even the bitch," he said with sneering emphasis. "I don't know, but I see no other choice," he added sadly. Lenihan gently drew his hands away from Sophie's. The moment was warm and sincere. He smiled and started toward the hallway that led to the apartment door. "I'll call you tomorrow morning, as soon as everything is worked out. If Leo can contact Fortescue today and make some headway, I'll let you know that as soon as I find out. Are you going to be okay?'

"I'll be fine," she answered confidently. "Pardon my French, but fuck them all."

Lenihan laughed and then whispered, "That's right, fuck 'em all." He left her in the living room and let himself out of the apartment.

Chapter Sixty-Two

Widelsky was carrying a brown paper bag in his right hand and a pint of milk in his left hand as he walked into the squad room, and, with surprise, said, "Where'd everybody go?"

Cairn was talking on the telephone and ignored Widelsky. Widelsky walked over to Cairn's desk and stuck his hand into the bag he was carrying, "Let's see," he mumbled, "bacon and egg, no ketchup, plenty of salt and pepper." His hand was deep in the bag, moving the wrapped sandwiches about when he found the one he was looking for and exclaimed, "Ah, here it is." He took the sandwich, wrapped in greasy wax paper, dropped it on Cairn's desk and draped it with a paper napkin. He then went to his desk and took another sandwich from the bag and dropped it on his desk. "I don't know where those other two went," he said, as much to himself as to Cairn, as he went over to the counter where the coffee urn was and laid the bag with the remaining sandwiches in it down, along with that the pint of milk he was also carrying. He then poured himself a cup of coffee and made his way back to his desk.

Cairn had just hung up the phone and said, "The boss just chased Slattery and Russo out the door."

It was the Monday before Labor Day. Ted Kreppell's permanent replacement had finally arrived in the person of Lieutenant Bill Allison. He had addressed the morning crew at eight-thirty, and it was nothing more than his name, his previous assignment—Robbery, and a notification that Wednesday at three-thirty he would convene a general staff meeting of the entire unit.

"What'd they do?" Widelsky asked.

"I was on the phone when the new boss came in and those two idiots were doing the jumble in the paper. Allison had a piece of paper in his hand and instead of showing him a little respect they ignored him," Cairn replied.

"Yeah, then what happened?" Widelsky inquired.

"Not much, except Allison went to the window and looked out to the yard where we park the unmarked cars and said, 'when was the last time those cars were washed?' Slattery, without missing a beat, said, 'Last time it rained,'" Cairn said, laughing.

Widelsky started to laugh too, then said, "You gotta be kidding. He said that to the new boss?"

"I had to bite my lip to keep from laughing. I had just called Gordon Alpert. You know, I wanted to get the full scoop on why the DA caved in to Sophie Cruz, and Alpert's secretary had me on hold, so I was paying attention. I couldn't fucking believe what Slattery said. What an asshole," Cairn said sourly.

"So what did the lieutenant do?" Widelsky asked.

"He did a double take, then said, 'I guess you're a better comedian than you are an investigator, since it's a well known fact I don't have sense of humor.'"

"I'd agree with that," Widelsky nodded.

"Alpert came on the line then, and I lost track of the conversation with the lieutenant and Slattery, but I'd say about now Russo and Slattery are ferrying our three cars back and forth from the garage for oil changes and washdowns."

"You think the new boss is going to be as tight in the pants as Kreppell was?" Widelsky asked.

"I don't think so. Slattery was way out of line, and I think the new guy handled it well. Shit, if I was a lieutenant and some sack of shit like Slattery blew me off like that I'd want to send him back to patrol."

"Well, that'll never happen," Widelsky replied sarcastically. "More importantly, what did Gordon have to say? Duffy's ears must have been ringing."

Cairn frowned and said, "I expected an earful, but they're all alike."

"He wasn't upset?" a puzzled Widelsky asked.

"Not at all," Cairn answered. "The first thing he does when he comes on the line is say, 'What's doing?' I say, 'You tell me because I can't believe what they're doing to you.' And he says, 'What're you talking about?'"

"That's cute," Widelsky added.

"Oh yeah, it was like pulling teeth. So I said, 'Sophie Cruz, Joe Daley, does that ring a bell?' And he goes into this long diatribe about Duffy having promoted Daley out of loyalty, then discovering how far over his head the guy was, he had no choice but to dump him, and as for Sophie Cruz there were a number of fundamental problems with the case that made it anything but a slam dunk. He went on and on with a lot of bullshit, but you have to give the man credit, he can talk a blue streak. Bottom line in the DA's office is that no one can speak ill of the boss," Cairn said with conviction.

"Shit, I would have bet a month's pay that Gordon would quit over this," Widelsky said with surprise that Gordon Alpert hadn't quit.

"I would have too, but think about it," Cairn mused. "Gordon's not there for life. Rumor is that he's been itching to leave for sometime and is waiting for the right opportunity. Last thing he wants is to be on the outs with the people in power. They're all in it together. He let it slip that Daley has a sweetheart job coming up with the state as an administrative judge."

"That figures." Widelsky sighed. "But what about Sophie Cruz? She's getting away with murder. He didn't say anything about it?"

"Stuck to the party line all the way," Cairn answered, with disappointment. "He thought in the end this was justice served since none of them thought she had ever intended to commit a murder."

"Justice served my ass!" Widelsky said with disgust as he crumbled the wax paper wrapper from his sandwich into a ball and fired it into the wastepaper basket by his desk. Widelsky licked his lips, then said, "That sandwich was so good I'm going to eat Slattery's. It'll be too cold to eat by the time he gets back, and if it's still here the cheap bastard will find some way to duck paying me the fifty cents it cost anyway."

"Excuses, excuses," Cairn said, laughing as Slattery's bacon and egg on a roll quickly disappeared from Widelsky's hand into his mouth.

Widelsky belched, and after he wiped his mouth, said, "I don't think the new boss likes the breakfast club. When I was going out to get the order I asked him if he wanted anything from the diner. He said, 'I eat at home,' and I figure after today we can eat on the road, you know?"

"If that's all we got to worry about, things are fine and dandy with me. Still, Alpert got my goat. He didn't give a shit," Cairn aid scornfully.

"We can't do nothing about that. Last week it was a fire drill to track down Monaghan and Cleary. This week it's history. We got to roll with the punches, Phil, just roll with the punches," Widelsky said in a relaxed tone.

Cairn stood up and put on his sport coat. "C'mon," he said as he waved his hand at Widelsky. He looked at his watch and waved his hand again. "Get your notebook. There was a stabbing in the Bon Amis Saturday night and the victim lost a kidney. Allison wants us to interview him this morning at the hospital, then track down the barmaid. I got all the info here," he said as he held up a folder with some loose sheets of papers sticking out from one end.

"What car are we gonna use for a car?" Widelsky asked as he followed Cairn out of the squad room.

"Our car is still parked outside. I'll tell the boss we'll get it serviced after we track this broad down," Cairn answered with little enthusiasm.

"You got all the bases covered today, don't you, Phil?" Widelsky replied cheerfully.

"You sound very chipper today, Francis," Cairn said sarcastically.

"I am," Widelsky said. "You know, unlike you, I hate going to trial on messy cases, and I bet that lawyer for Sophie Cruz would have been pulling every trick he could to make us look bad, and now that we ain't going to trial because Duffy threw in the towel I'm happy."

"So, if it suits you, then it don't make no difference if things ain't on the level," Cairn said, laughing.

"You're right," Widelsky sighed in agreement. "I'm just sick and tired of this case, that's all."

"I hear you, I hear you," Cairn answered.

Chapter Sixty-Three

Henry was sitting on the edge of the bed. Maria had left the paperwork and paint samples on the nightstand on his side of the bed. He was tired of looking at paint samples. They had closed on the house on August 18th, moved in on August 25th, and between Labor Day and Halloween Maria had consumed herself with the total renovation of a house that when it was offered for sale was advertised as "In Move-in Condition." All that was left to do was the painting of the dining room. It was November 5th, and Maria wanted everything done before Thanksgiving. She was leaning toward Linen White, but also liked a color identified as Meadow Yellow, and another one that was called White Oyster. She wanted Henry's input, but he knew she would make the final decision. What concerned him more was the paperwork she had left on top of the paint samples. He could hear the giggling from the bedroom down the hall, then Maria softly singing a song in a language he didn't recognize. He was still studying the paint samples when she slipped into the room and gently closed the door.

"Did you call him?" she asked.

Henry dropped the paint samples on the floor and reached for the two mimeographed pages that were on the nightstand. "He has a practice every Saturday for the next three weeks, then there are two games a week. And each Saturday there's a game. When does he go to visit his mother? We have an agreement," he said in a hushed, but angry tone.

Maria didn't answer. She opened her closet door, took a long flannel bathrobe off a hanger and tossed it unto the bed. She turned to the mirror over her dresser, ran her fingers through her hair and stretched her neck. "Tomorrow won't be a problem as long as long as Lucy keeps to the schedule. The practice isn't until three, and your nephew's taking him anyway." As she was talking she had taken off her sweater and bra. Her back was to Henry, and she lifted her breasts, studied herself in the mirror and sighed, "I'm getting old." She then unbuttoned her slacks and stepped out of them quickly and picked up her bathrobe and covered herself. Henry was staring at her and she glanced at him with annoyance, turned back to the mirror and said, "Stop leering at me."

Henry quickly replied with just as much annoyance, "I'll just take a picture next time, that's the way you like to be admired, isn't it?"

Maria's face reddened. That was the first reference he had ever made to the nude photographs Koch had taken of her, and the vitriol in his remark was stinging. "That was unnecessary. Sarcasm doesn't suit you well."

Henry wanted to restrain himself, but his anger had the best of him, and he replied, "Who said I was being sarcastic?"

Maria put her hands together, and feigning prayer, lamented in a cold whisper, "Dear God, forgive me but I've caused him some embarrassment." Then in a slightly louder voice, she continued, "You despicable son of a bitch. You humiliated me. You have the gall, the colossal gall, to be upset over those pictures? Pictures no one would have known about if your psychotic secretary hadn't pulled them out of my dresser when she broke into our home. Pictures no one would have ever known about, including you, if that whore hadn't murdered poor Millie." She took a breath, and before he could answer, took a step toward him and made a motion to slap him, but before she completed the act she withdrew her hand and said, "You selfish bastard."

Henry was stunned. "You were going to hit me." He laughed in disbelief. "What, are you crazy?"

"I'm angry," she said in a calmer tone as she went across the room, closed her closet door and then went and sat down on a chair next to her dresser. "I dragged myself back to work weeks sooner than I should have, and I did it because I didn't want people talking about us. I went to work, and despite whatever lies appeared in the newspapers, I carried myself with as much dignity as I could and no one, do you understand me," she angrily stressed, "no one dared even mention this horrible incident. People asked me how I was, but no one," she stressed again, "mentioned anything else, and that was exactly how I wanted them to act. And you," she hissed, "you're upset about those pictures. You, a man who slept with another woman for ten years, fathered a child by her and lived a lie all those years; you have the effrontery to be upset with me?" She was spent. Her mouth was open and she was shaking her head back and forth, breathing slowly in an attempt to regain her composure.

"Are you done?"

"I'm far from done. I told you after all of this happened that the past was behind us. That meant everything. It can't be any other way. You said what you said, and I said what I had to say. I don't want to have this conversation again. Anything that I may have done to hurt you was done before I ever met you. Everything you did to me was done after we were married. I know I'm not perfect, and I told you I was going to change. I want this marriage to work. What do you want?"

"I don't know," he said halfheartedly. "Too much has happened in too short a period of time. A little over four months ago I was trying to extract myself from the affair with Sophie. I wanted things to work out between us. I loved you and I still do, but now I'm confused."

"You want Sophie," she said in disbelief.

"It's not about wanting or not wanting anyone," he said as he leaned over and took her hand in his. "Do you realize that you were about to slap me. Is this what we're becoming?" He sighed anxiously.

She pulled her hand away from his. "You hurt me," she said in a choking voice.

"I know I did, and I'm sorry, but look at that has happened to us. In four month's time we've witnessed Millie's murder, Sophie's in prison, we left my apartment, bought this house and now I have an eight-year-old to deal with. I'm not up to it. I was looking at the paint samples and I hear the two of you giggling in the other room. He's been here a little over a month and he can barely look at me. We don't really know what he knows, do we?" he whispered earnestly.

Maria took his hand again and squeezed it. "I'm sorry. In some ways I'm more confused than you are. You're his father. Who am I?"

Henry let go of her hand and sat down on the bed. "You're trying, at least you're trying. Me, I'm lost, and every time I look at that boy I can't help but wonder what he's really thinking, especially about me."

"Dr. Fee and Sophie worked that out. Joseph knows you are his father. He knows his mother did something wrong and had to go away. Dr. Fee said in time it would all reveal itself, and as long as we gave the child the love and support he needed things would be fine. You heard him. He told you that children are remarkably resilient. He is a very capable child psychologist. We have to trust his judgment. Joseph is too old to lie to and too young to be told the truth. I think he's doing fine, It's you that I'm concerned about."

"You shouldn't have signed him up for the basketball program. What am I going to tell Ray Cruz? We had an agreement," he said with frustration.

Maria closed her eyes and tiredly replied, "Oh please, he's an eight-year-old boy. He's in a new home with people he hardly knows, a new school and neighborhood, and the one thing that has seemed to brighten him up is the chance to play on this little team at school. He doesn't appear very happy when he returns from visiting his mother in prison, I might add."

Henry released his hand from Maria's, jumped up from the bed and said loudly, "Precisely!"

Before he could continue, Maria interrupted, "Please, please don't raise your voice. I don't want him to hear us arguing."

"We're not arguing," Henry corrected. "We're having one of the most important conversations we've ever had. You just hit the nail on the head, by the way."

"Tell me," she inquired.

"He's not happy visiting his mother in jail. She's been in jail a little over two months. Doesn't that mean something to you?"

Maria uttered a disdainful little laugh, and replied, "It means he is adjusting to his new environment. If he misses a week or two here and there it isn't the end of the world. He knows his mother is safe. It doesn't mean he loves her any less. Maybe it means he's getting comfortable in this house. Did you think of it that way?"

"As I said before, I heard you two giggling, but he can't look me in the eye."

"Henry, he was raised by his mother and his aunt. He is used to women. A few months ago you were the man his mother worked for. Now you're his father. It is a lot to swallow for an eight-year-old. You could have stuck your head in the door tonight and said goodnight to him. You could address him as Joe or Joey or Joseph and not kid. You're a grown man. He's an eight-year-old boy. I believe it is up to you to make this work. Honestly," she said and paused, "your sister's family and your brother's family have already made more of a connection with him than you have. He's all excited that Marshall's taking him to his basketball practice tomorrow. Marshall even told him if he gets home in time they'll play some basketball in Gloria's yard before the practice. I wish he could get that excited about doing something with you."

"Well, Marshall's a good boy," he answered defensively. "And, anyway, he'd probably rather be with his cousin than me. After all, Marsh's a better ballplayer than I am."

"You're his father. Sooner or later you'll have to face that fact. I'm bending over backward to make this work. Gloria and Steven are doing their best too. But I said my piece. Everyone will be here for dinner tomorrow. What do we tell them?"

"Tell them what?" he said with some confusion.

"Henry, you hurt me to the core with what you said before. Either we move forward and make this work, or we end the marriage. I don't want to pretend that everything is okay, but know that just beneath the surface our marriage is distrust and resentment. I forgive you, and if you're mad at me and mad about things you don't even know about, things you never wanted to know about when I wanted to tell you, then there is no point going on because it will never work. You should care about me and your son. You should want nothing but the best for us. If you don't feel that way, then we can tell everyone it's over and I'll leave and you'll be on your own."

Henry laughed nervously and, in an attempt to lighten the moment, said, "Jesus, you said before that 'sarcasm' didn't suit me. Since when did you become so melodramatic?"

"Henry, you said so before. Our private lives have been laid bare in the newspapers, a woman was killed in our apartment and your mistress was the murderer, and now she's in jail. That's pretty dramatic if you ask me!"

"All right," he said calmly. "I don't get it, that's all. In one breath you love me and in the next you're ready to go out the door. You went out of your way to accept my son. You paid for this house; you went to special pains to make this a home for him. All the while I know you hate his mother. It doesn't add up."

"I hate her. She should be in jail for the rest of her life. Are you happy? Is that what you wanted to hear?"

"I knew that."

"I also love you. I love your family. They're my family too. I will never let your son know how I feel about his mother. He's your son, and I want him to be a part of your life, our life. He's a wonderful little boy. It's only five weeks he's been here, but in that time I've fallen in love with him. Does that answer your question?"

"I wish it were that easy for me, Maria, I really do."

"Henry, you have to try. You have to believe that we can make it work."

"I want to," he said, hoping to mollify her.

She smiled and sighed. "Let's go to bed," she said as she reached over and turned off the lamp by the bed and undid her robe. "Come to bed, I need you."

"I can't just now, Maria. I can't. I do love you, but I wish I could be like you, I do, I do. Go to bed. I'll go downstairs and call Ray, then I'll watch a little television or something. That's the best I can do right now, the best."

"You know how I feel," she whispered. "I'll see you in the morning."

Henry left their room, and as he headed toward the stairway he looked in on Joseph. There was a nightlight in the room. It cast a warm yellow glow over the child's bed. The boy was sleeping soundly. He had a thick head of dark hair and a fair face. His face was turned sideways on his pillow, and it was a picture of contentment. He admired him for a minute and suddenly understood Maria's feelings. With all the miserable things that happened in the past four months, the boy was a gift. Maria was right, he conceded, and with a slightly lighter heart he went downstairs to call Sophie's brother and endure what would surely be the second scolding he would receive that evening.

Chapter Sixty-Four

Was it someone attempting to break into the house? No, it was nothing more than a strong wind brushing the branches of the Rhododendron bushes against the window that wakened him with a start. It took a few seconds to fully wake up, and the crick in his neck was the first reminder that he had fallen asleep watching television. One scotch had turned into four scotches, and somewhere along the way the movie he was watching had failed to keep his attention and he drifted off into a restless slumber. He looked at his wristwatch. It was half past one and he was tired, but he didn't want to go upstairs to bed. He got up from the chair and turned off the television. He went over to the windows and looked out to the oversized backyard of his new home. There was no moon, and it was pitch black outside. He could hear the rustling of tree branches and bushes from the wind, but he couldn't see anything and felt homesick for the apartment on Lincoln Boulevard.

The two green leather chairs and the accompanying tea tables, along with the television and stereo console were all that remained from the apartment on Lincoln Boulevard. Henry stared at his reflection in the window and ran his fingers across the metal frames that held the individual lites of leaded glass in place. The view, as he recalled, from his eighth floor apartment was a snapshot of all the clutter and vitality of the Upper Borough. No matter how dark the night might be, the activity from other apartment houses and cars and buses and taxicabs running up and down the broad concourse of Lincoln Boulevard and the perfectly regimented columns of street lights and trees bordering the sidewalks and medians in the roadway kept the darkness at bay until the morning light returned. *You never felt alone on Lincoln Boulevard,* he thought. *There was always someone or something to catch your eye when you stood by the window and surveyed the world.* The view from the windows in his den in his new home on Seneca Avenue in Riverview provided the perfect metaphor for the wrong turn his life had taken. It wasn't a matter of acquiescence, but rather surrender. In his first conversation in the hospital with Maria, she had carefully set in motion her plan for revenge. That was how he interpreted it, and it wasn't until they had their flare up hours earlier that he finally realized what she was doing. Initially, the murder and all the revelations that followed had left him feeling guilty and humiliated. He felt responsible, not only for Millie's death, but also for the ruination of Sophie's life, and it was within that miasma of contrition and weakness and an overriding need for self redemption that he subordinated his will to hers and ruefully learned that absolution comes from within, and concessions and noble gestures, though well intentioned, only obfuscate the truth.

Henry Weiss finally understood the truth. Through most of his marriage to Maria they had survived in an environment of perpetual stalemate. Neither side wanted to win. Maria maintained her independence by acting aloof and uncaring, but she was clever enough to let her guard down occasionally and declare how much she loved and needed him. Those interludes proved captivating, and his vanity, his shallow appreciation of her physical beauty was all that was necessary to bind him to an emotional tether he had no desire to be free from. The greater balance of their marriage had existed in that condition and Maria's dominant trait was her lack of emotion. Maria didn't argue. Maria didn't stomp her feet and clench her fists in anger. There were no tantrums, no roiling rages at perceived slights or infidelities. She had acted as if those exhibitions of emotion were beneath her. Something insecure women did to attract attention or diminish the force of male domination. Maria dominated. Tonight that all fell apart, tonight she was humiliated and outraged, or was she? His instincts told him it was contrived. *We are what we are,* he thought. And the new Maria was too fragile, too labial, too Sophie like for him to accept.

He saw the half-filled tumbler of scotch and water, the remnants of ice floating in the glass and picked it up and swallowed heartily. He turned out the lights and made his way upstairs to the bedroom. He was troubled and confused, but there were no easy answers. She had taken control, and in doing so had won the approval of friends and family. Even Ray Cruz had surprised him. He had expected Ray to balk at the idea of the boy missing some of his scheduled visits with Sophie for something as trite as involvement in an after school basketball program, but Ray had treated it as if he had been expecting Henry's phone call. There was some relief in his voice, and perhaps even a hint of gratitude that Henry and Maria were exercising as much effort as they were to see that Joseph was well cared for and given every opportunity to feel loved and secure in his new home. Sophie was an afterthought, an embarrassment, a convicted and admitted criminal and while she was still Ray's sister, her happiness, her security and emotional well being were negotiable. Ray acted as if Sophie's feelings and needs were now secondary to everyone else's, and Henry found that attitude upsetting, but let it pass without comment. *After all*, he contemplated, *who was he to comment about the behavior of others when his own selfish indulgences had been so insensitive.*

He reached the upstairs hallway and stopped by his son's room. He looked the same as he had earlier, and in the warm yellow glow of the night light he was the picture of innocence and peaceful contentment. The child psychologist had explained in great detail the resiliency of children to traumatic events. The trick as he had put it was to help the child deal with the trauma so that the damage wouldn't be repressed, only to erupt at a later time in the child's life. His prescription in this special case was to give the boy as much access to his mother as he desired and was permitted, but to simultaneously keep his life well ordered and busy with positive experiences. Maria understood the concept completely. That was the impetus for family dinners every weekend for the past month. Joseph's immersion into the Weiss family couldn't have gone better. He was eight years younger in age than the next youngest cousin and because of that he was immediately adopted as one of their own without any sense of jealousy or competition from Steve and Muriel's three daughters and Gloria and Joel's two sons. Joseph was treated as a celebrity rather than a novelty and the attention he had received in little more than a month's time had put him at total ease with his cousins, aunts and uncles. Maria's tact in presenting herself, not as a stepmother or replacement for Sophie had been carried off with exceptional aplomb. Maria had asked Sophie's Aunt Lucy for pictures of Sophie and the boy so she could frame them and put them in his room. Lucy had given her three very nice photographs of Sophie and Joey, two from Christmas' past and one taken a summer ago at the beach. The framed photographs of his mother appeared to be the first things he noticed when Maria showed him his room. The next thing she did was tell him that none of them could ever replace his mother, and until they were reunited he was to understand that she and his father would protect him and let nothing happen to him. It was a simple and direct approach. Maria was right; the boy was used to women. She wasn't smothering, but she knew how to dole out the attention and affection so as not to overwhelm him, but give him that sense of security he had always known. Henry, for his part, was a bit player in all of this and believed that was the way Maria wanted it. For all her importuning that he bond with the boy, the opportunities to do so were limited. Being a father was much more than paying the bills or admiring a child because he had a pleasant disposition and a handsome face. Henry was at a loss at how to develop that bond and admittedly he wasn't certain he wanted to cross the divide between benign parenthood and actual parenthood.

He left the boy's doorway and headed to his bedroom as confused as he had been earlier when he went downstairs. He found Maria sleeping as peacefully and soundly as his son. He was certain Sophie was not resting as peacefully, and in an odd way he felt closer to her and more distant to Maria than he had ever felt before.

Chapter Sixty-Five

Maria was standing over the boy's shoulder, and in a disapproving voice, she said, "Are you having syrup for breakfast, or pancakes and grapefruit?"

Joseph laughed and ran a forkful of pancake through the pool of syrup on his plate and slowly lifted the fork to his mouth, "Umm," he said hungrily, "maybe I need a spoon."

Maria returned his laugh and went over to the sink and turned the faucet to fill the wash basin with water. "You are a wisenheimer, young man. Now hurry up and finish that glop. The taxi will be here in five minutes and you still have to brush your teeth."

"Why do you call it glop?" he asked.

"Because it is. That breakfast was nothing but sugar," she replied.

"Better than what you eat, ugh," he said with exaggeration.

"I'll make an exception for you on weekends but during the week it's cereal or poached eggs, and if you really wanted to be healthy and grow strong you should eat what I eat," Maria said as she bent her right arm and made a muscle.

"I'm never eating cottage cheese, even if you do put peaches in it," he said scornfully.

"You're very picky, did you know that?" Maria stated.

"Not as picky as you," he answered smartly.

"Why you precocious little monster," she said, feigning anger. "Go brush your teeth before I give you a plate of cottage cheese to eat."

"Never," he answered as he grabbed his throat with his hands and pretended he was choking.

"Wisenheimer," she said, laughing.

He smiled, then the smile faded and he sheepishly asked, "What do I tell Mommy about basketball?"

"Your father called your uncle last night. I don't know why he's still in bed, but go brush your teeth and I'll find out. I'm sure it will all be fine," she said reassuringly.

"I don't want her to get mad at me. It's not good for her. She cries too much," he said with grave concern.

Maria went over to him and placed her hand on his shoulder. "Don't worry, sweetheart, it will all be fine. I promise."

His face lit up again and he jumped from the chair and hurried out of the kitchen and up the stairs to the bathroom to brush his teeth.

Maria couldn't help but smile. The bond between them was growing stronger each day, and in an odd way her hatred for Sophie was weakening. She couldn't love Sophie's child and hate Sophie. Still, she couldn't let Henry know that. It was all too complicated, and the scene from the night before marked the first time in their marriage that she had lost control of her emotions. She couldn't believe that she had actually thought about hitting Henry, or that she had cried and carried on the way she had. It was totally out of character and nothing about her outburst had left her feeling any better. Ever since Koch she had prided herself on her ability to control her emotions, and by doing so get others to bend to her will. Yet, in one outburst it seemed as if she had lost control over her husband. Though not frequent, Henry had never spurned her advances, and his declaration the evening before when she went to remove her robe that he wasn't up to it was a dramatic moment in their relationship.

She heard the taxi's horn beeping and went to the front door. She opened the door, waved to the taxi driver and called out, "He'll be down in a minute." No sooner had she closed the door then the boy came bounding down the stairs two at a time.

"I'm ready," he exuberantly exclaimed. "What about the basketball?"

"It will all be fine, don't worry," she said without knowing if that was true or not.

"Great," he answered. "Marshall's taking me today, isn't he?"

"Yes, and he's as excited as you are," she said enthusiastically. He had his jacket on, and she bent down, zipped it up, lifted his chin and winked at him. He returned her wink and tilted his head and she responded by giving him a kiss on his cheek. He accepted the kiss, and without another word went out the door and down the walkway to the waiting taxi.

Henry had made a habit of avoiding his son whenever he could. On Sundays, Maria and Joseph went to church, then Henry took them for breakfast at the Riverview Diner, but on the other six days of the week Henry didn't come downstairs until the boy had left for school or to go visit his mother. Today was no different, and with the slamming of the door Henry appeared at the top of the stairs and said good morning to Maria. She would pretend that it was wrong of him to avoid the child, but that was just a fiction.

"I called you for breakfast before, but you didn't answer."

"I guess I didn't hear you," he said nonchalantly.

"I made pancakes for Joseph. There's some batter left over, would you like some?"

"Whatever, I have a handball game at eleven-thirty, but I have time. Yeah, pancakes will be fine. Did you make coffee?"

"Are you awake? You sound like you're having a conversation with yourself."

"One too many scotches last night," he said as he rubbed his temples with his fingers.

"That was my fault," she said contritely. "I don't know what came over me. I apologize."

"It's not your fault or my fault. We'll get past this. Put the hotcakes on, I'll be down in a few minutes," he said, changing the subject.

"I have some errands for you to run, but you can do them after you're finished at the Y."

He didn't reply, and she didn't wait for an answer, but headed to the kitchen to make his breakfast. She turned the burner on under the cast iron fry pan and let it heat for a minute. Once the pan was hot, she lowered the heat and dropped a half a teaspoon of Crisco into the pan and picked the pan up by the handle and rotated the pan so that the oil would heat and cover the entire cooking surface. She then placed the pan back on the burner and poured in a full ladle of pancake batter. The batter hit the fry pan and sizzled, and just as quickly bubbles appeared on the top surface of the batter as the downside browned. She watched it for about a minute, then turned the cake and left it for another minute before removing it from the fry pan and repeating the exercise again until she had three large browned cakes on a plate. She wiped the pan with a paper napkin and put the pancakes back into it to stay warm until Henry came downstairs.

"Pins and needles, needles and pins," she repeated to herself as she washed Joseph's breakfast plate and juice glass. The kitchen had two windows that provided a grand view of the backyard. Maria leaned over the sink and bathed her face in the stream of sunlight filtering through the window panes. The sky was blue bright, with a few soft white clouds and the trees branches waved in the autumn wind and carelessly shed gold and orange leaves over the lawn the gardener had raked clean a day earlier. The perimeter of the yard was guarded by a fieldstone wall, and at the back of the yard the gardener had planted rose bushes. They were small and thorny now, but he had promised her that they would flower and bloom this coming spring, and by the following spring you wouldn't see the wall. "Pins and needles, needles and pins," she repeated again disturbing her brief reverie. She laughed to herself. Her roommate Penny back in the old days in London, as she liked to call them, had used that phrase to brush away whatever disappointments life threw at her. Just the other day she was sewing a button on Joseph's shirt and he was playing with the pin cushion in her sewing basket and stuck his finger. "Pins and needles, needles and pins," she had said, laughing as she took his hand and kissed the finger where he had the pinprick. Now the phrase was stuck in her head, and she found herself repeating it whenever a troubling thought crossed her mind. However, it wasn't working today. A whirlwind of conflicting thoughts and emotions ruled her thought processes and she was powerless to stop them. Her new home, the beautiful yard, the presence of Henry's son under their roof were all blessings, and at times she felt giddy over how smoothly it was all going. Then, memories of the murder, Amos Koch, her dysfunctional marriage, Sophie's hatred of her, and every other hurt that had occurred in her life loomed in the background, foreboding and threatening, as a reminder that happiness had no place in her life. The fifteen minutes she spent with Joseph at breakfast was as blissful a time as she could recall. The bright kitchen, the easy banter back and forth, and his evident trust in whatever she said was more than she had imagined when she demanded of Henry that he fight for custody of his son. She didn't care, couldn't care a twit about the boy's relationship with his father. Henry was unwilling and that was fine with her. What mattered was that the boy trusted her, and in time would grow to love her. It was what had been missing in her life, and even if the happiness his company brought was temporary it was worth fighting for.

It always came down to what was missing instead of what was there, she reflected. Nothing had made her life unique, and much of it had been mired by her silent brooding over what should have been rather than what had been.

Perhaps she had been too philosophical and not honest enough to see herself for what she was. Why did she feel herself superior to Sophie? It was obvious to her now that Sophie had been as much a wife to Henry as she had been. Their bedroom may have been Henry's office, but according to what she gleaned from the district attorney's investigation of Henry and Sophie's affair, in addition to what she learned from Lee Futerman and his old tea bag of a secretary, Ruth Goolnick, they had a strong relationship. They got along well and despite Henry's deceit over the child and his determination not to be identified as the father he made it his business to meet every obligation. *Yes,* she thought, *he did all that and I never knew, I never suspected.* Claiming Sophie was a cheap whore was a misnomer. Whatever her mistake, she had stuck by her man for ten years and Maria sadly accepted that Henry's silence on the issue, his choice in the end to remain with her rather than Sophie didn't expunge his betrayal of their marriage. Maria had early on dismissed Sophie as crass and unattractive. The idea that she and Henry were having an affair was unimaginable, and when over time an accumulation of evidence pointed that way she still dismissed it. After all, Henry coveted beauty and sophistication. Wasn't that Maria's forte! It pained her to confront the truth and the pain brought the memory of Koch to the fore once again. Koch had ruined her in so many ways, and now she gladly recalled the denouement to their affair. The memory was intense and pleasurable. She felt neither guilt nor culpability. He had brought it on himself through arrogance and insatiable lust. She recalled with disgust his relentless obsession with her body. Constantly kissing her, feeling her breasts, nibbling on her ears and shoulders, licking her as a deer would a salt lick until he was sufficiently aroused and ready to fuck her. That was the word. "Fuck," she said to herself. She realized, too late, that in Koch's eyes she was something young and pleasant to fuck and nothing more. The other things they did, the things she foolishly thought created a bond between them were nothing more than pastimes. A day spent walking the city looking for an interesting inspiration for a photograph was a pastime. A favorite café or tea room again was nothing more than someplace to eat, and an afternoon in the park, however restful or invigorating, was the prelude to a bout of sex upon returning home. It was easy now to sum it all up and categorize each day's journey and itinerary. It was why the sex she first found so exhilarating quickly lost its ardor and became an effort she had to make and endure in solitude. "Fuck," she said again a little louder. *He knew he was leaving,* she bitterly thought, *and sick as I was he had to have me one more time and weak as I was I gave in.* It was the most shameful moment of her life. The trip to South Hampton had to be made. How could she not go? All she wanted to do was tell him what a selfish little pig he was. The idea of doing physical harm to him was ridiculous. She had been reared in a gentle and loving home. But, "Ah the eternal but," she quietly muttered as her heart raced and she was in that empty terminal once again. Suddenly and without premonition she attacked. The memory was so sweet; the look of shock on his face and the pathetic swinging of his wormy little penis as the piss sprayed out of it and he attempted to compose himself. The authorities had said it was the work of a professional. That gave her a laugh too. The strike was precise, but it was luck. The blunt tip of a steel umbrella lacked the precision of an ice pick, but in her blind fury her aim was exact or merely lucky, and with one powerful thrust he was gone. Amazingly, the police did little to follow-up the murder and she never heard from his family. What became of his belongings? Did the trunks go on to Argentina? Were the diamonds still hidden in the trunk handles? She had put that out of her mind long ago. Sadly, every man since who grunted over her in the throes of passion reminded her of Koch. She had tried hard to erase his memory, but he was too much like other men and that was why Henry had turned to Sophie. What Henry wanted from her and needed from her she never gave him. His weakness was his inability to understand how cold she was. He was like an infatuated schoolboy, and his love was indistinct from Koch's obsession. His desire for her, his lingering hope that she would change and embrace him was a wish he never turned from, and surely it was only through his affair with Sophie that he could continue to press that hope, certain that someday she would change. How could she hate the woman? Yes, the woman could hate her, but how could she return the venom. After all, Sophie was correct; it was she and not Maria who had been the faithful wife.

That was the source of her murderous urge on the subway platform. In an instant she knew the truth, and she was as ready to extinguish Sophie as she had Koch. Sophie's twisted face burned in her memory. When she awoke in the hospital it was one of the first things she remembered, not the incident on the platform, but her angry face. It was the same face she saw in the bedroom after she discovered Millie. She couldn't put the face on the body that ran from the closet. That image was too blurred, but somehow it was Sophie's face she recalled. These were thoughts she didn't gladly entertain, and she was relieved when she heard Henry's footsteps coming down the stairs.

"Hotcakes ready?" he asked pleasantly.

Maria smiled and said, "I thought you were never coming down, I tried to keep them warm."

"That's fine," he answered as he went over to the counter and poured himself a cup of coffee from the electric percolator.

"Do you want orange juice?" she asked.

"Of course," he replied as he poured a heavy layer of syrup over his pancakes.

"My God!" she exclaimed. "I know who your son takes after; you use more syrup than he does."

Henry frowned at the mention of "your son," and didn't directly respond, but as he was cutting his cakes he asked, "Did the paper come?"

"I'll go outside and look."

Henry devoured the pancakes, and by the time Maria returned with the newspaper he had pushed his chair back from the table and was sipping his coffee.

"Enjoyed the breakfast, didn't you? she said lightly, hoping to engage him in a pleasant but innocuous conversation.

"I did and I needed it, my stomach was a little queasy this morning."

She couldn't help herself, and replied testily, "Well, if you'd come to bed instead of going downstairs to drink scotch by yourself because you're upset over something that has nothing to do with you, maybe you wouldn't have a queasy stomach."

"You started it last night," he said just as testily.

"And I'm not going to put up with your petulance anymore. Whatever happened in my life that I might regret, not regret, but might regret, happened long before I met you," she lectured. "I'm sorry that photo album didn't go to South America with Amos, but it didn't, and I'm sorry I didn't throw it out long ago, but I didn't, and I don't ever want to talk about this again!"

"Amos," he muttered with disgust.

Maria regained her composure and replied icily, "Amos Koch, he was my lover. That was long before I met you. I won't ask you again, just let it go. I have. I let it go the day the man sailed away. They're just silly photographs and you, above all people…" she said without finishing the thought.

"Right," he said apologetically. "I cheat on you for ten years and it's okay, then I carry on about this. You tell me, you tell me," he said with a shake of his head.

Maria approached him, put her hands on his shoulders, leaned over and kissed his cheek. "I love you, Henry. I'm trying my best to show you I do."

"I know," he said, patting her hand.

"Good," she said calmly as she stood up. "I'm going to set the dining room table. Gloria's coming over around two-thirty. She's going to help me make the apple cobbler."

"That's nice, is Joel coming too?"

"I don't know. You really have his ear lately," she said inquisitively.

"I'm interested in his article. Some prestigious British quarterly is publishing it in their January issue. Joel's all excited. I like to indulge him at times. It seems Gloria and the boys don't share my enthusiasm," he said, chuckling.

"Yes, the professor," she said sarcastically. "I don't know if he's coming, but Marshall will be here to take Joseph to basketball. Which reminds me, did you call Ray Cruz last night?"

Henry let out a slight groan. "Yes, I did, and he was very cordial. He suggested maybe I could get the kid up there on a weekday on the weekends he misses visiting his mother. That'll cost me a small fortune in cab fares, but what could I say? He said he was going to visit Sophie today and he'd discuss it with her, but he thought it would all be fine, so the kid shouldn't worry."

"Joseph, his name is Joseph," she chided.

"How about Joey, I call him Joey?"

"It would be an improvement," she answered dryly.

"I'll try."

"You could drive him up there some afternoon after school," she suggested.

"Should I bring a Whitman sampler too," he replied sarcastically.

Maria frowned and answered, "If he has to go on a weekday, then you'll have to take him. At least give it some thought. I have things to do, but see me before you go to play handball. I have list of things I need you to pick up."

"Yes, dear," he answered as he picked up the newspaper and gave it his full attention.

Chapter Sixty-Six

It wasn't much of a workout. He played three games of handball, but it was doubles and his partner Jack Stern was such a finesse player that almost every serve or return he made ended in a point. He did work up a sweat in the steam room, and it was great to just be with the guys again; playing ball, talking sports and politics without ever a mention of work or home to muddy the conversation. Maria had asked him to stop at the bakery and pick up cookies, then to get beer and wine. He completed all his errands and was turning onto Seneca Avenue approaching his driveway when he saw Ray Cruz's cream-colored Chevrolet Bel Air in his rear view mirror.

Henry pulled into his driveway and Ray drew up in front of the house. He heard the car door to Ray's car slam shut and heard his son calling out, "Goodbye, Uncle Ray, Aunt Lucy, I'm gonna ask Maria now."

Henry was out of his car and walking with his packages toward the garage door. Joseph was running up the front walk. and Henry called over to him, "Hey, slow down, speedy."

Joseph stopped in his tracks. He wasn't sure if Henry was scolding him. and he breathlessly said, "Uncle Ray's going to take me to see the Jesuit Trapper's basketball game next Friday. Maria has to call Aunt Lucy and tell her. I can go, can't I?"

Henry gave him a big smile. and said, "Of course, you can go. That's nice, real nice."

Joseph returned the smile, then asked excitedly, "Is Marshall here?"

"Don't know, I just got home too, but I don't see that blue Volkswagen Joel lets him drive," Henry said as he looked up and down the empty street.

The boy looked up and down the street too, and without answering, Henry he bolted into the house. Henry opened the garage door and in the distance he could hear his son calling out to Maria and telling her he was home. He also heard him recount Ray Cruz's offer to take him to a Jesuit University basketball game and his plea, "Can I go, can I go?" *Why didn't he tell Maria I said he could go?* he asked himself. Of course, he knew the answer. Maria was the authority figure, and it was with Maria the boy had forged a relationship. He placed the beer in the refrigerator they kept in the garage and took several bottles of soda and seltzer from a shelf he stored them on and place them in the refrigerator too. He took the wine and cookies and went into the laundry room, then into the kitchen. Maria was standing at the counter preparing a cream cheese and jelly sandwich.

Maria looked up at him, but there was no smile on her face. "Ray Cruz took him home from the prison. That was nice. He's taking him to a basketball game Friday."

"Well, he's the uncle, nothing wrong with that," Henry answered defensively.

"I think that it's nice too. Have you thought about doing anything with your son?"

"When Dutchman's lake freezes, I'll take him skating."

Maria raised her eyebrows and shook her head, "That is not what I meant."

"Fine," he said, mocking her serious tone. "First sign of spring, we play catch in the backyard."

"Do you want a sandwich?" she asked.

"No thanks," he replied.

"What I meant," she said slowly, drawing the words out, "is that you could be a little more engaging."

"Well, he asked me outside if he could go, and I told him he could, but apparently he still needed your approval because he asked you the same question when he came in the house."

Maria laughed out loud and put her fingers to her lips. "You're jealous, I'm surprised. No, I am, but I feel better."

"I am not," he scoffed.

"I'm sorry. I shouldn't push you so hard."

"Whatever." He sighed. "I'm going to take a nap. Is that okay? What time's Gloria coming?"

"They should be here in a while."

"I just want a half hour, any longer and I get overtired."

"They won't be here for at least a half hour, and I want him to eat and digest his lunch before he goes; when you go upstairs send Joseph down."

"Yes, dear," he answered as he left the kitchen. On the way upstairs he was brooding. She had managed to work him into a corner once again over his relationship with the boy. He was a friendly man, but this was an eight-year-old, after all, and they hadn't much in common. His only hope he had told himself time and again was to let the clock run its course and eventually they would grow accustomed to one another and possibly something would grow from that. He came to the door to the boy's room, stopped and looked in. His son was seated at his desk, hunched over a piece of looseleaf paper. He had a pencil in his hand and had just finished printing a word when he heard Henry and looked up at him.

"Homework?" Henry said.

"Writing Mommy a letter," the boy cautiously answered.

"Didn't you just see her?"

"Yes, but if I write the letter today and Maria mails it on Monday, then Mommy gets it on Wednesday and that way she doesn't miss me too much," he said sadly.

"Makes sense," Henry said, shaking his head in agreement. He was about to go to his room when he impulsively asked the boy, "Did you tell her about the basketball practices and games?"

"Uncle Ray did. He said I could come on Thursdays when I can't on Saturday. Mommy said she didn't mind. Can I?"

"Sure thing, buddy, I'll take care of it."

"Maria said you would," he answered anxiously.

"You told her already?"

"Yes," he slightly stammered, fearful he had done something wrong.

"You two get along very well," Henry said, smiling, trying to put his son at ease.

"I like her," he said, hanging his head and avoiding making eye contact with his father.

"I like her too," Henry said, then without understanding why, he added, "How's your mom?"

"She cries when she first sees me. I cheer her up and we laugh a lot. It's not a nice place where she is," he answered self consciously.

Henry felt a pang of guilt. "You're a good kid, you know that, a good kid," he said as he stepped into the room and rubbed his son's shoulder lightly with his hand. "Your mother's only said good things about you, and I'm learning why."

"Thanks."

Henry could see that his son was uncomfortable with the conversation, and rather than prolong it, he said, "Maria's got your lunch ready and Marshall will be here soon, so you better get going."

There was a look of relief in his son's face and the boy put the pencil to the paper once more and drew a big heart and wrote, "I love you, Mommy" across the face of the heart. He folded the paper, left it on the desk, jumped up and slid past Henry, who was still standing in the doorway and ran down the stairs to Maria and his lunch.

Chapter Sixty-Seven

Henry never thought of himself as clever, and certainly not devious, but he had developed over the years an ability to steer a conversation toward an outcome favorable to his side of an argument. If patience was an art, than he was a master of it, and patience translated to being a good listener, and success came from letting your companion in the argument or conversation believe he was the master of the subject. It wasn't a question of how much you said, but when you spoke. Today was a longshot, but he couldn't wrest the subject of Amos Koch from his mind. Maria had banished him as a subject of conversation. Eighteen years ago she was willing to talk about him and about her past, but he had known that there were things there he didn't want to acknowledge, and indirectly he had feigned enough disinterest that she closed the subject. His reluctance to engage her past, or better, to allow her to share with him whatever transgressions she had committed created a fissure in the relationship that worsened over time. He was now ready to confront the past, and Maria would have none of it. Joel was his only hope.

"I'm surprised," Joel said amusingly.

Henry smiled at his brother-in-law and said, "Why?"

"I didn't think you'd have much interest spending the afternoon hiking."

"I wouldn't consider taking a walk down to the river promenade a hike," Henry answered in reply.

"I go along at a good pace, so I consider it a hike. Gloria did say you might be interested. She said you complained you were getting heavy."

"She's right," he said in agreement as he patted his stomach. "And I've noticed she's taken quite a few pounds off lately," Henry said in a complimentary voice.

"She has," Joel answered approvingly. "And I credit Maria for all the support she's given Gloria. Speaking of hiking, those two burned a lot of shoe leather over the last several months and it's paid off. Gloria's dropped twenty-five pounds since July."

"Yes, and she's starting to look like her old self."

"And acting more like her old self," Joel said happily as he pulled a tobacco pouch from his inside jacket pocket and a pipe from the side pocket of his jacket and went about filling the bowl with tobacco. They walked for several blocks without much conversation. Joel busied himself fiddling with his pipe; a new habit he had acquired after giving up cigarettes, and Henry's thoughts returned to his reason for accompanying Joel in the first place. The last thing Henry had wanted to do was a go for a walk. His nap had lasted no more than twenty minutes when he was awakened by his son's loud and happy whooping as he ran down the stairs to greet his cousin Marshall and his aunt and uncle. Minutes later Maria was at the bedroom door and announced that Joel and Gloria had arrived. Henry was never rude, and he obediently abandoned his nap and went downstairs to greet his sister and her husband. The handball game and the steamroom had tired him out, and the offer of taking a long walk with Joel wasn't inviting, but he needed to talk to Joel alone, and the long walk was the perfect pretense for his intended conversation. Joel made the invitation and was mildly surprised when Henry agreed to accompany him. Joel finally had the pipe lit, and after resuming the conversation about Gloria and Maria and their exercise program and their newfound sisterhood, Henry sensed that Joel was not only relaxed, but was in that mood where more intimate matters could be freely discussed.

"So I'm told some highbrow British journal is going to publish your piece on 'The Economics of War' in their January issue," Henry inquired.

Joel smiled with satisfaction, and replied, "Getting published is the academic's greatest challenge. I struck gold with this one," he said proudly.

"Make a little cabbage as they say," Henry said amusingly.

"It's not about money, it's about getting published, but it so happens that this does lead to money and getting published again."

"You'll have to explain," Henry replied.

"*The Historian* is publishing my article. *The Historian* is edited by Terrance Palmer. He's a respected scholar and author, and he also publishes under the pseudonym of Brendan Smart."

"Never heard of him either way," Henry said, interrupting.

"Terrance Palmer has published two serious books, and his alter ego, Brendan Smart, has published at least a dozen adventure novels. He has two series of books, *The Waleford Chronicles* and what else, *The Terrance Palmer Adventure* series. *The Waleford Chronicles* are based in the middle ages and the *Palmer* series is the colorful account of an 18ᵗʰ Century British naval captain. Each of them supplies equal amounts of adventure and history, and they're pretty entertaining. Anyway," he said, pausing to tamp down the tobacco in his pipe bowl and get it burning again, "Palmer wants to publish a series of college texts dealing with war in the twentieth century, and he's asked me to work on the project. I'm one of a half a dozen professors asked to work on this project, and Gloria and I will get a free trip to England out of this, and a few pennies too. The best part," he said with enthusiasm, "is that Mr. Palmer has an exceptional research team in place. His idea is not novel, but it is simple and highly saleable, which is the toughest part of the textbook business."

"How's that?" Henry asked.

"The textbook market is very competitive. Palmer has an established track record, so that gives him an edge. Say for instance we're discussing World War I. A chapter on my favorite subject outlining the economic consequences of war would open with an essay on the subject, then be followed by a comprehensive and largely chronological treatment of the topic, pretty much like an almanac, but not as dry. The trick is in getting the information across to the reader, you know, the facts, dates, numbers, names and so on would be presented not in paragraph form, but instead in bulleted entries. Digestible bits of data unadorned with all of the usual verbiage that puts students to sleep. The chapter then closes with a second essay that ties everything together. Think of it as a conceptual opening essay and a closing conceptual essay supported by the list of incontrovertible facts that should support each essay. I'm not making myself clear, am I?" Joel asked.

They were approaching the river promenade and the wind had picked up. Henry zippered the light jacket he was wearing, and answered, "You are. I gather these would be history books for students who don't like to read?"

"Yes, but for the serious student each chapter will have a reference source of additional books and articles for further enlightenment."

Henry nodded his head and said, "So you're writing the essays?"

"I outline the chapters I'm writing and the source material I want to cover. Palmer's team does additional research to support and verify my presentation of the subject material. My opening essay is a broad treatment of the subject that is supported by the fact pattern, and my closing essay ties it together. The short cut for the student is not reading endless paragraphs supplying the data. Retention of information is a problem for everyone. If you can grasp a concept quickly, than there is a greater chance you'll recall more of the facts that support that concept. Well, it's an idea, and I'm looking forward to the challenge," Joel said with satisfaction.

"Why you?" Henry asked seriously.

"Palmer likes my thesis, and he was impressed with my writing. Other than that, you could say I got lucky. And my area of scholarship is interesting. Much of history is about war. I see all war as an exercise in economics."

"It's always about the money, isn't it?" Henry remarked.

"Theoretically, yes." Joel replied. "What is war?" he asked and before Henry could reply, he answered his own question. "It is armed aggression against another for the primary purpose of taking the other's property and subjugating him to you. Belligerents cover their motives in a variety of ways, but in the end it comes down to filling your plate at the other poor bastard's expense," Joel said seriously as he sucked on the mouthpiece of his pipe in a failed attempt to keep the fire in the bowl going.

"That's a pretty simple theory for a serious scholar," Henry replied.

"Sure it's simple," Joel said with enthusiasm. "Why complicate what is natural to us. The art is in peeling away the veneer of deception that nations use to excuse the atrocities they wage on one another. My article deals with two subjects. I started with a brief overview of the First World War. A common argument is that the war was an aberration. A faulty result of an abomination of alliances and ententes that ostensibly existed to guarantee peace, but was nothing more than a house of cards..."

They had come to the end of Seneca Avenue where it entered the river promenade. Joel was a half step ahead of Henry, and at that point he might as well have been at a lectern at the university.

Goodness, he can drone on and on, Henry thought as he nodded his head in agreement every several seconds to indicate that he was listening to Joel's every word. Of course, he wasn't. What he was doing was waiting for the right moment to bring up Amos Koch and discern if Joel had made inquiries about him as Gloria had suggested at the hospital back in June.

The promenade was a mile and a half long path of crushed cinder that followed an uneven line along the ridge above the river up to the city line. A narrow two lane road bordered the promenade, on the east side and on the west side there was a three foot brick wall topped with an ornamental wrought iron railing. Below the wall was a steep drop of about twenty feet, then thirty yards or so of small trees and bushes which formed a straight edge of green and brown against the dark grey chain of gravel that lined the base of the elevation for the railroad tracks. Beyond the tracks there was a retaining wall that ran alongside the river for as far as the eye could see. The wind picked up as they marched up the promenade. Henry wished he had worn a warmer coat.

Joel stopped suddenly and knocked the bowl of his pipe against the brick wall. "And Napoleon," he said, sneering. "What do you think of him?"

Henry shrugged his shoulders and said, "I thought we were on World War I?"

"I'm talking generalities," Joel said with a touch of annoyance in his voice. "It doesn't matter whether it's Napoleon or Tamerlane. They're the same in my book, greedy, rapacious mass murderers with no respect for their fellow man. Do you think the murderous bunglers who made up the officers corps of the Allied forces were any better?"

"No," Henry conceded, not fully understanding what point his brother-in-law was attempting to make. If ten minutes earlier Henry had been congratulating himself on his ability to listen and tactfully enter the conversation at a point advantageous to himself, he recognized that his argument had just been dashed. In fact, Joel had lost him five minutes ago. There was no conversation. Joel wasn't much of a conversationalist and never had been. Given the opportunity to expound on those subjects dear to him he would do so exhaustively, otherwise he was a quiet and unimposing.

Joel put his pipe back in his coat pocket. He gave Henry a wry smile and his body language suggested that he knew Henry had lost interest in his lecture and rather than go on he changed the subject. He leaned over the iron railing and said, "What a beautiful view. I could stand here all day and take it in."

Henry smiled at Joel and looked up and down the river and rather abruptly said, "What about Argentina?"

"What about it?" Joel replied quizzically.

"During the first war, what role did it play?" Henry asked.

Joel didn't immediately respond to Henry's question, then it suddenly occurred to him that Henry asked the question for a reason and it was probably the prelude for why Henry went on the walk in the first place. He smiled knowingly, and said, "At the outbreak of the war Argentina was probably one of the ten wealthiest nations in the world. It was a major food producer. It is said there's no better beef on earth than a steak from the Argentine and, of course, there's the Tango." Joel then made several exaggerated dance steps as he turned around in a circle, then stopped abruptly and said, "Henry, I know you well enough to know that you aren't really interested in hearing me prattle on about history. I also know it's not like you go for a long walk. Handball or a little tennis is exercise, but a walk, come on now, you wouldn't go for a walk unless there was another reason besides exercise, and I don't believe you were listening to half of what I said before, so why don't you just ask me whatever it is you want to ask me?"

Henry felt foolish. It was out of character for Joel to be confrontational, but he had clearly discerned that Henry's interest in his scholarship was insincere and that there was another motive for his inquiry. It was an awkward moment, and Henry hesitated before he gave an answer. They had resumed walking, and Henry said, "I'm not anywhere as clever as I think I am, but I have some very serious concerns and I thought you could be of assistance."

Joel put his hand on Henry's elbow and said warmly, "Henry, you're family. You're my brother-in-law and I'd do anything for you. Just ask."

"You're right," Henry replied. "Back in June, the day after the murder I was at the hospital with Lee and Gloria. We were in a waiting area and I had just come from Maria's bedside. She'd regained consciousness that morning and I had to tell her about my son. It was a painful confession, but her reaction took me by surprise. There was no bitterness. She didn't seem all there, but at the same time she was very lucid and insisted right then and there that I take responsibility for my son. It was odd, and odder still was that she said if I didn't feel right about it I should ask Gloria because Gloria would know the right thing to do. You know their history," he said with a shrug of his shoulders. "Gloria?"

Joel smiled and said, "I know all that and, as you say, it is odd, but things have worked out. They're like sisters now."

"When we were in the hospital, Lee and Gloria and I were talking about the murder. The pictures came up. You know; the ones of Maria and I told them that Amos Koch's name was on the back of the pictures. That he was the photographer."

"Amos Koch, God, I'll never forget that name," Joel sighed. "I'll never be able to forget, though I'd like to, that dinner party at your apartment; Gloria at her worst."

"None of us have forgotten that night," Henry answered.

"I remember it as if it was last night. We were sitting there playing cards and the girls were in the living room, and Maria had taken out a photo album. Next thing I could feel the tension, and hard as I tried to ignore it, every word out of Gloria's mouth thundered in my ears. When she asked Maria if her father had been a Nazi I wanted to fade into the woodwork. Good God, I was mortified, and do you know that your sister didn't think she'd done a Goddamn thing wrong?"

"That's Gloria," a grateful Henry said, now that they had finally gotten around to talking about Amos Koch.

"It didn't stop there," Joel lamented. "I bet for at least six months I had to listen to Gloria carry on about Amos Koch. She was convinced Maria had led some secret criminal life before you met her. She'd torture me sometimes with these crazy theories. I used to ignore her, and finally the subject died out, but it was never the same between them. Not that it was ever that good."

"No, it wasn't, but Amos Koch is what I wanted to talk to you about."

Once again Joel gave Henry a puzzled look, and replied, "Amos Koch?"

"Yes," Henry said. "That day in the hospital Gloria told me that you were doing research for an article that was going to be printed. I guess it is this one in *The Historian* and that you were writing about Argentina during the first war, and that you were trying to locate some material about Amos Koch and his family business. They were meat exporters, I believe."

Joel's immediate reaction to Henry's statement was to laugh, then he quickly caught himself and said, "I apologize for laughing at you, but you have it all wrong. I was working on that article and I had asked Gloria to read my first draft. Probably a week or so before the murder I recall, but I never mentioned Amos Koch. There was a mention about the growth of Argentina's GDP during the war. They were shipping food to the Allies. She read that and asked about Amos Koch. I hadn't heard the name in years, but she was right back where'd we'd been fifteen years ago. All of a sudden she was after me to track down his company, did it exist and so on," he said with annoyance. "I know not to argue with her and I told her I'd see if anything turned up, but honestly, Henry, that was harebrained. First of all, the war was fifty years ago. Secondly, there were hundreds of businesses processing food for export. What would distinguish this man's business from anyone else's, and who would care in the first place, and it had no relevance to my subject?"

Henry couldn't hide his disappointment, and in a monotone voice, asked, "You don't know anything about Amos Koch?"

"Less than you do, I'm sure," Joel replied, then said. "What is it you want to know?"

"Everything, anything," Henry answered with emotion.

"I'm not your man, Henry, and why?" Joel asked.

"It's eating away at me," Henry conceded with sadness.

"What?" Joel asked.

"Who Maria is and was? Who this fucking Koch is, and, I don't know," he said with disgust as he threw his hands up in the air.

"I don't think I can help. If I could I would."

"Well, it was just what Gloria had said in the hospital. That thought was in my head, you were interested in him too."

"He's a name I heard too many times, and I guess Gloria was to a degree, I mean those pictures, I never saw them, obviously, but you have to ask yourself what was their relationship? Did you see them?" Joel asked.

"I initially learned from the police about Koch's name on the backs of the photographs and later I had a meeting with the assistant DA who was presenting the case before the grand jury. He let me see what they had recovered at the scene. Not the actual photographs, but copies of them, and I have to tell you, Joel," Henry said angrily. "It's insane, but I can't get them out of my head. I knew, I knew," he said emphatically. "I knew from the first time I set eyes on her that there was something not right. It was in my head, my subconscious, but I buried it and I've kept it buried ever since."

Joel was confused, and Henry's display of emotion was upsetting. "What wasn't right?"

"I had a buddy in the Army. Joe Listerneck was his name. He was dating this English girl, 'fun girl' was how he described her and 'fun' meant he was getting in her knickers. The girl, her name was Penny, well, Penny had a roommate and Joe said she was a real looker and why don't I take her out. Of course, Joe wanted to get the roommate out of the flat she was sharing with Joe's girl so they could have some fun. So, I agreed to take this girl out on a double date with Joe and his girl, knowing all along that at first chance Joe and his girl were going to leave us on our own."

"That other girl would be Maria?" Joel asked.

"Yes, and at the time I didn't have much interest in the opposite sex. The old man would never admit it, but I knew he was the reason I went directly to officer's school. He knew people," Henry said, shaking his head. "I went to OCS and a year and a half later I had bars on my collar. We were preparing for the invasion and while I didn't know where, I knew the combat engineers were going to lead the way and I was as green as they come and overcome with my responsibilities. Anyway, I liked Listerneck and I went on the date purely as a favor to him."

"So what happened?" Joel asked.

"I'm in front of the flat and Joe comes out with the two girls. His was blonde and skinny, kinda cute, but a dime a dozen. Walking behind them coming down the front steps is Maria. Joel, what can I say, she was a knockout, right off a magazine cover was how good she looked. The face, the figure, the hair, the dress, shoes, jewelry, all of it, perfect and she's living in this rundown flat with a girl that's got a run in her stockings and wearing a cotton dress she must have worn twenty times before. That was my impression, and it hasn't changed, and I knew the pieces didn't add up, but," he paused and shrugged his shoulders, "I didn't care. I didn't want to know."

"You think someone was keeping her?" Joel asked.

Henry grimaced. "Sounds melodramatic, but I do. Listen, she was incredible. She was funny, but not too talkative and very sophisticated. Everything was light, and she asked a lot of questions about me and where I came from and what I did and I was flattered. She told me a little about her childhood, but not much and I didn't ask many questions. We saw one another four or five times before I shipped out and I gave her my address in Huguenot City just in case, you know. It was a funny time and you didn't make plans. Who knew what was going to happen? She wasn't a 'fun girl,' not like her roommate. I never slept with her or anything, but there was something between us and when I got back to England, before I was shipped back home, I tried to look her up, but I couldn't locate her. That was it, I thought. I was in love, but I was so fucking battered by the war that I was happier to be going home, more than anything. She was a bittersweet memory, those are the best to have." He sighed with regret.

"She found you," Joel said.

"Let me retrace my steps," Henry answered. "What's got me so agitated is the fact that there was nothing ordinary about her. You never got out of the States during the war."

"Henry, I turned eighteen in November of 1944. They tried to get me there, but I was one of the lucky ones, I guess," Joel said apologetically.

Henry laughed. "No, I'm not being critical. I'm just saying that during the war, particularly in England, at least what I saw of it, people didn't have two shillings to rub together and you couldn't just trundle down to Woolworth's to buy a new pair of nylons. Maria was always well dressed. Top shelf dresses, good shoes and she always wore nylons. She had nice jewelry, too. She dressed and acted like someone with money, yet, she was living in some beatup flat and her roommate looked a hell of a lot more like the typical English working girl than Maria did. Something didn't fit, and I didn't want to think about it. Then she shows up in the States, gets in touch with me, and it was race to the finish and we're married and I didn't know a damn thing about her."

"Didn't you share the past with one another?" Joel asked incredulously.

"She tried, but I blew her off. She tried a couple of times, but I knew, subconsciously I knew there were things I didn't want to know. Damn!" he said angrily.

Joel put his hand on Henry's elbow and turned to face him. "Henry, we're family, and I can't recall when we've ever really acted like a family. Somehow, out of this tragedy and chaos we've all come together. The get togethers, the dinners, they're what families do, and it's been a Godsend. Don't you feel it too?" he asked earnestly.

They started walking again, and Henry blandly replied, "Joel, I'm numb to most of it, numb and in a daze."

Joel stepped ahead of him and leaned in Henry's direction as they kept up their pace. "Gloria and my boys are crazy about Joseph. Gloria and Maria have finally put aside whatever it was," he said as he waved his hands in front of his chest, "that kept them apart. Steve, Muriel, everyone's closer. Why can't you just accept it? What is it you're fighting?"

"I don't believe her. I don't believe her stories about Koch. I don't believe Sophie did it. I can't put it into words because it's a feeling, a hunch."

"What the hell are you thinking?" Joel replied testily. "This conversation started out with wanting to know about Koch and his business in World War I. How old could he have been? Maria was born in 1915. Sophie admitted she was guilty. Maria saw her in the apartment. You're not making any sense."

Henry was surprised by Joel's outburst. He didn't immediately answer him. Joel was right about the family. Since they had bought the house and taken custody of Joseph they had all grown closer. The dinners were pleasant and the tensions of the past had disappeared. They were all happier for it, but he couldn't shake his suspicions, and after a minute of silence he said, "I just wanted to verify if Amos Koch, Amos Koch as he was described to us, existed. Was there an Amos Koch in Buenos Aires? Did his family own a meat packing company? Was there such a thing as Garcia's Pride of the Pampas Beef or whatever the Goddamn brand was? It was a starting point. I don't believe Amos Koch was some benign businessman who took an avuncular interest in Maria. The more I think about it and what little I know and have since found out, I think he's some sort of criminal. I think Maria's involvement with him wasn't so innocent, and I can't accept all that has happened."

Joel listened to him intently. "For starters, if you're really determined to find out about Amos Koch, I have a suggestion."

577

"That's what I'm looking for," Henry answered.

"There are a number of legitimate investigations firms that could do a background on Amos Koch. It would cost you, but you hire someone reputable here and they in turn contact a reliable company in Buenos Aires and it wouldn't take more then a week to find out if his company ever existed, or for that fact, if he did. Newspapers library their past issues, master name indexes are maintained and most of this stuff nowadays has been microfilmed. I think you can find that much out, but what will it tell you?"

"I don't know," Henry answered. "All I know is that things have to add up and right now they don't."

Joel frowned and said, "What has to add up? What do you think you're going to find out? Say he does come from Argentina and there is or was a company and he lived to a ripe old age and died or is still with us, then what?"

"I don't know," Henry said with a laugh. "I just don't believe that is how it will turn out. I suspect the man was a criminal."

"Why?" Joel answered with a scowl. "Because he took some revealing photographs of Maria? You're not making any sense.'

"It doesn't make sense to you because you don't know Maria. You don't know Sophie," Henry said accusingly.

"You lost me," Joel answered tiredly.

Henry stopped walking. He leaned over the ornamental railing and stared at the river. "Joel, understand this," he said with conviction. "I'm no fool. Whatever I've done, I've done knowingly. The business between me and Sophie started out innocently. I was married, she had a boyfriend. When it comes to that sort of thing, maybe my morals aren't too strong. Whatever, I knew what I was doing. Sophie was a 'fun' girl," he said, alluding to Maria's English roommate. "We enjoyed one another and, honestly, there wasn't much enjoyment at my home, so I took advantage of the situation. I'm no fool," he said again. "But, I can be myopic when it suits my purposes, and when Sophie got pregnant it was just easier to think her boyfriend was the father. It was convenient. When I learned later on that I was the father I wasn't too happy about it, but I did what I had to do and things went along as they had been. I had a pretty good thing. Sophie was a great worker. I spent more time with her than I did with Maria, and as for the intimacy of our relationship, there was great deal more between us than between me and Maria. As it turns out, I know Sophie far better than I do my own wife. Sophie knew that too, and that's why she set her heart on marrying me. You have to understand, when I say I know Sophie, I mean I know her. She wouldn't hurt a fly. She's immature, I'll grant you. And she can have a tantrum from time to time, but she's all noise. The business about confronting Maria in front of our building and following her to the subway and throwing the kid's picture in her face is vintage Sophie. Same way she stormed out of the hotel in Montreal the night before. There's no guile with her. Why in God's name would she go to my apartment after she'd already confronted Maria? Something's terribly wrong. I feel it in my bones, I can't shake it, and to tell you the truth, I don't believe Maria."

"Do you think Maria killed Millie?" A shocked Joel asked.

"I don't think so, but I do think it very odd that shortly after regaining consciousness Maria was able to put the finger on Sophie and decide we had to gain custody of my son. I don't believe Maria's medical condition was as bad as it was initially portrayed. She's made a wonderful recovery, and I think she came to a lot sooner than anyone realized and she thought through this whole scenario. I think that on the morning I left for Montreal she finally seized on to the reality that there was something going on between me and Sophie and that she had to make a choice, and she chose to stay with me. That's what prompted the call to Montreal, and at the time I was grateful for it. The train ride up with Sophie was a disaster. She was dressed like a teenager, and most of her conversation was silly. Outside of the office work and the sex, we were no match, and leaving Maria for her would have been going from the frying pan to the fire. Maria couldn't have known what I was feeling when she called Montreal, and after the next day's events she was faced with a plate load of problems and Sophie was at the center of them. And I think," he said heavily. "I think," he repeated, "that Maria decided to start this marriage over and to do so she had to get rid of Sophie."

Joel laughed. "My goodness, that is insane. Who killed Millie? And," he paused for effect, "what does or how does Mr. Koch fit in?"

"I haven't figured all of that out yet," Henry said sheepishly. "Koch was a starting point. I have to figure out who Maria is first."

"Did you forget that Sophie pleaded guilty? They found her fingerprints in the elevator in your building. There's quite a bit of evidence, isn't there?'

Henry smiled and said, "Sophie's attorney was an incompetent loudmouth. He bullied her into accepting that deal, I'm sure of that."

"You know that for a fact?" Joel asked.

"No, this is all intuition, but it simply makes no sense for Maria to embrace my bastard son the way she has. Also, she said she had $80,000 in the bank. She's never earned more than $9,000 in a year. Where did the money come from? And there was a delivery to my apartment that same day, and some issues about the time the delivery boy spent in my apartment. I know this, Joel," Henry said with conviction. "It just doesn't add up, and that's why I sought your help."

"We better start home," Joel said, as he started walking again. "I understand your frustration. I also think you don't recognize how much stress this ordeal has put you through. I'm not a psychiatrist, but you've been through the mill and that can take its toll."

"You think this is all crazy talk," Henry said defensively.

"No, no," Joel said reassuringly. "You have a guilty conscience over Millie's death, and Sophie's complicity in it, and you feel responsible. And it seems, sadly I admit, that the marriage between you and Maria has been bad, and I do agree that her conduct is a little strange under the circumstances. She's never seemed the motherly kind, that's for certain."

"You're right about the guilt. I do feel responsible for everything, and I feel that in my current circumstance my life is more of a fraud than it was before. What's even worse is Maria and the kid are like that," he said as he crossed the middle finger and index finger of his left hand. "I'm shocked at how the kid has adjusted, but she's been magnificent. It's eerie; I'm like the third wheel. Maria is at me to do more to get closer to him, but I think it's an act. Don't ask me why."

"I guess I was mistaken when I gave my rosy assessment of family relations awhile ago, wasn't I?" Joel stated.

"From your perspective that's what you should be thinking. Tell me," Henry said, slightly changing the subject. "Before you mentioned that I could hire an investigations firm to research Amos Koch. Let me ask you this? You also said that newspapers keep name indexes and past issues on microfilm, didn't you?"

Joel was hesitant to reply because he knew Henry was going to ask him to do something and he didn't want to be involved, but he had no choice but to answer the question. "I did."

"Good, my real interest in Koch concerns when he and Maria were in France and England. It was 1936 if I remember. Now you said before that this historian you hooked up with, what was his name, Smart?"

"Terrance Palmer," Joel halfheartedly replied.

"Right, Palmer," Henry said. "You said that he has a research team that does crackerjack work, didn't you?"

"I don't recall the word crackerjack, but they're efficient."

"What would it cost me to have them do some research on Koch? Just a review of master name indexes in the London papers for 1936 or 1937 is all

I'm asking. Maybe they could check business listings for that same period? Could that be done? I'm willing to pay."

"Oh, for God's sake," Joel exclaimed. "What would that achieve?" he added caustically.

Henry ignored Joel's anger, and said, "Would you do it?"

"No, you're being ridiculous," Joel tersely replied.

It took twenty minutes for them to complete the loop and return to Seneca Avenue. Since Joel's last reply they had continued on in silence; each man uncomfortable with the other. Henry's ire was stronger and several times he had glanced at his brother-in-law with disgust, but said nothing. Joel was by nature a compromiser, and when they were within a block of Henry's house he stopped and put his hand on Henry's shoulder.

"Henry, I have great affection for you," he said sincerely. "I can tell that I've disappointed you, but what you're asking me to do is a waste of time. If I did do it, and had those inquiries made and they came back in the negative, as I'm sure they will, what will you want next?"

"I don't know? Maybe I'd try the Argentina connection. I'll probably do that anyway," Henry replied in a friendlier and warmer voice.

"Tell you what," Joel said. "This is between us and no one else. If I ask the gang over in London to do a little homework and they come up with nothing, will you put it to rest and not do anything else?"

Henry paused, took a breath, and then replied, "You mean don't do anything on my own?"

"I have to mail some papers tomorrow. The woman I'm dealing with I know fairly well. I'll add a letter asking her to research Koch's name and I'll give her Maria's maiden name. These people are very good. If they come up with nothing, then you have to promise me that you'll just let things go. Can I have your word?"

Henry smiled widely, put his arm around Joel's shoulders, and said, "You've got my word, brother."

"One more thing," Joel said dramatically. "If, on the remote chance I find out something untoward, you have to promise that you will not reveal to anyone that I helped you out."

"You have my word," Henry said as he gave Joel's shoulder a gentle squeeze.

Chapter Sixty-Eight

Henry was an agnostic, and prior to taking custody of his son he thought that Maria shared his lack of faith. He was wrong. The custody agreement required that Joseph continue his religious training in the Roman Catholic tradition, and Henry was surprised at how quickly and devotedly Maria resumed the religious practices of her youth. He doubted her sincerity. Lately, he questioned everything she did and recognized that they had undergone a role reversal. If in the past it was she who was sullen and aggrieved, though he didn't know why. He was now the aggrieved party and. in his case. he knew exactly why. Once again he was on the losing side of the argument. as no one else close to him shared his opinion. Maria was viewed as noble and loving. Her acceptance with open arms of his bastard son had earned her the respect of everyone they knew and within his family she had become the centerpiece of all activity. She was in control. and as her grip tightened he became more and more convinced that she was doing it to punish him. The few times he had suggested this, first to Joel, then later to his buddy Jack Stern, he was rebuked. Both men lauded Maria for her selflessness and dismissed Henry's concerns as the product of a guilty conscience. He had no one to turn to, and he longed for Sophie's company, finally realizing how important their relationship had been.

It was Sunday, December 12th. He had just returned home with the newspaper after dropping Maria and Joseph off at St. Brendan's Church for Sunday services. Maria preferred the 10:00 o'clock mass and between dropping them off at ten minutes to the hour and picking up the paper he had a good twenty-five minutes at home by himself where he could have a cigarette and a cup of coffee, and read over the sport's pages before returning to the church to pick them up and take them to the Riverview Diner for Sunday breakfast. This was his Sunday routine. After breakfast they would return home, then in the afternoon it was off to Gloria's for Sunday dinner with the rest of the family. He enjoyed going to the diner for breakfast. He didn't enjoy taking his wife and son to church. His own religious training as a child had been superficial, and while he was proud to be a Jew, his pride never extended into the realm of faith and religious observance. Nonetheless, he found it disturbing that Joseph was being raised as a Catholic without being given any opportunity to be exposed to Judaism. He had even mentioned his concerns to Maria, and her response was to laugh at him. "What would you know about your religion, or any one else's?" she had laughingly scoffed. Of course, she was right and it was nothing more than jealousy that left him feeling that way, but how you feel is what matters, he thought, and he was sorry he had ever agreed to take custody of the boy. It was obvious that the boy tolerated him. Every attempt at a prolonged conversation died, and it was only when they were in Maria's company or Gloria's or his nephews that the child acted happy. Alone with Henry he was quietly nervous. Henry knew it wouldn't get any better. He was uncomfortable in the new house, and even when there alone he found it hard to relax. Something wasn't right, and there was no one to turn to with his suspicions. He ignored the paper, drank his coffee, smoked his cigarette and felt sorry for himself; self pity had become his greatest comfort.

The phone rang and startled him from his sullen reverie. The wall phone was just inside the kitchen entrance and by the third ring he had the receiver in his hand.

"Hello," he dully inquired.

"Henry, it's Joel," his brother-in-law answered.

Henry perked up at the sound of his brother-in-law's voice, and replied, "You're up from your death bed, or are you calling to cancel dinner?"

"It was a forty-eight hour virus, I've recovered, and, in fact, I'm at my office."

"It's Sunday," a surprised Henry said.

"I was out Thursday and Friday, and yesterday was the first day I felt a little better, and tomorrow evening I'm on a panel at the University Club and I wanted to gather my notes. Also, I wanted to go through my mail."

"I'm happy to hear you're better. I guess dinner is on tonight?"

"Of course, I thought Gloria spoke to Maria yesterday."

"She may have, no one tells me anything," he lamented.

"No, we're all still on, but that isn't why I called," Joel said nervously.

Henry sensed Joel's nervousness and replied, "Is something up?"

Joel's breathing became a little heavier, and Henry could picture him with that worried look on his face, weighing whatever it was he was about to say. The pause was momentary, then Joel said in a cautious voice, "You remember, don't you that you gave me your word."

Henry was at a loss and had no clue as to what Joel was talking about, and rather than probe his mind to look for an answer, he simply said, "Joel, cut the horseshit, what is it you have to tell me?"

"You're right," Joel said with more confidence. "I was going through my mail and in the pile was a legal sized envelope from Gwen Davis. Do you remember the name?"

Henry did, and it was he who now sounded nervous. "Yes, that's the gal you mentioned who heads the research team for that fellow you're working with on the text book."

"Yes," Joel said, "and you'll never believe it, and," he added sternly, "you have to keep this strictly confidential. I offered to help, and if I knew what was going to happen I would not have, but I'm a man of my word and I expect you to be the same."

"Son of a bitch," Henry exclaimed. "She found out something about Koch, didn't she? I'll be a monkey's uncle, damn, I knew it."

"Well, it isn't much, but she has some ideas and…" Joel was saying when Henry cut him off.

"Joel, what in God's name did she find out. Spit it out, tell me," Henry said excitedly.

"He's dead for one thing," Joel said.

"It's 1965, that's surely possible," Henry replied.

"No, no," Joel corrected. "He's dead, and he's been dead since 1936. He was found murdered in a vacant ship terminal in Southampton in September of 1936."

Henry let out loud sigh. "1936," he said sadly.

"Yes, there's one and only one news story Gwen was able to dig up, and that doesn't give much information. Koch was in the import export business, and he was described as an Argentine, so Maria wasn't fibbing about that."

"Why was he killed?" Henry asked.

"There isn't much in the story. It says and I quote *'An undisclosed government source related that this may have been an assassination and that Mr. Koch had strong ties to several prominent Nazi Party officials in Berlin and he may have been involved in numerous financial improprieties. The manner of death has not been revealed, but this same source did assert that it was a quick, brutal and silent execution, and was clearly the handiwork of professional killers'* end quote."

"A Goddamn Nazi," Henry said with amazement. "Gloria was right all those years ago. Wrong man, but she was barking up the right tree."

"Hold on, Henry," Joel said calmly. "Gwen was nice enough to supply a little background information. Not about Koch, but about that time period and what was going on."

"Maria lied to us," Henry said with annoyance. "Can Gwen explain that?"

"No," Joel said harshly. "However, think about this, please. There is only one news story which suggests that the authorities were on to Koch and whoever he was dealing with, and they felt a need to close the door on this incident. I don't know how the authorities operate there, but I'm sure they're not as responsive to a persistent press as we are here. The probably fobbed it off as a security issue and the story died."

"But we don't know that?" Henry replied.

"We don't know anything," Joel answered peevishly.

"Nazis, financial improprieties, doesn't that tell you he was a criminal and Maria is a liar?" Henry replied just as peevishly.

"Gwen wrote a little synopsis, not of the incident obviously, but of the times, and I think she makes a valid point," Joel said calmly, not wanting to argue with Henry.

"What the hell do I care what she thinks?" Henry said with even more agitation. "Who asked for her opinion?"

"Calm down," Joel cautioned. "She was nice enough to do this errand for me, and since I had to give her some background information for why I was asking her to do this she was kind enough to offer a few suggestions to explain what happened to Koch and why."

"Another academic," Henry said with sarcasm.

"Just listen for a moment," Joel said in his calmest voice.

"You've got the floor, professor," an ever more sarcastic Henry answered.

"Bear in mind that Koch was from Argentina."

"He was born in Austria," Henry interrupted.

"Yes," Joel conceded, "but he was raised in Argentina and didn't get back to Europe until he was an adult. He was an outsider. And Gwen's point is simply that an affluent Jewish businessman in Germany at that time in its inglorious history would have had a clearer understanding of what was on the horizon, so to speak, than a born and bred German Jew or Austrian Jew would have."

"How does that decriminalize him?" Henry asked.

"Her point is that German Jews and Austrian Jews thought of themselves as Germans and Austrians first. I'm sure just as English Jews and French Jews thought of themselves as Englishmen and Frenchmen first. When they lined up against one another in the trenches in the first war the Jews weren't excluded. They fought too, and they fought as Frenchmen and Germans and not as Jews and gentiles. Will you accept that?" Joel asked.

"I'm really not in the mood for a history lesson, Joel," Henry said strongly. "I want to know about Koch."

"Excuse me," Joel said just as strongly. "I did you the favor and I don't appreciate your tone."

"Oh, give me a break please, Joel," Henry said with an edge still in his voice. "You know what's gone on and you know what I'm up against. Yes, I did ask a favor of you, and you helped me out, but you can't expect it to end there. I don't mean to be testy, but I'm not some kid sitting in your classroom. I fought my way across Europe. I know all about Hitler and Nazis and what they did. I saw some of the results firsthand, and not from pictures in a book or on a newsreel. Don't lecture me and don't make excuses. That bastard Koch was tied in with the worst people, and my wife was sleeping with him. And," he paused to take a breath, then continued with greater vehemence, "where did she get the money to buy this house? How much more does she have in the bank? Damned if I know, and now she won't even discuss Koch with me. I'm being played for a fool here, a damn fool!"

"Henry," Joel pleaded, "Gwen was attempting to put that time in history in perspective. We don't know what was going on in Koch's world, maybe he had no other choice. You want him to be a criminal. You want justification for how you feel about Maria, that's what I smell here and you're wrong. Take a few breaths and don't run off half cocked. This isn't you, it isn't you," he repeated.

"Are you going to give me what you have?" Henry asked.

"I will, but you have to keep me out of it. If Gloria finds out there'll be hell to pay."

"What makes you think that? Wasn't she after the same thing just months ago?" Henry answered.

"Months ago, Henry, months ago, things were different. I've finally figured out what was wrong between Maria and Gloria."

Henry looked at the kitchen clock. It was almost time to leave to pick Maria and Joseph up. "Listen, I have to get going. Can we talk later?"

"I don't think so. Henry, you must understand that up until a few months ago I never realized how intimidating Gloria found Maria. That business about Maria deferring to Gloria and telling you to ask for her guidance was enough to melt an iceberg. Right now, Maria is like a sister to Gloria. And that has made my life easier and made Gloria happier and benefited this entire family. I've told you this before. I did you a favor and answered your question. Please leave it there. Nothing good can come of this if you confront Maria with what you know," Joel said in a pleading voice.

"So what do I do? Forget what you told me, disregard it?" Henry asked.

"I should have never told you. What are you going to do?" he demanded.

"Nothing, let me see the papers. I'll send a messenger to pick them up at your office tomorrow. I won't say anything, I'll keep my word, I promise," Henry said.

"All right, I'll see you later today," a relieved Joel replied.

Henry put the phone back on the hook. He felt vindicated. Angry, but vindicated, and although he didn't know what he would do next he understood that it would be unfair to go back on his word to Joel and promised himself that later that day when they were at Gloria's he would take Joel aside and reaffirm his promise. She was a liar and a fraud, and for the time being that was enough lift him out of the doldrums.

Chapter Sixty- Nine

The black lace mantilla was carefully draped over her hair and fell to her shoulders and was lost against the deep black cashmere of her coat. Henry was puzzled by the mantilla, and the first time he saw her with it on he stared at her for a moment, then sniffed and wrinkled his nose in silent but visible disapproval. He readily deduced that the headdress was worn for religious services and his discomfort with the subject was obvious. She saw the look he gave her every Sunday when she came downstairs and, if for no reason than to further annoy him, she made it a habit to stand before the mirror in the foyer and readjust it before they left for church.

One of the perverse quirks of human nature is the tendency some people demonstrate to repeatedly engage in conduct simply to annoy another. Maria relished this new quirk in her behavior. They left for church at the appointed time, and as Henry glided the car to the curb in front of St. Brendan's Church, Maria cheerfully asked as her fingers fiddled with the lace edges of the mantilla, "Does my hair look all right?" Henry had to look at her to answer the question. "It looks fine," he had said in reply. Once again she had made his nose wrinkle in disdain and it brought her pleasure.

They were in church now, and the mass was ready to begin. She was in the first seat, fifth row, next to the middle aisle and Joseph was at her right hand. The black cashmere coat was perfectly tailored and she wore dark stockings and plain black high heeled shoes. Joseph was wearing a shirt and tie, dress slacks and a dark blue wool jacket. The two of them looked very smart, and that was the way she wanted it. Maria never failed to notice who noticed her, and if for no other reason than the sake of appearance she and Joseph set a standard few other church goers exceeded. She was pleased with herself, and as the bells rang announcing the beginning of the mass, she raised herself from the pew along with the other worshippers and stood in silence as the priest, followed by his acolytes, stepped from the sacristy and stood before the altar.

Monsignor Carmody said the ten o'clock mass every Sunday. Maria had briefly made his acquaintance back in October when she went to St. Brendan's rectory to register as a parishioner. Registration wasn't necessary, but she felt it was the thing to do since a condition of the custody agreement between Sophie and Henry was that Joseph would attend church and continue to receive religious instruction. She didn't remember the secretary's name, or much of what she said beyond stressing that Monsignor Carmody didn't make a big deal about parishioners participating in the weekly envelope system. Apparently it was a wealthy parish and the weekly collection exceeded the parish's needs, and the excess money was shipped off to the diocese for disbursement to less solvent parishes. It appeared that, unlike most clergymen, Monsignor Carmody wasn't interested in raising money. Just before she left the rectory the monsignor came into the secretary's office. Maria was introduced as a new parishioner and the monsignor shook her hand and welcomed her and her family to St. Brendan's. Maria's replied spontaneously that it wasn't much of a family, only her and her stepson.

She recalled how no sooner had the words left her mouth that she regretted saying what she said, but the monsignor didn't appear troubled by it at all, and cheerfully replied, "You and your stepson, that's family enough to me."

Maria remembered smiling, then saying, "My husband's not Catholic."

The monsignor's quick retort was, "We all can't be that lucky," then he laughed good-naturedly, announced he was running late, thanked her for registering with the parish and was out the door. She learned from the secretary that the monsignor said the ten o'clock mass on Sundays and his were the best sermons in Huguenot City. It was a memorable first impression, and the reference to his sermons was an understatement. Monsignor was a wonderful speaker. There was no thunder and lightening in his sermons. No desperate threats of damnation or hectoring on sin and all the vices people abide. Week after week he preached the gospel, referred to Jesus as the teacher, then implored his congregants to embrace the Good Life. That was his message. Christ, he instructed, was a teacher and the good word, as the gospel was called, was the introduction to the good life. The good life, in turn, was the realization that sin could not be avoided. Man as God created him was a fallen creature and the acceptance of that premise was the first step to salvation. He was the champion of Hate the Sin, Love the Sinner. To be human was to be weak. To learn to forgive others and to be humble was the road not only to salvation, but to peace of mind and contentment with existence.

Two months of church going and listening to the monsignor preach had delivered Maria to a new threshold in her life. Yes, she told herself, it was wrong to punish and needle Henry and she told herself at mass every Sunday that she would change, and when she fell back into those bad habits monsignor somehow through his ministry at the pulpit cleared her conscience. She felt better about herself than she could ever remember. Each Sunday she prepared for church. Each Sunday Joseph, her handsome, loving stepchild, sat next to her in the pew, and when the mass was ended and they exited the church, Monsignor Carmody was there to wish them well. She knew that very first Sunday she and Joseph attended mass that her life was changing for the better. After the mass ended they followed the procession from the church to where the priest stood on the top steps greeting his parishioners. She didn't think he would remember her, but he did, and with a warm smile, he said, "Mrs. Weiss, so good to see you again. This handsome young man must be your stepson?"

She said, "Yes," and the priest leaned down and introduced himself to Joseph and asked his name. The introductions were made, goodbyes offered until next week, then it was off to breakfast with Henry. It was a pleasant daydream, and through it all her eyes followed the priest as he stood at the altar and offered the opening prayers. She shifted her focus back to the mass, opened her prayer book and recited her responses. The prayer book was really a prop, as she knew the responses now by heart, and for most of the mass the book lay open in her hands while her eyes followed every movement at the altar. Today, however, something was amiss. She didn't immediately recognize it, but off to the left of the priest were two seats where the altar boys sat. The first seat was occupied by a chubby red-headed boy of about twelve. He was there every Sunday, and he was always accompanied by an Italian looking boy of about the same age. The Italian boy was missing. The boy seated next to the red-headed boy was older and much taller. He seemed out of place. The monsignor no longer held her attention. The new boy was an intruder. It was unsettling, and intuitively she sensed something was wrong.

They came to the part in the mass where the priest does the readings; first the epistle, then the gospel. Monsignor Carmody took a seat and the new altar boy stood up and went to the pulpit. This boy was much older than the other altar boys. He was taller, decidedly taller than the monsignor, and broader too. He walked slowly to the pulpit and ascended the stairs. He fidgeted with the microphone and, initially, with a tremor in his voice, but then with more confidence he read the epistle. Maria shuddered at the sound of his voice. Where had she heard it before? She recognized the boy's mannerisms. His nervousness had quickly given way to cockiness. His head was tilted slightly as he read, and when he was finished he smirked, or from where she was seated it looked like a smirk. All of a sudden she saw herself in the kitchen on Lincoln Blvd. She was wearing her nightgown and the delivery boy was there leering at her. He helped himself to a piece of candy and made some smart remark. The blood rushed to her face, and she put the prayer book back in its holder and steadied herself with both hands resting on the back of the pew in front of her. Since the episode with the homicide and her hospitalization for the leaking aneurysm she had been almost migraine free. The tingling in her spine had moved up to her temples, and a dull pain was throbbing on the right side of her head. She felt feint, but only momentarily, and as she breathed slowly and rhythmically the pain lessened some and the faintness diminished. He had finished the reading and stepped down from the pulpit. The monsignor took his place and read the gospel. Maria didn't listen. She watched the boy intently. It was the delivery boy. It was Danny Monaghan.

She never heard the gospel and paid no attention to the sermon, but before the monsignor left the pulpit he said he had several announcements to make. Maria breathed deeply and tried to clear her head. She looked up to the pulpit and saw the beaming face of the monsignor as he addressed the congregation and extended his outstretched hand toward the two altar boys seated behind him.

"And this morning we have with us a special altar boy. He did our first reading, is a senior at Cathedral High School, and is performing his service vocation here at St. Brendan's this Advent Season." He motioned for Daniel to stand up and be recognized. "Daniel Monaghan has been with us for several weeks and has been attending at various masses. He is also running our food pantry collection for the needy, and will be accepting donations in the church auditorium after each mass up until the Sunday before Christmas. So please be as generous as you can. Daniel's worked very hard and it is for a very good cause. And let me not forget that he has also offered to coach one of our C.Y.O. elementary level basketball teams this winter. Additional information concerning the food pantry and the C.Y.O. basketball program are in your parish bulletin." The monsignor left the pulpit, moved to the center of the altar and led the congregation in the recitation of the Apostle's Creed.

Maria unconsciously mouthed the words to the creed, but all she could visualize was the boy in her kitchen interspersed with the image of someone bolting from the closet in her bedroom and knocking her to the ground on that afternoon she found Millie Campos dead on the bedroom floor. Everything about church that had made her feel so good was dashed and crushed. The image had been there before, but she had dismissed it, even willed it from her mind, but now, standing there looking at him, it was impossible to deny. It wasn't Sophie who ran from that closet, it was that boy, that leering, smirking, fresh-mouthed kid.

The pain in her head subsided and was replaced by a dire feeling of anxiety. All the good that had happened over the past three months and the satisfaction and comfort she had enjoyed was dissipating quickly, and as she numbly participated in the church service, she came to the understanding that it was too late to admit the truth. Maria could no longer look at the altar. She was kneeling and had her face buried in her hands. Joseph gave her a gentle nudge and she looked up.

The monsignor was distributing Holy Communion and many of the parishioners in the row in front of her had left their seats and made their way down the aisle to receive the Eucharist. Several people to Maria's right were standing and ready to exit, but Maria was still kneeling and blocked their way. Joseph gave her another gentle nudge and she stood up, exited the pew and made her way down the aisle. Joseph was following right behind her. The two alter boys had already received communion and were kneeling at their station. Maria was in front of the Monsignor, and as he said, "Body of Christ," she responded by saying "Amen," and the monsignor placed the holy Eucharist on her outstretched tongue. She turned to the left and her eyes caught sight of Danny Monaghan and she stopped briefly to look at him. She was hoping it wouldn't be him, that possibly it would be some other boy with the same name, but it wasn't. Not only was it him, but he saw her looking at him and in the two or three seconds that passed she saw his head jerk back slightly and she knew that he was aware of her interest in him.

At the end of the mass she stood at her place in the pew until the monsignor and the altar boys proceeded down the aisle. She felt bolder now. There was nothing she could do to change the past, and she determined to give the boy a good hard look as he proceeded by. Strangely enough, he appeared as interested in her as she was in him, and from the moment he left the altar and marched down the aisle until he had come up to her and passed, his eyes were fixed on her and no one else. It was an exchange of recognition void of physical reaction. His face and hers were cold masks bearing no inference of feeling. They shared a secret, which if revealed, would only harm them. Maria filed out of the pew and followed the flow of parishioners down the aisle and out of the church. She didn't ever want to look at that boy again, nor even think of him. Monsignor Carmody was at the top of the stairs and the two altar boys were to his right. Normally she would exchange a few pleasantries with him, and he would shake Joseph's hand. It had started to sleet and rain, and as her turn came to greet the monsignor, she ignored him and tugged at Joseph's hand and made a quick step to the stairs.

The sleet had formed a thin shell of ice over the marble steps and she lost her footing and pitched forward. She felt herself going forward when two strong hands reached out and grabbed her arms from behind, steadying her and preventing her fall. Danny Monaghan was her rescuer. She was startled, and as she regained her balance she came face to face with him again. His cold mask had melted and he smiled at her meekly. She gave him no acknowledgement or thanks, and pulled away from his hands brusquely and made her ways down the church steps with Joseph following closely behind.

Henry was parked in front of the church and witnessed the incident with the altar boy. It evolved quickly, but from the moment he saw her exit the church doors it was clear that she was upset. There was no exchange with the monsignor. She was in a hurry and was almost pulling Joseph, then she slipped. There were two altar boys. One was older and bigger, and Henry hadn't seen him before, but it was a good thing he was there he thought. The boy reacted instantaneously and grabbed her with both of his hands and kept her from tumbling down the steps. Maria's response was shocking. Instead of thanking the boy, she pulled away from him with alarm. She didn't say, "Thank you" or show any appreciation for his quick reaction to what would have been a nasty and injurious tumble down the steep and hard marble steps of St. Brendan's Church. Her body language was distinct, and the verbal equivalent would have been a loud and resounding, "Don't touch me!"

Moments later she was in the car. "I have a terrible migraine. Take me home, you two go to breakfast without me," she commanded.

Henry put the car in gear and said, "You almost took a dive down the steps. Good thing that kid grabbed you."

"My head is killing me, I don't want to talk right now," was her response.

Henry wasn't feeling too sympathetic and replied, "That kid saved you from a nasty fall. You looked like you wanted to hit him instead of thanking him."

"I haven't had a migraine like this since before Millie died. If I lie down for a while with a cold compress maybe it will go away," she answered, refusing to discuss the incident on the church steps.

"Do you want to go to the doctor?" Henry asked.

"I want to lie down and rest, and I don't want to talk right now."

"Sure," Henry said quietly. "I'll take you home and me and the kid will go eat."

Two minutes later they were in the driveway. Maria got out of the car and Joseph remained in the back seat. Maria held the car door open and said, "You'll have to stop at Loesser's and pick up a cheesecake. I ordered one yesterday. Joseph can go in and get it." She turned her head to Joseph and continued, "Sweetheart, go straight to the back counter. You've been there with me before. Go to the counter and ask for Mrs. Weiss' order. Your father can park outside. Henry," she said redirecting her attention to him, "it's five dollars for the cake." She closed the car door and went up the walkway.

Henry didn't bother to watch her go into the house. "Did anything happen in church today? Maria seems a little upset," he asked his son as he pulled out of the driveway.

The boy shook his head and said, "No."

"Did she say anything to that kid?"

"Who?" Joseph asked.

"The altar boy, the one who kept her from falling down the steps," Henry said.

"She has a bad headache," the boy answered defensively.

Henry saw that his son was of no help, and in an effort to change the subject and keep a conversation going, he said, "Well, did we learn anything interesting in church today?"

Surprisingly, the boy immediately responded. "St. Brendan's has a basketball league. It's the C.Y.O.," he said enthusiastically, "and I can play in it 'cause I go there for religion."

"Doesn't your school have a team you play with?" Henry asked.

"That ends next week. The C.Y.O. starts soon. It's in the bulletin," he said as he took his copy of the Parish Weekly Bulletin and leaned over Henry's shoulder to show him.

Henry grabbed at the bulletin and said, "Sit down, you'll cause an accident."

Joseph sat back in his seat, and with added enthusiasm, asked, "Can I play? I didn't ask Maria, but can I?"

"We'll look into it," Henry said agreeably.

"I like basketball," the boy added eagerly.

"I do too," Henry answered. "We'll look into it, okay?"

"Okay," Joseph said.

Unexpectedly and spontaneously, Henry said, "How about, 'Okay, Pop' or 'Okay, Dad?'"

A good ten seconds went by, and Joseph sheepishly replied, "Daddy, please let me play on the C.Y.O. team."

"Sure, why not," Henry answered, quite bewildered by his initiation of the exchange between him and his son.

Chapter Seventy

Parking was at a premium in front of Loesser's Bakery on Sunday mornings. Henry pulled up in front of a fire hydrant and put the car in park. He handed Joseph a ten dollar bill and reiterated Maria's instructions. "Now don't go to the front counter, it'll be mobbed. Go all the way to the back counter. There's a big sign that says 'Pick Up.' Ask for Mrs. Weiss' order and give the man the ten dollars. He should give you five dollars change. Got it, junior?" Henry asked cheerfully.

"Yes," Joseph answered as he carefully put the ten dollar bill in his coat pocket.

"I'll be right here waiting, then will go for breakfast," Henry said as the boy opened the car door and headed toward the bakery.

Henry's cheeks reddened with embarrassment at the thought of his exchange with his son. The reality of fatherhood and actually being one had been a difficult subject. The boy wasn't comfortable with him, and he wasn't comfortable with the boy. However, and it was a big however, he couldn't deny his growing feelings for his son. He liked him, and he understood how difficult it was for the boy to be in his presence. Joseph seemed at ease with the rest of the family, and he had been completely seduced by Maria. It was Maria's obvious success at seduction that prompted Henry's surprising demand. Time would tell if Joseph's response was acceptance of the bribe or a breakthrough in their relationship.

The real issue was Maria. The news that Koch had been murdered and

Maria had lied about his demise was anti-climatic. Henry couldn't betray Joel and confront her with the truth, and even if he did she would coldly dismiss him. Cold and self-absorbed described her well, but when it was to her advantage she could be warm and engaging. He always succumbed to the warm and engaging Maria and weathered her cold and self-absorbed alter ego. Sophie had been the buffer and up until Millie's murder and his world coming apart that had been an acceptable arrangement. His infidelity was primarily one of the flesh, but Maria's was emotional. It wasn't that she didn't love him, she just couldn't love him all of the time. And that was fine, but what disturbed him was that she could willingly give her love to someone else. Finally, and only this morning, he saw the truth. He was jealous of his son. Maria loved the boy. How did it happen so quickly? How was it that the day after Millie's murder Maria was telling him he had to fight for his son? What had transpired on that subway platform between Sophie and Maria? How could a photograph of a child, something thrown in her face literally and figuratively, engender so much positive energy? How was it that she bore no anger toward him for the existence of the child? How was it that he allowed himself to be so easily manipulated by her? His protests were minimal, and he gave into her every demand: Fortescue, giving up his apartment, the payoff to Sophie, the purchase of the house, it was all done ostensibly for the boy's benefit. *Or was it?* he thought. Well, it wasn't and that was what had him so upset. She didn't do it for Joseph, not Joseph alone. She did it for herself, and that was as it should be for her because nothing was ever done by Maria that wouldn't bring her some benefit, perceived or real, in the end.

He would never know why, but something about the child, perhaps nothing more than knowing he existed and was within her grasp, awakened in her a pool of selfless love that had to be expressed. And the expression of that love was remarkable. In many ways her personality had changed, and changed for the better. That was good, he admitted, but it came at a price and the price was the boy. Henry finally realized that his endless distress with her wasn't about Koch or Maria's serial duplicity. It wasn't about years of coldness and indifference. It was Joseph, and it made perfect sense. It never occurred to him, the subject had been casually raised and quickly dispatched early on in their marriage and never pursued again. He expressed no intereest in having children, nor had she. They were completely compatible in that regard, and never once could he recall any display of regret from her on being childless.

Of course, he didn't know her, and that was why it was pointless to revisit the past. Together they had lived separate lives, and he was as much to blame as she was. Maria was a different woman. Whether she had reinvented herself, or merely allowed her real personality to surface was of little consequence and could not quell the stirring of emotion and jealousy he felt toward her successful usurpation of his place as Joseph's father. She had, he concluded, decided to be a mother to the boy; a decision that may very well have been made on a quiet subway platform last June. Again, motive didn't matter. It all fell into place. Every step had been calculated and here they were, six months later, playing father and mother to his son while the boy's real mother rotted in jail.

He took a deep breath and gripped the steering wheel. "What can I do?" he said aloud. "What can I do?" He looked toward the bakery for his son. Then the church bulletin Joseph had handed him caught his attention. "C.Y.O.," he muttered. "What's a C.Y.O.?" The front page had a picture of Christ tending a flock of sheep. The accompanying article discussed matters of religion that Henry had no inclination to read. He opened the bulletin, and on the third page saw an emboldened paragraph heading that read: *Parish News*. A series of sub-paragraphs followed with the listings Food Pantry, C.Y.O. Basketball League and Bingo highlighted. The information given was minimal and provided dates and times when the events would take place, and in the case of basketball, when registration would take place. He read on further just to see if there was any supporting information about the basketball program and he came to another highlighted section titled *Special Thanks*. He was going to skip over it until he saw another bold faced entry. That was a person's name and immediately upon seeing it he felt a pang of anxiety in his stomach. He went back to the beginning of the entry and read it slowly. It was a short paragraph authored by the monsignor. The subject was a high school student at Cathedral Prep named Daniel Monaghan who in fulfilling his vocational obligation, a requirement for graduation, was serving at mass each day through Advent and was operating the Food Pantry and would coach one of the C.Y.O. basketball teams. The monsignor went on to praise the boy's character and commitment to his church and community.

It had to be the same boy. It had to be the delivery boy, he thought. The name thundered in his ears. He had heard the name Monaghan all summer. Newspapers, Futerman, the assistant district attorney presenting the case to the grand jury, the boy was always a part of the picture. Wasn't it odd that Tim Cleary and Monaghan lived in the same building? How odd was it that just before Sophie took her plea there was a news story that the delivery boy's father, a hoodlum he was told, had threatened Tim Cleary. And wasn't it odd that Tim Cleary had initially pointed a finger of suspicion at Monaghan on the day of the murder and, of course, other than Millie and Maria, the only other person they definitely knew was in the apartment around the time of the murder was Daniel Monaghan. Up until this morning he knew all of this and had accepted it as coincidence. However, all had suddenly changed.

The scene with Maria on the church steps played through his mind. He admitted that there was much about his wife he didn't know, but there were some things, characteristics he understood thoroughly. Maria was careful of her image. Other than when she went for one of her long walks, she was meticulous about her dress and appearance. She had a graceful manner about her and was exceedingly cordial and polite in her exchanges with others in a social setting. She wasn't rude, although Sophie would dispute that, and she wasn't clumsy or sloppy.

Each Sunday morning for the past two months he had parked in front of the church and witnessed Maria and Joseph exit the church and greet the monsignor. It was the same polite exchange week after week. She shook the monsignor's hand and sincerely beamed at him, and he, in turn, beamed back and held her hand for that extra second, as if to signify there was a special bond between them. Joseph then received a perfunctory handshake or pat on the head from the monsignor, and when that was completed, Maria smiled and nodded at the altar boys before making her way down the steps to Henry's waiting car. That was the Sunday morning drill, but today was different. There was no smile on her face when she exited the church. There was no time to greet the monsignor. The regal way she carried herself with her head high and her back straight had been abandoned. Her head was bent and she was racing for the steps as if she was being pursued. He played the scene over and over in his head. Had the monsignor seen her? Had he leaned toward her, or did it happen too quickly? There was sleet and rain coming down, and in her haste to escape the church she slipped. The boy's reaction was instantaneous. He was a big healthy looking specimen, and as she pitched forward he caught her from behind and saved her. She looked at him, well, barely looked at him, and Henry saw her face wrench with disgust, and it was the look of shock on her face that solved the puzzle for him. Koch was a footnote from another time. The moment on the church steps with the altar boy was the key, and he felt his anger wane and a sense of satisfaction and purpose overcame him.

Monaghan was the murderer. It was so simple. Maria would never let a headache, no matter how severe, interfere with the image she had created for herself. The pain could have been blinding, but the monsignor and his acolytes would have never known because she would have pretended all was well, and the few seconds of courtesy would have been exchanged. Surely, he thought, she recognized the boy in church. She couldn't face him, and that explained her haste to leave church. Losing her balance and being touched by the boy disarmed her, and despite her best efforts to act as if nothing had occurred, she was exposed. She was in shock and he imagined, correctly, that it wasn't until she saw the boy in church and on the steps that she realized it was he and not Sophie who was in her bedroom that fateful day. Otherwise, it would have been Sunday as usual.

The car door opened and Joseph climbed in.

"Got the cake?" Henry asked.

"Yes," Joseph said as he handed Henry the five dollars change.

"Are you ready for breakfast?"

"Can I get French toast today?" he asked.

"Anything on the menu," Henry answered distractedly.

His mind was fixed on Maria. He had to be right, and he couldn't believe that everyone else had got it all wrong. He was sure that Maria's shocking epiphany this morning would have no effect on her official memory. There was no turning back now. She had the boy, and even if it was only for two years she wasn't prepared to give him up. Whatever her initial error, it had worked out to her liking. Seeing the murderer up close was a jolt, and it left her defenseless, but he was certain that by the time they returned home from the diner she would have made a recovery. A lie was as good as the truth if it benefited the liar, he concluded, and Maria had to have her way.

There was no advantage in confronting her. She would dismiss this accusation just as easily as she would dismiss the revelation about Koch. In each instance he knew her defense would be to mock him, then refuse to discuss the issue. He would go to Sophie. He would confront her with his observations. He would challenge Tim Cleary, the police and the district attorney. He had made his mind up, and as he pulled into the diner he looked at his son in the rearview mirror and pledged to himself that he'd do whatever it took to keep another Weiss from falling into Maria's web.

Chapter Seventy-One

He was numb. There was no panic. She recognized him and she knew what he did. It was evident from the look of fear and shock that registered on her face when he touched her. She would have rather fallen down the steps. He was certain of that, but there was nothing he could do. Right after he grabbed her and held her steady, for a second his impulse was to throw her down the steps. He wanted her dead. She was the only one who knew, and he wished he had let her fall, and maybe, just maybe, his twisted luck would have held out and she would have broken her neck and then the truth would have died with her. These were evil thoughts, but they were thoughts of survival and they comforted him.

It was his most successful collection day for the food pantry. He had expected to be done by two o'clock, but the volume was more than he expected and it wasn't until three o'clock that he had completed sorting and stocking all of the donated goods. He was putting on his coat when Father Carmody came into the auditorium.

"Danny," he said heartily, "I'm very impressed."

Danny smiled and said, "Thank you, Father. The people here at St. Brendan's are very generous."

"They are, but then they can afford it," the priest answered with a slight tone of disdain. "By the way," he said changing the subject, "I have to compliment you on your lightning reaction this morning. You're very quick."

"Oh, you mean the lady?" Danny replied innocently.

"Yes, Mrs. Weiss. She's a regular every Sunday at the ten o'clock mass. Funny thing, though, she always stops to greet me and exchange a few words. Today she blew right by me with her stepson, then she almost tumbled down the stairs. Good thing you grabbed her," he said as he shook his head, indicating that something wasn't right with that little scene.

Danny's stomach tightened up, and it was clear that the monsignor was attuned to Mrs. Weiss' distress, although Danny didn't believe the monsignor had the slightest knowledge of the genesis of that distress. "Just happened, you know," he answered diffidently.

"She didn't say anything to you, did she?" the monsignor asked.

"She looked upset, who knows," Danny said, offering no interest in the monsignor's questions.

"She's a lovely woman. Very polite and engaging, I'm sure there's an answer. Who knows, maybe you're right."

"Yeah, who knows," Danny said in agreement as he zipped up his jacket and pulled up the collar. "Is it still sleet and rain outside?" he asked, changing the subject.

"The sleet and rain stopped an hour ago, but it just started to snow. I don't think there'll be much accumulation. You take the bus home anyway, don't you?" the monsignor asked.

"I take the bus here because it's all uphill, but I'll probably walk home. I like to walk in the snow, as long as it isn't a blizzard."

"Youth," the monsignor cheerfully exclaimed. "You're serving the seven o'clock mass with me Tuesday morning?"

"Yes, Father, I'll be on time."

The monsignor winked and said, "See you then."

The sidewalk in front of St. Brendan's was covered in a light crust of snow. The wind had picked up and Danny could feel his cheeks redden. It was a long walk home. He enjoyed a snowy day just as much as he enjoyed a hot sunny one. Snow always had a softening effect on the cityscape, and despite the cold, it made everything appear warmer and friendlier. Once again he had to purge Mrs. Weiss from his mind. His thoughts raced back to where they were prior to Monsignor Carmody coming into the auditorium. Despite his futile desire to wish her dead, he knew nothing would come of today's encounter. Mrs. Weiss had her reasons, and Danny was a part of the effort. She was his accomplice, or perhaps he was hers, it didn't matter. His father had told him to forget about it and he had done a good job of it until this morning. Other instances would occur reminding him of what he had done, but then the moment would pass and his life would go on. That was what he told himself. Each time he remembered he felt numb. He had reasoned that it was an accident, an unfortunate one all the same, but an accident. He was at an age where it was hard to control his feelings, especially sexual ones. Mrs. Weiss had excited him and the discovery of those photographs caused events to spin out of control. He had entered into an act of personal fantasy. It was a harmless game, then that woman snuck in and caught him. His reaction was spontaneous. Nevertheless, it was unintentional and he never desired to harm anyone. He was convinced of his innocence, and as for Sophie Cruz, that was Mrs. Weiss' doing. There was nothing he could do about it now. His father was right, and as the snow and wind whipped at his face, he said aloud, "Fuck it, fuck it, fuck it."

He wanted to change the subject and think about something different, something pleasant and uncomplicated, but nothing currently in his life was going well. His involvement with Linda Kelly, an affection the timing of which could not have been planned better, and an affection that had literally rescued him from suffocating in guilt over Millie Campos' murder, was now unraveling and he was discontented with his place in her world. And it was her world, he lamented.

Over the summer the two had become closer and closer, and he had little time for his friends. Little Danny Coleman and Billy Shaw, along with the rest of the gang, saw less and less of him and they resented it. Pussy whipped was the expression they reserved for him. Danny took it in good humor, and while he understood the disappointment of his friends, Linda dominated him and there was little he could do to refute their teasing. He realized quickly that Linda was far worldlier than he was. She was smart and self assured. She knew where she was going, and she believed he was just as capable as she was. He had never thought that much of himself. Sure, he was athletic and not a bad looking boy, and he had some size to him, and some gracefulness too, but that was it. His self awareness was purely physical, and the idea that he was bright or could raise several stations above his family was alien to him. Alien, that is, until Linda massaged his confidence and convinced him he was shortchanging himself. Best of all, the murder never entered her conversation. She knew he had made the delivery to the apartment that day, but it was a mere coincidence, interesting conversation for a few minutes, but not much more. Fortuitously, when the papers carried the story about his father and Cleary, Linda and her family were out of the state. They had gone to New Hampshire for a ten day summer vacation. then on to Boston to look at Boston University and Northeastern. She had decided to attend one of those two schools, and by the time they returned just before Labor Day the case was over and Sophie Cruz was going to jail for a crime she didn't commit. Meanwhile, Linda was reconnecting with her girlfriends from school and Danny's social life was changing.

Linda had three good friends in school. All were from Riverview. Her closest friend of the three was Kathy McKay, and during the first week of school Linda introduced Kathy to Ernie Lombardi and they started dating. Weekends arrived and Danny and Linda and Ernie and Kathy doubled dated. Soon Linda's other good friends from school, Gerri Polito and Peggy McDonald and their respective boyfriends, Charlie Stroma and Vinny Calarco, came around regularly and the two couples grew to four couples. Most Saturday nights were spent at Linda's house. Viewed from the street level on Heath Avenue Linda's house appeared two stories high; however, the driveway sloped down at a steep pitch and revealed a third level and the home was actually three stories high. It was on that lower floor that years ago Linda's father had finished a room for entertaining, and it was where on most Saturday nights you'd find the four couples. Little Danny, Billy Shaw and the other guys weren't invited. Nor were any of the girls from the neighborhood.

Danny was now part of a new clique, and it was ruled by the teens from Riverview. All three girls, Kathy, Gerri and Peggy came from comfortable upper middle class families and the two boys, Charlie and Vinny, were wealthy. Charlie's father was a plastic surgeon and Vinny's a plumbing contractor. Because of the design of the house the room wasn't a conventional basement. It faced the rear yard of the house and the windows and door were at the normal level. The room had two small couches, a ping pong table a small kitchenette, and best of all, Linda's parents never ventured down for any parental inspections. It was indoors and private. Initially, Danny enjoyed his new friends, but it grew evident that none of them was interested in what he was interested in. It was nearing the end of 1965 and everything was changing fast. First it was the music. The British Invasion had conquered the music scene and now new American groups were making their way onto the scene and the music Danny coveted was taking a back seat. Pot was the new temptation, and Charlie Stroma was its messiah, and Ernie Lombardi had become his devout disciple.

His desire to change the subject and clean his mind of Maria Weiss' image had worked. The wind and snow were picking up, and as he trudged down Riverview Avenue toward Kingsbridge, he recalled with disgust the previous evening's shenanigans. Linda's parents were away for the night visiting her brother. They weren't comfortable leaving Linda alone, and the three girlfriends were staying over. There was no concern about the boyfriends visiting. The Kelly's trusted their daughter.

The evening started as usual. Linda put out potato chips, and 7-Up and Coke were in the refrigerator. Vinny always brought a bottle of Seagram's, and they mixed it with the 7-Up or Coke. Charlie displayed a handful of marijuana joints, and he and Peggy and Ernie and Kathy went out to the Kelly's back yard to get high. Dylan's *Highway 61 Revisited* was whining on Linda's portable stereo, and Danny recalled how out of place he felt. For the last seven Saturday nights the group had assembled at Linda's house and the only music that was played was Dylan, The Byrds, The Rolling Stones and endless Beatles.

Last week Charlie brought a record by a guy named Phil Ochs. He was a protest singer and that was another complaint. Everyone had something to say about the war. Danny didn't know there was a war, but they did. Charlie Stroma played guitar and that, too, was a headache. When Charlie got good and stoned, Kathy would get him to play. Charlie's voice was a clear and plaintive and his repertoire included many of the latest songs. He was good and Danny disliked him for it. It was more than just the music and pot smoking that got to him. The conversations were tiresome. Kathy McKay was especially talkative all the time, and not one thing she said registered with Danny and she knew it. Initially, she was warm to him, but over the weeks he sensed a growing enmity between them and it came from him as much as her.

Three things happened last night that irked him and almost caused a break up with Linda. Before he left his house for Linda's, he took three record albums from his collection. He had decided that he wasn't going to spend another Saturday night only listening to the music the other kids wanted to hear. He brought along the Beach Boys *All Summer Long* album, *Johnny Mathis' Greatest Hits* and the Four Seasons *Rag Doll* album. The albums were stacked near the stereo and right after Charlie and Ernie and the three girls came back inside from getting high Kathy went over to the records and picked up Danny's albums.

"What crap is this?" she said, laughing. "Linda where's the trash?" she shrieked mockingly as she dropped the three records back on the table.

Ernie had a goofy look on his face and was giggling as Kathy dropped the albums and acted as if they were contaminated. "Let me guess?" he said as he went over to her and picked up the top album. Is it Johnny Mathis?" He took Kathy in his arms and in an exaggerated waltz, he pushed her around the room while he cooingly crooned, "Oh chances are your chances are very good, your chances are your chances are very good." He held the final note, then took a bow. Everyone laughed hysterically.

Linda then got in on the act and said the music was passé, then Vinny asked what the other albums were and everyone laughed again. No one wanted to hear the Four Seasons, Johnny Mathis or The Beach Boys. Danny recalled how pissed off he was, but it was seven against one and he collected his three albums and set them aside. No one paid him much attention, then Linda told them that she had some music too, but it was new. She ran upstairs and a minute later she returned and announced theatrically, "Voila!" And from a bag that said Liberty Music she pulled out an album and showed it to the group.

The girls gushed with joy and Charlie Stoma called out, "That I want to hear."

Linda was preening, and she handed the album to Ernie and he slit the cellophane seal with his fingernail, withdrew the vinyl disc and carefully placed it on the spindle to the stereo. The record was The Beatle's latest release, *Rubber Soul*. They all settled in to listen to the music, and it was evident that the pot and whiskey had mellowed everyone. There was no conversation, then Vinny Calarco, who had appeared half drunk and asleep, suddenly popped off the couch and said, "Hey, Ernie, Charlie tells me you're going to Empire State?"

Ernie, who had nuzzled his head against Kathy's chest, laconically answered, "Why not?"

"Great," Vinny said with enthusiasm. "That's my first choice, too."

Empire State was the best of the state university schools, and when Danny heard Ernie say, "Why not," as if he thought he had a chance to get in there, he started laughing and chimed in, "Ernie, you're lucky if they let you into Borough Community."

Ernie Lombardi had never let a challenge from Danny Monaghan go unchecked, and he sat up and replied with a touch of malice, "What the fuck does that mean?"

Danny quickly replied, "That's the toughest state school to get into, who're you kidding?"

"My GPA's over 90 for three plus years, and my SAT score is closer to 1300 than it is to 1200. I guess that gets me in, so you'll have to go to Borough Community without me."

It was a stinging rebuke, a rebuke made more painful by the sneering look Kathy McKay gave him, and the added insult of being reprimanded by Linda when she said on the heels of Ernie's reply, "Danny, what is with you tonight? Go outside and have smoke and cool down."

That was what he did. He went outside and was on the verge of going home. Ernie's declaration that he was going to Empire, and his proud declaration of his scholastic achievement was stunning. They had been good friends since kindergarten. After the sixth grade they were in different classes, but Danny never knew that Ernie was a good student. Grades and school was something the guys never talked about. Little Danny and Billy Shaw went to summer school every year, but they were the dummies of the crowd. It was clear that Ernie wasn't, but he had deceived them and now that deception led to Danny's embarrassment.

Maria Weiss was the last thing on his mind now, and as the snowfall came faster plastering him in a rime of white he was aglow with anger. Ernie Lombardi had been one of his closest friends, and now he disliked him and relished the thought of that dislike. The remark about college was insignificant when compared to Ernie's greatest triumph. He had followed Linda's advice and gone out to the backyard. He was only there a minute when Charlie and Gerri and Peggy joined him.

Charlie lit up another joint and passed it around. This time Danny took the burning reefer when it was passed his way and inhaled deeply. The smoke had a sweet taste to it, and he held it in his lungs for as long as he could before he exhaled. He remembered Charlie smiling and saying, "Danny boy, you got to mellow out."

When they went back inside, Vinny Calarco was passed out on the couch. Linda was at the stereo and thankfully she was changing the record. Ernie and Kathy were missing, and Danny hoped they had left. Linda winked at him and he heard the riff of Southern California guitar licks introducing The Beach Boys singing *Little Deuce Coupe*.

For a moment he felt better. Charlie and the other girls were totally stoned and started singing along with the music. After listening to both sides of the album, Vinny Calarco roused from his stupor and merrily started chanting, "Four Seasons, Four Seasons."

Linda was standing by the stereo and she answered, "Okay, Four Seasons it is." She removed one album and put the other on. Once again the group sang along with the music. Their frivolity was redeeming, but the mood of reconciliation was aborted by the unexpected sounds of footsteps and laughter from the floor above and the reappearance of Kathy and Ernie into the downstairs room. All the while Danny believed they'd left for the evening when it was apparent they'd been upstairs. They settled back onto the couch and snuggled together quietly. Just thinking about it incensed him. It was unbelievable, and what was worse was the way Linda treated it. He had motioned to her to go outside and she followed him. Their exchange was brief. "Where were they?" he had asked her sharply.

"I let them use my bed, that's all," she replied.

That was that, he thought. *Ernie was banging Kathy and he was using Linda's bed to do it in.* Her parents weren't home and she was so casual about it made him sick. He still felt sick. "What about us?" was the next question he asked.

She gave him the same answer she'd been giving him every time he asked it. "I'll be eighteen in February. You'll be eighteen in January, when we're both eighteen and not until then."

And that was what she said every time, and he had no reason to disbelieve her, but he understood at that moment and better today than ever before that they had no future. It was clear and obvious. For what ever reason, Linda liked him and she felt comfortable and safe with him. Surely, she would give him her virginity, but that would be it. Losing it to him was safe. In less than a year she would be in Boston and he would be in Huguenot City. Father Dunphy was working hard to get him into Jesuit University, but in all likelihood he was going to Borough Community, and only after and if he improved his grades would he get to the university. Meanwhile, Linda and Ernie and the rest of them would be going away. They were in a different class and he knew it. He couldn't bear to be in her company any more that night and after she told him they would have to wait he gave her a kiss on the forehead, went back into the house, collected his records and jacket and left without saying anything else. As far as he was concerned, he was through with her and them.

As mad as he was, he didn't want to end it with Linda. She was calculating, and her plan, for it was a plan that he was a part of now but could be disposed of later, was to lose her virginity to him. Her crush on him started in the third grade and carried through to high school, and would end in her bedroom. He would call Linda and apologize. Her promise must be kept; it was something of value and he meant to have it. The steps to his building were covered with snow. It was way past three and he expected to find the apartment empty. The first order of business was to destroy the picture of Maria Weiss he had hidden so many months ago. He couldn't remember when he had last ogled her picture. Ogle was the word he liked to use, and that was just what he did. Using that particular word was a form of self punishment. His embarrassment over this infatuation he had with Maria Weiss gave him a creepy feeling, and he had now rationalized his behavior as nothing more than sexual immaturity; an immaturity that had lessened and would be extinguished when Linda fulfilled her promise.

Surprisingly, the front door to the apartment was unlocked. He entered and was met by his father in the foyer. Mike Monaghan was standing in front of the mirror that hung on the wall. He looked at Danny through the reflection in the mirror and said mirthfully, "You look like Frosty the fucking Snowman."

Danny brushed the snow from his hair and answered, "It's a long walk from St. Brendan's."

Mike was putting on his top coat, and said, "Your mother's still at church. Turn the roast off by 4:30 if she's not home. Tell her she doesn't have to save me dinner. I'll be eating out with my new partners."

Danny was puzzled by his father's demeanor. He seemed chipper and easygoing, which was in stark contrast to his usual gruff and surly manner. The reference to partners stymied him. He knew his father had a small interest in Bongos, but that was never mentioned. "You going into business?" he asked, not knowing what his father was talking about.

Mike buttoned up his overcoat and said, smiling, "My partners in the bar and me are buying two buildings on Riverview Avenue. They're located two blocks north of where you turn off for St. Brendan's, two storefronts and three apartments in each building. Things are looking up, Danny."

Danny was mildly stunned by his father's openness and friendliness. He seemed genuinely proud of himself. "Wow," was all he could say in response.

"Kid, you got to make the right friends in life."

Mike was at the door and unconsciously and spontaneously Danny blurted out what he was thinking, but didn't want to say, "I saw Mrs. Weiss today—she knows."

Mike still had his hand on the door. He looked at Danny with annoyance. "What?"

"I saw her today at church."

"The lady in the apartment?" his father asked.

"Yes, she saw me and she knows, I can just tell. Outside of church she almost slipped on the stairs and I grabbed her. She would have gotten hurt bad, but she pushed me away. Didn't say anything, just gave me a nasty look. I don't know what to do."

Mike frowned. "Danny, the last time the lady saw you were in her bedroom. She knows what happened, but she decided to pin it on her husband's girlfriend. She's just as guilty as you are, and she wants to forget it just as much as you do. I told you before, live with it."

"You don't think she'll say anything?"

Mike looked at Danny with disgust. "You got any brains?" he asked. "If she was going to say anything she would have said it months ago. She used you to get even with her husband. Forget it. And don't mention it to me anymore."

"Okay," Danny answered.

Mike said nothing else and left the apartment. Danny knew his father was angry with him for bringing it up, but he felt better. Mike was abrupt and blunt, but he was right. Danny went to his bedroom and opened the closet. He took out the game of Sorry and lifted the top off the box. Under the game board was Maria's picture. He didn't look at it. He started to tear at it, and when he was finished there was a pile of shredded paper on his bed. He gathered the paper in his cupped hands and went to the bathroom and dropped the pile in the toilet. He flushed twice, then went back to his bedroom and picked up the few remaining specks of paper and took them to the bathroom and flushed them. The act left him feeling cleansed. All the evidence was gone. That accomplished, he went back down the hallway to the telephone stand and dialed up Linda's number. He needed to talk to her and know she still cared.

Chapter Seventy-Two

Shoveling snow was a bad idea, and a foolishly bad idea when it was something you had never done before. It didn't look hard, at least when someone else was doing it. How many times had he seen Lunch or Cleary in front of the building on Lincoln Boulevard pushing snow to the curb? Granted, Lunch was well built, but Cleary had the definition of an egg and still Henry had seen him on many an occasion push away the snow with minimal effort. The ache was in the small of his back, and in retrospect he wished he had heeded Maria's warning. The snowstorm was unexpected. When he picked Maria and Joseph up at church there was sleet and rain. By three o'clock the sleet had changed to snow and the downfall was vigorous. He had expected it to drop an inch or two and move on. When they drove the few blocks to Gloria's house for dinner there was only a thin coating on the road. They left Gloria's at a little past nine in the evening and by that time the snow had stopped, but there was a good six inches on the ground and when he got home he shoveled snow for the first time in his life. He felt it now, but at the time it was as good an excuse as he could find to avoid being alone with his wife. It worked. When he got to bed she was already asleep, and as she faintly snored he stared at the ceiling and planned her undoing.

Today was Monday. The expression on her face as she pulled away from Danny Monaghan on the church steps the day before was a still life revelation of guilt imprinted in his mind. He went to work this morning and the first thing he did was call the Pinewood Correctional facility in Lichenville. Visiting hours for attorneys were from 10:00 a.m. to 3:00 p.m. daily and no appointment was necessary. The only stumbling block to an interview with an inmate concerned the inmate's work detail or unwillingness to see the attorney. He was on the highway going to Pinewood. The village of Lichenville bordered Washburn, and it wasn't more than a twenty-five minute ride. Along the way he stopped and bought Sophie two cartons of cigarettes. He had heard over the years that everyone in prison wanted cigarettes. The backache was constant, but not intolerable, and paled in contrast to the pain he would feel when Sophie confronted him. It would be harsh and ugly, and he wouldn't hold it against her. All night long he had lain in bed thinking about what to say to her. "Sorry" simply wasn't sufficient and, yet, he couldn't tell her he loved her because that wasn't the truth either. His feelings for Maria were as addled as ever, and by the time he had fallen asleep he found himself making excuses for her behavior.

The sky was as grey as it had been on Sunday and it mirrored his mood. All that mattered for the moment was making peace with Sophie and achieving her freedom. There were three exits along the highway for Washburn. He got off at the third exit and three blocks later he was crossing the railroad grade and approaching the parking lot for the Pinewood Women's Correctional Facility.

The parking lot was across the street from the compound. The entire facility was surrounded by a twenty-foot high chain link fence. The top of the fence was wreathed in barbed wire. The facility was comprised of four buildings, and they formed a rectangle. Between the angles formed by each building he could see green fields. If you removed the chain link fence and barbed wire, the facility would have looked like a high school.

Security at the front was minimal. The guard asked him his business, then opened the gate and directed him to the front entrance. The lobby was a shabby room with paint chipped walls and worn floor tiles. Two long wooden benches were lined up against the wall on either side of the entrance. Opposite the front door was a reception window. A large sign over the window directed visitors there. Henry approached the window.

An older woman, matronly looking, was at a desk on the other side. "Can I help you?" the woman pleasantly asked.

"Yes, I'm here to see a client of mine, Sophie Cruz."

The woman looked to her left and opened a three ringed-binder, casually flipped the pages and stopped and stared at a page, then turned several more pages until she stopped again, and said, "Here it is. Cruz, section 220. Your name, I need your name," she said to Henry.

"Mr. Weiss, I'm her attorney," he said, hoping she would focus on the word attorney and not the words Mr. Weiss. He had gambled correctly and couldn't help but smile as the receptionist spoke to someone over the phone.

"I have a lawyer here waiting to see Cruz in section 220. The log notation has her in class until 10:30 a.m." The woman paused, then resumed speaking. "Okay, I'll tell him you'll bring her here right after she's finished with the class." The woman hung up the phone, then looked up at Henry. "You have good timing, you must have known. She'll be through with her class in ten minutes. Take a seat over there," she said, pointing to the wooden benches. "They'll come and get you in a few minutes."

"I brought some cigarettes for her," he said, holding up the paper bag with the two cartons of cigarettes.

"When the guard comes for you, he'll take them and bring them to intake."

"Thank you," Henry said as he walked over to the bench to sit down. He wasn't seated for more than a few minutes when a door opened and he saw a uniformed officer approach the receptionist. They spoke quietly, then there was some muffled laughter and some additional conversation. Henry wasn't paying much attention, as he was framing in his mind what he would say to Sophie when he saw her. He was deep in thought, still unsure of what he would initially say to Sophie when he heard the receptionist call his name.

"Mr. Weiss, Mr. Weiss," she said twice, catching his attention on the second recitation of his name. "The guard will take you to the visiting area."

Henry stood up and approached the uniformed officer standing by the receptionist's window. The officer was tall and slim, about thirty or so he imagined, and his face was a picture of indifference. He didn't bother greeting Henry or introducing himself. He held out his hand and motioned with his fingers for Henry to hand him the paper bag with the two cartons of cigarettes. Henry handed over the cigarettes and the officer took them, looked at Henry and said, "Follow me."

It was a short walk. They went through a door and down a short corridor that was lined with offices. They went through a second door into what was the visiting area.

The officer escorting him said curtly, "Take a seat, she'll be out shortly." He then left and closed the door behind him. Six wooden chairs faced the interior wall. The lower section of the wall was made of concrete block and painted a pale pink. The upper section of the wall was a reinforced glass partition. Six stainless steel wings set about three feet apart were attached to the glass partitions at ninety degree angles. Attached to each wing was a telephone. The room on the other side of the partition was identical. Henry chose the third chair and sat down. A wooden shelf extended out a foot and was at table top height. He rested his arms on the shelf and waited for Sophie.

A door opened and Sophie stepped through it followed by a uniformed female officer. It was her, but it didn't look like Sophie, and as he leaned toward the glass to get a better look at her she locked her eyes with his, then covered her face. He saw her mouth open, but couldn't hear what she said. He realized that the glass partition had made the room Sophie was in soundproof.

She moved slowly toward him. She was shaking and he felt his heart start to race. She pulled out the chair and sat opposite him. She picked up the phone. He was frozen. She looked different. She had shortened her hair. She wore no makeup and, surprisingly, her skin looked healthier than he remembered, but the plainness about her face, basically unattractive, was highlighted and the baggy pants and oversized denim work shirt she was wearing diminished her figure to the extent that her femininity had evaporated. The only remaining feature was her eyes. Sophie had large expressive brown eyes, and it was in her eyes he felt such raw anger that he hesitated to pick his phone up. She was angry and shaking and he still sat there motionless.

Finally, she banged her phone on the glass partition and he took the phone off the hook.

Before he could speak, he heard her pleading with him, "Joey, Joey, did something happen to my baby? Please, don't tell me something happened."

"No, no, nothing happened," he replied as he touched the glass with his left hand attempting to soothe her. "He's a great kid and he's fine, just fine."

Sophie sighed. "I thought Mr. Lenihan was here. I didn't know why, but when I saw you all I could think of was my baby. He's all right?" she asked again.

"Fine, he's fine," Henry answered, and finding he was at a loss for something else to say he continued, "Oh, I brought you two cartons of cigarettes. The guard took them, but he has your name."

The emotion he had initially seen in her face was gone and replaced with a cold sullen scowl. "I stopped smoking," she said.

Henry jerked his head back with surprise. "You stopped smoking!" he said incredulously. "You loved to smoke."

"When I was in the Huguenot City jail that seemed to be the only thing that mattered. You know, having a cigarette, hoping the guard would come by every half hour and light you up. I told myself when I knew I was coming here that I wouldn't be in two prisons. One was enough, and the last cigarette I had was two days before I came here."

"Wow," Henry said with amazement. "You quit, just like that?"

Sophie put her phone receiver down on the counter in front of her and looked at him with disgust. He still had his receiver in his hand and he said to her, "Please Sophie, I came here to see you. It's important, please?"

She remained in her seat and stared at him. He kept the receiver to his ear, but had stopped talking. They remained fixed like that for five minutes. He looked past her and in the corner of her room the guard sat on a stool. The guard was watching them, and he was certain she had seen Sophie put the receiver down, but she demonstrated no inclination to interfere.

Finally, Henry put his receiver down on the counter and averted Sophie's cold stare. He wasn't going to leave until she did. He looked at his watch, pulled on his shirt cuffs, fidgeted with his tie and ran his fingers through his thinning hair. He picked up the receiver again and pleadingly said, "Sophie," and then in a louder voice, "Sophie, pick up the damn phone."

She gave in, slowly reached for the receiver, and said sharply, "What, what do you want from me?"

Henry was relieved. He smiled, and with as much encouragement as he could muster said, "I know you're innocent. I'm sorry for not acting sooner, but I know, I know now."

Sophie's face lit up with amusement, then she burst out laughing. "What did you say?" she howled.

Henry was stunned by her response and very soberly said, "You're innocent. I know that now."

"You bastard," she hissed. "You have the nerve to come here with cigarettes and an apology."

"Sophie, calm down," he pleaded. "It's a long story. Yes, I thought you did it at first. I admit it, but things aren't right. I see it with Maria, the way she is with Joey, and other things," he said, rambling.

Sophie had regained her composure and replied in an icy tone, "Henry, I spent the summer in hell. I didn't kill anyone. I don't know who did, and right now I don't care. I had no choice but to do what I did. I couldn't risk going to prison for twenty-five years. I'm here. I even have a job," she said with pride. "I'm a teaching assistant. They have a G.E.D. program and an office skills program here for the inmates. I'm teaching a typing class, and when I get out of here the agency that runs the program is going to hire me. My life isn't over, and I don't care about you or your wife. When the time comes, I'll get my son back and start over."

Henry shook his head in dismay, and in a soft voice said, "Sophie, you have every right to hate me, but please listen to me."

She sighed and closed her eyes, but the receiver was still close to her ear.

Henry said, "I found out some things about Maria. Things about her past and they were things I didn't know, things she had lied to me about. Yesterday, I went to St. Brendan's Church to pick her and Joey up after mass. It was very strange. She came out of church and was in a hurry. This wasn't like her because she always stops and talks to the priest, but yesterday she wanted no part of him. Well, it was raining and icy, and she almost fell down the steps but the altar boy grabbed her. He wasn't really a boy, it was a teenager, a big kid, and when he grabbed her she gave him such a look, a cold hateful look, and it was worse than any she's ever given me, and she pulled away from him so fiercely that I knew in my soul, I just knew that there was something else going on. She got in the car and said she had a migraine and I took her home. I took Joey out to breakfast, and when we got home she was fine, but I saw something and I learned later that the kid who grabbed her was the same kid that made the grocery delivery to my apartment the day of the murder. And," he stopped to take a breath, then went on, "it all fell into place. I mean all of it. Little things that have happened, and the way she is toward me, and especially Joey. I can't completely frame it, but I just know that when she saw that kid it turned her upside down, and I know he's the one, and I know she knows that too. The revelation may have only happened yesterday, but she knows. Does that make any sense?" he asked her.

"Joey loves her," she replied sadly and distantly, ignoring what he had just told her.

"He told you that?" Henry asked.

"No, he won't even mention her unless I ask, but when I ask him how everything is, or what he's doing I can see in his answers that he's happy. He doesn't want to be disloyal to me, but he's not unhappy. My aunt sees things too, and he tells her things, so I know." Sophie laughed, but it was a subdued laugh, then her eyes filled with tears. "She took my baby and he's happy with her. She put me in prison and you didn't care and that's why I don't care."

"That's part of it, at least I think it is, but did you listen to everything I had to say?"

Suddenly she was agitated and squirmed in her seat, then took the receiver from her ear and pounded it into the palm of her hand. "I don't care, I don't care. Really, I don't. When I get out, I'm going home and I want my baby back. That's all I want." She stood up and placed the receiver back on the hook. The line went dead and Henry looked at her with such sorrow that he felt the tears welling in his eyes. Sophie was defeated. She didn't care. She picked the phone off the hook. He still had his close to his ear and he said into the mouthpiece without looking at her. "I promise you I'll do what I can, everything I can to get you out of here."

Sophie listened to his words and allowed a moment of silence to pass before she answered him. "Henry, don't come here anymore. Leave me alone. If you have any feeling for me, any at all, you'll see that she doesn't steal my baby. That's all I ask."

"Sophie, Sophie," he pleaded to no avail. Her phone was back on the hook and she was walking toward the guard. They went through the door and disappeared. She never looked back.

No sooner had the door she and her guard gone through closed, than the door to the room he was in opened and the same guard who had brought him there reappeared and said, "Had a nice chat, I hope?"

Henry distractedly replied, "Yeah, fine chat, a very fine chat."

The ache in his back had grown sharper, and it was exacerbated by the sick feeling he had in his stomach after meeting with Sophie. He was speeding down the highway and in a hurry to get back to Huguenot City. He was upset with himself for thinking Sophie would have greeted him warmly, or at least been gracious for his acknowledgment that she was innocent. "What was I thinking?" he asked himself over and over. She didn't even look like Sophie. That was the first sign that things wouldn't go right. When she appeared through the doorway he was startled by her appearance. He didn't know why, but he had expected to see Sophie as he had always seen her. The woman who came through the door should have been dressed in heels, with a tight skirt and her chest pushed out, a blanket of dark hair hanging over her face, partially obscuring it, and full lips bright with lipstick with a cigarette waving from her painted fingertips. Her mood should have shifted from coarse condemnation of him to squealing bursts of affection. That was his Sophie. Today he was greeted by an imposter; a drab unattractive woman with a bad haircut and shapeless clothing, and what he felt and had to say to her mattered not a whit. How she felt about him, what she felt about him was unimportant. Her son, their son, was her life.

The lobby of the Lincoln Boulevard precinct was musty and unkempt. A disheveled American flag hung limply on an upright pole to the left of the front desk. Paint was peeling from the walls, and several pictures of police officers in dress uniforms were posted on the wall behind the front desk in a haphazard manner. To the right of the entrances were two rows of benches, and on the opposite side was a trophy case filled to capacity with dull tarnished cups of varying sizes. Henry looked at the benches, and thought, whether it was the district attorney's office, the correctional facility or a local precinct there would always be a drab waiting area with wooden benches.

He went straight ahead to the front desk. The desk was oversized and sat on a small platform. Sergeant John Callahan sat upright at the desk in a high leather backed chair. He was white-haired and bushy-browed, with a flat fighter's nose buried in a broad red face.

"Can I help you, sir?" he asked.

"I'd like to speak with Detective Widelsky. My name is Henry Weiss, and I have information about a homicide that occurred in my apartment on Lincoln Boulevard last June."

"Homicide," the sergeant said thoughtfully, then peered over the desk and gave Henry the once over.

"Is there a problem, Sergeant?" Henry asked sternly.

"Never a problem in my precinct, sir," he replied quickly as he turned his head and spoke to an officer Henry couldn't see. "Clay, call back to the squad and tell Widelsky there's a Mr. Weiss here to see him. Has information on a homicide." The sergeant then gave his attention to Henry, and said, "Let's hope they answer the phone."

Henry nodded his head and walked over to the trophy case. He examined the contents without any real interest, and no more than several minutes passed when he felt a mild tap on his shoulder.

"Mr. Weiss, I don't know if you remember me. I'm Detective Cairn. My partner Frank and I were the primary investigators on the Campos murder."

Henry smiled and answered, "Yes, of course I remember you."

"Good," Cairn replied. "Why don't you come with me and we can discuss whatever it is you have on your mind."

Cairn led the way, and Henry decided to hold off any further conversation until they arrived at Cairn's office. He followed Cairn into the squad room and saw that there was no else there except for Detective Widelsky, who was perched over a typewriter punching at the keys with his index fingers.

"Frank, Mr. Weiss," Cairn offered as an introduction.

"How are you?" Widelsky pleasantly asked.

Henry had decided to take an aggressive approach, and avoiding the initial courtesy of introduction the detectives had provided, he bluntly said, "You boys screwed up. Danny Monaghan's the murderer."

His statement didn't register much of a reaction from either of the two detectives. Cairn and Widelsky looked at one another, then Cairn smiled and

618

said, "Well, if we did perhaps you could share whatever information you have with us. Of course," he said with caution, "only the district attorney can reopen the case. We're out of it, but I'd like to hear what you have to say."

"Well, I don't put much stock in Mr. Duffy, that's for sure," Henry stated with annoyance. "You two know that kid made a delivery to my apartment around the time this thing happened. And you also know that he was seen leaving the building after my wife had returned. What you don't know is that my wife is a liar and, furthermore, yesterday she had an encounter with Danny Monaghan when she was leaving church and the look on her face told the whole story. You would have thought she'd seen the devil," he said emotionally.

"You know Danny Monaghan?" Widelsky asked.

"No, but read the parish bulletin," he answered as he took the folded newsletter from his inside jacket pocket and dropped it on Widelsky's desk. "It's the same kid."

Widelsky raised his eyebrows and frowned at Henry. He read the bulletin. "Chances are it's the same kid, but you're not making any sense. Do you agree, Phil?" he asked.

"Let me see that," Phil said as he approached Widelsky and took the folded newsletter from him. He read it, then echoed Widelsky's remark, "Yes, it is probably him, but so what?"

"Look," Henry said with annoyance, "the morning after the murder my wife miraculously exited her coma. Now, it turns out she didn't have a ruptured aneurysm, but she had a leaking one and she does suffer from migraines, and they have knocked her out for twelve, twenty hours at a time. I'm not going to dispute the doctors, but I don't think she was as bad off as she claimed or they thought. What occurs to me now is that on the morning she came to the only thing she was concerned about was my son. She wasn't mad at me. I don't think she was mad at Sophie. All she cared about, right from that time on was my getting custody of the kid. She wasn't concerned about poor Millie. Any sympathy in that direction was superficial. It was all about the kid, and she has him now, and I know she framed Sophie. It's as simple as that."

"Mr. Weiss," Cairn said sympathetically, "we're aware of the story. We know all about you and Sophie Cruz and your son."

"Bullshit, don't hand me that condescending crap," Henry interjected. "I'm telling you the truth, and you don't want to listen. That kid killed Millie. You didn't investigate him for more than five minutes. You were all over Sophie, smelled blood and made the kill. You're wrong! Flat out wrong, and I expect you to do something."

Widelsky remained impassive in the face of Henry's ranting, and calmly said, "You'll have to give us something more. All I hear is your gut feelings and they ain't going to get you anywhere with anyone, us or the D.A."

Henry laughed derisively, "Detective, we're ordinary people. You, me, all of us, and we think we have a leg up on the other guy because we go to work and do the same thing every day. We think we know better, but we don't. It's the ordinariness of life and there isn't an angel's hair's difference between a prince and a pauper. Have a little humility and retrace your steps. You fell into a trap and let a killer get away. Take my word for it."

Cairn looked at Widelsky and winked his eye at him. He took the parish bulletin that Henry had given them and folded it neatly. He approached Henry, handed him the bulletin and pointed his right hand to the squad room door. "It was very nice talking to you, Mr. Weiss, but we have some work to do. If you come up with anything else, take it to the district attorney. As far as we're concerned this case is closed, and like I said before, only the district attorney can reopen the case."

Henry offered a weak smile in return, and said, "I was in the Combat Engineers in the war. All the way across western Europe we led the way." He pointed the parish bulletin at Cairn and continued talking. "I was an officer, and I tried my best to do my best, but you know what I learned?"

Neither Cairn nor Widelsky responded, but their eyes were fixed on Henry.

"I learned that people make mistakes, mistakes all the time, and too often the consequences of those mistakes harm others. And the more confident a man is that he's in the right the greater the chance he'll wrong another. Hubris, gentleman, hubris," he repeated and stormed out of the office.

Cairn started laughing, then Widelsky joined in. "Get out your Webster's, Francis," Cairn said in between his laughter. "Hubris, gentlemen, hubris," he said mocking Henry's angry recitation of those very words.

"Nutty as a bed bug, that one is," Widelsky said in reply.

"Honestly, did he make any sense, any at all?" Cairn asked.

"Who knows? Who cares? Let him take it to the D.A. and see how far he gets with that scenario," Widelsky answered.

Chapter Seventy-Three

He was exhilarated. Keep the peace and make the deal, that was his personality. If someone or thing was unpleasant, avoid it. Change the subject, don't let tempers flare. All his practices catered to his proclivity for non-confrontation. *No more*, he thought, or at least no more on this subject until every principal in the story had heard from him. He didn't expect the police to do anything more than they did, and that was simply to spend a few minutes hearing him out. He stopped at the station house for one reason and that was to bait and insult them. He wasn't even going to bother with the district attorney's office, but Cleary, Monaghan and Maria were next in line.

It was meant to be. There in front of the apartment house on Lincoln Boulevard, the building he loved and that had been home to him for so long stood Tim Cleary. Henry went to the intersection, then wheeled a vicious U-turn and drove to the front of his old address. Cleary was on the sidewalk, staring at his shoes, smoking a cigarette. Henry double-parked his car, got out and slammed the door. Going from a sitting position to a standing one sent a sharp sting across his lower back and he winced in pain.

Cleary heard the door slam and picked his head up and looked around. He saw Henry purposely striding toward him and his face lit up with surprise. "Mr. Weiss," he said excitedly. "How are you?"

Henry scowled, and in a threatening voice dripping with venom, he said, "Tell me why you protected Danny Monaghan?"

Cleary took a step backward and replied, "What?"

"You heard me. Monaghan, what's going on with you and him? Why did you protect him?"

Cleary stammered, "Mi, mi, Mr. Weiss, I, I don't know what you're talking about. I ain't protecting nobody. I swear I ain't. You, you're my friend."

"I'm not your friend. I lived here. You work here. That kid killed Millie Campos, and I know you know it. His father put the fear of God in you and you lied. You're a coward, a dirty little coward," Henry said as he grabbed a handful of Cleary's coat and shook him. The hat fell from Cleary's head and a gust of wind caught it and it started to roll up the street.

Cleary batted Henry's hands away and once free set off in a mad dash after his hat. Henry stood and watched him scurry up the street. The hat rolled into the gutter, fell flat and stopped rolling. Cleary caught up with it, picked it up and brushed it against the sleeve of his coat. He was trembling and carefully watching Henry. He walked slowly to the sidewalk. Henry was still standing there mute and angry. Cleary yelled out to him, "You're a crazy bastard. You come near me again and I'll have you arrested."

He gave Henry a defiant look and walked into the alleyway of the building. He entered the building through the service door and went back up to the lobby. The lobby door was locked and he was hoping that somehow Henry hadn't entered the building. The lobby was quiet. He went to the front doors and looked out at the courtyard. He saw no sign of Henry, but from that location he was unable to tell if Henry was still standing in front of the building or if he had left. He didn't know what to make of the attack, and he was so shaken by the experience he began crying. All along he had thought of Henry as a friend, and now that belief was dashed and in its wake he felt only betrayal.

Henry's exhilaration increased. "I should have throttled the little bastard," he said aloud as he slapped the palm of his hand on the steering wheel. Cleary never saw it coming and the look on his face told Henry he was right and he felt better for it. It was in no one's interest to fight for Sophie. There was a murder and the police made an arrest and the district attorney was able to clean the slate and send a body to jail. His only hope was to shake the tree hard enough and pray he could loosen the fruit of truth from the branches of injustice and win Sophie her freedom. It was a noble thought destined to fail, and while he was well aware that his actions would come to naught, he owed it to Sophie to make the attempt.

The next step was to confront Danny Monaghan. Venue in this matter deserved thoughtful consideration. The teen's father was a thug. That much Henry had gleaned from the newspapers, and any attempt to confront him at his apartment would present the risk of Henry getting a beating, not that he was afraid of Monaghan, but the reality of that happening would abort any opportunity to challenge the teen and possibly get him to break. Similarly, waiting to catch him at St. Brendan's would present the obstacle of Monsignor Carmody, who, if present, would certainly interfere and prevent any interrogation from taking place. His only chance was the Associated Market, and in that regard Henry didn't know if Monaghan was still employed there or not.

He was back in his office. He looked up the number for the Associated Market in the phone book and dialed the number. A woman answered the phone on the second ring. "Associated Market," she said.

"Hello," Henry answered. "I wanted to stop by and drop something off for one of the boys that works there. Danny's his name. Is he on any day this week?"

"Sure, today at three o'clock, well, try 3:15, he's never on time."

"Excellent," Henry replied, then hung up.

It had been easier than he imagined. In front of him were several file folders, it was twelve-thirty and he decided to skip lunch and get his work done. He had a busy schedule for the week, and while his desire was the next confrontation, he gave in to discipline and dedicated the next three hours to his clients.

Three-thirty came quickly. His energy level was high, and what would have normally been a full day's worth of paperwork was history. Fifteen minutes later he was parked a block from the market. The delivery bike was nowhere in sight, and he didn't know if Monaghan was out on a delivery or if due to the snow and ice on the ground no deliveries were being made today. Also, it was Monday and the demand for that service was probably low. He was eager to start the next round and entered the store looking for his opponent. It was important to act natural, and he pulled a shopping cart from a line of empty carts and pushed it to the farthest aisle in the store. He turned up the aisle and saw several shoppers in front of him. He took a loaf of raisin bread and put it in his cart. A little further up was the dairy section and he took a container of cream and a small brick of cream cheese and added them to the cart. At the rear of the store was the produce section. He recalled Maria telling him that their old delivery boy Walter was now the produce manager. Henry didn't see him and that was fine. He was in no mood for small talk. The next aisle was empty and he passed it by. The aisle after that was the canned goods aisle, and halfway down the aisle, crouched on the floor deftly stamping cans with one hand and just as quickly putting them on the shelf was Danny Monaghan.

Henry pushed his cart to a stop before the box Danny was taking the cans from. He nudged the box and sternly said, "Do you know who I am?"

A startled Danny dropped a can from his hand. He looked at Henry for a moment and said, "No." Once again his heart was racing. Gina, one of the cashiers, had told him when he came to work that a man had called and made an inquiry about him. She teased him that he was going to get either a big tip or a punch in the mouth for messing around with some guy's wife. Gina was one of those busybody fat tub of lard women who laced everything they said with sexual innuendo. Talk around the store was Walter routinely gave her the business in the basement after closing hours. At first he thought she was just coming on to him, but after what had happened the day before his nerves were on edge and he had half expected Maria to show up with the police and accuse him of murder. The man behind the shopping cart wasn't Maria. It was her husband. He knew it and, more importantly, he knew that if he stuck to his story nothing would happen to him.

Danny said, "No," defiantly.

Henry stood there, hovering over him. He realized he couldn't physically intimidate him and bully him as he had bullied Cleary. "You don't know me? You were in my apartment. As a matter of fact, I know that you were in my bedroom. Does that refresh your memory?" Henry asked accusingly.

Danny dropped the price stamp on to the floor and stood up. He was slightly taller than Henry. He glared at Henry and said, "Who the fuck are you, old man?"

Henry wasn't intimidated. "Who the fuck am I?" He then laughed and licked his lips. "I know you murdered Millie Campos. I know Cleary covered for you, and I know my wife is terrified of you. I know it all, sonny. I know it all."

Danny was about to curse at Henry again when he heard the soft footsteps behind him, then Mr. Kimmel's voice. "What's going on, Danny, what's the argument about?" Before anyone could answer, Kimmel recognized Henry and said, "Henry Weiss, of course it's you, why are you harassing this boy?"

Henry frowned at Kimmel. "I'm not harassing him. I'm reminding him of what he's done."

"What's that?" Kimmel snapped.

"Murder," Henry testily replied.

Kimmel took hold of Henry's shopping cart and placed it behind him. He stepped aside and pointed toward the front of the store. "Please leave or I'll have you arrested for trespass. Danny, go down to the basement and help Walter unload the last delivery."

Danny nodded his head at Mr. Kimmel and brushed past Henry.

Henry went to grab his arm, but Danny was too quick and was beyond his grasp. Henry almost lost his balance and had to reach out and grab the shelf for support.

Kimmel was glaring at him, and repeated, "Please leave or I will call the police and have you arrested for trespass."

Henry stood tall and smoothed the lapels of his coat with his fingers. "That boy's a murderer."

Kimmel's face reddened, and he coldly replied, "You're embarrassing yourself, please leave."

Henry glowered at him, then said as he extended his arm behind a row of canned goods on the display shelf and tumbled them unto the floor, "Maybe I have."

Kimmel jumped out of the way as the cans hit the floor and rolled every which way. Henry didn't do or say anything else and walked down the aisle and out of the store.

"Lunatic, crazy lunatic," Kimmel said as he went down on his knees and collected the canned goods and placed them back on the shelf.

"That didn't go well," Henry muttered as he got back into his car. He hadn't even seen Kimmel when he entered the store, but Kimmel must have seen him and anticipated his reason for being there. Nonetheless, the exchange with Monaghan was brief, and Kimmel witnessed very little of it. Henry had wanted to confront Monaghan, not only with the accusation of murder, but also his chance meeting with Maria on the church steps. He was certain that would confuse the boy and possibly get him to say or do something that would indicate his involvement in the murder. Kimmel had foiled that plot, but there would be no one to run interference for Maria, and with that challenge in mind he headed home.

Maria was always home by 4:00 p.m. on Mondays, and on this day Joseph was attending a birthday party and wouldn't be home until after five. Henry parked in the driveway and entered his house through the front door. Chicken soup, salad and fresh rye bread were the standard Monday dinner, and the aroma of simmering soup was the first thing to greet Henry as he walked through the door. He went directly to the kitchen. Maria was standing by the sink rinsing lettuce leaves under the faucet.

"Hello dear," she said warmly. "How was your day?"

"Joseph's out?" Henry asked.

"Birthday party," Maria replied. "Carol Fenestron said she'd drop him off. She's very nice," Maria added. "So how was your day?" she asked again.

"Unusual, very unusual," Henry said with an air of mystery.

Maria smiled at him. "And what was so unusual?"

"For instance," he said as he walked to the stove and lifted the lid to the pot the soup was simmering in. "Smells good," he said approvingly.

"For instance, you were saying," Maria replied.

"Oh yes, I meant to tell you that I learned the most astonishing little fact today."

"Surprise me," she answered suspiciously.

"Surprise you." He laughed. "I was the one surprised."

"Henry," Maria now said with annoyance. "Stop talking silly and tell me."

"Amos Koch was murdered in Southampton, 1936, 1937, 1938, I've already forgotten the year, but then I'm sure you have too, since this must be very disturbing news. What was the year? Do you remember?"

Maria gave him a hurt look. Henry picked up a wooden spoon from the stove top and lightly tapped it on the lid of the soup pot. "Ta da!" he said, mocking her expression with a down turn of his lips.

Maria placed the last of the rinsed lettuce leaves on a clean dish towel and gently wrapped the leaves in the towel and shook it to release and absorb any excess water. When she was content she had drained most of the water from the leaves, she laid the towel back on the counter and picked up a leaf and shredded it into smaller pieces with her fingers and dropped them in a bowl.

She hadn't answered Henry, and finally said, "Hand me a cucumber from the refrigerator please." She then continued shredding the lettuce, refusing to acknowledge his mention of Amos Koch.

Henry got the cucumber and handed it to her. As he was doing so, he said, "You didn't think I'd ever find out, did you?"

"I told you I wasn't going to visit the past. It's done."

"No," he shot back angrily. "That was when you had a very different version of the past."

"Oh, for God sakes, Henry," she sighed, "where is your common sense, your decency?"

"My decency?" he said, laughing.

"My life before you is none of your business. What do you want me to tell you? I was his employee, his mistress, a prostitute a whore? I was all those things which, of course I wouldn't have been," she now said, laughing and holding up her left hand and waving the back of the hand at him, "if I'd been married to him. Why would I tell you anything about him? It was easier to say I worked for him and he went back to Argentina. When you saw those pictures I admitted we were lovers. I had no reason to tell you anything else, and it doesn't mean anything to begin with."

"Murder is interesting," he said sarcastically.

"We took a flat on Trevobir in London. It was small and he left most of his belongings in storage. One morning he left for Glasgow on business. What he was doing he kept from me. The next day the police came to the apartment to tell me he had been murdered and that he was about to board a ship for Bermuda. Wasn't that a nice ending to our affair?" she said indignantly.

Henry didn't initially reply. Maria was peeling the cucumber and he could see her lower lip quivering. He waited for her to say something else, then he said, "What was the secret?"

"There was no secret. He lied to me, he used me and then he abandoned me. He was a cold, selfish bastard and I was happy that he came to the end he did. That is not something I'm proud of, but it is the truth and there was never any reason to share it with you or anyone else."

"Well, then," he said accusingly. "What about yesterday, you're hiding that from me too?"

Maria was stunned. "Yesterday," she said, raising her voice. She immediately understood his accusation. He had witnessed the scene on the church steps. Not only had he witnessed it, but he had agreed to let Joseph participate in the St. Joseph's basketball program. A program Danny Monaghan was involved in. Joseph told her he gave the parish bulletin to Henry. She had not read the bulletin, but Joseph said the information about the program was in the bulletin. Surely, Henry had put two and two together and she had to react quickly and without suspicion.

"Yes, yesterday," Henry countered.

"We went to your sister's for dinner. Did I miss something?"

"You went to church first."

"Yes, and I had a migraine attack. You're concerned about my health? How sweet, how unlike you," she replied bitterly.

"You almost fell down the steps when you were running out of church, how unlike you," he said just as bitterly.

"And thank goodness the altar boy grabbed me. And do you know who he is, not that I'd think you would care."

It was Henry's turn to be stunned and said with apparent disappointment in his voice. "I think I do but?"

627

She cut him off, and said, "You think you do. What in God's name are you getting at? He's our delivery boy. Well," she said correcting herself, "he was our delivery boy when we lived on Lincoln Boulevard. He made the delivery the day Millie was murdered. Monsignor Carmody talked about him in church. He's in charge of the food pantry, and he's going to coach one of the basketball teams. I was quite surprised. I thought he was a bit of a wisenheimer, but he's a teenager and you know what they're like these days."

Maria's mood and tone had gone from anger and defiance to casual conversation, and Henry was uncertain about how to read her. "Why didn't you tell me that yesterday?"

"I had a migraine attack. Making small talk about the coincidence of this Monaghan boy wasn't very important to me. I haven't even thought about it until you brought it up, and while we're on that subject, why did you?"

"He murdered Millie and you know it."

Maria dropped the paring knife and the last of the cucumber she was slicing into the salad bowl, and in disbelief she nearly howled, "Have you lost your mind? Have you been interrogating me? Is this what you're doing?" She was angry, but it wasn't anger directed at his accusations. Rather, it was anger directed at his having figured so much out. How had he found out about Koch and why? How had he detected it was Danny Monaghan and not Sophie? Most importantly, how could she dissuade him from the truth?

"Tell the truth," he demanded.

Maria laughed. She left the kitchen and went into the dining room. Atop a mahogany server was a tray with two decanters. One contained scotch whiskey and the other dry sherry. She opened the door to the server and took out a small snifter and filled it with sherry. Henry had followed her into the room. "Help your self," she said. She went into the living room and sat down on the couch. Henry followed her into the living room and sat down in a wing chair that was one of two positioned across from the couch.

Maria sipped some sherry and said, "Joseph will be home soon. I don't want him to be a witness to this nonsense. So please tell me what this is all about? First you start in with Koch, then you make an accusation about Millie's murder. Are you investigating me and this murder? I'd like to know because you're are not only wrong, but you have hurt me beyond belief and I want an explanation. And you can start with Amos Koch. What gives you the right to go fishing into my past?"

Henry felt cowed by her anger. It had seemed clear to him, but suddenly he was tongue tied. He didn't want to betray Joel, and her reaction to his accusation about Danny Monaghan seemed so bland and innocent that he was now second guessing every move he had made. "I hired a private investigator. One in London, and he did a records search on the name Amos Koch. It was very simple, maybe a little underhanded on my part, but those pictures threw me for a loop," he said sheepishly.

Maria sipped at the sherry. "Are you satisfied now? Are there any more questions about Mr. Koch?"

"He was murdered."

"He was involved in a lot of shady dealings, Henry. I told you that once we left Berlin I had very little to do with him on a business level. He became very secretive, and I didn't pry. He ran out on me and the police left me with the feeling that he was a criminal of some type. They were satisfied that I wasn't and that was the end of it. Unlike you, I can let things go. If there was more to tell, I would tell you."

"Why did you lie to me about him?"

"Stop it," she demanded. "It was a painful relationship and all I wanted to do was forget it. Will you let me?"

Henry didn't know how to respond. He had humbled her, but Koch was only part of the story and there was still Monaghan to deal with. "All right, that takes care of Amos Koch, but I'm not satisfied. I saw what I saw yesterday and it is burned in my memory."

"Burned in your memory," she scoffed. "Why do you think that boy killed Millie? Why do you think I would know that and not have told it to the police if it were true?"

Henry didn't know what to say. She was calm. She was hurt, but in the face of it her demeanor was remarkable. She was talking to him as if he were a child who had unwittingly done something very hurtful, and that before she could punish him she had to spell out to him what it was he had done wrong. "It's the way everything has worked out. Your acceptance of my son, the way you looked at that kid when he grabbed you, the way you and Gloria get along now. I'm confused," he confessed.

"I tried to do what was best for everyone. Sophie was in our apartment. I saw her. You have a son. Why should he be punished? I met the delivery boy twice. Once when he came to our front door and surprised me. The police know that, and you do too. And another time when he was in the lobby being fresh to Tim Cleary. I didn't care for him. I am happy he was able to keep me from falling down the steps yesterday. I don't know what look I gave him, but your interpretation is wrong. It was Sophie and that is the truth. Any more questions, Detective Weiss?"

629

Henry stood up and rubbed his back. His head was hanging in shame. He had been so certain, and now the certainty that had burned so deeply all day was failing. He wanted to call her a liar, but she had trumped him at every turn and the shame he felt was over his inability to trap her. In his head it made perfect sense. As she described it his accusations were baseless. His lone success of the day was bullying Cleary, and even on that score, Cleary never wavered in his denial of Henry's accusations. *Maybe I am wrong,* he thought. *Maybe it is nothing more than guilt.*

Maria finished her sherry. She approached Henry and placed her hands around his waist. She massaged his lower back with her fingertips. "Your back hurts, doesn't it?" she asked.

He nodded his head. "Maybe I am crazy," he said sadly.

"Henry, we have gone through a very stressful time. I want to prove to you I love you, and I can't if you keep looking for reasons to deny my love. Whatever I hid about Amos Koch, I did out of shame. Millie's murder is what it is and you'll have to accept it. What else can I say?"

He brushed her forehead with his fingertips, "Forgive me, if you can, forgive me."

She hugged him briefly. "We have time before dinner. Take a hot bath and soak your back. When you're done, I'll rub Ben Gay on it."

"Okay," he answered in a defeated voice. The exhilaration was gone. The hope of exonerating Sophie had vanished. His detective work appeared pathetically overly dramatic and theatrical. Maria's calm graciousness in the face of his accusations was endearing. He had been prepared to cast her aside and declare their marriage dead, but the heated exchange and admissions of guilt never materialized. After all they had been through it appeared that she did love him. There wasn't much more he could ask for from her.

Chapter Seventy-Four

She was proud of him. The source of her pride was his intellect. He had threaded together the incongruent snippets of information from her history and the history of Millie's murder and made sense of it. Once the shock of Millie's murder had faded, his suspicions grew. Today was the watershed moment when he unleashed those suspicions. He had gotten it right, but no body of hard facts existed to support his accusations and it was, she mused, all thunder and no rain. She didn't appear threatened by his anger, nor did she even entertain a notion of guilt when he correctly identified Monaghan as the murderer, and by default her as a co-conspirator in that crime. There was no need to mount a defense, no need to take umbrage, nor engage in a demonstration of histrionics to make him back down. Conduct of that sort would have encouraged his interrogation. She had prevailed because he was a simple man to understand. At the core of his character was a belief in compromise. He liked people. He was gregarious and generous. Generous to a fault, but it made him feel good. If a waiter was slow or rude, or the food unsatisfactory he still left a good tip, and when she challenged him for doing so his usual answer was that "Maybe the fellow's had a bad day," or some other trite excuse to avoid finding fault. That was his nature, and it dominated his intellect and instincts. He would endure a slight and ignore an insult in the pursuit of harmony.

Her feelings of guilt were not over Millie's death or Sophie's wrongful incarceration, but her poor treatment of him for too many years of their marriage. It was a convenient fiction to place Sophie in her bedroom, thereby identifying her as Millie's murderer. At first it was what she believed, but soon after there was a nagging belief that Sophie was innocent. She denied that belief and so successful was her denial that it wasn't until she came face to face with Danny Monaghan that she had to admit the truth, and by then it was too late to undo what had been done.

The future had been decided, and it pleased her that Henry, a man she now loved, a man that she had perhaps never loved until today, had solved the riddle, then submitted to her denials. She had reacted calmly in the face of his threats. Amos Koch was easily explained away, and by naming Monaghan as the boy on the church steps before he could identify him as such left him speechless. It was a masterful performance, and it pleased her greatly that she had rendered his argument to the rank of meaningless conjecture. Suspicion could haunt him, but between them it was a dead issue. She had learned long ago that relationships and marriage, like life, were messy affairs, and it was futile to try and make sense of things. We are, she thought, driven by emotion more than anything else and at this time in her life she needed to be loved and it was the love of Henry and his son that mattered above all other things. Her plot to replace Sophie in Joseph's life was moving well, and just when she thought she had lost Henry, today's drama had favored her.

She finished making the salad and as she was putting the bowl in the refrigerator she heard the doorbell ring. It was probably Joseph, and as she went to let him in she recalled the feeling of conquest and satisfaction she had felt immediately after Koch's death and she realized that sensation again and she was happier for it.

Carol Fenestron was parked opposite the house. She honked the horn and waved to Maria and drove away. Joseph waved too and came into the house. Maria smiled at him and said, "Well, how was the birthday party?"

Joseph put down his book bag and opened it up. "Look what I got," he said exuberantly as he pulled a book, a comic book and an oversized candy cane from his book bag. He handed the items to Maria and she looked at each one. "I'll take charge of the candy cane," she said with disapproval. "You can have a small piece each night after dinner."

"You better hide it from Henry, or I won't get any of it," he dead-panned.

Maria laughed and led him into the living room. She placed the candy cane on the mantle of the fireplace. She looked at the comic book and said, "Little Archie's Christmas issue," and put that on the mantle. "You can look at that after you've completed your homework." Finally she looked at the book. *The Shore Road Mystery*, I bet it's a good story."

"It is, I want to start reading it tonight," Joseph answered excitedly. "We all got a book at the party. It's a Hardy Boys' mystery. Peter has read two of them already, and I want to get more. He says that they're great books."

She put the book on the mantle too, then sat down on the couch. "If you like it we can buy more. Are there many of them?"

"There's a ton of them," he said with added excitement.

"I didn't know a ton was a number," she said, laughing. "Now sit down next to me," she directed him. "We have to talk about something very important."

He obediently sat down on the couch next to her and said, "What?"

"Basketball," she said glumly. "Yesterday at Aunt Gloria's there was a lot of talk about basketball."

"Henry said I could play."

Your father," she said correcting him, "said you could play, but I spoke with Monsignor Carmody this morning and I found out that the program will be on Saturdays."

Joseph frowned and looked down to the floor. Maria reached over with her hand and placed it under his chin and gently tilted his face so that he was looking at her. "I was able to make an exception for the program at school, but it wouldn't be fair to do it again, would it?"

"Why can't I go after school like I did those two times?"

"We had to make special arrangements, it is winter, it gets dark early and it isn't fair to your Aunt Lucy, and I'm surprised at you," she said sadly.

"Surprised?" he said repeating her words.

"Yes, I'm a little disappointed in you. You aren't happy when you see your mother?"

His face flushed, then in a guilty voice, he said, "No, I love Mommy. She's so sad and I know I make her happy when I go to see her."

"Well," Maria said, and paused for a second, "I guess basketball is out. But," she said with enthusiasm in her voice, "tomorrow we're going to buy you a pair of ice skates, and on Thursday or Friday you are going for your first skating lesson."

His face lit up and he jumped off the couch and stood before her. "Peter skates at the Riverview rink every Sunday. Will you take me?"

"Of course we will. Did you know that your father and I can both skate?"

"Yes, you told me you could. Do I need lessons?"

"They would help, and now that we've settled all of this I have on more surprise, then you can go upstairs and start your homework."

"I'm getting something?"

"Mr. Perri is coming tomorrow."

"Who?"

"Our gardener, he's coming to put lights on the two fir trees out front and over the doorway. He's also going to hang a big Christmas wreath on the door and on Friday he's coming with a big Christmas tree and he'll put the lights on that too and put it up for us. Then you and I can decorate the tree. How's that?" she asked.

Joseph was beaming, and the disappointment about not being able to participate in St. Brendan's basketball program was already forgotten. "Why can't Henry put the lights on? Uncle Ray does it for us, but Mommy always fights with him until he gets it right."

"Your father has never had a Christmas tree. It will be easier if Mr. Perri does it, and by Friday we will be all lit up for Christmas."

"Can I have a piece of my candy cane now?" he asked.

"No," she said decisively. "After dinner, now get upstairs and start your homework. Your father's taking a bath and I have to rub his back."

"You told him not to shovel," Joseph said, laughing as he went ahead of her and ran up the stairs to his bedroom.

Maria took the candy cane and went to the kitchen with it and put it in a drawer under a stack of dish towels. Joseph's admonition that she should hide the candy from Henry was well founded. Henry had a sweet tooth, and any candy or cake left sitting around was fair game for his appetite. She turned off the flame on the soup to let it rest and set the table. After she was finished, she went up to her bedroom to change her clothes. She passed by Joseph's room and looked in. He was at his desk working on some arithmetic exercises. She smiled, closed his door and went to her bedroom. Henry was still in the bathroom. She took a pair of slacks and a sweater from her closet and laid them on the bed and started to undress. She could hear the water draining from the tub. Moments later Henry was in the doorway with a towel wrapped around his waist. She was in a full slip and had the pair of slacks and a sweater in her hand. She put down the clothes, looked at him and remarked sharply. "You're all wet; don't you know how to dry yourself?"

He reached over and opened the linen closet door and took out a second towel. "I was going for reinforcements," he answered dryly.

Maria laughed and approached him, and took the towel from his hand. "Let me rub you down and get you good and dry. Then you can lie down on the bed and I'll rub some Ben Gay into your back," she said affectionately.

"Whatever," he said lightly.

The towel was thick, and she started with his head and gently rubbed his hair and ears and neck. As she moved to his shoulders and back, she massaged with greater effort. The towel he had wrapped around his waist was damp and she undid it and let if fall to the floor. She continued to dry his body right down to his ankles and when she was complete, she brought the towel back up and lightly rubbed his genitals. He didn't say anything, but she could feel him harden and she uncharacteristically remarked, "We haven't seen that for a while." She let that towel drop to the floor too and gently fondled him. She was right up against him and his hands stretched behind him and he slid them up and down over the silky slip that draped her hips. She let go of him and kissed his back and then he turned around and they kissed. It was all spontaneous, and they danced from the threshold of the bathroom to their bed. Koch flashed in her mind and she recalled the night she went to his room. It had been so long since she had felt the pangs of desire, and it happened quickly and ended happily. Henry went down on his back, and she lifted her slip and mounted him. She smiled and put her finger to her lips praying for silence.

He whispered, "The kid's home?"

"Don't worry, just be quiet," she said lovingly.

When they were done, she slid off him and slapped his thigh. "Roll over, for a bonus I'll rub your back."

He rolled over. He heard her go into the bathroom. He felt as if he had woken from a bad dream. All of the anger that had been building for six months had dissipated in the long breath of his accusations, her calm denials and the sweet balm of sex. She came back into the room. She was dressed and had the tube of Ben Gay in her hand. She applied a small tab to her fingers and rubbed it into his lower back. "How does that feel?" she said gently.

"Good, good." He sighed.

She dug her fingers in and massaged him deeply for another minute, then said, "That should do it. Get dressed. Dinner will be ready in five minutes."

"Honey."

"Yes, Henry."

"I'm sorry. My mind's been spinning out of control for so long. I worked myself into a lather, and I can't explain it, but I am sorry."

"Oh, Henry," she said sweetly. "I keep telling you that this has been very stressful for you, for us. I want to make up for all the bad times. I love you." She bent over and squeezed his shoulders and kissed the back of his head. "I love you. No more talk about the past, we can't change it, so why worry about it."

"You're right. I love you too."

Maria said nothing else and left the room.

Henry put on his pants and shirt. He thought about Sophie for a moment and all that had transpired since he had gone to work in the morning. His back felt a little better. He still believed Sophie was innocent, but the thought of Maria being involved was washed from his mind. He had put her to the test and it was evident she was innocent. Surprisingly, she was obviously unaware of how close he was to denouncing her. It was best to leave well enough alone. The police wouldn't act, and Sophie had made her own bed, and though the thought that Monaghan was the killer lingered, he realized that he was powerless to affect circumstances and he would have to let it go. *She loves me and I made her feel good,* he thought as he headed to the kitchen. On a day that had begun with so much anger he felt at peace and was in a better place than he had been for some time. Sophie had asked of him only one thing and that was to care for their child and protect him from Maria, and that plea had lost its appeal. Nothing would ever permit Sophie's hatred of Maria to retreat. The contestants had changed, but not the target of her vendetta. First Sophie fought Maria for Henry, and now she was fighting her for Joseph and the irony was that Maria never knew she had been engaged. His assessment of his wife had been terribly misguided, and he was determined evermore to stand by her side.

Maria put the rye bread in the breadbasket. She ladled soup into bowls and set the salad bowl on the table. The steam from the soup was pervasive, and it revived a nostalgic memory of life with Rudy and her family. That sense of family had escaped her for decades, and now it had returned and she pulsed with silent joy as Henry and Joseph came into the kitchen for dinner.

Chapter Seventy-Five

Tim Cleary sucked the ice out of his drink glass and crushed it with his teeth. The taste of icy water overshadowed the remnants of rye whiskey and ginger ale, and as he put the drink glass back down on the bar he motioned to the bartender to fill the glass again. "One more for the road, Pop," he said to Pop Degnan, the Monday night bartender at Pete's Bridge Lounge.

"What's the hurry?" Pop asked as he poured a measure of whiskey into a shot glass and dumped it into Cleary's empty glass.

"No hur, hurry," Cleary stammered. "You know, it's the season to be jolly."

"It's Monday, that's all," Pop replied as he topped off the drink with a few lumps of ice and a splash of ginger ale.

Cleary, uncharacteristically, didn't answer. The bar was nearly empty. It was seven o'clock and the working men who frequented the bar for a few quick drinks on the way home had cleared out and all that was left was Cleary and a few stragglers on the other side of the room. He fumbled in his pocket for his cigarettes and realized the pack was on the bar. This was his sixth rye and ginger and with each fresh drink he lit a cigarette. He was hoping Mike Monaghan would come in, but it didn't look like that was going to happen and he knew that if he didn't find his way home soon his mother would find her way to Pete's and lead him out by his ear. Ever since she assaulted him with the broomstick back in August he had made every effort to give her no good reason to publicly embarrass him again. "What to do, what to do," he mumbled to himself.

The whiskey had worked its magic, he was emboldened and before his customary lack of nerve resurfaced he downed the drink, magnanimously dropped a dollar bill on the bar, picked up his cigarettes and announced to Pop Degnan that he'd be on his way. "Maybe I'll see you next week, Pop," he slightly slurred as he stepped down from the barstool and headed for the exit.

The wind was whipping down Bailey Avenue, and it swirled in the courtyard as he climbed the two levels of steps and entered the 2810 side of the building. The steam radiators were hissing in the lobby and the air was warm and moist. The Monaghan's apartment was on the left side of the lobby just before the stairwell that led to the upper floors. The lobby was quiet. The hissing radiators and the soft din of music coming from the apartment next to the Monaghans was the only noise in the lobby. Cleary stood before Monaghan's door and listened. The kitchen was at the front of the apartment and he thought he detected the sound of running water and clinking dishes. The toughest part was getting by Mary Monaghan. He knew she'd answer the door. He took a deep breath and rang the bell. An unseen hand pulled open the peephole and he saw an eye and heard a woman's voice, "Tim Cleary, what could you want?" The peephole snapped shut and the door opened. "Tim, can I help you?" Mary Monaghan asked.

"Ye,ye, yes," he stammered. "Is Mike home? I need to ta, ta, talk to him."

Mary gave him a queer look and said, "Are you all right? Would you like to come in, maybe a cup of coffee or something?"

"I need to talk to him," he answered in a more composed voice.

"He's taking a nap before dinner, but I'll get him," she said with a tinge of annoyance in her voice. "Please come in."

"No, I can wait here."

Mary closed the door and he heard her calling her husband. "Mike, there's someone here to see you. Mike, are you up, did you hear me?"

Her voice grew fainter, then there was silence. The lobby was el shaped on the Monaghan's side of the building and Cleary walked to the furthest recess and opened the window that looked over the lower courtyard. He had played in every corner of the building as a child and was familiar with the way conversations echoed off the tiled walls and marble floors so that a whisper offered on one side of the lobby was clear to the ear on the other side. If they leaned slightly toward the window opening and spoke quietly their voices wouldn't carry. Cleary did worry that Monaghan might take the information the wrong way and exercise his anger by tossing him out the window. He still possessed his whiskey nerve, but the feelings of warmth and peacefulness that were with him in the bar were fading, and the nervous edginess that had dominated his mood since the encounter with Henry Weiss was resurfacing with greater sharpness as he waited for Mike Monaghan. Finally the door to Monaghan's apartment opened and a glowering Monaghan looked about for a moment, then seeing Cleary, strode purposely toward him and barked, "What the fuck are you up to?"

Cleary gave Monaghan a serious look and took a deep breath, mustered up his nerve and said, "Something happened to me today that you ought to know."

"What happened?"

"Hen, Henry Weiss stopped at the building today and he was crazy," Cleary said with a little excitement in his voice.

At the mention of Henry's name Monaghan felt a chill. Cleary was staring at him, waiting for a reaction. Monaghan didn't want to appear alarmed, but he was, and it was for him an odd and unusual reaction. "What are you getting at?" he asked.

Cleary nodded his head and said, "I'm getting ahead of myself. Today I was out in front catching a smoke when I hear this car door slam and next thing I know Henry Weiss is grabbing me by my coat and yelling at me. Telling me I'm a liar and he knows that Danny is the killer."

Monaghan knew precisely what Cleary was talking about, and in conjunction with his son's experience with Mrs. Weiss the day before he feared that something he believed had been put to rest was going to resurrect itself with a vengeance. He had to play it cool and after giving the appearance of mulling over what Cleary had just said he casually replied, "Weiss is the same guy whose girlfriend killed that woman in your building?"

"Yeah, him," he said angrily. "And the crazy bastard was going to hit me and was accusing Danny, but I told him he was nuts and not to bother me."

"That's it?" Monaghan said with no real concern in his voice.

"Yeah, but I know him and this wasn't like him, not him at all, the fucking guy was on fire," he whispered.

"Give me a smoke," Monaghan ordered. Cleary took the pack from his shirt pocket and handed one to Monaghan. He reached into his coat pocket and took out a pack of matches, lit a match and held the match while Monaghan lit the cigarette. Monaghan took a drag on the burning stick, and after exhaling, casually said, "Who knows what his problem is? Maybe he ain't getting any nooky no more. The girlfriend's in jail and the wife don't put out. Fuck him, and if he bothers you again call the cops." Monaghan laughed, and added with menace, "And you can tell him if you see him again to knock on my door. I'd be happy to hear what he has to say."

Cleary was relieved by Monaghan's easy acceptance of what had happened. "I just wanted you to know, just in case there's any trouble. I told him the truth, just li, like I told everybody else."

"Thanks," Monaghan said as he closed the window. Cleary nodded his head and left without further comment. Monaghan watched him leave the lobby. It was hard to contain his anger. Danny had come home minutes before Cleary rang their bell. He had to talk to the boy, but it was going to be difficult with his wife around. Something had to have set Henry Weiss off, and he imagined it was Mrs. Weiss. Only yesterday he had dismissed Danny's fears over Mrs. Weiss, as he believed she had intentionally fingered Sophie Cruz. It made no sense for her to refute her story, but why else would Henry Weiss have accosted Cleary today, and why else would he have accused Danny?

He dropped the cigarette on the floor and crushed it with his foot. His blood was boiling, and he was helpless to do anything about it. He went back into the apartment and Mary was waiting in the foyer. "What was that all about?" she asked.

"Bobby Watts has been picking on him. Bullshit, but I told him I'd speak to Watts. That's all. When's dinner?" he asked, changing the subject.

"I don't like him."

"Cleary?"

"Him too, but I don't like Bobby Watts. He beats his wife," Mary said disapprovingly.

"I don't know about that, but I get along with him."

"He's a little crazy, you better be careful," she warned.

Monaghan frowned and answered her, "I'm a little crazy too, and I think Bobby Watts knows that. When's dinner?"

She answered his frown with one of her own. "Get Danny, it's ready."

Danny was sitting on his bed rubbing his hands together. Monaghan could see the boy was upset. "Something happen today?" he asked.

"You're not going to believe what happened."

"Henry Weiss?" Monaghan asked his son.

The boy gave him a startled look, and replied, "Yeah, the son of a bitch came to the store today and accused me of killing that woman."

Mike Monaghan looked at his son sympathetically, and said, "He paid Cleary a visit too."

"What am I going to do?" Danny said as he started to cry.

Monaghan cuffed his son in the back of the head and said sternly, "Don't start fucking crying for starters. You're going to do what I've told you to do since this happened."

Danny sniffed and wiped his eyes. "Yeah, I know, keep my mouth shut," he said grudgingly.

"Listen," his father said in a calmer less threatening voice, "did Mr. McKee give you his card?"

Danny got off the bed and went to his bureau. There was a wooden box that had originally contained an English Leather cologne and after shave set. He used the box to store his money and other incidentals. He separated a few slips of paper and some dollar bills he had in the box and pulled out Roger McKee's business card. "It's here," he said showing the card to his father.

"Put it in your wallet," Monaghan instructed his son. "The cops come to your job," he paused, then continued, "or pick you up on the street, you tell them to talk to Mr. McKee. They bring you in, you say nothing except to ask for Mr. McKee. I know they won't come here, and if they want you they'll grab you when your mother or me ain't around. The important thing is you stay clammed up. They hit you, you take it. They threaten you with the electric chair, life in prison or any other shit, you just keep your fucking trap shut. Do you understand?"

"Yes, I'm just scared."

"Get over that too, or your mother will be on your case. You never told anybody about this, did you?"

"No one," he answered.

"Not even your girlfriend?" Monaghan asked suspiciously.

"No one, just like you told me."

"Boys," Mary Monaghan called out as she came down the hallway. "Dinner's going to get cold. What are you two up to?"

"C'mon," Monaghan said to his son.

Mary Monaghan was puzzled. It was rare for Mike and Danny to converse at length, and they'd been in Danny's room for a good five minutes. A little sports now and then was all they ever talked about, and that was about the extent of the father son relationship. However, she thought, something about her husband had changed recently and it was for the better. She didn't approve of Bongos. Father Dunphy claimed it was a sinful place, and if ever a bar deserved to be described as a "den of iniquity," Bongos was the place. Yet, she knew the bar did well and now her husband was buying real estate. Also, his drinking habits had slowed down considerably, and he wasn't keeping the late hours he'd kept for so long. Finally, Carla Rink had gone back to her husband Eddie and moved to the Lower Borough. Maybe there was a chance Mike would come back to her, she thought. Most importantly the bar and now this real estate business might put them in a far stronger financial position than they'd ever been in before, and that was important because she wanted Danny to go to Jesuit University, and for that she would need her husband's help.

"What was so interesting it kept you two from dinner?" she asked coyly.

Monaghan looked at his son and said, "We were talking basketball, that's all. The Jesuit Trappers are off to a good start."

Mary's heart leapt at the mention of the Jesuit University basketball team. Now was her opportunity and she made her pitch. "Father Dunphy can get him into Jesuit," she said.

Danny looked at his mother blankly, and Mike smiled as she handed him a dinner plate loaded with mashed potatoes, spinach and meat loaf. "I thought that was out of our league, his and ours."

Mary smiled back at him and reached into the pocket of her housecoat and took out a bank book. "I've been saving for years," she said as she handed the book to Monaghan. He dropped his fork, took the bank book from her and opened it up. "Two thousand and two hundred dollars," he said impressively. "That's a lot of money." He gave his son a sour look, and said, "My money too, isn't it?"

Mary snatched the bank book from his hand and put it back into her housecoat. "I've scrimped and saved for ten years for that money."

Monaghan laughed and cut of a generous piece of meat loaf and balanced it on his fork in front of his mouth and said before he deposited the meat, "It was my money. Anyway, how is Danny getting into the school? All you've done is complain to me about his school work for years."

"He's doing excellent work this year, so far, and his college boards were a little better than we expected. I think we can thank Linda for that," she said confidently.

Monaghan looked at his son and said, "What do you think?"

Danny instantly remembered the scene in Linda's basement with Ernie Lombardi and how Ernie had sneered at him and crowed about his grades and bragged that he would get into Empire State without any problem. It was a challenge, and entry into Jesuit University was just the thing to shut Ernie up, and his snotty girlfriend too. Once again the walls were closing in on him and he needed relief. The idea of being admitted to Jesuit suddenly thrilled him, and he said with enthusiasm, "If I can get in, I'll go."

Mary went over and hugged Danny about his shoulders. "Father Dunphy said that they would accept you on academic probation, and if you maintain an average of at least 2.5 for your fist year, you're in." She pulled a slip of paper from her pocket and read from some notes she had penciled in. "He called this afternoon, 2.5 that's the grade average. I think it's about a C+, but I know you can do better. But you have to do well next semester in school because they want those grades too."

"When will I officially be in?" Danny asked.

"I guess when they send out the acceptance letters, but Father said you're in and I have no reason to doubt him," Mary answered confidently. "I can pay for all of the first year and part of the second, but I'll need some help from you, Mike," she said sternly.

"What about Dunphy? He's done this much, why can't he help with the money too. That's what boyfriends are for, aren't they?" he said sarcastically.

"Why must you always be so crude," she said as she put her plate down on the table. "I know Danny hasn't done as well as he should, but he's improved, and those College Board scores count. You should be proud, and if you're going to be such a Goddamned big shot with your bar and now this real estate stuff you could share something with your family."

He didn't initially respond. He ate his dinner and watched her and Danny play with their food. The reference to the bar and the potential real estate deal were sensitive matters. This past year he had felt very lucky. Vince LoBianco and Chick Nathan had taken him under their wings and were rewarding him for years of risk and service. He had been lucky, and by all accounts should have done jail time. Life was changing. Carla had moved on and he'd met a new woman. He was on the Bongos bowling team and they played on Tuesday nights. Borough Bowling was a combination bowling lane, diner and cocktail lounge. Most bowlers when they were done with the evening's competition either went to the diner or the lounge. Mike liked the lounge, and had recently met a divorcee who was the answer to Carla's exit from his life. The new woman was in her forties, but well preserved and without children and no desire to remarry. She'd been married twice and they both failed. She lived in a new highrise in Riverview, and Mike was just what she was looking for in a boyfriend. Two dates a week was all she needed, and she'd never been in Bongos and knew very few of the people he knew. Best of all, both Vince and Chick complimented him on his new diversion. Everything had been going his way.

The murder was history and while he was never a hundred percent certain of how it happened, he knew the kid's involvement was accidental and felt it was an unfortunate, but blameless crime. His feeling for Mary had been dull for years, but he admired her pluck and tenacity. He was silently proud when she showed him the bank book. It was all going well, and now he had to deal with Henry Weiss. He knew Danny would do as he instructed and if he had been asked to make a wager his bet would have been that the police, had Weiss even gone to them with his accusations, would have shown little interest in opening a case where the suspect had already pleaded guilty and gone to jail. Nonetheless, Weiss was a threat and he would have to be dealt with. He finished his meal, turned to his wife and said, "If he gets in and stays in I'll help out. But you spend your money first before you get anymore of mine." Having made his decision, he got up from the table and left the room.

Mary was beaming. "He can be such a bastard," she whispered to Danny. The telephone rang and she sprang up from the table and went into the foyer to answer it.

Danny immediately tensed up with alarm. What if it was the police or Henry Weiss? When would the other shoe drop? It turned out to be his mother's sister and as his mother prattled over the phone and the sound of the television blared from the living room he stared at his half eaten dinner and pondered his fate.

Chapter Seventy-Six

The steel bar he held in his hand was twelve inches long and weighed about two pounds. It was called re-bar and was used to reinforce concrete fabrications. The piece he was holding was scrap from the last job he had worked on. He had carefully wrapped the bar in electrical tape. He used the type that had adhesive on one side and a clear black finish on the other. He wrapped the two ends, first filling in the spaces between the raised ridges on the bar. The ridges increased the bond between the steel bar and the concrete mixture it reinforced and as a result exponentially strengthened whatever structure it was being built. For his purposes he wanted to erase those ridges and end up with a smooth round length of steel. He neatly wound the tape around the hard metal cylinder until he had increased the diameter from three quarters of an inch to a full inch. He gripped the bar from one end with his right hand and lightly tapped it against the palm of his left hand. The dull slap of the taped steel bar against his palm was soothing to him and he rhythmically drummed his palm while he sat behind the wheel of his car killing time while weighing the potential consequences of the decision he had made.

January 1966 was cold and snowy. The building trades came to a halt by mid-month and no outside work would begin again until late February or early March. That was fine with Mike Monaghan. The real estate deal with Vince LoBianco and Chick Nathan was settled the second week of January. Mike Monaghan now owned property. This was a watershed accomplishment for him. All his life he had been a worker and a renter. After fifteen years of being involved with LoBianco and Nathan he was a silent partner in a very successful bar, and now the part owner of two buildings in Riverview. He was getting somewhere in life, and although they had to help him discover his ambition, he was aware of it now and he wanted more.

Chick Nathan's wife owned and operated a discount beauty supply store on Monmouth Road. Vince and Chick wanted to open a second shop in one of the storefronts in the building they and Mike just bought. Mike would be a partner too. Vince suggested that Mary Monaghan could run the store. Chick's wife would train her. Mary would earn a salary and they'd all make a profit. Mike at first balked, but his newfound ambitions gave caution to his initial cynicism and he agreed to make a proposal to his wife. After all, if Danny was accepted to Jesuit University, as Mary insisted he would, then this was a surefire way to cover the tuition. Ambition was a powerful drug, and once he was struck it was no longer just about him. Mike Monaghan had lived much of his life in the present tense, but things were changing. He didn't want to spend his remaining years of productivity stooped over at a construction site tying lengths of metal wire together.

Vince LoBianco and Chick Nathan lived well. If a quick buck could be made, they were first in line, but that was candy to them. They had good business sense and they earned far more honest dollars than dishonest ones. Vince had let him in the door, and he had to make the best of it. He had always kept his own counsel and confided in no one, and it was now clear to him that it was that quality that Vince admired most. Whatever he'd been asked to do, he did, and there were never any questions afterward no matter how things turned out. On the occasions when the police had picked him up, he maintained his silence. The police were always more interested in connecting whatever it was they accused him of to Vince and Chick, but he never so much as acknowledged the reference to his two benefactors.

He had earned his place and the only thing that was surprising was Vince's admission that he and Chick were fringe players in Huguenot City's criminal environment. Much of what they earned from gambling and loan sharking went elsewhere, just as most of the jobs Mike had performed for them over the years were done at the request of persons unknown to Mike, but with a much greater stake in Huguenot City's underworld. They were small time criminals and very successful businessmen. In Kingsbridge, many people thought they were big time hoods and they did nothing to dissuade anyone from that belief. Vince thought it was good for business and gave him a certain color and reputation he enjoyed. Chick liked it because people left him alone. The important thing was to make money and take care of your own. That was Vince LoBianco's credo and it was seconded by Chick Nathan.

Money didn't mean pocket money. Money meant a better life for you and yours. Mike Monaghan was in that frame of mind now, and whatever his vices were, he was responsible for his wife, his son and his daughter. In his daughter Kathleen's eyes he was a bum. Kathleen, who couldn't bear the sight of him was coming home to Huguenot City from Liverpool in May. Upon graduation from nursing school she would be coming home to work at Huguenot City Hospital. Nothing would please him more than to be living in one of the new high rises in Riverview and having her brother on his way to Jesuit University. These were the plans he was making and he was determined to succeed. There was one wrinkle and he was going to take care of that soon.

The car was cold. He had turned it off when he parked, and the moisture from his breath had iced over the windows. The light from the street lamps was dim, but he was able to read the numbers on his watch dial, and the clock read five-thirty. Every evening the man left his office at five-thirty. Mike left nothing to chance. He had staked the man out on four evenings over the last two weeks and each evening the man followed the same schedule. He put on his brown cotton work gloves and exited his car. The metal pipe was pushed up the sleeve of his right arm. He was parked a half a block east of Lincoln Boulevard. He walked up to Lincoln Boulevard and turned south. Two blocks later he turned left. One full block, then halfway down the next block was the parking lot. The lot was fenced in, but the rolling entrance gate from 163rd Street and the exit gate to 164th Street were both open. The lot was poorly lit except for the spotlight on the sign that highlighted the monthly rates, and a second sign advertising vacancies and the phone number for the management company that operated the lot and the towing company that patrolled the lot and towed all unauthorized vehicles. Monaghan crossed the street and started back toward Lincoln Boulevard.

Henry was wearing his good camel hair overcoat. Maria had given him a cashmere scarf for Christmas. The scarf was soft and warm. He hadn't expected the gift, and in return had bought no present for her. Up until the arrival of his son into their lives, Christmas was a holiday spent away from Huguenot City. Early on in the marriage Maria had made a few attempts to observe the holiday, but it wasn't his day and eventually it wasn't her day either. Working in a department store during the holidays diminished some of the glow of the season. Sable's Department Store began the Christmas season the day after Thanksgiving, and by Christmas Day Maria was thankful for their annual secular vacation. That was history now; Joseph's presence in their lives changed everything. Henry was now a Jew who celebrated Christmas. They had a tree and decorations, Christmas dinner and Gloria and Steven and their families all came to visit, and it was a day they enjoyed. Henry walked away from it with his Christmas scarf and Joseph had a ball, and Maria regaled them all with tales of her own childhood and how very different the celebrations were then. It was a wonderful day and no time was wasted by him worrying over Sophie, the delivery boy, the blindness of the police and district attorney, or any of his other recent obsessions with Millie Campos' murder and Maria's murky past. He had closed the book on those two subjects and was happier for it. Family was growing in importance to him. Maria was more attentive and loving, and Joseph was a delight. He was happy to be on his way home.

The wind was picking up on Lincoln Boulevard as he made his way to the parking lot where he kept his car. Since the move to Riverview he needed his car every day and was thankful to find adequate parking two and a half blocks from his office. Maria was making stuffed cabbage for dinner, and he was looking forward to a good meal on this very cold January evening. The cold made his eyes water and his nose felt slightly numb. He picked up his pace and turned right onto 163rd Street. He didn't notice the big man walking up the hill who had momentarily stopped to bend down and tie his shoe. The street went downhill slightly and he crossed over to the north side and entered the lot. His car was parked in the far corner on the 164th Street side. He reached into his coat pocket for his keys and headed for his car.

Monaghan tightened the laces on his work boots. He felt his chest tighten with anticipation and felt a surge of violent energy. He stood up and watched Henry as he crossed the street. Monaghan looked down as a man and woman passed him on the sidewalk. He crossed the street and picked up his pace, and followed Henry into the lot. There was snow and ice everywhere and his boots made a crunching sound as he closed the gap between them. Henry reached his car and unlocked it and opened the door. Just as he was doing that he heard the sound of footsteps close behind him. He had heard them in the distance only moments ago, but he thought little of it and now in this dark corner of the parking lot there was someone coming up behind him, and in the brief second that it took to contemplate what was happening he was frightened and turned to meet the intruder. It was too late. He would never remember what happened.

Monaghan had the pipe in his right hand. Henry was turning his head to him. Monaghan's right hand came sweeping down from his right shoulder and struck Henry across the back of his skull. The pipe landed with a heavy thud and Henry crumbled to the ground. Monaghan reached into the car and knocked out the interior light with the pipe. He bent down and tossed the pipe into a small mound of snow. He pulled up the back of Henry's overcoat and felt for the wallet in Henry's pants. He ripped open the left rear pocket and the wallet fell to the ground. He put the wallet in his coat pocket. He put his left hand up to his mouth and with his teeth pulled the glove tips finger by finger until the empty glove was held hanging from his mouth by his teeth and his left hand was free. He put his left hand in Henry's front left pocket and felt a packet of money wrapped in a rubber band. He took out the money and put that in his pocket too. He put the glove back on his left hand and fished in the snow pile for his pipe. He found the pipe and wiped it on Henry's coat. He stood up and slipped the pipe up his right sleeve and left the lot via the 164th Street exit. Henry was left unconscious, lying on the ground in front of the open door to his car.

It was over in a matter of seconds. Monaghan went up 164th Street with his head down and his chin buried in his chest and the collar of his coat pulled as high as it could go. The weather was perfect, and every pedestrian he passed was as bundled up as he was and just as intent at keeping out the cold wind. He took no notice of anyone and no one took any notice of him. He didn't bother to go through Henry's wallet, and when he turned onto Lincoln Boulevard he tossed the wallet into a small row of hedges that graced the front of an apartment building that stood between 164th Street and a 165th Street. He turned off the boulevard at a 165th Street and went to his car. He was very confident that no one had noticed him. He had hit him hard, as hard as he'd ever hit a man before, and it would not have surprised him if the blow was fatal. If he was dead, then so be it, and if not, it would be awhile before he was whole again. Monaghan had given this job a lot of thought. Back in December after the confrontations with Cleary and Danny he expected the police to bring Danny in for questioning. He reasoned at that time Maria Weiss had told her husband the truth. It was the only conceivable explanation for Henry's behavior. By New Year's Monaghan had come to the conclusion and, it was a startling conclusion, that Henry Weiss had figured the crime out without his wife revealing anything to him. It was the only reasonable conclusion that would explain why Henry attacked Cleary and Danny. If Maria Weiss had told the truth, then the police and district attorney would surely have reopened the case. No inquiries came from the police or the district attorney. Henry Weiss had solved the crime, and Mike Monaghan was convinced that he had not heard the last from him. Henry Weiss was responsible for his actions and Monaghan had to protect his family. Vince LoBianco was a good teacher.

Tuesday night was bowling night. He had spent the better part of the day working on one of the apartments, and along with Tommy Kendricks he had put a new sink in a kitchen and laid down a linoleum floor. He let Kendricks go at four-thirty, but that was the beginning of an alibi if he needed one. The Huguenot Lanes was a block from the Broadway Bridge. He parked across the street from the bowling alley and walked up to the bridge. About midway across the bridge he stopped and lit up a cigarette. The wind was vicious and it took several tries with his lighter before he could get the cigarette lit. He leaned over the railing and looked at the swirling waters below. He stretched his right arm downward over the rail and the length of re-bar he had used to assault Henry Weiss slid from his sleeve and fell to the river below. It made a small splash and was gone. He headed back to the bowling alley and as he was walking he tossed the brown cotton work gloves over the railing too and watched them toss and twist in the wind until they landed in the water and floated away. It was close to six in the evening. He had told Mary he was going to eat at the bowling alley instead of coming home for dinner, and that was exactly what he was going to do, not that he often bothered to tell her in advance whether he'd be home for supper or not, but on this important day he needed to be on the same page with everyone else. He would have a beer and a hamburger, bowl with his team, and if his new girlfriend was in the mood he would go with her to her apartment for a quick lay. He put his hand in his pocket and took out the wad of bills he had stolen from Henry Weiss. He took off the rubber band and dropped it into the gutter. He counted the bills and there was a total of two hundred and ten dollars. He added it to his own roll of bills. He was proud of himself.

He opened the trunk to his car and took out the bag with his bowling ball and shoes in it. He took of his heavy work coat and dropped it in the trunk. He closed the trunk and opened the back door to the car. On a hangar were his bowling shirt and leather coat. He took the leather coat off the hangar and put it on. He took the hangar with the shirt and dropped the shirt between the handles of the bowling ball bag and started toward the bowling alley. As he approached the fronts doors to the bowling alley, he stopped to look in the display window. Several spotlights illuminated gleaming balls and multi-colored leather bags and shoes. He felt in his pocket for the thick packet of bills he was carrying and decided that after he ate he would purchase a new ball and bag. *Compliments of Henry Weiss*, he thought. He caught his reflection in the glass doors of the bowling alley as he walked through them and smiled at himself. He had handled the problem decisively and felt neither guilt, nor shame for his actions. The hollow report of bowling balls striking wooden pins echoed throughout the bowling alley. He liked that sound, and he liked to bowl, and at that moment in his life he couldn't recall a time when he'd felt more satisfaction than he did then.

Chapter Seventy-Seven

The sound of the incoming enemy artillery was deafening. They had started construction of the pontoon bridges over the Roer River in late February of '45. The colonel usually dictated the daily diary, but he had delegated the job to the lieutenant. He had a terrible headache, and he didn't want to think, but the image of him standing over the corporal wouldn't fade, and he could hear himself talking: "…23 Feb 6 to 8 floats Bridge #5 knocked out by enemy aircraft." He could see the corporal typing his words. "…24 Feb 171 Engineer C battalion reports 3 men killed, 18 wounded, 32 missing in construction of bridges over the Roer River." On and on it went. He would attempt to open his eyes, but the light was blinding, followed by the concussive thunder of exploding ordnance that created such an ache in his head that only complete stillness and faint breathing seemed to muffle the pain. He was in two worlds. There was nothing more frightening to him than the sound of incoming artillery fire. The devastation of exploding shells, the indiscriminate damage and carnage they caused was a miserable memory that would never fade, and an experience so terrifying that it was only understood by those who witnessed it. The pain in his head brought back those memories, but he knew that it was a poor correlation to what caused that pain. The wound he was suffering from had no connection to the war. It was not a result of war and he was not a victim of the battlefield's lottery. The war was over more than twenty years ago. Something far more sinister had occurred.

He wanted to talk, but the energy wasn't there. Maria was holding his hand.

There was no recollection of consciousness, either losing it or regaining it. An evil act had been perpetrated. What it was or who it was did not matter for the moment. All he knew was that the pounding in his head was similar to the preparations for crossing the Roer River. An explosion would go off in his head and would propel him back in time to the war, and bits and pieces of that horrible time would pass through his consciousness like the frames in a movie, then the pain would subside and he would feel her hand holding his, gently squeezing his fingers and he would feel safe.

A thousand thoughts and scenes spilled over his imagination, and like soup through a colander he held onto very few of them. There was a recent dinner at his sister's that he recalled. Someone, perhaps his sister Gloria, but he wasn't sure, was talking about near death experiences and a question was posed to Maria about her brush with death. That moment was clear in his memory. Maria said that her bleeding aneurysm had not been life-threatening and there were no unusual experiences except for what she was thinking of when she woke up. She laughed. He could hear her laughter and the way she smiled and explained that there was something about one of the doctors attending to her that reminded her of a friend in London during the war, and how odd it was that she would regain consciousness and think about people and places she'd thought were long forgotten. The pain had subsided and he was lucid and the irony of their circumstances could not be denied. He was in a hospital, and like his wife, his mind had traveled back in time to the war and he didn't know why. And he didn't know if she was being truthful. Didn't she tell him when he first saw her in the hospital that he had to acknowledge his son? Or had she dreamt about one thing and upon seeing him at her bedside she moved on to a more pressing topic, and what did it matter? His head hurt.

He didn't want to open his eyes. He squeezed Maria's hand and attempted to talk. The words came easily and, surprisingly, little pain was associated with speaking. "Turn off the light," he said weakly. She let go of his hand and he felt her lean over his bed and heard her pulling on something and then a click. His eyes were still closed. He opened them slightly and turned his head to the left. Maria bent down and kissed his hands, "Henry, sweetheart," she softly cooed. "You poor thing. If I had lost you I don't know what I would have done."

"Last time we were in a hospital, you were in the bed and I was holding your hand," he said as he winced in pain.

"Don't talk if it hurts."

"I thought I was back in the service. It was the Roer River all over again."

"You're very lucky."

"What happened?"

"You were beaten and robbed. The police said that somebody snuck up on you from behind while you were getting into your car last night and hit you over the head and stole your wallet and money."

"Did they catch him?"

"They have an idea. They said there have been a number of muggings down around the courthouse and the business district the last month. They say they are drug addicts, junkies they call them, and they're working on it."

Henry opened his eyes wider, "I don't remember anything. I was in the war again and then I remembered that when you were in here you were thinking about the war too. Isn't that odd?"

"Who knows why we think what we think? I'm just happy they didn't kill you."

"I don't even remember being at work or what I was doing. It's all a blur to me."

"When they brought you in, you were unconscious and the doctors thought you were going into a coma, but that didn't happen. I've been here since last night. The police were nice enough to bring me over. Joseph is with Gloria. She was here too, but left, and by the time I got here you were in and out of consciousness. The doctors said that was good, but all night you were moaning. I cried and cried and I'm just thankful right now that you're not dead," she said with much emotion, as she started to cry again.

"I don't know what time it is, or how long I've been here. It is one big blur except for the artillery," he said painfully.

"Artillery," she asked.

"Inside my head is like being back in the war and under fire. Damn, it's starting again," he almost cried as he closed his eyes and kept his head as still as he could. Flashes of light and jolts of pain echoed in his head. He clenched his teeth and slowed his breathing. She was still holding his hand and stroking the back of it. She said something about junkies, but that didn't sound right to him. The pain was ebbing and he squeezed her hand a little tighter. He felt safe with Maria. She was a survivor, she would protect him. He was tired and weak, and it took too much effort to think any more about what had happened, though he tried until sleep came and his mind went blank.

Maria sat holding his hand for another ten minutes until she was certain that he was sleeping. It was ten in the morning and she had been at his side since eight o'clock the evening before. She was exhausted. Gloria had taken charge of Joseph and was going to get him off to school and come back after school to see Henry. Maria felt comfortable that Henry's condition would improve and decided to go home. Their conversation told her there was no permanent damage, and for that she was grateful. She stood up and pulled back the curtain to the cubicle they had placed him in the night before. The area he was in was attached to the emergency room, and Henry's condition was still being closely monitored by the medical staff. The doctor had told her that once they felt his condition was stable they would move him to a regular room. It was expected that he would remain in the hospital for at least two more days before he went home. The prognosis was positive, although the doctor had told her that Henry would be susceptible to severe headaches that would abate with time. She was anxious to go home and take a bath and a nap.

On her way out she stopped at the front desk to tell the nurse she was leaving. Before she could get the nurse's attention, two men approached her and one of them said, "Excuse me, Mrs. Weiss."

It was Detective Cairn. He smiled at her. Behind him was standing Detective Widelsky. Widelsky nodded his head at her, but didn't smile. She looked at them with surprise and simply replied, "Yes?"

"We're happy to hear your husband is going to be all right," Cairn said pleasantly.

She was suspicious of them, and again she kept her answer brief. "Yes, thank you."

"We were wondering if we could talk to you for a minute or two, if you're up to it," Cairn said with a sympathetic smile.

"I thought Detective Ruggerio was investigating this case."

"He is," Cairn said defensively. "I just have a couple of questions, and the doctor said it will be a day or two before we can speak to your husband. If it's an inconvenience we could schedule it for some other time."

"I've been up all night. I was going home to go to bed."

"Do you need a ride home? We could talk in the car."

"No," she said abruptly. "Someone is picking me up and I have to go."

Widelsky could see that Cairn was getting nowhere with her, and he edged in front of Cairn and gently placed his hand on Maria's elbow. He guided her to a corner away from the front desk and said bluntly and accusingly, "Did you know that your husband came to see us at the precinct in December? Would you like to know what he said?"

Maria stiffened and cocked her head slightly. She took a step backward, not wanting to be too close to Widelsky, and answered, "Was it the Monday after that snowstorm?"

Cairn interjected with surprise in his voice, "Yes, it was."

Widelsky shot him an annoyed look and said to Maria, "He told you he came to see us?"

Maria half smiled and replied, "Oh, he told me about his visit to the precinct. He told me that the boy who made the delivery to our apartment was the real murderer and he told me in so many words that I was a liar."

The two detectives looked at one another, and Cairn took the lead again. "Well, we didn't put much stock in what he said that day, but we did tell our boss and he told his boss, and in light of what happened last evening our captain thought it would be a good idea to interview you, you know, just to find out who else he was talking to or accusing and if there was, you know, some connection between last evening and everything else, I guess."

Maria listened to Cairn intently, and when he was finished speaking she gave him a cold smile and said, "I didn't put any stock in what Henry had to say that day. I've told my story, and I'm not going to tell it anymore." With that said she turned and headed for the exit.

Cairn took a step to follow her, but Widelsky reached out and grabbed his arm. "Let her go for Christ's sake. This was a fucking wild goose chase and you know it."

Cairn spoke softly and said, "That fucking broad leaves me cold. Right now I believe her husband. It's like the murder never happened."

"Come on," Widelsky ordered, "let's go get some coffee, then will go back and write up a little report for the captain. Tell him she knew about her husband's accusations in December, and as far as she was concerned they were farfetched and her story was her story and that's it. I'm tired of this fucking case and these fucking people. She looked at us like we were two pieces of shit on the sidewalk. She can rot, and for my money we put the right person in jail and she can fucking rot too."

"Yeah," Cairn sighed, "Henry Weiss feels guilty and we're supposed to do it all over again."

They were on the sidewalk in front of the hospital. Widelsky looked across the street and there at the bus stop stood Maria. "Hey, Phil," he said laughing. "She said someone was picking her up and there she is at the bus stop. What a cold bitch she is."

"You're right," Cairn said angrily. "To her we ain't nothing more than two pieces of shit on the sidewalk."

Chapter Seventy-Eight

Maria saw the two detectives. It pleased her when the shorter one, Widelsky, the Slav with a pumpkin for a head, that was how she described him to herself, poked at his partner and pointed at her. She was happy they saw her, happy that they knew she chose the bus rather than go with them. Cairn was tolerable. He was the pro-typical Irish charmer, she thought. Smiling, winking his eye, pretending to be a friend was his game, but it wasn't sincere. It was just an act. Widelsky presented more of a problem. He was a brutal Slav, and not too far removed from his lowly peasant roots. His kind was tougher to fool and couldn't be flattered. She wasn't sure if they were acting on their own, or if their captain had sent them to interview her. Drawing a connection between Henry's accusations of Danny Monaghan's guilt in Millie's murder and the robbery and assault last evening made no sense to her. She was satisfied with how she handled them. She was cold and indifferent, and she wanted them to see her at the bus stop. The police, by nature, were cynical and suspicious. It was an effort to not treat them rudely, but it was equally important to let them know that they were insignificant in her eyes, and she was confident that the message had been delivered. She watched them as they turned the corner and walked out of her sight.

The bus arrived a minute later and as she took her seat her she realized how tired she was. She planned on taking a warm bath, then taking a three hour nap. Joseph would be arriving home from school at three-thirty, and she was determined to take him for his ice skating lesson. She had prearranged it with

Gloria to pick Joseph up after the lesson and she would go back to the hospital to visit Henry. Her brother-in-law Joel would go to the hospital this evening too, then drive her home. She was surprised at how she reacted when she saw Henry in the hospital. Her tears were real. What would she have done if he had been killed? The very thought ripped her apart because it meant that Joseph would exit her life. Henry was the tether that kept Joseph attached to her. Of course, that attack and Henry's subsequent injuries did give her an advantage.

Ever since that dramatic scene in December Henry had been very quiet. She was never sure if she had completely convinced him that his take, his keenly accurate version of who killed Millie Campos, was wrong. The doctor had told her it would be months before he was a hundred percent again and that meant it would put that much more time between the murder, Sophie's incarceration and whatever lingering doubts Henry held about her guilt. Time was on her side, and she harbored no doubt that she would prevail. Family life, warm and rewarding, would continue as it had for the last four months, and she would allow nothing to disrupt it.

Life was almost as full as it had been with Rudy and the rest of her family so very long ago. Rarely did a day pass when she didn't think of Rudy. Every time she looked at Joseph she saw the resemblance, and even though that resemblance was a mere coincidence it pleased her so much that she had decided that when the time came for Joseph to leave her house and join his mother she would leave Henry, leave Huguenot City and start over because to be apart from Joseph, to allow his mother to pollute his mind against her would be too much to bear. *What else could she do?* she thought. Henry and the boy would never be close. They were trying, but they were trying for her sake and not theirs. She would push Joseph to Henry, and Henry to Joseph, and each in his own way wanted her between them. The thought of Joseph leaving her life was as painful as the memory of Rudy's death. Henry would support him and that would be the extent of his relationship with his son. Sophie would welcome the challenge of distancing the child from them and all that would remain for her was the empty journey of growing old with Henry.

Life without the boy would be overwhelming, and her decision was made. When the time came she would go away. She had finally learned to love Henry; however, that love, she realized, was an outgrowth of her affection for his son, and without the child their relationship would sink to the natural level it endured through most of their marriage. Guy Roberts was an option, but she suspected any union between them would be short lived. Her tolerance for men was limited, yet she didn't want to be alone. She still had time. She anticipated it would be two more years before Sophie would be free to claim her child. Maria was intent on enjoying those years and Joseph's portended absence like death was inevitable. She was in control of her destiny, and neither Henry, nor the police, nor anyone else could change that. She felt herself nodding off to sleep. Her head fell to the side and rested against the window of the bus. Soon she was snoring lightly in rhythm with the vibrations of the bus's engine. A dribble of spit seeped from the corner of her closed mouth and ran down her chin unto the black leather handbag she clutched in her fingers. The harsh winter sunlight pierced the glass windows of the bus, accenting every emerging wrinkle on her face and strand of gray hair on her head. Three decades of adversity and the fatigue and stress of the past year had finally undone her. She was worn out and tired. The bus was warm and the heat felt good. At that moment she was content to sleep. The perfect posture and the radiance had dissipated and there slumped in the seat was a non-descript middle-aged woman taking a catnap; thoughts or dreams, it didn't matter, of Joseph and Rudy combed through her mind and she was at peace with herself and that was all that mattered.

Chapter Seventy-Nine

It was finally going to happen and the anticipation had him giddy. He was lying on the bed with two pillows under his head. He had no appetite. He was tuned to WHUG on the radio. The Simon and Garfunkel hit song *Sounds of Silence* was playing, but it didn't get him down. Nothing could get him down right now, and when his mother called to him that his father was home and dinner would be ready in ten minutes he didn't answer, but instead closed the door to his bedroom and stared at the ceiling.

Linda had met him at the CYO basketball practice. She was still a terrific free throw shooter, and one by one she took his young players to the foul line and instructed them on the proper way to plant the feet, place a hand on each side of the ball and gently loft it to the basket. She had a great time, the kids loved her, and it was a good balance to his gruff treatment of a band of noisy and non-attentive third and fourth graders.

They locked up the gym and took the bus home. She started giggling and told him she had a secret. They went back and forth for a bit, then she opened her handbag. The bag was oversized and had books and other things in it, and sitting at the bottom was a rectangular square box. "One dozen, lubricated," he recalled her whispering. She repeated the word 'lubricated' slowly and salaciously, and giggled uncontrollably for a minute. There it was in the bottom of her bag. A dozen lubricated condoms. Her parents were going to her brother's on Saturday and were staying overnight. It was one week past his birthday and two weeks before hers, but the timing was right and "a promise was a promise," she had reminded him, and Saturday was to be the night.

Mary Monaghan was working the masher with great vigor as she pushed and twisted it in the lumpy mush of boiled potatoes. She added a little more milk and rested her hand for a moment. Mike Monaghan was leaning against the kitchen counter with the newspaper tucked under his arm.

"Mary," he said earnestly, "I have to tell Vince tomorrow. You asked me yesterday to give you a day to think about it. What's the answer?"

She started mashing again, and without making eye contact, said rather meekly, "I don't know anything about business. I might screw things up."

"You'll work in the other store with Chick's wife for a few weeks. This is easy."

"What will I tell Father Dunphy? He depends on me."

"What they pay you isn't even pin money for Christ's sake," he replied dismissively.

"I know, but it leaves me time to keep up the house and shop and cook. When will I have time to do those things if I'm in a store six days a week."

"Danny was accepted to Jesuit. You can pay for the first year, but what about after that? Face it, sweetheart," he said warmly and sincerely, if uncharacteristically, "that's a tough school and I don't believe he could work his way through college and keep his grades up at the same time. You're gonna have to pay his college and what St. John's pays you isn't going to foot the bill."

"I thought you said you'd help out?"

"I did and the store is the answer."

The potatoes were done, and she placed the bowl on the stove on an empty burner. She took the chicken from the roasting pan and placed it on the cutting board. "Cut some meat, please, while I make the gravy." She poured the drippings from the roasting pan into a pot and added some leftover water from the boiled potatoes and added a tablespoon of Kitchen Bouquet seasoning and a few ounces of corn starch mixed with water. She was stirring the gravy, and finally said, "Let me talk with Father Dunphy."

"Mary, I know you and the priest are good friends. I have plans for us, and I think he'd agree. There's no reason you can't visit him, damn, invite him over for dinner once a week, I don't care, and don't you and the rest of the girls in the altar society go to dinner with him once a month?"

She looked at him skeptically. "Invite him to dinner? Where will I put him, on the fire escape?" she answered sarcastically as she swept her hand about the small kitchen. "It gets claustrophobic when the three of us eat in here."

"I'm taking care of that too," he said.

"We're moving?" She laughed after she said it.

"There are two new buildings opening up in Riverview. One will be finished next month, and the other by the end of the summer. I worked on the first one for a few weeks. That's the Riverview Edge. Big apartments, two bedrooms, parquet floors, modern appliances and sleeves built into the walls for air conditioning and wiring fit to support it."

"We can't afford that," she scoffed.

Mike smiled, approached his wife and placed his hands on her shoulders. He looked at her and smirked. "Mary, I'm gonna turn forty next year. I ain't a kid no more. My fucking hands and my back and my knees ache from bending over all day working like a fucking coolie. Half the guys that drink on the job don't drink 'cause they're drunks, they drink to dull the pain and get through the day. It's a young man's job, and I'm not gonna be doing it much longer. Vince and me and Chick took most of the profit from the bar and used it as a down payment to buy those buildings. There's money left to start the store, and we have plans to open another bar in Riverview. A much better place than Bongos, and it will make money too. Those guys know what they're doing and I'm just happy they included me."

"They're criminals," she said nervously. "All the problems you had with the police were because of them. How can you trust them?"

"Mary, whatever problems I had with the police was my doing. I did some bad things, and I kept my mouth shut and what happened? Nothing, that's what happened."

"That makes it okay?"

"Listen," he said quietly, "I never killed anybody, and most of what I did the assholes had it coming to them. There's a lot of money out there, and we can make it honestly. Look, look at the ceiling," he said as he pointed to the area above the stove. "How many times has that been plastered? It's ready to crumble again. How many mice we catch? When you turn on the light in the kitchen, what's the first thing you see? Roaches, that's what."

Mary was busy stirring the gravy. He was making a good argument, and she was enjoying the exchange between them. Finally, there was give and take instead of his normal "take it or leave it" answer to every argument they had. "Parquet floors and an apartment that no one has ever lived in before," she said wistfully.

"And a doorman too, and it'll run about three hundred a month."

"That's three times what we pay here," she said in shock.

"We'll have money coming in from the bar, the beauty supply store, the rents from the apartments and other stores, the new bar, and your salary and my salary. The money is there."

"Well, if it's that good why can't you just hire someone?"

"Vince likes to keep everything in the family. He don't trust outsiders, and Chick is the same way. You gotta do this for us, Mary."

It was a reversal in roles, and for the life of her she couldn't remember when, if ever, he had pleaded with her to do anything. Suddenly money and being important, that was how she saw it, had changed her man. She turned off the gravy and said spitefully, "For us, there is no us. Last Saturday night was one of the nicest evenings I've ever had with you. We went to the dance at St. John's, you stayed with me the entire evening, didn't drink too much and we danced and you were the life of the party and then we came home," and she stopped and blushed, and then in a whisper she continued, "It was like it was a long time ago and I thought you were changing, but I was wrong."

"We did have a nice night."

"What about your girlfriend?"

"Carla's been out of the picture for months; she went back to Eddie," he said with neither shame nor embarrassment."

"I mean the new one."

"What?" he said, feigning ignorance.

"Tuesday you went bowling right after work and then you didn't come home until after midnight, well after, and I could smell her on you. It wasn't Carla's smell, it's someone new."

"I was hanging out at the bar after our league bowled. There's a bunch of broads hang out there too. That's all."

"I can't believe you."

"Mary," he said slowly and tenderly, "I'm really trying. Saturday night was very nice and we should go out more often. I want to move you out of this dump, and I want Danny to go to Jesuit and God willing I'd like to see Kathleen come home and be happy to see me. I'd also like to have air conditioning in the summer when it's ninety fucking degrees out and not have to walk around in my skivvies sweating my ass off."

"Parquet floors," she said. "Will we have a river view, or one of downtown Huguenot City?"

"You can pick the view and the floor, and you'll have a dining area where we can put a regular table and nice chairs. Then you can invite Father Dunphy for dinner, proper like you would like to do."

She turned the gas back on under the gravy. "I'll do it. Go get Danny, tell him dinner's ready. Can we tell him?"

Mike smiled. "Yeah, I want him to help out at the store too. He can quit the supermarket job and work for you."

"I'd like that," she said, smiling.

Mike left the kitchen. She knew the tuition was an issue, and all along she was going to agree with him, but she wanted to see if he would cave a little and give in to her. He did, although it was only to the degree that he was capable of doing so, but it was progress. There would always be other women, and as hard as that was to accept it would be much easier with money in her pocketbook, her son's tuition paid and a brand new apartment. *Parquet floors, new appliances and air conditioning*, she thought happily. *How long before we can get a color television?*

It had been a tough sale's pitch, but she bought it, and he was pleased with himself. Vince had told him that they would only open the beauty supply store if Mary would run it. A great deal depended on Mary, and it was obvious to Mike that Vince was determined to curb his appetites. Whether it was age, or just the realization that a little compromise made life easier, he was taking Vince's direction.

Danny's bedroom door was closed. Mike pushed it open and turned on the overhead light. Danny's head bounced off the pillow and he appeared startled. "Dinner's ready, sport," Mike said. Mike then dropped the newspaper on the bed. There's a story on page one about your friend. I don't think you'll have to worry about him anymore." Mike left the bedroom and went to the bathroom to wash his hands.

Danny heard the water running. He picked up the paper and scanned the headlines. "What friend?" he wondered. In the lower left hand corner he saw the headline *Local Attorney Beaten, Robbed and Left for Dead*. It was Henry Weiss, and the first paragraph after the headline gave a brief rehash of the Millie Campos murder. The story went on to describe how Henry was found unconscious with his head split open in his car in a parking lot near his law office. It concluded that he would survive, but he was expected to have a long recovery.

His father had initially startled him, but the combination of menace and nonchalance was unmistakable, and Danny had heard it correctly. "I don't think you'll have to worry about him anymore," meant exactly that. Henry had threatened Danny in December, and Mike Monaghan couldn't abide by that. His initial instructions to Danny were to keep his mouth shut under all circumstances and, obviously, he couldn't immediately strike at Henry Weiss without drawing attention to himself or Danny. Whether or not anyone listened to Henry Weiss, or was going to do something on his behalf became meaningless. Henry Weiss didn't know Mike Monaghan. Henry Weiss didn't know that it was a mistake to threaten Mike Monaghan. The threat may have been indirect, but it left Mike Monaghan no choice and he had to take care of business, and he did. Danny was proud of his father, and the fears he had harbored these last seven months evaporated. He was safe.

Linda had a promise to keep and Henry Weiss was no longer someone to fear. The murder happened so long ago that he had absolved himself of all guilt. His father was on his side, and the aroma from the roasting chicken and his mother's homemade gravy assured him that God was on his side too and life right now would be good.

Epilogue

March 6, 1966

Joseph laughed in return, and lifted two more letter tiles from the letter rack and said, "E-N and that spells GARDEN. How many points, Aunt Lucy?"

Lucy pointed the tip of the pencil at the letters, mumbled to herself, then announced triumphantly, "Twenty points, you have a double word and a double letter for the G." She wrote the score down and said to Sophie, "You're losing again."

Sophie sighed and smiled and looked at her son with wonder. "You're only in the third grade, how did you get so smart?"

Joseph returned her smile. "I play Scrabble all the time. I'm getting good at it."

"Last year you were still playing Candyland. You must have some very new smart friends."

"My friends don't play Scrabble," he blurted out, then quickly changed the subject and said, "I'm thirsty. Can I go get a drink of water from the fountain?"

Sophie nodded her head and looked at her aunt. Joseph got up from his chair and walked across the gym to where the water fountain was located. The gym floor was a maze of tables and chairs with women and children huddled together at every table, some playing games and others talking, and some just holding hands. It was a vibrant mosaic of white and brown and black faces, and in another place it would have painted a warm representation of racial and family harmony and unity, except that the gym was a part of the Pinewood Woman's Correctional Facility, and at each table there was one woman distinct from everyone else at the table; that woman was dressed in denim pants and a rough sweatshirt and she was an inmate.

Lucy patted Sophie's hand. "He talks about you all the time. He misses you so and ties so hard to be strong."

"Tia, don't lie," she sadly replied. "Every week I hear or see something else, and I know he misses me less and less."

Lucy puckered her lips and shook her head, "Have faith in him, he's just a little boy."

Sophie's eyes swelled with tears and she bit her lip. "You're right. I have to be strong. Twenty more minutes and the bell will ring, then he's gone for another week, and if something comes up, then it's a week and a half or two weeks. Tia, tia," she whispered, "he's all I want, I can't lose him."

Lucy bent over, took Sophie's hand in hers and brought it to her lips and kissed Sophie's fingers. "You worry too much, he loves you. Ask him."

Sophie wiped her tears away. Joseph was at the table, and he stopped and looked at Sophie, "Mommy, Mommy, why are you crying?"

"Nothing, honey." Sophie sniffed and smiled. "I just love you so and don't want to lose you, that's all."

Tears filled the boy's eyes, and he went to his mother and put his arms around her and sat on her lap. "I cry for you too, every night, but I hide in the pillow and no one hears me. They don't know and I just pretend. I do everything you told me to do." He stood up and went back to his seat. "Can we finish the game?"

Sophie was too emotional. His words had made her cry openly. "Put it away, we'll play next week, I promise." They sat there silently as he put the tiles and the racks back in the box and put the big rubber band Maria had given him around the outside of the box so none of the pieces would fall out. Sophie took a big breath and said, "You love me more than them, you still do, don't you?"

He gave her a guilty look. "Mommy, you know I love you."

"I know. I'm being silly. I'm sorry. I guess I think Maria is going to steal you from me."

He looked away and said, "Maria's nice to me."

"How's your father?"

"He's nice to me too, but we don't talk much."

Sophie laughed. "You act so grownup I forget you're only eight. I meant how is he doing?"

"Oh," Joseph said, realizing that his mother wanted to know about Henry's recovery. "He's s'posed to go back to work Monday. Maria yells at him all the time. She makes him walk and do other stuff so he gets better. She said he almost died and I think he's very sad."

"We can walk out to the gate and wait for the bell. It's too stuffy in here," Sophie said sadly. She looked at her son adoringly, put her arm around his shoulder and pulled him close to her. They started walking, with Lucy following behind carrying the box with the Scrabble game. Joseph nestled against his mother. "Mommy, when you come home, will I still go to the same school?"

"If you want to, sweetheart," she said sweetly.

"I want to," he answered as he put his arm around her waist and pulled her even closer to him.

The gymnasium doors opened to a wire enclosed walkway that led to the main gate. Prisoners were allowed to the yellow line and no further. Sophie and Joseph stood near the yellow line. No one was talking. The bell rang. It was time to go. Sophie bent down and pulled her son close and hugged him tightly. If she held him too long he would have stopped breathing. He pushed her back ever so lightly, smiled, and with tears in his eyes, said, "Mommy, don't be so sad. It makes me sad."

"I know, I know. You're all I have. Don't ever leave me." She stood up, hugged him once more, then turned to her aunt. "Tia, watch over him." Joseph had started down the path and Sophie reached out, grabbed Lucy's hand and stopped her from following Joseph. "You see what's happening, don't you? She's taking him away from me. You have to let me know everything, everything," she said strongly.

"Sophie, my little baby," Lucy said, near tears. "He's fine. I know you hate her, but she's being good to your son. Trust him, I know he loves you. Trust him." Lucy gently slipped her hand from Sophie's and headed for the gate.

The second bell rang and Sophie returned to the gymnasium. Ever since Henry's visit, her life in prison had been sheer turmoil. The peace she had found had vanished, and in its place were a host of unsettling thoughts. Was Henry correct? Was it the delivery boy? Why didn't he trust Maria? Why had he not done anything else? Yes, she had told him to leave her alone, but that was out of pride. She had expected him to do something, but he had done nothing. And then there was the robbery and assault. Was that just another coincidence, or was someone else involved? Did Henry try to get her case reopened and did somebody get in his way? There were endless questions, and the only thing that made any sense was Maria's culpability. Whether it was to punish Sophie or fill some void in her life, Maria had made a bid to take Joseph from her. Lucy didn't see it, but Sophie saw it in her son's eyes. The Scrabble games, the skating lessons, the hikes and books they read, along with the Spanish lessons were in each and every instance time spent alone with each other. Maria had immersed herself in the boy's life, and it was a competition Sophie couldn't enter. It would be at least two more years before she would be free, and her great fear was that Joseph would return home with her, but yearn for his father's house. Despite what Lucy and her brother Ray said, she knew what she was up against. She was trapped in prison and there was nothing she could do, and eventually the child would tire of his mother's tears. Eventually, too, as he got older he would grow uncomfortable with the weekly visits and the hard edged reality that his mother was in prison.

The prisoners were lined up and accounted for and led back to their secure rooms. She got into bed and doubled up her pillow and faced the wall. She had resolved that she would lose him, and for consolation she returned to her favorite pastime. Hours were wasted on her bed dreaming of revenge. She was a survivor. She told herself that every day. *I have two years to figure it out*, she thought. *Two years to put it all in order. It didn't have to happen right away, but in time Maria and Henry would pay a price. After all*, she mused, every story has to have a happy ending and that would be the happy end to hers.